W9-BRS-927

Detective Duos

Detective Duos

Edited by
Marcia Muller and Bill Pronzini

NEW YORK   OXFORD
OXFORD UNIVERSITY PRESS
1997

Oxford University Press

Oxford   New York

Athens   Auckland   Bangkok   Bogotá   Bombay   Buenos Aires
Calcutta   Cape Town   Dar es Salaam   Delhi   Florence   Hong Kong
Istanbul   Karachi   Kuala Lumpur   Madras   Madrid   Melbourne
Mexico City   Nairobi   Paris   Singapore   Taipei   Tokyo   Toronto   Warsaw

and associated companies in
Berlin   Ibadan

Copyright © 1997 by Marcia Muller and Bill Pronzini

Published by Oxford University Press, Inc.,
198 Madison Avenue, New York, New York 10016-4314

Library of Congress Cataloging-in-Publication Data
Detective duos / edited by Marcia Muller and Bill Pronzini
p. cm.
Includes index.
ISBN 0-19-510214-2
1. Detective and mystery stories, American 2. Detective and mystery stories,
English 3. Partnership — Fiction. I. Muller, Marcia. II. Pronzini, Bill.
PS648.D4D48 1997 813'.087208 — dc21   97-10562

Since this page cannot legibly accommodate the acknowledgments, pages
441–42 constitute an extension of the copyright page.

3 5 7 9 8 6 4 2

Printed in the United States of America
n acid-free paper

CONTENTS

CONTENTS

INTRODUCTION

Fictional characters who work together in one capacity or another to solve a mystery have been a staple of the crime-fiction genre since Edgar Allan Poe wrote the first detective story in the early 1840s. Such characters may be amateur or professional or a combination of the two; of either gender; of any sort of ethnic, religious, or social background; and of any period in history. They need not function as equal partners in order to qualify, for the umbrella designation of "detective duos" is a broad one. Indeed, there are almost as many types and variations of sleuthing partnerships as there are types and variations of mystery and detective fiction itself.

The first and most influential type is that in which the celebrated cases of a master detective are chronicled by a close friend or relative who is either present during the investigation or provided ex post facto with all the details necessary to the case's solution. In this kind of story, the narrator generally contributes little or nothing to the solution, although he (for they're usually male) may be allowed to say or do something that triggers his idol's ratiocinative powers. Hence, critic H. R. F. Keating's term "trailing-behind narrator" for the passive member of the team. Despite his nonparticipant role, the narrator's presence is important for several reasons: He functions as a camera for the setting of scene, the establishment of the dramatis personæ, and the noting of clues; he serves as a sounding board for the musings of the detective; the telling of the story from his viewpoint permits the inner workings of the detective's mind to remain a tantalizing mystery; and the relative shallowness of his own thoughts, plus his eagerness to extol the other's virtues (the trailing-behind narrator is usually a self-effacing individual), makes the sleuth seem all that much more clever, wise, and imposing.

Poe's 1841 tale, "The Murders in the Rue Morgue," was both the first detective story and the first to feature such a duo. The master detective is, of course, C. Auguste Dupin; the narrator of this and the four other Dupin stories is so dwarfed by the Parisian sleuth's virtuosity that Poe did not even bother to provide him with a name. Though this method of detective storytelling was copied by other writers in the United States, chiefly the perpetrators of dime novels and story-paper weeklies, and by writers in England and France, it was not until British physician Arthur Conan Doyle penned the first Dr. Watson–narrated Sherlock Holmes story, *A Study in Scarlet,* in 1887 that the form achieved its highest level of excellence.

Aside from the unique character and deductive prowess of Holmes, the element that made the series the most popular and most imitated in the genre's history is Doyle's handling of Dr. John Watson. No trailing-behind cipher is he. Even though Watson is content to bask in Holmes' shadow, he is every bit as real and engaging a personage, and his friendship with the Great Man has a depth of feeling unlike that of any other nineteenth—and few twentieth—century detecting teams. Watson's eye is far keener than that of any of his counterparts; when he reports, often with journalistic precision, on the sights, sounds, and smells of London and the English countryside, we feel as if we have been transported back in time to that fascinating Victorian era.

Only a few of the many Holmes–Watson imitations and variations are of sufficient quality to have endured. The earliest and best of the strict pastiches are Arthur Morrison's tales of Martin Hewitt, a blander version of Holmes, which are narrated by his friend, the journalist Brett; the adventures originally appeared in *The Strand Magazine,* just as the Holmes–Watson stories did, and were first collected in *Martin Hewitt, Investigator* (1894). The most effective of this century's pastiches are the Solar Pons stories of August Derleth, begun in the late 1920s. They are not only faithful to the tone and spirit of Doyle's tales, but are likewise set in a well-depicted re-creation of Holmes's and Watson's gaslit London; Pons and his companion, Dr. Lyndon Parker, reside at 7B Praed Street and undertake to solve mysteries reminiscent in plot and even title ("The Adventure of the Limping Man," "The Adventure of the Sotheby Salesman") of the originals. Eleven collections of Solar Pons stories, beginning with *In Re: Sherlock Holmes,* appeared between 1945 and 1973.

Among the more significant of the early variations is E. W. Hornung's A. J. Raffles, gentleman, cricketeer, and notorious thief, who also sometimes functions as a sleuth and whose exploits are narrated in fawning style by his former school chum Bunny Manders. The popularity of such Raffles collections as *The Amateur Cracksman* (1899) led to several films, as well as a new series of Raffles and Bunny Manders tales by Barry Perowne that continued into the 1980s. Conan Doyle's success with Sherlock Holmes was one reason Hornung chose to emulate him; another was the fact that he was Doyle's brother-in-law.

The Red Thumb Mark, the first of R. Austin Freeman's stories about Dr. John Thorndyke, the most accomplished of the "scientific detectives," and his chronicler, Dr. Christopher Jervis, appeared in 1907. In 1918, Melville Davisson Post published *Uncle Abner: Master of Mysteries,* called by author and editor Ellery Queen "the finest book of detective short stories written by an American author since Poe." Uncle Abner is "a grimly austere and supremely righteous countryman who smites wrongdoers and mends destinies like a biblical prophet transplanted to the New World," in another critic's description; his detections, set in rural West Virginia in the mid-nineteenth century, are narrated by his nephew, Martin, though Martin's role in some stories is quite minor.

Madame Rosika Storey and her secretary and chronicler, Bella, were the first important two-woman detective duo; they debuted in Hulbert Footner's 1926 collection, *Madame Storey.* Nero Wolfe and Archie Goodwin, Rex Stout's extraordinary team of private investigators, immediately made their mark in *Fer-de-Lance* (1934). Although Archie serves as narrator of Wolfe's deductive triumphs he also plays an active role in their cases and is portrayed in greater depth—and not incidentally treats the master detective with far less reverence—than any other narrator-partner. Lillian de la Torre's *Dr. Sam: Johnson, Detector* (1946) features the eighteenth-century lexicographer and sage in a series of tales narrated by his real-life biographer, James Boswell. Boswell's journals and his personal relationship with Dr. Johnson were surely influences on both Poe and Doyle in the choice of format for their detective stories, and in Lillian de la Torre's capable hands they made fitting detective-story heroes in their own right.

William MacHarg's Detective O'Malley, known as "the smartest dumb cop in detective fiction," was introduced in 1930 in a series of *Collier's* short-shorts narrated by MacHarg himself. A collection of these, *The Affairs of O'Malley,* was published in 1940. Yet another variation was the long-running series of novels by Aaron Marc Stein writing as George Bagby, which began with *Murder at the Piano* (1935) and feature Inspector Schmidt, Chief of Manhattan's Homicide Squad, and his "Watson," Bagby, whom a publisher allegedly assigned to travel with Schmidt and then write a book about his career. A second Stein series likewise makes use of the Holmes–Watson formula: Manhattan District Attorney Jeremiah X. Gibson and his coworker and friendly chronicler, Mac, partners-in-crime in eighteen books published under the pseudonym Hampton Stone. The first of these, *The Corpse in the Corner Saloon,* appeared in 1948.

Another popular type of detecting duo is the husband-and-wife team. The earliest of significance was an amusing pair of detective-agency owners, Tommy and Tuppence Beresford, who debuted in Agatha Christie's *The Secret Adversary* (1922). Two other Tommy-and-Tuppence novels were published, *N or M?* (1941) and *Postern of Fate* (1973), and a collection of their short cases, *Partners in Crime,* appeared in 1929. The first notable American married duo was Dashiell Hammett's Nick and Nora Charles; despite the fact that they starred in only one novel, *The Thin Man* (1934), the film version of the book (starring William Powell and Myrna Loy) and its five sequels established a lasting niche for the pair in American popular culture.

Patrick Quentin's Peter and Iris Duluth, a New York theater couple who detect in six novels, were the next major husband-and-wife team; their career debuted with *A Puzzle for Fools* (1936). Frances and Richard Lockridge's Pam and Jerry North started their extremely successful detective partnership four years later, in *The Norths Meet Murder.* Kelley Roos's Jeff and Haila Troy also began detecting in 1940, in *Made Up to Kill;* and in 1941 Frances Crane created the first of her color-titled Pat and Jean Abbott mysteries, *The Turquoise Shop.* The Norths and Troys do most of their sleuthing in New York City and environs; the Duluths traveled wider afield, to California and Mexico, for example, while the Abbotts are a globe-trotting pair whose cases occur in such exotic locales as Tangier and Hong Kong, as well as in various U.S. and European cities. Typical of all four series is bright, witty dialogue, mostly bloodless murders, and breathless chases during which the wife is placed at considerable peril. Only the Duluths were allowed on occasion to depart from the light-and-breezy formula, with the realistic introduction of personal and marital problems.

Four major husband-and-wife series were established in the 1970s and 1980s. The first two are Victorian-era historicals. Elizabeth Peters's archeological mysteries, set in both England and Egypt, feature Amelia Peabody and Radcliffe Emerson, colleagues who first meet in *Crocodile on the Sandbank* (1975) and later marry. The archeological backgrounds in each title are authentic in every detail, for like her duo, Peters has a Ph.D. in the field. Anne Perry's novels set in late-nineteenth-century England, begun with *The Cater Street Hangman* (1979), carry on the detections of Charlotte Pitt and her husband, Inspector (later Superintendent) Thomas Pitt. The Pitts are an odd couple, she a gentlewoman whose family considers her marriage beneath her and he a no-nonsense, hardworking police officer. The background differences between the two characters allow Perry to explore class and social issues of the period.

The husband-and-wife formula is also fully adaptable to the modern milieu, as proven by Herbert Resnicow's Norma and Alexander Gold. Born in *The Gold Solution* (1983), they were the first Jewish detecting couple—a sort of married version of Nero Wolfe and Archie Goodwin in that the husband is sedentary as the result of a heart attack and the wife does his legwork. A second Jewish team, Faye Kellerman's Peter Decker and Rina Lazarus, were unmarried when they debuted in *The Ritual Bath* (1985) and took their vows only after sharing three cases. Their partnership, like that of Anne Perry's Charlotte and Thomas Pitt, is one of a professional detective—Decker is a member of the Los Angeles Police Department—working in tandem with an amateur sleuth. Kellerman's depiction of this sort of relationship, and of the world of Orthodox Judaism, is particularly good.

The partnership of a police professional and an amateur is not limited to husband and wife (or unmarried lovers), of course. The earliest example of this type of pairing is Anna Katharine Green's *That Affair Next Door* (1897), in which elderly Miss Amelia Butterworth is teamed with New York policeman Ebenezer Gryce. This combination of nosy spinster and methodical law officer served as a prototype for numerous other detecting duos, most prominently Stuart Palmer's Hildegarde Withers and Inspector Oscar Piper. *The Notorious Sophie Lang* (1925) by Frederick Irving Anderson brought together detective-story writer Oliver Armiston and Deputy Parr of the New York police, who are also featured in a collection of eight excellent short stories, *The Book of Murder* (1930). Other professional-and-amateur duos include Inspector Arnold of Scotland Yard and his friend, avocational criminologist Desmond Merrion, who star in more than sixty novels by Miles Burton (Cecil John Charles Street) published between 1931 *(The Secret of High Eldersham)* and 1960 *(Legacy of Death)*; and Hildegard

Dolson's Inspector McDougal of Wingate, Connecticut, and his landlady, Lucy Ramsdale, who always managed to end up in the middle of such investigations as *Please Omit Funeral* (1975).

The fact that actual police officers often work in pairs has led to several fictional duos whose cases tend to be much more realistic than those in which the police enlist the aid of an amateur. One of the best known professional partnerships is that of black Pasadena, California, plainclothesman Virgil Tibbs and white Carolina police chief Bill Gillespie; John Ball's 1965 novel, *In the Heat of the Night,* explores serious racial issues set against the background of a murder investigation in a small Southern town and was the inspiration for the 1967 film of the same title, starring Sidney Poitier and Rod Steiger, as well as the episodic television series featuring Carroll O'Connor and Howard Rollins. (In both film and TV versions Tibbs's homebase became Philadelphia, and the small Southern town was relocated to Mississippi and renamed from Wells to Sparta.) Carolyn Weston's three-book series featuring the Santa Monica Police Department's investigative team of Casey Kellog and Al Krug, introduced in *Poor, Poor Ophelia* (1972), are not nearly as well known as the television show that was based on the series — *The Streets of San Francisco,* starring Karl Malden and Michael Douglas — but they stand on their own as incisive studies of the relationship between partners separated by the generation gap. The same is true of Reginald Hill's excellent series about Yorkshire, England's Superintendent Andrew Dalziel and Sergeant Peter Pascoe, who were inaugurated in *A Clubbable Woman* (1970).

Peter Lovesey's novels featuring Sergeant Cribb and Constable Thackeray of Scotland Yard's Criminal Investigation Department, which began with *Wobble to Death* (1970), combine the procedural with the historical tale; each illuminate some aspect of Victorian England, such as the popular stage or marathon racing. James McClure created an unusual duo, the South African team of Lieutenant Tromp Kramer of the Trekkersburg Murder and Robbery Squad and his Bantu assistant, Detective Sergeant Mickey Zondi, in *The Steam Pig* (1971); the pair battle the specter of apartheid as well as criminal elements in six additional novels. *A Choice of Crimes* (1980) by Leslie Egan (a pseudonym of Elizabeth Linington) brings together yet another pair who would eventually marry: Vic Varallo and Delia Riordan of the Glendale, California, police force. The Varallo-Riordan books provide solid insight into what life is like for both a policewoman and two-officer family.

The most popular of the current professional teams is also a duo in which both partners are ethnic. Tony Hillerman began his fine series about the Navajo Tribal Police by focusing on a single, seasoned officer, Lieutenant Joe Leaphorn, in *The Blessing Way* (1970); in *People of Darkness* (1980), he introduced a second series character, Sergeant Jim Chee, who is much younger and less disillusioned than Leaphorn; and in the 1987 novel *Skinwalkers,* he brought the pair together with considerable success. The contrasts between the older man, who has lost his faith in the traditional Native American ways, and the younger one, studying to become a shaman, reveal the inner conflicts of a culture that has been damaged by encroachments from the outside and feels a desperate need to preserve its customs.

A similar study in contrasts is that of an earlier pairing of men of different ethnic and religious backgrounds, Roman Catholic priest Father Joseph Shanley and Jewish Detective-Sergeant Sammy Golden; Jack Webb's nine-novel series featuring this affecting duo commenced with *The Big Sin* (1952). A few years after the Shanley–Golden duo appeared, the first team of African-American detectives was created by mainstream black novelist Chester Himes in *For Love of Imabelle* (1957): tough and violent Harlem policemen Coffin Ed Johnson and Grave Digger Jones. Himes knew whereof he wrote, having lived in Harlem and having spent seven years in prison, yet he finally ended the series after a seventh title, *Blind Man with a Pistol* (1969), because, as he put it, "the violence shocks even me."

A much less hard-boiled collaboration is *Beyond the Grave* (1986), in which Marcia Muller and Bill Pronzini combined two of their individual series characters, contemporary Hispanic museum curator Elena Oliverez and 1890s San Francisco–based private investigator John Quincannon, in a unique blend of the modern and the historical mystery; the story bridges a nearly hundred-year span of time, with Oliverez in 1986 resolving a partially unsolved 1894 case of Quincannon's through a combination of the private detective's case reports and her own legwork and deduction. Barbara D'Amato's half Hispanic, half Italian Chicago policewoman, Susannah (Suze) Maria Figueroa, teams with black officer Norm Bennis in the 1996 novel of high-tech crime, *Killer.app*. The engaging pair, who first appeared in a series of short stories, are highly entertaining and provide readers with a realistic look at day-to-day urban police work.

Until recent years, gay and lesbian detectives have been few and far between in crime fiction. The first duo to include a homosexual was introduced in 1980's *Vermillion* by Nathan Aldyne, a joint pseudonym of Michael McDowell and Dennis Schuetz; in this and three subsequent color-coded titles, gay bartender Dan Valentine and his straight woman friend, Clarisse Lovelace, joined forces to solve mysteries set in Boston and on Cape Cod. In the late 1980s Ellen Dearmore (a pseudonym of Erlene Hubly) combined the lesbian mystery with the historical mystery in a pair of novelettes featuring Gertrude Stein and Alice B. Toklas as crime-solvers and peopled with numerous other historical figures. The author's sudden death tragically ended plans for additional Stein-Toklas mysteries.

The various types and combinations of wholly amateur duos are wide-ranging, husband-and-wife teams being just one of many. E. Phillips Oppenheim introduced one of the more unusual pairings in *A Pulpit in the Grill Room* (1938): Milan hotel maître d' Louis, who solves mysteries from his table in the grill room with the aid of retired army officer and journalist Lyson. In the same year, married collaborators G. D. H. and Margaret Cole published a collection of short stories, *Mrs. Warrender's Profession,* in which the mother of their series sleuth, James Warrender, outdetects her professional son. James Yaffe's delightful series of "Mom" stories—two novels and numerous short tales, the best of which were collected in 1997 under the title *My Mother, the Detective* —are built along the same lines as the Coles' Mrs. Warrender.

Aaron Marc Stein's *The Sun Is a Witness* (1940) introduced archeological sleuths Tim Mulligan and Elsie Mae Hunt, colleagues and platonic friends who apply their understanding of history and nuances of various cultures to resolve mysteries in such far-flung and well-depicted locales as Mexico, Greece, and Yugoslavia. George Baxt, known for his novels about gay New York police detective Pharoah Love, began a second series in 1967's *A Parade of Cockeyed Creatures,* this one starring eccentric lovers and amateur detectives Sylvia Plotkin and Max Van Larsen. John D. MacDonald's immensely popular Travis McGee often detected with a partner, his economist friend, Meyer; McGee, whose self-described profession of "salvage consultant" hides a darker side to his work, enlists Meyer's aid in several titles, notably *Darker Than Amber* (1966). Another well-regarded amateur team, journalist Maggie Rome and cantankerous New England newspaper editor C. B. Greenfield, was established by Lucille Kallen in her 1979 novel, *Introducing C. B. Greenfield.* Though frequently at odds, the pair is always gruffly affectionate, with Rome doing most of the legwork and Greenfield applying his intellect to the information she gathers in order to bring about a solution.

The private-eye story is a subgenre typified by heroes who are loners. Nevertheless, a surprising number of fictional private investigators have worked with others in their profession, as well as with amateurs and members of different professions—a tradition that extends back to the dime novels of the nineteenth century and the tandem exploits of such characters as Old Sleuth and Young Sleuth, and Nick Carter. Carter, who detected with his father and a variety of other partners, was the most popular of all the dime-novel sleuths; first introduced to the American public in 1886, his career lasted through several incarnations, the last of them as a James Bondian secret agent, well into the 1980s.

Dime-novel detectives were in effect superheroes, possessing vast amounts of arcane knowledge, abnormal physical abilities, and a talent for assuming almost any identity and disguise. Much more realistic were the detectives who populated the offspring of the dime novels, the pulp-paper magazines that flourished during the first half of the twentieth century. Such upper-echelon titles as *Black Mask, Dime Detective, Detective Fiction Weekly,* and *Street and Smith's Detective Story* were training grounds for some of the more important names in the crime-fiction genre, among them Dashiell Hammett, Raymond Chandler, Erle Stanley Gardner, Cornell Woolrich, and Fredric Brown. The hard-edged stories that were the pulps' staple fare displayed a wide variety of series char-

9

acters, including such private-eye duos as Roger Torrey's Marge Chalmers and Pat McCarthy; Merle Constiner's The Dean and his "Watson," Ben Mathews; and D. L. Champion's Rex Sackler and Joey Graham. (Non-private-eye duos were also a mainstay of the pulps. Two of the best known are Erle Stanley Gardner's Ed Jenkins, the Phantom Crook, who is joined in many *Black Mask* stories by his wife, Helen Chadwick; and Frederick Nebel's Police Captain Steve McBride and alcoholic reporter Kennedy of the *Free Press,* who were likewise showcased in a long-running *Black Mask* series.)

The most famous private detective team is certainly Rex Stout's Nero Wolfe and Archie Goodwin. Almost as renowned in their day were Bertha Cool and Donald Lam, an unlikely pair of Los Angeles operatives; first seen in *The Bigger They Come* (1939), they were featured in another thirty novels over an equal number of years. Originally an underpaid assistant and later Bertha's partner, Lam does most of the active detecting because, we're told, private investigation is an unseemly profession for a woman. In fact, Bertha is a mountain of a woman who loves to watch Donald work and can seldom be moved by anything other than a large fee. Lam, on the other hand, is a former lawyer who knows "just how far he can stick his neck out . . . a romantic at heart, but hard as a diamond and a man who never forgets a favor or an injury."

Geoffrey Homes (Daniel Mainwaring) launched the careers of chubby, unconventional Humphrey Campbell and his fat, lazy, and corrupt partner, Oscar Morgan, in *Then There Were Three* (1938) and brought them back in four more fast, furious, and witty mysteries set primarily in central California. Otis Beagle and Joe Peel, "two of the most upright and fearless heels ever to run a detective agency," were the invention of former pulp writer Frank Gruber; the southern California–based partners starred in two novels, *Beagle Scented Murder* (1946) and *The Lonesome Badger* (1954). (Gruber's primary series also utilized a duo, Johnny Fletcher and his muscular stooge, Sam Cragg, itinerant book salesmen and amateur sleuths in *The French Key,* 1940, and a dozen subsequent novels.) Fredric Brown's Ed Hunter and his uncle, Am Hunter, joined forces in *The Fabulous Clipjoint* (1947) to investigate the murder of Ed's father, and worked so well together that they later opened a detective agency; their exploits are chronicled in a total of seven novels and one short story. New York City detective agency owners Schuyler Cole and Luke Speare, the protagonists of *The Deadly Miss Ashley* (1950) and five other novels by Frederick C. Davis, are an appealing pair whose cases' solutions, like those of the Hunters, depend far more on legwork and deduction than on the violent tactics utilized by so many fictional private eyes.

Examples of investigators joining forces with police officers, lawyers, and other professional and nonprofessional individuals are more numerous. Erle Stanley Gardner's Paul Drake detected with attorney Perry Mason in many novels, such as *The Case of the Moth-Eaten Mink* (1952), as well as in the original *Perry Mason* television show

(1957–1966) starring Raymond Burr, William Hopper, and Barbara Hale. Thomas B. Dewey's series of paperback originals featuring Los Angeles investigator Pete Schofield and his sultry wife, Jeannie, is one of the few examples of a husband-and-wife duo in which one of the team is a private eye; the series began with *Go to Sleep, Jeannie* (1959) and continued through seven additional novels. Marvin Kaye's series about publicist Hilary Quayle and private operative Gene (a man so colorless that Kaye did not see fit to give him a last name) is a variation on the theme in that Hilary would rather be a private detective, but feels she would have difficulty succeeding because of her gender. In the first of their adventures, *A Lively Game of Death* (1972), she thus co-opts Gene to provide the proper legal umbrella under which she can operate. A similar rationale and ploy were used as the basis for the 1980s television series *Remington Steele*, starring Stephanie Zimbalist and Pierce Brosnan. A 1978 novel by Bill Pronzini and Collin Wilcox, *Twospot*, teamed the "Nameless Detective" and Lieutenant Frank Hastings of the San Francisco Police Department. Working together, the two professionals solve a complex series of crimes and narrowly avert a political assassination.

Easily the most offbeat pairing in this category is that of Norbert Davis's Doan and Carstairs, whose unique talents are displayed in three novels—*The Mouse in the Mountain* (1943), *Sally's in the Alley* (1943), and *Oh Murderer Mine!* (1946)—and two long pulp novelettes. Doan is a private eye who looks fat but isn't, and who, despite a great fondness for alcohol, has never suffered a hangover; Carstairs is an aloof, fawn-colored Great Dane whom Doan won in a crap game and who considers Doan a low, uncouth person, not at all the sort *he* would have chosen for a master. Their adventures are both hard-boiled and funny.

Fictional espionage agents, like private eyes, tend to be loners, but there are a number of duos of this type as well. The earliest are two young men from the British Foreign Office, Carruthers and Davies, who stumble across German plans to invade England in Erskine Childers' highly acclaimed novel *The Riddle of the Sands* (1903). John Buchan's British intelligence agent, Richard Hannay, is aided by the American agent Blenkiron in thwarting the Kaiser in *Greenmantle* (1916). Two operatives of an unnamed American intelligence organization, Harrigan and Hoeffler, help preserve national security in a series of tales by Patrick O'Malley (a pseudonym of Frank O'Rourke); the first of these, *The Affair of the Red Mosaic*, appeared in 1961.

Ross Thomas's *The Cold War Swap* (1966) teamed undercover agent McCorkle with an able amateur, Padillo; he brought them back for three encores, all set in Washington, D.C. Michael Gilbert's team of deadly British counterintelligence agents, Mr. Calder and Mr. Behrens, appears in numerous short stories. In perhaps the most unusual twist on spy duo, Dorothy Dunnett's Johnson Johnson, skipper of the yacht *Dolly*, teams with different woman (or "bird") in each of six titles set in such locales as Scotland, Spain, and the Bahamas; the first of these, *Dolly and the Singing Bird* (U.S. title· *The Photogenic Soprano*), was published in 1968. All titles in the series originally appeared in England under the author's real name, Dorothy Halliday.

Yet another variation on the duo theme is the teaming of two authors and their individual series characters on common cases. Stuart Palmer's New York–based spinster schoolteacher, Hildegarde Withers, and Craig Rice's hard-drinking Chicago lawyer, John J. Malone, joined forces in six novelettes collected in *People vs. Withers and Malone* (1963). Richard S. Prather and Stephen Marlowe united their best-selling softcover private eyes, Shell Scott and Chester Drum, in the wild and woolly *Double in Trouble* (1959). In the only prominent two-author, two-gender pairing to date, Marcia Muller's Sharon McCone and Bill Pronzini's "Nameless Detective" shared a case in *Double* (1984) that takes place not in San Francisco, where both sleuths normally operate, but at a private-eye convention in San Diego.

Finally, there are the pairings of two different series characters created by one author. A few examples among many: Carter Brown's sheriff's investigator Al Wheeler and his flashy female private eye, Mavis Seidlitz, in *Lament for a Lousy Lover* (1960); Michael Innes' John Appleby of Scotland Yard and portrait artist and amateur sleuth Charles Honeybath, in *Appleby and Honeybath* (1983); and the aforementioned joining of Tony Hillerman's Navajo Tribal Policemen, Joe Leaphorn and Jim Chee.

Detecting duos have also been prominently featured in other forms of popular culture: films, radio and television shows, even comic books and comic strips. Such superhero teams as Superman (Clark Kent) and Lois Lane, Batman and Robin the Boy Wonder, The Green Hornet and his faithful valet, Kato, and The Shadow (Lamont Cranston) and Margo Lane certainly qualify. As do Sherlock Holmes and Dr. Watson as portrayed by Basil Rathbone and Nigel Bruce in numerous films; and such other cinematic pairs as Nick and Nora Charles, Charlie Chan and his Number One (or Number Two or Number Three) son, Hildegarde Withers and Oscar Piper, and Agatha Christie's Miss Marple and her friend Jimmy in the amusing trio of novel adaptations starring Margaret Rutherford (e.g., *Murder at the Gallop,* 1963). In addition, such celluloid sleuths as The Saint, The Falcon, Torchy Blane, Ellery Queen, The Crime Doctor, and Boston Blackie had recurring sidekicks and foils who both helped and hindered their investigations.

Among the more prominent radio series duos were George Harmon Coxe's Flashgun Casey and his girlfriend, Annie Williams *(Casey, Crime Photographer)*; Havana charter boat owner Slate Shannon and his lady love, Sailor Duval (*Bold Venture,* starring Humphrey Bogart and Lauren Bacall); Mr. Keen and his intelligence-challenged sidekick, Mike Clancy *(Mr. Keen, Tracer of Lost Persons)*; and Jack, Doc, and Reggie of the A-1 Detective Agency, technically a trio, though Jack and Doc did most of the investigating *(I Love a Mystery)*. The list of television duos is even longer. In the 1950 there were *Mr. and Mrs. North,* starring Richard Denning and Barbara Britton, an

12

Dragnet, in which Jack Webb's Sergeant Joe Friday of the Los Angeles Police Department worked with such partners as Frank Smith (Ben Alexander) and Bill Gannon (Harry Morgan). In the 1960s there were Kelly Robinson (Robert Culp) and Alexander Scott (Bill Cosby), the globe-trotting espionage agents in *I Spy*; Napoleon Solo (Robert Vaughan) and Illya Kuryakin (David McCallum), who battled the international crime syndicate THRUSH in *The Man from U.N.C.L.E.*; and private eye Joe Mannix (Mike Connors) and his African-American secretary, Peggy Fair (Gail Fisher), in *Mannix*. In the 1970s and 1980s there were San Francisco police commissioner Stuart McMillan (Rock Hudson) and his wife Sally (Susan St. James) in *McMillan and Wife*; San Francisco Police Lieutenant Mike Stone (Karl Malden) and Inspector Steve Keller (Michael Douglas) in *The Streets of San Francisco*; southern California–based amateur crime-solvers Jonathan and Jennifer Hart (Robert Wagner and Stephanie Powers) in *Hart to Hart*; and New York police officers Christine Cagney (Sharon Gless) and Mary Beth Lacey (Tyne Daly) in *Cagney & Lacey*.

The stories gathered in these pages cover most of the broad spectrum of detective duos, both in historical development and in types of partnerships. Edgar Allan Poe's "The Purloined Letter" is one of the first detective stories and also features the first example of a duo, that of the master detective and his chronicler. The selections by Sir Arthur Conan Doyle (Sherlock Holmes and Dr. Watson), R. Austin Freeman (Dr. John Thorndyke and Christopher Jervis), and Hulbert Footner (Madame Rosika Storey and Bella) are also examples of this type. Husband-and-wife teams are well represented by Frances and Richard Lockridge's Mr. and Mrs. North, Kelley Roos's Jeff and Haila Troy, and Patrick Quentin's Peter and Iris Duluth, as are pairs of male and female private investigators by P. G. Wodehouse's Paul Snyder and Elliot Oakes, Rex Stout's Nero Wolfe and Archie Goodwin, Fredric Brown's Ed and Am Hunter, and Marcia Muller's Sharon McCone and Rae Kelleher. And Bill Pronzini's Sabina Carpenter and John Quincannon story offers a look at both a two-gender and an 1890s private-eye duo. Barbara D'Amato's Suze Figueroa and Norm Bennis are police officers as well as ethnic detectives. Another ethnic pairing is Jack Webb's Father Joseph Shanley and Detective-Sergeant Sammy Golden. Agatha Christie's Mr. Satterthwaite and the mysterious Harley Quin may be classified as amateur sleuths, and Julie Smith's Skip Langdon and Steve Steinman are a police officer–amateur duo. There are forensic pathologists (Lawrence G. Blochman's Dr. Daniel Coffee and Dr. Motilal Mookerji, another ethnic character), Interpol agents (Edward D. Hoch's Sebastian Blue and Laura Charme), spies (Michael Gilbert's Mr. Calder and Mr. Behrens), and actual historical figures (Ellen Dearmore's Gertrude Stein and Alice B. Toklas). Also represented is the collaboration between two writers and their individual series characters (Stuart Palmer's Hildegarde Withers and Craig Rice's John J. Malone), and, just for fun, a detective association between an animal and a human (Lilian Jackson Braun's Siamese cat Phut Phat and one of its owners, known as Two).

These stories also cover a wide range of detective fiction types: pure deduction, impossible crime, cozy, dark comedy, espionage, procedural, historical. Their locales are likewise varied: England, Europe, Antarctica, and such U.S. settings as New York, Chicago, San Francisco, Los Angeles, and a pair of fast-moving trains—one heading from Chicago to New York and the other across California's Mojave Desert a hundred years ago.

Readers will note the absence of a story featuring any African American detective other than Barbara D'Amato's Norm Bennis. This is because no suitable work exists. Chester Himes' Harlem police detectives Coffin Ed Johnson and Grave Digger Jones appear only in novels, as do Ed Lacy's Touissant Moore and other individuals who detect alone; and while there are short stories featuring such notable black detectives as Walter Mosley's Easy Rawlins and Gar Anthony Haywood's Aaron Gunner, these characters also do not work with partners. Hawk, a featured player in Robert B. Parker's series of novels about Boston private eye Spenser, does not function in the capacity of a detective, or figure in the one Spenser short story.

Similarly, Tony Hillerman's Joe Leaphorn and Jim Chee, among other ethnic detectives, appear together in novels but no shorter work. The same is true of such famous nonethnic duos cited in this introduction as Dashiell Hammett's Nick and Nora Charles, Erle Stanley Gardner's Perry Mason and Paul Drake, A. A. Fair's Bertha Cool and Donald Lam, Ross Thomas's McCorkle and Padillo, Anne Perry's Charlotte and Thomas Pitt, and Elizabeth Peters's Amelia Peabody and Radcliffe Emerson. Nor are there any short stories featuring a gay male duo (or a gay male and a heterosexual partner), nor any duo stories by such best-selling crime-fiction writers as Patricia D. Cornwell, Sue Grafton, John Grisham, Elmore Leonard, and Sara Paretsky.

There are, of course, many detective partnerships past and present not mentioned in the preceding pages. Space limitations precluded the listing of every established series and individual novel, and at the present rate with which detective series are being inaugurated in the booming mystery fiction market, it is quite probable that more than one new detective duo will have been launched between the time these words are being written and their publication. The possible variations on the types of partnership sleuths, as we've endeavored to point out, are dependent only upon an author's—or team of authors'—ingenuity, and therefore are virtually infinite.

Marcia Muller   Bill Pronzini

Edgar Allan Poe

(1809-1849)

Edgar Allan Poe was the founding father of the mystery and detective story as we know it today. In just five famous tales, he anticipated almost every conceivable type of crime-fiction plot: the sensational thriller and the locked-room "miracle problem" in "The Murders in the Rue Morgue" (1841); the analytic exercise and the fictional extrapolation of a real-life crime in "The Mystery of Marie Roget" (1842); the puzzle story in general and the code and cipher tale in particular in "The Gold Bug" (1843); the secret-agent adventure and the classic tale of ratiocination (a word Poe himself invented) in "The Purloined Letter" (1844); and the solving of a small-town murder mystery by the narrator in "'Thou Art the Man'" (1844).

Poe also originated the first important series sleuth, C. Auguste Dupin —a character very much modeled on François-Eugène Vidocq, the reformed thief and forger who became the first chief of the Surete in 1811 and who later wrote a highly glamorized autobiography. By choosing to provide Dupin with an unnamed friend and biographer who narrates the accounts of his cases, after the fashion of Dr. Samuel Johnson's Boswell, Poe by extension invented the first detective duo. The use of this Boswellian device in the Dupin stories surely influenced Sir Arthur Conan Doyle in his creation of Sherlock Holmes and Dr. Watson nearly half a century later.

The life of Edgar Allan Poe has been so distorted by academics and filmmakers that it is difficult to obtain a true sense of the man. Until recently he was widely believed to have been a tortured genius suffering from dementia and beset by alcohol and drug problems; while there is still some doubt as to the state of his mental health, extensive research by modern scholars has determined that his alcohol and drug use was grossly exaggerated by a rival who sought to discredit him after his death, and that in fact Poe died not of substance abuse but of rabies. Of his literary worth there can be little dispute. The poet W. H. Auden once lamented the fact that in his own country, "Poe is taught as a respectable rival to the pulps," as a consequence of the subject matter—murder, madness, supernatural horror —of much of his fiction and poetry. In fact, his voice and vision were serious, unique, enlightening, and quintessentially American—a true original in the keenest literary sense of the term.

THE PURLOINED LETTER

C. AUGUSTE DUPIN AND AN UNNAMED NARRATOR
PARIS, FRANCE
1844

Nil sapientiæ odiosius acumine nimio.

—*Seneca*

At Paris, just after dark one gusty evening in the autumn of 18——, I was enjoying the twofold luxury of meditation and a meerschaum, in company with my friend, C. Auguste Dupin, in his little back library, or book-closet, *au troisiéme*, No. 33 *Rue Dunôt, Faubourg St. Germain*. For one hour at least we had maintained a profound silence; while each, to any casual observer, might have seemed intently and exclusively occupied with the curling eddies of smoke that oppressed the atmosphere of the chamber. For myself, however, I was mentally discussing certain topics which had formed matter for conversation between us at an earlier period of the evening; I mean the affair of the Rue Morgue, and the mystery attending the murder of Marie Rogêt. I looked upon it, therefore, as something of a coincidence, when the door of our apartment was thrown open and admitted our old acquaintance, Monsieur G——, the Prefect of the Parisian police.

We gave him a hearty welcome; for there was nearly half as much of the entertaining as of the contemptible about the man, and we had not seen him for several years. We had been sitting in the dark, and Dupin now arose for the purpose of lighting a lamp, but sat down again, without doing so, upon G.'s saying that he had called to consult us, or rather to ask the opinion of my friend, about some official business which had occasioned a great deal of trouble.

"If it is any point requiring reflection," observed Dupin, as he forbore to enkindle the wick, "we shall examine it to better purpose in the dark."

"That is another of your odd notions," said the Prefect, who had the fashion of calling everything "odd" that was beyond his comprehension, and thus lived amid an absolute legion of "oddities."

"Very true," said Dupin, as he supplied his visitor with a pipe, and rolled toward him a comfortable chair.

"And what is the difficulty now?" I asked. "Nothing more in the assassination way I hope?"

"Oh, no; nothing of that nature. The fact is, the business is *very* simple indeed, and I make no doubt that we can manage it sufficiently well ourselves; but then I thought Dupin would like to hear the details of it, because it is so excessively *odd.*"

"Simple and odd," said Dupin.

"Why, yes; and not exactly that either. The fact is, we have all been a good deal puzzled because the affair *is* so simple, and yet baffles us altogether."

"Perhaps it is the very simplicity of the thing which puts you at fault," said my friend.

"What nonsense you *do* talk!" replied the Prefect, laughing heartily.

"Perhaps the mystery is a little *too* plain," said Dupin.

"Oh, good heavens! who ever heard of such an idea?"

"A little *too* self-evident."

"Ha! ha! ha!—ha! ha! ha!—ho! ho! ho!" roared our visitor, profoundly amused, "oh, Dupin, you will be the death of me yet!"

"And what, after all, *is* the matter on hand?" I asked.

"Why, I will tell you," replied the Prefect, as he gave a long, steady, and contemplative puff, and settled himself in his chair. "I will tell you in a few words; but, before I begin, let me caution you that this is an affair demanding the greatest secrecy, and that I should most probably lose the position I now hold, were it known that I confided it to any one."

"Proceed," said I.

"Or not," said Dupin.

"Well, then; I have received personal information, from a very high quarter, that a certain document of the last importance has been purloined from the royal apartments. The individual who purloined it is known; this beyond a doubt; he was seen to take it. It is known, also, that it still remains in his possession."

"How is this known?" asked Dupin.

"It is clearly inferred," replied the Prefect, "from the nature of the document, and from the non-appearance of certain results which would at once arise from its passing *out* of the robber's possession—that is to say, from his employing it as he must design in the end to employ it."

"Be a little more explicit," I said.

"Well, I may venture so far as to say that the paper gives its holder a certain power in a certain quarter where such power is immensely valuable." The Prefect was fond of the cant of diplomacy.

"Still I do not quite understand," said Dupin.

"No? Well; the disclosure of the document to a third person, who shall be nameless, would bring in question the honor of a personage of most exalted station; and this fact gives the holder of the document an ascendancy over the illustrious personage whose honor and peace are so jeopardized."

"But this ascendancy," I interposed, "would depend upon the robber's knowledge of the loser's knowledge of the robber. Who would dare——"

"The thief," said G., "is the Minister D——, who dares all things, those unbecoming as well as those becoming a man. The method of the theft was not less ingenious than bold. The document in question—a letter, to be frank—had been received by the personage robbed while alone in the royal *boudoir*. During its perusal she was suddenly interrupted by the entrance of the other exalted personage from whom especially it was her wish to conceal it. After a hurried and vain endeavor to thrust it in a drawer, she was forced to place it, open as it was, upon a table. The address, however, was uppermost, and the contents thus unexposed, the letter escaped notice. At this junction enters the Minister D——. His lynx eye immediately perceives the paper, recognizes the handwriting of the address, observes the confusion of the personage addressed, and fathoms her secret. After some business transactions, hurried through in his ordinary manner, he produces a letter somewhat similar to the one in question, opens it, pretends to read it, and then places it in close juxtaposition to the other. Again he converses, for some fifteen minutes, upon the public affairs. At length, in taking leave, he takes also from the table the letter to which he had no claim. Its rightful owner saw, but, of course, dared not call attention to the act, in the presence of the third personage who stood at her elbow. The minister decamped; leaving his own letter—one of no importance—on the table."

"Here, then," said Dupin to me, "you have precisely what you demand to make the ascendancy complete—the robber's knowledge of the loser's knowledge of the robber."

"Yes," replied the Prefect; "and the power thus attained has, for some months past, been wielded, for political purposes, to a very dangerous extent. The personage robbed is more thoroughly convinced, every day, of the necessity of reclaiming her letter. But this, of course, cannot be done openly. In fine, driven to despair, she has committed the matter to me."

"Than whom," said Dupin, amid a perfect whirlwind of smoke, "no more sagacious agent could, I suppose, be desired, or even imagined."

"You flatter me," replied the Prefect; "but it is possible that some such opinion may have been entertained."

"It is clear," said I, "as you observe, that the letter is still in the possession of the minister; since it is this possession, and not any employment of the letter, which bestows the power. With the employment the power departs."

"True," said G.; "and upon this conviction I proceeded. My first care was to make thorough search of the minister's hotel; and here my chief embarrassment lay in the necessity of searching without his knowledge. Beyond all things, I have been warned of the danger which would result from giving him reason to suspect our design."

"But," said I, "you are quite *au fait* in these investigations. The Parisian police have done this thing often before."

"Oh, yes; and for this reason I did not despair. The habits of the minister gave me, too, a great advantage. He is frequently absent from home all night. His servants are by no means numerous. They sleep at a distance from their master's apartment, and, being chiefly Neapolitans, are readily made drunk. I have keys, as you know, with which I can open any chamber or cabinet in Paris. For three months a night has not passed, during the greater part of which I have not been engaged, personally, in ransacking the D—— Hotel. My honor is interested, and, to mention a great secret, the reward is enormous. So I did not abandon the search until I had become fully satisfied that the thief is a more astute man than myself. I fancy that I have investigated every nook and corner of the premises in which it is possible that the paper can be concealed."

"But is it not possible," I suggested, "that although the letter may be in possession of the minister, as it unquestionably is, he may have concealed it elsewhere than upon his own premises?"

"This is barely possible," said Dupin. "The present peculiar condition of affairs at court, and especially of those intrigues in which D—— is known to be involved, would render the instant availability of the document—its susceptibility of being produced at a moment's notice—a point of nearly equal importance with its possession."

"Its susceptibility of being produced?" said I.

"That is to say, of being *destroyed*," said Dupin.

"True," I observed; "the paper is clearly then upon the premises. As for its being upon the person of the minister, we may consider that as out of the question."

"Entirely," said the Prefect. "He has been twice waylaid, as if by footpads, and his person rigidly searched under my own inspection."

"You might have spared yourself this trouble," said Dupin. "D——, I presume, is not altogether a fool, and, if not, must have anticipated these waylayings, as a matter of course."

"Not *altogether* a fool," said G., "but then he is a poet, which I take to be only one remove from a fool."

"True," said Dupin, after a long and thoughtful whiff from his meerschaum, "although I have been guilty of certain doggerel myself."

"Suppose you detail," said I, "the particulars of your search."

"Why, the fact is, we took our time, and we searched *everywhere*. I have had long experience in these affairs. I took the entire building, room by room;

devoting the nights of a whole week to each. We examined, first, the furniture of each apartment. We opened every possible drawer; and I presume you know that, to a properly trained police-agent, such a thing as a *secret* drawer is impossible. Any man is a dolt who permits a 'secret' drawer to escape him in a search of this kind. The thing is *so* plain. There is a certain amount of bulk — of space — to be accounted for in every cabinet. Then we have accurate rules. The fiftieth part of a line could not escape us. After the cabinets we took the chairs. The cushions we probed with the fine long needles you have seen me employ. From the tables we removed the tops."

"Why so?"

"Sometimes the top of a table, or other similarly arranged piece of furniture, is removed by the person wishing to conceal an article; then the leg is excavated, the article deposited within the cavity, and the top replaced. The bottoms and tops of bedposts are employed in the same way."

"But could not the cavity be detected by sounding?" I asked.

"By no means, if, when the article is deposited, a sufficient wadding of cotton be placed around it. Besides, in our case, we were obliged to proceed without noise."

"But you could not have removed — you could not have taken to pieces *all* articles of furniture in which it would have been possible to make a deposit in the manner you mention. A letter may be compressed into a thin spiral roll, not differing much in shape or bulk from a large knitting-needle, and in this form it might be inserted into the rung of a chair, for example. You did not take to pieces all the chairs?"

"Certainly not; but we did better — we examined the rungs of every chair in the hotel, and, indeed, the jointings of every description of furniture, by the aid of a most powerful microscope. Had there been any traces of recent disturbance we should not have failed to detect it instantly. A single grain of gimlet-dust, for example, would have been as obvious as an apple. Any disorder in the gluing — any unusual gaping in the joints — would have sufficed to insure detection."

"I presume you looked to the mirrors, between the boards and the plates, and you probed the beds and the bedclothes, as well as the curtains and carpets."

"That of course; and when we had absolutely completed every particle of the furniture in this way, then we examined the house itself. We divided its entire surface into compartments, which we numbered, so that none might be missed; then we scrutinized each individual square inch throughout the premises, including the two houses immediately adjoining, with the microscope, as before."

"The two houses adjoining!" I exclaimed; "you must have had a great deal of trouble."

"We had; but the reward offered is prodigious."

"You include the *grounds* about the houses?"

"All the grounds are paved with brick. They gave us comparatively little trouble. We examined the moss between the bricks, and found it undisturbed."

"You looked among D——'s papers, of course, and into the books of the library?"

"Certainly; we opened every package and parcel; we not only opened every book, but we turned over every leaf in each volume, not contenting ourselves with a mere shake, according to the fashion of some of our police officers. We also measured the thickness of every book-*cover*, with the most accurate admeasurement, and applied to each the most jealous scrutiny of the microscope. Had any of the bindings been recently meddled with, it would have been utterly impossible that the fact should have escaped observation. Some five or six volumes, just from the hands of the binder, we carefully probed, longitudinally, with the needles."

"You explored the floors beneath the carpets?"

"Beyond doubt. We removed every carpet, and examined the boards with the microscope."

"And the paper on the walls?"

"Yes."

"You looked into the cellars?"

"We did."

"Then," I said, "you have been making a miscalculation, and the letter is *not* upon the premises, as you suppose."

"I fear you are right there," said the Prefect. "And now, Dupin, what would you advise me to do?"

"To make a thorough research of the premises."

"That is absolutely needless," replied G——. "I am not more sure that I breathe than I am that the letter is not at the hotel."

"I have no better advice to give you," said Dupin. "You have, of course, an accurate description of the letter?"

"Oh, yes!"—And here the Prefect, producing a memorandum-book, proceeded to read aloud a minute account of the internal, and especially of the external, appearance of the missing document. Soon after finishing the perusal of this description, he took his departure, more entirely depressed in spirits than I had ever known the good gentleman before.

In about a month afterward he paid us another visit, and found us occupied very nearly as before. He took a pipe and a chair and entered into some ordinary conversation. At length I said:

"Well, but G., what of the purloined letter? I presume you have at last made up your mind that there is no such thing as overreaching the Minister?"

"Confound him, say I—yes; I made the re-examination, however, as Dupin suggested—but it was all labor lost, as I knew it would be."

"How much was the reward offered, did you say?" asked Dupin.

"Why, a very great deal—a *very* liberal reward—I don't like to say how much, precisely; but one thing I *will* say, that I wouldn't mind giving my individual check for fifty thousand francs to any one who could obtain me that letter. The fact is, it is becoming of more and more importance every day; and the reward has been lately doubled. If it were trebled, however, I could do no more than I have done."

"Why, yes," said Dupin, drawlingly, between the whiffs of his meerschaum, "I really—think, G., you have not exerted yourself—to the utmost in this matter. You might—do a little more, I think, eh?"

"How?—in what way?"

"Why—puff, puff—you might—puff, puff—employ counsel in the matter, eh?—puff, puff, puff. Do you remember the story they tell of Abernethy?"

"No; hang Abernethy!"

"To be sure! hang him and be welcome. But, once upon a time, a certain rich miser conceived the design of sponging upon this Abernethy for a medical opinion. Getting up, for this purpose, an ordinary conversation in a private company, he insinuated his case to the physician, as that of an imaginary individual.

"'We will suppose,' said the miser, 'that his symptoms are such and such; now, doctor, what would *you* have directed him to take?'

"'Take!' said Abernethy, 'why, take *advice*, to be sure.'"

"But," said the Prefect, a little discomposed, "I *am perfectly* willing to take advice, and to pay for it. I would *really* give fifty thousand francs to any one who would aid me in the matter."

"In that case," replied Dupin, opening a drawer, and producing a check-book, "you may as well fill me up a check for the amount mentioned. When you have signed it, I will hand you the letter."

I was astounded. The Prefect appeared absolutely thunder-stricken. For some minutes he remained speechless and motionless, looking incredulously at my friend with open mouth, and eyes that seemed starting from their sockets; then apparently recovering himself in some measure, he seized a pen, and, after several pauses and vacant stares, finally filled up and signed a check for fifty thousand francs, and handed it across the table to Dupin. The latter examined it carefully and deposited it in his pocketbook; then, unlocking an *escritoire*, took thence a letter and gave it to the Prefect. This functionary grasped it in a perfect agony of joy, opened it with a trembling hand, cast a rapid glance at its contents, and then, scrambling and struggling to the door, rushed at length unceremoniously from the room and from the house, without having uttered a syllable since Dupin had requested him to fill up the check.

When he had gone, my friend entered into some explanations.

"The Parisian police," he said, "are exceedingly able in their way. They are persevering, ingenious, cunning, and thoroughly versed in the knowledge which their duties seem chiefly to demand. Thus, when G—— detailed to us his mode of searching the premises at the Hotel D——, I felt entire confidence in his having made a satisfactory investigation—so far as his labors extended."

"So far as his labors extended?" said I.

"Yes," said Dupin. "The measures adopted were not only the best of their kind, but carried out to absolute perfection. Had the letter been deposited within the range of their search, these fellows would, beyond a question, have found it."

I merely laughed—but he seemed quite serious in all that he said.

"The measures, then," he continued, "were good in their kind, and well executed; their defect lay in their being inapplicable to the case and to the man. A certain set of highly ingenious resources are, with the Prefect, a sort of Procrustean bed, to which he forcibly adapts his designs. But he perpetually errs by being too deep or too shallow for the matter in hand; and many a school-boy is a better reasoner than he. I knew one about eight years of age, whose success at guessing in the game of 'even and odd' attracted universal admiration. This game is simple, and is played with marbles. One player holds in his hand a number of these toys, and demands of another whether that number is even or odd. If the guess is right, the guesser wins one; if wrong, he loses one. The boy to whom I allude won all the marbles of the school. Of course he had some principle of guessing; and this lay in mere observation and admeasurement of the astuteness of his opponents. For example, an arrant simpleton is his opponent, and, holding up his closed hand, asks, 'Are they even or odd?' Our school-boy replies, 'Odd,' and loses; but upon the second trial he wins, for he then says to himself: 'The simpleton had them even upon the first trial, and his amount of cunning is just sufficient to make him have them odd upon the second; I will therefore guess odd';—he guesses odd, and wins. Now, with a simpleton a degree above the first, he would have reasoned thus: 'This fellow finds that in the first instance I guessed odd, and, in the second, he will propose to himself, upon the first impulse, a simple variation from even to odd, as did the first simpleton; but then a second thought will suggest that this is too simple a variation, and finally he will decide upon putting it even as before. I will therefore guess even';—he guesses even, and wins. Now this mode of reasoning in the school-boy, whom his fellows termed 'lucky,'—what, in its last analysis, is it?"

"It is merely," I said, "an identification of the reasoner's intellect with that of his opponent."

"It is," said Dupin; "and, upon inquiring of the boy by what means he effected the *thorough* identification in which his success consisted, I received answer as follows: 'When I wish to find out how wise, or how stupid, or how good, or how wicked is any one, or what are his thoughts at the moment, I fashion the expression of my face, as accurately as possible, in accordance with the expression of his, and then wait to see what thoughts or sentiments arise in my mind or heart, as if to match or correspond with the expression.' This response of the school-boy lies at the bottom of all the spurious profundity which has been attributed to Rochefoucauld, to La Bougive, to Machiavelli, and to Campanella."

"And the identification," I said, "of the reasoner's intellect with that of his opponent, depends, if I understand you aright, upon the accuracy with which the opponent's intellect is admeasured."

"For its practical value it depends upon this," replied Dupin; "and the Prefect and his cohort fail so frequently, first, by default of this identification, and, secondly, by ill-admeasurement, or rather through non-admeasurement, of the intellect with which they are engaged. They consider only their *own* ideas of ingenuity; and, in searching for any thing hidden, advert only to the modes in which *they* would have hidden it. They are right in this much—that their own ingenuity is a faithful representative of that of *the mass*; but when the cunning of the individual felon is diverse in character from their own, the felon foils them, of course. This always happens when it is above their own, and very usually when it is below. They have no variation of principle in their investigations; at best, when urged by some unusual emergency—by some extraordinary reward—they extend or exaggerate their old modes of *practice*, without touching their principles. What, for example, in this case of D———, has been done to vary the principle of action? What is all this boring, and probing, and sounding, and scrutinizing with the microscope, and dividing the surface of the building into registered square inches—what is it all but an exaggeration *of the application* of the one principle or set of principles of search, which are based upon the one set of notions regarding human ingenuity, to which the Prefect, in the long routine of his duty, has been accustomed? Do you not see he has taken it for granted that *all* men proceed to conceal a letter, not exactly in a gimlet-hole bored in a chair-leg, but, at least, in *some* out-of-the-way hole or corner suggested by the same tenor of thought which would urge a man to secrete a letter in a gimlet-hole bored in a chair-leg? And do you not see also, that such *recherchés* nooks for concealment are adapted only for ordinary occasions, and would be adopted only by ordinary intellects; for, in all cases of concealment, a disposal of an article concealed24 25

—a disposal of it in this *recherché* manner,—is, in the very first instance, presumable and presumed; and thus its discovery depends, not at all upon the acumen but altogether upon the mere care, patience, and determination of the seekers; and where the case is of importance—or, what amounts to the same thing in the political eyes, when the reward is of magnitude,—the qualities in question have *never* been known to fail. You will now understand what I meant in suggesting that, had the purloined letter been hidden anywhere within the limits of the Prefect's examination—in other words, had the principle of its concealment been comprehended within the principles of the Prefect—its discovery would have been a matter altogether beyond question. This functionary, however, has been thoroughly mystified; and the remote source of his defeat lies in the supposition that the Minister is a fool, because he has acquired renown as a poet. All fools are poets; this the Prefect *feels*; and he is merely guilty of a *non distributio medii* in thence inferring that all poets are fools."

"But is this really the poet?" I asked. "There are two brothers, I know; and both have attained reputation in letters. The Minister I believe has written learnedly on the Differential Calculus. He is a mathematician, and no poet."

"You are mistaken; I know him well; he is both. As poet *and* mathematician, he would reason well; as mere mathematician, he could not have reasoned at all, and thus would have been at the mercy of the Prefect."

"You surprise me," I said, "by these opinions, which have been contradicted by the voice of the world. You do not mean to set at naught the well-digested idea of centuries. The mathematical reason has long been regarded as *the* reason *par excellence.*"

"'*Il y a á parier,*'" replied Dupin, quoting from Chamfort, "'*que toute idée publique, toute convention reçue, est une sottise, car elle a convenue au plus grand nombre.*' The mathematicians, I grant you, have done their best to promulgate the popular error to which you allude, and which is none the less an error for its promulgation as truth. With an art worthy a better cause, for example, they have insinuated the term 'analysis' into application to algebra. The French are the originators of this particular deception; but if a term is of any importance—if words derive any value from applicability—then 'analysis' conveys 'algebra' about as much as, in Latin, '*ambitus*' implies 'ambition,' '*religio*' 'religion,' or *homines honesti'* a set of *honorable* men."

"You have a quarrel on hand, I see," said I, "with some of the algebraists of Paris; but proceed."

"I dispute the availability, and thus the value, of that reason which is cultivated in any especial form other than the abstractly logical. I dispute, in particular, the reason educed by mathematical study. The mathematics are the science of form and quantity; mathematical reasoning is merely logic applied to observation upon form and quantity. The great error lies in supposing that even the truths of what is called *pure* algebra are abstract or general truths. And this error is so egregious that I am confounded at the universality with which it has been received. Mathematical axioms are *not* axioms of general truth. What is true of *relation*—of form and quantity—is often grossly false in regard to morals, for example. In this latter science it is very usually *un*true that the aggregated parts are equal to the whole. In chemistry also the axiom fails. In the consideration of motive it fails; for two motives, each of a given value, have not, necessarily, a value when united, equal to the sum of their values apart. There are numerous other mathematical truths which are only truths within the limits of *relation*. But the mathematician agues from his *finite truths*, through habit, as if they were of an absolutely general applicability—as the world indeed imagines them to be. Bryant, in his very learned 'Mythology,' mentions an analogous source of error, when he says that 'although the pagan fables are not believed, yet we forget ourselves continually, and make inferences from them as existing realities.' With the algebraists, however, who are pagans themselves, the 'pagan fables' *are* believed, and the inferences are made, not so much through lapse of memory as through an unaccountable addling of the brains. In short, I never yet encountered the mere mathematician who would be trusted out of equal roots, or one who did not clandestinely hold it as a point of his faith that $x^2 + px$ was absolutely and unconditionally equal to q. Say to one of these gentlemen, by way of experiment, if you please, that you believe occasions may occur where $x^2 + px$ is *not* altogether equal to q, and, having made him understand what you mean, get out of his reach as speedily as convenient, for, beyond doubt, he will endeavor to knock you down.

"I mean to say," continued Dupin, while I merely laughed at his last observations, "that if the Minister had been no more than a mathematician, the Prefect would have been under no necessity of giving me this check. I knew him, however, as both mathematician and poet, and my measures were adapted to his capacity, with reference to the circumstances by which he was surrounded. I knew him as a courtier, too, and as a bold *intriguant*. Such a man, I considered, could not fail to be aware of the ordinary policial modes of action. He could not have failed to anticipate—and events have proved that he did not fail to anticipate—the waylayings to which he was subjected. He must have foreseen, I reflected, the secret investigations of his premises. His frequent absences from home at night, which were hailed by the Prefect as certain aids to his success, I regarded only as *ruses*, to afford opportunity for thorough search to the police, and thus the sooner to impress them with the conviction to which G——, in fact, did finally arrive—the conviction that the letter was not upon the premises. I felt, also, that the whole train of thought, which I was at some pains in detailing to you just now, concerning the invariable principle of policial action in searches for articles concealed—I felt that this whole train of thought would necessarily pass through the mind of the minister. It would imperatively lead him to despise all the ordinary *nooks* of concealment. *He* could not, I reflected, be so weak as not to see that the most intricate and remote recess of his hotel would be as open as his commonest closets to the eyes, to the probes, to the gimlets, and to the microscopes of the Prefect. I saw, in fine, that he would be driven, as a matter of course, to *simplicity*, if not deliberately induced to it as a matter of choice. You will remember, perhaps, how desperately the Prefect laughed when I suggested, upon our first interview, that it was just possible this mystery troubled him so much on account of is being so *very* self-evident."

"Yes," said I, "I remember his merriment well. I really thought he would have fallen into convulsions."

"The material world," continued Dupin, "abounds with very strict analogies to the immaterial; and thus some color of truth has been given to the rhetorical dogma, that metaphor, or simile, may be made to strengthen an argument as well as to embellish a description. The principle of the *vis inertiæ*, for example, seems to be identical in physics and metaphysics. It is not more true in the former, that a large body is with more difficulty set in motion than a smaller one, and that its subsequent *momentum* is commensurate with this difficulty, than it is, in the latter, that intellects of the vaster capacity, while more forcible, more constant, and more eventful in their movements than those of inferior grade, are yet the less readily moved, and more embarrassed, and full of hesitation in the first steps of their progress. Again: have you ever noticed which of the street signs, over the shop doors, are the most attractive of attention?"

"I have never given the matter a thought," I said.

"There is a game of puzzles," he resumed, "which is played upon a map. One party playing requires another to find a given word—the name of town, river, state, or empire—any word, in short, upon the motley and perplexed surface of the chart. A novice in the game generally seeks to embarrass his opponents by giving them the most minutely lettered names; but the adept selects such words as stretch, in large characters, from one end of the chart to the other. These, like the over-largely lettered signs and placards of the street, escape observation by dint of being excessively obvious; and here the physical oversight is precisely analogous with the moral inapprehension by which the intellect suffers to pass unnoticed those considerations which are too obtrusively and too palpably self-evident. But this is a point, it appears, somewhat above or beneath the understanding of the Prefect. He never once thought it probable, or possible, that the minister had deposited the letter immediately beneath the nose of the whole world, by way of best preventing any portion of that world from perceiving it.

"But the more I reflected upon the daring, dashing, and discriminating ingenuity of D——; upon the fact that the document must always have been *at hand*, if he intended to use it to good purpose; and upon the decisive evidence, obtained by the Prefect, that it was not hidden within the limits of that dignitary's ordinary search——the more satisfied I became that, to conceal this letter, the minister had resorted to the comprehensive and sagacious expedient of not attempting to conceal it at all.

"Full of those ideas, I prepared myself with a pair of green spectacles, and called one fine morning, quite by accident, at the Ministerial hotel. I found D—— at home, yawning, lounging, and dawdling, as usual, and pretending to be in the last extremity of *ennui*. He is, perhaps, the most really energetic human being now alive —but that is only when nobody sees him.

"To be even with him, I complained of my weak eyes, and lamented the necessity of spectacles, under cover of which I cautiously and thoroughly surveyed the whole apartment, while seemingly intent only upon the conversation of my host.

"I paid especial attention to a large writing-table near which he sat, and upon which lay confusedly, some miscellaneous letters and other papers, with one or two musical instruments and a few books. Here, however, after a long and very deliberate scrutiny, I saw nothing to excite particular suspicion.

"At length my eyes, in going the circuit of the room, fell upon a trumpery filigree card-rack of pasteboard, that hung dangling by a dirty blue ribbon, from a little brass knob just beneath the middle of the mantelpiece. In this rack, which had three or four compartments, were five or six visiting cards and a solitary letter. This last was much soiled and crumpled. It was torn nearly in two, across the middle— as if a design, in the first instance, to tear it entirely up as worthless, had been altered, or stayed, in the second. It had a large black seal, bearing the D—— cipher *very* conspicuously, and was addressed, in a diminutive female hand, to D——, the minister, himself. It was thrust carelessly, and even, as it seemed, contemptuously, into one of the uppermost divisions of the rack.

"No sooner had I glanced at this letter than I concluded it to be that of which I was in search. To be sure, it was, to all appearance, radically different from the one of which the Prefect had read us so minute a description. Here the seal was large and black, with the D—— cipher; there it was small and red, with the ducal arms of the S—— family. Here, the address, to the minister, was diminutive and feminine; there the superscription, to a certain royal personage, was markedly bold and decided; the size alone formed a point of correspondence. But, then, the *radicalness* of these differences, which was excessive; the dirt; the soiled and torn condition of the paper, so inconsistent with the *true* methodical habits of D——, and so suggestive of a design to delude the beholder into an idea of the worthlessness of the document;—these things, together with the hyperobtrusive situation of this document, full in the view of every visitor, and thus exactly in accordance with the conclusions to which I had previously arrived; these things, I say, were strongly corroborative of suspicion, in one who came with the intention to suspect.

"I protracted my visit as long as possible, and, while I maintained a most animated discussion with the minister, upon a topic which I knew well had never failed to interest and excite him, I kept my attention really riveted upon the letter. In this examination, I committed to memory its external appearance and arrangement in the rack; and also fell, at length, upon a discovery which set at rest whatever trivial doubt I might have entertained. In scrutinizing the edges of the paper, I observed them to be more *chafed* than seemed necessary. They presented the *broken* appearance which is manifested when a stiff paper, having been once folded and pressed with a folder, is refolded in a reversed direction, in the same creases or edges which had formed the original fold. This discovery was sufficient. It was clear to me that the letter had been turned, as a glove, inside out, re-directed and resealed. I bade the minister good-morning, and took my departure at once, leaving a gold snuff-box upon the table.

"The next morning I called for the snuff-box, when we resumed, quite eagerly, the conversation of the preceding day. While thus engaged, however, a loud report, as if of a pistol, was heard immediately beneath the windows of the hotel, and was succeeded by a series of fearful screams, and the shoutings of a terrified mob. D—— rushed to a casement, threw it open, and looked out. In the meantime I stepped to the card-rack, took the letter, put it in my pocket, and replaced it by a *fac-simile*, (so far as regards externals) which I had carefully prepared at my lodgings—imitating the D—— cipher, very readily, by means of a seal formed of bread.

"The disturbance in the street had been occasioned by the frantic behavior of a man with a musket. He had fired it among a crowd of women and children. It proved, however, to have been without ball, and the fellow was suffered to go his way as a lunatic or a drunkard. When he had gone, D—— came from the window, whither I had followed him immediately upon securing the object in view. Soon afterward I bade him farewell. The pretended lunatic was a man in my own pay."

"But what purpose had you," I asked, "in replacing the letter by a *fac-simile*? Would it not have been better, at the first visit, to have seized it openly, and departed?"

"D——," replied Dupin, "is a desperate man, and a man of nerve. His hotel, too, is not without attendants devoted to his interests. Had I made the wild attempt you suggest, I might never have left the Ministerial presence alive. The good people of Paris might have heard of me no more. But I had an object apart from these considerations. You know my political prepossessions. In this matter, I act as a partisan of the lady concerned. For eighteen months the Minister has had her in his power. She has now him in hers—since, being unaware that the letter is not in his possession, he will proceed with his exactions as if it was. Thus will he inevitably commit himself, at once, to his political destruction. His downfall, too, will not be more precipitate than awkward. It is all very well to talk about the *facilis descensus Averni*; but in all kinds of climbing, as Catalani said of singing, it is far more easy to get up than to come down. In the present instance I have no sympathy—at least no pity—for him who descends. He is that *monstrum horrendum*, an unprincipled man of genius. I confess, however, that I should like very well to know the precise character of his thoughts, when, being defied by her whom the Prefect terms 'a certain personage,' he is reduced to opening the letter which I left for him in the card-rack."

"How? did you put any thing particular in it?"

"Why—it did not seem altogether right to leave the interior blank—that would have been insulting. D——, at Vienna once, did me an evil turn, which I told him, quite good-humoredly, that I should remember. So, as I knew he would feel some curiosity in regard to the identity of the person who had outwitted him, I thought it a pity not to give him a clew. He is well acquainted with my MS., and I just copied into the middle of the blank sheet the words

"'————*Un dessein si fueneste,*
S'il n'est digne d'Atrée, est digne de Thyeste.'
They are to be found in Crébillon's 'Atrée.'"

Sir Arthur Conan Doyle

(1859–1930)

Inarguably, the most famous detective in literature is Sherlock Holmes. By the same token, Holmes and his biographer, Dr. John Watson, are the most famous literary detective duo. *A Study in Scarlet* (1887), the debut novel of a young Southsea physician, brought the pair together, established them in their rooms at 221B Baker Street, and set them forth on their first successful investigation, that of the Lauriston Garden mystery. A second novel, *The Sign of the Four,* followed two years later. Both books are minor, however, when compared to the brilliant short stories—and the equally brilliant novel *The Hound of the Baskervilles* (1902)—which followed.

It has been written that judged solely as a writer of detective fiction, Arthur Conan Doyle rarely played fair with the reader. Doyle withholds key facts in many of the tales, including some of the best known, and the reader has little opportunity to match wits with Holmes in his dazzling feats of deduction. Logic does not always prevail, and there are repetitions of certain plot devices as well as numerous implausibilities that often have to do with impenetrable disguises.

Be this as it may, it is not the plots so much as the characters of Holmes and Watson—and to a lesser degree, Doyle's ability to evoke vividly the London of gaslight and hansom cabs—that have kept the stories alive for more than a century. Curiously enough, the same may be said of the long-running series of Holmes–Watson films starring Basil Rathbone and Nigel Bruce: It is the interplay and screen presence of the two actors in their roles that overshadow what are generally trite storylines and make the series as enjoyable as it is today, half a century after it ended.

In all, over a period of more than thirty years, Doyle wrote just four Holmes–Watson novels and enough short stories to fill five volumes. The first of the collections, *The Adventures of Sherlock Holmes* (1892), is justifiably the most renowned book of detective short stories; almost as important is *The Memoirs of Sherlock Holmes* (1894). The present selection, one of the lesser-known tales in the canon, is from the third collection, *The Return of Sherlock Holmes* (1905). The best of the novels, of course, is *The Hound of the Baskervilles*; it is both a classic book of detection and a story so well known outside the field that it has achieved legendary status: There are

31

more than a few individuals who believe the giant hound that roamed the moors near Baskerville Hall actually existed.

The Sherlock Holmes stories were only a small portion of Doyle's prodigious output after he abandoned his medical practice in 1892 to write full-time. He published dozens of novels and story collections of various types, including some rather startling fantasy and horror tales: plays, books of verse, and nonfiction works. He was deeply interested in the occult and wrote six books on spiritualism, notably a definitive two-volume study, *History of Spiritualism* (1926). It is both ironic and a measure of Doyle's aesthetic discernment that he valued many of these works far more than he did the exploits of Holmes and Watson.

THE ADVENTURE OF THE EMPTY HOUSE

SHERLOCK HOLMES AND DR. WATSON
LONDON, ENGLAND
1894

I t was in the spring of the year 1894 that all London was interested, and the fashionable world dismayed, by the murder of the Honourable Ronald Adair under most unusual and inexplicable circumstances. The public has already learned those particulars of the crime which came out in the police investigation, but a good deal was suppressed upon that occasion, since the case for the prosecution was so overwhelmingly strong that it was not necessary to bring forward all the facts. Only now, at the end of nearly ten years, am I allowed to supply those missing links which make up the whole of that remarkable chain. The crime was of interest in itself, but the interest was as nothing to me compared to the inconceivable sequel, which afforded me the greatest shock and surprise of any event in my adventurous life. Even now, after this long interval, I find myself thrilling as I think of it, and feeling once more that sudden flood of joy, amazement, and incredulity which utterly submerged my mind. Let me say to that public, which has shown some interest in those glimpses which I have occasionally given them of the thoughts and actions of a very remarkable man, that they are not to blame me if I have not shared my knowledge with them, for I should have considered it my first duty to do so, had I not been barred by a positive prohibition from his own lips, which was only withdrawn upon the third of last month.

It can be imagined that my close intimacy with Sherlock Holmes had interested me deeply in crime, and that after his disappearance I never failed to read with care the various problems which came before the public. And I even attempted, more than once, for my own private satisfaction, to employ his methods in their solution, though with indifferent success. There was none, however, which appealed to me like this tragedy of Ronald Adair. As I read the evidence at the inquest, which led up to a verdict of wilful murder against some person or persons unknown, I realized more clearly than I had ever done the loss which the community had sustained by the death of Sherlock Holmes. There were points about this strange business which would, I was sure, have especially appealed to him, and the efforts of the police would have been supplemented, or more probably anticipated, by the trained observation and the alert mind of the first criminal agent in Europe. All day, as I drove upon my round, I turned over the case in my mind and found no explanation which appeared to me to be adequate. At the risk of telling a twice-told tale, I will recapitulate the facts as they were known to the public at the conclusion of the inquest.

The Honourable Ronald Adair was the second son of the Earl of Maynooth, at that time governor of one of the Australian colonies. Adair's mother had returned from Australia to undergo the operation for cataract, and she, her son Ronald, and her daughter Hilda were living together at 427 Park Lane. The youth moved in the best society—had, so far as was known, no enemies and no particular vices. He had been engaged to Miss Edith Woodley, of Carstairs, but the engagement had been broken off by mutual consent some months before, and there was no sign that it had left any very profound feeling behind it. For the rest of the man's life moved in a narrow and conventional circle, for his habits were quiet and his nature unemotional. Yet it was upon this easy-going young aristocrat that death came, in most strange and unexpected form, between the hours of ten and eleven-twenty on the night of March 30, 1894.

Ronald Adair was fond of cards—playing continually, but never for such stakes as would hurt him. He was a member of the Baldwin, the Cavendish, and the Bagatelle card clubs. It was shown that, after dinner on the day of his death, he had played a rubber of whist at the latter club. He had also played there in the afternoon. The evidence of those who had played with him—Mr. Murray, Sir John Hardy, and Colonel Moran—showed that the game was whist, and that there was a fairly equal fall of the cards. Adair might have lost five pounds, but not more. His fortune was a considerable one, and such a loss could not in any way affect him. He had played nearly every day at one club or other, but he was a cautious player, and usually rose a winner. It came out in evidence that, in partnership with Colonel Moran, he had actually won as much as four hundred and twenty pounds in a sitting, some weeks before, from Godfrey Milner and Lord Balmoral. So much for his recent history as it came out at the inquest.

On the evening of the crime, he returned from the club exactly at ten. His mother and sister were out spending the evening with a relation. The servant deposed that she heard him enter the front room on the second floor, generally used as his sitting-room. She had lit a fire there, and as it smoked she had opened the window. No sound was heard from the room until eleven-twenty, the hour of the return of Lady Maynooth and her daughter. Desiring to say good-night, she attempted to enter her son's room. The door was locked on the inside, and no answer could be got to their cries and knocking. Help was obtained, and the door forced. The unfortunate young man was found lying near the table. His head had been horribly mutilated by an expanding revolver bullet, but no weapon of any sort was to be found in the room. On the table lay two banknotes for ten pounds each and seventeen pounds ten in silver and gold, the money arranged in little piles of varying amount. There were some figures also upon a sheet of paper, with the names of some club friends opposite to them, from which it was conjectured that before his death he was endeavouring to make out his losses or winnings at cards.

A minute examination of the circumstances served only to make the case more complex. In the first place, no reason could be given why the young man should have fastened the door upon the inside. There was the possibility that the murderer had done this, and had afterwards escaped by the window. The drop was at least twenty feet, however, and a bed of crocuses in full bloom lay beneath. Neither the flowers nor the earth showed any sign of having been disturbed, nor were there any marks upon the narrow strip of grass which separated the house from the road. Apparently, therefore, it was the young man himself who had fastened the door. But how did he come by his death? No one could have climbed up to the window without leaving traces. Suppose a man had fired through the window, he would indeed be a remarkable shot who could with a revolver inflict so deadly a wound. Again, Park Lane is a frequented thoroughfare; there is a cab stand within a hundred yards of the house. No one had heard a shot. And yet there was the dead man, and there the revolver bullet, which had mushroomed out, as soft-nosed bullets will, and so inflicted a wound which must have caused instantaneous death. Such were the circumstances of the Park Lane Mystery, which were further complicated by entire absence of motive, since, as I have said, young Adair was not known to have any enemy, and no attempt had been made to remove the money or valuables in the room.

All day I turned these facts over in my mind, endeavouring to hit upon some theory which could reconcile them all, and to find that line of least resistance which my poor friend had declared to be the starting-point of every investigation. I confess that I made little progress. In the evening I strolled across the Park, and found myself about six o'clock at the Oxford Street end of Park Lane. A group of loafers upon the pavements, all staring up at a particular window, directed me to the house which I had come to see. A tall, thin man with coloured glasses, whom I strongly suspected of being a plain-clothes detective, was pointing out some theory of his own, while the others crowded round to listen to what he said. I got as near him as I could, but his observations seemed to me to be absurd, so I withdrew again in some disgust. As I did so I struck against an elderly, deformed man, who had been behind me, and I knocked down several books which he was carrying. I remember that as I picked them up, I observed the title of one of them, *The Origin of Tree Worship*, and it struck me that the fellow must be some poor bibliophile, who, either as a trade or as a hobby, was a collector of obscure volumes. I endeavoured to apologize for the accident, but it was evident that these books which I had so unfortunately maltreated were very precious objects in the eyes of their owner. With a snarl of contempt he turned upon his heel, and I saw his curved back and white side-whiskers disappear among the throng.

My observations of No. 427 Park Lane did little to clear up the problem in which I was interested. The house was separated from the street by a low wall and railing, the whole not more than five feet high. It was perfectly easy, therefore, for anyone to get into the garden, but the window was entirely inaccessible, since there was no waterpipe or anything which could help the most active man to climb it. More puzzled than ever, I retraced my steps to Kensington. I had not been in my study five minutes when the maid entered to say that a person desired to see me. To my astonishment it was none other than my strange old book collector, his sharp, wizened face peering out from a frame of white hair, and his precious volumes, a dozen of them at least, wedged under his right arm.

"You're surprised to see me, sir," said he, in a strange, croaking voice.

I acknowledged that I was.

"Well, I've a conscience, sir, and when I chanced to see you go into this house, as I came hobbling after you, I thought to myself, I'll just step in and see that kind gentleman, and tell him that if I was a bit gruff in my manner there was not any harm meant, and that I am much obliged to him for picking up my books."

"You make too much of a trifle," said I. "May I ask how you knew who I was?"

"Well, sir, if it isn't too great a liberty, I am a neighbour of yours, for you'll find my little bookshop at the corner of Church Street, and very happy to see you, I am sure. Maybe you collect yourself, sir. Here's *British Birds*, and *Catullus*, and *The*

Holy War—a bargain, every one of them. With five volumes you could just fill that gap on that second shelf. It looks untidy, does it not, sir?"

I moved my head to look at the cabinet behind me. When I turned again, Sherlock Holmes was standing smiling at me across my study table. I rose to my feet, stared at him for some seconds in utter amazement, and then it appears that I must have fainted for the first and the last time in my life. Certainly a gray mist swirled before my eyes, and when it cleared I found my collar-ends undone and the tingling after-taste of brandy upon my lips. Holmes was bending over my chair, his flask in his hand.

"My dear Watson," said the well-remembered voice, "I owe you a thousand apologies. I had no idea that you would be so affected."

I gripped him by the arms.

"Holmes!" I cried. "Is it really you? Can it indeed be that you are alive? Is it possible that you succeeded in climbing out of that awful abyss?"

"Wait a moment," said he. "Are you sure that you are really fit to discuss things? I have given you a serious shock by my unnecessarily dramatic reappearance."

"I am all right, but indeed, Holmes, I can hardly believe my eyes. Good heavens! to think that you—you of all men—should be standing in my study." Again I gripped him by the sleeve, and felt the thin, sinewy arm beneath it. "Well, you're not a spirit, anyhow," said I. "My dear chap, I'm overjoyed to see you. Sit down, and tell me how you came alive out of that dreadful chasm."

He sat opposite to me, and lit a cigarette in his old, nonchalant manner. He was dressed in the seedy frockcoat of the book merchant, but the rest of that individual lay in a pile of white hair and old books upon the table. Holmes looked even thinner and keener than of old, but there was a dead-white tinge in his aquiline face which told me that his life recently had not been a healthy one.

"I am glad to stretch myself, Watson," said he. "It is no joke when a tall man has to take a foot off his stature for several hours on end. Now, my dear fellow, in the matter of these explanations, we have, if I may ask for your coöperation, a hard and dangerous night's work in front of us. Perhaps it would be better if I gave you an account of the whole situation when that work is finished."

"I am full of curiosity. I should much prefer to hear now."

"You'll come with me to-night?"

"When you like and where you like."

"This is, indeed, like the old days. We shall have time for a mouthful of dinner before we need go. Well, then, about that chasm. I had no serious difficulty in getting out of it, for the very simple reason that I never was in it."

"You never were in it?"

"No, Watson, I never was in it. My note to you was absolutely genuine. I had little doubt that I had come to the end of my career when I perceived the some-what sinister figure of the late Professor Moriarty standing upon the narrow path-way which led to safety. I read an inexorable purpose in his gray eyes. I exchanged some remarks with him, therefore, and obtained his courteous permission to write the short note which you afterwards received. I left it with my cigarette-box and my stick, and I walked along the pathway, Moriarty still at my heels. When I reached the end I stood at bay. He drew no weapon, but he rushed at me and threw his long arms around me. He knew that his own game was up, and was only anx-ious to revenge himself upon me. We tottered together upon the brink of the fall. I have some knowledge, however, of baritsu, or the Japanese system of wrestling, which has more than once been very useful to me. I slipped through his grip, and he with a horrible scream kicked madly for a few seconds, and clawed the air with both his hands. But for all his efforts, he could not get his balance, and over he went. With my face over the brink, I saw him fall for a long way. Then he struck a rock, bounded off, and splashed into the water."

I listened with amazement to this explanation, which Holmes delivered between the puffs of his cigarette.

"But the tracks!" I cried. "I saw, with my own eyes, that two went down the path and none returned."

"It came about in this way. The instant that the Professor had disappeared, it struck me what a really extraordinarily lucky chance Fate had placed in my way. I knew that Moriarty was not the only man who had sworn my death. There were at least three others whose desire for vengeance upon me would only be increased by the death of their leader. They were all most dangerous men. One or other would certainly get me. On the other hand, if all the world was convinced that I was dead they would take liberties, these men, they would soon lay themselves open, and sooner or later I could destroy them. Then it would be time for me to announce that I was still in the land of the living. So rapidly does the brain act that I believe I had thought this all out before Professor Moriarty had reached the bottom of the Reichenbach Fall.

"I stood up and examined the rocky wall behind me. In your picturesque ac-count of the matter, which I read with great interest some months later, you assert that the wall was sheer. That was not literally true. A few small footholds presented themselves, and there was some indication of a ledge. The cliff is so high that to climb it all was an obvious impossibility, and it was equally impossible to make my way along the wet path without leaving some tracks. I might, it is true, have re-versed my boots, as I have done on similar occasions, but the sight of three sets of tracks in one direction would certainly have suggested a deception. On the whole, then, it was best that I should risk the climb. It was not a pleasant business,

Watson. The fall roared beneath me. I am not a fanciful person, but I give you my word that I seemed to hear Moriarty's voice screaming at me out of the abyss. A mistake would have been fatal. More than once, as tufts of grass came out in my hand or my foot slipped in the wet notches of the rock, I thought that I was gone. But I struggled upward, and at last I reached a ledge several feet deep and covered with soft green moss, where I could lie unseen, in the most perfect comfort. There I was stretched, when you, my dear Watson, and all your following were investigating in the most sympathetic and inefficient manner the circumstances of my death.

"At last, when you had all formed your inevitable and totally erroneous conclusions, you departed for the hotel, and I was left alone. I had imagined that I had reached the end of my adventures, but a very unexpected occurrence showed me that there were surprises still in store for me. A huge rock, falling from above, boomed past me, struck the path, and bounded over into the chasm. For an instant I thought that it was an accident, but a moment later, looking up, I saw a man's head against the darkening sky, and another stone struck the very ledge upon which I was stretched, within a foot of my head. Of course, the meaning of this was obvious. Moriarty had not been alone. A confederate—and even that one glance had told me how dangerous a man that confederate was—had kept guard while the Professor had attacked me. From a distance, unseen by me, he had been a witness of his friend's death and of my escape. He had waited, and then making his way round to the top of the cliff, he had endeavoured to succeed where his comrade had failed.

"I did not take long to think about it, Watson. Again I saw that grim face look over the cliff, and I knew that it was the precursor of another stone. I scrambled down on to the path. I don't think I could have done it in cold blood. It was a hundred times more difficult than getting up. But I had no time to think of the danger, for another stone sang past me as I hung by my hands from the edge of the ledge. Halfway down I slipped, but, by the blessing of God, I landed, torn and bleeding, upon the path. I took to my heels, did ten miles over the mountains in the darkness, and a week later I found myself in Florence, with the certainty that no one in the world knew what had become of me.

"I had only one confidant—my brother Mycroft. I owe you many apologies, my dear Watson, but it was all-important that it should be thought I was dead, and it is quite certain that you would not have written so convincing an account of my unhappy end had you not yourself thought that it was true. Several times during the last three years I have taken up my pen to write to you, but always I feared lest your affectionate regard for me should tempt you to some indiscretion which would betray my secret. For that reason I turned away from you this evening when you upset my books, for I was in danger at the time, and any show of surprise and emotion upon your part might have drawn attention to my identity and led to the most de plorable and irreparable results. As to Mycroft, I had to confide in him in order to obtain the money which I needed. The course of events in London did not run so well as I had hoped, for the trial of the Moriarty gang left two of its most dangerous members, my own most vindictive enemies, at liberty. I travelled for two years in Tibet, therefore, and amused myself by visiting Lhassa, and spending some days with the head lama. You may have read of the remarkable explorations of a Norwegian named Sigerson, but I am sure that it never occurred to you that you were receiving news of your friend. I then passed through Persia, looked in at Mecca, and paid a short but interesting visit to the Khalifa at Khartoum, the results of which I have communicated to the Foreign Office. Returning to France, I spent some months in a research into the coal-tar derivatives, which I conducted in a laboratory at Montpellier, in the south of France. Having concluded this to my satisfaction and learning that only one of my enemies was now left in London, I was about to return when my movements were hastened by the news of this very remarkable Park Lane Mystery, which not only appealed to me by its own merits, but which seemed to offer some most peculiar personal opportunities. I came over at once to London, called in my own person at Baker Street, threw Mrs. Hudson into violent hysterics, and found that Mycroft had preserved my rooms and my papers exactly as they had always been. So it was, my dear Watson, that at two o'clock to-day I found myself in my old armchair in my own old room, and only wishing I could have seen my old friend Watson in the other chair which he has so often adorned."

Such was the remarkable narrative to which I listened on that April evening—a narrative which would have been utterly incredible to me had it not been confirmed by the actual sight of the tall, spare figure and the keen, eager face, which I had never thought to see again. In some manner he had learned of my own sad bereavement, and his sympathy was shown in his manner rather than in his words. "Work is the best antidote to sorrow, my dear Watson," said he; "and I have a piece of work for us both to-night which, if we can bring it to a successful conclusion, will in itself justify a man's life on this planet." In vain I begged him to tell me more. "You will hear and see enough before morning," he answered. "We have three years of the past to discuss. Let that suffice until half-past nine, when we start upon the notable adventure of the empty house."

It was indeed like old times when, at that hour, I found myself seated beside him in a hansom, my revolver in my pocket, and the thrill of adventure in my heart. Holmes was cold and stern and silent. As the gleam of the street-lamps flashed upon his austere features, I saw that his brows were drawn down in thought and his thin lips compressed. I knew not what wild beast we were about to hunt down in the dark jungle of criminal London, but I was well assured, from the bearing of this master huntsman, that the adventure was a most grave one—while the sardonic smile which occasionally broke through his ascetic gloom boded little good for the object of our quest.

I had imagined that we were bound for Baker Street, but Holmes stopped the cab at the corner of Cavendish Square. I observed that as he stepped out he gave a most searching glance to right and left, and at every subsequent street corner he took the utmost pains to assure that he was not followed. Our route was certainly a singular one. Holmes's knowledge of the byways of London was extraordinary, and on this occasion he passed rapidly and with an assured step through a network of mews and stables, the very existence of which I had never known. We emerged at last into a small road, lined with old, gloomy houses, which led us into Manchester Street, and so to Blandford Street. Here he turned swiftly down a narrow passage, passed through a wooden gate into a deserted yard, and then opened with a key the back door of a house. We entered together, and he closed it behind us.

The place was pitch dark, but it was evident to me that it was an empty house. Our feet creaked and crackled over the bare planking, and my outstretched hand touched a wall from which the paper was hanging in ribbons. Holmes's cold, thin fingers closed round my wrist and led me forward down a long hall, until I dimly saw the murky fanlight over the door. Here Holmes turned suddenly to the right, and we found ourselves in a large, square, empty room, heavily shadowed in the corners, but faintly lit in the centre from the lights of the street beyond. There was no lamp near, and the window was thick with dust, so that we could only just discern each other's figures within. My companion put his hand upon my shoulder and his lips close to my ear.

"Do you know where we are?" he whispered.

"Surely that is Baker Street," I answered, staring through the dim window.

"Exactly. We are in Camden House, which stands opposite to our own old quarters."

"But why are we here?"

"Because it commands so excellent a view of that picturesque pile. Might I trouble you, my dear Watson, to draw a little nearer to the window, taking every precaution not to show yourself, and then to look up at our old rooms—the starting-point of so many of your little fairy-tales? We will see if my three years of absence have entirely taken away my power to surprise you."

I crept forward and looked across at the familiar window. As my eyes fell upon it, I gave a gasp and a cry of amazement. The blind was down, and a strong light was burning in the room. The shadow of a man who was seated in a chair within was thrown in hard, black outline upon the luminous screen of the window. There was no mistaking the poise of the head, the squareness of the shoulders, the sharpness of the features. The face was turned half-round, and the effect was that of one of those black silhouettes which our grandparents loved to frame. It was a perfect reproduction of Holmes. So amazed was I that I threw out my hand to make sure that the man himself was standing beside me. He was quivering with silent laughter.

"Well?" said he.

"Good heavens!" I cried. "It is marvellous."

"I trust that age doth not wither nor custom stale my infinite variety," said he, and I recognized in his voice the joy and pride which the artist takes in his own creation. "It really is rather like me, is it not?"

"I should be prepared to swear that it was you."

"The credit of the execution is due to Monsieur Oscar Meunier, of Grenoble, who spent some days in doing the moulding. It is a bust in wax. The rest I arranged myself during my visit to Baker Street this afternoon."

"But why?"

"Because, my dear Watson, I had the strongest possible reason for wishing certain people to think that I was there when I was really elsewhere."

"And you thought the rooms were watched?"

"I *knew* that they were watched."

"By whom?"

"By my old enemies, Watson. By the charming society whose leader lies in the Reichenbach Fall. You must remember that they knew, and only they knew, that I was still alive. Sooner or later they believed that I should come back to my rooms. They watched them continuously, and this morning they saw me arrive."

"How do you know?"

"Because I recognized their sentinel when I glanced out of my window. He is a harmless enough fellow, Parker by name, a garroter by trade, and a remarkable performer upon the jew's-harp. I cared nothing for him. But I cared a great deal for the much more formidable person who was behind him, the bosom friend of Moriarty, the man who dropped the rocks over the cliff, the most cunning and dangerous criminal in London. That is the man who is after me to-night, Watson, and that is the man who is quite unaware that we are after *him*."

My friend's plans were gradually revealing themselves. From this convenient retreat, the watchers were being watched and the trackers tracked. That angular shadow up yonder was the bait, and we were the hunters. In silence we stood together in the darkness and watched the hurrying figures who passed and repassed in front of us. Holmes was silent and motionless; but I could tell that he was keenly alert, and that his eyes were fixed intently upon the stream of passers-by. It was a bleak and boisterous night, and the wind whistled shrilly down the long street. Many people were moving to and fro, most of them muffled in their coats and cravats. Once or twice it seemed to me that I had seen the same figure before, and I especially noticed two men who appeared to be sheltering themselves from the wind in the doorway of a house some distance up the street. I tried to draw my companion's attention to them; but he gave a little ejaculation of impatience, and continued to stare into the street. More than once he fidgeted with his feet and tapped rapidly with his fingers upon the wall. It was evident to me that he was becoming uneasy, and that his plans were not working out altogether as he had hoped. At last, as midnight approached and the street gradually cleared, he paced up and down the room in uncontrollable agitation. I was about to make some remark to him, when I raised my eyes to the lighted window, and again experienced almost as great a surprise as before. I clutched Holmes's arm, and pointed upward.

"The shadow has moved!" I cried.

It was indeed no longer the profile, but the back, which was turned towards us.

Three years had certainly not smoothed the asperities of his temper or his impatience with a less active intelligence than his own.

"Of course it has moved," said he. "Am I such a farcical bungler, Watson, that I should erect an obvious dummy, and expect that some of the sharpest men in Europe would be deceived by it? We have been in this room two hours, and Mrs. Hudson has made some change in that figure eight times, or once in every quarter of an hour. She works it from the front, so that her shadow may never be seen. Ah!" He drew in his breath with a shrill, excited intake. In the dim light I saw his head thrown forward, his whole attitude rigid with attention. Outside the street was absolutely deserted. Those two men might still be crouching in the doorway, but I could no longer see them. All was still and dark, save only that brilliant yellow screen in front of us with the black figure outlined upon its centre. Again in the utter silence I heard that thin, sibilant note which spoke of intense suppressed excitement. An instant later he pulled me back into the blackest corner of the room, and I felt his warning hand upon my lips. The fingers which clutched me were quivering. Never had I known my friend more moved, and yet the dark street still stretched lonely and motionless before us.

But suddenly I was aware of that which his keener senses had already distinguished. A low, stealthy sound came to my ears, not from the direction of Baker Street, but from the back of the very house in which we lay concealed. A door opened and shut. An instant later steps crept down the passage—steps which were meant to be silent, but which reverberated harshly through the empty house. Holmes crouched back against the wall, and I did the same, my hand closing upon the handle of my revolver. Peering through the gloom, I saw the vague outline of a man, a shade blacker than the blackness of the open door. He stood for an instant, and then he crept forward, crouching, menacing, into the room. He was within three yards of us, this sinister figure, and I had braced myself to meet his spring, before I realized that he had no idea of our presence. He passed close beside us, stole over to the window, and very softly and noiselessly raised it for half a foot. As he sank to the level of this opening, the light of the street, no longer dimmed by the dusty glass, fell full upon his face. The man seemed to be beside himself with excitement. His two eyes shone like stars, and his features were working convulsively. He was an elderly man, with a thin, projecting nose, a high, bald forehead, and a huge grizzled moustache. An opera hat was pushed to the back of his head, and an evening dress shirt-front gleamed out through his open overcoat. His face was gaunt and swarthy, scored with deep, savage lines. In his hand he carried what appeared to be a stick, but as he laid it down upon the floor it gave a metallic clang. Then from the pocket of his overcoat he drew a bulky object, and he busied himself in some task which ended with a loud, sharp click, as if a spring or bolt had fallen into its place. Still kneeling upon the floor he bent forward and threw all his weight and strength upon some lever, with the result that there came a long whirling, grinding noise, ending once more in a powerful click. He straightened himself then, and I saw that what he held in his hand was a sort of gun, with a curiously misshapen butt. He opened it at the breech, put something in, and snapped the breechlock. Then, crouching down, he rested the end of the barrel upon the ledge of the open window, and I saw his long moustache droop over the stock and his eye gleam as it peered along the sights. I heard a little sigh of satisfaction as he cuddled the butt into his shoulder, and saw that amazing target, the black man on the yellow ground, standing clear at the end of his foresight. For an instant he was rigid and motionless. Then his finger tightened on the trigger. There was a strange, loud whiz and a long, silvery tinkle of broken glass. At that instant Holmes sprang like a tiger on to the marksman's back, and hurled him flat upon his face. He was up again in a moment, and with convulsive strength he seized Holmes by the throat, but I struck him on the head with the butt of my revolver, and he dropped again upon the floor. I fell upon him, and as I held him my comrade blew a shrill call upon a whistle. There was the clatter of running feet upon the pavement, and two policemen in uniform, with one plain-clothes detective, rushed through the front entrance and into the room.

"That you, Lestrade?" said Holmes.

"Yes, Mr. Holmes. I took the job myself. It's good to see you back in London, sir."

"I think you want a little unofficial help. Three undetected murders in one year won't do, Lestrade. But you handled the Molesey Mystery with less than your usual — that's to say, you handled it fairly well."

We had all risen to our feet, our prisoner breathing hard, with a stalwart constable on each side of him. Already a few loiterers had begun to collect in the street.

Holmes stepped up to the window, closed it, and dropped the blinds. Lestrade had produced two candles, and the policemen had uncovered their lanterns. I was able at last to have a good look at our prisoner.

It was a tremendously virile and yet sinister face which was turned towards us. With the brow of a philosopher above and the jaw of a sensualist below, the man must have started with great capacities for good or for evil. But one could not look upon his cruel blue eyes, with their drooping, cynical lids, or upon the fierce, aggressive nose and the threatening, deep-lined brow, without reading Nature's plainest danger-signals. He took no heed of any of us, but his eyes were fixed upon Holmes's face with an expression in which hatred and amazement were equally blended. "You fiend!" he kept on muttering. "You clever, clever fiend!"

"Ah, Colonel!" said Holmes, arranging his rumpled collar. "'Journeys end in lovers' meetings,' as the old play says. I don't think I have had the pleasure of seeing you since you favoured me with those attentions as I lay on the ledge above the Reichenbach Fall."

The colonel still stared at my friend like a man in a trance. "You cunning, cunning fiend!" was all that he could say.

"I have not introduced you yet," said Holmes. "This, gentlemen, is Colonel Sebastian Moran, once of Her Majesty's Indian Army, and the best heavy-game shot that our Eastern Empire has ever produced. I believe I am correct, Colonel, in saying that your bag of tigers still remains unrivalled?"

The fierce old man said nothing, but still glared at my companion. With his savage eyes and bristling moustache he was wonderfully like a tiger himself.

"I wonder that my very simple stratagem could deceive so old a *shikari*," said Holmes. "It must be very familiar to you. Have you not tethered a young kid under a tree, lain above it with your rifle, and waited for the bait to bring up your tiger? This empty house is my tree, and you are my tiger. You have possibly had other guns in reserve in case there should be several tigers, or in the unlikely supposition of your own aim failing you. These," he pointed around, "are my other guns. The parallel is exact."

Colonel Moran sprang forward with a snarl of rage, but the constables dragged him back. The fury upon his face was terrible to look at.

"I confess that you had one small surprise for me," said Holmes. "I did not anticipate that you would yourself make use of this empty house and this convenient front window. I had imagined you as operating from the street, where my friend Lestrade and his merry men were awaiting you. With that exception, all has gone as I expected."

Colonel Moran turned to the official detective.

"You may or may not have just cause for arresting me," said he, "but at least there can be no reason why I should submit to the gibes of this person. If I am in the hands of the law, let things be done in a legal way."

"Well, that's reasonable enough," said Lestrade. "Nothing further you have to say, Mr. Holmes, before we go?"

Holmes had picked up the powerful air-gun from the floor, and was examining its mechanism.

"An admirable and unique weapon," said he, "noiseless and of tremendous power: I knew Von Herder, the blind German mechanic, who constructed it to the order of the late Professor Moriarty. For years I have been aware of its existence, though I have never before had the opportunity of handling it. I commend it very specially to your attention, Lestrade, and also the bullets which fit it."

"You can trust us to look after that, Mr. Holmes," said Lestrade, as the whole party moved towards the door. "Anything further to say?"

"Only to ask what charge you intend to prefer?"

"What charge, sir? Why, of course, the attempted murder of Mr. Sherlock Holmes."

"Not so, Lestrade. I do not propose to appear in the matter at all. To you, and to you only, belongs the credit of the remarkable arrest which you have effected. Yes, Lestrade, I congratulate you! With your usual happy mixture of cunning and audacity, you have got him."

"Got him! Got whom, Mr. Holmes?"

"The man that the whole force has been seeking in vain—Colonel Sebastian Moran, who shot the Honourable Ronald Adair with an expanding bullet from an air-gun through the open window of the second-floor front of No. 427 Park Lane, upon the thirtieth of last month. That's the charge, Lestrade. And now, Watson, if you can endure the draught from a broken window, I think that half an hour in my study over a cigar may afford you some profitable amusement."

Our old chambers had been left unchanged through the supervision of Mycroft Holmes and the immediate care of Mrs. Hudson. As I entered I saw, it is true, an unwonted tidiness, but the old landmarks were all in their place. There were the chemical corner and the acid-stained, deal-topped table. There upon a shelf was the row of formidable scrap-books and books of reference which many of our fellow-citizens would have been so glad to burn. The diagrams, the violin-case, and the pipe-rack—even the Persian slipper which contained the tobacco—all met my eyes as I glanced round me. There were two occupants of the room—one, Mrs. Hudson, who beamed upon us both as we entered—the other, the strange dummy which had played so important a part in the evening's adventures. It was a wax-coloured model of my friend, so admirably done that it was a perfect facsimile. It stood on a small pedestal table with an old dressing-gown of Holmes's so draped round it that the illusion from the street was absolutely perfect.

"I hope you observed all precautions, Mrs. Hudson?" said Holmes.

"I went to it on my knees, sir, just as you told me."

"Excellent. You carried the thing out very well. Did you observe where the bullet went?"

"Yes, sir. I'm afraid it has spoilt your beautiful bust, for it passed right through the head and flattened itself on the wall. I picked it up from the carpet. Here it is!"

Holmes held it out to me. "A soft revolver bullet, as your perceive, Watson. There's genius in that, for who would expect to find such a thing fired from an airgun? All right, Mrs. Hudson. I am much obliged for your assistance. And now, Watson, let me see you in your old seat once more, for there are several points which I should like to discuss with you."

He had thrown off the seedy frockcoat, and now he was the Holmes of old in the mouse-coloured dressing-gown which he took from his effigy.

"The old *shikari's* nerves have not lost their steadiness, nor his eyes their keenness," said he, with a laugh, as he inspected the shattered forehead of his bust.

"Plumb in the middle of the back of the head and smack through the brain. He was the best shot in India, and I expect there are few better in London. Have you heard the name?"

"No, I have not."

"Well, well, such is fame! But, then, if I remember right, you had not heard the name of Professor James Moriarty, who had one of the great brains of the century. Just give me down my index of biographies from the shelf."

He turned over the pages lazily, leaning back in his chair and blowing great clouds from his cigar.

"My collection of M's is a fine one," said he. "Moriarty himself is enough to make any letter illustrious, and here is Morgan the prisoner, and Merridew of abominable memory, and Mathews, who knocked out my left canine in the waiting-room at Charing Cross, and, finally, here is our friend of to-night."

He handed over the book, and I read:

> *Moran, Sebastian, Colonel.* Unemployed. Formerly 1st Bangalore Pioneers. Born London, 1840. Son of Sir Augustus Moran, C.B., once British Minister to Persia. Educated Eton and Oxford. Served in Jowaki Campaign, Afghan Campaign, Charasiab (despatches), Sherpur, and Cabul. Author of *Heavy Game of the Western Himalayas* (1881); *Three Months in the Jungle* (1884). Address: Conduit Street. Clubs: The Anglo-Indian, the Tankerville, the Bagatelle Card Club.

On the margin was written, in Holmes's precise hand:

The second most dangerous man in London.

"This is astonishing," said I, as I handed back the volume. "The man's career is that of an honourable soldier."

"It is true," Holmes answered. "Up to a certain point he did well. He was always a man of iron nerve, and the story is still told in India how he crawled down a drain after a wounded man-eating tiger. There are some trees, Watson, which grow to a certain height, and then suddenly develop some unsightly eccentricity. You will see it often in humans. I have a theory that the individual represents in his development the whole procession of his ancestors, and that such a sudden turn to good or evil stands for some strong influence which came into the line of his pedigree. The person becomes, as it were, the epitome of the history of his own family."

"It is surely rather fanciful."

"Well, I don't insist upon it. Whatever the cause, Colonel Moran began to go wrong. Without any open scandal, he still made India too hot to hold him. He retired, came to London, and again acquired an evil name. It was at this time that he was sought out by Professor Moriarty, to whom for a time he was chief of the staff. Moriarty supplied him liberally with money, and used him only in one or two very high-class jobs, which no ordinary criminal could have undertaken. You may have some recollection of the death of Mrs. Stewart, of Lauder, in 1887. Not? Well, I am sure Moran was at the bottom of it, but nothing could be proved. So cleverly was the colonel concealed that, even when the Moriarty gang was broken up, we could not incriminate him. You remember at that date, when I called upon you in your rooms, how I put up the shutters for fear of air-guns? No doubt you thought me fanciful. I knew exactly what I was doing, for I knew of the existence of this remarkable gun, and I knew also that one of the best shots in the world would be behind it. When we were in Switzerland he followed us with Moriarty, and it was undoubtedly he who gave me that evil five minutes on the Reichenbach ledge.

"You may think that I read the papers with some attention during my sojourn in France, on the look-out for any chance of laying him by the heels. So long as he was free in London, my life would really not have been worth living. Night and day the shadow would have been over me, and sooner or later his chance must have come. What could I do? I could not shoot him at sight, or I should myself be in the dock. There was no use appealing to a magistrate. They cannot interfere on the strength of what would appear to them to be a wild suspicion. So I could do nothing. But I watched the criminal news, knowing that sooner or later I should get him. Then came the death of this Ronald Adair. My chance had come at last. Knowing what I did, was it not certain that Colonel Moran had done it? He had played cards with the lad, he had followed him home from the club, he had shot him through the open window. There was not a doubt of it. The bullets alone are enough to put his head in a noose. I came over at once. I was seen by the sentinel, who would, I knew, direct the colonel's attention to my presence. He could not fail to connect my sudden return with his crime, and to be terribly alarmed. I was sure that he would make an attempt to get me out of the way *at once*, and would bring round his murderous weapon for that purpose. I left him an excellent mark in the window, and, having warned the police that they might be needed—by the way, Watson, you spotted their presence in that doorway with unerring accuracy—I took up what seemed to me to be a judicious post for observation, never dreaming that he would choose the same spot for his attack. Now, my dear Watson, does anything remain for me to explain?"

"Yes," said I. "You have not made it clear what was Colonel Moran's motive in murdering the Honourable Ronald Adair?"

"Ah! my dear Watson, there we come into those realms of conjecture, where the most logical mind may be at fault. Each may form his own hypothesis upon the present evidence, and yours is as likely to be correct as mine."

"You have formed one, then?"

"I think that it is not difficult to explain the facts. It came out in evidence that Colonel Moran and young Adair had, between them, won a considerable amount of money. Now, Moran undoubtedly played foul—of that I have long been aware. I believe that on the day of the murder Adair had discovered that Moran was cheating. Very likely he had spoken to him privately, and had threatened to expose him unless he voluntarily resigned his membership of the club, and promised not to play cards again. It is unlikely that a youngster like Adair would at once make a hideous scandal by exposing a well known man so much older than himself. Probably he acted as I suggest. The exclusion from his clubs would mean ruin to Moran, who lived by his ill-gotten card-gains. He therefore murdered Adair, who at the time was endeavouring to work out how much money he should himself return, since he could not profit by his partner's foul play. He locked the door lest the ladies should surprise him and insist upon knowing what he was doing with these names and coins. Will it pass?"

"I have no doubt that you have hit upon the truth."

"It will be verified or disproved at the trial. Meanwhile, come what may, Colonel Moran will trouble us no more. The famous air-gun of Von Herder will embellish the Scotland Yard Museum, and once again Mr. Sherlock Holmes is free to devote his life to examining those interesting little problems which the complex life of London so plentifully presents."

P. G. Wodehouse

(1881–1975)

The creator of the wonderfully witty and urbane stories about addlepated aristocrat Bertie Wooster and his valet, Jeeves, was a lifelong devotee of mystery and detective fiction. One of P(elham) G(renville) Wodehouse's early novels, The Little Nugget, is a genuine (if minor) detective yarn narrated by Peter Burns, a "rich, good looking, amiable, brave, and certainly not stupid" amateur sleuth. It was published in the United States in 1914, the same year "Death at the Excelsior" appeared in the English magazine Pearson's under the title "The Education of Detective Oakes" and in slightly different form. This, too, is a true detective story, the only other written by Wodehouse. Its featured players are a young operative named Elliot Oakes and his boss, Mr. Paul Snyder of the Paul Snyder Detective Agency, who undertake to untangle a case that baffles everyone involved, including the coroner, who can't quite make up his mind if a murder has been committed or not. Although it cannot be said to be among Wodehouse's finest tales, it does have a clever locked-room gimmick that makes use of a unique weapon, and both Oakes and Snyder are engaging enough to make one wish the author had seen fit to provide additional samples of their talents.

P. G. Wodehouse published close to one hundred novels and more than a score of short-story collections during his remarkable seventy-year career. He was once called "the best living writer of English"; true or not, he was certainly one of the foremost humorists in any language. The world he created was one entirely his own, peopled by such endearing characters as Jeeves and Bertie, Mr. Mulliner, Lord Emsworth, Stanley Featherstonehaugh Ukridge, and the members of the Drones Club. It is a measure of Wodehouse's genius that he was able to freeze time in that world at about 1927, where it remained in crystalline tranquillity even in his final book, which he was working on at the time of his death in 1975 at the age of ninety-three.

Despite his fascination with the detective story and his early excursion into the form, his broad fictional world is generally crime-free. A few of his novels have elements of mystery and detection, among them Piccadilly Jim (1918) and such later efforts as Ice in the Bedroom (1961) and Do Burglars Burgle Banks? (1968), but those elements are all relatively minor. A number of his short stories may be classified as criminous, particularly the Lord

Emsworth novelette and title story of his 1937 collection, *The Crime Wave at Blandings*. Most of the best of these were posthumously collected under the title *Wodehouse on Crime: A Dozen Tales of Fiendish Cunning* (1981) The collection is a delight, though more so for its characters and its gentle and nostalgic humor than for its rather thin links to the mystery genre.

DEATH AT THE EXCELSIOR

PAUL SNYDER AND ELLIOT OAKES
ENGLAND
1914

I

The room was the typical bedroom of the typical boarding-house, furnished, insofar as it could be said to be furnished at all, with a severe simplicity. It contained two beds, a pine chest of drawers, a strip of faded carpet, and a wash basin. But there was that on the floor which set this room apart from a thousand rooms of the same kind. Flat on his back, with his hands tightly clenched and one leg twisted oddly under him and with his teeth gleaming through his grey beard in a horrible grin, Captain John Gunner stared up at the ceiling with eyes that saw nothing.

Until a moment before, he had had the little room all to himself. But now two people were standing just inside the door, looking down at him. One was a large policeman, who twisted his helmet nervously in his hands. The other was a tall, gaunt old woman in a rusty black dress, who gazed with pale eyes at the dead man. Her face was quite expressionless.

The woman was Mrs. Pickett, owner of the Excelsior Boarding-House. The policeman's name was Grogan. He was a genial giant, a terror to the riotous element of the waterfront, but obviously ill at ease in the presence of death. He drew in his breath, wiped his forehead, and whispered: "Look at his eyes, ma'am!"

Mrs. Pickett had not spoken a word since she had brought the policeman into the room, and she did not do so now. Constable Grogan looked at her quickly. He was afraid of Mother Pickett, as was everybody else along the waterfront. Her silence, her pale eyes, and the quiet decisiveness of her personality cowed even the tough old salts who patronized the Excelsior. She was a formidable influence in that little community of sailormen.

"That's just how I found him," said Mrs. Pickett. She did not speak loudly, but her voice made the policeman start.

He wiped his forehead again. "It might have been apoplexy," he hazarded.

Mrs. Pickett said nothing. There was a sound of footsteps outside, and a young man entered, carrying a black bag.

"Good morning, Mrs. Pickett. I was told that—Good Lord!" The young doctor dropped to his knees beside the body and raised one of the arms. After a moment he lowered it gently to the floor, and shook his head in grim resignation.

"He's been dead for hours," he announced. "When did you find him?"

"Twenty minutes back," replied the old woman. "I guess he died last night. He never would be called in the morning. Said he liked to sleep on. Well, he's got his wish."

"What did he die of, sir?" asked the policeman.

"It's impossible to say without an examination," the doctor answered. "It looks like a stroke, but I'm pretty sure it isn't. It might be a coronary attack, but I happen to know his blood pressure was normal, and his heart sound. He called in to see me only a week ago, and I examined him thoroughly. But sometimes you can be deceived. The inquest will tell us." He eyed the body almost resentfully. "I can't understand it. The man had no right to drop dead like this. He was a tough old sailor who ought to have been good for another twenty years. If you want my honest opinion—though I can't possibly be certain until after the inquest—I should say he had been poisoned."

"How would he be poisoned?" asked Mrs. Pickett quietly.

"That's more than I can tell you. There's no glass about that he could have drunk it from. He might have got it in capsule form. But why should he have done it? He was always a pretty cheerful sort of old man, wasn't he?"

"Yes, sir," said the Constable. "He had the name of being a joker in these parts. Kind of sarcastic, they tell me, though he never tried it on me."

"He must have died quite early last night," said the doctor. He turned to Mrs. Pickett. "What's become of Captain Muller? If he shares this room he ought to be able to tell us something about it."

"Captain Muller spent the night with some friends at Portsmouth," said Mrs. Pickett. "He left right after supper, and hasn't returned."

The doctor stared thoughtfully about the room, frowning.

"I don't like it. I can't understand it. If this had happened in India I should have said the man had died from some form of snakebite. I was out there two years, and

I've seen a hundred cases of it. The poor devils all looked just like this. But the thing's ridiculous. How could a man be bitten by a snake in a Southampton water-front boarding-house? Was the door locked when you found him, Mrs Pickett?"

Mrs. Pickett nodded. "I opened it with my own key. I had been calling to him and he didn't answer, so I guessed something was wrong."

The Constable spoke: "You ain't touched anything, ma'am? They're always very particular about that. If the doctor's right, and there's been anything up, that's the first thing they'll ask."

"Everything's just as I found it."

"What's that on the floor beside him?" the doctor asked.

"Only his harmonica. He liked to play it of an evening in his room. I've had some complaints about it from some of the gentlemen, but I never saw any harm, so long as he didn't play it too late."

"Seems as if he was playing it when—it happened," Constable Grogan said. "That don't look much like suicide, sir."

"I didn't say it was suicide."

Grogan whistled. "You don't think—"

"I'm not thinking anything—until after the inquest. All I say is that it's queer."

Another aspect of the matter seemed to strike the policeman. "I guess this ain't going to do the Excelsior any good, ma'am," he said sympathetically.

Mrs. Pickett shrugged her shoulders.

"I suppose I had better go and notify the coroner," said the doctor.

He went out, and after a momentary pause the policeman followed him. Constable Grogan was not greatly troubled with nerves, but he felt a decided desire to be somewhere where he could not see the dead man's staring eyes.

Mrs. Pickett remained where she was, looking down at the still form on the floor. Her face was expressionless, but inwardly she was tormented and alarmed. It was the first time such a thing as this had happened at the Excelsior, and, as Constable Grogan had hinted, it was not likely to increase the attractiveness of the house in the eyes of possible boarders. It was not the threatened pecuniary loss which was troubling her. As far as money was concerned, she could have lived comfortably on her savings, for she was richer than most of her friends supposed. It was the blot on the escutcheon of the Excelsior—the stain on its reputation—which was tormenting her.

The Excelsior was her life. Starting many years before, beyond the memory of the oldest boarder, she had built up the model establishment, the fame of which had been carried to every corner of the world. Men spoke of it as a place where you were fed well, cleanly housed, and where petty robbery was unknown.

Such was the chorus of praise that it is not likely that much harm could come to the Excelsior from a single mysterious death, but Mother Pickett was not consoling herself with such reflections. She looked at the dead man with pale, grim eyes. Out in the hallway the doctor's voice further increased her despair. He was talking to the police on the telephone, and she could distinctly hear his every word.

II

The offices of Mr. Paul Snyder's Detective Agency in New Oxford Street had grown in the course of a dozen years from a single room to an impressive suite bright with polished wood, clicking typewriters, and other evidences of success. Where once Mr. Snyder had sat and waited for clients and attended to them himself, he now sat in his private office and directed eight assistants.

He had just accepted a case—a case that might be nothing at all or something exceedingly big. It was on the latter possibility that he had gambled. The fee offered was, judged by his present standards of prosperity, small. But the bizarre facts, coupled with something in the personality of the client, had won him over. He briskly touched the bell and requested that Mr. Oakes should be sent in to him.

Elliot Oakes was a young man who both amused and interested Mr. Snyder, for though he had only recently joined the staff, he made no secret of his intention of revolutionizing the methods of the agency. Mr. Snyder himself, in common with most of his assistants, relied for results on hard work and plenty of common sense. He had never been a detective of the showy type. Results had justified his methods, but he was perfectly aware that young Mr. Oakes looked on him as a dull old man who had been miraculously favored by luck.

Mr. Snyder had selected Oakes for the case in hand principally because it was one where inexperience could do no harm, and where the brilliant guesswork which Oakes preferred to call his inductive reasoning might achieve an unexpected success.

Another motive actuated Mr. Snyder in his choice. He had a strong suspicion that the conduct of this case was going to have the beneficial result of lowering Oakes' self-esteem. If failure achieved this end, Mr. Snyder felt that failure, though it would not help the Agency, would not be an unmixed ill.

The door opened and Oakes entered tensely. He did everything tensely, partly from a natural nervous energy, and partly as a pose. He was a lean young man, with dark eyes and a thin-lipped mouth, and he looked quite as much like a typical detective as Mr. Snyder looked like a comfortable and prosperous stock broker.

"Sit down, Oakes," said Mr. Snyder. "I've got a job for you."

Oakes sank into a chair like a crouching leopard, and placed the tips of his fingers together. He nodded curtly. It was part of his pose to be keen and silent.

"I want you to go to this address"—Mr. Snyder handed him an envelope—"and look around. The address on that envelope is of a sailors' boarding-house down in Southampton. You know the sort of place—retired sea captains and so on live there. All most respectable. In all its history nothing more sensational has ever happened than a case of suspected cheating at halfpenny nap. Well, a man had died there."

"Murdered?" Oakes asked.

"I don't know. That's for you to find out. The coroner left it open. 'Death by Misadventure' was the verdict, and I don't blame him. I don't see how it could have been murder. The door was locked on the inside, so nobody could have got in."

"The window?"

"The window was open, granted. But the room is on the second floor. Anyway, you may dismiss the window. I remember the old lady saying there was a bar across it, and that nobody could have squeezed through."

Oakes' eyes glistened. He was interested. "What was the cause of death?" he asked.

Mr. Snyder coughed. "Snake bite," he said.

Oakes' careful calm deserted him. He uttered a cry of astonishment. "Why, that's incredible!"

"It's the literal truth. The medical examination proved that the fellow had been killed by snake poison—cobra, to be exact, which is found principally in India."

"Cobra!"

"Just so. In a Southampton boarding-house, in a room with a locked door, this man was stung by a cobra. To add a little mystification to the limpid simplicity of the affair, when the door was opened there was no sign of any cobra. It couldn't have got out through the door, because the door was locked. It couldn't have got out of the window, because the window was too high up, and snakes can't jump. And it couldn't have gotten up the chimney, because there was no chimney. So there you have it."

He looked at Oakes with a certain quiet satisfaction. It had come to his ears that Oakes had been heard to complain of the infantile nature and unworthiness of the last two cases to which he had been assigned. He had even said that he hoped some day to be given a problem which should be beyond the reasoning powers of a child of six. It seemed to Mr. Snyder that Oakes was about to get his wish.

"I should like further details," said Oakes, a little breathlessly.

"You had better apply to Mrs. Pickett, who owns the boarding-house," Mr. Snyder said. "It was she who put the case in my hands. She is convinced that it is murder. But, if we exclude ghosts, I don't see how any third party could have taken a hand in the thing at all. However, she wanted a man from this agency, and was prepared to pay for him, so I promised her I would send one. It is not our policy to turn business away."

He smiled wryly. "In pursuance of that policy I want you to go and put up at Mrs. Pickett's boarding house and do your best to enhance the reputation of our agency. I would suggest that you pose as a ship's chandler or something of that sort. You will have to be something maritime or they'll be suspicious of you. And if your visit produces no other results, it will, at least, enable you to make the acquaintance of a very remarkable woman. I commend Mrs. Pickett to your notice. By the way, she says she will help you in your investigations."

Oakes laughed shortly. The idea amused him.

"It's a mistake to scoff at amateur assistance, my boy," said Mr. Snyder in the benevolently paternal manner which had made a score of criminals refuse to believe him a detective until the moment when the handcuffs snapped on their wrists. "Crime investigation isn't an exact science. Success or failure depends in a large measure on applied common sense, and the possession of a great deal of special information. Mrs. Pickett knows certain things which neither you nor I know, and it's just possible that she may have some stray piece of information which will provide the key to the entire mystery."

Oakes laughed again. "It is very kind of Mrs. Pickett," he said, "but I prefer to trust to my own methods." Oakes rose, his face purposeful. "I'd better be starting at once," he said. "I'll send you reports from time to time."

"Good. The more detailed the better," said Mr. Snyder genially. "I hope your visit to the Excelsior will be pleasant. And cultivate Mrs. Pickett. She's worth while."

The door closed, and Mr. Snyder lighted a fresh cigar. "Dashed young fool," he murmured, as he turned his mind to other matters.

III

A day later Mr. Snyder sat in his office reading a typewritten report. It appeared to be of a humorous nature, for, as he read, chuckles escaped him. Finishing the last sheet he threw his head back and laughed heartily. The manuscript had not been intended by its author for a humorous effort. What Mr. Snyder had been reading was the first of Elliot Oakes' reports from the Excelsior. It read as follows:

> I am sorry to be unable to report any real progress. I have formed several theories which I will put forward later, but at present I cannot say that I am hopeful.

Directly I arrived here I sought out Mrs. Pickett, explained who I was, and requested her to furnish me with any further information which might be of service to me. She is a strange, silent woman, who impressed me as having very little intelligence. Your suggestion that I should avail myself of her assistance seems more curious than ever, now that I have seen her.

The whole affair seems to me at the moment of writing quite inexplicable. Assuming that this Captain Gunner was murdered, there appears to have been no motive for the crime whatsoever. I have made careful inquiries about him, and find that he was a man of fifty-five; had spent nearly forty years of his life at sea, the last dozen in command of his own ship; was of a somewhat overbearing disposition, though with a fund of rough humour; had travelled all over the world, and had been an inmate of the Excelsior for about ten months. He had a small annuity, and no other money at all, which disposes of money as the motive for the crime.

In my character of James Burton, a retired ships' chandler, I have mixed with the other boarders, and have heard all they have to say about the affair. I gather that the deceased was by no means popular. He appears to have had a bitter tongue, and I have not met one man who seems to regret his death. On the other hand, I have heard nothing which would suggest that he had any active and violent enemies. He was simply the unpopular boarder—there is always one in every boarding house—but nothing more.

I have seen a good deal of the man who shared his room—another sea captain, named Muller. He is a big, silent person, and it is not easy to get him to talk. As regards the death of Captain Gunner he can tell me nothing. It seems that on the night of the tragedy he was away at Portsmouth with some friends. All I have got from him is some information as to Captain Gunner's habits, which leads nowhere. The dead man seldom drank, except at night when he would take some whiskey. His head was not strong, and a little of the spirit was enough to make him semi-intoxicated, when he would be hilarious and often insulting. I gather that Muller found him a difficult roommate, but he is one of those placid persons who can put up with anything. He and Gunner were in the habit of playing draughts together every night in their room, and Gunner had a harmonica which he played frequently. Apparently, he was playing it very soon before he died, which is significant, as seeming to dispose of the idea of suicide.

As I say, I have one or two theories, but they are in a very nebulous state. The most plausible is that on one of his visits to India—I have ascertained that he made several voyages there—Captain Gunner may in some way have fallen foul of the natives. The fact that he certainly died of the poison of an Indian snake supports this theory. I am making inquiries as to the movements of several Indian sailors who were here in their ships at the time of the tragedy.

I have another theory. Does Mrs. Pickett know more about this affair than she appears to? I may be wrong in my estimate of her mental qualities. Her apparent stupidity may be cunning. But here again, the absence of motive brings me up against a dead wall. I must confess that at present I do not see my way clearly. However, I will write again shortly.

Mr. Snyder derived the utmost enjoyment from the report. He liked the substance of it, and above all, he was tickled by the bitter tone of frustration which characterized it. Oakes was baffled, and his knowledge of Oakes told him that the sensation of being baffled was gall and wormwood to that high-spirited young man. Whatever might be the result of this investigation, it would teach him the virtue of patience.

He wrote his assistant a short note:

Dear Oakes,

Your report received. You certainly seem to have got the hard case which, I hear, you were pining for. Don't build too much on plausible motives in a case of this sort. Fauntleroy, the London murderer, killed a woman for no other reason than that she had thick ankles. Many years ago, I myself was on a case where a man murdered an intimate friend because of a dispute about a bet. My experience is that five murderers out of ten act on the whim of the moment, without anything which, properly speaking, you could call a motive at all.

Yours very cordially,
Paul Snyder

P.S. I don't think much of your Pickett theory. However, you're in charge. I wish you luck.

IV

Young Mr. Oakes was not enjoying himself. For the first time in his life, the self-confidence which characterized all his actions seemed to be failing him. The change had taken place almost overnight. The fact that the case had the appearance of presenting the unusual had merely stimulated him at first, But then doubts had crept in and the problem had begun to appear insoluble.

True, he had only just taken it up, but something told him that, for all the progress he was likely to make, he might just as well have been working on it steadily for a month. He was completely baffled. And every moment which he spent in the Excelsior Boarding-House made it clearer to him that that infernal old woman with the pale eyes thought him an incompetent fool. It was that, more than anything, which made him acutely conscious of his lack of success. His nerves were being sorely troubled by the quiet scorn of Mrs. Pickett's gaze. He began to think that perhaps he had been a shade too self-confident and abrupt in the short interview which he had had with her on his arrival.

As might have been expected, his first act, after his brief interview with Mrs. Pickett, was to examine the room where the tragedy had taken place. The body was gone, but otherwise nothing had been moved.

Oakes belonged to the magnifying-glass school of detection. The first thing he did on entering the room was to make a careful examination of the floor, the walls, the furniture, and the windowsill. He would have hotly denied the assertion that he did this because it looked well, but he would have been hard put to it to advance any other reason.

If he discovered anything, his discoveries were entirely negative, and served only to deepen the mystery of the case. As Mr. Snyder had said, there was no chimney, and nobody could have entered through the locked door.

There remained the window. It was small, and apprehensiveness, perhaps, of the possibility of burglars, had caused the proprietress to make it doubly secure with an iron bar. No human being could have squeezed his way through it.

It was late that night that he wrote and dispatched to headquarters the report which had amused Mr. Snyder.

Two days later Mr. Snyder sat at his desk, staring with wide, unbelieving eyes at a telegram he had just received. It read as follows:

HAVE SOLVED GUNNER MYSTERY. RETURNING.... OAKES

Mr. Snyder narrowed his eyes and rang the bell.

"Send Mr. Oakes to me directly he arrives," he said.

He was pained to find that his chief emotion was one of bitter annoyance. The swift solution of such an apparently insoluble problem would reflect the highest credit on the Agency, and there were picturesque circumstances connected with the case which would make it popular with the newspapers and lead to its being given a great deal of publicity.

Yet, in spite of all this, Mr. Snyder was annoyed. He realized now how large a part the desire to reduce Oakes' self-esteem had played with him. He further realized, looking at the thing honestly, that he had been firmly convinced that the young man would not come within a mile of a reasonable solution of the mystery. He had desired only that his failure would prove a valuable educational experience for him. For he believed that failure at this particular point in his career would make Oakes a more valuable asset to the Agency. But now here Oakes was, within a ridiculously short space of time, returning to the fold, not humble and defeated, but triumphant. Mr. Snyder looked forward with apprehension to the young man's probable demeanor under the intoxicating influence of victory.

His apprehensions were well grounded. He had barely finished the third of the series of cigars, which, like milestones, marked the progress of his afternoon, when the door opened and young Oakes entered. Mr. Snyder could not repress a faint moan at the sight of him. One glance was enough to tell him that his worst fears were realised.

"I got your telegram," said Mr. Snyder.

Oakes nodded. "It surprised you, eh?" he asked.

Mr. Snyder resented the patronizing tone of the question, but he had resigned himself to be patronized, and keep his anger in check.

"Yes," he replied, "I must say it did surprise me. I didn't gather from your report that you had even found a clue. Was it the Indian theory that turned the trick?"

Oakes laughed tolerantly. "Oh, I never really believed that preposterous theory for one moment. I just put it in to round out my report. I hadn't begun to think about the case then—not really think."

Mr. Snyder, nearly exploding with wrath, extended his cigar-case. "Light up, and tell me all about it," he said, controlling his anger.

"Well, I won't say I haven't earned this," said Oakes, puffing away. He let the ash of his cigar fall delicately to the floor—another action which seemed significant to his employer. As a rule, his assistants, unless particularly pleased with themselves, used the ashtray.

"My first act on arriving," Oakes said, "was to have a talk with Mrs. Pickett. A very dull old woman."

"Curious. She struck me as rather intelligent."

"Not on your life. She gave me no assistance whatever. I then examined the room where the death had taken place. It was exactly as you described it. There was no chimney, the door had been locked on the inside, and the one window was

59

very high up. At first sight, it looked extremely unpromising. Then I had a chat with some of the other hoarders. They had nothing of any importance to contribute. Most of them simply gibbered. I then gave up trying to get help from the outside, and resolved to rely on my own intelligence."

He smiled triumphantly. "It is a theory of mine, Mr. Snyder, which I have found valuable that, in nine cases out of ten, remarkable things don't happen."

"I don't quite follow you there," Mr. Snyder interrupted.

"I will put it another way, if you like. What I mean is that the simplest explanation is nearly always the right one. Consider this case. It seemed impossible that there should have been any reasonable explanation of the man's death. Most men would have worn themselves out guessing at wild theories. If I had started to do that, I should have been guessing now. As it is—here I am. I trusted to my belief that nothing remarkable ever happens, and I won out."

Mr. Snyder sighed softly. Oakes was entitled to a certain amount of gloating, but there could be no doubt that his way of telling a story was downright infuriating.

"I believe in the logical sequence of events. I refuse to accept effects unless they are preceded by causes. In other words, with all due respect to your possibly contrary opinions, Mr. Snyder, I simply decline to believe in a murder unless there was a motive for it. The first thing I set myself to ascertain was—what was the motive for the murder of Captain Gunner? And, after thinking it over and making every possible inquiry, I decided that there was no motive. Therefore, there was no murder."

Mr. Snyder's mouth opened, and he obviously was about to protest. But he appeared to think better of it and Oakes proceeded: "I then tested the suicide theory. What motive was there for suicide? There was no motive. Therefore, there was no suicide."

This time Mr. Snyder spoke. "You haven't been spending the last few days in the wrong house by any chance, have you? You will be telling me next that there wasn't any dead man."

Oakes smiled. "Not at all. Captain John Gunner was dead, all right. As the medical evidence proved, he died of the bite of a cobra. It was a small cobra which came from Java."

Mr. Snyder stared at him. "How do you know?"

"I do know, beyond any possibility of doubt."

"Did you see the snake?"

Oakes shook his head.

"Then, how in heaven's name—"

"I have enough evidence to make a jury convict Mr. Snake without leaving the box."

"Then suppose you tell me this. How did your cobra from Java get out of the room?"

"By the window," replied Oakes, impassively.

"How can you possibly explain that? You say yourself that the window was high up."

"Nevertheless, it got out by the window. The logical sequence of events is proof enough that it was in the room. It killed Captain Gunner there, and left traces of its presence outside. Therefore, as the window was the only exit, it must have escaped by that route. It may have climbed or it may have jumped, but somehow it got out of that window."

"What do you mean—it left traces of its presence outside?"

"It killed a dog in the backyard behind the house," Oakes said. "The window of Captain Gunner's room projects out over it. It is full of boxes and litter and there are a few stunted shrubs scattered about. In fact, there is enough cover to hide any small object like the body of a dog. That's why it was not discovered at first. The maid at the Excelsior came on it the morning after I sent you my report while she was emptying a box of ashes in the yard. It was just an ordinary stray dog without collar or license. The analyst examined the body, and found that the dog had died of the bite of a cobra."

"But you didn't find the snake?"

"No. We cleaned out that yard till you could have eaten your breakfast there, but the snake had gone. It must have escaped through the door of the yard, which was standing ajar. That was a couple of days ago, and there has been no further tragedy. In all likelihood it is dead. The nights are pretty cold now, and it would probably have died of exposure."

"But, I just don't understand how a cobra got to Southampton," said the amazed Mr. Snyder.

"Can't you guess it? I told you it came from Java."

"How did you know it did?"

"Captain Muller told me. Not directly, but I pieced it together from what he said. It seems that an old shipmate of Captain Gunner's was living in Java. They corresponded, and occasionally this man would send the captain a present as a mark of his esteem. The last present he sent was a crate of bananas. Unfortunately, the snake must have got in unnoticed. That's why I told you the cobra was a small one. Well, that's my case against Mr. Snake, and short of catching him with the goods, I don't see how I could have made out a stronger one. Don't you agree?"

It went against the grain for Mr. Snyder to acknowledge defeat, but he was a fair-minded man, and he was forced to admit that Oakes did certainly seem to have solved the impossible.

"I congratulate you, my boy," he said as heartily as he could. "To be completely frank, when you started out, I didn't think you could do it. By the way, I suppose Mrs. Pickett was pleased?"

"If she was, she didn't show it. I'm pretty well convinced she hasn't enough sense to be pleased at anything. However, she has invited me to dinner with her tonight. I imagine she'll be as boring as usual, but she made such a point of it, I had to accept."

VI

For some time after Oakes had gone, Mr. Snyder sat smoking and thinking, in embittered meditation. Suddenly there was brought the card of Mrs. Pickett, who would be grateful if he could spare her a few moments. Mr. Snyder was glad to see Mrs. Pickett. He was a student of character, and she had interested him at their first meeting. There was something about her which had seemed to him unique, and he welcomed this second chance of studying her at close range.

She came in and sat down stiffly, balancing herself on the extreme edge of the chain in which a short while before young Oakes had lounged so luxuriously.

"How are you, Mrs. Pickett?" said Mr. Snyder genially. "I'm very glad that you could find time to pay me a visit. Well, so it wasn't murder after all."

"Sir?"

"I've just been talking to Mr. Oakes, whom you met as James Burton," said the detective. "He has told me all about it."

"He told *me* all about it," said Mrs. Pickett dryly.

Mr Snyder looked at her inquiringly. Her manner seemed more suggestive than her words.

"A conceited, headstrong young fool," said Mrs. Pickett.

It was no new picture of his assistant that she had drawn. Mr. Snyder had often drawn it himself, but at the present juncture it surprised him. Oakes, in his hour of triumph, surely did not deserve this sweeping condemnation.

"Did not Mr. Oakes' solution of the mystery satisfy you, Mrs. Pickett?"

"No!"

"It struck me as logical and convincing," Mr. Snyder said.

"You may call it all the fancy names you please, Mr. Snyder. But Mr. Oakes' solution was not the right one."

"Have you an alternative to offer?"

Mrs. Pickett tightened her lips.

"If you have, I should like to hear it."

"You will—at the proper time."

"What makes you so certain that Mr. Oakes is wrong?"

"He starts out with an impossible explanation, and rests his whole case on it. There couldn't have been a snake in that room because it couldn't have gotten out. The window was too high."

"But surely the evidence of the dead dog?"

Mrs. Pickett looked at him as if he had disappointed her. "I had always heard *you* spoken of as a man with common sense, Mr. Snyder."

"I have always tried to use common sense."

"Then why are you trying now to make yourself believe that something happened which could not possibly have happened just because it fits in with something which isn't easy to explain?"

"You mean that there is another explanation of the dead dog?" Mr. Snyder asked.

"Not *another*. What Mr. Oakes takes for granted is not an explanation. But there is a common sense explanation, and if he had not been so headstrong and conceited he might have found it."

"You speak as if you had found it," chided Mr. Snyder.

"I have," Mrs. Pickett leaned forward as she spoke, and stared at him defiantly. Mr. Snyder started. "*You* have?"

"Yes."

"What is it?"

"You will know before tomorrow. In the meantime try and think it out for yourself. A successful and prosperous detective agency like yours, Mr. Snyder, ought to do something in return for a fee."

There was something in her manner so reminiscent of the school teacher reprimanding a recalcitrant pupil that Mr. Snyder's sense of humor came to his rescue. "We do our best, Mrs. Pickett," he said. "But you mustn't forget that we are only human and cannot guarantee results."

Mrs. Pickett did not pursue the subject. Instead, she proceeded to astonish Mr. Snyder by asking him to swear out a warrant for the arrest of a man known to them both on a charge of murder.

Mr. Snyder's breath was not often taken away in his own office. As a rule, he received his clients' communications calmly, strange as they often were. But at her words he gasped. The thought crossed his mind that Mrs. Pickett might well be mentally unbalanced. The details of the case were fresh in his memory, and he distinctly recollected that the person she mentioned had been away from the boarding house on the night of Captain Gunner's death, and could, he imagined, produce witnesses to prove it.

Mrs. Pickett was regarding him with an unfaltering stare. To all outward appearances, she was the opposite of unbalanced.

"But you can't swear out a warrant without evidence," he told her.

"I have evidence," she replied firmly.

"Precisely what kind of evidence?" he demanded.

"If I told you now you would think that I was out of my mind."

"But, Mrs. Pickett, do you realize what you are asking me to do? I cannot make this agency responsible for the arbitrary arrest of a man on the strength of a single individual's suspicions. It might ruin me. At the least it would make me a laughing stock."

"Mr. Snyder, you may use your own judgment whether or not to make the arrest on that warrant. You will listen to what I have to say, and you will see for yourself how the crime was committed. If after that you feel that you cannot make the arrest I will accept your decision. I know who killed Captain Gunner," she said. "I knew it from the beginning. It was like a vision. But I had no proof. Now things have come to light and everything is clear."

Against his judgment, Mr. Snyder was impressed. This woman had the magnetism which makes for persuasiveness.

"It—it sounds incredible." Even as he spoke, he remembered that it had long been a professional maxim of his that nothing was incredible, and he weakened still further.

"Mr. Snyder, I ask you to swear out that warrant."

The detective gave in. "Very well," he said.

Mrs. Pickett rose. "If you will come and dine at my house tonight I think I can prove to you that it will be needed. Will you come?"

"I'll come," promised Mr. Snyder.

VII

When Mr. Snyder arrived at the Excelsior and shortly after he was shown into the little private sitting room where he found Oakes, the third guest of the evening unexpectedly arrived.

Mr. Snyder looked curiously at the newcomer. Captain Muller had a peculiar fascination for him. It was not Mr. Snyder's habit to trust overmuch to appearances. But he could not help admitting that there was something about this man's aspect which brought Mrs. Pickett's charges out of the realm of the fantastic into that of the possible. There was something odd—an unnatural aspect of gloom—about the man. He bore himself like one carrying a heavy burden. His eyes were dull, his face haggard. The next moment the detective was reproaching himself with allowing his imagination to run away with his calmer judgment.

The door opened, and Mrs. Pickett came in. She made no apology for her lateness.

To Mr. Snyder one of the most remarkable points about the dinner was the peculiar metamorphosis of Mrs. Pickett from the brooding silent woman he had known to the gracious and considerate hostess.

Oakes appeared also to be overcome with surprise, so much so that he was unable to keep his astonishment to himself. He had come prepared to endure a dull evening absorbed in grim silence, and he found himself instead opposite a bottle of champagne of a brand and year which commanded his utmost respect. What was even more incredible, his hostess had transformed herself into a pleasant old lady whose only aim seemed to be to make him feel at home.

Beside each of the guests' plates was a neat paper parcel. Oakes picked his up, and stared at it in wonderment. "Why, this is more than a party souvenir, Mrs. Pickett," he said. It's the kind of mechanical marvel I've always wanted to have on my desk."

"I'm glad you like it, Mr. Oakes," Mrs. Pickett said, smiling. "You must not think of me simply as a tired old woman whom age has completely defeated. I am an ambitious hostess. When I give these little parties, I like to make them a success. I want each of you to remember this dinner."

"I'm sure I will."

Mrs. Pickett smiled again. "I think you all will. You, Mr. Snyder." She paused. "And you, Captain Muller."

To Mr. Snyder there was so much meaning in her voice as she said this that he was amazed that it conveyed no warning to Muller. Captain Muller, however, was already drinking heavily. He looked up when addressed and uttered a sound which might have been taken for an expression of polite acquiescence. Then he filled his glass again.

Mr. Snyder's parcel revealed a watch-charm fashioned in the shape of a tiny, candid-eye camera. "That," said Mrs. Pickett, "is a compliment to your profession." She leaned toward the captain. "Mr. Snyder is a detective, Captain Muller."

He looked up. It seemed to Mr. Snyder that a look of fear lit up his heavy eyes for an instant. It came and went, if indeed it came at all, so swiftly that he could not be certain.

"So?" said Captain Muller. He spoke quite evenly, with just the amount of interest which such an announcement would naturally produce.

"Now for yours, Captain," said Oakes. "I guess it's something special. It's twice the size of mine, anyway."

It may have been something in the old woman's expression as she watched Captain Muller slowly tearing the paper that sent a thrill of excitement through Mr. Snyder. Something seemed to warn him of the approach of a psychological moment. He bent forward eagerly.

There was a strangled gasp, a thump, and onto the table from the captain's hands there fell a little harmonica. There was no mistaking the look on Muller's face now. His cheeks were like wax, and his eyes, so dull till then, blazed with a panic and horror which he could not repress. The glasses on the table rocked as he clutched at the cloth.

Mrs. Pickett spoke. "Why, Captain Muller, has it upset you? I thought that, as his best friend, the man who shared his room, you would value a memento of Captain Gunner. How fond you must have been of him for the sight of his harmonica to be such a shock."

The captain did not speak. He was staring fascinated at the thing on the table. Mrs. Pickett turned to Mr. Snyder. Her eyes, as they met his, held him entranced.

"Mr. Snyder, as a detective, you will be interested in a curious and very tragic affair which happened in this house a few days ago. One of my boarders, Captain Gunner, was found dead in his room. It was the room which he shared with Captain Muller. I am very proud of the reputation of my house, Mr. Snyder, and it was a blow to me that this should have happened. I applied to an agency for a detective, and they sent me a stupid boy, with nothing to recommend him except his belief in himself. He said that Captain Gunner had died by accident, killed by a snake which had come out of a crate of bananas. I knew better. I knew that Captain Gunner had been murdered. Are you listening, Captain Muller? This will interest you, as you were such a friend of his."

The captain did not answer. He was staring straight before him, as if he saw something invisible in eyes forever closed in death.

"Yesterday we found the body of a dog. It had been killed, as Captain Gunner had been, by the poison of a snake. The boy from the agency said that this was conclusive. He said that the snake had escaped from the room after killing Captain Gunner and had in turn killed the dog. I knew that to be impossible, for, if there had been a snake in that room it could not have made its escape."

Her eyes flashed, and became remorselessly accusing. "It was not a snake that killed Captain Gunner. It was a cat. Captain Gunner had a friend who hated him. One day, in opening a crate of bananas, this friend found a snake. He killed it, and extracted the poison. He knew Captain Gunner's habits. He knew that he played a harmonica. This man also had a cat. He knew that cats hated the sound of a harmonica. He had often seen this particular cat fly at Captain Gunner and scratch him when he played. He took the cat and covered its claws with the poison. And then he left it in the room with Captain Gunner. He knew what would happen."

Oakes and Mr. Snyder were on their feet. Captain Muller had not moved. He sat there, his fingers gripping the cloth. Mrs. Pickett rose and went to a closet. She unlocked the door. "Kitty!" she called. "Kitty! Kitty!"

A black cat ran swiftly out into the room. With a clatter and a crash of crockery and a ringing of glass the table heaved, rocked and overturned as Muller staggered to his feet. He threw up his hands as if to ward something off. A choking cry came from his lips. "Gott! Gott!"

Mrs. Pickett's voice rang through the room, cold and biting: "Captain Muller, you murdered Captain Gunner!"

The captain shuddered. Then mechanically he replied: "Gott! Yes, I killed him."

"You heard, Mr. Snyder," said Mrs. Pickett. "He has confessed before witnesses. Take him away."

Muller allowed himself to be moved toward the door. His arm in Mr. Snyder's grip felt limp. Mrs. Pickett stopped and took something from the debris on the floor. She rose, holding the harmonica.

"You are forgetting your souvenir, Captain Muller," she said.

R. Austin Freeman

(1862–1943)

Dr. John Evelyn Thorndyke has been called the only convincing scientific investigator in detective fiction, with considerable justification. Joined by his associate, Christopher Jervis, M.D., who narrates his idol's investigations in the classic manner pioneered by Poe and refined by Doyle, Dr. Thorndyke draws on a wealth of scientific knowledge—everything from anatomy to zoology—to solve his cases. Although many of the plots involve technical explanations, R. Austin Freeman (like Doyle, a former physician) was a master at making science and its jargon explicable to the lay reader.

Thorndyke and Jervis were introduced in the novel *The Red Thumb Mark* (1907), notable for its first use of fingerprint forgery in detective fiction. But it was in Freeman's 1912 collection of five novelettes, *The Singing Bone,* that he provided his greatest contribution to the genre. In such stories as "The Case of Oscar Brodski," he invented the "inverted" detective story, a device much copied by other writers and utilized to cinematic perfection in the TV series *Columbo.* In the first part of this type of tale, the reader is permitted to witness the commission of a crime and furnished with all the facts necessary to solve it; in the second part, the reader is led through each of the steps used by the investigator to gather clues and correctly interpret them. The question of "whodunit" is thus eliminated, though there is a challenge of sorts to match wits with the sleuth and spot the clues in advance; but the main pleasure is in watching a superior intellect at work—using scientific methods in Dr. Thorndyke's case, rather than pure deduction as in the Sherlock Holmes stories.

Freeman's most celebrated work is *Mr. Pottermack's Oversight* (1930), which critic Anthony Boucher called "a leisurely, gentle novel, yet an acute one. No other detective in fiction has ever equaled Thorndyke in the final section of explication [and] the scene is especially effective in this novel," offering an intellectual stimulus often attributed to the detective story but rarely found. The same is applicable to "The Puzzle Lock," the title story of a 1925 collection of Thorndyke stories. A variation of the inverted form in that the detailed methodology of the crime is presented to Thorndyke and the reader through an ex post facto exchange of dialogue, it is a pretty brainteaser involving an ingenious locking mechanism on a strongroom door. Editor and anthologist Raymond T. Bond considered it "close to being the most exciting single episode in the Doctor's long and varied career," adding that no other story in the Thorndyke annals puts such an immediate and terrifying demand on his mental powers or promises "so completely breathless an ending."

THE PUZZLE LOCK

DR. JOHN THORNDYKE AND CHRISTOPHER JERVIS
LONDON, ENGLAND
1926

I do not remember what was the occasion of my dining with Thorndyke at Giamborini's on the particular evening that is now in my mind. Doubtless, some piece of work completed had seemed to justify the modest festival. At any rate, there we were, seated at a somewhat retired table, selected by Thorndyke, with our backs to the large window through which the late June sunlight streamed. We had made our preliminary arrangements, including a bottle of Barsac, and were inspecting dubiously a collection of semi-edible *hors d'œuvres*, when a man entered and took possession of a table just in front of ours, which had apparently been reserved for him, since he walked directly to it and drew away the single chair that had been set aslant against it.

I watched with amused interest his methodical procedure, for he was clearly a man who took his dinner seriously. A regular customer, too, I judged by the waiter's manner and the reserved table with its single chair. But the man himself interested me. He was out of the common and there was a suggestion of character, with perhaps a spice of oddity, in his appearance. He appeared to be about sixty years of age, small and spare, with a much wrinkled, mobile and rather whimsical face, surmounted by a crop of white, upstanding hair. From his waistcoat pocket protruded the ends of a fountain-pen, a pencil and a miniature electric torch such as surgeons use; a silver-mounted Coddington lens hung from his watchguard and the middle finger of his left hand bore the largest seal ring that I have ever seen.

"Well," said Thorndyke, who had been following my glance, "what do you make of him?"

"I don't quite know," I replied. "The Coddington suggests a naturalist or a scientist of some kind, but that blatant ring doesn't. Perhaps he is an antiquary or a numismatist or even a philatelist. He deals with small objects of some kind."

At this moment a man who had just entered strode up to our friend's table and held out his hand, which the other shook, with no great enthusiasm, as I thought. Then the newcomer fetched a chair, and setting it by the table, seated himself and picked up the menu card, while the other observed him with a shade of disapproval. I judged that he would rather have dined alone, and that the personality of the new arrival—a flashy, bustling, obtrusive type of man—did not commend him.

From this couple my eye was attracted to a tall man who had halted near the door and stood looking about the room as if seeking some one. Suddenly he spied an empty, single table, and, bearing down on it, seated himself and began anxiously to study the menu under the supervision of a waiter. I glanced at him with slight disfavor. One makes allowances for the exuberance of youth, but when a middle-aged man presents the combination of heavily greased hair parted in the middle, a waxed moustache of a suspiciously intense black, a pointed imperial and a single eye-glass, evidently ornamental in function, one views him with less tolerance. However, his get-up was not my concern, whereas my dinner was, and I had given this my undivided attention for some minutes when I heard Thorndyke emit a soft chuckle.

"Not bad," he remarked, setting down his glass.

"Not at all," I agreed, "for a restaurant wine."

"I was not alluding to the wine," said he, "but to our friend Badger."

"The inspector!" I exclaimed. "He isn't here, is he? I don't see him."

"I am glad to hear you say that, Jervis," said he. "It is a better effort than I thought. Still, he might manage his properties a little better. That is the second time his eyeglass has been in the soup.

Following the direction of his glance, I observed the man with the waxed moustache furtively wiping his eyeglass; and the temporary absence of the monocular grimace enabled me to note a resemblance of the familiar features of the detective officer.

"If you say that is Badger, I suppose it is," said I. "He is certainly a little like our friend. But I shouldn't have recognized him."

"I don't know that I should," said Thorndyke, "but for the little unconscious tricks of movement. You know the habit he has of stroking the back of his head and of opening his mouth and scratching the side of his chin. I saw him do it just now. He had forgotten his imperial until he touched it, and then the sudden arrest of movement was very striking. It doesn't do to forget a false beard."

"I wonder what his game is," said I. "The disguise suggests that he is on the look-out for somebody who might know him; but apparently that somebody has not turned up yet. At any rate, he doesn't seem to be watching anybody in particular."

"No," said Thorndyke. "But there is somebody whom he seems rather to avoid watching. Those two men at the table in front of ours are in his direct line of vision, but he hasn't looked at them once since he sat down, though I noticed that he gave them one quick glance before he selected his table. I wonder if he has observed us. Probably not, as we have the strong light of the window behind us and his attention is otherwise occupied."

I looked at the two men and from them to the detective, and I judged that my friend was right. On the inspector's table was a good-sized fern in an ornamental pot, and this he had moved so that it was directly between him and the two strangers, to whom he must have been practically invisible; and now I could see that he did, in fact, steal an occasional glance at them over the edge of the menu card. Moreover, as their meal drew to an end, he hastily finished his own and beckoned to the waiter to bring his bill.

"We may as well wait and see them off," said Thorndyke, who had already settled our account. "Badger always interests me. He is so ingenious and he has such shockingly bad luck."

We had not long to wait. The two men rose from the table and walked slowly to the door, where they paused to light their cigars before going out. Then Badger rose, with his back towards them and his eyes on the mirror opposite; and as they went out, he snatched up his hat and stick and followed. Thorndyke looked at me inquiringly.

"Do we indulge in the pleasures of the chase?" he asked, and as I replied in the affirmative, we, too, made our way out and started in the wake of the inspector.

As we followed Badger at a discreet distance, we caught an occasional glimpse of the quarry ahead, whose proceedings evidently caused the inspector some embarrassment, for they had a way of stopping suddenly to elaborate some point that they were discussing, whereby it became necessary for the detective to drop farther in the rear than was quite safe, in view of the rather crowded state of the pavement. On one of these occasions, when the older man was apparently delivering himself of some excruciating joke, they both turned suddenly and looked back, the joker pointing to some object on the opposite side of the road. Several people turned to see what was being pointed at, and, of course, the inspector had to turn, too, to avoid being recognized. At this moment the two men popped into an entry, and when the inspector once more turned they were gone.

71

As soon as he missed them, Badger started forward almost at a run, and presently halted at the large entry of the Celestial Bank chambers, into which he peered eagerly. Then, apparently sighting his quarry, he darted in, and we quickened our pace and followed. Half-way down the long hall we saw him standing at the door of a lift, frantically pressing the call-button.

"Poor Badger!" chuckled Thorndyke, as we walked past him unobserved. "His usual luck! He will hardly run them to earth now in this enormous building. We may as well go through to the Blenheim Street entrance."

We pursued our way along the winding corridor and were close to the entrance when I noticed two men coming down the staircase that led to the hall.

"By Jingo! Here they are!" I exclaimed. "Shall we run back and give Badger the tip?"

Thorndyke hesitated. But it was too late. A taxi had just driven up and was discharging its fare. The younger man, catching the driver's eye, ran out and seized the door-handle; and when his companion had entered the cab, he gave an address to the driver, and, stepping in quickly, slammed the door. As the cab moved off, Thorndyke pulled out his note-book and pencil and jotted down the number of the vehicle. Then we turned and retraced our steps; but when we reached the lift-door, the inspector had disappeared. Presumably, like the incomparable Tom Bowling, he had gone aloft."

"We must give it up, Jervis," said Thorndyke. "I will send him—anonymously—the number of the cab, and that is all we can do. But I am sorry for Badger."

With this we dismissed the incident from our minds—at least, I did; assuming that I had seen the last of the two strangers. Little did I suspect how soon and under what strange and tragic circumstances I should meet with them again!

It was about a week later that we received a visit from our old friend, Superintendent Miller of the Criminal Investigation Department. The passing years had put us on a footing of mutual trust and esteem, and the capable, straightforward detective officer was always a welcome visitor.

"I've just dropped in," said Miller, cutting off the end of the inevitable cigar, "to tell you about a rather queer case that we've got in hand. I know you are always interested in queer cases."

Thorndyke smiled blandly. He had heard that kind of preamble before, and he knew, as did I, that when Miller became communicative we could safely infer that the Millerian bark was in shoal water.

"It is a case," the superintendent continued, "of a very special brand of crook. Actually there is a gang, but it is the managing director that we have particularly got our eye on."

"Is he a regular 'habitual,' then?" asked Thorndyke.

"Well," replied Miller, "as to that, I can't positively say. The fact is that we haven't actually seen the man to be sure of him."

"I see," said Thorndyke, with a grim smile. "You mean to say that you have got your eye on the place where he isn't."

"At the present moment," Miller admitted, "that is the literal fact. We have lost sight of the man we suspected, but we hope to pick him up again presently. We want him badly, and his pals too. It is probably quite a small gang, but they are mighty sly, a lot too smart to be at large. And they'll take some catching, for there is some one running the concern with a good deal more brains than crooks usually have."

"What is their lay?" I asked.

"Burglary," he replied. "Jewels and plate, but principally jewels; and the special feature of their work is that the swag disappears completely every time. None of the stuff has ever been traced. That is what drew our attention to them. After each robbery we made a round of all the fences, but there was not a sign. The stuff seemed to have vanished into smoke. Now that is very awkward. If you never see the men and you can't trace the stuff, where are you? You've got nothing to go on."

"But you seem to have got a clue of some kind," I said.

"Yes. There isn't a lot in it; but it seemed worth following up. One of our men happened to travel down to Colchester with a certain man, and when he came back two days later, he noticed this same man on the platform at Colchester and saw him get out at Liverpool Street. In the interval there had been a jewel robbery at Colchester. Then there was a robbery at Southampton, and our man went at once to Waterloo and saw all the trains in. On the second day, behold! the Colchester sportsman turns up at the barrier, so our man, who had a special taxi waiting, managed to track him home and afterwards got some particulars about him. He is a chap named Shemmonds; belongs to a firm of outside brokers. But nobody seems to know much about him and he doesn't put in much time at the office.

"Well, then, Badger took him over and shadowed him for a day or two, but just as things were looking interesting, he slipped off the hook. Badger followed him to a restaurant, and, through the glass door, saw him go up to an elderly man at a table and shake hands with him. Then he took a chair at the table himself, so Badger popped in and took a seat near them where he could keep them in view. They went out together and Badger followed them, but he lost them in the Celestial Bank Chambers. They went up in the lift just before he could get to the door and that was the last he saw of them. But we have ascertained that they left the building in a taxi and that the taxi set them down at Great Turnstile."

"It was rather smart of you to trace the cab," Thorndyke remarked.

"You've got to keep your eyes skinned in our line of business," said Miller. "But now we come to the real twister. From the time those two men went down Great Turnstile, nobody has set eyes on either of them. They seem to have vanished into thin air.

"You found out who the other man was, then?" said I.

"Yes. The restaurant manager knew him; an old chap named Luttrell. And we knew him, too, because he has a thumping burglary insurance, and when he goes out of town he notifies his company. They make arrangements with us to have the premises watched."

"What is Luttrell?" I asked.

"Well, he is a bit of a mug, I should say, at least that's his character in the trade. Goes in for being a dealer in jewels and antiques, but he'll buy anything—furniture, pictures, plate, any blooming thing. Does it for hobby, the regular dealers say. Likes the sport of bidding at the sales. But the knock-out men hate him; never know what he's going to do. Must have private means, for though he doesn't often drop money, he can't make much. He's no salesman. It is the buying that he seems to like. But he is a regular character, full of cranks and oddities. His rooms in Thavies Inn look like the British Museum gone mad. He has got electric alarms from all the doors up to his bedroom and the strong-room in his office is fitted with a puzzle lock instead of keys."

"That doesn't seem very safe," I remarked.

"It is," said Miller. "This one has fifteen alphabets. One of our men has calculated that it has about forty billion changes. No one is going to work that out, and there are no keys to get lost. But it is that strong-room that is worrying us, as well as the old joker himself. The Lord knows how much valuable stuff there is in it. What we are afraid of is that Shemmonds may have made away with the old chap and be lying low, waiting to swoop down on that strong-room."

"But you said that Luttrell goes away sometimes," said I.

"Yes; but then he always notifies his insurance company and he seals up his strong-room with a tape round the door-handle and a great seal on the door-post. This time he hasn't notified the company and the door isn't sealed. There's a seal on the door-post—left from last time, I expect—but only the cut ends of tape. I got the caretaker to let me see the place this morning; and, by the way, Doctor, I have taken a leaf out of your book. I always carry a bit of squeezing wax in my pocket now and a little box of French chalk. Very handy they are, too. As I had 'em with me this morning, I took a squeeze of the seal. May want it presently for identification.

He brought out of his pocket a small tin box from which he carefully extracted an object wrapped in tissue paper. When the paper had been tenderly removed there was revealed a lump of moulding wax, one side of which was flattened and bore a sunk design.

"It's quite a good squeeze," said Miller, handing it to Thorndyke. "I dusted the seal with French chalk so that the wax shouldn't stick to it."

My colleague examined the "squeeze" through his lens, and passing it and the lens to me, asked:

"Has this been photographed, Miller?"

"No," was the reply, "but it ought to be before it gets damaged."

"It ought, certainly," said Thorndyke, "if you value it. Shall I get Polton to do it now?"

The superintendent accepted the offer gratefully and Thorndyke accordingly took the squeeze up to the laboratory, where he left it for our assistant to deal with. When he returned, Miller remarked:

"It is a baffling case, this. Now that Shemmonds has dropped out of sight, there is nothing to go on and nothing to do but wait for something else to happen; another burglary or an attempt on the strong-room."

"Is it clear that the strong-room has not been opened?" asked Thorndyke.

"No, it isn't," replied Miller. "That's part of the trouble. Luttrell has disappeared and he may be dead. If he is, Shemmonds will probably have been through his pockets. Of course there is no strong-room key. That is one of the advantages of a puzzle lock. But it is quite possible that Luttrell may have kept a note of the combination and carried it about him. It would have been risky to trust entirely to memory. And he would have had the keys of the office about him. Any one who had those could have slipped in during business hours without much difficulty. Luttrell's premises are empty, but there are people in and out all day going to the other offices. Our man can't follow them all in. I suppose you can't make any suggestion, Doctor?"

"I am afraid I can't," answered Thorndyke. "The case is so very much in the air. There is nothing against Shemmonds but bare suspicion. He has disappeared only in the sense that you have lost sight of him, and the same is true of Luttrell— though there is an abnormal element in his case. Still, you could hardly get a search-warrant on the facts that are known at present."

"No," Miller agreed, "they certainly would not authorize us to break open the strong-room, and nothing short of that would be much use."

Here Polton made his appearance with the wax squeeze in a neat little box such s jewellers use.

"I've got two enlarged negatives," said he; "nice clear ones. How many prints shall I make for Mr. Miller?"

"Oh, one will do, Mr. Polton," said the superintendent. "If I want any more I'll ask you." He took up the little box, and slipping it in his pocket, rose to depart. "I'll let you know, Doctor, how the case goes on, and perhaps you wouldn't mind turning it over a bit in the interval. Something might occur to you."

Thorndyke promised to think over the case, and when we had seen the superintendent launched down the stairs, we followed Polton up to the laboratory, where we each picked up one of the negatives and examined it against the light. I had already identified the seal by its shape—a *vesica piscis* or boat-shape—with the one that I had seen on Mr. Luttrell's finger. Now, in the photograph enlarged three diameters I could clearly make out the details. The design was distinctive and curious rather than elegant. The two triangular spaces at the ends were occupied respectively by a *memento mori* and a winged hour-glass and the central portion was filled by a long inscription in Roman capitals, of which I could at first make nothing.

"Do you suppose this is some kind of cryptogram?" I asked.

"No," Thorndyke replied. "I imagine the words were run together merely to economize space. This is what I make of it."

He held the negative in his left hand, and with his right wrote down in pencil on a slip of paper the following four lines of doggerel verse:

"Eheu alas how fast the dam fugaces
Labuntur anni especially in the cases
Of poor old blokes like you and me Posthumus
Who only waits for vermes to consume us."

"Well," I exclaimed, "it is a choice specimen; one of old Luttrell's merry conceited jests, I take it. But the joke was hardly worth the labor of engraving on a seal."

"It is certainly a rather mild jest," Thorndyke admitted. "But there may be something more in it than meets the eye."

He looked at the inscription reflectively and appeared to read it through once or twice. Then he replaced the negative in the drying rack, and, picking up the paper, slipped it into his pocketbook.

"I don't quite see," said I, "why Miller brought this case to us or what he wants you to think over. In fact, I don't see that there is a case at all."

"It is a very shadowy case," Thorndyke admitted. "Miller has done a good deal of guessing, and so has Badger; and it may easily turn out that they have found a mare's nest. Nevertheless there is something to think about."

"As, for instance—?"

"Well, Jervis, you saw the men; you saw how they behaved; you have heard Miller's story and you have seen Mr. Luttrell's seal. Put all those data together and you have the material for some very interesting speculation, to say the least. You might even carry it beyond speculation."

I did not pursue the subject, for I knew that when Thorndyke used the word "speculation," nothing would induce him to commit himself to an opinion. But later, bearing in mind the attention that he seemed to bestow on Mr. Luttrell's schoolboy verses, I got a print from the negative and studied the foolish inscription exhaustively. But if it had any hidden meaning—and I could imagine no reason for supposing that it had—that meaning remained hidden; and the only conclusion at which I could arrive was that a man of Luttrell's age might have known better than to write such nonsense.

The superintendent did not leave the matter long in suspense. Three days later he paid us another visit and half-apologetically reopened the subject.

"I am ashamed to come badgering you like this," he said, "but I can't get this case out of my head. I've a feeling that we ought to get a move of some kind on. And, by the way—though that is nothing to do with it—I've copied out the stuff on that seal and I can't make any sense of it. What the deuce are fugaces? I suppose 'vermes' are worms, though I don't see why he spelt it that way."

"The verses," said Thorndyke, "are apparently a travesty of a Latin poem; one of the odes of Horace which begins:

'Eheu! fugaces, Postume, Postume,

Labuntur anni,'

which means, in effect, 'Alas! Postume, the flying years slip by.'"

"Well," said Miller, "any fool knows that—any middle-aged fool, at any rate. No need to put it into Latin. However, it's of no consequence. To return to this case; I've got an authority to look over Luttrell's premises—not to pull anything about, you know, just to look round. I called in on my way here to let the caretaker know that I should be coming in later. I thought that perhaps you might like to come with me. I wish you would, Doctor. You've got such a knack of spotting things that other people overlook."

He looked wistfully at Thorndyke, and as the latter was considering the proposal, he added:

"The caretaker mentioned a rather odd circumstance. It seems that he keeps an eye on the electric metres in the building and that he has noticed a leakage of current in Mr. Luttrell's. It is only a small leak; about thirty watts an hour. But he can't account for it in any way. He has been right through the premises to see if any lamp has been left on in any of the rooms. But all the switches are off everywhere, and it can't be a short circuit. Funny, isn't it?"

It was certainly odd, but there seemed to me nothing in it to account for the expression of suddenly awakened interest that I detected in Thorndyke's face. However, it evidently had some special significance for him, for he asked almost eagerly:

"When are you making your inspection?"

"I am going there now," replied Miller, and he added coaxingly: "Couldn't you manage to run round with me?"

Thorndyke stood up. "Very well," said he. "Let us go together. You may as well come, too, Jervis, if you can spare an hour."

I agreed readily, for my colleague's hardly disguised interest in the inspection suggested a definite problem in his mind; and we at once issued forth and made our way by Mitre Court and Fetter Lane to the abode of the missing dealer, an old-fashioned house near the end of Thavies Inn.

"I've been over the premises once," said Miller, as the caretaker appeared with the keys, "and I think we had better begin the regular inspection with the offices. We can examine the stories and living-rooms afterwards."

We accordingly entered the outer office, and as this was little more than a waiting-room, we passed through into the private office, which had the appearance of having been used also as a sitting-room or study. It was furnished with an easy-chair, a range of book-shelves and a handsome bureau book-case, while in the end wall was the massive iron door of the strong-room. On this, as the chief object of interest, we all bore down, and the superintendent expounded its peculiarities.

"It is quite a good idea," said he, "this letter-lock. There's no keyhole—though a safe-lock is pretty hopeless to pick even if there was a keyhole—and no keys to get lost. As to guessing what the 'open sesame' may be—well, just look at it. You could spend a lifetime on it and be no forrader."

The puzzle lock was contained in the solid iron doorpost, through a slot in which a row of fifteen A's seemed to grin defiance on the would-be safe-robber. I put my finger on the milled edges of one or two of the letters and rotated the discs, noticing how easily and smoothly they turned.

"Well," said Miller, "It's no use fumbling with that. I'm just going to have a look through his ledger and see who his customers were. The book-case is unlocked. I tried it last time. And we'd better leave this as we found it."

He put back the letters that I had moved, and turned away to explore the book-case; and as the letter-lock appeared to present nothing but an insoluble riddle, I followed him, leaving Thorndyke earnestly gazing at the meaningless row of letters.

The superintendent glanced back at him with an indulgent smile.

"The doctor is going to work out the combination," he chuckled. "Well, well. There are only forty billion changes and he's a young man for his age."

With this encouraging comment, he opened the glass door of the book-case, and reaching down the ledger, laid it on the desk-like slope of the bureau.

"It is a poor chance," said he, opening the ledger at the index, "but some of these people may be able to give us a hint where to look for Mr. Luttrell, and it is worth while to know what sort of business he did."

He ran his finger down the list of names and had just turned to the account of one of the customers when we were startled by a loud click from the direction of the strong-room. We both turned sharply and beheld Thorndyke grasping the handle of the strong-room door, and I saw with amazement that the door was now slightly ajar.

"God!" exclaimed Miller, shutting the ledger and starting forward, "he's got it open!" He strode over to the door, and directing an eager look at the indicator of the lock, burst into a laugh. "Well, I'm hanged!" he exclaimed. "Why, it was unlocked all the time! To think that none of us had the sense to tug the handle! But isn't it just like old Luttrell to have a fool's answer like that to the blessed puzzle!"

I looked at the indicator, not a little astonished to observe the row of fifteen A's, which apparently formed the key combination. It may have been a very amusing joke on Mr. Luttrell's part, but it did not look very secure. Thorndyke regarded us with an inscrutable glance and still grasped the handle, holding the door a bare half-inch open.

"There is something pushing against the door," said he. "Shall I open it?"

"May as well have a look at the inside," replied Miller. Thereupon Thorndyke released the handle and quickly stepped aside. The door swung slowly open and the dead body of a man fell out into the room and rolled over on to its back.

"Mercy on us!" gasped Miller, springing back hastily and staring with horror and amazement at the grim apparition. "That is not Luttrell." Then, suddenly starting forward and stooping over the dead man, he exclaimed: "Why, it is Shemmonds. So that is where he disappeared to. I wonder what became of Luttrell."

"There is somebody else in the strong-room," said Thorndyke; and now, peering in through the doorway, I perceived a dim light, which seemed to come from a hidden recess, and by which I could see a pair of feet projecting round the corner. In a moment Miller had sprung in, and I followed. The strong-room was L-shaped in plan, the arm of the L formed by a narrow passage at right angles to the main room. At the end of this a single small electric bulb was burning, the light of which showed the body of an elderly man stretched on the floor of the passage. I recognized him instantly in spite of the dimness of the light and the disfigurement caused by a ragged wound on the forehead.

"We had better get him out of this," said Miller, speaking in a flurried tone, partly due to the shock of the horrible discovery and partly to the accompanying physical unpleasantness, "and then we will have a look round. This wasn't just a mere robbery. We are going to find things out."

With my help he lifted Luttrell's corpse and together we carried it out, laying it on the floor of the room at the farther end, to which we also dragged the body of Shemmonds.

"There is no mystery as to how it happened," I said, after a brief inspection of the two corpses. "Shemmonds evidently shot the old man from behind with the pistol close to the back of the head. The hair is all scorched round the wound of entry and the bullet came out at the forehead."

"Yes," agreed Miller, "that is all clear enough. But the mystery is why on earth Shemmonds didn't let himself out. He must have known that the door was un-locked. Yet instead of turning the handle, he must have stood there, like a fool, bat-tering at the door with his fists. Just look at his hands."

"The further mystery," said Thorndyke, who, all this time, had been making a minute examination of the lock both from without and within, "is how the door came to be shut. That is quite a curious problem."

"Quite," agreed Miller. "But it will keep. And there is a still more curious prob-lem inside there. There is nearly all the swag from the Colchester robbery. Looks as if Luttrell was in it."

Half-reluctantly he re-entered the strong-room and Thorndyke and I followed. Near the angle of the passage he stooped to pick up an automatic pistol and a small, leather-bound book, which he opened and looked into by the light of the lamp. At the first glance he uttered an exclamation and shut the book with a snap.

"Do you know what this is?" he asked, holding it out to us. "It is the nominal roll, address book and journal of the gang. We've got them in the hollow of our hand; and it is dawning upon me that old Luttrell was the managing director whom I have been looking for so long. Just run your eyes along those shelves. That's loot; every bit of it. I can identify the articles from the lists that I made out."

He stood looking gloatingly along the shelves with their burden of jewellery, plate and other valuables. Then his eye lighted on a drawer in the end wall just under the lamp; an iron drawer with a disproportionately large handle and bearing a very legible label inscribed "unmounted stones."

"We'll have a look at his stock of unmounted gems," said Miller; and with that he bore down on the drawer, and seizing the handle, gave a vigorous pull. "Funny," said he. "It isn't locked, but something seems to be holding it back."

He planted his foot on the wall and took a fresh purchase on the handle.

"Wait a moment, Miller," said Thorndyke; but even as he spoke, the superinten-dent gave a mighty heave; the drawer came out a full two feet; there was a loud click, and a moment later the strong-room door slammed.

"Good God!" exclaimed Miller, letting go the drawer, which immediately slid in with another click. "What was that?"

"That was the door shutting," replied Thorndyke. "Quite a clever arrangement; like the mechanism of a repeater watch. Pulling out the drawer wound up and released a spring that shut the door. Very ingenious."

"But," gasped Miller, turning an ashen face to my colleague, "we're shut in!"

"You are forgetting," said I—a little nervously, I must admit—"that the lock is as we left it."

The superintendent laughed, somewhat hysterically. "What a fool I am!" said he. "As bad as Shemmonds. Still we may as well——" Here he started along the passage and I heard him groping his way to the door, and later heard the handle turn. Suddenly the deep silence of the tomb-like chamber was rent by a yell of terror.

"The door won't move. It's locked fast!"

On this I rushed along the passage with a sickening fear at my heart. And even as I ran, there rose before my eyes he horrible vision of the corpse with the battered hands that had fallen out when we opened the door of this awful trap. He had been caught as we were caught. How soon might it not be that some stranger would be looking in on our corpses.

In the dim twilight by the door I found Miller clutching the handle and shaking it like a madman. His self-possession was completely shattered. Nor was my own condition much better. I flung my whole weight on the door in the faint hope that the lock was not really closed, but the massive iron structure was as immovable as a stone wall. I was, nevertheless, gathering myself up for a second charge when I heard Thorndyke's voice close behind me.

"That is no use, Jervis. The door is locked. But there is nothing to worry about."

As he spoke, there suddenly appeared a bright circle of light from the little electric lamp that he always carried in his pocket. Within the circle, and now clearly visible, was a second indicator of the puzzle lock on the inside of the door-post. Its appearance was vaguely reassuring, especially in conjunction with Thorndyke's calm voice; and it evidently appeared so to Miller, for he remarked, almost in his natural tones:

"But it seems to be unlocked still. There is the same AAAAAA that it showed when we came in."

It was perfectly true. The slot of the letter-lock still showed the range of fifteen A's, just as it had when the door was open. Could it be that the lock was a dummy and that there was some other means of opening the door? I was about to put this question to Thorndyke when he put the lamp into my hand, and, gently pushing me aside, stepped up to the indicator.

"Keep the light steady, Jervis," said he, and forthwith he began to manipulate the milled edges of the letter discs, beginning, as I noticed, at the right, or reverse end of the slot and working backwards. I watched him with feverish interest and curiosity, as also did Miller, looking to see some word of fifteen letters develop in the slot. Instead of which, I saw, to my amazement and bewilderment, my colleague's finger transforming the row of A's into a succession of M's, which however, were presently followed by an L and some X's. When the row was completed it looked like some remote, antediluvian date set down in Roman numerals.

"Try the handle now, Miller," said Thorndyke.

The superintendent needed no second bidding. Snatching at the handle, he turned it and bore heavily on the door. Almost instantly a thin line of light appeared at the edge; there was a sharp click, and the door swung right open. We fell out immediately—at least the superintendent and I did—thankful to find ourselves outside and alive. But, as we emerged, we both became aware of a man, white-faced and horror-stricken of aspect, stooping over the two corpses at the other end of the room. Our appearance as so sudden and unexpected—for the massive solidity of the safe-door had rendered our movements inaudible outside—that, for a moment or two, he stood immovable, staring at us, wild-eyed and open-mouthed. Then, suddenly, he sprang up erect, and, darting to the door, opened it and rushed out with Miller close on his heels.

He did not get very far. Following the superintendent, I saw the fugitive wriggling in the embrace of a tall man on the pavement, who, with Miller's assistance, soon had a pair of handcuffs snapped on the man's wrists and then departed with his captive in search of a cab.

"That's one of 'em, I expect," said Miller, as we returned to the office; then, as his glance fell on the open strong-room door, he mopped his face with his handkerchief. "That door gives me the creeps to look at it," said he. "Lord! what a shakeup that was! I've never had such a scare in my life. When I heard that door shut and I remembered how that poor devil, Shemmonds, came tumbling out—phoo!" He wiped his brow again, and, walking towards the strong-room door asked: "By the way, what was the magic word after all?" He stepped up to the indicator, and, after a quick glance, looked around at me in surprise. "Why!" he exclaimed, "blow me if it isn't AAAA still! But the doctor altered it, didn't he?"

At this moment Thorndyke appeared from the strongroom, where he had apparently been conducting some exploration, and to him the superintendent turned for an explanation.

"It is an ingenious device," said he; "in fact, the whole strong-room is a monument of ingenuity, somewhat misapplied, but perfectly effective, as Mr. Shemmonds's corpse testifies. The key-combination is a number expressed in Roman numerals, but the lock has a fly-back mechanism which acts as soon as the door begins to open. That was how Shemmonds was caught. He, no doubt purposely, avoided watching Luttrell set the lock—or else Luttrell didn't let him—but as he went in with his intended victim, he looked at the indicator and saw a row of A's, which he naturally assumed to be the key-combination. Then, when he tried to let himself out, of course, the lock wouldn't open."

"It is rather odd that he didn't try some other combinations," said I.

"He probably did," replied Thorndyke; "but when they failed he would naturally come back to the A's, which he had seen when the door was open, this is how it works."

He shut the door, and then, closely watched by the superintendent, and me, turned the milled rims of the letter-discs until the indicator showed a row of numerals thus: MMMMMMMCCCLXXXV. Grasping the handle, he turned it and gave a gentle pull, when the door began to open. But the instant it started from its bed, there was a loud click and all the letters of the indicator flew back to A.

"Well, I'm jiggered!" exclaimed Miller. "It must have been an awful suck in for that poor blighter, Shemmonds. Took me in, too. I saw those A's and the door open, and I thought I knew all about it. But what beats me, Doctor, is how you managed to work it out. I can't see what you had to go on. Would it be allowable to ask how it was done?"

"Certainly," replied Thorndyke; "but we had better defer the explanation. You have got those two bodies to dispose of and some other matters, and we must get back to our chambers. I will write down the key-combination, in case you want it, and then you must come and see us and let us know what luck you have had."

He wrote the numerals on a slip of paper, and when he had handed it to the superintendent, we took our leave.

"I find myself," said I, as we walked home, "in much the same position as Miller. I don't see what you had to go on. It is clear to me that you not only worked out the lock-combination—from the seal inscription, as I assume—but that you identified Luttrell as the director of the gang. I don't, in the least, understand how you did it."

"And yet, Jervis," said he, "it was an essentially simple case. If you review it and cast up the items of evidence, you will see that we really had all the facts. The problem was merely to co-ordinate them and extract their significance. Take first the character of Luttrell. We saw the man in company with another, evidently a fairly intimate acquaintance. They were being shadowed by a detective, and it is pretty clear that they detected the sleuth, for they shook him off quite neatly. Later, we learn from Miller that one of these men is suspected to be a member of a firm of swell burglars and that the other is a well-to-do, rather eccentric and very miscellaneous dealer, who has a strong-room fitted with a puzzle lock. I am astonished that the usually acute Miller did not notice how well Luttrell fitted the part of the managing director whom he was looking for. Here was a dealer who bought and sold all sorts of queer but valuable things, who must have had unlimited facilities for getting rid of stones, bullion and silver, and who used a puzzle lock. Now, who uses a puzzle lock? No one, certainly, who can conveniently use a key. But to the manager of a gang of thieves it would be a valuable safeguard, for he might at any moment be robbed of his keys, and perhaps made away with. But he could not be robbed of the secret passport, and his possession of it would be a security against murder. So you see that the simple probabilities pointed to Luttrell as the head of the gang.

"And now consider the problem of the lock. First, we saw that Luttrell wore on his left hand a huge, cumbrous seal ring, that he carried a Coddington lens on his watchguard, and a small electric lamp in his pocket. That told us very little. But when Miller told us about the lock and showed us the squeeze of the seal, and when we saw that the seal bore a long inscription in minute lettering, a connection began to appear. As Miller justly observed, no man — and especially no elderly man — would trust the key-combination exclusively to his memory. He would carry about him some record to which he could refer in case his memory failed him. But that record would hardly be one that anybody could read, or the secrecy and safety of the lock would be gone. It would probably be some kind of cryptogram; and when we saw this inscription and considered it in conjunction with the lens and the lamp, it seemed highly probable that the key-combination was contained in the inscription; and that probability was further increased when we saw the nonsensical doggerel of which the inscription was made up. The suggestion was that the verses had been made for some purpose independent of their sense. Accordingly I gave the inscription very careful consideration.

"Now we learned from Miller that the puzzle lock had fifteen letters. The key might be one long word, such as 'superlativeness,' a number of short words, or some chemical or other formula. Or it was possible that it might be of the nature of a chronogram. I have never heard of chronograms being used for secret records or messages, but it has often occurred to me that they would be extremely suitable. And this was an exceptionally suitable case."

"Chronogram," said I. "Isn't that something connected with medals?"

"They have often been used on medals," he replied. "In effect, a chronogram is an inscription of some letters of which form a date connected with the subject of the inscription. Usually the date letters are written or cut larger than the others for convenience in reading, but, of course, this is not essential. The principle of a chronogram is this. The letters of the Roman alphabet are of two kinds: those that are simply letters and nothing else, and those that are numerals as well as letters.

The numeral letters are M = a thousand, D = five hundred, C = one hundred, L = fifty, X = ten, V = five, and I = one. Now, in deciphering a chronogram, you pick out all the numeral letters and add them up without regard to their order. The total gives you the date.

"Well, as I said, it occurred to me that this might be of the nature of a chronogram; but as the lock had letters and not figures, the number, if there was one, would have to be expressed in Roman numerals, and it would have to form a number of fifteen numeral letters. As it was thus quite easy to put my hypothesis to the test, I proceeded to treat the inscription as a chronogram and decipher it; and behold! it yielded a number of fifteen letters, which, of course, was as nearly certainty as was possible, short of actual experiment."

"Let us see how you did the decipherment," I said, as we entered our chambers and shut the door. I procured a large notebook and pencil, and, laying them on the table, drew up two chairs.

"Now," said I, "fire away."

"Very well," he said. "We will begin by writing the inscription in proper chronogram form with the numeral letters double size and treating the U's as V's and the W's as double V's according to the rules."

Here he wrote out the inscription in Roman capitals thus:

"eheV aLas hoVV fast the DaM fVgaCes
LabVntVr annI especCIaLLy In the Cases
of poor oLD bLokes Like yoV anD Me postHVMVs
VVho onLy VVaIt for VerMes to ConsVMe Vs"

"Now," said he, "let us make a column of each line and add them up, thus:

1			2			3			4		
V	=	5	L	=	50	L	=	50	VV	=	10
L	=	50	V	=	5	D	=	500	L	=	50
VV	=	10	V	=	5	L	=	50	VV	=	10
D	=	500	I	=	1	L	=	50	I	=	1
M	=	1000	C	=	100	I	=	1	V	=	5
V	=	5	I	=	1	V	=	5	M	=	1000
C	=	100	L	=	50	D	=	500	C	=	100
			L	=	50	M	=	1000	V	=	5
			I	=	1	V	=	5	M	=	1000
			C	=	100	M	=	1000	V	=	5
						V	=	5			
		1670			363			3166			2186

"Now," he continued, "we take the four totals and add them together, thus:

$$1670$$
$$363$$
$$3166$$
$$2186$$
$$\overline{7385}$$

and we get the grand total of seven thousand three hundred and eighty-five, and this, expressed in Roman numbers, is MMMMMMMCCCLXXXV. Here, then, is a number consisting of fifteen letters, the exact number of spaces in the indicator of the puzzle lock; and I repeat that this striking coincidence, added to, or rather multiplied into, the other probabilities, made it practically certain that this was the key-combination. It remained only to test it by actual experiment."

"By the way," said I, "I noticed that you perked up rather suddenly when Miller mentioned the electric metre."

"Naturally," he replied. "It seemed that there must be a small lamp switched on somewhere in the building, and the only place that had not been examined was the strong-room. But if there was a lamp alight there, some one had been in the strong-room. And, as the only person who was known to be able to get in was missing, it seemed probable that he was in there still. But if he was, he was pretty certainly dead; and there was quite a considerable probability that some one else was in there with him, since his companion was missing, too, and both had disappeared at the same time. But I must confess that that spring drawer was beyond my expectations, though I suspected it as soon as I saw Miller pulling at it. Luttrell was an ingenious old rascal; he almost deserved a better fate. However, I expect his death will have delivered the gang into the hands of the police."

Events fell out as Thorndyke surmised. Mr. Luttrell's little journal, in conjunction with the confession of the spy who had been captured on the premises, enabled the police to swoop down on the disconcerted gang before any breath of suspicion had reached them; with the result that they are now secured in strong-rooms of another kind whereof the doors are fitted with appliances as effective as, though less ingenious than, Mr. Luttrell's puzzle lock.

Agatha Christie

(1890–1976)

Agatha Christie was the grande dame of the Golden Age of mystery fiction, and her name is virtually synonymous with those of her main series detectives, Miss Jane Marple and Hercule Poirot. Lesser known, however, are the two pairs of detecting duos she created: Tuppence and Tommy Beresford, and Mr. Satterthwaite and Harley Quin. The Beresfords are an amusing pair of detective-agency owners whose exploits are chronicled in such titles as *The Secret Adversary* (1922) and *Postern of Fate* (1973). A much more unusual duo are Mr. Satterthwaite and his sidekick, Harley Quin.

The short stories collected in *The Mysterious Mr. Quin* (1930) are among Christie's best and most ambiguous. While Mr. Satterthwaite is the type of upper-class Englishman that peoples much of her work, Quin is an enigmatic individual who appears and disappears at will, his arrival always coinciding with a mystery that Satterthwaite must solve. The Quin character poses an intriguing question: Is he in fact a harlequin, a supernatural being? It is a question Christie, who claimed the Quin stories among her favorites, chose not to answer, and he will forever remain an elusive and fascinating figure. In "The Love Detectives," Quin aids Satterthwaite in an inquiry into matters of the heart.

Christie's career spanned many decades, beginning with the introduction of Hercule Poirot in *The Mysterious Affair at Styles* (1920) and culminating in *Sleeping Murder,* Miss Jane Marple's last case, in 1976. In between she produced more than eighty novels, utilizing an astounding array of misdirection, red herrings, and cleverly planted clues. Locked rooms, missing corpses, unshakable alibis, cryptic messages—all were employed in order to bamboozle the readers, while providing enough information so that the most diligent of them could solve the mystery along with her sleuths. The internal logic of her plots is always solid; while Miss Marple is an English gentlewoman with little experience beyond her village at St. Mary Mead, and Poirot is a more worldly Belgian gentleman, both rely on sound reasoning to reach their correct conclusions. (Or, as Poirot would have it, they rely on their "little grey cells.") Other of her lesser-known series characters, Colonel Race and Superintendent Battle, detect in a similar deductive manner.

In addition to novels featuring these characters, Christie also wrote non-series mysteries, such as *And Then There Were None* (first published in Britain in 1939 under the title *Ten Little Niggers,* which was quite justly deemed unsuitable for the American audience), *Sparkling Cyanide* (1945), and *Endless Night* (1967). First produced in 1952, her play *The Mousetrap*—one of more than a dozen she wrote—is still drawing audiences in London. In all of her work, she created a world in which the guilty party was nearly always punished—a world of English villages, manor houses with perfect gardens, afternoon teas, and a clear delineation between "upstairs" and "downstairs." With the exception of the latter—servants did not fare particularly well in Christie's work—one cannot help but agree with critic Michael Seward's comment upon the occasion of Dame Agatha's death: "If Christie's world didn't really exist, it should have."

THE LOVE DETECTIVES

MR. SATTERTHWAITE AND HARLEY QUIN
ENGLAND
1930

L ittle Mr. Satterthwaite looked thoughtfully across at his host. The friendship between these two men was an old one. The colonel was a simple country gentleman whose passion in life was sport. The few weeks that he spent perforce in London, he spent unwillingly. Mr. Satterthwaite, on the other hand, was a town bird. He was an authority on French cooking, on ladies' dress, and on all the latest scandals. His passion was observing human nature, and he was an expert in his own special line—that of an onlooker at life.

It would seem, therefore, that he and Colonel Melrose would have little in common, for the colonel had no interest in his neighbors' affairs, and a horror of any kind of emotion. The two men were friends mainly because their fathers before them had been friends. Also they knew the same people, and had reactionary view about *nouveaux riches.*

It was about half-past seven. The two men were sitting in the colonel's comfortable study, and Melrose was describing a run of the previous winter with a kee hunting man's enthusiasm. Mr. Satterthwaite, whose knowledge of horses consisted chiefly of the time honored Sunday morning visit to the stables which still obtains in old-fashioned country houses, listened with his invariable politeness.

The sharp ringing of the telephone interrupted Melrose. He crossed to the table and took up the receiver.

"Hello, Yes—Colonel Melrose speaking. What's that?"

His whole demeanor altered—became stiff and official. It was the magistrate speaking now, not the sportsman.

He listened for some moments, then said laconically:

"Right, Curtis. I'll be over at once."

He replaced the receiver and turned to his guest.

"Sir James Dwighton has been found in his library—murdered."

"What?"

Mr. Satterthwaite was startled—thrilled.

"I must go over to Alderway at once. Care to come with me?"

Mr. Satterthwaite remembered that the colonel was chief constable of the county.

"If I shan't be in the way—" He hesitated.

"Not at all. That was Inspector Curtis telephoning. Good honest fellow, but no brains. I'd be glad if you would come with me, Satterthwaite. I've got an idea this is going to turn out a nasty business."

"Have they got the fellow who did it?"

"No," replied Melrose, shortly.

Mr. Satterthwaite's trained ear detected a *nuance* of reserve behind the curt negative. He began to go over in his mind all that he knew of the Dwightons.

A pompous old fellow, the late Sir James, brusque in his manner. A man that might easily make enemies. Veering on sixty, with grizzled hair and a florid face. Reputed to be tightfisted in the extreme.

His mind went on to Lady Dwighton. Her image floated before him, young, auburn haired, slender. He remembered various rumors, hints, odd bits of gossip. So that was it—that was why Melrose looked so glum. Then he pulled himself up —his imagination was running away with him.

Five minutes later Mr. Satterthwaite took his place beside his host in the latter's little two seater, and they drove off together into the night.

The colonel was a taciturn man. They had gone quite a mile and a half before he spoke. Then he jerked out abruptly:

"You know 'em, I suppose?"

"The Dwightons? I know all about them, of course." Who was there Mr. Satterthwaite didn't know all about? "I've met him once, I think, and her rather oftener."

"Pretty woman," said Melrose.

"Beautiful!" declared Mr. Satterthwaite.

"Think so?"

"A pure Renaissance type," declared Mr. Satterthwaite, warming up to his theme. "She acted in those theatricals—the charity *matineé*, you know, last spring. I was very much struck. Nothing modern about her—a pure survival. One can imagine her in the Doge's palace, or Lucretia Borgia."

The colonel let the car swerve slightly, and Mr. Satterthwaite came to an abrupt stop. He wondered what fatality had brought the name of Lucretia Borgia to his tongue. Under the circumstances —

"Dwighton was not poisoned, was he?" he asked abruptly.

Melrose looked at him sideways, somewhat curiously.

"Why do you ask that, I wonder?" he said.

"Oh, I—I don't know." Mr. Satterthwaite was flustered. "I—it just occurred to me."

"Well, he wasn't," said Melrose gloomily. "If you want to know, he was crashed on the head."

"With a blunt instrument," murmured Mr. Satterthwaite, nodding his head sagely.

"Don't talk like a damned detective story, Satterthwaite. He was hit on the head with a bronze figure."

"Oh," said Satterthwaite, and relapsed into silence.

"Know anything of a chap called Paul Delangua?" asked Melrose after a minute or two.

"Yes. Good-looking young fellow."

"I dare say women would call him so," growled the colonel.

"You don't like him?"

"No, I don't."

"I should have thought you would have. He rides very well."

"Like a foreigner at the horse show. Full of monkey tricks."

Mr. Satterthwaite suppressed a smile. Poor old Melrose was so very British in his outlook. Agreeably conscious himself of a cosmopolitan point of view, Mr. Satterthwaite was able to deplore the insular attitude toward life.

"Has he been down in this part of the world?" he asked.

"He's been staying at Alderway with the Dwighton's. The rumor goes that Sir James kicked him out a week ago."

"Why?"

"Found him making love to his wife, I suppose. What the hell—"

There was a violent swerve, and a jarring impact.

"Most dangerous crossroads in England," said Melrose. "All the same, the other fellow should have sounded his horn. We're on the main road. I fancy we've damaged him rather more than he has damaged us."

He sprang out. A figure alighted from the other car and joined him. Fragments of speech reached Satterthwaite.

"Entirely my fault, I'm afraid," the stranger was saying. "But I do not know this part of the country very well, and there's absolutely no sign of any kind to show you're coming onto the main road."

The colonel, mollified, rejoined suitably. The two men bent together over the stranger's car which a chauffeur was already examining. The conversation became highly technical.

"A matter of half an hour, I'm afraid," said the stranger. "But don't let me detain you. I'm glad your car escaped injury as well as it did."

"As a matter of fact——" the colonel was beginning, but he was interrupted.

Mr. Satterthwaite, seething with excitement, hopped out of the car with a bird-like action, and seized the stranger warmly by the hand.

"It *is!* I thought I recognized the voice," he declared excitedly. "What an extraordinary thing."

"Eh?" said Colonel Melrose.

"Mr. Harley Quin. Melrose, I'm sure you've heard me speak many times of Mr. Quin?"

Colonel Melrose did not seem to remember the fact, but he assisted politely at the scene while Mr. Satterthwaite was chirruping gayly on.

"I haven't seen you—let me see——"

"Since the night at the Bells and Motley," said the other quietly.

"The Bells and Motley, eh?" said the colonel.

"An inn," explained Mr. Satterthwaite.

"What an odd name for an inn."

"Only an old one," said Mr. Quin. "There was a time, remember, when Bells and Motley were more common in England than they are nowadays."

"I suppose so; yes, no doubt you are right," said Melrose vaguely.

He blinked. By a curious effect of light—the headlights of one car and the red taillight of the other—Mr. Quin seemed for a moment to be dressed in motley himself. But it was only the light.

"We can't leave you here stranded on the road," continued Mr. Satterthwaite. "You must come along with us. There's plenty of room for three, isn't there, Melrose?"

"Oh, rather."

But the colonel's voice was a little doubtful.

"The only thing is," he remarked, "the job we're on. Eh, Satterthwaite?"

Mr. Satterthwaite stood stock still. Ideas leaped and flashed over him. He positively shook with excitement.

"No," he cried. "No, I should have known better! There is no chance where you are concerned, Mr. Quin. It was not an accident that we all met tonight at the crossroads."

Colonel Melrose stared at his friend in astonishment. Mr. Satterthwaite took him by the arm.

"You remember what I told you—about our friend Derek Capel? The motive for his suicide, which no one could guess? It was Mr. Quin who solved that problem—and there have been others since. He shows you things that are there all the time, but which you haven't seen. He's marvelous."

"My dear Satterthwaite, you are making me blush," said Mr. Quin, smiling. "As far as I can remember, these discoveries were all made by you, not by me."

"They were made because you were there," said Mr. Satterthwaite with intense conviction.

"Well," said Colonel Melrose, clearing his throat uncomfortably. "We mustn't waste any more time. Let's get on."

He climbed into the driver's seat. He was not too well pleased at having the stranger foisted upon him through Mr. Satterthwaite's enthusiasm, but he had no valid objection to offer, and he was anxious to get on to Alderway as fast as possible.

Mr. Satterthwaite urged Mr. Quin in next, and himself took the outside seat. The car was a roomy one, and took three without undue squeezing.

"So you are interested in crime, Mr. Quin?" said the colonel, doing his best to be genial.

"No, not exactly in crime."

"What, then?"

Mr. Quin smiled.

"Let us ask Mr. Satterthwaite. He is a very shrewd observer."

"I think," said Satterthwaite slowly, "I may be wrong, but I think—that Mr. Quin is interested in—lovers."

He blushed as he said the last word, which is one no Englishman can pronounce without self-consciousness. Mr. Satterthwaite brought it out apologetically, and with an effect of inverted commas.

"By gad!" said the colonel, startled and silenced.

He reflected inwardly that this seemed to be a very rum friend of Satterthwaite's. He glanced at him sideways. The fellow looked all right—quite a normal young chap. Rather dark, but not at all foreign-looking.

"And now," said Satterthwaite importantly, "I must tell you all about the case." He talked for some ten minutes. Sitting there in the darkness, rushing through the night, he had an intoxicating feeling of power. What did it matter if he were only a looker-on at life? He had words at his command, he was master of them, he could string them to a pattern—a strange Renaissance pattern composed of the beauty of Laura Dwighton, with her white arms and red hair—and the shadowy dark figure of Paul Delangua, whom women found handsome.

Set that against the background of Alderway—Alderway that had stood since the days of Henry VII, and some said before that. Alderway that was English to the core, with its clipped yew, and its old beak barn and the fish pond, where monks had kept their carp for Fridays.

In a few deft strokes he had etched in Sir James, a Dwighton who was a true descendant of the old De Wittons, who long ago had wrung money out of the land and locked it fast in coffers, so that whoever else had fallen on evil days, the masters of Alderway had never become impoverished.

At last Mr. Satterthwaite ceased. He was sure, had been sure all along, of the sympathy of his audience. He waited now the word of praise which was his due. It came.

"You are an artist, Mr. Satterthwaite."

"I—I do my best." The little man was suddenly humble.

They had turned in at the lodge gates some minutes ago. Now the car drew up in front of the doorway, and a police constable came hurriedly down the steps to meet them.

"Good evening, sir. Inspector Curtis is in the library."

"Right."

Melrose ran up the steps followed by the other two. As the three of them passed across the wide hall, an elderly butler peered from a doorway apprehensively. Melrose nodded to him.

"Evening, Miles. This is a sad business."

"It is, indeed," the other quavered. "I can hardly believe it, sir; indeed I can't. To think that anyone should strike down the master."

"Yes, yes," said Melrose, cutting him short. "I'll have a talk with you presently."

He strode on to the library. There a big, soldierly-looking inspector greeted him with respect.

"Nasty business, sir. I have not disturbed things. No fingerprints on the weapon. Whoever did it knew his business."

Mr. Satterthwaite looked at the bowed figure sitting at the big writing table, and looked hurriedly away again. The man had been struck down from behind, a smashing blow that had crashed in the skull. The sight was not a pretty one.

93

The weapon lay on the floor—a bronze figure about two feet high, the base of it stained and wet. Mr. Satterthwaite bent over it curiously.

"A Venus," he said softly. "So he was struck down by Venus."

He found food for poetic meditation in the thought.

"The windows," said the inspector, "were all closed and bolted on the inside."

He paused significantly.

"Making an inside job of it," said the chief constable reluctantly. "Well—well, we'll see."

The murdered man was dressed in plus fours, and a bag of golf clubs had been flung untidily across a big leather couch.

"Just come in from the links," explained the inspector, following the chief constable's glance. "At five-fifteen, that was. Had tea brought here by the butler. Later he rang for his valet to bring him down a pair of soft slippers. As far as we can tell, the valet was the last person to see him alive."

Melrose nodded, and turned his attention once more to the writing table.

A good many of the ornaments had been overturned and broken. Prominent among these was a big dark enamel clock, which lay on its side in the very center of the table.

The inspector cleared his throat.

"That's what you might call a piece of luck, sir," he said. "As you see, it's stopped. *At half-past six.* That gives us the time of the crime. Very convenient.

The colonel was staring at the clock.

"As you say," he remarked. "Very convenient." He paused a minute, and then added: "Too damned convenient! I don't like it, inspector."

He looked around at the other two. His eye sought Mr. Quin's with a look of appeal in it.

"Damn it all," he said. "It's too neat. You know what I mean. Things don't happen like that."

"You mean," murmured Mr. Quin, "that clocks don't fall like that?

Melrose stared at him for a moment, then back at the clock, which had that pathetic and innocent look familiar to objects which have been suddenly bereft of their dignity. Very carefully Colonel Melrose replaced it on its legs again. He struck the table a violent blow. The clock rocked, but it did not fall. Melrose repeated the action, and very slowly, with a kind of unwillingness, the clock fell over on its back.

"What time was the crime discovered?" demanded Melrose sharply.

"Just about seven o'clock, sir."

"Who discovered it?"

"The butler."

"Fetch him in," said the chief constable. "I'll see him now. Where is Lady Dwighton, by the way?"

"Lying down, sir. Her maid says that she's prostrated and can't see anyone."

Melrose nodded, and Inspector Curtis went in search of the butler. Mr. Quin was looking thoughtfully into the fireplace. Mr. Satterthwaite followed his example. He blinked at the smoldering logs for a minute or two, and then something bright caught his eye lying in the grate. He stopped and picked up a little sliver of curved glass.

"You wanted me, sir?"

It was the butler's voice, still quavering and uncertain. Mr. Satterthwaite slipped the fragment of glass into his waistcoat pocket and turned round.

The old man was standing in the doorway.

"Sit down," said the chief constable kindly. "You're shaking all over. It's been a shock to you, I expect."

"It has indeed, sir."

"Well, I shan't keep you long. Your master came in just after five, I believe?"

"Yes, sir. He ordered tea to be brought to him here. Afterward, when I came to take it away, he asked for Jennings to be sent to him—that's his valet, sir."

"What time was that?"

"About ten minutes past six, sir."

"Yes—well?"

"I sent word to Jennings, sir. And it wasn't till I came in here to shut the windows and draw the curtains at seven o'clock that I saw—"

Melrose cut him short.

"Yes, yes, you needn't go into all that. You didn't touch the body, or disturb anything, did you?"

"Oh! No indeed, sir! I went as fast as I could go to the telephone to ring up the police."

"And then?"

"I told Janet—her ladyship's maid, sir—to break the news to her ladyship."

"You haven't seen your mistress at all this evening?"

Colonel Melrose put the question casually enough, but Mr. Satterthwaite's keen ears caught anxiety behind the words.

"Not to speak to, sir. Her ladyship has remained in her own apartments since the tragedy."

"Did you see her before?"

The question came sharply, and everyone in the room noted the hesitation before the butler replied.

"I—I just caught a glimpse of her, sir, descending the staircase."

"I—I just caught a glimpse of her, sir, descending the staircase."

"Did she come in here?"

Mr. Satterthwaite held his breath.

"I—I think so, sir."

"What time was that?"

You might have heard a pin drop. Did the old man know, Mr. Satterthwaite wondered, what hung on his answer?

"It was just upon half-past six, sir."

Colonel Melrose drew a deep breath.

"That will do, thank you. Just send Jennings, the valet, to me, will you?"

Jennings answered the summons with promptitude. A narrow-faced man with a catlike tread. Something sly and secretive about him.

A man thought Mr. Satterthwaite, *who would easily murder his master if he could be sure of not being found out.*

He listened eagerly to the man's answers to Colonel Melrose's questions. But his story seemed straight-forward enough. He had brought his master down some soft hide slippers and removed the brogues.

"What did you do after that, Jennings?"

"I went back to the stewards' room, sir."

"At what time did you leave your master?"

"It must have been just after a quarter past six, sir."

"Where were you at half-past six, Jennings?"

"In the stewards' room, sir."

Colonel Melrose dismissed the man with a nod. He looked across at Curtis inquiringly.

"Quite correct, sir, I checked that up. He was in the stewards' room from about six twenty until seven o'clock."

"Then that lets him out," said the chief constable a trifle regretfully. "Besides, there's no motive."

They looked at each other.

There was a tap at the door.

"Come in," said the colonel.

A scared-looking lady's maid appeared.

"If you please, her ladyship has heard that Colonel Melrose is here and she would like to see him."

"Certainly," said Melrose. "I'll come at once. Will you show me the way?"

But a hand pushed the girl aside. A very different figure now stood in the doorway. Laura Dwighton looked like a visitor from another world.

She was dressed in a clinging medieval tea gown of dull blue brocade. Her auburn hair parted in the middle and brought down over her ears. Conscious of the fact she had a style of her own, Lady Dwighton had never had her hair shingled. It was drawn back into a simple knot in the nape of her neck. Her arms were bare. One of them was outstretched to steady herself against the frame of the doorway, the other hung down by her side, clasping a book. *She looked,* Mr. Satterthwaite thought, *like a Madonna from an early Italian canvas.*

She stood there, swaying slightly from side to side. Colonel Melrose sprang toward her.

"I've come to tell you—to tell you—"

Her voice was low and rich. Mr. Satterthwaite was so entranced with the dramatic value of the scene that he had forgotten its reality.

"Please, Lady Dwighton—"

Melrose had an arm round her, supporting her. He took her across the hall into a small anteroom, its walls hung with faded silk. Quin and Satterthwaite followed. She sank down on the low settee, her head resting back on a rust-colored cushion, her eyelids closed. The three men watched her. Suddenly she opened her eyes and sat up. She spoke very quietly:

"*I killed him,*" she said. "That's what I came to tell you. *I killed him!*"

There was a moment's agonized silence. Mr. Satterthwaite's heart missed a beat.

"Lady Dwighton," said Melrose. "You've had a great shock—you're unstrung. I don't think you quite know what you're saying."

Would she draw back now—while there was yet time?

"I know perfectly what I'm saying. It was I who shot him."

Two of the men in the room gasped, the other made no sound. Laura Dwighton leaned still farther forward.

"Don't you understand? I came down and shot him. I admit it."

The book she had been holding in her hand clattered to the floor. There was a paper cutter in it, a thing shaped like a dagger with a jeweled hilt. Mr. Satterthwaite picked it up mechanically and placed it on the table. As he did so he thought: *That's a dangerous toy. You could kill a man with that.*

"Well—" Laura Dwighton's voice was impatient—"what are you going to do about it? Arrest me? Take me away?"

Colonel Melrose found his voice with difficulty.

"What you have told me is very serious, Lady Dwighton. I must ask you to go to your room till I have—er—made arrangements."

She nodded and rose to her feet. She was quite composed now, grave and cold.

As she turned toward the door, Mr. Quin spoke: "What did you do with the revolver, Lady Dwighton?"

A flicker of uncertainty passed across her face.

"I—I dropped it there on the floor. No, I think I threw it out of the window oh! I can t remember now. What does it matter? I hardly knew what I was doing. It doesn't matter, does it?"

"No," said Mr. Quin. "I hardly think it matters."

She looked at him in perplexity with a shade of something that might have been alarm. Then she flung back her head and went imperiously out of the room. Mr. Satterthwaite hastened after her. She might, he felt, collapse at any minute. But she was already halfway up the staircase, displaying no sign of her earlier weakness. The scared-looking maid was standing at the foot of the stairway, and Mr. Satterthwaite spoke to her authoritatively:

"Look after your mistress," he said.

"Yes, sir." The girl prepared to ascend after the blue-robed figure. "Oh, please sir, they don't suspect him, do they?"

"Suspect whom?"

"Jennings, sir. Oh! Indeed, sir he wouldn't hurt a fly."

"Jennings? No, of course, not. Go and look after your mistress."

"Yes, sir."

The girl ran quickly up the staircase. Mr. Satterthwaite returned to the room he had just vacated.

Colonel Melrose was saying heavily:

"Well, I'm jiggered. There's more in this than meets the eye. It—it's like those dashed silly things heroines do in many novels."

"It's unreal," agreed Mr. Satterthwaite. "It's like something on the stage."

Mr. Quin nodded. "Yes, you admire the drama, do you not? You are a man who appreciates good acting when you see it."

Mr. Satterthwaite looked hard at him.

In the silence that followed a far-off sound came to their ears.

"Sounds like a shot," said Colonel Melrose. "One of the keepers, I dare-say. That's probably what she heard. Perhaps she went down to see. She wouldn't go close or examine the body. She'd leap at once to the conclusion —"

"Mr. Delangua, sir."

It was the old butler who spoke, standing apologetically in the doorway.

"Eh?" said Melrose. "What's that?"

"Mr. Delangua is here, sir, and would like to speak to you if he may."

Colonel Melrose leaned back in his chair.

"Show him in," he said grimly.

A moment later Paul Delangua stood in the doorway. As Colonel Melrose had hinted, there was something un-English about him—the easy grace of his movements, the dark handsome face, the eyes set a little too near together. There hung about him the air of the Renaissance. He and Laura Dwighton suggested the same atmosphere.

"Good evening, gentlemen," said Delangua. He made a little theatrical bow.

"I don't know what your business may be, Mr. Delangua," said Colonel Melrose sharply, "but if it is nothing to do with the matter at hand——"

Delangua interrupted him with a laugh.

"On the contrary," he said, "it has everything to do with it."

"What do you mean?"

"I mean," said Delangua quietly, "that I have come to give myself up for the murder of Sir James Dwighton."

"You know what you are saying?" said Melrose gravely.

"Perfectly."

The young man's eyes were riveted to the table.

"I don't understand——"

"Why I give myself up? Call it remorse—call it anything you please. I stabbed him right enough—you may be quite sure of that." He nodded toward the table. "You've got the weapon there, I see. A very handy little tool. Lady Dwighton unfortunately left it lying around in a book, and I happened to snatch it up."

"One minute," said Colonel Melrose. "Am I to understand that you admit stabbing Sir James with this?"

He held the dagger aloft.

"Quite right. I stole in through the window, you know. He had his back to me. It was quite easy. I left the same way."

"Through the window?"

"Through the window, of course."

"And what time was this?"

Delangua hesitated.

"Let me see—I was talking to the keeper fellow—that was at a quarter past six. I heard the church tower chime. It must have been—well, say somewhere about half-past."

A grim smile came to the colonel's lips.

"Quite right, young man," he said. "Half-past six was the time. Perhaps you've heard that already? But this is altogether a most peculiar murder!"

"Why?"

"So many people confess to it," said Colonel Melrose.

They heard the sharp intake of the other's breath.

"Who else has confessed to it?" he asked in a voice that he vainly strove to render steady.

"Lady Dwighton."

Delangua threw back his head and laughed in rather a forced manner.

"Lady Dwighton is apt to be hysterical," he said lightly. "I shouldn't pay any attention to what she says if I were you."

"I don't think I shall." said Melrose. "But there's another odd thing about this murder."

"What's that?"

"Well," said Melrose, "Lady Dwighton has confessed to having shot Sir James, and you have confessed to having stabbed him. But luckily for both of you, he wasn't shot or stabbed, you see. His skull was smashed in."

"My God!" cried Delangua. "But a woman couldn't possibly do that——"

He stopped, biting his lip. Melrose nodded with the ghost of a smile.

"Often read of it," he volunteered. "Never seen it happen."

"What?"

"Couple of young idiots each accusing themselves because they thought the other one had done it," said Melrose. "Now we've got to begin at the beginning."

"The valet," cried Mr. Satterthwaite. "That girl just now——I wasn't paying any attention at the time."

He paused, striving for coherence.

"She was afraid of our suspecting him. There must be some motive that he had and which we don't know, but she does."

Colonel Melrose frowned, then he rang the bell. When it was answered, he said: "Please ask Lady Dwighton if she will be good enough to come down again?"

They waited in silence until she came. At sight of Delangua she started and stretched out a hand to save herself from falling. Colonel Melrose came quickly to the rescue.

"It's quite all right, Lady Dwighton. Please don't be alarmed."

"I don't understand. What is Mr. Delangua doing here?"

Delangua came over to her.

"Laura——Laura——why did you do it?"

"Do it?"

"I know. It was for me——because you thought that I——after all, it was natural, I suppose. But, oh! You angel!"

Colonel Melrose cleared his throat. He was a man who disliked emotion and had a horror of anything approaching a "scene."

"If you'll allow me to say so, Lady Dwighton, both you and Mr. Delangua, have had a lucky escape. He had just arrived in his turn to 'confess' to the murder—— oh, it's quite all right, he didn't do it! But what we want to know is the truth. No more shillyshallying. The butler says you went into the library at half-past six—— is that so?"

Laura looked at Delangua. He nodded.

"The truth, Laura," he said. "That is what we want now."

She breathed a deep sigh.

"I will tell you."

She sank down on a chair that Mr. Satterthwaite had hurriedly pushed forward.

"I did come down. I opened the library door and I saw——"

She stopped and swallowed. Mr. Satterthwaite leaned forward and patted her hand encouragingly.

"Yes," he said. "Yes. You saw?"

"My husband was lying across the writing table. I saw his head—the blood—oh!"

She put her hands to her face. The chief constable leaned forward.

"Excuse me, Lady Dwighton. You thought Mr. Delangua had shot him?"

She nodded.

"Forgive me, Paul," she pleaded. "But you said—you said ——"

"That I'd shoot him like a dog," said Delangua grimly. "I remember. That was the day I discovered he'd been ill-treating you."

The chief constable kept sternly to the matter in hand.

"Then I am to understand, Lady Dwighton, that you went upstairs again and—er—said nothing. We needn't go into your reason. You didn't touch the body or go near the writing table?'

She shuddered.

"No, no. I ran straight out of the room."

"I see, I see. And what time was this exactly? Do you know?"

"It was just half-past six when I got back to my bedroom."

"Then at—say five and twenty past six, Sir James was already dead." The chief constable looked at the others,. "That clock—it was faked, eh? We suspected that all along. Nothing easier than to move the hands to whatever time you wished, but they made a mistake to lay it down on its side like that. Well, that seems to narrow it down to the butler or the valet, and I can't believe it's the butler. Tell me, Lady Dwighton, did this man Jennings have any grudge against your husband?"

Laura lifted her face from her hands.

"Not exactly a grudge, but—well James told me only this morning that he'd dismissed him. He'd found him pilfering."

"Ah! Now we're getting at it. Jennings would have been dismissed without a character. A serious matter for him."

"You said something about a clock," said Laura Dwighton. "There's just a chance—if you want to fix the time—James would have been sure to have his little golf watch on him. Mightn't that have been smashed too when he fell forward?"

"It's an idea," said the colonel slowly. "But I'm afraid—Curtis!"

The inspector nodded in quick comprehension and left the room. He returned a minute later. On the palm of his hand was a silver watch marked like a golf ball, the kind that are sold for golfers to carry loose in a pocket with balls.

"Here it is, sir," he said, "but I doubt if it will be any good. They're tough, these watches."

The colonel took it from him and held it to his ear.

"It seems to have stopped anyway," he observed.

He pressed with his thumb and the lid of the watch flew open. Inside the glass was cracked across.

"Ah!" he said exultantly.

The hand pointed to exactly a quarter past six.

"A very good glass of port Colonel Melrose," said Mr. Quin.

It was half-past nine, and the three men had just finished a belated dinner at Colonel Melrose's house. Mr. Satterthwaite was particularly jubilant.

"I was quite right," he chuckled. "You can't deny it, Mr. Quin. You turned up tonight to save two absurd young people who were both bent on putting their heads into a noose."

"Did I?" said Mr. Quin. "Surely not. I did nothing at all."

"As it turned out, it was not necessary," agreed Mr. Satterthwaite. "But it might have been. It was touch and go, you know. I shall never forget the moment when Lady Dwighton said 'I killed him.' I've never saw anything on the stage half as dramatic."

"I'm inclined to agree with you," said Mr. Quin.

"Wouldn't have believed such a thing could happen outside a novel," declared the colonel, for perhaps the twentieth time that night.

"Does it?" asked Mr. Quin.

The colonel stared at him.

"Damn it, it happened tonight."

"Mind you," interposed Mr. Satterthwaite, leaning back and sipping his port. "Lady Dwighton was magnificent, quite magnificent, but she made one mistake. She shouldn't have leaped to the conclusion that her husband had been shot. In the same way Delangua was a fool to assume that he had been stabbed just because the dagger happened to be lying on the table in front of us. It was a mere coincidence that Lady Dwighton should have brought it down with her."

"Was it?" asked Mr. Quin.

"Now if they'd only confined themselves to saying that they'd killed Sir James without particularizing how——" went on Mr. Satterthwaite——"what would have been the result?"

"They might have been believed," said Mr. Quin with an odd smile.

"The whole thing was exactly like a novel," said the colonel.

"That's where they got the idea from, I daresay," said Mr. Quin.

"Possibly," agreed Mr. Satterthwaite. "Things one has read do come back to one in the oddest way."

He looked across at Mr. Quin.

"Of course," he said. "The clock really looked suspicious from the first. One ought never to forget how easy it is to put the hands of a clock or watch forward or back."

Mr. Quin nodded and repeated the words.

"Forward," he said, and paused. *"Or back."*

There was something encouraging in his voice. His bright dark eyes were fixed on Mr. Satterthwaite.

"The hands of the clock were put forward," said Mr. Satterthwaite. "We know that."

"Were they?" asked Mr. Quin.

Mr. Satterthwaite stared at him.

"Do you mean," he said slowly, "that it was the watch which was put back? But that doesn't make sense. It's impossible."

"Not *impossible*," murmured Mr. Quin.

"Well—absurd. To whose advantage could that be?"

"Only, I suppose, to some one who had an *alibi* for that time."

"By gad!" cried the colonel. "That's the time young Delangua said he was talking to the keeper."

"He told us that very particularly," said Mr. Satterthwaite.

They looked at each other. They had an uneasy feeling as of solid ground failing beneath their feet. Facts went spinning round, turning new and unexpected faces and in the center of the kaleidoscope was the dark smiling face of Mr. Quin.

"But in that case——" began Melrose——"in that case——"

Mr. Satterthwaite, nimble witted, finished his sentence for him.

"It's all the other way round. A plant just the same—but a plant against the valet. Oh, but it can't be! It's impossible. Why each of them accused themselves of the crime."

"Yes," said Mr. Quin. "Up till then you suspected them, didn't you?"

His voice went on, placid and dreamy:

"Just like something out of a book, you said, colonel. They got the idea there.

It's what the innocent hero and heroine do. Of course it made you think *them* innocent—there was the force of tradition behind them. Mr. Satterthwaite has been saying all along it was like something on the stage. You were both right. *It wasn't real.* You've been saying so all along without knowing what you were saying. They'd have told a much better story than that if they'd *wanted* to be believed."

The two men looked at him helplessly.

"It would be clever," said Mr. Satterthwaite slowly. "It would be diabolically clever. And I've thought of something else. The butler said he went in at seven to shut the windows—so he must have expected them to be open."

"That's the way Delangua came in," said Mr. Quin. "He killed Sir James with one blow, and he and she together did what they had to do—"

He looked at Mr. Satterthwaite, encouraging him to reconstruct the scene. He did so, hesitatingly.

"They smashed the clock and put it on its side. Yes. They altered the watch and smashed it. Then he went out of the window and she fastened it after him. But there's one thing I don't see. Why bother with the watch at all? Why not simply put back the hands of the clock?"

"The clock was always a little obvious,'" said Mr. Quin. "Any one might have seen through a rather transparent device like that."

"But surely the watch was too far-fetched. Why, it was pure chance that we ever thought of the watch."

"Oh, no," said Mr. Quin. "It was the lady's suggestion, remember."

Mr. Satterthwaite stared at him fascinated.

"And yet, you know," said Mr. Quin dreamily, "the one person who wouldn't be likely to overlook the watch would be the valet. Valets know better than anyone what their masters carry in their pockets. If he altered the clock, the valet would have altered the watch too. They don't understand human nature, those two. They are not like Mr. Satterthwaite."

Mr. Satterthwaite shook his head.

"I was all wrong," he murmured humbly. "I thought that you had come to save them."

"So I did," said Mr. Quin. "Oh! Not those two—the others. Perhaps you didn't notice the lady's maid? She wasn't wearing blue brocade, or acting a dramatic part. But she's really a very pretty girl, and I think she loves that man Jennings very much. I think that between you, you'll be able to save her man from getting hanged."

"We've no proof of any kind," said Colonel Melrose heavily.

Mr. Quin smiled.

"Mr. Satterthwaite has."

"I?"

Mr. Satterthwaite was astonished.

Mr. Quin went on: "You've got a proof that that watch wasn't smashed in Sir James's pocket. You can't smash a watch like that without opening the case. Just try it and see. Some one took the watch out and opened it, set back the hands, smashed the glass, and then shut it and put it back. *They never noticed that a fragment of glass was missing.*"

"Oh!" cried Mr. Satterthwaite. His hand flew to his waistcoat pocket. *He drew out a fragment of curved glass.*

It was his moment.

"With this," said Mr. Satterthwaite importantly, "I shall save a man from death."

Hulbert Footner

(1879–1944)

Madame Rosika Storey was among the earliest of the fully realized female sleuths, a professional detective who was not above using her voluptuous charm to inspire awe in other people. The hard-headed police inspector in "The Sealed Room," for instance, is "floored by her beauty (and) brains." Yet in the private company of Bella, her assistant and "Watson," she could often be keen, human, lovable, and full of laughter. Together, Mme. Storey and Bella, who sometimes contributed to the solution of a particular case, formed the first major two-woman detective duo. They appeared in four novels, among them *The Under Dogs* (1925), *The Doctor Who Held Hands* (1929), and *Dangerous Cargo* (1934), and four volumes of short stories, beginning with *Madame Storey* (1926) and concluding with *The Almost Perfect Murder* (1933). Despite the relative brevity of their ten-year joint career, Mme. Storey and Bella made a small but significant contribution to both the development of partnership sleuthing and to the Golden Age (i.e., between the two world wars) of fictional detectives.

The same is not quite true of their creator. William Hulbert Footner was a Canadian actor and novelist who wrote adventure and "modern romance" fiction as well as detective stories. From 1911 to 1945 he produced upward of fifty novels and half a dozen collections of short stories; more than two-thirds of these are criminous in nature, yet except for Mme. Storey—and, arguably, his 1930 novel, *The Mystery of the Folded Paper*, with his other principal series detective, Amos Lee Mappin—he wrote little of interest or merit. Mappin appeared in ten novels, but despite a resemblance to Dickens's Mr. Pickwick, he was a rather colorless character and his cases other than *The Mystery of the Folded Paper* were pedestrian. Footner's non-series crime novels, notably *The Island of Fear* (1936) and *The Obeah Murders* (1937), are better than the Mappins and some of the Storeys, but still lack any lasting qualities. As one critic has noted, his style is undistinguished. However, the Mme. Storey tales have a certain period charm that makes them, unlike most of his other work, quite readable today.

THE SEALED HOUSE

MME. ROSIKA STOREY AND BELLA
NEW YORK
C. 1930

M y job as secretary to Madame Storey has always been an exciting one (sometimes too exciting for my own comfort), but the most active period was during the time when my employer was retained by the Washburn legislative committee in connection with their investigation of the Police Department. Mme. Storey's particular job was to examine into the methods used in detecting crime and to make a report.

Our first interview with Inspector Barron who was in charge of the detective force at that time, had its humorous side. Barron was a big, red-faced man, a magnificent physical specimen, quite honest I believe, but somewhat bullheaded. The sight of Mme. Storey threw him into confusion, and I could not help but feel a little sorry for him. He was floored by her beauty and he resented her brains. He objected to my presence at the conference.

"Miss Brickley is my memory," said Mme. Storey with that baffling smile which has capsized so many men honest and otherwise; "she is my card-index, my prompt-book, almost I might say my other self. I cannot move without her."

He shrugged and let the matter go. "Well, Madame," he said with a sour face, "I need hardly say that the police welcome your co-operation in any shape, manner or form. Everything is open here. How do you propose to begin?"

"I am not interested in your office routine," she said; "let us work out one or two typical cases together."

"Fine!" he said. "I will let you know just as soon as anything important breaks, so that you can be in on it from the beginning."

"But why wait for a crime to be committed?" said Mme. Story. "Surely there is plenty of unfinished business on hand."

He scowled at her in an injured way as if he was thinking: "You're too darn good-looking! It's not fair!"

"The Ada Rousseau case, for instance," she added quietly.

"That's not unfinished business!" he said, all hot immediately. "That was closed up a week ago. There never was anything for the police to do there."

"I wonder!" said Mme. Storey thoughtfully.

"Ada Rousseau committed suicide!" he cried, slapping his desk. "There can be no question or doubt about that. She was a damned ... excuse me, Madame ... she

107

was a bad woman. She lived in luxury in a fine house without any visible means of support. She was known in all the flashy speakeasies in town as a souse—and worse! She was found dead under some shrubbery in Central Park with an empty bottle of veronal in her hand, and the autopsy proved that she died from an overdose. She had bought the veronal herself. What more do you want?"

"Somebody may have given her the veronal in a drink," suggested Mme. Storey. "She was seen earlier that night in Raffaello's speakeasy on Fifty-third Street. She picked up a young man there and left the place with him. Did you find that young man?"

"Why should I?" demanded Barron. "She was found lying in a mink coat that was worth three thousand dollars, and she had diamonds on her worth ten thousand. As for its being a crime of jealousy, the woman was getting old; she had lost her looks and attractiveness. That's ridiculous."

"But there are other motives for murder besides robbery and jealousy," said Mme. Storey quietly.

"What are they?"

"Well, there is . . . fear!"

Inspector Barron puffed out his red cheeks and fussed amongst the papers on his desk. Then his sullen eyes like a schoolboy's crept back to Mme. Storey's face. He wanted to stand in well with so handsome a woman, but she exasperated him. "What do you know?" he muttered.

"Not a thing!" she said with a wave of her hand. "Except what I have read in the newspapers. . . . But it struck me as very strange that a woman like Ada Rousseau, as luxurious as a cat, should go and creep under a bush on a wet winter's night to kill herself. If she wanted to end it all, why didn't she do it in her own comfortable house?"

"You can search me!" said Barron.

"Another thing," Mme. Storey went on, "in the published list of articles that were found on her there was no mention of keys or a key, yet her maid testified at the inquest that she was not accustomed to wait up for her mistress. What became of Ada Rousseau's latchkey?"

The burly Inspector merely scowled and made marks on his desk pad.

"How did she live, anyhow?" my employer continued. "A woman whose beauty was fading, as you have pointed out. It has been shown that she spent money with the greatest freedom, yet no property has been found except the furnishings of her house and her jewels. Somebody was paying, and paying heavily."

"Some things are best not stirred up," muttered the Inspector.

"Oh, quite!" said Mme. Storey. "But it's up to you and me to ferret out murder if murder has been done."

"Whom do you suspect?" he growled.

Mme. Storey laughed candidly. "My dear man! How do I know? I'm no magician. I have merely pointed out one or two suspicious circumstances. Let's go up and look over the woman's house together, and we'll see what we see."

"Can't get in," he said. "The house has been sealed up by the Surrogate's court until the woman's estate is adjudged."

"Under the circumstances you could obtain an order from the Surrogate to view it."

"I suppose I could, if the husband was willing."

"Husband?" said Mme. Storey. "I didn't know Ada Rousseau had a husband."

"He doesn't figure," said Inspector Barron. "They've been parted for twenty-five years. He turned up when he read of her death in the newspapers, and there appears to be no other heir."

"He could hardly object to our going over the house," said Mme. Storey. "Let him come along with us if he is afraid that we might pinch something."

Barron picked up his telephone muttering something that sounded like: "All damn nonsense!" But his eye kindled when it dwelt on Mme. Storey sitting there smiling delightfully in a chic little hat and speckless white gloves. The Inspector part of him was disgusted, but the man was charmed by the idea of going on an expedition with her.

The house was a smallish brownstone front on East Thirty-Sixth Street where it slides down Murray Hill. Not very grand on the outside, but when you considered the value of property in that neighbourhood, an impressive residence for a lone woman. Ada Rousseau had lived there for twenty years and the rent was four hundred dollars a month.

Our party comprised Inspector Barron and his men, the Surrogate's clerk who cut the seals on the front door, Maggie Dolan, the dead woman's former maid, and Thomas Jackman, her long discarded husband. The last-named was a middle-aged man, meek and crushed-looking, painfully anxious to please. His seedy attire suggested the actor long out of work.

Inside there was something horrible in the air. The rooms expressed a kind of slatternly luxury; cushioned furniture, stuffy hangings, gilt ornaments; none of it too clean. There was a faint smell of cigarette smoke and stale whiskey everywhere; the silence and chill were like an old cemetery vault.

Beginning with the basement kitchen which had a door on the backyard, Mme. Storey immediately set about one of her whirlwind examinations of the premises. It is beautiful to watch her exactitude and concentration. With her magnifying glass she lingered long over the yard door.

From the basement she proceeded direct to the second floor, boudoir in front, bedroom in the rear. These rooms were full of ghastly reminders of the dead. No-body had troubled to tidy up, and the woman's clothes still lay where she had flung them, though she herself was under the sod. The grimmest touch was the expensive mink coat that somebody had brought in and dropped on a chair. One could picture the dead body lying wrapped in it on the sodden ground under a leafless bush. These rooms were drugged with perfume.

Mme. Storey with her glass was led like a sleuth hound to a little steel safe built into the side of a writing desk in the boudoir. She dropped to her knees in front of it, and holding her ear close to the lock, turned the knob this way and that, closing her eyes and listening with intense concentration.

The door of the safe presently swung open. It contained but a single compartment. In it lay a confused heap of glittering jewellery; bracelets, rings, necklets. She disregarded the jewels. After examining the inside of the compartment with the utmost care, she closed the door again, and gave the knob a twirl to lock it.

Afterwards she stood thinking hard, piecing out a pattern of reasoning in her mind. Suddenly she went to a handsome silver tea service on a small table between the windows. Amongst the pieces was an antique silver tea-caddy. Removing the top, she emptied the tea into the tray. Inserting two fingers into the caddy, she drew out a folded paper.

"It's a lone woman's pet hiding-place," she murmured with a grim smile. "Quick! Put the tea back into the caddy!"

I hastily obeyed. Meanwhile Mme. Storey, removing an outer wrapper of plain paper, revealed an old letter, folded small. She spread it out, taking care not to injure it. As she read it her face became as grave as marble.

"Let's go down," she said quietly. "I want to ask the maid a question or two."

The others were in the drawing-room. Maggie Dolan was a woman of forty odd all rigged out in her mistress's cast-off finery; an easy-going creature like most of her kind.

"Did your mistress carry a latchkey?" asked Mme. Storey.

"Sure, Ma'am," answered Maggie. "She wouldn't wait on the step."

"Last Monday, that is the night she didn't come home, were you disturbed at all?"

The woman stared at her, startled. "Sure I was so," she said. "How did you know? I sleep in the front basement. I hear a noise upstairs, and I run up because often when she come home late she wanted helping. I could swear I heard the door close, but there wasn't nobody there. I was scared. I put the chain on the door and sit down to wait for her. But she never come, and at eight o'clock the police telephoned . . ."

"Why didn't you tell this at the inquest?" put in Barron sharply.

"Nobody asked me, sir," said Maggie.

"One more question," said Mme. Storey. "Where did Miss Rousseau's income come from?"

Maggie shook her head. "It wouldn't be Ada to tell anybody that. All I know is she got five hundred in cash every week. Went out a Saturday morning and fetched it. I don't know where she got it."

Mme. Storey blew a cloud of cigarette smoke, and studied Maggie through it; a trick she has with a witness.

"Wait now!" said Maggie. "I recollect the money was brought to her once a couple of years ago when she was sick abed. Young fellow brought it and took her receipt."

"Would you know him again?" asked Mme. Storey carelessly.

"I sure would, Ma'am. He was a pretty fellow."

"That's all," said Mme. Storey. She turned to Barron. "On the night of Ada Rousseau's death somebody entered the house with her key. He couldn't get in that way again, because on Tuesday night the police were here, and on Wednesday it was sealed up by the court."

"Well?" said Barron as she paused.

"On Wednesday night," said Mme. Storey, flicking the ash off her cigarette, "somebody forced an entrance through the door on the yard."

There was a general exclamation. "How do you know?" demanded Barron.

"The evidence is in the door. He broke a pane of glass, and put his hand in to draw the bolt and turn the key. He brought a new pane with him, puttied it in, and painted the putty to match the other panes. When he left, he locked the door and carried the key with him."

"How do you know this was Wednesday night?"

"The paint has dried, and a certain amount of dust has fallen on it."

Jackman, the woman's ex-husband and her heir who had scarcely spoken up to now, became violently agitated. The seedy old actor did not appear to be acting now. The cry was forced from him. "Broke in? Broke in? For what?"

"Obviously to search for something," said Mme. Storey. "A cool hand. He wore cotton gloves. He went direct to the safe in the boudoir."

"Oh, my God!" gasped Jackman, clutching his head. "Ada's jewels! That's all there is of any value!"

"How could he know the combination of the safe?" put in Barron.

"He didn't have to know it. It is a simple lock. If he knew the kind of lock it was, he could have taught himself to open such a lock before he came. All you have to do is to turn the knob and listen for the tumblers to engage. I have just opened it myself. I saw the marks of the cotton gloves in the dust inside, but the jewels have not been disturbed."

"How do you know he didn't take something else ... something else?" stuttered Jackman.

"He didn't find what he was after," said Mme. Storey coolly, "because he came back on Thursday night and searched further. Also Friday night, Saturday night, and last night. He hasn't found it yet."

Jackman passed a handkerchief over his sweating face.

"How can you reconstruct his movements so exactly?" demanded Barron.

"The nocturnal visitor is a man," answered Mme. Storey, smiling. "He overlooked the marks he was leaving everywhere in the dust. Any woman who has ever kept house in New York can figure pretty exactly how much dust falls in twenty-four hours."

"What is he after?" cried Barron.

She shrugged. "How can I tell? One might guess that it was some piece of evidence in the possession of Ada Rousseau that enabled her to collect five hundred dollars a week for twenty years. Twenty-five thousand dollars a year. That's the interest on half a million. It's a good round sum."

Barron drove his fist into his palm. "By God, yes!" he cried. "And that's why the woman was murdered!"

My employer glanced at me privately, and pulled a droll face. Here was a sudden change of front.

"What do you propose to do next?" asked Barron.

"Lie in wait for our friend to-night," she said, turning a ring on her finger.

At midnight, Mme Storey and I were concealed in the passage leading from the foot of the basement stairs back to the kitchen. It was as black as your hat there. My employer had chosen the spot because the electric light switch was within reach of her hand. Inspector Barron was crouched down below the table under the kitchen window, and his secretary, young Slosson, was in a sort of broom closet alongside the door from the yard. Slosson, a husky specimen, was supposed to pop out and cut off the man's retreat.

Jackman, the heir-at-law, had insisted on being present in the house and the Surrogate's clerk was there in the way of duty. These two and several plain clothes men were waiting upstairs in the dark drawing-room.

I ought to mention that during the afternoon our man, Crider, had succeeded in finding the taxi-driver who had picked up Ada Rousseau and the unknown young man outside Raffaello's. He had driven them to a point in Fifty-Sixth Street where they got out of his cab and entered a private car that was waiting. The woman appeared to be too drunk to realize what she was doing. The taxi-driver thought there was another man in the back of the private car, but did not get a good look at him.

Mme. Storey had not brought Crider with us to the sealed house. He had been sent away with some instructions that were as yet unknown to me.

It was so still throughout the house that I could hear the mice scrabbling and squeaking behind the plaster. The smell of the old foul gas-cooker filled the kitchen. I am no good at such times. I can face actual danger well enough; but to have to wait for the unknown demoralizes me. I felt as if there was a hard hand closing around my throat.

Mme. Storey whispered: "Move around a bit. It lets down the strain."

So I started pacing the linoleum-covered passage between the stairs and the kitchen door, feeling my way along the wall.

Once as I approached Mme. Storey, she touched me lightly, and I froze where I stood. "Listen!" she whispered.

I heard some slight sounds from the yard in the rear, and the thud of a hard body on the earth. A faint light came from outside, and presently a shadow darkened the panes of the door; shoulders and a head with a soft hat pulled down. The key turned in the lock and he opened the door. For a moment he stood there listening, then came in.

It was all over in a second. The kitchen light flooded on; Barron rose from beside the table pointing a gun. Slosson stepped out of the closet. "Put 'em up!" growled Barron.

The new-comer did not so much as flinch at the gun. A handsome young man with dark, keen eyes and a resolute mouth. He was well-dressed. The gloved hands were empty. He looked at Barron unafraid, and turning his head coolly, took in Slosson and his gun. When he saw Mme. Storey and me in the doorway, his eyes widened in astonishment, but he said nothing. Whatever he may be, you can't but respect a man who keeps his mouth shut.

"Put 'em up!" repeated Barron, making an ugly move with the gun.

The young man smiled contemptuously. "Put away your guns," he said. "I'm not armed. I'm no killer."

Barron and his man seized him and patted him all over. All they found on him was an electric torch, and they returned their guns to their pockets. Slosson shot the bolt in the door.

"Who are you?" demanded Barron.

"I'll never tell you," said the young man coolly.

"You fool!" cried Barron angrily. "You're caught! The game is up! Give an account of yourself!" He showed the badge under his coat.

A desperate look came into the young man's face, but it was not fear. "Sure, the game is up!" he muttered bitterly. "But I'm not talking."

Barron cursed him savagely. Mme. Storey came forward with a more conciliatory air. "We know you're no common thief," she said.

He took off his hat when she addressed him. He had a shapely, well-poised head. "Who are you?" he asked warily.

"I don't know if it means anything to you," my employer replied; "I am Rosika Storey."

He softened a little. "Yes, I know who you are," he said. "I wish you were on my side instead of against me."

Barron launched out at him again. "You had better come clean!"

His loud voice brought the other men running down into the kitchen. Jackman, whose property was threatened, bored into the young man with his frightened suspicious eyes, but he could make no more of him than Barron.

The young housebreaker suddenly changed his tactics. "My name is Lawrence Lowe," he said to Barron with a mocking grin, "or anything else you like. I read in the papers that this woman had left a small fortune in jewels, and the house was empty, and I came to lift them, that's all. I hired a room in the house that backs up on this, and made a portable ladder to throw over the fence."

"You're lying!" shouted Barron. "There's more to it than that. You'll be charged with murder!"

"You'll have a tough job hanging that on me, old man," the other answered coolly. "You'd better be satisfied with a charge of attempted burglary, or unlawful entry or whatever it is, you call it. I'll plead guilty to that, and take the rap."

"I'll make you talk!" cried Barron.

The young man's dark eyes blazed up. "Sure!" he said. "I've heard of the rubber hose and the water cure, and the brass knucks and all. But they'll never fetch anything out of me. You can kill me sooner!"

Mme. Storey lit a cigarette and, keenly watching the young man through the smoke, pursued her own train of thought. She presently whispered to me to call up Maggie Dolan and tell her to come at once.

When I returned to the kitchen, Barron was still storming. The dark young man was leaning back, half-sitting on the table, with his hands down at each side gripping the edge. His unafraid glance travelled around from one to another, sizing us up. Though he had not a friend there, he kept his head, and coolly parried Barron's questions.

"You're lying!" cried the Inspector. "We know that you've been into the safe, and that you left the jewels there."

"That's foolish," came the smiling answer. "What should a thief be looking for but jewels!" He steadily faced Barron out.

And then he suddenly collapsed. He heard sounds from the yard. He stiffened, a look of agony came into his face and his eyes bolted. "Oh, for God's sake, keep her out of this!" he cried brokenly. "Keep her out! Keep her out!"

At the same moment the door was violently rattled, and a woman's voice cried out: "Let me in!" Slosson threw the bolt back, and a bareheaded blonde girl ran into the light.

She was perfectly blind to all of us there in the kitchen except one. She ran to him and slipping her arm under his, caught it hard against her breast. Her eyes piteously searched his face. "Oh, Ralph, what has happened?" she gasped.

He turned away his head. "Why did you have to come!" he groaned.

"From my window I saw the lights go up," she protested. "I saw people moving about; I knew you were in danger; I couldn't stay away. I'm not made of wood!"

He was unable to speak.

"What has happened? What has happened?" she cried, shaking his arm.

"I'm caught," he said in a low bitter voice. "These are police. This one—" pointing to Barron—"appears to be an Inspector because he wears a gold badge. The lady yonder is the celebrated Madame Storey!"

"Well, if you're caught I might as well be caught too," she murmured. She turned and faced us defiantly.

Life came back into the young man's face. He threw an arm around the girl's shoulders and drew her hard against his side. His dark face brooded over her with a kind of desperate fondness. "You *have* upset the apple-cart!" he murmured.

I now had my first good look at her. About twenty years old I should say, fair and sensitive as one of Rossetti's models, but with a power of emotion that was absent in those lackadaisical misses. She was wearing an expensively simple one-piece dress of blue serge with odd narrow bands of greed suede. Her thin hands spoke a language of their own.

She addressed Barron indignantly. "He's not a criminal! Are you blind! Can't you see it for yourself?"

"I've seen 'em of all kinds," answered the Inspector with a hard smile. "And when a man breaks into a house in the middle of the night. . . ."

"He did it for me!" the girl cried. "To save me and somebody who is dear to me. Is that the act of a criminal?"

"Well, tell us all about it, Miss," said Barron cajolingly.

"Not a word, Nora!" cried the young man sharply. "I forbid it."

Barron flushed angrily. "You'd better let her tell the truth," he growled. "We'll find it out anyhow. The truth never hurt anybody."

"Neither did keeping your mouth shut!" retorted the young man.

Jackman, needless to say, was terribly excited by this scene. He pulled nervously at his lower lip, and his bleary eyes kept darting from one to another of the pair. He could make nothing of it. Finally he could hold his tongue no longer.

"Who the hell are you?" he demanded of the young man. "What's your game? What are you after in this house?"

"I don't know you," came the cool answer.

"This is my house," cried Jackman, slapping his chest. "That is, everything in it is mine. What are you after here? I guess I've got a right to know!"

"Do you think I'm going to tell you?" said the young man smiling.

The girl put herself in front of him as if to protect him from the angry proprietor. "He's no thief," she said. "He wants nothing of yours."

Barron thoroughly angered, cried out: "Maybe he's worse than a thief! Maybe he'll have to answer to a charge of murder!"

It was a sickening blow to the girl. She fell back against her lover's breast paperwhite and gasping. "Oh! No! No! ... I never thought ... Oh, it can't be! ... Why, he never started until after the woman. . . ."

The young man clapped his hand over her mouth.

"I want the truth," shouted Barron. "And by God! I'm going to get it! . . ."

My employer was not going to stand for bull-dozing. "They have a right to refuse to answer our questions, Inspector," she said quickly. "Because anything they say may be used against them later. You and I have other ways of arriving at the truth. Have patience for a moment. I have sent for Maggie Dolan."

Even while she was speaking there was a ring at the front door. One of the detectives ran upstairs to answer it. He returned, bringing the woman who had served Ada Rousseau for so many years. Maggie had thrown on her absurd finery anyhow; and her hat was askew and her homely face puffy with sleep. She looked around blinking and confused.

"What's up ... what's up?" she stuttered.

"Maggie," said Mme. Storey, "look at this young man and tell us if you have ever seen him before. Think before you answer."

Maggie gave her hat a shove which sent it over too far on the other side. But none of us laughed; there was an electric tension in the air. The young man stared at her scornfully. Maggie looked at him and dumbly shook her head.

"I don't recollect ..." she began. Then something stirred in her. "Wait a minute! Seems like I seen his face somewheres. . . . Yes. Now I've got it! That's the young fella as brought the money to Ada, time she was sick abed and couldn't fetch it herself."

"Ha!" cried Barron slapping his thigh.

The young fellow stared at Maggie with absolute blankness.

"Are you sure, Maggie?" asked Mme. Storey sternly. "Could you go on the stand and swear to it?"

"Sure I could, Ma'am. Because I was scared when he come. I watched him good. I couldn't be mistaken."

"What scared you?"

"Because Ada, Ma'am, when she told me he was coming, she said I must bring him upstairs and wait in the room as long as he was there. It would be too good a chance, Ada says, for him to stick a knife in her and save the five hundred a week."

This piece of testimony came with the force of a thunderbolt. There was complete silence in the kitchen followed by a confused outbreak. "There's your motive!" shouted Barron. "That will send you to the chair!" Jackman, the old actor, looked stupidly from one to another with his lip hanging. "I don't get it! I just don't get it!"

The young girl broke down utterly; clung to her lover and hid her face in his breast, convulsed with sobs. He was badly shaken himself, but it was of her he was thinking. The dark head bent low over the blonde one as he tried to find words of comfort to whisper to her.

A distressing business all around. I hated my job. I looked to Mme. Storey to do something, but she seemed to be satisfied that the case was proven. Barron sent one of his men to telephone for a car to take the prisoners to Headquarters. The young fellow made a despairing plea for his girl.

"Let her go back the way she came, sir. You've got me. I'm the principal in this affair. I take the full responsibility."

The girl jerked her head up. "No! No!" she protested. "I won't leave you! This is *my* business!"

"She has confessed that she is your accomplice," said Barron.

The young man turned to my employer. "Madame Storey . . ."

She shook her head compassionately. "Inspector Barron is the boss," she said. "I can do nothing."

We all trooped up to the drawing-room to wait for the car. There was a ring at the door, and my heart sank, but it was not the police; it was Crider come to report the result of his mission. I judged from his pleased face that he had been successful.

"Thank God!" said Mme. Storey. "You found it!"

"Yes, Madam." He produced a silver key ring with four keys hanging from it. We all stared. I thought Barron's eyes would pop out of his head.

Mme. Storey handed the keys to Maggie. "Do you know these?"

It was a moment or two before the woman could concentrate her scattered faculties. Her eyes widened. "Why sure," she said. "Them's Ada's keys! This here is the front door; this is the middle drawer of her desk; this is the liquor closet and this the iron-bound trunk in the packing-room. I know them well."

"Crider," said Mme. Storey, "tell the Inspector where you found them."

Everybody waited for the answer as if life hung on it.

In his matter-of-fact way Crider said: "I found them in this fellow Jackman's room, sir. Mme. Storey instructed me to search it while he was out of the way with you here. The keys were hidden in the toe of an old shoe."

Again that terrific silence. A choking cry was forced from Jackman. He clutched at his throat and pitched headlong to the carpet. A couple of stalwart plain clothes men jerked him to his feet and planted him in an arm-chair. He had not lost consciousness, but his control had gone. His head rolled from side to side on the back of the chair, he writhed and whined and the truth came tumbling out.

"I didn't aim to kill her! As God is my judge I didn't mean it! ... Twenty-five years ago she turned me out. She framed the divorce! ... All these years, wouldn't see me, wouldn't give me a cent! Though I was starving! ... Was that right? Was that right? ... I knew she was collecting five hundred dollars a week on an incriminating letter that she had. And I was her rightful husband. Wasn't I entitled to a part of it? ...

"I brooded on it. Sometimes I didn't have a place to lay my head! She wouldn't give me a cent! ... She drove me crazy! And I made up my mind I would get the letter. I was entitled to it.... I got a fellow to help me. It was easy. He got her drunk and brought her to me. Why, the poison, the veronal, was in her own handbag. I just poured it in her whiskey.... I didn't aim to kill her, I tell you. I just wanted to put her out for a while so I could come to the house and get the letter. Once I had it she'd have to treat with me.... But she died on me and I had to leave her in the park....

"I took her keys and came to the house. But I was scared off. In a few days I'd have had the run of the house anyhow...."

Inspector Barron shut him off with a gesture of disgust. "This is the lowest wretch I have ever had before me," he said. "Take him away! Take him away!"

By this time the police car had arrived. Jackman was yanked to his feet and hustled out.

The young couple, Ralph and Nora, had listened to his story with wondering faces. Barron now turned to them scowling, and the young man threw his arm around the girl.

"What shall I do with these two?" said Barron. "The fellow is a housebreaker just the same. What was *he* after?"

"He was after the letter too," said Mme. Storey. "He was acting for the man who has been blackmailed for twenty-five years. He works for that man, and this girl is the man's daughter. When they read of Ada Rousseau's death they feared that the letter would be found, and that they would all be ruined. It was a crime, of course, but surely there was a good deal of justification. Can't you let him go, Inspector?"

"I can't act in the dark," he said scowling. "I must know what is behind it all."

"Let's not mention any names," said Mme. Storey. "As a young man this girl's father had the misfortune to become infatuated with Ada Rousseau. He was foolish enough to write her a letter confessing that he had stolen money from his employer for her sake. She saved the letter for future use. Since that time the stolen money has been paid back a hundred times over, and the writer of the letter has become one of our best citizens. It would be a shame, wouldn't it, to drag him down now? And the innocent with him?"

"How did you learn so much?" demanded Barron.

"Oh, just by a process of deduction," she said blandly. "Just by piecing all the little bits together."

"Where is the damned letter anyhow?"

"How should I know? Maybe Ada destroyed it after all.... Let them go, Inspector," she went on in her most persuasive voice. "You have the real murderer. This will be a big feather in your cap!"

He looked at her with a sharp inquiry in his eyes.

"I don't want any of the glory of this case," she said demurely.

Barron let out a breath of relief. "All right," he said, "I'll take the responsibility of letting them go." He offered Mme. Storey his hand. "You're a wonderful woman," he said with the grand condescension of a full-blooded male, "and I count it a privilege to have you working with me!"

"How nice of you," said Mme. Storey sweetly. She put her foot out and trod on my toe.

"Can I put you down anywhere?" he asked.

"No, thanks," she said. "You had better go with your prisoner. I'll take these young people home. I want to give them some good advice. I'll be seeing you tomorrow."

He bowed gallantly and went out with his men. The rest of us followed. Last of all came the Surrogate's clerk, who locked the front door with a padlock, and put fresh seals on it

Mme. Storey and I shared a taxi with Ralph and Nora. On the way home she would not talk about what had happened, but just made jokes. When we reached her place she made me get out first and open the gate that admits to her maisonette. Standing by the door of the cab, she opened her handbag and produced the letter she had found in Ada Rousseau's tea-caddy. Pressing it into Ralph's hand, she said:

"A little wedding present from a well-wisher."

She ran in without waiting for them to thank her. As I closed the gate behind her I heard Ralph's joyful voice ring out:

"Nora, I have it! We are safe!"

Dorothy L. Sayers

(1893–1957)

One of the most singular creations in detective fiction is Dorothy L. Sayers's Lord Peter Wimsey, the stylish and urbane English aristocrat who detected with alacrity in eleven novels and twenty-one short stories. Lord Peter did not detect in a vacuum, however. Sayers peopled his world with a full cast of well-delineated characters: mystery writer Harriet Vane (who later became Wimsey's wife); Detective-Inspector Charles Parker; the efficient Miss Climpson; and, of course, Wimsey's valet, Mr. Bunter. This ongoing cast frequently aided and abetted Lord Peter in his investigations. Harriet Vane, for example, assumed a large role in *Have His Carcase* (1932) and *Gaudy Night* (1935); Detective-Inspector Parker (who eventually married Wimsey's sister, the Lady Mary) is of great assistance in *Clouds of Witness* (1926). In "The Footsteps That Ran," Mr. Bunter—without whom the Wimsey household would surely grind to a halt—detects alongside His Lordship in a mystery that proves "Jealousy is cruel as the grave." Ellery Queen considered the story one of the most affecting in Sayers' 1928 collection, *Lord Peter Views the Body*.

Although Sayers adhered firmly to the fair-play conventions of the Golden Age mystery, she chose to create a milieu and characters that were less static than many of her contemporaries'. Lord Peter first appeared (in *Whose Body?*, 1923) as an attractive but somewhat effete and frivolous young man, but as he evolved he took on larger dimensions, changing in response to the situations and people he encountered. More than just a collection of eccentricities—the monocle, the top hat—he is a thinking and feeling individual who matures over time. Similarly, Harriet Vane evolves from a brash and somewhat prickly young woman into an admirable character who is more than a match for Wimsey. Sayers' writing is stylish and of high literary quality, and the tales are set against a variety of interesting backgrounds: a trial in the House of Lords (*Clouds of Witness*); the advertising industry, which Sayers knew well, having worked for an agency (*Murder Must Advertise*, 1933); bell-ringing (*The Nine Tailors*, 1934); and an Oxford college (*Gaudy Night*). While Sayers also created a series of eleven stories about Montague Egg, a commercial traveler in wines and spirits (five of which may be found in the 1939 collection *In the Teeth of the Evidence and Other Stories*), Lord Peter Wimsey remains her most enduring creation.

THE FOOTSTEPS THAT RAN

LORD PETER WIMSEY AND MR. BUNTER
LONDON, ENGLAND
1928

M r. Bunter withdrew his head from beneath the focusing cloth.

"I fancy that will be quite adequate, sir," he said deferentially, "unless there are any further patients, if I may call them so, which you would wish to put on record."

"Not today," replied the doctor. He took the last stricken rat gently from the table, and replaced it in its cage with an air of satisfaction. "Perhaps on Wednesday, if Lord Peter can kindly spare your services once again——"

"What's that?" murmured his lordship, withdrawing his long nose from the investigation of a number of unattractive-looking glass jars. "Nice old dogs," he added vaguely. "Wags his tail when you mention his name, what? Are these monkey-glands, Hartman, or a southwest elevation of Cleopatra's duodenum?"

"You don't know anything, do you" said the young physician, laughing. "No use playing your bally-fool-with-an-eyeglass tricks on me, Wimsey. I'm up to them. I was saying to Bunter that I'd be no end grateful if you'd let him turn up again three days hence to register the progress of the specimens—always supposing they do progress, that is."

"Why ask, dear old thing?" said his lordship. "Always a pleasure to assist a fellow-sleuth, don't you know. Trackin' down murderers—all in the same way of business and all that. All finished? Good egg! By the way, if you don't have that cage mended you'll lose one of your patients—Number 5. The last wire but one is workin' loose—assisted by the intelligent occupant. Jolly little beasts, ain't they? No need of dentists—wish I was a rat—wire much better for the nerves than that fizzlin' drill."

Dr. Hartman uttered a little exclamation.

"How in the world did you notice that, Wimsey? I didn't think you'd even looked at the cage."

"Built noticin'—improved by practice," said Lord Peter quietly. "Anythin' wrong leaves a kind of impression on the eye; brain trots along afterward with the warnin'. I saw that when we came in. Only just grasped it. Can't say my mind was glued on the matter. Shows the victim's improvin', anyhow. All serene, Bunter?"

"Everything perfectly satisfactory, I trust, my lord," replied the manservant. He had packed up his camera and plates, and was quietly restoring order in the little laboratory, whose fittings—compact as those of an ocean liner—had been disarranged for the experiment.

"Well," said the doctor, "I am enormously obliged to you, Lord Peter, and to Bunter too. I am hoping for a great result from these experiments, and you cannot imagine how valuable an assistance it will be to me to have a really good series of photographs. I can't afford this sort of thing—yet," he added, his rather haggard young face wistful as he looked at the great camera, "and I can't do the work at the hospital. There's no time; I've got to be here. A struggling G.P. can't afford to let his practice go, even in Bloomsbury. There are time when even a half-crown visit makes all the difference between making both ends meet and having an ugly hiatus."

"As Mr. Micawber said," replied Wimsey, "'Income twenty pounds, expenditure nineteen, nineteen, six—result: happiness; expenditure twenty pounds, ought, six—result: misery. Don't prostrate yourself in gratitude, old bean; nothin' Bunter loves like messin' round with pyro and hyposulphite. Keeps his hand in. All kinds of practice welcome. Fingerprints and process plates spell seventh what-you-may-call-it of bliss, but focal-plane work on scurvy-ridden rodents (good phrase!) acceptable if no crime forthcoming. Crimes have been rather short lately. Been eatin' our heads off, haven't we, Bunter? Don't know what's come over London. I've taken to prying into my neighbor's affairs to keep from goin' stale. Frightened the postman into a fit the other day by askin' him how his young lady at Croydon was. He's a married man, livin' in Great Ormond Street."

"How did you know?"

"Well, I didn't really. But he lives just opposite to a friend of mine—inspector Parker; and his wife—not Parker's; he's unmarried; the postman's; I mean—asked Parker the other day whether the flyin' shows at Croydon went on all night. Parker, bein' flummoxed, said 'No,' without thinkin'. Bit of a give-away, what? Thought I'd give the poor devil a word in season, don't you know. Uncommonly thoughtless of Parker."

The doctor laughed. "You'll stay to lunch, won't you?" he said. "Only cold meat and salad, I'm afraid. My woman won't come Sundays. Have to answer my own door. Deuced unprofessional, I'm afraid, but it can't be helped."

"Pleasure," said Wimsey, as they emerged from the laboratory and entered the dark little flat by the back door. "Did you build this place on?"

"No," said Hartman; "the last tenant did that. He was an artist. That's why I took the place. It comes in very useful, ramshackle as it is, though this glass roof is a bit sweltering on a hot day like this. Still, I had to have something on the ground floor, cheap, and it'll do till times get better."

"Till your vitamin experiments make you famous, eh?" said Peter cheerfully. "You're goin' to be the comin' man, you know. Feel it in my bones. Uncommonly neat little kitchen you've got, anyhow."

"It does," said the doctor. "The lab makes it a bit gloomy, but the woman's only here in the daytime."

He led the way into a narrow little dining-room, where the table was laid for a cold lunch. The one window at the end farthest from the kitchen looked out into Great James Street. The room was little more than a passage, and full of doors — the kitchen door, a door in the adjacent wall leading into the entrance-hall, and a third on the opposite side, through which his visitor caught a glimpse of a moderate-sized consulting-room.

Lord Peter Wimsey and his host sat down to table, and the doctor expressed a hope that Mr. Bunter would sit down with them. That correct person, however, deprecated any such suggestion.

"If I might venture to indicate my own preference, Sir," he said, "it would be to wait upon you and his lordship in the usual manner."

"It's no use," said Wimsey. "Bunter likes me to know my place. Terrorizin' sort of man, Bunter. Can't call my soul my own. Carry on, Bunter; we wouldn't presume for the world."

Mr. Bunter handed the salad, and poured out the water with a grave decency appropriate to a crusted old tawny port.

It was a Sunday afternoon in that halcyon summer of 1921. The sordid little street was almost empty. The ice-cream man alone seemed thriving and active. He leaned luxuriously on the green post at the corner, in the intervals of driving a busy trade. Bloomsbury's swarm of able-bodied and able-voiced infants was still; presumably within-doors, eating steamy Sunday dinners inappropriate to the tropical weather. The only disturbing sounds came from the flat above, where heavy footsteps passed rapidly to and fro.

"Who's the merry-and-bright bloke above?" enquired Lord Peter presently. "Not an early riser, I take it. Not that anybody is on a Sunday mornin'. Why an inscrutable Providence ever inflicted such a ghastly day on people livin' in town I can't imagine. I ought to be in the country, but I've got to meet a friend at Victoria this afternoon. Such a day to choose.... Who's the lady? Wife or accomplished friend? Gather she takes a properly submissive view of woman's duties in the home, either way. That's the bedroom overhead, I take it."

Hartman looked at Lord Peter in some surprise.

"'Scuse my beastly inquisitiveness, old thing," said Wimsey. "Bad habit. Not my business."

"How did you—?"

"Guesswork," said Lord Peter, with disarming frankness. "I heard the squawk of an iron bedstead on the ceiling and a heavy fellow get out with a bump, but it may quite well be a couch or something. Anyway, he's been potterin' about in his stocking feet over these few feet of floor for the last half-hour, while the woman has been clatterin' to and fro, in and out of the kitchen and away into the sittin'-room, with her high heels on, ever since we've been here. Hence deduction as to domestic habits of the first-floor tenants."

"I thought," said the doctor, with an aggrieved expression, "you'd been listening to my valuable exposition of the beneficial effects of Vitamin B, and Lind's treatment of scurvy with fresh lemons in 1755."

"I was listenin'," agreed Lord Peter hastily, "but I heard the footsteps as well. Fellow's toddled into the kitchen—only wanted the matches, though; he's gone off into the sittin'-room and left her to carry on the good work. What was I sayin'? Oh, yes! You see, as I was sayin' before, one hears a thing or sees it without knowin' or thinkin' about it. Then afterwards one starts meditatin', and it all comes back, and one sorts out one's impressions. Like those plates of Bunter's. Picture's all there, l—la—what's the word I want, Bunter?"

"Latent, my lord."

"That's it. My right-hand man, Bunter; couldn't do a thing without him. The picture's latent till you put the developer on. Same with the brain. No mystery. Little grey matter's all you want to remember things with. As a matter of curiosity, was I right about those people above?"

"Perfectly. The man's a gas-company's inspector. A bit surly, but devoted (after his own fashion) to his wife. I mean, he doesn't mind hulking in bed on a Sunday morning and letting her do the chores, but he spends all the money he can spare on giving her pretty hats and fur coats and what not. They've only been married about six months. I was called in to her when she had a touch of 'flu in the spring, and he was almost off his head with anxiety. She's a lovely little woman, I must say—Italian. He picked her up in some eating-place in Soho, I believe. Glorious dark hair and eyes: Venus sort of figure; proper contours in all the right places; good skin—

all that sort of thing. She was a bit of a draw to that restaurant while she was there, I fancy. Lively. She had an old admirer round here one day—awkward little Italian fellow, with a knife—active as a monkey. Might have been unpleasant, but I happened to be on the spot, and her husband came along. People are always laying one another out in these streets. Good for business, of course, but one gets tired of tying up broken heads and slits in the jugular. Still, I suppose the girl can't help being attractive, though I don't say she's what you might call stand-offish in her manner. She's sincerely fond of Brotherton, I think, though—that's his name."

Wimsey nodded inattentively. "I suppose life is a bit monotonous here," he said.

"Professionally, yes. Births and drunks and wife-beatings are pretty common. And all the usual ailments, of course. God!" cried the doctor explosively, "if only I could get away, and do my experiments!"

"Ah!" said Peter, "where's that eccentric old millionaire with a mysterious disease, who always figures in the novels? A lightning diagnosis—a miraculous cure—'God bless you doctor; here are five thousand pounds'—Harley Street—"

"That sort doesn't live in Bloomsbury," said the doctor.

"It must be fascinatin', diagnosin' things," said Peter thoughtfully. "How d'you do it? I mean, is there a regular set of symptoms for each disease, like callin' a club to show you want your partner to go no trumps? You don't just say: 'This fellow's got a pimple on his nose, therefore he has fatty degeneration of the heart—'"

"I hope not," said the doctor drily.

"Or is it more like gettin' a clue to a crime?" went on Peter. "You see somethin'—a room, or a body, say, all knocked about anyhow, and there's a damn sight of symptoms of somethin' wrong, and you've got just to pick out the ones which tell the story?"

"That's more like it," said Dr. Hartman. "Some symptoms are significant in themselves—like the condition of the gums in scurvy, let us say—others in conjunction with—"

He broke off, and both sprang to their feet as a shrill scream sounded suddenly from the flat above, followed by a heavy thud. A man's voice cried out lamentably, feet ran violently to and fro; then, as the doctor and his guests stood frozen in consternation, came the man himself—falling down the stairs in his haste, hammering at Hartman's door.

"Help! Help! Let me in! My wife! He's murdered her!"

They ran hastily to the door and let him in. He was a big, fair man, in his shirt sleeves and stockings. His hair stood up, and his face was set in bewildered misery.

"She is dead—dead. He was her lover," he groaned. "Doctor! I have lost my wife! My Maddalena—" He paused, looked wildly for a moment, and then said hoarsely, "Someone's been in—somehow—stabbed her—murdered her. I'll have the law on him, doctor. Come quickly—she was cooking the chicken for my dinner—Ah-h-h!"

He gave a long, hysterical shriek, which ended in a hiccupping laugh. The doctor took him roughly by the arm and shook him. "Pull yourself together, Mr. Brotherton," he said sharply. "Perhaps she is only hurt. Stand out of the way!"

"Only hurt?" said the man, sitting heavily down on the nearest chair. "No—no —she is dead—little Maddalena—Oh, my God!"

Dr. Hartman had snatched a roll of bandages and a few surgical appliances from the consulting-room, and he ran upstairs, followed closely by Lord Peter. Bunter remained for a few moments to combat hysterics with cold water. Then he stepped across to the dining-room window and shouted.

"Well, wot is it?" cried a voice from the street.

"Would you be so kind as to step in here a minute, officer?" said Mr. Bunter. "There's been murder done."

When Brotherton and Bunter arrived upstairs with the constable, they found Dr. Hartman and Lord Peter in the little kitchen. The doctor was kneeling beside the woman's body. At their entrance he looked up, and shook his head.

"Death instantaneous," he said. "Clean though the heart. Poor child. She cannot have suffered at all. Oh, constable, it is very fortunate you are here. Murder appears to have been done—though I'm afraid the man has escaped. Probably Mr. Brotherton can give us some help. He was in the flat at the time."

The man had sunk down on a chair, and was gazing at the body with a face from which all meaning seemed to have been struck out. The policeman produced a notebook.

"Now, sir," he said, "don't let's waste any time. Sooner we can get to work the more likely we are to catch our man. Now, you was 'ere at the time, was you?"

Brotherton stared a moment, then, making a violent effort, he answered steadily:

"I was in the sitting-room, smoking and reading the paper. My—she—was getting the dinner ready in here. I heard her give a scream, and I rushed in and found her lying on the floor. She didn't have time to say anything. When I found she was dead, I rushed to the window, and saw the fellow scrambling away over the glass roof there. I yelled at him, but he disappeared. Then I ran down—"

"'Arf a mo'," said the policeman. "Now, see 'ere, sir, didn't you think to go after 'im at once?"

"My first thought was for her," said the man. "I thought maybe she wasn't dead. I tried to bring her round—" His speech ended in a groan.

"You say he came in through the window," said the policeman.

"I beg your pardon, officer," interrupted Lord Peter, who had been apparently making a mental inventory of the contents of the kitchen. "Mr Brotherton suggested that the man went *out* through the window. It's better to be accurate."

"It's the same thing," said the doctor. "It's the only way he could have come in. These flats are all alike. The staircase door leads into the sitting-room, and Mr. Brotherton was there, so the man couldn't have come that way."

"And," said Peter, "he didn't get in through the bedroom window, or we should have seen him. We were in the room below. Unless, indeed, he let himself down from the roof. Was the door between the bedroom and the sitting-room open?" he asked suddenly, turning to Brotherton.

The man hesitated a moment. "Yes," he said finally. "Yes, I'm sure it was."

"Could you have seen the man if he had come through the bedroom window?"

"I couldn't have helped seeing him."

"Come, come, sir," said the policeman, with some irritation, "better let *me* ask the questions. Stands to reason the fellow wouldn't get in through the bedroom window in full view of the street."

"How clever of you to think of that," said Wimsey. "Of course not. Never occurred to me. Then it must have been this window, as you say."

"And, what's more, here's his marks on the window-sill," said the constable triumphantly, pointing to some blurred traces among the London soot. "That's right. Down he goes by that drain-pipe, over the glass roof down there—what's that the roof of?"

"My laboratory," said the doctor. "Heavens! to think that while we were at dinner this murdering villain——"

"Quite so, sir," agreed the constable. "Well, he'd get away over the wall into the court be'ind. 'E'll 'ave been seen there, no fear; you needn't anticipate much trouble in layin' 'ands on 'im, sir. I'll go round there in 'arf a tick. Now then, sir"—turning to Brotherton—"'ave you any idea wot this party might have looked like?"

Brotherton lifted a wild face, and the doctor interposed.

"I think you ought to know, constable," he said, "that there was—well, not a murderous attack, but what might have been one, made on this woman before—about eight weeks ago—by a man named Marincetti—an Italian waiter—with a knife."

"Ah!" The policeman licked his pencil eagerly. "Do you know this party as 'as been mentioned?" he enquired of Brotherton.

"That's the man," said Brotherton, with concentrated fury. "Coming here after my wife—God curse him! I wish to God I had him dead here beside her!"

"Quite so," said the policeman. "Now, sir"—to the doctor—"'ave you got the weapon wot the crime was committed with?"

"No," said Hartman, "there was no weapon in the body when I arrived."

"Did *you* take it out?" pursued the constable, to Brotherton.

"No," said Brotherton, "he took it with him."

"Took it with 'im," the constable entered the fact in his notes. "Phew! Wonderful 'ot it is in 'ere, ain't it, sir?" he added, mopping his brow.

"It's the gas-oven, I think," said Peter mildly. "Uncommon hot thing, a gas-oven, in the middle of July. D'you mind if I turn it out? There's the chicken inside, but I don't suppose you want—"

Brotherton groaned, and the constable said: "Quite right, sir. A man wouldn't 'ardly fancy 'is dinner after a thing like this. Thank you, sir. Well now, doctor, wot kind of weapon do you take this to 'ave been?"

"It was a long, narrow weapon—something like an Italian stiletto, I imagine," said the doctor, "about six inches long. It was thrust in with great force under the fifth rib, and I should say it had pierced the heart centrally. As you see, there has been practically no bleeding. Such a wound would cause instant death. Was she lying just as she is now when you first saw her, Mr. Brotherton?"

"On her back, just as she is," replied the husband.

"Well, that seems clear enough," said the policeman. "This 'ere Marinetti, or wotever 'is name is, 'as a grudge against the poor young lady—"

"I believe he was an admirer," put in the doctor.

"Quite so," agreed the constable. "Of course, these foreigners are like that— even the decentest of 'em. Stabbin' and such-like seems to come nateral to them, as you might say. Well this 'ere Marinetti climbs in 'ere, sees the poor young lady standin' 'ere by the table all alone, gettin' the dinner ready; 'e comes in be'ind, catches 'er—easy job, you see; no corsets nor nothing—she shrieks out, 'e pulls 'is stiletty out of 'er an' makes tracks. Well, now we've got to find 'im, and by your leave, sir, I'll be gettin' along. We'll 'ave 'im by the 'eels before long, sir, don't you worry. I'll 'ave to put a man in charge 'ere, sir, to keep folks out, but that needn't worry you. Good mornin', gentlemen."

"May we move the poor girl now?" asked the doctor.

"Certainly. Like me to 'elp you, sir?"

"No. Don't lose any time. We can manage." Dr. Hartman turned to Peter as the constable clattered downstairs. "Will you help me, Lord Peter?"

"Bunter's better at that sort of thing," said Wimsey, with a hard mouth.

The doctor looked at him in some surprise, but said nothing, and he and Bunter carried the still form away. Brotherton did not follow them. He sat in a grief-stricken heap, with his head buried in his hands. Lord Peter walked about the little kitchen, turning over the various knives and kitchen utensils, peering into the sink bucket, and apparently taking an inventory of the bread, butter, condiments, vegetables, and so forth which lay about in preparation for the Sunday meal. There were potatoes in the sink, half peeled, a pathetic witness to the quiet domestic life which had been so horribly interrupted. The colander was filled with green peas. Lord Peter turned these things over with an inquisitive finger, gazed into the smooth surface of a bowl of dripping as though it were a divining-crystal, ran his hands several times right through a bowl of flour—then drew his pipe from his pocket and filled it slowly.

The doctor returned, and put his hand on Brotherton's shoulder.

"Come," he said gently, "we have laid her in the other bedroom. She looks very peaceful. You must remember that, except for that moment of terror when she saw the knife, she suffered nothing. It is terrible for you, but you must try not to give way. The police—"

"The police can't bring her back to life," said the man savagely. "She's dead. Leave me alone, curse you! Leave me alone, I say!"

He stood up, with a violent gesture.

"You must not sit here," said Hartman firmly. "I will give you something to take, and you must try to keep calm. Then we will leave you, but if you don't control yourself—"

After some further persuasion, Brotherton allowed himself to be led away.

"Bunter," said Lord Peter, as the kitchen door closed behind them, "do you know why I am doubtful about the success of those rat experiments?"

"Meaning Dr. Hartman's, my lord?"

"Yes. Dr. Hartman has a theory. In any investigation, my Bunter, it is most damnably dangerous to have a theory."

"I have heard you say so, my lord."

"Confound you—you know it as well as I do! What is wrong with the doctor's theories, Bunter?"

"You wish me to reply, my lord, that he only sees the facts which fit in with the theory."

"Thought-reader!" exclaimed Lord Peter bitterly.

"And that he supplied them to the police, my lord."

"Hush!" said Peter, as the doctor returned.

"I have got him to lie down," said Dr. Hartman, "and I think the best thing we can do is to leave him to himself."

"D'you know," said Wimsey, "I don't cotton to that idea, somehow."

"Why? Do you think he's likely to destroy himself?"

"That's as good a reason to give as any other, I suppose," said Wimsey, "when you haven't got any reason which can be put into words. But my advice is, don't leave him for a moment."

"But why? Frequently, with a deep grief like this, the presence of other people is merely an irritant. He begged me to leave him."

"Then for God's sake go back to him," said Peter.

"Really, Lord Peter," said the doctor, "I think I ought to know what is best for my patient."

"Doctor," said Wimsey, "this is not a question of your patient. A crime has been committed."

"But there is no mystery."

"There are twenty mysteries. For one thing, when was the window-cleaner here last?"

"The window-cleaner?"

"Who shall fathom the ebony-black enigma of the window-cleaner?" pursued Peter lightly, putting a match to his pipe. "You are quietly in your bath, in a state of more or less innocent nature, when an intrusive head appears at the window, like the ghost of Hamilton Tighe, and a gruff voice, suspended between earth and heaven, says, 'Good morning, sir.' Where do window-cleaners go between visits? Do they hibernate, like busy bees? Do they——"

"Really, Lord Peter," said the doctor, "don't you think you're going a bit beyond the limit?"

"Sorry you feel like that," said Peter, "but I really want to know about the window-cleaner. Look how clear these panes are."

"He came yesterday, if you want to know," said Dr. Hartman, rather stiffly.

"You are sure?"

"He did mine at the same time."

"I thought as much," said Lord Peter. "In that case, it is absolutely imperative that Brotherton should not be left alone·for a moment. Bunter! Confound it all, where's that fellow got to?"

The door into the bedroom opened.

"My lord?" Mr. Bunter unobtrusively appeared, as he had unobtrusively stolen out to keep an unobtrusive eye upon the patient.

"Good," said Wimsey. "Stay where you are." His lackadaisical manner had gone, and he looked at the doctor as four years previously he might have looked at a refractory subaltern.

"Dr. Hartman," he said, "something is wrong. Cast your mind back. We were talking about symptoms. Then came the scream. Then came the sound of feet running. *Which direction did they run in?*"

"I'm sure I don't know."

"Don't you? Symptomatic though, doctor. They have been troubling me all the time, subconsciously. Now I know why. They ran *from the kitchen.*"

131

"Well?"

"Well! And now the window-cleaner——"

"What about him?"

"Could you swear that it wasn't the window-cleaner who made those marks on the sill?"

"And the man Brotherton saw——"

"Have we examined your laboratory roof for his footsteps?"

"But the weapon? Wimsey, this is madness! Someone took the weapon."

"I know. But did you think the edge of the wound was clean enough to have been made by a smooth stiletto? It looked ragged to me."

"Wimsey, what are you driving at?"

"There's a clue here in the flat—and I'm damned if I can remember it. I've seen it—I know I've seen it. It'll come to me presently. Meanwhile, don't let Brotherton——"

"What?"

"Do whatever it is he's going to do."

"But what is it?"

"If I could tell you that I could show you the clue. Why couldn't he make up his mind whether the bedroom door was open or shut? Very good story, but not quite thought out. Anyhow—I say, doctor, make some excuse, and strip him, and bring me his clothes. And send Bunter to me."

The doctor stared at him, puzzled. Then he made a gesture of acquiescence and passed into the bedroom. Lord Peter followed him, casting a ruminating glance at Brotherton as he went. Once in the sitting-room, Lord Peter sat down on a red velvet armchair, fixed his eyes on a gilt-framed oleograph, and became wrapped in contemplation.

Presently Bunter came in, with his arms full of clothing. Wimsey took it, and began to search it, methodically enough, but listlessly. Suddenly he dropped the garments, and turned to the manservant.

"No," he said, "this is a precaution, Bunter mine, but I'm on the wrong tack. It wasn't here I saw—whatever I did see. It was in the kitchen. Now, what was it?"

"I could not say, my lord, but I entertain a conviction that I was also, in a manner of speaking, conscious—not consciously conscious, my lord, if you understand me, but still conscious of an incongruity."

"Hurray!" said Wimsey suddenly. "Cheer-oh! for the subconscious what's-his-name! Now let's remember the kitchen. I cleared out of it because I was gettin' obfuscated. Now then. Begin at the door. Fryin'-pans and sauce-pans on the wall Gas-stove—oven goin'—chicken inside. Rack of wooden spoons on the wall gas-lighter, pan-lifter. Stop me when I'm gettin' hot. Mantelpiece. Spice-boxes and stuff. Anything wrong with them? No. Dresser. Plates. Knives and forks—all clean; flour dredger—milk-jug—sieve on the wall—nutmeg-grater. Three-tier steamer. Looked inside—no grisly secrets in the steamer."

"Did you look in all the dresser drawers, my lord?"

"No. That could be done. But the point is, I *did* notice somethin'. What did I notice? That's the point. Never mind. On with the dance—let joy be unconfined! Knife-board. Knife-powder. Kitchen table. Did you speak?"

"No," said Bunter, who had moved from his attitude of wooden deference.

"Table stirs a chord. Very good. On table. Choppin'-board. Remains of ham and herb stuffin'. Packet of suet. Another sieve. Several plates. Butter in a glass dish. Bowl of drippin'—"

"Ah!"

"Drippin'—! Yes, there was—"

"Something unsatisfactory, my lord—"

"About the drippin'! Oh, my head! What's that they say in *Dear Brutus*, Bunter? 'Hold on to the workbox.' That's right. Hold on to the drippin'. Beastly slimy stuff to hold on to— Wait!"

There was a pause.

"When I was a kid," said Wimsey, "I used to love to go down into the kitchen and talk to old cookie. Good old soul she was, too. I can see her now, gettin' chicken ready, with me danglin' my legs on the table. *She* used to pluck an' draw 'em herself. I revelled in it. Little beasts boys are, ain't they, Bunter? Pluck it, draw it, wash it, stuff it, tuck its little tail through its little what-you-may-call-it, truss it, grease the dish—Bunter?"

"My lord!"

"Hold on to the dripping!"

"The bowl, my lord—"

"The bowl—visualize it—what was wrong?"

"It was full, my lord!"

"Got it—got it— *got* it! The bowl was full—smooth surface. Golly! I knew here was something queer about it. Now why shouldn't it be full? Hold on to he—"

"The bird was in the oven."

"Without dripping!"

"Very careless cookery, my lord."

"The bird—in the oven—no dripping. Bunter! Suppose it was never put in till ter she was dead? Thrust in hurriedly by someone who had something to hide— orrible!"

"But with what object, my lord?"

"Yes, why? That's the point. One more mental association with the bird. It's just coming. Wait a moment. Pluck, draw, wash, stuff, tuck up, truss— By God!"

"My lord?"

"Come on, Bunter. Thank Heaven we turned off the gas!"

He dashed through the bedroom, disregarding the doctor and the patient, who sat up with a smothered shriek. He flung open the oven door and snatched out the baking-tin. The skin of the bird had just begun to discolour. With a little gasp of triumph, Wimsey caught the iron ring that protruded from the wing, and jerked out —*the six-inch spiral skewer*.

The doctor was struggling with the excited Brotherton in the doorway. Wimsey caught the man as he broke away, and shook him into the corner with a jiu-jitsu twist.

"Here is the weapon," he said.

"Prove it, blast you!" said Brotherton savagely.

"I will," said Wimsey. "Bunter, call in the policeman at the door. Doctor, we shall need your microscope."

In the laboratory the doctor bent over the microscope. A thin layer of blood from the skewer had been spread upon the slide.

"Well?" said Wimsey impatiently.

"It's all right," said Hartman. "The roasting didn't get anywhere near the middle. My God, Wimsey, yes, you're right—round corpuscles, diameter $1/3621$—mammalian blood—probably human—"

"Her blood," said Wimsey.

"It was very clever, Bunter," said Lord Peter, as the taxi trundled along on the way to his flat in Piccadilly. "If that fowl had gone on roasting a bit longer the blood-corpuscles might easily have been destroyed beyond all hope of recognition. It all goes to show that the unpremeditated crime is usually the safest."

"And what does your lordship take the man's motive to have been?"

"In my youth," said Wimsey meditatively, "they used to make me read the Bible Trouble was, the only books I ever took to naturally were the ones they weren' over and above keen on. But I got to know the Song of Songs pretty well by heart Look it up, Bunter; at your age it won't hurt you; it talks sense about jealousy."

"I have perused the work in question, your lordship," replied Mr. Bunter, with sallow blush. "It says, if I remember rightly: '*Jealousy is cruel as the grave.*'"

Frances Lockridge

(1896–1963)

Richard Lockridge

(1898–1982)

The husband-and-wife team of detecting duos is a particularly popular one, having reached its peak in the 1940s and 1950s. The prototype couple, Dashiell Hammett's Nick and Nora Charles, appeared in just one novel, *The Thin Man* (1934), and yet it so captured the public's imagination that it inspired a series of six Thin Man films starring William Powell and Myrna Loy (1936–1947). In 1940, another major couple arrived on the mystery scene: Frances and Richard Lockridge's Pam and Jerry North *(The Norths Meet Murder)*, who were soon to rival the Charleses in popularity. Ironically, the pair first saw publication in a noncriminous book of amusing domestic sketches by Richard Lockridge, *Mr. and Mrs. North* (1936). Jerry, a publisher, and Pam, his intuitive and intrepid wife, lived and did the bulk of their crime-solving in New York City; more than a score of their adventures appeared between 1940 and 1963. The 1952–1953 television series *Mr. and Mrs. North* starring Richard Denning and Barbara Britton, earned the couple an even wider audience.

The Norths did not detect alone; they were often aided and abetted by such other characters as Bill Weigand and Sergeant Mullins of the New York Police Department. (In 1957 Weigand starred in a case of his own, *The Tangled Cord.*) It is characteristic of the Lockridges' work that individuals from one series appear in another, thus creating a highly realistic world of interlocking relationships. While their strength did not lie in plotting (Pam's intuitions are often far-fetched, and nearly every novel predictably ends with her being terrorized by the criminal and then saved by her husband), the Lockridges excelled at witty repartee, evocative description, and strong characterization.

The Lockridges together, and Richard Lockridge alone after his wife's death in 1963, were extremely prolific writers who produced four series. While the Norths are their most enduring creations, their novels about Captain/Inspector Merton Heimrich of the New York State Police are particularly good in terms of plotting and characterization. Heimrich first appeared in *Think of Death* (1947) as a single man, but as the series continued he matured and eventually married. His territory, Putnam County and the village of The Corners, are as much of a character in the sixteen-book series as Heimrich himself.

Other series characters by the Lockridges are Nathan Shapiro, an NYPD officer who works for Bill Weigand (*Murder Can't Wait,* 1964; *The Old Die Young,* 1980) and assistant New York City District Attorney Bernie Simmons (*Squire of Death,* 1965; *Death on the Hour,* 1974). In addition, Richard Lockridge wrote nonseries suspense novels, such as *A Matter of Taste* (1949) and *Troubled Journey* (1970).

In "Pattern for Murder," the only Mr. and Mrs. North criminous short story, Pam attends a reunion of old schoolmates and is confronted by much more than mere memories. It has all the qualities of the duo's longer and more involved investigations.

PATTERN FOR MURDER

PAM AND JERRY NORTH
NEW YORK
1955

Fern Hartley came to New York to die, although that was far from her intention. She came from Centertown, in the Middle West, and died during a dinner party—given in her honor, at a reunion of schoolmates. She died at the bottom of a steep flight of stairs in a house on West Twelfth Street. She was a little woman and she wore a fluffy white dress. She stared at unexpected death through strangely bright blue eyes. . . .

There had been nothing to foreshadow so tragic an ending to the party—nothing, at any rate, on which Pamela North, who was one of the schoolmates, could precisely put a finger. It was true that Pam, as the party progressed, had increasingly felt tenseness in herself; it was also true that, toward the end, Fern Hartley had seemed to behave somewhat oddly. But the tenseness, Pam told herself, was entirely her own fault, and as for Fern's behavior—well, Fern *was* a little odd. Nice, of course, but—trying. Pam had been tried.

She had sat for what seemed like hours with a responsive smile stiffening her lips and with no comparable response stirring in her mind. It was from that, surely, that the tenseness—the uneasiness—arose. Not from anything on which a finger could be put. It's my own fault, Pam North thought. This is a reunion, and I don't reunite. Not with Fern, anyway.

It had been Fern on whom Pam had responsively smiled. Memories of old days, of schooldays, had fluttered from Fern's mind like pressed flowers from the yellowed pages of a treasured book. They had showered about Pam North, who had been Fern's classmate at Southwest High School in Centertown. They had showered also about Hortense Notson and about Phyllis Pitt. Classmates, too, they had been those years ago—they and, for example, a girl with red hair.

"—*red* hair," Fern Hartley had said, leaning forward, eyes bright with memory. "Across the aisle from you in Miss Burton's English class. Of *course* you remember, Pam. She went with the boy who stuttered."

I *am* Pamela North, who used to be Pamela Britton, Pam told herself, behind a fixed smile. I'm not an imposter; I did go to Southwest High. If only I could prove it by remembering something—anything. Any *little* thing.

"The teacher with green hair?" Pam North said, by way of experiement. "Streaks of, anyway? Because the dye—"

Consternation clouded Fern's bright eyes. "*Pam!*" she said. "That was another one entirely. Miss Burton was the one who—"

It had been like that from the start of the party—the party of three couples and Miss Fern Hartley, still of Centertown. They were gathered in the long living room of the Stanley Pitts' house—the gracious room which ran the depth of the small, perfect house—an old New York house, retaining the charm (if also something of the inconvenience) of the previous century.

As the party started that warm September evening, the charm was uppermost. From open casement windows at the end of the room there was a gentle breeze. In it, from the start, Fern's memories had fluttered.

And none of the memories had been Pam North's memories. Fern has total recall; I have total amnesia, Pam thought, while keeping the receptive smile in place, since one cannot let an old schoolmate down. Did the others try as hard? Pam wondered. Find themselves as inadequate to recapture the dear, dead days?

Both Hortense Notson and Phyllis Pitt had given every evidence of trying, Pam thought, letting her mind wander. Fern was now reliving a perfectly wonderful picnic, of their junior year. Pam was not.

Pam did not let the smile waver; from time to time she nodded her bright head and made appreciative sounds. Nobody had let Fern down; all had taken turns in listening—even the men. Jerry North was slacking now, but he had been valiant.

His valor had been special, since he had never even been in Centertown. And Stanley Pitt had done his bit, too; of course, he was the host. Of course, Fern was the Pitts' house guest; what a lovely house to be a guest in, Pam thought, permitting her eyes briefly to accompany her mind in its wandering.

Stanley—what a distinguished-looking man he is, Pam thought—was with Jerry, near the portable bar. She watched Jerry raise his glass as he listened. Her own glass was empty, and nobody was doing anything about it. An empty glass to go with an empty mind, Pam thought, and watched Fern sip ginger ale. Fern never drank anything stronger. Not that she had anything against drinking. Of course not. But even one drink made her feel all funny.

"Well," Pam had said, when Fern had brought the subject up, earlier on. "Well, that's more or less the idea, I suppose. This side of hilarious, of course."

"You know," Fern said then, "you always did talk funny. Remember when we graduated and you—"

Pam didn't remember. Without looking away from Fern, or letting the smile diminish, Pam nevertheless continued to look around the room. How lovely Phyllis is, Pam thought—really is. Blonde Phyllis Pitt was talking to Clark Notson, blond also, and sturdy, and looking younger than he almost certainly was.

Clark had married Hortense in Centertown. He was older—Pam remembered that he had been in college when they were in high school. He had married her when she was a skinny, dark girl, who had had to be prouder than anyone else because her parents lived over a store and not, properly, in a house. And look at her now, Pam thought, doing so. Dark still—and slim and quickly confident, and most beautifully arrayed.

Well, Pam thought, we've all come a long way. (She nodded, very brightly, to another name from the past—a name signifying nothing.) Stanley Pitt and Jerry—neglecting his own wife, Jerry North was—had found something of fabulous interest to discuss, judging by their behavior. Stanley was making points, while Jerry listened and nodded. Stanley was making points one at a time, with the aid of the thumb and the fingers of his right hand. He touched thumbtip to successive fingertips, as if to crimp each point in place. And Jerry—how selfish could a man get—ran a hand through this hair, as he did when he was interested.

"Oh," Pam said. "Of course I remember *him*, Fern."

A little lying is a gracious thing.

What a witness Fern would make, Pam thought. Everything that had happened —beginning, apparently, at the age of two—was brightly clear in her mind, not muddy as in the minds of so many. The kind of witness Bill Weigand, member in good standing of the New York City Police Department, always hoped to find and almost never did—never had, that she could remember, in all the many investigations she and Jerry had shared since they first met Bill years ago.

Fern would be a witness who really remembered. If Fern, Pam thought, knew something about a murder, or where a body was buried, or any of the other important things which so often come up, she would remember it precisely and remember it whole. A good deal of sifting would have to be done, but Bill was good at that.

Idly, her mind still wandering, Pam hoped that Fern did not, in fact, know anything of buried bodies. It could, obviously, be dangerous to have so total a recall and to put no curb on it. She remembered, and this from asssociation with Bill, how often somebody did make that one revealing remark too many. Pam sternly put a curb on her own mind and imagination. What could Fern—pleasant, bubbling Fern, who had not adventured out of Centertown, excepting for occasional trips like these—know of dangerous things?

Pam North, whose lips ached, in whose mind Fern's words rattled, looked hard at Jerry, down the room, at the bar. Get me out of this, Pam willed across the space between them. Get me out of this! It had been known to work or had sometimes seemed to work. It did not now. Jerry concentrated on what Stanley Pitt was saying. Jerry ran a hand through his hair.

"Oh, dear," Pam said, breaking into the flow of Fern's words, as gently as she could. "Jerry wants me for something. You know how husbands are."

She stopped abruptly, remembering that Fern didn't, never having had one. She got up—and was saved by Phyllis, who moved in. What a hostess, Pam thought, and moved toward Jerry and the bar. The idea of saying that to poor Fern, Pam thought. This is certainly one of my hopeless evenings. She went toward Jerry.

"I don't" she said when she reached him, "remember anything about anything. Except one teacher with green hair, and that was the wrong woman."

Jerry said it seemed very likely.

"There's something a little ghoulish about all this digging up of the past," Pam said. "Suppose some of it's still alive?" she added.

"Huh?" Jerry said.

He was told not to bother. And that Pam could do with a drink. Jerry poured, for them both, from a pitcher in which ice tinkled.

"Some time," Pam said, "She's going to remember that one thing too many. That's what I mean. You see?"

"No," Jerry said, simply.

"Not everybody," Pam said, a little darkly, "wants everything remembered about everything. Because—"

Stanley Pitt, who had turned away, turned quickly back. He informed Pam that she had something there.

"I heard her telling Hortense—" Stanley Pitt said, and stopped abruptly, since Hortense, slim and graceful (and *so* beautifully arrayed) was coming toward them.

"How Fern doesn't change," Hortense said. "Pam, do you remember the boy next door?"

"I don't seem to remember anything," Pam said. "Not anything at all."

"You don't remember," Hortense said. "I don't remember. Phyllis doesn't. And with it all, she's so—sweet." She paused. "Or is she?" she said. "Some of the things she brings up—always doing ohs, the boy next door was. How does one do an oh?"

"Oh," Jerry said, politely demonstrating, and then, "Was he the one with green hair?" The others looked blank at that, and Pam said it was just one of the things she'd got mixed up, and now Jerry was mixing it worse. And Pam said, did Hortense ever feel she hadn't really gone to Southwest High School at all and was merely pretending she had? Was an imposter?

"Far as I can tell," Hortense said, "I never lived in Centertown. Just in a small, one-room vacuum. Woman without a past." She paused. "Except," she said, in another tone, "Fern remembers me in great detail."

Stanley Pitt had been looking over their heads—looking at his wife, now the one listening to Fern. In a moment of silence, Fern's voice fluted. "Really, a dreadful thing to happen," Fern said. There was no context.

"Perhaps," Stanley said, turning back to them, "it's better to have no past than to live in one. Better all around. And safer."

He seemed about to continue, but then Clark Notson joined them. Clark did not, Pam thought, look like a man who was having a particularly good time. "Supposed to get Miss Hartley her ginger ale," he said. He spoke rather hurriedly.

Jerry, who was nearest the bar, said, "Here," and reached for the innocent bottle —a bottle, Pam thought, which looked a little smug and virtuous among the other bottles. Jerry used a silver opener, snapped off the bottle cap. The cap bouced off, tinkled against a bottle.

"Don't know your own strength," Clark said, and took the bottle and, with it, a glass into which Jerry dropped ice. "Never drinks anything stronger, the lady doesn't," Clark said, and bore away the bottle.

"And doesn't need to," Hortense Notson said, and drifted away. She could drift immaculately.

"She buys dresses," Pam said. "Wouldn't you know?"

"As distinct—?" Jerry said, and was told he knew perfectly well what Pam meant.

"Buys them for, not from," Pam said.

To this, Jerry simply said, "Oh."

It was then a little after eight, and there was a restless circulation in the long room. Pam was with Phyllis Pitt. Phyllis assured her that food would arrive soon. And hadn't old times come flooding back?

"Mm," Pam said. Pam was then with Clark Notson and, with him, talked unexpectedly of tooth paste. One never knows what will come up at a party. It appeared that Clark's firm made tooth paste. Stanley Pitt joined them. He said Clark had quite an operation there. Pam left them and drifted, dutifully, back to Fern, who sipped ginger ale. Fern's eyes were very bright. They seemed almost to glitter. (But that's absurd, Pam thought. People's don't, only cats.)

"It's so exciting," Fern said, and looked around the room, presumably at "it." "To meet you all again, and your nice husbands and——" she paused. "Only," she said, "I keep wondering . . ."

Pam waited. She said, "What, Fern?"

"Oh," Fern said, "Nothing dear. Nothing really. Do you remember——"

Pam did not. She listened for a time, and was relieved by Hortense, and drifted on again. For a minute or two, then, Pam North was alone and stood looking up and down the softly lighted room. Beyond the windows at the far end, lights glowed up from the garden below. The room was filled, but not harshly, with conversation —there seemed, somehow, to be more than the seven of them in it. Probably, Pam thought, memories crowded it—the red-haired girl, the stuttering boy.

Fern laughed. Her laughter was rather high in pitch. It had a little "hee" at the end. That little "hee," Pam thought idly, would identify Fern—be something to remember her by. As Jerry's habit of running his hand through his hair would identify him if, about all else, she suddenly lost her memory. (As I've evidently begun to do, Pam North thought.) Little tricks. And Fern puts her right index finger gently to the tip of her nose, presumably when she's thinking. Why, Pam thought, she did that as a girl, and was surprised to remember.

Her host stood in front of her, wondering what he could get her. She had, Pam told him, everything.

"Including your memories?" Stanley Pitt asked her. Pam noticed a small scar on his chin. But it wasn't, of course, the same thing as—as running a hand through your hair. But everybody has something, which is one way of telling them apart.

"I seem," Pam said, "a little short of memories."

"By comparison with Miss Hartley," Stanley said, "who isn't? A pipe line to the past. Can't I get you a drink?"

He could not. Pam had had enough. So, she thought, had all of them. Not that anybody was in the least tight. But still . . .

Over the other voices, that of Fern Hartley was raised. There was excitement in it. So it isn't alcohol, Pam thought, since Fern hadn't had any. It's just getting keyed up at the party. She looked toward Fern, who was talking, very rapidly, to Jerry. No doubt, Pam thought, about what I was like in high school. Not that there's any thing he shouldn't know. But still . . .

Fern was now very animated. If, Pam thought, I asked whether anyone here was one cocktail up I'd—why, I'd say Fern. Fern, of all people. Or else, Pam thought, she has some exciting surprise.

It was not eight thirty. A maid appeared at the door, waited to be noticed, and nodded to Phyllis Pitt, who said, at once, "Dinner, everybody." The dining room was downstairs, on a level with the garden. "These old stairs," Phyllis said. "Everybody be careful."

The stairs were, indeed, very steep, and the treads very narrow. But there were handrails and a carpet. The stairway ended in the dining room, where candles glowed softly on the table, among flowers.

"If you'll sit—" Phyllis said, starting with Pam North. "And you and—" They moved to the places indicated. "And Fern—" Phyllis said, and stopped. "Why," she said, "where is—"

She did not finish, because Fern Hartley stood at the top of the steep staircase. She was a slight figure in a white dress. She seemed to be staring fixedly down at them, her eyes strangely bright. Her face was flushed and she made odd, uncertain movements with her little hands.

"I'm—" Fern said, and spoke harshly, loudly, and so that the word was almost a shapeless sound. "I'm—

And then Fern Hartley, taking both hands from the rails, pitched headfirst down the staircase. In a great moment of silence, her body made a strange, soft thudding on the stairs. She did not cry out.

At the bottom of the red-carpeted stairs she lay quite still. Her head was at a hideous angle to her body. That was how she died.

Fern Hartley died of a broken neck. There was no doubt. Six people had seen her fall. Now she lay at the bottom of the stairs and no one would ever forget her soft quick falling down that steep flight. An ambulance surgeon confirmed the cause of her death and another doctor from up the street—called when it seemed the ambulance would never get there—confirmed it, too.

But after he had knelt for some time by the body the second doctor beckoned the ambulance surgeon and they went out into the hallway. Then the ambulance surgeon beckoned one of the policemen who had arrived with the ambulance, and the policeman went into the hall with them. After a few minutes, the policeman returned and asked, politely enough, that they all wait upstairs. There were, he said meaninglessly, a few formalities.

They waited upstairs, in the living room. They waited for more than two hours, puzzled and in growing uneasiness. Then a thinnish man of medium height, about whom there was nothing special in appearance, came into the room and looked around at them.

"Why, *Bill!*" Pam North said.

The thinnish man looked at her, and then at Jerry North, and said, "Oh." Then he said there were one or two points.

And then Pam said, "Oh," on a note strangely flat.

How one introduces a police officer, who happens to be an old and close friend, to other friends who happen to be murder suspects—else why was Bill Weigand there?—had long been a moot question with Pam and Jerry North. Pam said, "This is Bill Weigand, everybody. Captain Weigand. He's—he's a policeman. So there must be—" And stopped.

"All right, Pam," Bill Weigand said. Then, "you all saw her fall. Tell me about it." He looked around at them, back at Pam North. It was she who told him.

Her eyes had been "staring"? Her face flushed? Her movements uncertain? Her voice hoarse? "Yes," Pam said, confirming each statement. Bill Weigand looked from one to another of the six in the room. He received nods of confirmation. One of the men—tall, dark-haired but with gray coming, a little older than the others—seemed about to speak. Bill waited. The man shook his head. Bill got them identified then. The tall man was Stanley Pitt. This was his house.

"But," Bill said, "she hadn't been drinking. The medical examiner is quite certain of that." He seemed to wait for comment.

"She said she never did," Pam told him.

"So—" Bill said.

Then Hortense Notson spoke, in a tense voice. "You act," she said, "as if you think one of us pushed her."

Weigand looked at her carefully. He said, "No. That didn't happen, Mrs. Notson. How could it have happened? You were all in the dining room, looking up at her. How could any of you have pushed her?"

"Then," Clark Notson said, and spoke quickly, with unexpected violence. "Then why all this? She . . . what? Had a heart attack?"

"Possibly," Bill said. "But the doctors—"

Again he was interrupted.

"I've heard of you," Notson said, and leaned forward in the chair. "Aren't you homicide?"

"Right," Bill said. He looked around again, slowly. "As Mr. Notson said, I'm homicide." And he waited

Phyllis Pitt—the pretty, the very pretty, light-haired woman—had been crying. More than the rest, in expression, in movements, she showed the shock of what had happened. "Those dreadful stairs," she said, as if to herself. "Those dreadful stairs."

Her husband got up and went to her and leaned over her. He touched her bright hair and said, very softly, "All right, Phyl. All right."

"Bill," Pam said. "Fern fell downsteairs and—and died. What more is there?"

"You all agree," Bill said, "that she was flushed and excited and uncertain—as if she had been drinking. But she hadn't been drinking. And . . . the pupils of her eyes were dilated. That was why she seemed to be staring. Because, you see, she couldn't see where she was going. So . . ." He paused. "She walked off into the air. I have to find out why. So what I want . . ."

It took him a long time to get what he wanted, which was all they could remember, one memory reinforcing another, of what had happened from the start of the dinner party until it ended with Fern Hartley, at the foot of the staircase, all her memories dead. Pam, listening, contributing what she could, could not see that a pattern formed—a pattern of murder.

Fern had seemed entirely normal—at least, until near the end. They agreed on that. She had always remembered much about the past and talked of it. Meeting old school friends, after long separation, she had seemed to remember everything—far more than any of the others.

"Most of it, to be honest, wasn't very interesting." That was Hortense Notson. Hortense Notson looked at Pam, at Phyllis Pitt.

"She was so sweet," Phyllis said, in a broken voice.

"So—so interested herself." Pam said, "A good deal of it was pretty long ago, Bill."

Fern had shared her memories chiefly with the other women. But she had talked of the past, also, with the men.

"It didn't mean much to me," Stanley Pitt said. "It seemed to be all about Centertown, and I've never been in Centertown. Phyllis and I met in New York." He paused. "What's the point of this?" he said.

"I don't know," Bill Weigand told him. "Not yet. Everything she rememberd seemed to be trivial? Nothing stands out? To any of you?"

"She remembered I had a black eye the first time she saw me," Clark Notson said. "Hortense and I—when we were going together—ran into her at a party. It was a long time ago. And I had a black eye, she said. I don't remember anything about it. I don't even remember the party, actually. Yes, I'd call it pretty trivial."

"My God," Stanley Pitt said. "*Is* there some point to this?"

"I don't know," Bill said again, and was patient. "Had you known Miss Hartley before, Mr. Pitt?"

"Met her for the first time yesterday," Stanley told him. "We had her to dinner and she stayed the night. Today I took her to lunch, because Phyl had things to do about the party. And——" He stopped. He shrugged and shook his head, seemingly at the futility of everything.

"I suppose," Jerry North said, "the point is——did she remember something that somebody——one of us——wanted forgotten?"

"Yes," Bill said. "It may be that."

Then it was in the open. And with it in the open, the six looked at one another; and there was a kind of wariness in the manner of their looking. Although what on earth I've got to be wary about I don't know, Pam thought. Or Jerry, she added in her mind. She couldn't have told Jerry anything about me. Well, not anything important. At least not very . . .

"I don't understand," Phyllis said, and spoke dully. "I just don't understand at all. Fern just——just fell down those awful stairs."

It became like a game of tennis, with too many players, played in the dark. "Try to remember," Bill had told them; and it seemed they tried. But all they remembered was apparently trivial.

"There was something about a boy next door," Phyllis Pitt remembered. "A good deal older than she was——than we all were. Next door to Fern. A boy named ——" She moved her hands helplessly. "I've forgotten. A name I'd never heard before. Something——she said something dreadful——happened to him. I suppose he died of something."

"No," Hortonse Notson said. "She told me about him. He didn't die. He went to jail. He was always saying 'oh.'" She considered. "I think," she said, "he was named Russell something." She paused again. "Never in my life, did I hear so much about people I'd never heard of. Gossip about the past."

Stanley Pitt stood up. His impatience was evident.

"Look," he said. "This is my house, Captain. These people are my guests. Is any of this badgering getting you anywhere? And . . . where is there to get? Maybe she had a heart attack. Maybe she ate something that——" He stopped, rather abruptly; rather as if he had stumbled over something.

Weigand waited, but Pitt did not continue. Then Bill said they had thought of that. The symptoms——they had all noticed the symptoms——including the dilation of the pupils, might have been due to acute food poisoning. But she had eaten almost nothing during the cocktail period. The maid who had passed canapés was sure of that. Certainly she had eaten nothing the rest had not. And she had drunk only ginger ale, from a freshly opened bottle.

"Which," Bill said, "apparently you opened, Jerry."

Jerry North ran his right hand through his hair. He looked at Bill blankly.

"Of course you did," Pam said. "So vigorously the bottle cap flew off. Don't you——"

"Oh," Jerry said. Everybody looked at him. "Is that supposed——"

But he was interrupted by Pitt, still leaning forward in his chair. "Wait," Pitt said, and put right thumb and index finger together, firmly, as if to hold a thought pinched between them. They waited.

"This place I took her to lunch," Stanley said. "It's a little place——little downstairs place, but wonderful food. I've eaten there off and on for years. But ... I don't suppose it's too damned sanitary. Not like your labs are, Clark. And the weather's been hot. And——" He seemed to remember something else and held this new memory between thumb and finger. "Miss Hartley ate most of a bowl of ripe olives. Said she never seemed to get enough of them. And ... isn't there something that can get into ripe olives? That can poison people?" He put the heel of one hand to his forehead. "God," he said. "Do you suppose it was that?"

"You mean food poisoning?" Weigand said. "Yes——years ago people got it from ripe olives. But not recently, that I've heard of. New methods and——"

"The olives are imported," Pitt said. "From Italy, I think. Yes. Dilated pupils——"

"Right," Bill said. "And the other symptoms match quite well. You may——"

But now he was interrupted by a uniformed policeman, who brought him a slip of paper. Bill Weigand looked at it and put it in his pocket and said, "Right," and the policeman went out again.

"Mr. Notson," Bill said, "you're the production manager of the Winslow Pharmaceutical Company, aren't you?"

Notson looked blank. He said, "Sure."

"Which makes all kinds of drug products?"

Notson continued to look blank. He nodded his head.

"And Mr. Pitt," Bill Weigand said. "You're——"

He's gone off on a tangent, Pam North thought, half listening. What difference can it make that Mr. Notson makes drugs——or that Mr. Pitt tells people how to run offices and plants better——is an "efficiency engineer"? Because just a few minutes ago, somebody said something really important. Because it was wrong. Because——Oh! Pam thought. It's on the tip of my mind. If people would only be quiet, so I could think. If Bill only wouldn't go off on these——

"All kinds of drugs," Bill was saying, from his tangent, in the distance. "Including preparations containing atropine?"

She heard Clark Notson say, "Yes. Sure."

"Because," Bill said, and now Pam heard him clearly—very clearly—"Miss Hartley had been given atropine. It might have been enough to have killed her, if she had not had quick and proper treatment. She'd had enough to bring on dizziness and double vision. So that, on the verge of losing consciousness, she fell downstairs and broke her neck. Well?"

He looked around.

"The ginger ale," Jerry said. "The ginger ale I opened. That ... opened so easily. Was that it?"

"Probably," Bill said. "The cap taken off carefully. Put back on carefully. After enough atropine sulphate had been put in. Enough to stop her remembering." Again he looked around at them; and Pam looked, too, and could see nothing—except shock—in any face. There seemed to be fear in none.

"The doctors suspected atropine from the start," Bill said, speaking slowly. "But the symptoms of atropine poisoning are very similar to those of food poisoning—or ptomaine. If she had lived to be treated, almost any physician would have diagnosed food poisoning—particularly after Mr. Pitt remembered the olives—and treated for that. Not for atropine. Since the treatments are differeent, she probably would not have lived." He paused. "Well," he said, "what did she remember? So that there was death for remembrance?"

Phyllis Pitt covered her eyes with both hands and shook her head slowly, dully. Hortense Notson looked at Weigand with narrowed eyes and her husband with—Pam thought—something like defiance. Stanley Pitt looked at the floor and seemed deep in thought, to be planning each through between thumb and finger, when Weigand turned from them and said, "Yes?" to a man in civilian clothes. He went to talk briefly with the man. He returned. He said the telephone was a useful thing; he said the Centertown police were efficient.

"The boy next door," Weigand said, "was named Russell Clarkson. He was some years—fifteen, about—older than Fern Hartley. Not a boy any more, when she was in high school, but still 'the boy next door.' He did go to jail, as you said, Mrs. Notson. He helped set up a robbery of the place he worked in. A payroll messenger was killed. Clarkson got twenty years to life. And—he escaped in two years, and was never caught. And—*he was a chemist*. Mr. Notson. As you are. Mr. *Clark* Notson."

Notson was on his feet. His face was very red and he no longer looked younger han he was. He said, "You're crazy! I can prove—" His voice rose until he was houting across the few feet between himself and Weigand.

And then it came to Pam—came with a kind of violent clarity. "Wait, Bill. *Wait!*" Pam shouted. "It wasn't 'ohs' at all. Not *saying* them. That's what was wrong."

They were listening. Bill was listening.

Then Pam pointed at Hortense. "You," she said, "the first time you said *doing* ohs. Not saying 'Oh.' You even asked how one *did* an oh. We thought it was the—the o-h kind of O. But—it was the *letter* O. And—*look at him now!* He's doing them now. *With his fingers.*"

And now she pointed at Stanley Pitt, who was forming the letter O with the thumb and index finger of his right hand; who now, violently, closed into fists his betraying hands. A shudder ran through his body. But he spoke quietly without looking up from the floor.

"She hadn't quite remembered," he said, as if talking of something which had happened a long time ago. "Not quite." And he put the thumb and index finger tip to tip again, to measure the smallness of a margin. "But—she would have. She remembered everything. I've changed a lot and she was a little girl, but . . ."

He looked at his hands. "I've always done that, I guess," he said. He spread his fingers and looked at his hands. "Once it came up," he said, "There would be fingerprints. So—I had to try." He looked up, then, at his wife. "You see, Phyl, that I had to try?"

Phyllis covered her face with her hands.

After a moment Stanley Pitt looked again at his hands, spreading them in front of him. Slowly he began to bring together the fingertips and thumbtips of both hands; and he studied the movements of his fingers intently, as if they were new to him. He sat so, his hands moving in patterns they had never been able to forget, until Weigand told him it was time to go.

Rex Stout

(1886–1975)

Rex Stout was a successful businessman and part-time writer—for the first twenty years of his career he sold serials and short fiction to such pulp magazines as *All-Story* and *Black Cat* and later such mainstream novels as *How Like a God* (1929) and *Forest Fire* (1933)—before turning his hand to detective fiction. It was here that he found his true metier and forged a lasting niche in literary history. His 1934 novel, *Fer-de-Lance*, introduced two of the most engaging characters ever to grace the printed page, the obese private investigator Nero Wolfe and his thin, handsome legman, Archie Goodwin. It has been said that Wolfe and Goodwin represented the two diverse facets of Stout's personality, which may or may not be a valid assessment. In any case the pair are what one critic has called "a unique hybrid of the classic [i.e., ratiocinative] and hardboiled schools of detective fiction."

Wolfe is remarkably erudite, a misogynist, and the possessor of a huge appetite for gourmet food and beer; his grand passion is the care and nurturing of rare orchids, ten thousand plants of which he keeps in the rooftop plant room of his Manhattan brownstone. He can be induced to leave these West Thirty-fifth Street premises, where he lives with Archie and his chef and majordomo, Fritz Brenner, only on infrequent occasions and then with a great deal of grumbling reluctance. Goodwin, twenty years younger and the owner of a roving eye (he is mystery fiction's premier skirt-chaser), does whatever physical activity is required to bring one of Wolfe's cases to a successful conclusion, though he uses intelligence and cunning far more often than brawn. He also takes delight in goading, prodding, and manipulating his employer, particularly when Wolfe's bank account becomes dangerously low and a new case is required for replenishment. The delightfully witty and often pungent dialogue between the two (they sometimes spat like feisty marriage partners) is the centerpiece of the series. Other characters recur, each a well-drawn but minor player: Inspector Cramer, Wolfe's police department foil; the fashionable sophisticate, Lily Rowan, who almost succeeds in making a husband of Archie on more than one occasion; and Saul Panzer, a freelance private detective.

The second novel to feature the distinguished duo, *The League of Frightened Men*, appeared in 1935; thirty more followed over the next forty years, as well as thirteen collections of long novelettes. Prominent among the novels are those in which Wolfe is forced by circumstances to leave West Thirty-fifth Street for short periods. In *Too Many Cooks* (1930), widely considered to be the team's finest case, he forces himself to board a train in order to attend a meeting of the great chefs of the world at a West Virginia spa—and finds murder along with his quest for a secret recipe for *saucisse minuit*. In *Some Buried Caesar* (1939), Wolfe's desire to exhibit his albino orchids at an upstate New York fair leads him and Archie on a highly eventful 250-mile car trip, the highlight of which is a hilarious scene in which the two are chased by a none-too-social bull. The story that follows also takes Wolfe away from home, this time to make an unprecedented speech at the Independence Day picnic of the United Restaurant Workers of America.

Stout's literary success was never matched by the numerous radio, film, and television adaptations of his dueling duo's exploits. No actors ever quite captured the essence of either character, perhaps because Wolfe and Archie are sui generis—made so starkly real by Stout's evocative portrayals that we would know both men instantly if we were ever to meet them. Anyone else, like the many imitators they spawned over the past sixty-plus years, is merely an impostor.

FOURTH OF JULY PICNIC

NERO WOLFE AND ARCHIE GOODWIN
LONG ISLAND, NEW YORK
C. 1958

I

Flora Korby swiveled her head, with no hat hiding any of her dark brown hair, to face me with her dark brown eyes. She spoke.

"I guess I should have brought my car and led the way."

"I'm doing fine," I assured her. "I could shut one eye too."

"Please don't," she begged. "I'm stupefied as it is. May I have your autograph— I mean when we stop?"

Since she was highly presentable I didn't mind her assuming that I was driving with one hand because my right arm wanted to stretch across her shoulders, though she was wrong. I had left the cradle long ago. But there was no point in explaining to her that Nero Wolfe, who was in the back seat, had a deep distrust of moving vehicles and hated to ride in one unless I drove it, and therefore I was glad to have an excuse to drive with one hand because that would make it more thrilling for him.

Anyway, she might have guessed it. The only outside interest that Wolfe permits to interfere with his personal routine of comfort, not to mention luxury, is Rusterman's restaurant. Its founder, Marko Vukcic, was Wolfe's oldest and closest friend; and when Vukcic died, leaving the restaurant to members of the staff and making Wolfe executor of his estate, he also left a letter asking Wolfe to see to it that the restaurant's standards and reputation were maintained; and Wolfe had done so, making unannounced visits there once or twice a week, and sometimes even oftener, without ever grumbling—well, hardly ever. But he sure did grumble when Felix, the maître d'hôtel, asked him to make a speech at the Independence Day picnic of the United Restaurant Workers of America. Hereafter I'll make it URWA.

He not only grumbled, he refused. But Felix kept after him, and Wolfe finally gave in when Felix came to the office one day with reinforcements: Paul Rago, the sauce chef at the Churchill; James Korby, the president of URWA; H. L. Griffin, a food and wine importer who supplied hard-to-get items not only for Rusterman's but also for Wolfe's own table; and Philip Holt, URWA's director of organization. They also were to be on the program at the picnic, and their main appeal was that they simply had to have the man who was responsible for keeping Rusterman's the best restaurant in New York after the death of Marko Vukcic. Since Wolfe is only as vain as three peacocks, and since he had loved Marko if he ever loved anyone, that got him. There had been another inducement: Philip Holt had agreed to lay off of Fritz, Wolfe's chef and housekeeper. For three years Fritz had been visiting the kitchen at Rusterman's off and on as a consultant, and Holt had been pestering him, insisting that he had to join URWA. You can guess how Wolfe liked that.

Since I do everything that has to be done in connection with Wolfe's business and his rare social activities, except that he thinks he does all the thinking, and we won't go into that now, it would be up to me to get him to the scene of the picnic, Culp's Meadows on Long Island, on the Fourth of July. Around the end of June James Korby phoned and introduced his daughter Flora. She told me that the directions to Culp's Meadows were very complicated, and I said that all directions on Long Island were very complicated, and she said she had better drive us out in her car.

I liked her voice, that is true, but also I have a lot of foresight, and it occurred to me immediately that it would be a new and exciting experience for my employer to watch me drive with one hand, so I told her that, while it must be Wolfe's car and I must drive, I would deeply appreciate it if she would come along and tell me the way. That was how it happened, and that was why, when we finally rolled through the gate at Culp's Meadows, after some thirty miles of Long Island parkways and another ten of grade intersections and trick turns, Wolfe's lips were pressed so tight he didn't have any. He had spoken only once, around the fourth or fifth mile, when I had swept around a slowpoke.

"Archie. You know quite well."

"Yes, sir." Of course I kept my eyes straight ahead. "But it's an impulse, having my arm like this, and I'm afraid to take it away because if I fight an impulse it makes me nervous, and driving when you're nervous is bad."

A glance in the mirror showed me his lips tightening, and they stayed tight.

Passing through the gate at Culp's Meadows, and winding around as directed by Flora Korby, I used both hands. It was a quarter to three, so we were on time, since the speeches were scheduled for three o'clock. Flora was sure a space would have been saved for us back of the tent, and after threading through a few acres of parked cars I found she was right, and rolled to a stop with the radiator only a couple of yards from the canvas. She hopped out and opened the rear door on her side, and I did likewise on mine. Wolfe's eyes went right to her, and then left to me. He was torn. He didn't want to favor a woman, even a young and pretty one, but he absolutely had to show me what he thought of one-hand driving. His eyes went right again, the whole seventh of a ton of him moved, and he climbed out on her side.

II

The tent, on a wooden platform raised three feet above the ground, not much bigger than Wolfe's office, was crowded with people, and I wormed through to the front entrance and on out, where the platform extended into the open air. There was plenty of air, with a breeze dancing in from the direction of the ocean, and plenty of sunshine. A fine day for the Fourth of July. The platform extension was crammed with chairs, most of them empty. I can't report on the condition of the meadow's grass because my view was obstructed by ten thousand restaurant workers and their guests, maybe more. A could of thousand of them were in a solid mass facing the platform, presumably those who wanted to be up front for the speeches, and the rest were sprayed around all over, clear across to a fringe of trees and a row of sheds.

Flora's voice came from behind my shoulder. "They're coming out, so if there's a chair you like, grab it. Except the six up front; they're for the speakers."

Naturally I started to tell her I wanted the one next to hers, but didn't get it out because people came jostling out of the tent onto the extension. Thinking I had better warn Wolfe that the chair he was about to occupy for an hour or so wa about half as wide as his fanny, to give him time to fight his impulses, I worked past to the edge of the entrance, and when the exodus had thinned out I entered the tent. Five men were standing grouped beside a cot which was touching the canvas of the far side, and a man was lying on the cot. To my left Nero Wolfe was bending over to peer at the contents of a metal box there on a table with its lid open. I stepped over for a look and saw a collection of bone-handled knives, eight of them, with blades varying in length from six inches up to twelve. They weren't shiny, but they looked sharp, worn narrow by a lot of use for a lot of years. I asked Wolfe whose throat he was going to cut.

"They are Dubois," he said. "Real old Dubois. The best. They belong to Mr. Korby. He brought them to use in a carving contest, and he won, as he should. I would gladly steal them." He turned. "Why don't they let that man alone?"

I turned too, and through a gap in the group saw that the man on the cot was Philip Holt, URWA's director of organization. "What's the matter with him?" I asked.

"Something he ate. They think snails. Probably the wrong kind of snails. A doctor gave him something to help his bowels handle them. Why don't they leave him alone with his bowels?"

"I'll go ask," I said, and moved.

As I approached the cot James Korby was speaking. "I say he should be taken to a hospital, in spite of what the doctor said. Look at his color!"

Korby, short, pudgy, and bald, looked more like a restaurant customer than a restaurant worker, which may have been one reason he was president of URWA.

"I agree," Dick Vetter said emphatically. I had never seen Dick Vetter in person, but I had seen him often enough on his TV show—in fact, a little too often. If I quit dialing his channel he wouldn't miss me, since twenty million Americans, mostly female, were convinced that he was the youngest and handsomest MC on the waves. Flora Korby had told me he would be there, and why. His father had been a bus boy in a Broadway restaurant for thirty years, and still was because he wouldn't quit.

Paul Rago did not agree, and said so. "It would be a pity," he declared. He made it "peety," his accent having tapered off enough not to make it "peetee." With his broad shoulders and six feet, his slick black hair going gray, and his moustache with pointed tips that was still all black, he looked more like an ambassador from below the border than a sauce chef. He was going on. "He is the most important man in the union—except, of course, the president—and he should make an appearance on the platform. Perhaps he can before we are through."

"I hope you will pardon me." That was H. L. Griffin, the food and wine importer. He was a skinny little runt, with a long narrow chin and something wrong with one eye, but he spoke with the authority of a man whose firm occupied a whole floor in one of the midtown hives. "I may have no right to an opinion, since I am not a member of your great organization, but you have done me the honor of inviting me to take part in your celebration of our country's independence, and I do know of Phil Holt's high standing and wide popularity among your members. I would merely say that I feel that Mr. Rago is right, that they will be disappointed not to see him on the platform. I hope I am not being presumptuous."

From outside the tent, from the loudspeakers at the corners of the platform, a booming vice had been calling to the picnickers scattered over the meadow to close in and prepare to listen. As the group by the cot went on arguing, a state trooper in uniform, who had been standing politely aside, came over the joined them and took a look at Philip Holt, but offered no advice. Wolfe also approached for a look. Myself, I would have said that the place for him was a good bed with an attractive nurse smoothing his brow. I saw him shiver all over at least three times. He decided it himself, finally, by muttering at them to let him alone and turning on his side to face the canvas. Flora Korby had come in, and she put a blanket over him, and I noticed that Dick Vetter made a point of helping her. The breeze was sweeping through and one of them said he shouldn't be in a draft, and Wolfe told me to lower the flap of the rear entrance, and I did so. The flap didn't want to stay down, so I tied the plastic tape fastening to hold it, in a single bowknot. Then they all marched out through the front entrance to the platform, including the state trooper, and I brought up the rear. As Korby passed the table he stopped to lower the lid on the box of knives, real old Dubois.

The speeches lasted an hour and eight minutes, and the ten thousand URWA members and guests took them standing like ladies and gentlemen. You are probably hoping I will report them word for word, but I didn't take them down and I didn't listen hard enough to engrave them on my memory. At that, the eagle didn't scream as much or as loud as I had expected. From my seat in the back row I could see most of the audience, and it was quite a sight.

The first speaker was a stranger, evidently the one who had been calling on them to gather around while we were in the tent, and after a few fitting remarks he introduced James Korby. While Korby was orating, Paul Rago left his seat, passed down the aisle in the center, and entered the tent. Since he had plugged for an appearance by Philip Holt I though his purpose might be to drag him out alive or dead, but it wasn't. In a minute he was back again, and just in time, for he had just sat down when Korby finished and Rago was introduced.

The faces out front had all been serious for Korby, but Rago's accent through the loudspeakers had most of them grinning by the time he warmed up. When

Korby left his chair and started down the aisle I suspected him of walking out on Rago because Rago had walked out on him, but maybe not, since his visit in the tent was even shorter than Rago's had been. He came back out and returned to his chair, and listened attentively to the accent.

Next came H. L. Griffin, the importer, and the chairman had to lower the mike for him. His voice took the loudspeakers better than any of the others, and in fact he was darned good. It was only fair, I thought, to have the runt of the bunch take the cake, and I was all for the cheers from the throng that kept him on his feet a full minute after he finished. He really woke them up, and they were still yelling when he turned and went down the aisle to the tent, and it took the chairman a while to calm them down. Then, just as he started to introduce Dick Vetter, the TV star suddenly bounced up and started down the aisle with a determined look on his face, and it was easy to guess why. He thought Griffin was going to take advantage of the enthusiasm he had aroused by hauling Philip Holt out to the platform, and he was going to stop him. But he didn't have to. He was still two steps short of the tent entrance when Griffin emerged alone. Vetter moved aside to let him pass and then disappeared into the tent. As Griffin proceeded to his chair in the front row there were some scattered cheers from the crowd, and the chairman had to quiet them again before he could go on. Then he introduced Dick Vetter, who came out of the tent and along to the mike, which had to be raised again, at just he right moment.

As Vetter started to speak, Nero Wolfe arose and headed for the tent, and I raised my brows. Surely, I thought, he's not going to involve himself in the Holt problem; and then, seeing the look on his face, I caught on. The edges of the wooden chair seat had been cutting into his fanny for nearly an hour and he was in a tantrum, and he wanted to cool off a little before he was called to the mike. I grinned at him sympathetically as he passed and then gave my ear to Vetter. His soapy voice (I say soapy) came through the loudspeakers in a flow of lather, and after a couple of minutes of it I was thinking that it was only fair for Griffin, the runt, to sound like a man, and for Vetter, the handsome young idol of millions, to sound like whipped cream, when my attention was called. Wolfe was at the tent entrance, crooking a finger at me. As I got up and approached he backed into the tent, and I followed. He crossed to the rear entrance, lifted the flap, maneuvered his bulk through the hole, and held the flap for me. When I had made it he descended the five steps to the ground, walked to the car, grabbed the handle of the rear door, and pulled. Nothing doing. He turned to me.

"Unlock it."

I stood. "Do you want something?"

"Unlock it and get in and get the thing started. We're going."

"We are like hell. You've got a speech to make."

He glared at me. He knows my tones of voice as well as I know his "Archie," he said, "I am not being eccentric. There is a sound and cogent reason and I'll explain on the way. Unlock this door."

I shook my head. "Not till I hear the reason. I admit it's your car." I took the keys from my pocket and offered them. "Here. I resign."

"Very well." He was grim. "That man on the cot is dead. I lifted the blanket to adjust it. One of those knives is in his back, clear to the handle. He is dead. If we are still here when the discovery is made you know what will happen. We will be here all day, all night, a week, indefinitely. That is intolerable. We can answer questions at home as well as here. Confound it, unlock the door!"

"How dead is he?"

"I have told you he is dead."

"Okay. You ought to know better. You do know better. We're stuck. They wouldn't ask us questions at home, they'd haul us back out here. They'd be waiting for us on the stoop and you wouldn't even get inside the house." I returned the keys to my pocket. "Running out when you're next on the program, that would be nice. The only question is do we report it now or do you make your speech and let someone else find it, and you can answer that."

He had stopped glaring. He took in a long, deep breath, and when it was out again he said, "I'll make my speech."

"Fine. It'd be a shame to waste it. A question. Just now when you lifted the flap to come out I didn't see you untie the tape fastening. Was it already untied?"

"Yes."

"The makes it nice." I turned and went to the steps, mounted, raised the flap for him, and followed him into the tent. He crossed to the front and on out, and I stepped to the cot. Philip Holt lay facing the wall, with the blanket up to his neck, and I pulled it down far enough to see the handle of the knife, an inch to the right of the point of the shoulder blade. The knife blade was all buried. I lowered the blanket some more to get at a hand, pinched a fingertip hard for ten seconds, released it, and saw it stay white. I picked some fluff from the blanket and dangled it against his nostrils for half a minute. No movement. I put the blanket back as I had found it, went to the metal box on the table and lifted the lid, and saw that the shortest knife, the one with the six-inch blade, wasn't there.

As I went to the rear entrance and raised the flap, Dick Vetter's lather or whipped cream, whichever you prefer, came to an end through the loudspeakers, and as I descended the five steps the meadowful of picnickers was cheering.

Our sedan was the third car on the right from the foot of the steps. The second car to the left of the steps was a 1955 Plymouth, and I was pleased to see that it still had an occupant, having previously noticed her—a woman with careless gray hair topping a wide face and a square chin, in the front seat but not behind the wheel.

I circled around to her side and spoke through the open window. "I beg your pardon. May I introduce myself?"

"You don't have to, young man. Your name's Archie Goodwin, and you work for Nero Wolfe, the detective." She had tired gray eyes. "You were just out here with him."

"Right. I hope you won't mind if I ask you something. How long have you been sitting here?"

"Long enough. But it's all right, I can hear the speeches. Nero Wolfe is just starting to speak now."

"Have you been here since the speeches started?"

"Yes, I have. I ate too much of the picnic stuff and I didn't feel like standing up in that crowd, so I came to sit in the car."

"Then you've been here all the time since the speeches began?"

"That's what I said. Why do you want to know?"

"I'm just checking on something. If you don't mind. Has anyone gone into the tent or come out of it while you've been here?"

Her tired eyes woke up a little. "Ha," she said, "so something's missing. I'm not surprised. What's missing?"

"Nothing, as far as I know. I'm just checking a certain fact. Of course you saw Mr. Wolfe and me come out and go back in. Anyone else, either going or coming?"

"You're not fooling me, young man. Something's missing, and you're a detective."

I grinned at her. "All right, have it your way. But I do want to know, if you don't object."

"I don't object. As I told you, I've been right here ever since the speeches started, I got here before that. And nobody has gone into the tent, nobody but you and Nero Wolfe, and I haven't either. I've been right here. If you want to know about me, my name is Anna Banau, Mrs. Alexander Banau, and my husband is a captain at Zoller's—"

A scream came from inside the tent, an all-out scream from a good pair of lungs. I moved, to the steps, up, and past the flap into the tent. Flora Korby was standing near the cot with her back to it, her hand covering her mouth. I was disappointed in her. Granting that a woman has a right to scream when she finds a corpse, she might have kept it down until Wolfe had finished his speech.

III

It was a little after four o'clock when Flora Korby screamed. It was 4:34 when a glance outside through a crack past the flap of the tent's rear entrance, the third such glance I had managed to make, showed me that the Plymouth containing Mrs. Alexander Banau was gone. It was 4:39 when the medical examiner arrived with his bag and found that Philip Holt was still dead. It was 4:48 when the scientists came, with cameras and fingerprint kits and other items of equipment, and Wolfe and I and the others were herded out to the extension, under guard. It was 5:16 when I counted a total of seventeen cops, state and county, in uniform and out, on the job. It was 5:30 when Wolfe muttered at me bitterly that it would certainly be all night. It was 5:52 when a chief of detectives named Baxter got so personal with me that I decided, finally and definitely, not to play. It was 6:21 when we all left Culp's Meadows for an official destination. There were four in our car: one in uniform with Wolfe in the back seat, and one in his own clothes with me in front. Again I had someone beside me to tell me the way, but I didn't put my arm across his shoulders.

There had been some conversing with us separately, but most of it had been a panel discussion, open air, out on the platform extension, so I knew pretty well how things stood. Nobody was accusing anybody. Three of them—Korby, Rago, and Griffin—gave approximately the same reason for their visits to the tent during the speechmaking: that they were concerned about Philip Holt and wanted to see if he was all right. The fourth, Dick Vetter, gave the reason I had guessed, that he thought Griffin might bring Holt out to the platform, and he intended to stop him. Vetter, by the way, was the only one who raised a fuss about being detained. He said that it hadn't been easy to get away from his duties that afternoon, and he had a studio rehearsal scheduled for six o'clock, and he absolutely had to be there. At 6:21, when we all left for the official destination, he was fit to be tied.

None of them claimed to know for sure that Holt had been alive at the time he visited the tent; they all had supposed he had fallen asleep. All except Vetter said they had gone to the cot and looked at him, at his face, and had suspected nothing wrong. None of them had spoken to him. To the question, "Who do you think did it and why?" they all gave the same answer: someone must have entered the tent by the rear entrance, stabbed him, and departed. The fact that the URWA director of organization had got his stomach into trouble and had been attended by a doctor in the tent had been no secret, anything but.

I have been leaving Flora out, since I knew and you know she was clear, but the cops didn't. I overheard one of them tell another one it was probably her, because stabbing a sick man was more like something a woman would do than a man.

Of course the theory that someone had entered by the back door made the fastening of the tent flap an important item. I said I had tied the tape before we left the tent, and they all agreed that they had seen me do so except Dick Vetter, who said he hadn't noticed because he had been helping to arrange the blanket over Holt; and Wolfe and I both testified that the tape was hanging loose when we had entered the tent while Vetter was speaking. Under this theory the point wasn't who had untied it, since the murderer could have easily reached through the crack from the outside and jerked the knot loose; the question was when. On that none of them was any help. All four said they hadn't noticed whether the tape was tied or not when they went inside the tent.

That was how it stood, as far as I knew, when we left Culp's Meadows. The official destination turned out to be a building I had been in before a time or two, not as a murder suspect—a county courthouse back of a smooth green lawn with a couple of big trees. First we were collected in a room on the ground floor, and, after a long wait, were escorted up one flight and through a door that was inscribed DISTRICT ATTORNEY.

At least 91.2 per cent of the district attorneys in the State of New York think they would make fine tenants of the governor's mansion at Albany, and that should be kept in mind in considering the conduct of DA James R. Delaney. To him at least four of that bunch, and possibly all five, were upright, important citizens in positions to influence segments of the electorate. His attitude as he attacked the problem implied that he was merely chairing a meeting of a community council called to deal with a grave and difficult emergency—except, I noticed, when he was looking at or speaking to Wolfe or me. Then his smile quit working, his tone sharpened, and his eyes had a different look.

With a stenographer at a side table taking it down, he spent an hour going over it with us, or rather with them, with scattered contributions from Chief of Detectives Baker and others who had been at the scene, and then spoke his mind.

"It seems," he said, "to be the consensus that some person unknown entered the tent from the rear, stabbed him, and departed. There is the question, how could such a person have known the knife would be there at hand? but he need not have known. He might have decided to murder only when he saw the knives, or he might have had some other weapon with him, and, seeing the knives, thought one of them would better serve his purpose and used it instead. Either is plausible. It must be admitted that the whole theory is plausible, and none of the facts now known are in contradiction to it. You agree, Chief?"

"Right," Baxter conceded. "Up to now. As long as the known facts are facts."

Delaney nodded. "Certainly. They have to be checked." His eyes took in the audience. "You gentlemen, and you, Miss Korby, you understand that you are to re-main in this jurisdiction, the State of New York, until further notice, and you are to be available. With that understood, it seems unnecessary at present to put you under bond as material witnesses. We have your addresses and know where to find you."

He focused on Wolfe, and his tone changed. "With you, Wolfe, the situation is somewhat different. You're a licensed private detective, and so is Goodwin, and the record of your high-handed performances does not inspire confidence in your—uh —candor. There may be some complicated and subtle reasons why the New York City authorities have stood for your tricks, but out here in the suburbs we're more simple-minded. We don't like tricks."

He lowered his chin, which made his eyes slant up under his heavy brows. "Let's see if I've got your story right. You say that as Vetter started to speak you felt in your pocket for a paper on which you had made notes for your speech, found it wasn't there, thought you had left it in your car, went to get it, and when, after you had en-tered the tent, it occurred to you that the car was locked and Goodwin had the keys, you summoned him and you and he went out to the car. Then Goodwin remem-bered that the paper had been left on your desk at your office, and you and he re-turned to the tent, and you went out to the platform and resumed your seat. Another item: when you went to the rear entrance to leave the tent to go out to the car, the tape fastening of the flap was hanging loose, not tied. Is that your story?"

Wolfe cleared his throat. "Mr. Delaney. I suppose it is pointless to challenge your remark about my candor or to ask you to phrase your question less offensive-ly." His shoulders went up an eighth of an inch, and down. "Yes, that's my story."

"I merely asked you the question."

"I answered it."

"So you did." The DA's eyes came to me. "And of course, Goodwin, your story is the same. If it needed arranging, there was ample time for that during the hubbub that followed Miss Korby's scream. But with you there's more to it. You say that after you and Wolfe re-entered the tent, and he continued through the front en-trance to the platform, it occurred to you that there was a possibility that he had taken the paper from his desk and put it in his pocket, and had consulted it during the ride, and had left it in the car, and you went out back again to look, and you were out there when Miss Korby screamed. Is that correct?"

As I had long since decided not to play, when Baxter had got too personal, I merely said, "Check."

Delaney returned to Wolfe. "If you object to my being offensive, Wolfe, I'll put it this way: I find some of this hard to believe. Anyone as glib as you are needing notes for a little speech like that? And you thinking you had left the paper in the car, and Goodwin remembering it had been left at home on your desk and then thinking it might be in the car after all? Also there are certain facts. You and Goodwin were the last people inside the tent before Miss Korby entered and found the body. You admit it. The others all state that they don't know whether the tape was tied or not when they visited the tent; you and Goodwin can't very well say that, since you went out that way, so you say you found it untied."

He cocked his head. "You admit you had had words with Philip Holt during the past year. You admit he had become obnoxious to you—your word, obnoxious— by his insistence that your personal chef must join his union. The record of your past performances justifies me in saying that a man who renders himself obnoxious to you had better watch his step. I'll say this, if it weren't for the probability that some unknown person entered from the rear, and I concede that it's quite possible, you and Goodwin would be held in custody until a judge could be found to issue a warrant for your arrest as material witnesses. As it is, I'll make it easier for you." He looked at his wristwatch. "It's five minutes to eight. I'll send a man with you to a restaurant down the street, and we'll expect you back here at nine-thirty. I want to cover all the details with you, thoroughly." His eyes moved. "The rest of you may go for the present, but you are to be available."

Wolfe stood up. "Mr. Goodwin and I are going home," he announced. "We will not be back this evening."

Delaney's eyes narrowed. "If that's the way you feel about it, you'll stay. You can send out for sandwiches."

"Are we under arrest?"

The DA opened his mouth, closed it, and opened it again. "No."

"Then we're going." Wolfe was assured but not belligerent. "I understand your annoyance, sir, at this interference with your holiday, and I'm aware that you don't like me—or what you know, or think you know, of my record. But I will not sur- render my convenience to your humor. You can detain me only if you charge me, and with what? Mr. Goodwin and I have supplied all the information we have. Your intimation that I am capable of murdering a man, or of inciting Mr. Goodwin to murder him, because he has made a nuisance of himself, is puerile. You concede that the murderer could have been anyone in that throng of thousands. You have no basis whatever for any supposition that Mr. Goodwin and I are concealing any knowledge that would help you. Should such a basis appear, you know where to find us. Come, Archie."

He turned and headed for the door, and I followed. I can't report the reaction because Delaney at his desk was behind me, and it would have been bad tactics to look back over my shoulder. All I knew was that Baxter took two steps and stopped, and none of the other cops moved. We made the hall, and the entrance, and down the path to the sidewalk, without a shot being fired; and half a block to where the car was parked. Wolfe told me to find a phone booth and call Fritz to tell him when we would arrive for dinner, and I steered for the center of town.

As I had holiday traffic to cope with, it was half past nine by the time we got home and washed and seated at the dinner table. A moving car is no place to give Wolfe bad news, or good news either for that matter, and there was no point in spoiling his dinner, so I waited until after we had finished with the poached and truffled broilers and broccoli and stuffed potatoes with herbs, and salad and cheese, and Fritz had brought coffee to us in the office, to open the bag. Wolfe was reaching for the remote-control television gadget, to turn it on so as to have the pleasure of turning it off again, when I said, "Hold a minute. I have a report to make. I don't blame you for feeling self-satisfied, you got us away very neatly, but there's a catch. It wasn't somebody that came in the back way. It was one of them."

"Indeed." He was placid, after-dinner placid, in the comfortable big made-to-order chair back of his desk. "What is this, flummery?"

"No, sir. Nor am I trying to show that I'm smarter than you are for once. It's just that I know more. When you left the tent to go to the car your mind was on a quick getaway, so you may not have noticed that a woman was sitting there in a car to the left, but I did. When we returned to the tent and you went on out front, I had an idea and went out back again and had a talk with her. I'll give it to you verbatim, since it's important."

I did so. That was simple, compared with the three-way and four-way conversations I have been called on to report word for word. When I finished he was scowling at me, as black as the coffee in his cup.

"Confound it," he growled.

"Yes, sir. I was going to tell you, there when we were settling the details of why we went out to the car, the paper with your notes, but as you know we were interrupted, and after that there was no opportunity that I liked, and anyway I had seen that Mrs. Banau and the car were gone, and that baboon named Baxter had hurt my feelings, and I had decided not to play. Of course the main thing was you, your wanting to go home. If they had known it was one of us six, or seven counting Flora, we would all have been held as material witnesses, and you couldn't have got bail on the Fourth of July, and God help you. I can manage in a cell, but you're too big. Also if I got you home you might feel like discussing a raise in pay. Do you?"

"Shut up." He closed his eyes, and after a moment opened them again. "We're in a pickle. They may find that woman any moment, or she may disclose herself. What about her? You have given me her words, but what about her?"

"She's good. They'll believe her. I did. You would. From where she sat the steps and tent entrance were in her minimum field of vision, no obstructions, less than ten yards away."

"If she kept her eyes open."

"She thinks she did, and that will do for the cops when they find her. Anyhow, I think she did too. When she said nobody had gone into the tent but you and me she meant it."

"There's the possibility that she herself, or someone she knew and would pro-tect—No, that's absurd, since she stayed there in the car for some time after the body was found. We're in a fix."

"Yes, sir." Meeting his eyes, I saw no sign of the gratitude I might reasonably have expected, so I went on. "I would like to suggest, in considering the situation don't bother about me. I can't be charged with withholding evidence because I didn't re-port my talk with her. I can just say I didn't believe her and saw no point in making it tougher for us by dragging it in. The fact that someone might have come in the back way didn't eliminate us. Of course I'll have to account for my questioning her, but that's easy. I can say I discovered that he was dead after you went back out to the platform to make your speech, and, having noticed her there in the car, I went out to question her before reporting the discovery, and was interrupted by the scream in the tent. So don't mind me. Anything you say. I can phone Delaney in the morning, or you can, and spill it, or we can just sit tight and wait for the fireworks."

"Pfui," he said.

"Amen," I said.

He took in air, audibly, and let it out. "That woman may be communicating with them at this moment, or they may be finding her. I don't complain of your performance; indeed, I commend it. If you had reported that conversation we would both be spending tonight in jail." He made a face. "Bah. As it is, at least we can try something. What time is it?"

I looked at my wristwatch. He would have had to turn his head almost to a right angle to glance at the wall clock, which was too much to expect. "Eight after eleven."

"Could you get them here tonight?"

"I doubt it. All five of them?"

"Yes."

"Possibly by sunup. Bring them to your bedroom?"

He rubbed his nose with a fingertip. "Very well. But you can call them now, as many as you can get. Make it eleven in the morning. Tell them I have a disclosure to make and must consult with them."

"That should interest them," I granted, and reached for the phone.

IV

By the time Wolfe came down from the plant rooms to greet the guests, at two minutes past eleven the next morning, there hadn't been a peep out of the Long Island law. Which didn't mean there couldn't be one at three minutes past eleven. According to the morning paper, District Attorney Delaney and Chief of Detectives Baxter had both conceded that anyone could have entered the tent from the back and therefore it was wide open. If Anna Banau read newspapers, and she probably did, she might at any moment be going to the phone to make a call.

I had made several, both the night before and that morning, getting the guests lined up; and one special one. There was an address and phone number for an Alexander Banau in the Manhattan book, but I decided not to dial it. I also decided not to ring Zoller's restaurant on Fifty-second Street. I hadn't eaten at Zoller's more than a couple of times, but I knew a man who had been patronizing it for years, and I called him. Yes, he said, there was a captain at Zoller's named Alex, and yes, his last name was Banau. He liked Alex and hoped that my asking about him didn't mean that he was headed for some kind of trouble. I said no trouble was contemplated, I just might want to check a little detail, and thanked him. Then I sat and looked at the slip on which I had scribbled the Banau home phone number, with my finger itching to dial it, but to say what? No.

I mention that around ten-thirty I got the Marley .38 from the drawer, saw that it was loaded, and put it in my side pocket, not to prepare for bloodshed, but just to show that I was sold on Mrs. Banau. With a murderer for a guest, and an extremely nervy one, there was no telling.

H. L. Griffin, the importer, and Paul Rago, the sauce chef, came alone and separately, but Korby and Flora had Dick Vetter with them. I had intended to let Flora have the red leather chair, but when I showed them to the office, Rago, the six-footer with the mustache and the accent, had copped it, and she took one of the yellow chairs in a row facing Wolfe's desk, with her father on her right and Vetter on her left. Griffin, the runt who had made the best speech, was at the end of the row nearest my desk. When Wolfe came down from the plant rooms, entered, greeted them, and headed for his desk, Vetter spoke up before he was seated.

"I hope this won't last long, Mr. Wolfe. I asked Mr. Goodwin if it couldn't be earlier, and he said it couldn't. Miss Korby and I must have an early lunch because I have a script conference at one-thirty."

I raised a brow. I had been honored. I had driven a car with my arm across the shoulders of a girl whom Dick Vetter himself thought worthy of a lunch.

Wolfe, adjusted in his chair, said mildly, "I won't prolong it beyond necessity, sir. Are you and Miss Korby friends?"

"What's that got to do with it?"

"Possibly nothing. But now, nothing about any of you is beyond the bounds of my curiosity. It is a distressing thing to have to say, in view of the occasion of our meeting yesterday, the anniversary of the birth of this land of freedom, but I must. One of you is a miscreant. One of you people killed Philip Holt."

The idea is to watch them and see who faints or jumps up and runs. But nobody did. They all stared.

"One of us?" Griffin demanded.

Wolfe nodded. "I thought it best to begin with that bald statement, instead of leading up to it. I thought——"

Korby cut in. "This is funny. This is a joke. After what you said yesterday to that district attorney. It's a *bad* joke."

"It's no joke, Mr. Korby. I wish it were. I thought yesterday I was on solid ground, but I wasn't. I now know that there is a witness, a credible and confident witness, to testify that no one entered the tent from the rear between the time that the speeches began and the discovery of the body. I also know that neither Mr. Goodwin nor I killed him, so it was one of you. So I think we should discuss it."

"You say a witness?" Rago made it "weetnuss."

"Who is he?" Korby wanted to know. "Where is he?"

"It's a woman, and she is available. Mr. Goodwin, who has spoken with her, is completely satisfied of her competence and bona fides, and he is hard to satisfy. It is highly unlikely that she can be impeached. That's all I——"

"I don't get it," Vetter blurted. "If they've got a witness like that why haven't they come for us?"

"Because they haven't got her. They know nothing about her. But they may find her at any moment, or she may go to them. If so you will soon be discussing the matter not with me but with officers of the law——and so will I. Unless you do discuss it with me, and unless the discussion is productive, I shall of course be constrained to tell Mr. Delaney about her. I wouldn't like that and neither would you. After hearing her story his manner with you, and with me, would be quite difference from yesterday. I want to ask you some questions."

"Who is she?" Korby demanded. "Where is she?"

Wolfe shook his head. "I'm not going to identify her or place her for you. I note our expressions——especially yours, Mr. Korby, and yours, Mr. Griffin. You are keptical. But what conceivable reason could there be for my getting you here to oint this weapon at you except the coercion of events? Why would I invent or ontrive such a dilemma? I, like you, would vastly prefer to have it as it was, that murderer came from without, but that's no good now. I concede that you may suspect me too, and Mr. Goodwin, and you may question us as I may question you. But one of us killed Philip Holt, and getting answers to questions is clearly in the interest of all the rest of us."

They exchanged glances. But they were not the kind of glances they would have exchanged five minutes earlier. They were glances of doubt, suspicion, and surmise, and they weren't friendly.

"I don't see," Griffin objected, "what good questions will do. We were all there together and we all know what happened. We all know what everybody said."

Wolfe nodded. "But we were all supporting the theory that excluded us. Now we're not. We can't. One of us has something in his background which, if known, would account for his determination to kill that man. I suggest beginning with autobiographical sketches from each of us, and here is mine. I was born in Montenegro and spent my early boyhood there. At the age of sixteen I decided to move around, and in fourteen years I became acquainted with most of Europe, a little of Africa, and much of Asia, in a variety of roles and activities. Coming to this country in nineteen-thirty, not penniless, I bought this house and entered into practice as a private detective. I am a naturalized American citizen. I first heard of Philip Holt about two years ago when Fritz Brenner, who works for me, came to me with a complaint about him. My only reason for wishing him harm, but not the extremity of death, was removed, as you know, when he agreed to stop annoying Mr. Brenner about joining your union if I would make a speech at your blasted picnic. Mr. Goodwin?"

I turned my face to the audience. "Born in Ohio. Public high school, pretty good at geometry and football, graduated with honor but no honors. Went to college two weeks, decided it was childish, came to New York and got a job guarding a pier, shot and killed two men and was fired, was recommended to Nero Wolfe for a chore he wanted done, did it, was offered a full-time job by Mr. Wolfe, took it, still have it. Personally, was more entertained than bothered by Holt's trying to get union dues out of Fritz Brenner. Otherwise no connection with him or about him."

"You may," Wolfe told them, "question us later if you wish. Miss Korby?"

"Well—" Flora said. She glanced at her father, and, when he nodded, she aimed at Wolfe and went on, "My autobiography doesn't amount to much. I was born in New York and have always lived here. I'm twenty years old. I didn't kill Phil Holt and had no reason to kill him." She turned her palms up. "What else?"

"If I may suggest," H. L. Griffin offered, "if there's a witness as Wolfe says, if there is such a witness, they'll dig everything up. For instance, about you and Phil."

She gave him an eye. "What about us, Mr. Griffin?"

"I don't know. I've only heard talk, that's all, and they'll dig up the talk."

"To hell with the talk," Dick Vetter blurted, the whipped cream sounding sou

Flora looked at Wolfe. "I can't help talk," she said. "It certainly is no secret that Phil Holt was — well, he liked women. And it's no secret that I'm a woman, and I guess it's not a secret that I didn't like Phil. For me he was what you called him, a nuisance. When he wanted something."

Wolfe grunted. "And he wanted you?"

"He thought he did. That's all there was to it. He was a pest, that's all there is to say about it."

"You said you had no reason to kill him."

"Good heavens, I didn't! A girl doesn't kill a man just because he won't believe her when she says no!"

"No to what? A marriage proposal?"

Her father cut in. "Look here," he told Wolfe, "you're barking up the wrong tree. Everybody knows how Phil Holt was about women. He never asked one to marry him and probably he never would. My daughter is old enough and smart enough to take care of herself, and she does, but not by sticking a knife in a man's back." He turned to Griffin. "Much obliged, Harry."

The importer wasn't fazed. "It was bound to come out, Jim, and I thought it ought to be mentioned now."

Wolfe was regarding Korby. "Naturally it raises the question how far a father might go to relieve his daughter of a pest."

Korby snorted. "If you're asking it, the answer is no. My daughter can take care of herself. If you want a reason why I might have killed Phil Holt you'll have to do better than that."

"Then I'll try, Mr. Korby. You are the president of your union, and Mr. Holt was an important figure in it, and at the moment the affairs of unions, especially their financial affairs, are front-page news. Have you any reason to fear an investigation, or had Mr. Holt?"

"No. They can investigate as much as they damn please."

"Have you been summoned?"

"No."

"Had Mr. Holt been summoned?"

"No."

"Have any officials of your union been summoned?"

"No." Korby's pudgy face and bald top were pinking up a little. "You're barking up the wrong tree again."

"But at least another tree. You realize, sir, that if Mr. Delaney starts after us in earnest, the affairs of the United Restaurant Workers of America will be one of his major concerns. For the murder of Philip Holt we all had opportunity, and the means were there at hand; what he will seek is the motive. If there was a vulnerable spot in the operation of your union, financial or otherwise, I suggest that it would be wise for you to disclose it now for discussion."

"There wasn't anything." Korby was pinker. "There's nothing wrong with my union except rumors. That's all it is, rumors, and where's a union that hasn't got rumors with all the stink they've raised? We're not vulnerable to anything or anybody."

"What kind of rumors?"

"Any kind you want to name. I'm a crook. All the officers are crooks. We've raided the benefit fund. We've sold out to the big operators. We steal lead pencils and paper clips."

"Can you be more specific? What was the most embarrassing rumor?"

Korby was suddenly not listening. He took a folded handkerchief from his pocket, opened it up, wiped his face and his baldness, refolded the handkerchief at the creases, and returned it to his pocket. Then his eyes went back to Wolfe.

"If you want something specific," he said, "it's not a rumor. It's a strictly internal union matter, but it's sure to leak now and it might as well leak here first. There have been some charges made, and they're being looked into, about kickbacks from dealers to union officers and members. Phil Holt had something to do with some of the charges, though that wasn't in his department. He got hot about it."

"Were you the target of any of the charges?"

"I was not. I have the complete trust of my associates and my staff."

"You said 'dealers.' Does that include importers?"

"Sure, importers are dealers."

"Was Mr. Griffin's name mentioned in any of the charges?"

"I'm not giving any names, not without authority from my board. Those things are confidential."

"Much obliged, Jim," H. L. Griffin said, sounding the opposite of obliged. "Even exchange?"

"Excuse me." It was Dick Vetter, on his feet. "It's nearly twelve o'clock and Miss Korby and I have to go. We've got to get some lunch and I can't be late for that conference. Anyway, I think it's a lot of hooey. Come on, Flora."

She hesitated a moment, then left her chair, and he moved. But when Wolfe snapped out his name he turned. "Well?"

Wolfe swiveled his chair. "My apologies. I should have remembered that you are pressed for time. If you can give us, say five minutes?"

The TV star smiled indulgently. "For my autobiography? You can look it up. It's in print—*TV Guide* a couple of months ago, or *Clock* magazine, I don't remember the date. I say this is hooey. If one of us is a murderer, okay, I wish you luck, bu this isn't getting you anywhere. Couldn't I just tell you anything I felt like?"

"You could indeed, Mr. Vetter. But if inquiry reveals that you have lied or have omitted something plainly relevant that will be of interest. The magazine articles you mentioned—do they tell of your interest in Miss Korby?"

"Nuts." Many of his twenty million admirers wouldn't have liked either his tone or his diction.

Wolfe shook his head. "If you insist, Mr. Vetter, you may of course be disdainful about it with me, but not with the police once they get interested in you. I asked you before if you and Miss Korby are friends, and you asked what that had to do with it, and I said possibly nothing. I now say possibly something, since Philip Holt was hounding her—how savagely I don't know yet. Are you and Miss Korby friends?"

"Certainly we're friends. I'm taking her to lunch."

"Are you devoted to her?"

His smile wasn't quite so indulgent, but it was still a smile. "Now that's a delicate question," he said. "I'll tell you how it is. I'm a public figure and I have to watch my tongue. If I said yes, I'm devoted to Miss Korby, it would be in all the columns tomorrow and I'd get ten thousand telegrams and a million letters. If I said no, I'm not devoted to Miss Korby, that wouldn't be polite with her here at my elbow. So I'll just skip it. Come on, Flora."

"One more question. I understand that your father works in a New York restaurant. Do you know whether he is involved in any of the charges Mr. Korby spoke of?"

"Oh, for God's sake. Talk about hooey." He turned and headed for the door, taking Flora with him. I got up and went to the hall and on to the front door, opened it for them, closed it after them, put the chain-bolt on, and returned to the office. Wolfe was speaking.

"... and I assure you, Mr. Rago, my interest runs with yours—with all of you except one. You don't want the police crawling over you and neither do I."

The sauce chef had straightened up in the red leather chair, and the points of his mustache seemed to have straightened up too. "Treeks," he said.

"No, sir," Wolfe said. "I have no objection to tricks, if they work, but this is merely a forthright discussion of a lamentable situation. No trick. Do you object to telling us what dealings you had with Philip Holt?"

"I am deesappointed," Rago declared. "Of course I knew you made a living with detective work, everybody knows that, but to me your glory is your great contributions to cuisine—your *sauce printemps*, your oyster pie, your *artichauts drigants*, and others. I know what Pierre Mondor said of you. So it is a deesappointment when I am in your company that the only talk is of the ugliness of murder."

"I don't like it any better than you do, Mr. Rago. I am pleased to know that ~re Mondor spoke well of me. Now about Philip Holt?"

"If you insist, certainly. But what can I say? Nothing."

"Didn't you know him?"

Rago spread his hands and raised his shoulders and brows. "I had met him. As one meets people. Did I know him? Whom does one know? Do I know you?"

"But you never saw me until two weeks ago. Surely you must have seen something of Mr. Holt. He was an important official of your union, in which you were active."

"I have not been active in the union."

"You were a speaker at its picnic yesterday."

Rago nodded and smiled. "Yes, that is so. But that was because of my activity in the kitchen, not in the union. It may be said, even by me, that in sauces I am supreme. It was for that distinction that it was thought desirable to have me." His head turned. "So, Mr. Korby?"

The president of URWA nodded yes. "That's right," he told Wolfe. "We thought the finest cooking should be represented, and we picked Rago for it. So far as I know, he has never come to a union meeting. We wish he would, and more like him."

"I am a man of the kitchen," Rago declared. "I am an artist. The business I leave to others."

Wolfe was on Korby. "Did Mr. Rago's name appear in any of the charges you spoke of?"

"No. I said I wouldn't give names, but I can say no. No, it didn't."

"You didn't say no when I asked about Mr. Griffin." Wolfe turned to the importer. "Do you wish to comment on that, sir?"

I still hadn't decided exactly what was wrong with Griffin's left eye. There was no sign of an injury, and it seemed to function okay, but it appeared to be a little off center. From an angle, the slant I had from my desk, it looked normal.

He lifted his long narrow chin. "What do you expect?" he demanded.

"My expectations are of no consequence. I merely invite comment."

"On that, I have none. I know nothing about any charges. What I want, I want to see that witness."

Wolfe shook his head. "As I said, I will not produce the witness—for the present. Are you still skeptical?"

"I'm always skeptical." Griffin's voice would have suited a man twice his size. "I want to see that witness and hear what she has to say. I admit I can see no reason why you would invent her—if there is one it's too deep for me, since it puts you in the same boat with us—but I'm not going to believe her until I see her. Maybe I will then, and maybe I won't."

"I think you will. Meanwhile, what about your relations with Philip Holt? How long and how well did you know him?"

"Oh, to hell with this jabber!" Griffin bounced up, not having far to bounce. "If there was anything in my relations with him that made me kill him, would I be telling you?" He flattened his palms on Wolfe's desk. "Are you going to produce that witness? No?" He wheeled. "I've had enough of this! You, Jim? Rago?"

That ended the party. Wolfe could have held Korby and Rago for more jabber, but apparently he didn't think it worth the effort. They asked some questions, what was Wolfe going to do now, and what was the witness going to do, and why couldn't they see her, and why did Wolfe believe her, and was he going to see her and question her, and of course nobody got anything out of that. The atmosphere wasn't very cordial when they left. After letting them out I returned to the office and stood in front of Wolfe's desk. He was leaning back with his arms folded.

"Lunch in twenty minutes," I said cheerfully.

"Not in peace," he growled.

"No, sir. Any instructions?"

"Pfui. It would take an army, and I haven't got one. To go into all of them, to trace all their connections and dealings with the man one of them murdered . . ." He unfolded his arms and put his fists on the desk. "I can't even limit it by assuming that it was an act of urgency, resulting from something that had been said or done that day or in the immediate past. The need or desire to kill him might have dated from a week ago, or a month, or even a year, and it was satisfied yesterday in that tent only because circumstances offered the opportunity. No matter which one it was—Rago, who visited the tent first, or Korby or Griffin or Vetter, who visited it after him in that order—no matter which, the opportunity was tempting. The man was there, recumbent and disabled, and the weapon was there. He had a plausible excuse for entering the tent. To spread the cloud of suspicion to the multitude, all he had to do was untie the tape that held the flap. Even if the body were discovered soon after he left the tent, even seconds after, there would be no question he couldn't answer."

He grunted. "No. Confound it, no. The motive may be buried not only in a complexity of associations but also in history. It might take months. I will have to contrive something."

"Yeah. Any time."

"There may be none. That's the devil of it. Get Saul and Fred and Orrie and have them on call. I have no idea for what, but no matter, get them. And let me alone."

I went to my desk and pulled the phone over.

V

There have been only five occasions in my memory when Wolfe has cut short his afternoon session with the orchids in the plant rooms, from four o'clock to six, and that was the fifth.

If there had been any developments inside his skull I hadn't been informed. There had been none outside, unless you count my calling Saul and Fred and Orrie, our three best bets when we needed outside help, and telling them to stand by. Back at his desk after lunch, Wolfe fiddled around with papers on his desk, counted the week's collection of bottle caps in his drawer, rang for Fritz to bring beer and then didn't drink it, and picked up his current book, *The Fall* by Albert Camus, three or four times, and put it down again. In between he brushed specks of dust from his desk with his little finger. When I turned on the radio for the four-o'clock newscast he waited until it was finished to leave for his elevator trip up to the roof.

Later, nearly an hour later, I caught myself brushing a speck of dust off my desk with my little finger, said something I needn't repeat here, and went to the kitchen for a glass of milk.

When the doorbell rang at a quarter past five I jumped up and shot for the hall, realized that was unmanly, and controlled my legs to a normal gait. Through the one-way glass panel of the front door I saw, out on the stoop, a tall lanky guy, narrow from top to bottom, in a brown suit that needed pressing and a brown straw hat. I took a breath, which I needed apparently, and went and opened the door the two inches allowed by the chain-bolt. His appearance was all against it, but there was no telling what kind of a specimen District Attorney Delaney or Chief of Detectives Baxter might have on his staff.

I spoke through the crack. "Yes, sir?"

"I would like to see Mr. Nero Wolfe. My name is Banau, Alexander Banau."

"Yes, sir." I took the bolt off and swung the door open, and he crossed the sill. "You hat, sir?" He gave it to me and I put it on the shelf. "This way, sir." I waited until I had him in the office and in the red leather chair to say, "Mr. Wolfe is engaged at the moment. I'll tell him you're here."

I went to the hall and on to the kitchen, shutting doors on the way, buzzed the plant rooms on the house phone, and in three seconds, instead of the usual fifteen or twenty, had a growl in my ear. "Yes?"

"Company. Captain Alexander Banau."

Silence, then: "Let him in."

"He's already in. Have you any suggestions how I keep him occupied until six o'clock?"

"No." A longer silence. "I'll be down."

As I said, that was the fifth time in all the years I have been with him. I went back to the office and asked the guest if he would like something to drink, and he said no, and in two minutes there was the sound of Wolfe's elevator descending and stopping, the door opening and shutting, and his tread. He entered, circled around the red leather chair, and offered a hand.

"Mr. Banau? I'm Nero Wolfe. How do you do, sir?"

He was certainly spreading it on. He doesn't like to shake hands, and rarely does. When he adjusted in his chair he gave Banau a look so sociable it was damn close to fawning, for him.

"Well, sir?"

"I fear," Banau said, "that I may have to make myself disagreeable. I don't like to be disagreeable. Is that gentleman"—he nodded at me—"Mr. Archie Goodwin?"

"He is, yes, sir."

"Then it will be doubly disagreeable, but it can't be helped. It concerns the tragic event at Culp's Meadows yesterday. According to the newspaper accounts, the police are proceeding on the probability that the murderer entered the tent from the rear, and left that way after he had performed the deed. Just an hour ago I telephoned to Long Island to ask if they still regard that as probable, and was told that they do."

He stopped to clear his throat. I would have liked to get my fingers around it to help. He resumed.

"It is also reported that you and Mr. Goodwin were among those interviewed, and that compels me to conclude, reluctantly, that Mr. Goodwin has failed to tell you of a conversation he had with my wife as she sat in our car outside the tent. I should explain that I was in the crowd in front, and when your speech was interrupted by the scream, and confusion resulted, I made my way around to the car, with some difficulty, and got in and drove away. I do not like tumult. My wife did not tell me of her conversation with Mr. Goodwin until after we got home. She regards it as unwise to talk while I am driving. What she told me was that Mr. Goodwin approached the car and spoke to her through the open window. He asked her if anyone—"

"If you please." Wolfe wiggled a finger. "Your assumption that he hasn't reported the conversation to me is incorrect. He has."

"What! He has?"

"Yes, sir. If you will—"

"Then you know that my wife is certain that no one entered the tent from the rear while the speeches were being made? No one but you and Mr. Goodwin? Absolutely certain? You know she told him that?"

"I know what she told him, yes. But if you will—"

"And you haven't told the police?"

"No, not yet. I would like——"

"Then she has no choice." Banau was on his feet. "It is even more disagreeable than I feared. She must communicate with them at once. This is terrible, a man of your standing, and the others too. It is terrible, but it must be done. In a country of law the law must be served."

He turned and headed for the door.

I left my chair. Stopping him and wrapping him up would have been no problem, but I was myself stopped by the expression on Wolfe's face. He looked relieved; he even looked pleased. I stared at him, and was still staring when the sound came of the front door closing. I stepped to the hall, saw that he was gone and hadn't forgotten his hat, and returned and stood at Wolfe's desk.

"Goody," I said. "Cream? Give me some."

He took in air, all the way, and let it out. "This is more like it," he declared. "I've had all the humiliation I can stand. Jumping out of my skin every time the phone rang. Did you notice how quickly I answered your ring upstairs? Afraid, by heaven, afraid to go into the tropical room to look over the Renanthera imschootiana! Now we know where we are."

"Yeah. Also where we soon will be. If it had been me I would have kept him at least long enough to tell him——"

"Shut up."

I did so. There are certain times when it is understood that I am not to badger, and the most important is when he leans back in his chair and shuts his eyes and his lips start to work. He pushes them out, pulls them in, out and in, out and in.... That means his brain has crashed the sound barrier. I have seen him, dealing with a tough one, go on with that lip action for up to an hour. I sat down at my desk, thinking I might as well be near the phone.

That time he didn't take an hour, not having one. More like eight minutes. He opened his eyes, straightened up, and spoke.

"Archie. Did he tell you where his wife was?"

"No. He told me nothing. He was saving it for you. She could have been in the drugstore at the corner, sitting in the phone booth."

He grunted. "Then we must clear out of here. I am going to find out which of them killed that man before we are all hauled in. The motive and the evidence will have to come later; the thing now is to identify him as a bone to toss to Mr. Delaney. Where is Saul?"

"At home, waiting to hear. Fred and Orrie——"

"We need only Saul. Call him. Tell him we are coming there at once. Where would Mr. Vetter have his conference?"

"I suppose at the MXO studio."

"Get him. And if Miss Korby is there, her also. And the others. You must get them all before they hear from Mr. Delaney. They are all to be at Saul's place without delay. At the earliest possible moment. Tell them they are to meet and question the witness, and it is desperately urgent. If they balk I'll speak to them and——"

I had the phone, dialing.

VI

After they were all there and Wolfe started in, it took him less than fifteen minutes to learn which one was it. I might have managed it in fifteen days, with luck. If you like games you might lean back now, close your eyes and start pushing your lips out and in, and see how long it takes you to decide how you would do it. Fair enough, since you know everything that Wolfe and I knew. But get it straight; don't try to name him or come up with evidence that would nail him; the idea is, how do you use what you now know to put the finger on him? That was what Wolfe did, and I wouldn't expect more of you than of him.

Saul Panzer, below average in size but miles above it in savvy, lived alone on the top floor—living room, bedroom, kitchenette, and bath—of a remodeled house on Thirty-eighth Street between Lexington and Third. The living room was big, lighted with two floor lamps and two table lamps, even at seven o'clock of a July evening, because the blinds were drawn. One wall had windows, another was solid with books, and the other two had pictures and shelves that were cluttered with everything from chunks of minerals to walrus tusks. In the far corner was a grand piano.

Wolfe sent his eyes around and said, "This shouldn't take long."

He was in the biggest chair Saul had, by a floor lamp, almost big enough for him. I was on a stool to his left and front, and Saul was off to his right, on the piano bench. The chairs of the five customers were in an arc facing him. Of course it would have been sensible and desirable to arrange the seating so that the murderer was next to either Saul or me, but that wasn't practical since we had no idea which one it was, and neither did Wolfe.

"Where's the witness?" Griffin demanded. "Goodwin said she'd be here."

Wolfe nodded. "I know. Mr. Goodwin is sometimes careless with his pronouns. The witness is present." He aimed a thumb at the piano bench. "There. Mr. Saul Panzer, who is not only credible and confident but——"

"You said it was a woman!"

"There is another witness who is a woman; doubtless there will be others when one of you goes on trial. The urgency Mr. Goodwin spoke of relates to what Mr. Panzer will tell you. Before he does so, some explanation is required."

"Let him talk first," Dick Vetter said, "and then explain. We've heard from you already."

"I'll make it brief." Wolfe was unruffled. "It concerns the tape fastening on the flap of the rear entrance of the tent. As you know, Mr. Goodwin tied it before we left to go to the platform, and when he and I entered the tent later and left by the rear entrance it had been untied. By whom? Not by someone entering from the outside, since there is a witness to testify that no one had——"

James Korby cut in. "That's the witness we want to see. Goodwin said she'd be here."

"You'll see her, Mr. Korby, in good time. Please bear with me. Therefore the tape had been untied by someone who had entered from the front—by one of you four men. Why? The presumption is overwhelming that it was untied by the murderer, to create and support the probability that Philip Holt had been stabbed by someone who entered from the rear. It is more than a presumption; it approaches certainty. So it seemed to me that it was highly desirable, if possible, to learn who had untied the tape; and I enlisted the services of Mr. Panzer." His head turned. "Saul, if you please?"

Saul had his hand on a black leather case beside him on the bench. "Do you want it all, Mr. Wolfe? How I got it?"

"Not at the moment, I think. Later, if they want to know. What you have is more important than how you got it."

"Yes, sir." He opened the lid of the case and took something from it. "I'd rather not explain how I got it because it might make trouble for somebody."

I horned in. "What do you mean 'might'? You know damn well it would make trouble for somebody."

"Okay, Archie, okay." His eyes went to the audience. "What I've got is these photographs of fingerprints that were lifted from the tape on the flap of the rear entrance of the tent. There are some blurry ones, but here are four good ones. Two of the good ones are Mr. Goodwin's, and that leaves two unidentified." He turned to the case and took things out. He cocked his head to the audience. "The idea is, I take your prints and——"

"Not so fast, Saul." Wolfe's eyes went right, and left again. "You see how it is, and you understand why Mr. Goodwin said it was urgent. Surely those of you who did *not* untie the tape will not object to having your prints compared with the photographs. If anyone does object he cannot complain if an inference is made. Of course there is the possibility that none of your prints will match the two unidentified ones in the photographs, and in that case the results will be negative and not conclusive. Mr. Panzer has the equipment to take your prints, and he is an expert. Will you let him?"

Glances were exchanged.

"What the hell," Vetter said. "Mine are on file anyway. Sure."

"Mine also," Griffin said. "I have no objection."

Paul Rago abruptly exploded. "Treeks again!"

All eyes went to him. Wolfe spoke. "No, Mr. Rago, no tricks. Mr. Panzer would prefer not to explain how he got the photographs, but he will if you insist. I assure you—"

"I don't mean treeks how he gets them." The sauce chef uncrossed his legs. "I mean what you said, it was the murderer who untied the tape. That is not necessary. I can say that was a lie! When I entered the tent and looked at him it seemed to me he did not breathe good, there was not enough air, and I went and untied the tape so the air could come through. So if you take my print and find it is like the photograph, what will that prove? Nothing at all. Nuh-theeng! So I say it is treeks again, and in this great land of freedom—"

I wasn't trying to panic him. I wasn't even going to touch him. And I had the Marley .38 in my pocket, and Saul had one too, so if he had tried to start something he would have got stopped quick. But using a gun, especially in a crowd, is always bad management unless you have to, and he was twelve feet away from me, and I got up and moved merely because I wanted to be closer. Saul had the same notion at the same instant, and the sight of us two heading for him, with all that he knew that we didn't know yet, was too much for him. He was out of his chair and plunging toward the door as I took my second step.

Then, of course, we had to touch him. I reached him first, not because I'm faster than Saul but because he was farther off. And the damn fool put up a fight, although I had him wrapped. He kicked Saul where it hurt, and knocked a lamp over, and bumped my nose with his skull. When he sank his teeth in my arm I thought, That will do for you, mister, and jerked the Marley from my pocket and slapped him above the ear, and he went down.

Turning, I saw that Dick Vetter had also wrapped his arms around someone, and she was neither kicking nor biting. In moments of stress people usually show what is really on their minds, even important public figures like TV stars. There wasn't a word about it in the columns next day.

VII

have often wondered how Paul Rago felt when, at his trial a couple of months later, no evidence whatever was introduced about fingerprints. He knew then, of course, that it had been a treek and nothing but, that no prints had been lifted from the tape by Saul or anyone else, and that if he had kept his mouth shut and played along he might have been playing yet.

I once asked Wolfe what he would have done if that had happened.

He said, "It didn't happen."

I said, "What if it had?"

He said, "Pfui. The contingency was too remote to consider. It was as good as certain that the murderer had untied the tape. Confronted with the strong probability that it was about to be disclosed that his print was on the tape, he had to say something. He had to explain how it got there, and it was vastly preferable to do so voluntarily instead of waiting until evidence compelled it."

I hung on. "Okay, it was a good trick, but I still say what if?"

"And I still say it is pointless to consider remote contingencies. What if your mother had abandoned you in a tiger's cage at the age of three months? What would you have done?"

I told him I'd think it over and let him know.

As for motive, you can have three guesses if you want them, but you'll never get warm if you dig them out of what I have reported. In all the jabber in Wolfe's office that day, there wasn't one word that had the slightest bearing on why Philip Holt died, which goes to show why detectives get ulcers. No, I'm wrong; it was mentioned that Philip Holt liked women, and certainly that had a bearing. One of the women he had liked was Paul Rago's wife, an attractive blue-eyed number about half as old as her husband, and he was still liking her, and, unlike Flora Korby, she had liked him and proved it.

Paul Rago hadn't liked that.

Kelley Roos

pseudonym of
Audrey Roos (1912–1982)
William Roos (1911–)

Kelley Roos is the pseudonym of a husband-and-wife writing team, William Roos and Audrey (née Kelley) Roos. As is the case with the Lockridges' Mr. and Mrs. North, Kelley Roos's Jeff and Haila Troy are an attractive, sophisticated New York City couple; he works in a photography studio, while she, a former aspiring actress, tends the home fires. The Troy novels, beginning with *Made Up to Kill* (1940), are typical of the subgenre in the 1940s and 1950s: amusing, bloodless, spiced with witty dialogue, and often relying on the formula of the imperiled wife being saved at the last minute by her husband. Their adventures are set against such diverse backdrops as the theater *(Made Up to Kill)*; model yachting (*Sailor Take Warning*, 1944); and a strange snowbound lodge in Westchester County, New York (*Ghost of a Chance*, 1947). Four films were inspired by the Roos novels, the first and best being *A Night to Remember* (1942), starring Loretta Young and Brian Aherne, based on the 1942 title *The Frightened Stiff*. In addition to their full-length adventures, the Troys appeared in a number of novelettes, three of which are collected in *Triple Threat* (1949).

While the Troy novels were somewhat superficial and conformed to the conventions of the time, their carefree good humor and refreshing characterization made them popular with readers, and the Roos team proved that they were willing to try other types of collaborative detective fiction. In 1956 they broke away from their main series to present another detecting duo, Steve and Connie Barton, who appeared in only one novel, *The Blond Died Dancing*. They also made forays into psychological suspense and intrigue, with such novels as *Cry in the Night* (1966), *What Did Hattie See?* (1970), and *Bad Trip* (1971). Even the final Troy novel (*One False Move*, 1966) was a departure: The setting is not New York, but a small Texas town, and the couple have recently been divorced—although they do reconcile at the end. In "Two Over Par," the couple are at their amusing best as they solve a mystery on the golf links.

TWO OVER PAR

JEFF AND HAILA TROY
LONG ISLAND, NEW YORK
1949

J eff stepped back from teeing up my ball and handed me the family driver. I kept my head down and swung. The ball, obviously a faulty one, curved into a thicket not far away. Jeff teed his ball, kept his head down, and swung. His ball sliced into the same thicket. The Troys, as they say around the club, were in the rough.

"Are you sure," I said, "that you're really supposed to keep your head down?"

"I don't know," Jeff said dismally. "But I couldn't raise mine now even if I wanted to. I'm too ashamed."

"Those are our last two balls."

"Yeah." Jeff picked up our bag, slung it over his shoulder. "If we didn't spend so much money on balls we could afford a caddy."

"Couldn't we alternate? Hire a caddy one day, use balls the next?"

"Women," Jeff said, "shouldn't be allowed on a golf course."

We trudged toward the thicket and plunged into it. We separated and began looking for our balls. It wasn't very interesting work. Perhaps I had done too much of it in this week since we had taken up golf. I kicked aimlessly at the thick grass as I walked around, I—

"Jeff!"

"Did you find your ball?" Jeff yelled.

"No," I said. "No, I—I found a caddy!"

Then Jeff was at my side. He saw what I had seen. He crouched down beside the young man, reaching for his wrist. But he didn't test his pulse; he didn't need to. As Jeff touched the arm, the body rolled onto its back and we saw the bullet hole in Eddie Riorden's head.

I turned away. "I'll go back to the clubhouse. I'll phone—"

"Wait," Jeff said.

He moved deeper into the thicket. I had taken one step after him when he stopped. I saw his shoulders go rigid. Then he turned and came back to me.

He took me by the arm and led me out onto the fairway.

"Jeff," I said, "what is it? What did you see?"

"Eddie was caddying for Mrs. Carleton."

"For Mrs.—Oh," I said.

"Yes. Just like Eddie. Shot through the head."

•

I never got it straight just what Joe Hinkle's official title was—chief of police, sheriff, constable, what? But when murder was committed at the Ocean Country Club on Long Island, Joe Hinkle was the man who represented the law. He was a pleasant, large-faced man. He seemed a little put out that there had been two murders; he seemed to feel that somebody had overdone it.

Joe talked to Jeff and me in a private dining room off the club's bar. He kept looking over our heads toward the bar. I got the impression that Joe would have liked to forget the whole thing and have a drink, then another, followed by a few more—even though it was still only nine-thirty in the morning.

Joe Hinkle sighed and put the palms of his hands on the bare dining table. He looked at us.

"You found the bodies," he said.

"We're sorry," Jeff said.

"That's all right." The policeman sighed again. "If you hadn't, somebody else would have. You two play golf pretty early in the morning."

"We're self-conscious about our golf," I explained.

"Was there anyone else on the course while you were playing?"

"We didn't see anyone," I said.

"What difference would that make?" Jeff asked. "It looked to me as though Mrs. Carleton and Eddie had been lying there all night long."

"Yeah, that's right," Joe said. "Doc Grandle says they been dead about twelve hours or so. That's what I figure, too. It gets dark around nine these nights. So Mrs. Carleton was playing her round of golf some time before then. I expect to set the time of the shooting pretty close by asking questions around the club. I wish whoever did it would confess."

"I wouldn't bank on that," Jeff said.

"No, I guess I shouldn't. If I killed two people, I wouldn't admit it." Joe slouched down in his chair and closed his eyes. "Mrs. Carleton and Eddie Riorden —who would have a motive to kill them two? I figure nobody would. I figure that the killer shot Eddie, then had to shoot Mrs. Carleton, too, because she was a witness to Eddie's murder. Or vice versa. By that I mean, there is the alternative that Mrs. Carleton was the intended victim, and Eddie the innocent bystander. How does that sound to you, Troy?"

"Logical," Jeff said.

"I'm glad to hear you say that. You've had some experience with murder cases, I understand."

"A little," Jeff admitted.

"Well, that's more than I've had. Thank the Lord."

Jeff said, "Did you find anything interesting in that thicket?"

"We found Eddie's cap. And Mrs. Carleton's golf bag. That's about all so far."

"You must have found a lot of balls. Mrs. Carleton and Haila and I aren't the only ones with a slice around here."

"You're right. We did find some balls." Hinkle extracted three balls from his jacket pocket and rolled them across the table to Jeff. "Maybe one of them belongs to you."

"This one is Haila's. Mine isn't here." Jeff looked closely at the third one. "This ball's monogrammed. L.K."

"Yeah, probably Louis Kling. I'll see he gets it. All Mrs. Carleton's balls are initialed, too—J.T.C. We found two of them in her bag, still wrapped in tissue paper."

Jeff said, "You didn't find the ball she was playing with?"

"Not yet. We haven't had much time to do any real looking around in that thicket. I'm having the place roped off for a hundred yards around the spot the bodies were. I plan to have the boys go through it with a fine-comb."

"That's the idea," Jeff said. "With a fine-comb."

"I hope we find more than a bunch of golf balls." Hinkle heaved another of his sighs. "I wish we'd find a gun with the killer's fingerprints on it. I'd like that— that'd be nice, wouldn't it?"

"It would even be rather surprising," Jeff said. "Did you know Eddie Riorden?"

"Sure. Everybody knew Eddie. He was our high school football hero four or five years ago. Eddie must be about twenty-two now and as far as I know he never did a lick of work except enough to keep him in cigarette money. Caddying, pin boy— —that kind of stuff. Nice kid, though, just lazy. Well, I got to go over and talk to Mrs. Carleton's husband. I want to get that over with. If there's anything you can do for me, Troy, I'll let you know."

"Thanks," Jeff said.

Jeff and I walked back to the cottage that was teaching us never again to rent a cottage for the summer. Automatically, with our minds still in a thicket on a golf course, we started on our morning chores. I made the bed while Jeff put fresh adhesive tape on the screen door. Jeff tried to talk the hot-water heater into justifying its existence while I spray-gunned the joint. I was about to start my daily campaign against the ants in the icebox when the girl slammed into the house.

"I'm Fran Leslie," she said. "Where's your husband?"

"Jeff!" I yelled.

I had seen Fran Leslie around the club. She was a pretty girl, in a rather wild, excited way, who seemed continually to be in motion. I finally realized the reason for it. Fran considered herself too sophisticated for the younger set, but she found the older set a bit stuffy. So she spent most of her time shuttling between sets. This, however, seemed to be good for her figure. It was, in fact, developed far beyond her mind.

Impatiently, she said, "This is terribly important!"

I shouted for Jeff again. He came into the room, saw Fran Leslie inside our cottage, then looked at the screen door as if he were reproaching himself for having put adhesive tape in the wrong places.

"Hello," he said.

"Mr. Troy!" Fran said. "How much do you charge?"

"Different prices," Jeff said. "Three dollars for fixing a flat, five for taking down an old Christmas tree, six——"

"I mean for your services as a detective!"

"Is it you who needs a detective?" Jeff asked.

"Yes."

"Why?"

"Because I'm going to be arrested for killing Janet Carleton, that's why! You've got to save me, Mr. Troy. I didn't kill Janet—or that caddy, either; but everyone on Long Island has thought for years that some day I would—kill Janet, I mean."

"Sit down, Miss Leslie," Jeff suggested.

"Please, Mr. Troy!" Fran turned to me in exasperation. "I'm practically on my way to the electric chair, and the man asks me to sit down!"

"All right," Jeff said. "What's your motive?"

"Oh, I've got one—and a jury would just eat it up! I wouldn't stand a chance. Janet stole the man I love. I've been insanely jealous for ages."

"A fairly good motive," Jeff said unenthusiastically. "The man you love is Mr. Carleton?"

"Yes. Tom Carleton. Tom's always been my man, if you know what I mean. Then, four years ago, Janet came along—glamorous, exciting, beautiful Janet! You can see how much I hate her! She took Tom. He never looked at me again."

"Fran," Jeff said, "how old are you?"

"Seventeen. Why?"

"Then Janet took Tom Carleton away from you when you were thirteen."

"Yes! That's how ruthless she was! She knew Tom and I couldn't get married right away and——"

"I suppose," Jeff said, "that your parents insisted you finish grammar school first."

"I knew that I would mature quickly," Fran said. She threw back her shoulders to prove it, and she did prove it. Jeff modestly lowered his eyes. "Tom is only twelve years older than I am," she said, "and we have so much in common."

"What?"

"Well, for one thing——"

"Go on," Jeff said.

"Well, for one thing, we both belong to the Country Club."

"Oh," Jeff said "Frannie, could you see it in Tom's eyes that some day he would marry you?"

"He would have married me, he would have!" Fran cried. "And I've wanted to kill Janet for years! Everybody knows that! Mr. Troy, you've got to save me by finding the real murderer. I'll give you five hundred dollars!"

"Frannie, why don't you go to a movie or something?"

"If you won't take this case, you know what I'll do? I'll—"

"Stop," Jeff said. "Don't even tell me what you'll do. I'll take the case. I'll try to prove, Frannie, that you didn't commit two murders."

"Oh, thank you so much!"

"Good-by, Frannie," Jeff said.

She pouted. "Aren't you going to ask me about my alibi?"

"All right. Where were you at the time of the crime?"

"I was walking on the beach, alone."

"Did anybody see you?"

"Not a soul!" Frannie said happily. "I absolutely cannot prove that it wasn't me who committed those murders! I have no alibi."

"Good-by, Frannie," Jeff said sternly.

A little later I asked Jeff if he really meant to take Fran's five hundred dollars. He thought he might as well. She would probably just spend it on bubble gum. I told him I thought that he was underestimating a woman of seventeen. At seventeen a woman has all her faculties; that is, she's a woman. He said he agreed with me but, he said, let's not discuss this any further, let's go and see Mrs. Carleton's husband, Tom.

We found Tom Carleton sitting on the steps of the side porch of his big, year-round house. The fears we had that he might rather see us at some later time he quickly dispelled. He needed someone to talk with, someone, preferably, who was not a friend of the family paying a duty call. We filled his need admirably, he insisted.

He said, "Joe Hinkle told me about you. He's glad you're around. Shall we sit here on the steps, or would you rather—"

"This is fine," Jeff said.

We sat down with Carleton. He was lean and tall and very attractive in a strong, rugged way. The wrinkles of good humor and laughter stood out now in his pale, somber face like tiny, drained stream-beds. He was in complete control of himself. It would be he who would console his wife's friends, not they him.

"I might have prevented it," he said.

Jeff said, "Almost anybody can always figure out that they—"

"No," Tom said, "this is real. You see, I haven't played much golf this year—in the past month none at all. I just went sour on it. Yesterday Janet tried to talk me into playing a round with her before dinner. We used to do that all the time. But I said no, and I wouldn't let her talk me into it. To tell the truth, she got pretty sore about it, in her funny way. Humorous way, I mean. She made some remarks about me and my fishing and fish in general that were classics. Lately, you see, I'd rather fish than golf. So Janet went to the club alone. When she didn't come back for dinner I didn't think anything of it. She often stayed at the club, especially when she was a little sore at me. I went to bed about nine. To get to Montauk Point for fishing by five, I have to be on my way at four. So I slept in my study—as I always do when I'm getting up early and don't want to waken Janet when I roll out of bed. That's how I got out of the house this morning without knowing she wasn't at home. I'd left my car in front of the house; I took for granted that Janet's was in the garage. But what I started to say was ... if I'd played golf with her as she wanted me to ... but I see your point, Troy. It's no good—that kind of figuring."

"I don't suppose," Jeff said, "you've had any time to think about who might have killed your wife."

"Yes, I have. It doesn't take very many minutes to do a lot of thinking about a thing like that. Nobody could have wanted to kill Janet, no one had any reason to. Nobody had anything to gain in the way of money or anything. And as far as anyone hating her—well, Janet lived an ordinary, suburban life. You don't make enemies living like that. She ran the house, she played golf in the summer, bridge in the winter—she never did anything that would have made an enemy for her."

"What about Fran Leslie?"

Tom Carleton looked at Jeff and smiled wanly. "I think," he said, "that's a foolish question."

"So do I, but I had to know that you thought so, too."

"Frannie's been an embarrassment to me for years. I realize that you should take adolescents and their emotions seriously. But Frannie—there's nothing deep or psychological about her. She's a good, healthy extrovert. I spanked her when she was fourteen and if she hadn't enjoyed it so much, I would have kept on spanking her. No, Troy, nobody wanted to kill my wife."

"I think," Jeff said, "I know what you mean."

"Yes. I mean that someone must have been gunning for Eddie Riorden. And Janet was killed because she saw who murdered Eddie."

"Do you know where Eddie lived?"

"No. But the caddy master at the club would know."

"We'll ask him—and thanks."

•

Jamestown, Long Island, was as Colonial American as anything you saw on the way to Booton. There was a white church, a cannon in the square, a Town Hall beside the Super-Market. The Riorden house was on the edge of the town—a two story frame building, a yard without a lawn in front of it, a collection of shabby sheds and coops behind it. Eddie's sister answered Jeff's knock. She was a little younger than Eddie, a beautiful girl with shining black hair, dark eyes, an appealing mouth. There was no doubt she was Eddie's sister.

Jeff said, "We'd like to talk to you about Eddie—for just a moment."

"Are you from the police?" She looked at me. "Or a newspaper . . . or what?"

"We're working with the police," Jeff said.

"I suppose you want to know who Eddie ran around with . . . things like that?

"Yes."

"I'll have to tell you what I told the rest of them. We don't know. We hardly knew Eddie any more. He wasn't ever home, except to sleep. He just—well, drifted away from us lately. We didn't see him much, he never brought any of his friends home."

"Who were his friends?"

She shook her head. "I don't even know if there was anyone special. I—I don't like to say this, but it's true. Except for the country club in the summer, Eddie spent more time in Andrew's Bar than he did at home. I wish I could help you, but . . ."

"You have helped us," Jeff said.

Andrew's Bar took up half the ground floor of a tourist hotel that apparently had never lived up to its original owner's hopes. There were only three cars in the parking space meant for twenty or thirty. The bar was not filled with vacationists sopping up before-lunch cocktails; four male natives were spending dimes on beers.

When the bartender placed our beers before us, Jeff said, "My name's Troy, I—"

"Troy," the bartender said. He glanced down at his group of four customers. They all looked at Jeff. "Troy," the bartender said again. "I've heard about you. You're helping Joe Hinkle with the murders."

"Yes," Jeff said. "News travels fast around here."

"Yes, it does. A little place, Jamestown, but a nice place."

The tallest of the four beer drinkers said, "We've just been talking about it, the murder."

"I guess you all knew Eddie," Jeff said.

"He was in here every night," the shortest drinker said.

"He missed once a week," the third one said. "The night of the midget auto races."

"He came in then. Late, though," Shorty said.

The third one nodded. "After I went home, I guess."

"Well, more or less you could just about say," the bartender said, "that Eddie was in here every night." He turned to Jeff. "What's that got to do with the murder?"

"You've just been talking about the murder," Jeff said.

"Naturally," the bartender said.

"Eddie was a popular boy, wasn't he?"

"He was a sweet kid," Shorty said.

"A sweet kid," the third man said. "A great ball player, any kind of ball. He was going to go places if he ever got a break. He had everything to live for."

"Everybody liked Eddie, I guess," Jeff said.

A moment died away. Then, carefully, the bartender said, "Yeah, everybody liked Eddie. I can't think of a single exception to that rule."

For the first time the fourth man spoke up, and he spoke up angrily. "The hell with it!" he said. "I can think of somebody who didn't like Eddie!"

"Now, wait, Mel," the bartender said. "Take it easy."

"The hell with it!" Mel said. "Listen here, Troy. George Carey didn't like Eddie and everybody here knows it!"

"George Carey," Jeff said. "You mean the golf pro at the Country Club?"

"That's right. I've no idea what it was between Carey and Eddie, but——"

"Mel," the bartender said, "I'm not sure it's up to you to——"

"Eddie's dead, murdered! Listen, Troy, for the past month or so Carey used to come in here—to see Eddie. They'd go back there to the corner table and talk— no, not talk, argue! We never could hear what it was all about and Eddie would never tell us, but it wasn't good. They got pretty hot, the two of them, Eddie and Carey. Well, the other night was the blow-up. For a minute it looked like they were going to start swinging at each other. When Carey went out of here he looked just about mad enough to——"

"Now, take it easy, Mel," the bartender said.

"Mad enough," Jeff said, "to kill Eddie?"

"Yes, blast it! That's what I was going to say and I am saying it! Mad enough to kill Eddie! And Eddie was killed."

We had seen George Carey around the club, of course, but we had never said more than hello to each other. He was a genial, nice-looking fellow in his forties. When Jeff and I walked into his little office in the caddy house, he knew at once why we were calling on him. He wasn't the sort of person you had to handle with care, and Jeff went straight to the point.

"We've just come from Andrew's Bar," Jeff said. "We heard that you and Eddie Riorden nearly slugged it out a couple of nights ago. We didn't hear what it was you disagreed about—or maybe that isn't important."

Carey thought that over for a moment. "It is important," he said, "because I'm sure you're not going to find anyone else, anyone at all, who ever tangled with Eddie in the slightest degree."

"Everybody loved Eddie," Jeff said. "He hadn't an enemy in the world."

"That's true—literally."

"But the other night you were ready to take him apart. That could mean that Eddie had one enemy in the world."

"Yes," Carey said. "That's why it's important you understand why I was fighting with Eddie."

He opened a drawer of his desk; he found what he was looking for. He slid the letter out of its envelope and handed it to Jeff. Jeff held it so that I could see.

It was a short note, written without the aid of a secretary, on the stationery of Randall College, Randall, Ohio. It said: "Dear George; I've got everything set for your boy, Eddie Riorden. He'd better be as good as you say he is. In haste, Carl."

"That's Carl Moss," Carey said. "He coaches football at Randall."

"He got Eddie an athletic scholarship," Jeff said.

"Yes."

"But Eddie didn't want to go to college," Jeff said. "No matter how much you tried to persuade him, he wouldn't agree to go."

"That's it," Carey said. "I've known Eddie since he was caddying up here in his bare feet. He was quite a kid. He was the best high school athlete I've ever seen. For the last three years I've been after him to go to college. But he was tired of school, he said. Actually, he was lazy. I'm afraid Eddie was well on his way to being a bum. I decided finally to go ahead and get him a scholarship at my old school ... I though maybe that would turn the trick. But it didn't. Eddie'd been slopping around for so long that his ambition was all gone. He used to avoid me here at the club. The only place I could corner him was at that bar. I talked myself hoarse to him, and the other night I lost my temper. It made me sore to see a boy like Eddie turning into a bum."

"But you still liked him," Jeff said.

"How could I help it? How could anybody not like Eddie?"

"Well," Jeff said, "I guess that's that."

"Even if it isn't," Carey said, "I'll have to leave you now. Joe Hinkle seems to be holding a little meeting that I'm invited to."

"We'll go with you," Jeff said.

Hinkle was holding his meeting in the same room where we had seen him that morning. The meeting was a small, intimate affair. Carey, Jeff, and I joined Hinkle, Fran Leslie, Tom Carleton, and the club's woman champ, Arlene Miller. The meeting didn't look as though it had started; Joe Hinkle didn't look as though he wanted to start it. He was a morose, discouraged man.

"Troy," he said, "tell me something."

"Sure," Jeff said.

"Tell me who killed them. So we can all go home."

"I know how you feel," Jeff said. "Did you find anything more in the thicket?"

"We found a lot. The two halves of a broken niblick, some empty bottles—mostly half-pints—a couple of old tin cans, a dozen or so trees, a watch that Mac Small lost seven years ago, a fifty-cent piece, and nine golf balls."

"Did you find Mrs. Carleton's ball?"

"Not yet. We had to knock off because it was getting dark in the thicket. But frankly, I think we found everything there is in it."

"But of course," Jeff said, "you'll look some more tomorrow."

"Of course. I'm nothing else, but I'm thorough."

"Mr. Carleton," Jeff said, "is there any chance that Mrs. Carleton wouldn't have been playing with one of her own balls?"

Arlene Miller gave a short laugh. She said, "Janet Carleton would no more think of using any ball but those special ones of hers than she would think of using someone else's clubs. Janet was a real golfer, not a Sunday player."

"I see," Jeff said. He turned back to Hinkle. "Have you found anyone who saw Mrs. Carleton playing her first nine holes?"

"Her last nine holes," Arlene Miller said.

Hinkle cleared his throat. "I been all through that, Troy. Mr. Carleton says that, considering the time his wife left home, she would have been lucky to get much more than nine holes played before dark. It seems like she was the last one to start around. Nobody seen her park her car or tee off."

"That isn't unusual," Carey said. "At that time of day everybody at the club is either in the dining room or the bar. There's as much drinking as golf around this place, you all know that."

"Anyway," Hinkle said, "nobody saw her. She must have walked straight from her car to the first tee, or whatever you call it. Eddie must have met her there. He always caddied for her. He was probably waiting for her."

"Somebody," Jeff said, "the last person who left the club last night must have noticed Mrs. Carleton's car was still here. Why didn't they worry about her?"

"That was Al Frost," Hinkle said. "He admits seeing the car. He also admits that after an evening at the bar here he never worries or wonders about anything. Nice fellow though, Al."

"Well," Jeff said, "I won't hold up your meeting any longer."

"I wish you'd stay, Troy."

"No, I couldn't add anything to the proceedings. Call me tomorrow, will you, if you find Mrs. Carleton's ball?"

"Why don't you come and help us?"

"I will," Jeff said.

It was beginning to grow dark when Jeff and I left our cottage that night. It was very dark when we walked through the empty parking lot of the locked-up, deserted clubhouse. I followed Jeff through the gap in the hedge, then I stopped.

"Darling," I said, "I won't go another step until you tell me where we're going and why."

"Haila, if I told you, you wouldn't go with me. Come on now, quietly."

I went on quietly. We walked across the start of the fairway of the first hole. We went another fifty yards and we were crossing the ninth hole's fairway. Then, in another minute or two, we were groping our way into the thicket. I could touch Jeff, but I couldn't see him. I held on to his jacket and shuffled blindly forward. Jeff stopped and sat down; he pulled me down beside him. He put his arm around me. But he didn't kiss me. I still didn't know what we were doing in this hell-black hole.

"May I smoke?" I whispered.

"No. From now on don't even breathe unless it's absolutely necessary."

We sat there for so long that I began to be convinced that I had slept through a day and was not sitting through my second night. I was uncomfortable, cold. I was something else. I found Jeff's ear and whispered into it.

"I'm scared," I said.

"Naturally," Jeff whispered back.

That reassurance did me a lot of good. I wasn't cold any longer, or uncomfortable—I was just frightened. Jeff's hand touched my wrist and tightened on it. I stopped breathing. I had heard it, too.

Through the thicket something was moving toward us. It might have been slithering along on its stomach, it might have been edging along on two feet, or more——but it was coming toward us. Now a piece of foliage brushed my face as it moved back in place. The shuffling sound came closer, and then stopped.

I felt Jeff move. I heard the click of his flashlight and saw a beam of light shoot through the blackness. For a moment it searched wildly, then it hit and held. I saw a man's outstretched arm, his had six inches above the ground. Clutched in the hand was a golf ball.

Jeff pulled the light up the man's arm until it flashed full in his face. Tom Carleton straightened up. I saw his arm back out of the ray of light, then swing forward through it. . . .

When people regain consciousness, they usually start life again by asking a silly question. My question didn't seem silly to me at the time, but that's exactly what it turned out to be. I looked at Jeff and Joe Hinkle for a moment before I spoke.

I said, "How could Tom Carleton find his wife's golf ball in the dark like that?"

"He didn't find it," Jeff said. "He was losing it."

"Oh," I said. "Where am I?"

"In our cottage," Jeff said.

"Where is Tom Carleton?"

"In my jail," Joe Hinkle said. "Are you all right, Mrs. Troy? He hit you with a golf ball, you know."

"Yes, I know, Mr. Hinkle. But I'm fine. That's just what I needed."

"Well, then, Troy——"

"Sure, Joe, listen. You and your boys couldn't find that ball—because there was no ball. There was no ball because Mrs. Carleton wasn't playing golf. Eddie Riorden was not her caddy—he was her lover.

"Eddie and Mrs. Carleton . . ."

"That thicket was their rendezvous. If anyone had wandered into it unexpectedly, Eddie would have gone though the motions of caddying for a lady with a bad slice. It was a nice setup while it lasted. And it lasted until Tom Carleton got wise."

"So I was wrong," Joe said, "when I figured that one of them got killed because he saw the other one murdered."

"Everybody liked Mrs. Carleton," Jeff said. "Everybody loved Eddie. Nobody had a reason to kill either of them. But maybe, I thought, somebody had a reason to kill *both* of them. And then, when you couldn't find the ball Janet Carleton should have been playing with . . ."

"Yeah," Joe said. "I guess that proved it to you. And when Tom heard you talking about the ball this afternoon, he figured he'd better get one there in a hurry."

"Oh, now I see," I said. "He didn't find that ball. He was putting it there."

"That's right. I'm sorry he hit you with it, Haila."

"Oh, I don't mind. That's a hazard of the game, getting hit. But I don't think it was very sporting the way he did it."

"What, darling?"

"It's a rule, Jeff! You're supposed to yell 'Fore!'"

Margery Allingham

(1904–1966)

The Golden Age of mystery fiction saw the creation of many an English gentleman-sleuth, and a good proportion of them were imbued with colorful eccentricities, rather than any genuine depth of characterization. A reading of Margery Allingham's early Albert Campion novels (*The Crime at Black Dudley*, 1929; *Death of a Ghost*, 1934) might convey the false impression that this is true of her series detective. In these books, the protagonist appears as a two-dimensional figure with vague connections to the British royal family, an action-adventurer and dabbler in mysteries—or, as critic H. R. F. Keating states, "a cleverly updated version of Baroness Orczy's Scarlet Pimpernel, the indolent man-about-town." Allingham, a stylish writer with outstanding powers of description, soon tired of the convention, and Campion underwent the first of two transformations—to a man who was little more than a camera observing the world around him, after the fashion of Ross Macdonald's Lew Archer.

It can be argued that Campion is the perfect character to act as uninvolved observer: His appearance and manner are unremarkable and bland. And had it not been for World War II and its effect on Allingham, he may very well have remained on the emotional sidelines. But the war affected Allingham strongly, and thus Campion changed, even in his physical description: "There were new lines on his over-thin face and with their appearance some of his old misleading vacancy of expression had vanished." Allingham's novels took on a greater sense of realism; no longer were they tales of bloodless murders, romance, and genteel puzzles, but depictions of love, death, and crime as it actually happens. In such titles as *The Tiger in the Smoke* (1952), *The Beckoning Lady* (1955), and *Hide My Eyes* (1958), Allingham employed her full talents to comment on the world and human relationships.

Albert Campion appeared in a number of short stories, collected in *Mr. Campion and Others* (1939) and *The Case Book of Mr. Campion* (1947). In "One Morning They'll Hang Him," we see him paired with Detective Inspector Kenny of the Criminal Investigation Department. Allingham once wrote of the piece that it was an attempt to "combine a human story with careful detection," and called Kenny "a less sympathetic police officer than I like to write about in the ordinary way." The resultant interplay between the two leads them to a startling solution to what appears an open-and-shut case.

ONE MORNING THEY'LL HANG HIM

ALBERT CAMPION AND DETECTIVE INSPECTOR KENNY
ENGLAND
1950

I t was typical of Detective Inspector Kenny, at that time D.D.I. of the L. Division, that, having forced himself to ask a favor, he should set about it with the worst grace possible. When at last he took the plunge, he heaved his two hundred pounds off Mr. Campion's fireside couch and set down his empty glass with a clatter.

"I don't know if I needed that at three in the afternoon," he said ungratefully, his small blue eyes baleful, "but I've been up since two this morning dealing with women, tears, minor miracles and this perishing rain." He rubbed his broad face, and presented it scarlet and exasperated at Mr. Campion's back. "If there's one thing that makes me savage it's futility!" he added.

Mr. Albert Campion, who had been staring idly out of the window watching the rain on the roofs, did not glance around. He was still the lean, somewhat ineffectual-looking man to whom the Special Branch had turned so often in the last twenty years. His very fair hair had bleached into whiteness and a few lines had appeared round the pale eyes which were still, as always, covered by large horn-rimmed spectacles, but otherwise he looked much as Kenny first remembered him——"Friendly and a little simple—the old snake!"

"So there's futility in Barraclough Road too, is there?" Campion's light voice sounded polite rather than curious.

Kenny drew a sharp breath of annoyance.

"The Commission has 'phoned you? He suggested I should look you up. It's not a great matter—just one of those stupid little snags which has some perfectly obvious explanation. Once it's settled, the whole case is open-and-shut. As it is, we can't keep the man at the station indefinitely."

Mr. Campion picked up the early edition of the evening paper from his desk.

"This is all I know," he said holding it out, "Mr. Oates didn't 'phone. There you are, in the Stop Press, *Rich Widow shot in Barraclough Road West. Nephew at police station helping investigation.* What's the difficulty? His help is not altogether whole hearted, perhaps?"

To his surprise an expression remarkably like regret flickered round Kenny's narrow lips.

"Ruddy young fool," he said, and sat down abruptly. "I tell you, Mr. Campion, this thing is in the bag. It's just one of those ordinary, rather depression little stories which most murder cases are. There's practically no mystery, no chase—nothing but a wretched little tragedy. As soon as you've spotted what I've missed, I shall charge this chap and he'll go before the magistrates and be committed for trial. His counsel will plead insanity and the jury won't have it. The Judge will sentence him, he'll appeal, their Lordships will dismiss it. The Home Secretary will sign the warrant and one morning they'll take him out and they'll hang him." He sighed. "All for nothing," he said. "All for nothing at all. It'll probably be raining just like it is now," he added inconsequentially.

Mr. Campion's eyes grew puzzled. He knew Kenny for a conscientious officer, and, some said, a hard man. This philosophic strain was unlike him.

"Taken a fancy to him?" he inquired.

"Who? I certainly haven't." The Inspector was grim. "I've got no sympathy for youngsters who shoot up their relatives however selfish the old bottoms may be. No, he's killed her and he must take what's coming to him, but it's hard on—well, on some people. Me, for one." He took out a large old-fashioned notebook and folded it carefully in half. "I stick to one of these," he remarked virtuously, "None of your backs of envelopes for me. My record is kept as neatly as when I was first on the beat, and it can be handed across the court whenever a know-all counsel asks to see it." He paused. "I sound like an advertisement, don't I? Well, Mr. Campion, since I'm here, just give me your mind to this, if you will. I don't suppose it'll present any difficulty to you."

"One never knows," murmured Mr. Campion idiotically. "Start with the victim."

Kenny returned to his notebook.

"Mrs. Mary Alice Cibber, aged about seventy or maybe a bit less. She had heart trouble which made her look frail, and, of course, I didn't see her until she was dead. She had a nice house in Barraclough Road, a good deal too big for her, left her by her husband who died ten years ago. Since then she's been alone except for a maid who cleared off in the war and now for another old party who calls herself a companion. *She* looks older still, poor old girl, but you can see she's been kept well under—" he put his thumb down expressively—"by Mrs. C. who appears to have been a dictator in her small way. She was the sort of woman who lived for two chairs and a salad bowl."

"I beg your pardon?"

"Antiques." He was mildly contemptuous. "The house is crammed with them, all three floors and the attic, everything kept as if it was brand-new. The old companion says she loved it more than anything on earth. Of course she hadn't much else *to* love, not a relation in the world except the nephew—"

"Whose future you see so clearly?"

"The man who shot her," the Inspector agreed. "He's a big nervy lad, name of Woodruff, the son of the old lady's brother. His mother, father, and two young sisters all got theirs in the blitz on Portsmouth. Whole family wiped out."

"I see." Campion began to catch some of Kenny's depression. "Where was he when that happened?"

"In the Western Desert." The D.D.I.'s protuberant eyes were dark with irritation. "I told you this was just an ordinary miserable slice of life. It goes on the same way. This boy, Richard Woodruff—he's only twenty-eight now—did very well in the war. He was in the landings in Sicily and went through the fighting in Italy where he got the M.C. and was promoted major. Then he copped in for the breakthrough in France and just before the finish he became a casualty. A bridge blew up with him on it—or something of the sort, my informant didn't know exactly—and he seems to have become what the boys call 'bomb happy.' It used to be 'shell shock' in my day. As far as I can gather, he always had been quick-tempered, but this sent him over the edge. He sounds to me as if he wasn't sane for a while. That may help him in his defense, of course."

"Yes." Campion sounded depressed. "Where's he been since then?"

"On a farm mostly. He was training to be an architect before the war but the motherly old army knew what was best for him and when he came out of the hospital they bunged him down to Dorset. He's just got away. Some wartime buddy got him a job in an architect's office under the old pals' act and he was all set to take it up." He paused and his narrow mouth, which was not entirely insensitive, twisted bitterly. "Ought to have started Monday," he said.

"Oh dear," murmured Mr. Campion inadequately. "Why did he shoot his aunt? Pure bad temper?"

Kenny shook his head.

"He had a reason. I mean one can see why he was angry. He hadn't anywhere to live, you see. As you know London is crowded, and rents are fantastic. He and his wife paying through the nose for a cupboard of a bed-sitting room off the Edgeware Road."

"His wife?" The lean man in the horn rims was interested. "Where did she come from? You're keeping her very quiet."

To Campion's surprise the Inspector did not speak at once. Instead he grunted, and there was regret, and surprise at it, in his little smile. "I believe I would if I could," he said sincerely. "He found her on the farm. They've been married six weeks. I don't know if you've ever seen love, Mr. Campion? It's very rare—the kind I mean." He put out his hands deprecatingly. "It seems to crop up—when it does—among the most unexpected people, and when you do see it, well, it's very impressive." He succeeded in looking thoroughly ashamed of himself. "I shouldn't call myself a sentimental man," he said.

"No." Campion was reassuring. "You got his war history from her, I suppose?"

"I had to but we're confirming it. He's as shut as a watch—or a hand grenade. 'Yes' and 'No' and 'I did not shoot her'—that's about all his contribution amounted to, and he's had a few hours of expert treatment. The girl is quite different. She's down there too. Won't leave. We put her in the waiting room finally. She's not difficult—just sits there."

"Does she know anything about it?"

"No." Kenny was quite definite. "She's nothing to look at," he went on presently, as if he felt the point should be made. "She's just an ordinary nice little country girl, a bit too thin and a bit too brown, natural hair and inexpert make-up, and yet with this—this blazing radiant steadfastness about her!" He checked himself. "Well, she's fond of him," he amended.

"Believes he's God," Campion suggested.

Kenny shook his head. "She doesn't care if he isn't," he said sadly. "Well, Mr. Campion, some weeks ago these two approached Mrs. Cibber about letting them have a room or two at the top of the house. That must have been the girl's idea; she's just the type to have old-fashioned notions about blood being thicker than water. She made the boy write. The old lady ignored the question but asked them both to an evening meal last night. The invitation was sent a fortnight ago, so you can see there was no eager bless-you-my-children about it."

"Any reason for the delay?"

"Only that she had to have notice if she were giving a party. The old companion explained that to me. There was the silver to get out and clean, and the best china to be washed, and so on. Oh, there was nothing simple and homely about that household!" He sounded personally affronted. "When they got there, of course there was a blazing row."

"Hard words or flying crockery?"

Kenny hesitated. "In a way, both," he said slowly. "It seems to have been a funny sort of flare-up. I had two accounts of it—one from the girl and one from the companion. I think they are both trying to be truthful but they both seem to have been completely foxed by it. They both agree that Mrs. Cibber began it. She waited until there were three oranges and a hundredweight of priceless early Worcester dessert service on the table, and then let fly. Her theme seems to have been the impudence of Youth in casting its eye on its inheritance before Age was in its grave, and so on and so on. She then made it quite clear that they hadn't a solitary hope of getting what they wanted, and conveyed that she did not care if they slept in the street so long as her precious furniture was safely housed. There's no doubt about it that she was very aggravating and unfair."

"Unfair?"

"Ungenerous. After all she knew the man quite well. He used to go and stay with her by himself when he was a little boy." Kenny returned to his notes. "Woodruff then lost his temper in his own way which, if the exhibition he gave in the early hours of this morning is typical, is impressive. He goes white instead of red, says practically nothing, but looks as if he's about to 'incandesce'—if I make myself plain."

"Entirely." Mr. Campion was deeply interested. This new and human Kenny was an experience. "I take it he then fished out a gun and shot her?"

"Lord, no! If he had, he'd have a chance at least of Broadmoor. No. He just got up and asked her if she had any of his things, because if so he'd take them and not inconvenience her with them any longer. It appears that when he was in the hospital some of his gear had been sent to her, as his next of kin. She said yes, she had, and it was waiting for him in the boot cupboard. The old companion, Miss Smith, was sent trotting out to fetch it and came staggering in with an old officer's hold-all, bursted at the sides and filthy. Mrs. Cibber told her nephew to open it and see if she'd robbed him, and he did as he was told. Of course, one of the first things he saw among the ragged bush shirts and old photographs was a revolver and a clip of ammunition." He paused and shook his head. "Don't ask me how it got there. You know what hospitals were like in the war. Mrs. Cibber went on taunting the man in her own peculiar way, and he stood there examining the gun and presently loading it, almost absently. You can see the scene?"

Campion could. The pleasant, perhaps slightly overcrowded room was vivid in his mind, and he saw the gentle light on the china and the proud, bitter face of the woman.

"After that," said Kenny, "the tale gets more peculiar, although both accounts agree. It was Mrs. C. Who laughed and said, 'I suppose you think I ought to be shot?' Woodruff did not answer but he dropped the gun in his side pocket. Then he packed up the hold-all and said, 'Good-bye.'" He hesitated. "Both statements say that he then said something about *the sun having gone down.* I don't know what that meant, or if both women mistook him. Anyway, there's nothing to it. He had no explanation to offer. Says he doesn't remember saying it. However, after that he suddenly picked up one of his aunt's beloved china fruit bowls and simply dropped it on the floor. It fell on a rug, as it happened, and did not break, but old Mrs. Cibber nearly passed out, the companion screamed, and the girl hurried him off home."

"With the gun?"

"With the gun." Kenny shrugged his heavy shoulders. "As soon as the girl heard that Mrs. Cibber had been shot, she jumped up with a tale that he had *not* taken it. She said she'd sneaked it out of his pocket and put it on the window sill. The lamest story you ever heard! She's game and she's ready to say absolutely anything, but she won't save him, poor kid. He was seen in the district at midnight."

Mr. Campion put a hand through his sleek hair. "Aah. That rather tears it."

"Oh, it does. There's no question that he did it. It hardly arises. What happened was this. The young folk got back to their bed-sitting room about ten to nine. Neither of them will admit it, but it's obvious that Woodruff was in one of those boiling but sulky rages which made him unfit for human society. The girl left him alone—I should say she has a gift for handling him—and she says she went to bed while he sat up writing letters. Quite late, she can't or won't say when, he went out to the post. He won't say anything. We may or may not break him down, he's a queer chap. However, we have a witness who saw him somewhere about midnight at the Kilburn end of Barraclough Road. Woodruff stopped him and asked if the last eastbound 'bus had gone. Neither of them had a watch, but the witness is prepared to swear it was just after midnight—which is important because the shot was fired at two minutes before twelve. We've got that time fixed."

Mr. Campion, who had been taking notes, looked up in mild astonishment.

"You got that witness very promptly," he remarked. "Why did he come forward?"

"He was a plainclothesman off duty," said Kenny calmly. "One of the local men who had been out to a reunion dinner. He wasn't right but he had decided to walk home before his wife saw him. I don't know why he hadn't a watch"—Kenny frowned at this defect—"anyway, he hadn't, or it wasn't going. But he was alert enough to notice Woodruff. He's a distinctive chap you know. Very tall and dark, and his manner was so nervy and excitable that the dick thought it worth reporting."

Campion's teeth appeared in a brief smile.

"In fact, he recognized him at once as a man who looked as though he'd done a murder?"

"No." The Inspector remained unruffled. "No, he said he looked like a chap who had just got something off his mind and was pleased with himself."

"I see. And meanwhile the shot was fired at two minutes to twelve."

"That's certain." Kenny brightened and became businesslike. "The man next door heard it and looked at his watch. We've got his statement and the old lady's companion. Everyone else in the street is being questioned. But nothing has come in yet. It was a cold wet night and most people had their windows shut; besides, the room where the murder took place was heavily curtained. So far, these two are the only people who seem to have heard anything at all. The man next door woke up and nudged his wife who had slept through it. But then he may have dozed again, for the next thing he remembers is hearing screams for help. By the time he got to the window, the companion was out in the street in her dressing gown, wedged in between the lamp post and the mail box, screeching her little gray head off. The rain was coming down in sheets."

"When exactly was this?"

"Almost immediately after the shot, according to the companion. She had been in bed for some hours and had slept. Her room is on the second floor, at the back. Mrs. Cibber had not come up with her but had settled down at her bureau in the drawing-room, as she often did in the evening. Mrs. C. was still very upset by the scene at the meal, and did not want to talk. Miss Smith says she woke up and thought she heard the front door open. She won't swear to this, and at any rate she thought nothing of it, for Mrs. Cibber often slipped out to the mail box with letters before coming to bed. Exactly how long it was after she woke that she heard the shot she does not know, but it brought her scrambling out of bed. She agrees she might have been a minute or two finding her slippers and a wrapper, but she certainly came down right away. She says she found the street door open, letting in the rain, and the drawing-room door, which is next to it, wide open as well, and the lights in there full on." He referred to his notes and began to read out loud. "'I smelled burning'"—she means cordite—"'and I glanced across the room to see poor Mrs. Cibber on the floor with a dreadful hole in her forehead. I was too frightened to go near her, so I ran out of the house shouting "Murder! Thieves!"'"

"That's nice and old-fashioned. Did she see anybody?"

"She says not, and I believe her. She was directly under the only lamp post for fifty yards and it certainly was raining hard."

Mr. Campion appeared satisfied but unhappy. When he spoke his voice was very gentle.

"Do I understand that your case is that Woodruff came back, tapped on the front door, and was admitted by his aunt? After some conversation, which must have taken place in lowered tones since the companion upstairs did not hear it, he shot her and ran away, leaving all the doors open?"

"Substantially, yes. Although he may have shot her as soon as he saw her."

"In that case she'd have been found dead in the hall."

Kenny blinked. "Yes, I suppose she would. Still, they couldn't have talked much."

"Why?"

The Inspector made a gesture of distaste. "This is the bit which gets under my skin," he said. "They could hardly have spoken long—*because she'd forgiven him.* She had written to her solicitor—the finished letter was on her writing pad ready for the post. She'd written to say she was thinking of making the upper part of her house into a home for her nephew, and asked if there was a clause in her lease to prevent it. She also said she wanted the work done quickly, as she had taken a fancy to her new niece and hoped in time there might be children. It's pathetic, isn't it?" His eyes were wretched. "That's what I meant by futility. She'd forgiven him, see? She wasn't a mean old harridan, she was just quick-tempered. I told you this isn't a mystery tale, this is ordinary sordid life."

Mr. Campion looked away.

"Tragic," he said. "Yes. A horrid thing. What do you want me to do?"

Kenny sighed. "Find the gun," he murmured.

The lean man whistled.

"You'll certainly need that if you're to be sure of a conviction. How did you lose it?"

"He's ditched it somewhere. He didn't get rid of it in Barraclough Road because the houses come right down to the street, and our chaps were searching for it within half an hour. At the end of the road he caught the last 'bus, which ought to come along at midnight but was a bit late last night, I'm morally certain. These drivers make up time on the straight stretch by the park; it's more than their jobs are worth, so you never get them to admit it. Anyhow, he didn't leave the gun on the 'bus, and it's not in the house where his room is. It's not in the old lady's house at 81 Barraclough Road because I've been over the house myself." He peered at the taller man hopefully. "Where would you hide a gun in this city at night, if you were all that way from the river? It's not so easy, is it? If it had been anywhere obvious it would have turned up by now."

"He may have given it to someone."

"And risked blackmail?" Kenny laughed. "He's not as dumb as that. You'll have to see him. He says he never had it—but that's only natural. Yet where did he put it, Mr. Campion? It's only a little point but, as you say, it's got to be solved."

Campion grimaced.

"Anywhere, Kenny. Absolutely anywhere. In a drain—"

"They're narrow gratings in Barraclough Road."

"In a sandbin or a static water tank—"

"There aren't any in that district."

"He threw it down in the street and someone, who felt he'd rather like to have a gun, picked it up. Your area isn't peopled solely with the law-abiding, you know." Kenny became more serious. "That's the real likelihood," he admitted gloomily. "But all the same, I don't believe he's the type to throw away a gun casually. He's too intelligent, too cautious. Do you know how this war has made some men cautious even when they're being the most reckless? He's one of those. He's hidden it. Where? Mr. Oates said you'd know if anyone did."

Campion ignored this blatant flattery. He stood staring absently out of the window for so long that the Inspector was tempted to nudge him, and when at last he spoke, his question did not sound promising.

"How often did he stay with his aunt when he was a child?"

"Quite a bit, I think, but there's no kid's hiding-place there that only he could have known, if that's what you're after." Kenny could hardly conceal his disappointment. "It's not that kind of house. Besides, he hadn't the time. He got back about twenty past twelve: a woman in the house confirms it—she met him on the stairs. He was certainly spark out when we got there at a quarter after four this morning. They were both sleeping like kids when I first saw them. She had one skinny brown arm around his neck. He just woke up in a rage, and she was more astounded than frightened. I swear—"

Mr. Campion had ceased to listen.

"Without the gun the only real evidence you've got is the plainclothesman's story of meeting him," he said. "And even you admit that gallant officer was walking for his health after a party. Imagine a good defense lawyer enlarging on that point."

"I have," the Inspector agreed, dryly. "That's why I'm here. You must find the gun for us, sir. Can I fetch you a raincoat? Or," he added, a faintly smug expression flickering over his broad face, "will you just sit in your armchair and do it from there?"

To his annoyance his elegant host appeared to consider the question.

"No, perhaps I'd better come with you," he said at last. "We'll go to Barraclough Road first, if you don't mind. And if I might make a suggestion, I should send Woodruff and his wife back to their lodgings—suitably escorted, of course. If the young man was going to crack, I think he would have done so by now, and the gun, wherever it is, can hardly be at the police station."

Kenny considered. "He may give himself away and lead us to it." He agreed although without enthusiasm. "I'll telephone. Then we'll go anywhere you say, but as I told you I've been over the Barraclough Road house myself and if there's anything there it's high time I retired."

Mr. Campion merely looked foolish, and the Inspector sighed and let him have his way.

He came back from the telephone smiling wryly.

"That's settled," he announced. "He's been behaving like a good soldier interrogated by the enemy, silly young fool—after all, we're only trying to hang him! The girl has been asking for him to be fed, and reporters are crawling up the walls. Our boys won't be sorry to get rid of them for a bit. They'll be looked after. We shan't lose 'em. Now, if you've set your heart on the scene of the crime, Mr. Campion, we'll go."

In the taxi he advanced a little idea.

"I was thinking of that remark he is alleged to have made," he said, not without shame. "You don't think that it could have been 'Your sun has gone down,' and that we could construe it as a threat within meaning of the act?"

Campion regarded him owlishly.

"We could, but I don't think we will. That's the most enlightening part of the whole story, don't you think?"

If Inspector Kenny agreed, he did not say so, and they drove to the top of Barraclough Road in silence. There Campion insisted on stopping at the first house next to the main thoroughfare. The building had traded on its proximity to the shopping center and had been converted into a dispensing chemist's. Campion was inside for several minutes, leaving Kenny in the cab. When he came out he offered no explanation other than to observe fatuously that they had a "nice time" and settled back without troubling to look out at the early Victorian stucco three-story houses which lined the broad road.

A man on duty outside, and a handful of idlers gaping apathetically at the drawn blinds, distinguished 81 Barraclough Road. Kenny rang the bell and the door was opened after a pause by a flurried old lady with a duster in her hand.

"Oh, it's you, Inspector," she said hastily. "I'm afraid you've found me in a muddle. I've been trying to tidy up a little. *She* couldn't have born the place left dirty after everyone had been trampling over it. Yet I don't mean to say that you weren't all very careful."

She led them into a spotless dining-room which glowed with old mahogany and limpid silver, and the wan afternoon light showed them her reddened eyes and worn navy-blue housedress. She was a timid-looking person, not quite so old as Kenny had suggested, with very neat gray hair and a skin which had never known cosmetics. Her expression was closed and secret with long submission, and her shoulder blades stuck out a little under the cloth of her dress. Her hands still trembled slightly from the shock of the evening before.

Kenny introduced Campion. "We shan't be long, Miss Smith," he said cheerfully. "Just going to have another look around. We shan't make a mess."

Campion smiled at her reassuringly. "It's difficult to get help these days?" he suggested pleasantly.

"Oh, it is," she said earnestly. "And Mrs. Cibber wouldn't trust just anyone with her treasures. They are so very good." Her eyes filled with tears. "She was so fond of them."

"I daresay she was. That's a beautiful piece, for instance." Campion glanced with expert interest at the serpentine sideboard with its genuine handles and toilet cupboard.

"Beautiful," echoed Miss Smith dutifully. "And the chairs, you see?"

"I do." He eyed the Trafalgar set with the cherry-leather seats. "Is this where the quarrel took place?"

She nodded and trembled afresh. "Yes. I——I shall never forget it, never."

"Was Mrs. Cibber often bad-tempered?"

The woman hesitated, and her firm small mouth moved without words.

"Was she?"

She shot a swift unhappy glance at him.

"She was quick," she said. "Yes I think I ought to say she was quick. Now, would you like to see the rest of the house or——?"

Campion glanced at his watch and compared it with the Tompion bracket clock on the mantelshelf.

"I think we've just time," he said, idiotically. "Upstairs first, Inspector."

The next thirty-five minutes reduced Kenny to a state of jitters rare to him. After watching Campion with breathless interest for the first five, it slowly dawned on him that the expert had forgotten the crime in his delight at discovering a treasure-trove. Even Miss Smith, who betrayed a certain proprietorial pride, flagged before Campion's insatiable interest. Once or twice she hinted that perhaps they ought to go down, but he would not hear of it. By the time they had exhausted the third floor and were on the steps to the attic, she became almost firm. There was really nothing there but some early Georgian children's toys, she said.

"But I must just see the toys. I've got a 'thing' on toys, Kenny." Campion sounded ecstatic. "Just a minute——"

A vigorous tattoo on the front door interrupted him and Miss Smith, whose nerves were suffering, emitted a little squeak.

"Oh, dear. Somebody at the door. I must go down."

"No, no." Campion was uncharacteristically effusive. "I'll see who it is and come back. I shan't be a moment."

He flung himself downstairs with boyish enthusiasm, Miss Smith behind him, and Kenny, seeing escape at last, following as quickly as the narrow stairs would permit.

They reached the hall just in time to see him closing the door. "Only the post," he said, holding out a package. "Your library book, Miss Smith."

"Oh, yes," she came forward, hand outstretched. "I was expecting that."

"I rather thought you were." His voice was very soft and suddenly menacing. He held the cardboard book box high over his head with one hand, and with the other released the flap which closed it. The soft gleam of metal appeared in the light from the transom, and a service revolver crashed heavily to the parquet floor.

For a long minute there was utter silence. Even Kenny was too thunderstruck to swear.

Miss Smith appeared frozen in mid-air, her hands clawing at the box.

Then, most dreadfully, she began to scream. . . .

A little over an hour later Kenny sat on a Trafalgar chair in a room which seemed to quiver and shudder with terrible sound. He was pale and tired-looking. His shirt was torn and there were three livid nail scratches down his face.

"God," he said, breathing hard. "God, can you beat that?"

Mr. Campion sat on the priceless table and scratched his ear.

"It was a bit more than I bargained for," he murmured. "It didn't occur to me that she'd become violent. I'm afraid they may be having trouble in the van. Sorry, I ought to have thought of it."

The C.I.D. man grunted. "Seems to me you thought of plenty," he muttered. "It came as a shock to me—I don't mind admitting it since I can't very well help it. When did it come to you? From the start?"

"Oh, Lord, no." Campion sounded apologetic. "It was that remark of Woodruff's you quoted about the sun going down. That's what set me on the train of thought. Weren't you ever warned as a kid, Kenny, and by an aunt perhaps, never to let the sun go down on your wrath?"

"I've heard it, of course. What do you mean? It was a sort of saying between them?"

"I wondered if it was. They knew each other well when he was a child, and they were both quick-tempered people. It seemed to me that he was reminding her that the sun *had* gone down, and he showed her he could have smashed her precious bowl if he had liked. It would have broken, you know, if he hadn't taken care it shouldn't. I wondered if, like many quick-tempered people, they got sorry just as quickly. Didn't you think it odd, Kenny, that directly after the row they should *both* have settled down to write letters?"

The detective stared at him.

"She wrote to her solicitor," he began slowly. "And he——? Good Lord! You think he wrote to her to say he was sorry?"

"Almost certainly, but we shall never find his letter. That's in the kitchen stove by now. He came back to deliver it, pushed it through the door, and hurried off looking just as your plainclothesman said, as if he'd got something off his chest. Then he could sleep. The sun had not gone down on his wrath." He slid off the table and stood up. "The vital point is, of course, that *Mrs. Cibber knew he would.* She sat up waiting for it."

Kenny sucked in his breath.

"And Miss Smith knew?"

"Of course, she knew. Mrs. Cibber hadn't the kind of temperament one can keep a secret. Miss Smith knew from the moment that Mrs. Cibber received the initial letter that the nephew would get his way in the end—*unless she could stop it somehow!* She was the one with the bee in her bonnet about the furniture. I realized that as soon as you said the whole house was kept like a bandbox. No woman with a weak heart can keep a three-story house like a palace, or compel another to do it—unless the other wants to. Miss Smith was the one with the mania. Who was to get the house if the nephew died in the war? Mrs. Cibber must have made some provision."

Kenny rubbed his head with both hands. "I knew!" he exploded. "The lawyer's clerk told me this morning when I rang up to find out if Woodruff was the heir. I was so keen to confirm that point that I discounted the rest. If he died the companion was to have it for her lifetime."

Campion looked relieved.

"I thought so. There you are, you see. She had to get rid of them both—Woodruff and his new wife. With a young and vigorous woman in the house there was a danger of the companion becoming—well redundant. Don't you think?"

Kenny was fingering his notebook.

"You think she'd planned it for a fortnight?"

"She'd thought of it for a fortnight. She didn't see how to do it until the row occurred last night. When she found the gun on the window sill, where young Mrs. Woodruff left it, and Mrs. Cibber told her that the boy would come back, the plan was obvious." He shivered. "Do you realize that she must have been waiting, probably on the stairs, with the gun in her hand and the book box addressed to herself in the other, listening for Woodruff's letter to slide under the door? As soon as she heard it, she had to fly down and get it and open the door. Then she had to walk into the drawing room, shoot the old lady as she turned to see who it was, and put the gun in the book box. The instant she was certain Mrs. Cibber was dead, she then had to run out screaming to her place between the lamp post and the mail box and—*post the package!*"

Kenny put down his pencil and looked up.

"Now here," he said with honest admiration, "there I hand it to you. How in the world did you get on to that?"

"You suggested it."

"*I* did?" Kenny was pleased in spite of himself. "When?"

"When you kept asking me where one could hide a gun in a London street with no wide gratings and no sandbins. There was only the mail box. I guessed she'd posted it to herself—no one else would have been safe. Even the dead letter office eventually gives up its dead. That's why I was so keen to get her to the top of the house—as far away from the front door as possible." He sighed. "The book box was misguided genius. The gun was an old Luger, did you notice? Loot. That's why he never had to turn it in. It just fitted in the box. She must have had a thrill when she discovered that."

Kenny shook his head wonderingly. "Well, blow me down!" he said inelegantly, "Funny that *I* put you onto it!"

Mr. Campion was in bed that night when the telephone rang. It was Kenny again.

"I say, Mr. Campion?"

"Yes?"

"Sorry to bother you at this time of night but there's something worrying me. You don't mind, do you?"

"Think nothing of it."

"Well. Everything is all right. Smith had been certified by three medicos. The little girl is very happy comforting her boy, who seems to be upset about his aunt's death. The Commissioner is very pleased. But I can't get off to sleep. Mr. Campion, *how did you know what time the afternoon post is delivered in Barraclough Road?*"

The lean man stifled a yawn.

"Because I went into the chemist's shop on the corner and asked," he said. "Elementary, my dear Kenny."

Patrick Quentin

pseudonym of

Hugh Wheeler (1912–1987)

Richard Wilson Webb (1901–)

Peter and Iris Duluth were another husband-and-wife detecting duo of the 1930s and 1940s, but with a difference: Neither they nor the mysteries in which they became embroiled followed a consistently established pattern. While such teams as Mr. and Mrs. North and Jeff and Haila Troy seemed to lead mostly pleasant, trouble-free domestic lives, the Duluths were beset by all sorts of personal difficulties. In the first novel in the series, *A Puzzle for Fools* (1936), Peter—a former Broadway producer with a serious drinking problem—checks himself into an expensive private sanatorium to dry out. The ensuing murder muddle has him doubting his own sanity. In *Puzzle for Puppets* (1944), Iris, a glamorous stage and film star, and Peter are blamed for the killing of a maker of life-size puppets and spend much of the novel squabbling with circus folk and each other while on the run from the police. The couple is also plagued by the specters of infidelity and divorce, though the phantoms are eventually vanquished. Their investigations are not confined to New York City, their home base; they also do their amateur sleuthing in Mexico City, San Francisco, Reno, and in the following story, the southern California beach town of La Jolla. Nor are the tones of the six "Puzzle" novels the same; some are light, others much darker, as befit their various plots. The only constants throughout the series are expert plotting, well-drawn characters, and polished prose.

"Puzzle for Poppy" was the first short story featuring the Duluths, originally published in *Ellery Queen's Mystery Magazine* in early 1946. It is one of the lighter series entries, called by Ellery Queen "a delightfully wacky yarn" in which a huge fortune is left to a fat St. Bernard whose life is then imperiled by jealous human heirs. As Iris Duluth says, "Really, this shouldn't happen to a dog!"

Patrick Quentin was the joint pseudonym of Hugh Wheeler and Richard Wilson Webb, who also wrote as Q. Patrick, Quentin Patrick, and Jonathan Stagge. From 1936 to 1952 the pair produced numerous series mystery novels; these include four featuring Lieutenant Timothy Trant of the New York City police, the best of which is probably *Death and the Maiden*

(1939), and nine Jonathan Stagges starring Dr. Hugh Westlake and his bratty daughter, Dawn, the most noteworthy being *The Scarlet Circle* (1943). Prior to 1936, Richard Webb wrote four collaborative Q. Patrick novels, two each with Mary Louise Aswell and Martha Mott Kelley. One of these, the Aswell–Webb thriller *The Grindle Nightmare* (1935), is a harrowing and memorable tale of child murder that caused considerable controversy when it was first published. From 1953 until 1965, Hugh Wheeler wrote seven solo nonseries mysteries under the Patrick Quentin name; they include *The Man in the Net* (1956), filmed with Alan Ladd in what many consider his worst acting role, and *Family Skeletons* (1965).

PUZZLE FOR POPPY

PETER AND IRIS DULUTH
LA JOLLA, CALIFORNIA
1946

"Yes, Miss Crump," snapped Iris into the phone. "No, Miss Crump. Oh, nuts, Miss Crump."

My wife flung down the receiver.

"Well?" I asked.

"She won't let us use the patio. It's that dog, that great fat St. Bernard. It mustn't be disturbed."

"Why?"

"It has to be alone with its beautiful thoughts. It's going to become a mother. Peter, it's revolting. There must be something in the lease."

"There isn't," I said.

When I'd rented our half of this La Jolla hacienda for my shore leave, the lease specified that all rights to the enclosed patio belonged to our eccentric co-tenant. It oughtn't to have mattered, but it did because Iris had recently skyrocketed to fame as a movie star and it was impossible for us to appear on the streets without being mobbed. For the last couple of days we had been virtually beleaguered in our apartment. We were crazy about being beleaguered together, but even Héloise and Abelard needed a little fresh air once in a while.

That's why the patio was so important.

Iris was staring through the locked French windows at the forbidden delights of the patio. Suddenly she turned.

"Peter, I'll die if I don't get things into my lungs—ozone and things. We'll just have to go to the beach."

"And be torn limb from limb by your public again?"

"I'm sorry, darling. I'm terribly sorry." Iris unzippered herself from her housecoat and scrambled into slacks and a shirt-waist. She tossed me my naval hat. "Come, Lieutenant—to the slaughter."

When we emerged on the street, we collided head on with a man carrying groceries into the house. As we disentangled ourselves from celery stalks, there was a click and a squeal of delight followed by a powerful whistle. I turned to see a small girl who had been lying in wait with a camera. She was an unsightly little girl with sandy pigtails and a brace on her teeth.

"Geeth," she announced. "I can get two buckth for thith thnap from Barney Thtone. He'th thappy about you, Mith Duluth."

Other children, materializing in response to her whistle, were galloping toward us. The grocery man came out of the house. Passers-by stopped, stared and closed in—a woman in scarlet slacks, two sailors, a flurry of bobby-soxers, a policeman.

"This," said Iris grimly, "is the end."

She escaped from her fans and marched back to the two front doors of our hacienda. She rang the buzzer on the door that wasn't ours. She rang persistently. At length there was the clatter of a chain sliding into place and the door opened wide enough to reveal the face of Miss Crump. It was a small, faded face with a most uncordial expression.

"Yes?" asked Miss Crump.

"We're the Duluths," said Iris. "I just called you. I know about your dog, but . . ."

"Not *my* dog," corrected Miss Crump. "Mrs Wilberframe's dog. The late Mrs. Wilberframe of Glendale who has a nephew and a niece-in-law of whom I know a great deal in Ogden Bluffs, Utah. At least, they *ought* to be in Ogden Bluffs."

This unnecessary information was flung at us like a challenge. Then Miss Crump's face flushed into sudden, dimpled pleasure.

"Duluth! Iris Duluth. You're *the* Iris Duluth of the movies?"

"Yes," said Iris.

"Oh, why didn't you tell me over the phone? My favorite actress! How exciting! Poor thing—mobbed by your fans. Of course you may use the patio. I will give you the key to open your French windows. Any time."

Miraculously the chain was off the door. It opened halfway and then stopped. Miss Crump was staring at me with a return of suspicion.

"You *are* Miss Duluth's husband?"

"Mrs. Duluth's husband," I corrected her. "Lieutenant Duluth."

She still peered. "I mean, you have proof?"

I was beyond being surprised by Miss Crump. I fumbled from my wallet a dog-earned snapshot of Iris and me in full wedding regalia outside the church. Miss Crump studied it carefully and then returned it.

"You must please excuse me. What a sweet bride! It's just that I can't be too careful—for Poppy."

"Poppy?" queried Iris. "The St. Bernard?"

Miss Crump nodded. "It is Poppy's house, you see. Poppy pays the rent."

"The dog," said Iris faintly, "pays the rent?"

"Yes, my dear. Poppy is very well-to-do. She is hardly more than a puppy, but she is one of the richest dogs, I suppose, in the whole world."

Although we entertained grave doubts as to Miss Crump's sanity, we were soon in swimming suits and stepping through our open French windows into the sunshine of the patio. Miss Crump introduced us to Poppy.

In spite of our former prejudices, Poppy disarmed us immediately. She was just a big, bouncing, natural girl unspoiled by wealth. She greeted us with great thumps of her tail. She leaped up at Iris, dabbing at her cheek with a long, pink tongue. Later, when we had settled on striped mattresses under orange trees, she curled into a big clumsy ball at my side and laid her vast muzzle on my stomach.

"Look, she likes you." Miss Crump was glowing. "Oh, I knew she would!"

Iris, luxuriating in the sunshine, asked the polite question. "Tell us about Poppy. How did she make her money?"

"Oh, she did not make it. She inherited it." Miss Crump sat down on a white iron chair. "Mrs. Wilberframe was a very wealthy woman. She was devoted to Poppy."

"And left her all her money?" I asked.

"Not quite all. There was a little nest egg for me. I was her companion, you see, for many years. But I am to look after Poppy. That is why I received the nest egg. Poppy pays me a generous salary too." She fingered nondescript beads at her throat. "Mrs. Wilberframe was anxious for Poppy to have only the best and I am sure I try to do the right thing. Poppy has the master bedroom, of course. I take the little one in front. And then, if Poppy has steak for dinner, I have hamburger." She stared intensely, "I would not have an easy moment if I felt that Poppy did not get the best."

Poppy, her head on my stomach, coughed. She banged her tail against the flagstones apologetically.

Iris reached across me to pat her. "Has she been rich for long?"

"Oh, no, Mrs Wilberframe passed on only a few weeks ago." Miss Crump paused. "And it has been a great responsibility for me." She paused again and then blurted: "You're my friends, aren't you? Oh, I am sure you are. Please, please, won't you help me? I am all alone and I am so frightened."

"Frightened?" I looked up and, sure enough, her little bird face was peaked with fear.

"For Poppy." Miss Crump leaned forward. "Oh, Lieutenant, it is like a nightmare. Because I know. I just know they are trying to murder her!"

"They?" Iris sat up straight.

"Mrs. Wilberframe's nephew and his wife. From Ogden Bluffs, Utah."

"You mentioned them when you opened the door."

"I mention them to everyone who comes to the house. You see, I do not know what they look like and I do not want them to think I am not on my guard."

I watched her. She might have looked like a silly spinster with a bee in her bonnet. She didn't. She looked nice and quite sane, only scared.

"Oh, they are not good people. Not at all. There is nothing they would not stoop to. Back in Glendale, I found pieces of meat in the front yard. Poisoned meat, I know. And on a lonely road, they shot at Poppy. Oh, the police laughed at me. A car backfiring, they said. But I know differently. I know they won't stop till Poppy is dead." She threw her little hands up to her face. "I ran away from them in Glendale. That is why I came to La Jolla. But they have caught up with us. I know. Oh, dear, poor Poppy who is so sweet without a nasty thought in her head."

Poppy, hearing her name mentioned, smiled and panted.

"But this nephew and his wife from Ogden Bluffs, why should they want to murder her?": My wife's eyes were gleaming with a detective enthusiasm I knew of old. "Are they after her money?"

"Of course," said Miss Crump passionately. "It's the will. The nephew is Mrs. Wilberframe's only living relative, but she deliberately cut him off and I am sure I do not blame her. All the money goes to Poppy and—er—Poppy's little ones."

"Isn't the nephew contesting a screwy will like that?" I asked.

"Not yet. To contest a will takes a great deal of money—lawyers fees and things. It would be much, much cheaper for him to kill Poppy. You see, one thing is not covered by the will. If Poppy were to die before she became a mother, the nephew would inherit the whole estate. Oh, I have done everything in my power. The moment, the—er—suitable season arrived, I found a husband for Poppy. In a few weeks now, the—the little ones are expected. But these next few weeks ..."

Miss Crump dabbed at her eyes with a small handkerchief. "Oh, the Glendale police were most unsympathetic. They even mentioned the fact that the sentence for shooting or killing a dog in this state is shockingly light—a small fine at most.

I called the police here and asked for protection. They said they'd send a man around some time but they were hardly civil. So you see, there is no protection from the law and no redress. There is no one to help me."

"You've got us," said Iris in a burst of sympathy.

"Oh ... oh ..." The handkerchief fluttered from Miss Crump's face. "I knew you were my friends. You dear, dear things. Oh, Poppy, they are going to help us."

Poppy, busy licking my stomach, did not reply. Somewhat appalled by Iris' hasty promise but ready to stand by her, I said:

"Sure, we'll help, Miss Crump. First, what's the nephew's name?"

"Henry. Henry Blodgett. But he won't use that name. Oh, no, he will be too clever for that."

"And you don't know what he looks like?"

"Mrs. Wilberframe destroyed his photograph many years ago when he bit her as a small boy. With yellow curls, I understand. That is when the trouble between them started."

"At least you know what age he is?"

"He should be about thirty."

"And the wife?" asked Iris.

"I know nothing about her," said Miss Crump coldly, "except that she is supposed to be a red-headed person, a former actress."

"And what makes you so sure one or both of them have come to La Jolla?

Miss Crump folded her arms in her lap. "Last night. A telephone call."

"A telephone call?"

"A voice asking if I was Miss Crump, and then—silence." Miss Crump leaned toward me. "Oh, now they know I am here. They know I never let Poppy out. They know every morning I search the patio for meat, traps. They must realize that the only possible way to reach her is to enter the house."

"Break in?"

Miss Crump shook her tight curls. "It is possible. But I believe they will rely on guile rather than violence. It is against that we must be on our guard. You are the only people who have come to the door since that telephone call. Now anyone else that comes to your apartment or mine, whatever their excuse ..." She lowered her voice. "Anyone may be Henry Blodgett or his wife and we will have to outwit them."

A fly settled on one of Poppy's valuable ears. She did not seem to notice it. Miss Crump watched us earnestly and then gave a self-scolding cluck.

"Dear me, here I have been burdening you with Poppy's problems and you must be hungry. How about a little salad for luncheon? I always feel guilty about eating

in the middle of the day when Poppy has her one meal at night. But with guests—
yes, and allies—I am sure Mrs. Wilberframe would not have grudged the expense."
With a smile that was half-shy, half-conspiratorial, she fluttered away.

I looked at Iris. "Well," I said, "is she a nut or do we believe her?"

"I rather think," said my wife, "that we believe her."

"Why?"

"Just because." Iris' face wore the entranced expression which had won her so
many fans in her last picture. "Oh, Peter, don't you see what fun it will be? A beautiful St. Bernard in peril. A wicked villain with golden curls who bit his aunt."

"He won't have golden curls any more," I said. "He's a big boy now."

Iris, her body warm from the sun, leaned over me and put both arms around
Poppy's massive neck.

"Poor Poppy," she said. "Really, this shouldn't happen to a dog!"

The first thing happened some hours after Miss Crump's little salad luncheon while
Iris and I were still sunning ourselves. Miss Crump, who had been preparing Poppy's dinner and her own in her apartment, came running to announce:

"There is a man at the door! He claims he is from the electric light company to
read the meter. Oh, dear, if he is legitimate and we do not let him in, there will be
trouble with the electric light company and if . . ." She wrung her hands. "Oh, what
shall we do?"

I reached for a bathrobe. "You and Iris stay here. And for Mrs. Wilberframe's
sake, hang on to Poppy."

I found the man outside the locked front door. He was about thirty with thin-
ning hair and wore an army discharge button. He showed me his credentials. They
seemed in perfect order. There was nothing for it but to let him in. I took him into
the kitchen where Poppy's luscious steak and Miss Crump's modest hamburger
were lying where Miss Crump had left them on the table. I hovered over the man
while he located the meter. I never let him out of my sight until he had departed. In
answer to Miss Crump's anxious questioning, I could only say that if the man had
been Henry Blodgett he knew how much electricity she'd used in the past month
—but that was all.

The next caller showed up a few minutes later. Leaving Iris, indignant at being
out of things, to stand by Poppy, Miss Crump and I handled the visitor. This time it
was a slim, brash girl with bright auburn hair and a navy-blue slack suit. She was, she
said, the sister of the woman who owned the hacienda. She wanted a photograph for
the newspapers—a photograph of her Uncle William who had just been promoted
to Rear Admiral in the Pacific. The photograph was in a trunk in the attic.

Miss Crump, reacting to the unlikeliness of the request, refused entry. The red-head wasn't the type that wilted. When she started talking darkly of eviction, I overrode Miss Crump and offered to conduct her to the attic. The girl gave me one quick, experienced look and flounced into the hall.

The attic was reached by the back stairs through the kitchen. I conducted the red-head directly to her claimed destination. There were trunks. She searched through them. At length she produced a photograph of a limp young man in a rac-coon coat.

"My Uncle William," she snapped, "as a youth."

"Pretty," I said.

I took her back to the front door. On the threshold she gave me another of her bold, appraising stares.

"You know something?" she said. "I was hoping you'd make a pass at me in the attic."

"Why?" I asked.

"So's I could tear your ears off."

She left. If she had been Mrs. Blodgett, she knew how to take care of herself, she knew how many trunks there were in the attic—and that was all.

Iris and I had dressed and were drinking Daiquiris under a green and white striped umbrella when Miss Crump appeared followed by a young policeman. He had come, she said, in answer to her complaint. She showed him Poppy; she bab-bled out her story of the Blodgetts. He obviously thought she was a harmless lu-natic, but she didn't seem to realize it. After she had let him out, she settled beam-ingly down with us.

"I suppose," said Iris, "you asked for his credentials?"

"I ..." Miss Crump's face clouded. "My dear, you don't think that perhaps he wasn't a real police....?"

"To me," said Iris, "everyone's a Blodgett until proved to the contrary."

"Oh, dear," said Miss Crump.

Nothing else happened. By evening Iris and I were back in our part of the house. Poppy had hated to see us go. We had hated to leave her. A mutual crush had de-veloped between us.

But now we were alone again, the sinister Blodgetts did not seem very substan-tial. Iris made a creditable *Boeuf Stroganov* from yesterday's leftovers and changed into a lime green négligée which would have inflamed the whole Pacific Fleet. I was busy being a sailor on leave with his girl when the phone rang. I reached over Iris for the receiver, said "Hello," and then sat rigid listening.

It was Miss Crump's voice. But something was horribly wrong with it. It came across hoarse and gasping.

"Come," it said. "Oh, come. The French windows. Oh, please ..."
The voice faded. I heard the clatter of a dropped receiver.
"It must be Poppy," I said to Iris. "Quick."
We ran out into the dark patio. Across it, I could see the light French windows
to Miss Crump's apartment. They were half open, and as I looked Poppy squirmed
through to the patio. She bounded toward us, whining.
"Poppy's all right," said Iris. "Quick!"
We ran to Miss Crump's windows. Poppy barged past us into the living room.
We followed. All the lights were on. Poppy had galloped around a high-backed davenport. We went to it and looked over it.

Poppy was crouching on the carpet, her huge muzzle dropped on her paws. She
was howling and staring straight at Miss Crump.

Poppy's paid companion was on the floor too. She lay motionless on her back,
her legs twisted under her, her small, grey face distorted, her lips stretched in a
dreadful smile.

I knelt down by Poppy. I picked up Miss Crump's thin wrist and felt for the
pulse. Poppy was still howling. Iris stood, straight and white.

"Peter, tell me. Is she dead?"

"Not quite. But only just not quite. Poison. It looks like strychnine...."

We called a doctor. We called the police. The doctor came, muttered a shocked
diagnosis of strychnine poisoning and rushed Miss Crump to the hospital. I asked if
she had a chance. He didn't answer. I knew what that meant. Soon the police came
and there was so much to say and do and think that I hadn't time to brood about
poor Miss Crump.

We told Inspector Green the Blodgett story. It was obvious to us that somehow
Miss Crump had been poisoned by them in mistake for Poppy. Since no one had
entered the house that day except the three callers, one of them, we said, must have
been a Blodgett. All the Inspector had to do, we said, was to locate those three
people and find out which was a Blodgett.

Inspector Green watched us poker-faced and made no comment. After he'd left,
we took the companionless Poppy back to our part of the house. She climbed on
the bed and stretched out between us, her tail thumping, her head flopped on the
pillows. We didn't have the heart to evict her. It was not one of our better nights.

Early next morning, a policeman took us to Miss Crump's apartment. Inspector
Green was waiting in the living room. I didn't like his stare.

"We've analyzed the hamburger she was eating last night," he said. "There was
enough strychnine in it to kill an elephant."

"Hamburger!" exclaimed Iris. "Then that proves she was poisoned by the
Blodgetts!"

"Why?" asked Inspector Green.

"They didn't know how conscientious Miss Crump was. They didn't know she always bought steak for Poppy and hamburger for herself. They saw the steak and the hamburger and they naturally assumed the hamburger was for Poppy, so they poisoned that."

"That's right," I cut in. "The steak and the hamburger were lying right on the kitchen table when all three of those people came in yesterday."

"I see," said the Inspector.

He nodded to a policeman who left the room and returned with three people — the balding young man from the electric light company, the red-headed vixen, and the young policeman. None of them looked happy.

"You're willing to swear," the Inspector asked us, "that these were the only three people who entered this house yesterday."

"Yes," said Iris.

"And you think one of them is either Blodgett or his wife?"

"They've got to be."

Inspector Green smiled faintly. "Mr. Burns here has been with the electric light company for five years except for a year when he was in the army. The electric light company is willing to vouch for that. Miss Custis has been identified as the sister of the lady who owns this house and the niece of Rear Admiral Moss. She has no connection with any Blodgetts and has never been in Utah." He paused. "As for Officer Patterson, he has been a member of the police force here for eight years. I personally sent him around yesterday to follow up Miss Crump's complaint."

The Inspector produced an envelope from his pocket and tossed it to me. "I've had these photographs of Mr. and Mrs. Henry Blodgett flown from the files of the Ogden Bluffs *Tribune*."

I pulled the photographs out of the envelope. We stared at them. Neither Mr. or Mrs. Blodgett looked at all the sort of person you would like to know. But neither of them bore the slightest resemblance to any of the three suspects in front of us.

"It might also interest you," said the Inspector quietly, "that I've checked with the Ogden Bluffs police. Mr. Blodgett has been sick in bed for over a week and his wife has been nursing him. There is a doctor's certificate to that effect."

Inspector Green gazed down at his hands. They were competent hands. "It looks to me that the whole Blodgett story was built up in Miss Crump's mind — or yours." His grey eyes stared right through us. "If we have to eliminate the Blodgetts and these three people from suspicion, that leaves only two others who had the slightest chance of poisoning the hamburger."

Iris blinked. "Us?"

"You," said Inspector Green almost sadly.

·

They didn't arrest us, of course. We had no conceivable motive. But Inspector Green questioned us minutely and when he left there was a policeman lounging outside our door.

We spent a harried afternoon racking our brains and getting nowhere. Iris was the one who had the inspiration. Suddenly, just after she had fed Poppy the remains of the *Stroganov*, she exclaimed:

"Good heavens above, of course!"

"Of course, what?"

She spun to me, her eyes shining.

"Barney Thtone," she lisped. "Why didn't we realize? Come on!"

She ran out of the house into the street. She grabbed the lounging policeman by the arm.

"You live here," she said. "Who's Barney Stone?"

"Barney Stone?" The policeman stared. "He's the son of the druggist on the corner."

Iris raced me to the drugstore. She was attracting quite a crowd. The policeman followed, too.

In the drugstore, a thin young man with spectacles stood behind the prescription counter.

"Mr. Stone?" asked Iris.

His mouth dropped open. "Gee, Miss Duluth. I never dreamed ... Gee, Miss Duluth, what can I do for you? Cigarettes? An alarm clock?

"A little girl," said Iris. "A little girl with sandy pigtails and a brace on her teeth. What's her name? Where does she live?

Barney Stone said promptly: "You mean Daisy Kornfeld. Kind of homely. Just down the block. 712. Miss Duluth, I certainly ..."

"Thanks," cut in Iris and we were off again with our ever growing escort.

Daisy was sitting in the Kornfeld parlor, glumly thumping the piano. Ushered in by an excited, cooing Mrs. Kornfeld, Iris interrupted Daisy's rendition of *The Jolly Farmer*.

"Daisy, that picture you took of me yesterday to sell to Mr. Stone, is it developed yet?"

"Geeth no, Mith Duluth. I ain't got the developing money yet. Theventy-five thenth. Ma don't give me but a nickel an hour for practithing thith gothdarn piano."

"Here." Iris thrust a ten-dollar bill into her hand. "I'll buy the whole roll. Run get the camera. We'll have it developed right away."

"Geeth." The mercenary Daisy stared with blank incredulity at the ten-dollar bill. I stared just as blankly myself. I wasn't being bright at all.

I wasn't much brighter an hour later. We were back in our apartment, waiting for Inspector Green. Poppy, all for love, was trying to climb into my lap. Iris, who had charmed Barney Stone into developing Daisy's films, clutched the yellow envelope of snaps in her hand. She had sent our policeman away on a secret mission, but an infuriating passion for the dramatic had kept her from telling or showing me anything. I had to wait for Inspector Green.

Eventually Iris' policeman returned and whispered with her in the hall. Then Inspector Green came. He looked cold and hostile. Poppy didn't like him. She growled. Sometimes Poppy was smart.

Inspector Green said: "you've been running all over town. I told you to stay here."

"I know." Iris' voice was meek. "It's just that I wanted to solve poor Miss Crump's poisoning."

"Solve it?" Inspector Green's query was skeptical.

"Yes. It's awfully simple really. I can't imagine why we didn't think of it from the start."

"You mean you know who poisoned her?"

"Of course." Iris smiled, a maddening smile. "Henry Blodgett."

"But . . ."

"Check with the airlines. I think you'll find that Blodgett flew in from Ogden Bluffs a few days ago and flew back today. As for being sick in bed under his wife's care, I guess that'll make Mrs. Blodgett an accessory before the fact, won't it?"

Inspector Green was pop-eyed.

"Oh, it's my fault really," continued Iris. "I said no one came to the house yesterday except those three people. There was someone else, but he was so ordinary, so run-of-the-mill, that I forgot him completely."

I was beginning to see then, Inspector Green snapped: "And this run-of-the-mill character?"

"The man," said Iris sweetly, "who had the best chance of all to poison the hamburger, *the man who delivered it*—the man from the Supermarket."

"We don't have to guess. We have proof." Iris fumbled in the yellow envelope. "Yesterday morning as we were going out, we bumped into the man delivering Miss Crump's groceries. Just at that moment, a sweet little girl took a snap of us. This snap."

She selected a print and handed it to Inspector Green. I moved to look at it over his shoulder.

"I'm afraid Daisy is an impressionistic photographer," murmured Iris. "That hip on the right is me. The buttocks are my husband. But the figure in the middle— quite a masterly likeness of Henry Blodgett, isn't it? Of course, there's the grocery apron, the unshaven chin . . ."

She was right. Daisy had only winged Iris and me but with the grocery man she had scored a direct hit. And the grocery man was unquestionably Henry Blodgett.

Iris nodded to her policeman, "Sergeant Blair took a copy of the snap around the neighborhood groceries. They recognized Blodgett at the Supermarket. They hired him day before yesterday. He made a few deliveries this morning, including Miss Crump's, and took a powder without his pay."

"Well . . ." stammered Inspector Green. "Well . . ."

"Just how many charges can you get him on?" asked my wife hopefully. "At- tempted homicide, conspiracy to defraud, illegal possession of poisonous drugs. . . . The rat, I hope you give him the works when you get him."

"We'll get him all right," said Inspector Green.

Iris leaned over and patted Poppy's head affectionately.

"Don't worry, darling. I'm sure Miss Crump will get well and we'll throw a lovely christening party for your little strangers. . . ."

Iris was right about the Blodgetts. Henry got the works. And his wife was held as an accessory. Iris was right about Miss Crump too. She is still in the hospital but improving steadily and will almost certainly be well enough to attend the christen- ing party.

Meanwhile, at her request, Poppy is staying with us, awaiting maternity with rollicking unconcern.

It's nice having a dog who pays the rent.

Stuart Palmer

(1905-1968)

Craig Rice

(1908-1957)

Over a fifteen-year span from the late 1940s to the early 1960s, Stuart Palmer and his good friend and fellow mystery writer Craig Rice (Georgiana Ann Randolph Craig), who had worked together on the scripting of the 1942 film *The Falcon's Brother,* collaborated on half a dozen novelettes for *Ellery Queen's Mystery Magazine.* Each story teamed Palmer's crusty New York schoolteacher, Hildegarde Withers, that "tall, angular person who somehow suggested a fairly well-dressed scarecrow," with Rice's hard-drinking, womanizing Chicago lawyer, John J. Malone. All six were collected in *People vs. Withers and Malone* (1963).

Working in tandem, the pair solve what the book's dust-jacket blurb describes as "hectic, hilarious homicides." Both Palmer and Rice wrote cleverly constructed, fair-play whodunits flavored with sometimes wacky humor, and the blending of their talents produced some memorable stories. One is the present selection, a jolly spoof of the intrigue-on-the—Orient Express genre, which takes place on the *Super-Century* en route from Chicago to New York. It features a dead man lurking sans clothing in Miss Withers's compartment, the murder weapon having been planted in Malone's adjoining compartment, and a combination of quick thinking on the lawyer's part and a bizarre dream on the spinster's that unmasks the culprit. The story was one of two Withers and Malone tales sold to MGM —"resulting finally," in Stuart Palmer's words, "in *Mrs. O'Malley and Mr. Malone,* a starring vehicle for James Whitmore, in which Miss Withers changed into Ma Kettle [Marjorie Main]." Palmer and Rice were two of the scriptwriters on that deservedly obscure 1951 film.

Stuart Palmer was the author of fourteen novels featuring Miss Withers and her friend and foil, New York police inspector Oscar Piper; notable among them are *The Penguin Pool Murder* (1931), *Murder on the Blackboard* (1932), *The Puzzle of the Red Stallion* (1936), and *The Puzzle of the Happy Hooligan* (1941). Several of the early novels were filmed in the 1930s with Edna May Oliver, then Helen Broderick, and finally ZaSu Pitts as Miss Withers and James Gleason as Oscar Piper. The pair also appears in two collections, *The Riddles of Hildegarde Withers* (1947) and *The Monkey Murder and Other Hildegarde Withers Stories* (1950).

Craig Rice introduced John J. Malone in *Eight Faces at Three* (1939), in which he shares the crime-solving spotlight with the husband-and-wife team of Jake and Helen Justus. Several other novels featuring Malone and the Justuses followed, including *Trial by Fury* (1941), which many aficionados consider her best novel. A second well-regarded series also starred a detective duo, street photographers Bingo Riggs and Handsome Kusak, who appeared in such lethal romps as *The Sunday Pigeon Murders* (1942) and *The Thursday Turkey Murders* (1943). A versatile writer, Rice also penned a somewhat autobiographical mystery, *Home Sweet Homicide* (1944), in which thinly disguised versions of her own children serve as sleuths; and a trio of nonhumorous psychological crime novels published under the pseudonym Michael Venning. Her work was so popular in the 1940s that she was the subject of an article in *Time* and her photo was on the magazine's cover.

ONCE UPON A TRAIN

HILDEGARDE WITHERS AND JOHN J. MALONE
TRAIN EN ROUTE FROM CHICAGO TO NEW YORK
C. 1950

t was nothing, really," said John J. Malone with weary modesty. "After all, I never lost a client yet."

The party in Chicago's famed Pump Room was being held to celebrate the miraculous acquittal of Stephen Larsen, a machine politician accused of dipping some thirty thousand dollars out of the municipal till. Malone had proved to the jury and to himself that his client was innocent—at least, innocent of that particular charge.

It was going to be a nice party, the little lawyer kept telling himself. By the way Larsen's so-called friends were bending their elbows, the tab would be colossal. Malone hoped fervently that his fee for services rendered would be taken care of today, before Larsen's guests bankrupted him. Because there was the matter of two months' back office rent. . . .

"Thank you, I will," Malone said, as the waiter picked up his empty glass. He wondered how he could meet the redhead at the next table, who looked sultry and bored in the midst of a dull family party. As soon as he got his money from Larsen he would start a rescue operation. The quickest way to make friends, he always said, was to break a hundred-dollar bill in a bar, and that applied even to curvaceous redheads in Fath models.

But where *was* Steve Larsen? Lolly was here, wearing her most angelic expression and a slinky gown which she overflowed considerably at the top. She was hinting that the party also celebrated a reconciliation between herself and Stevie; that the divorce was off. She had hocked her bracelet again, and Malone remembered hearing that her last show had closed after six performances. If she got her hand back into Steve's pocket, Malone reflected, goodbye to his fee of three grand.

He'd made elaborate plans for that money. They not only included the trip to Bermuda which he'd been promising himself for twenty years, but also the redhead he'd been promising himself for twenty minutes.

Others at the table were worrying too. "Steve is late, even for him!" spoke up Allen Roth suddenly.

Malone glanced at the porcine paving contractor who was rumored to be Larsen's secret partner, and murmured, "Maybe he got his dates mixed."

"He'd *better* show," Roth said, in a voice as cold as a grave-digger's shovel.

The little lawyer shivered, and realized that he wasn't the only guest who had come here to make a collection. But he simply had to have that money. $3,000 — $30,000. He wondered, half musing, if he shouldn't have made his contingent fee, say, $2,995. This way it almost looked like . . .

"What did you say about ten per cent, counselor?" Bert Glick spoke up wisely.

Malone recovered himself. "You misunderstood me. I merely said, 'When on pleasure bent, never muzzle the ox when he treadeth out the corn.' I mean rye." He turned to look for the waiter, not solely from thirst. The little lawyer would often have been very glad to buy back his introduction to Bert Glick.

True, the City Hall hanger-on had been helpful during the trial. In fact, it had been his testimony as a prosecution witness that had clinched the acquittal, for he had made a surprise switch on several moot points of the indictment. Glick was a private detective turned bail-bondsman, clever at tapping wires and dipping his spoon into any gravy that was being passed.

Glick slapped Malone on the back and said, "If you knew what I know, you wouldn't be looking at your watch all the time. Because this ain't a coming out party, it's a surprise party. And the surprise is that the host ain't gonna be here!"

Malone went cold—as cold as Allen Roth's gray eyes across the table. "Keep talking," he said, adding in a whisper a few facts which Glick might not care to have brought to the attention of the district attorney.

"You don't need to be so nasty," Glick said. He rose suddenly to his feet, lifting his glass. "A toast! A toast to good ol' Stevie, our pal, who's taking the Super-Century for New York tonight, next stop Paris or Rio. And with him, my fine feathered friends, he's taking the dough he owes most of us, and a lot more too. Bon voyage!" The man absorbed the contents of his glass and slowly collapsed in his chair.

There was a sudden hullabaloo around the table. Malone closed his eyes for just five seconds, resigning himself to the certainty that his worst suspicions were true. When he opened his eyes again, the redhead was gone. He looked at his watch. There was still a chance of catching that New York train, with a quick stop at Joe the Angel's bar to borrow the price of a ticket. Malone rushed out of the place, wasting no time in farewells. Everybody else was leaving too, so that finally Glick was left alone with the waiter and with the check.

As Malone had expected, Joe the Angel took a very dim view of the project, pointing out that it was probably only throwing good money after bad. But he handed over enough for a round trip, plus Pullman. By the time his cab had dumped him at the I.C. station, Malone had decided to settle for one way. He needed spending money for the trip. There were poker games on trains.

Suddenly he saw the redhead! She was jammed in a crowd at the gate, crushed between old ladies, noisy sailors, and a bearded patriarch in the robes of the Greek Orthodox Church. She struggled with a mink coat, a yowling cat in a traveling case, and a caged parrot.

Malone leaped gallantly to her rescue, and for a brief moment was allowed to hold the menagerie, before a Redcap took over. The moment was just long enough for the lawyer to have his hand clawed by the irate cat, and for him and the parrot to develop a lifelong dislike. But he did hear the girl say, "Compartment B in Car 10, please." And her warm grateful smile sent him racing off in search of the Pullman conductor.

Considerable eloquence, some trifling liberties with the truth, and a ten-dollar bill got him possession of the drawing room next to a certain compartment. That settled, he paused to make a quick deal with a roving Western Union boy, and more money changed hands. When he finally swung aboard the already moving train, he felt fairly confident that the trip would be pleasant and eventful. And lucrative, of course. The minute he got his hands on Steve Larsen . . .

Once established in the drawing room, Malone studied himself in the mirror, whistling a few bars of "The Wabash Cannonball." For the moment the primary target could wait. He was glad he was wearing his favorite Finchley suit, and his new green-and-lavender Sulka tie.

"A man of distinction," he thought. True, his hair was slightly mussed, a few cigar ashes peppered his vest, and the Sulka tie was beginning to creep toward one ear, but the total effect was good. Inspired, he sat down to compose a note to Operation Redhead, in the next compartment. He knew it was the right compartment, for the parrot was already giving out with imitations of a boiler factory, assisted by the cat.

He wrote:

> *Lovely lady,*
> *Let's not fight Fate. We were destined to have dinner together. I am*
> *holding my breath for your yes.*
>
> > *Your unknown admirer,*
> > *J.J.M*

He poked the note under the connecting door, rapped lightly, and waited.

After a long moment the note came back, with an addition in a surprisingly precise hand.

> *Sir, You have picked the wrong girl. Besides, I had dinner in the Pump*
> *Room over an hour ago, and so, I believe, did you.*

Undaunted, Malone whistled another bar of the song. Just getting any answer at all was half the battle. So she'd noticed him in the Pump Room! He sat down and wrote swiftly:

> *Please, an after-dinner liqueur with me, then?*

This time the answer was:

> *My dear sir: MY DEAR SIR!*

But the little lawyer thought he heard sounds of feminine laughter, though of course it might have been the parrot. He sat back, lighted a fresh cigar, and waited. They were almost to Gary now, and if the telegram had got through . . .

It had, and a messenger finally came aboard with an armful of luscious *Gruss von Teplitz* roses. Malone intercepted him long enough to add a note which really should be the clincher.

> *To the Rose of Tralee, who makes all other women look like withered*
> *dandelions. I'll be waiting in the club car. Faithfully, John J. Malone*

That was the way, he told himself happily. Don't give her a chance to say *No* again.

After a long and somewhat bruising trip through lurching Pullman cars, made longer still because he first headed fore instead of aft, Malone finally sank into a chair in the club-car lounge, facing the door. Of course, she would take time to arrange the roses, make a corsage out of a couple of buds, and probably shift into an even more startling gown. It might be quite a wait. He waved at the bar steward and said, "Rye, please, with a rye chaser."

"You mean rye with a beer chaser, Mr. Malone?"

"If you know my name, you know enough not to confuse me. I mean beer with a rye chaser!" When the drink arrived Malone put it where it would do the most good, and then for lack of anything better to do fell to staring in awed fascination at the lady who had just settled down across the aisle.

She was a tall, angular person who somehow suggested a fairly well-dressed scarecrow. Her face seemed faintly familiar, and Malone wondered if they'd met before. Then he decided that she reminded him of a three-year-old who had winked at him in the paddock at Washington Park one Saturday and then run out of the money.

Topping the face—as if anything could—was an incredible headpiece consisting of a grass-green crown surrounded by a brim of nodding flowers, wreaths and ivy. All it seemed to need was a nice marble tombstone.

She looked up suddenly from her magazine. "Pardon me, but did you say something about a well-kept grave?" Her voice reminded Malone of a certain Miss Hackett who had talked him out of quitting second-year high school. Somehow he found himself strangely unable to lie to her.

"Madam, do you read minds?"

"Not minds, Mr. Malone. *Lips*, sometimes." She smiled. "Are you really *the* John J. Malone?"

He blinked. "How in the—of, of course! The *magazine!* Those fact-detective stories *will* keep writing up my old cases. Are you a crime-story fan, Mrs.—?"

"Miss. Hildegarde Withers, schoolteacher by profession and meddlesome old snoop by avocation, at least according to the police. Yes, I've read about you. You solve crimes and right wrongs, but usually by pure accident while chasing through saloons after some young woman who is no better than she should be. Are you on a case now?"

"Working my way through the second bottle," he muttered, suddenly desperate. It would never do for the redhead to come in and find him tied up with this character.

"I didn't mean that kind of a case," Miss Withers explained. "I gather that even though you've never lost a client, you have mislaid one at the moment?"

Malone shivered. The woman had second sight, at least. He decided that it would be better if he went back through the train and met the Rose of Tralee, who

225

must certainly be on her way here by this time. He could also keep an eye open for Steve Larsen. With a hasty apology he got out of the club car, pausing only to purchase a handy pint of rye from the bar steward, and started on a long slow prowl of mile after mile of wobbling, jerking cars. The rye, blending not unpleasantly with the champagne he had taken on earlier, made everything a little hazy and unreal. He kept getting turned around and blundering into the long-deserted diner. Two or three times he bumped into the Greek Orthodox priest with the whiskers, and similarly kept interrupting four sailors shooting craps in a men's lounge.

But—no redhead. And no Larsen. Finally the train stopped—could it be Toledo already? Malone dashed to the vestibule and hung over the step, to make sure that Steve didn't disembark. When they were moving again he resumed his pilgrimage, though by this time he had resigned himself to the fact that he was being stood up by the Rose of Tralee. At last, he turned mournfully back toward where his own lonesome cubicle ought to be—and then suddenly found himself back in the club car!

No redheaded Rose. Even The Hat had departed, taking her copy of *Official Fact Detective Stories* with her. The car was deserted except for a bridge game going on in one corner and a sailor—obviously half-seas over—who was drowsing in a big chair with a newspaper over his face.

The pint was empty. Malone told the steward to have it buried with full military honors, and to fetch him a cheese on rye. "On second thought, skip the cheese and make it just straight rye, please."

The drink arrived, and with it a whispered message. There was a lady waiting down the corridor.

Malone emptied his glass and followed the steward, trying to slip him five dollars. It slipped right back. "Thanks, Mr. Malone, but I can't take money from an old classmate. Remember, we went through the last two years of Kent College of Law together?"

Malone gasped. "Class of '45. And you're Homer—No, *Horace* Lee Randolph. But—"

"What am I doing here? The old story. Didn't know my place, and got into Chicago Southside politics. Bumped up against the machine, and got disbarred on a phony charge of subornation of perjury. It could have been squared by handing a grand to a certain sharper at City Hall, but I didn't have the money." Horace shrugged. "This pays better than law, anyway. For instance, that lady handed me five dollars just to unlock the private lounge and tell you she's waiting to see you there."

The little lawyer winced. "She—was she a queer old maid in a hat that looked like she'd made it herself?"

"Oh, no. No hat."

Malone breathed easier. "Was she young and lovely?"

"My weakness is the numbers game, but I should say the description is accurate."

Humming "But 'twas not her beauty alone that won me; oh, no, 'twas the truth . . ." Malone straightened his tie and opened the door.

Lolly Larsen exploded in his face with all the power of a firecracker under a tin can. She grabbed his lapels and yelped: "Well, where is the dirty ————?"

"Be more specific. Which dirty ————?" Malone said, pulling himself loose.

"*Steve,* of course!"

"I don't know, but I still hope he's somewhere on this train. You joining me in the search? Nice to have your pretty face among us."

Lolly had the face of a homesick angel. Her hair was exactly the color of a twist of lemon peel in a glass of champagne brut, her mouth was an overripe strawberry, and her figure might have inspired the French bathing suit, but her eyes were cold and strange as a mermaid's. "Are you in this with Steve?" she demanded.

Malone said, "In simple, one-syllable words that even you can understand— No!"

Lolly suddenly relaxed, swaying against him so that he got a good whiff of brandy, nail polish and Chanel Number 5. "I'm sorry. I guess I'm just upset. I feel so terribly helpless—"

For Malone's money, she was as helpless as an eight-button rattlesnake. "You see," Lolly murmured, "I'm partly to blame for Steve's running away. I should have stood by him at the trial, but I hadn't the courage. Even afterward—I didn't actually promise to come back to him, I just said I'd come to his party. I meant to tell him—in the Pump Room. So, please, please help me find him—so I can make him see how much we really *need* each other!"

Malone said, "Try it again, and flick the eyelashes a little bit more when you come to 'need each other.'"

Lolly jerked away and called him a number of things, of which "dirty little shyster!" was the most complimentary. "All right," she finally said in a matter-of-fact tone. "Steve's carrying a hundred grand, and you can guess how he got it. I happen to know —Glick isn't the *only* one who's been spying on him since he got out of jail yesterday. I don't want Steve back, but I do want a fat slice for keeping my mouth shut. One word from me to the D.A. or the papers, and not even you can get him off."

"Go on," Malone said wearily. "But you interest me in less ways than one."

"Find Steve!" she told him. "Make a deal and I'll give you ten per cent of the take. But work fast, because we're not the only ones looking for him. Steve double-crossed everybody who was at that party this afternoon. He's somewhere on this train, but he's probably shaved off his moustache, or put on a fright-wig, or—"

Malone yawned and said, "Where can I get in touch with you?"

"I couldn't get a reservation of any kind." Her strange eyes warmed hopefully. "But I hear you have a drawing room?"

"Don't look at me in that tone of voice," Malone said hastily. "Besides, I snore. Maybe there'll be something available for you at the next stop."

He was out of there and back in the club car before Lolly could turn on any more of the charm. He decided to have one for the road—the New York Central Road, and one for the Pennsy too. The sensible thing was to find Steve Larsen, collect his own hard-earned fee, and leave Lolly alone. Her offer of ten per cent of the blackmail take touched on a sore spot.

Malone began to work his way through the train again, this time desperately questioning porters. The worst of it was, there was nothing remarkable about Larsen's appearance except curly hair, which he'd probably had straightened and dyed, a mustache that could have been shaved off, and a briefcase full of money, which he'd probably hidden. In fact, the man was undoubtedly laughing at everybody from behind a false set of whiskers.

Such were Malone's thoughts as he suddenly came face to face again with the Greek Orthodox priest, who stared past him through thick, tinted spectacles. The little lawyer hesitated and was lost. Throwing caution to the winds, he yanked vigorously at the beard. But it was an orthodox beard, attached in the orthodox manner. Its owner let loose a blast which just possibly might have been an orthodox Greek blessing. Malone didn't wait to find out.

His ears were still burning when he stepped into a vestibule and ran head on into Miss Hildegarde Withers. He nodded coldly and started past her.

"Ah, go soak your fat head!"

Malone gasped.

"It's the parrot," Miss Withers explained, holding up the caged monstrosity. "It's been making such a racket that I'm taking it to the baggage car for the night."

"Where—where did you get that—bird?" Malone asked weakly.

"Why, Sinbad is a legacy from the aunt whose funeral I just went back to attend. I'm taking him back to New York with me."

"New York!" Malone moaned. "We'll be there before I find that—"

"You mean that Mr. Larsen?" As he stood speechless, she went briskly on. "You see, I happened to be at a family farewell party at the table next to yours in the Pump Room, and my hearing is very acute. So, for that matter, is my eyesight. Has it occurred to you that Larsen may be wearing a disguise of some sort?"

"That it has," admitted Malone sadly, thinking of the Greek priest.

The schoolteacher lowered her voice. "You remember that when we had our little chat in the club car sometime ago, there was an obviously inebriated sailor dozing behind a newspaper?"

"There's one on every train," Malone said. "One or more."

"Exactly. Like Chesterton's postman, you never notice them. But somehow that particular sailor managed to stay intoxicated without ordering a single drink or nipping at a private bottle. More than that, when you suddenly left he poked his head out from behind the paper and stared after you with a very odd expression, rather as if he suspected you had leprosy. I couldn't help noticing—"

"Madam, I love you," the lawyer said fervently. "I love you because you remind me of Miss Hackett back in Dorchester High, and because of your hat, and because you are sharper than a tack."

Miss Withers sniffed, but it was a mollified sniff. "Sorry to interrupt, but that same sailor entered our car just as I left it with the parrot. I just happened to look back, and I rather think he was trying the door of your drawing room."

Malone clasped her hand fondly. Unfortunately it was the hand that held the cage, and the parrot took advantage of the long-awaiting opportunity to nip viciously at his thumb. "Thank you so very much—some day I'll wring your silly neck" was Malone's sincere but somewhat garbled exit line.

"Go boil your head in lard!" the bird screamed after him.

The maiden schoolteacher sighed. "Come on, Sinbad, you're going into durance vile. And I'm going to retire to my lonely couch, drat it all." She looked wistfully over her shoulder. "Some people have all the fun!"

But twelve cars, ten minutes, and four drinks later, Malone was lost again. A worried porter was saying, "If you could only remember your car number, sah?" A much harassed Pullman conductor added, "If you'd just show us your ticket stub, we'd locate you."

"You don't need to locate *me*," Malone insisted. "I'm right here."

"Maybe you haven't got a stub."

"I have so a stub. It's in my hatband." Crafty as an Indian guide, Malone backtracked them unerringly to his drawing room. "Here's the stub—now where was I?"

The porter looked out the window and said, "just coming into Altoona, sah."

"They lay in the wreck when they found them. They had died when the engine had fell . . ." sang Malone happily. But the conductor winced and said they'd be going.

"You might as well," Malone told him. "If neither one of you can sing baritone."

The door closed behind them, and a moment later a soft voice called, "Mr. Malone?"

He stared at the connecting door. *The Rose of Tralee*, Malone told himself happily. He adjusted his tie, and tried the door. Miraculously, it opened. Then he saw that it was Miss Hildegarde Withers, looking very worried, who stared back at him.

Malone said, "What have you done with my redhead?"

"If you refer to my niece Joannie," the schoolteacher said sharply, "she only helped me get my stuff aboard and rode as far as Englewood. But never mind that now. I'm in trouble."

"I knew there couldn't be two parrots like that on one train," Malone groaned. "Or even in one world."

"There's worse than parrots on this train," snapped Miss Withers. "This man Larsen for whom you were looking so anxiously—"

The little lawyer's eyes narrowed. "Just what is your interest in Larsen?"

"None whatever, except that he's here in my compartment. It's very embarrassing, because he's not only dead, he's *undressed!*"

"Holy St. Vitus!" gulped Malone. "Quiet! Keep *calm*. Lock your door and *don't* talk!"

"My door is locked, and who's talking?" The schoolteacher stepped aside and Malone peered gingerly past her. The speed with which he was sobering up probably established a new record. It was Larsen, all right. He was face down on the floor, dressed only in black shoes, blue socks, and a suit of long underwear. There was also a moderate amount of blood.

At last Malone said hoarsely, "I suspect foul play!"

"Knife job," said Miss Withers with professional coolness. "From the back, through the *latissimus dorsi*. Within the last twenty minutes, I'd say. If I hadn't had some difficulty in convincing the baggage men that Sinbad should be theirs for the night, I might have walked in on the murderer at work." She gave Malone a searching glance. "It wasn't *you*, by any chance?"

"Do you think I'd murder a man who owed me three thousand dollars?" Malone demanded indignantly. He scowled. "But a lot of people are going to jump to that conclusion. Nice of you not to raise an alarm."

She sniffed. "You didn't think I'd care to have a man—even a dead man— found in my room in this state of undress? Obviously, he hasn't your money on his person. So—what is to be done about it?"

"I'll defend you for nothing," John J. Malone promised. "Justifiable homicide. Besides, you were framed. He burst in upon you and you stabbed in defense of your honor ..."

"*Just* a minute! The corpse was *your* client. You've been publicly asking for him all through the train. I'm only an innocent bystander." She paused. "In my opinion, Larsen was lured to your room purposely by someone who had penetrated his disguise. He was stabbed, and dumped here. Very clever, because if the body had been left in your room, you could have got rid of it or claimed that you were framed. But this way, to the police mind at least, it would be obvious that you did the job and then tried to palm it off on the nearest neighbor."

Malone sagged weakly against the berth. His hand brushed against the leather case, and something slashed viciously at his fingers. "But I thought you got rid of that parrot!" he cried.

"I did," Miss Withers assured him. "That's Precious in his case. A twenty-pound Siamese, also part of my recent legacy. Don't get too close, the creature dislikes train travel and is in a foul temper."

Malone stared through the wire window and said, "It's father must have been either a bobcat or a buzz saw."

"My aunt left me her mink coat, on condition that I take both her pets," Miss Withers explained wearily. "But I'm beginning to think it would be better to shiver through these cold winters. And speaking of cold—I'm a patient woman, but not very. You have one minute, Mr. Malone, to get your dead friend out of here!"

"He's no friend of mine, dead or alive," Malone began. "And I suggest—"

There was a heavy knocking on the corridor door "Open up in there!"

"Say something!" whispered Malone. "Say you're undressed!"

"You're undressed—I mean, I'm undressed," she cried obediently.

"Sorry, ma'am," a masculine voice said on the other side of the door. "But we're searching this train for a fugitive from justice. Hurry, please."

"Just a minute," sang out the schoolteacher, making frantic gestures at Malone.

The little lawyer shuddered, then grabbed the late Steve Larsen and tugged him through the connecting door into his drawing room. Meanwhile, Miss Withers cast aside maidenly modesty and tore pins from her hair, the dress from her shoulders. Clutching a robe around her, she opened the door a crack and announced, "This is an *outrage!*"

The train conductor, a Pullman conductor, and two Altoona police detectives crowded in, ignoring her protest. They pawed through the wardrobe, peered into every nook and cranny.

Miss Withers stood rooted to the spot, in more ways than one. There was a damp brownish-red spot on the carpet, and she had one foot firmly holding it down. At last the delegation backed out, with apologies. Then she heard a feeble, imploring tapping on the connecting door, and John J. Malone's voice whispering "Help!"

The maiden schoolteacher stuck her head out into the corridor again, where the search party was already waiting for Malone to open up. "Oh, officer!" she cried tremulously. "Is there any danger?"

"No, ma'am."

"Was the man you're looking for a burly, dark-complexioned cutthroat with dark glasses and a pronounced limp in the left leg?"

"No, lady. Get lost, please, lady."

"Because on my way back from the diner I saw a man like that. He leered, and then followed me through three cars."

"The man we're looking for is an embezzler, not a mental case." They hammered on Malone's door again. "Open up in there!"

Over her shoulder Miss Withers could see the pale, perspiring face of John J. Malone as he dragged Steve Larsen back into her compartment again.

"But, officer," she improvised desperately, "I'm sure that the awful dark man who followed me was a distinct criminal type——" There was a reassuring whisper of "Okay" from behind her, and the sound of a softly closing door. Miss Withers backed into her compartment, closed and locked the connecting door, and then sank down on the edge of her berth, trying to avoid the blankly staring eyes of the dead man.

Next door there was a rumble of voices, and then suddenly Malone's high tenor doing rough justice to "Did Your Mother Come from Ireland?" The schoolteacher heard no more than the first line of the chorus before the Jello in her knees melted completely. When she opened her eyes again, she saw Malone holding a dagger before her, and she very nearly fainted again.

"You were so right," the little lawyer told her admiringly. "It was a frame-up all right—but meant for me. *This* was tucked into the upholstery of my room. I sat on it while they were searching, and had to burst into song to cover my howl of anguish."

"Oh, dear!" said Miss Withers.

He sat down beside her, patted her comfortingly on the shoulder, and said, "Maybe I can shove the body out the window!"

"We're still in the station," she reminded him crisply. "And from what experience I've had with train windows, it would be easier to solve the murder than open one. Why don't we start searching for clues?"

Malone stood up so quickly that he rapped his head on the bottom of the upper berth. "Never mind *clues*. Let's just find the murderer!"

"Just as easy as that?"

"Look," he said. "This train was searched at the request of the Chicago police because somebody—probably Bert Glick—tipped them off that Larsen and a lot of stolen money were on board. The word has got around. Obviously, somebody else knew—somebody who caught the train and did the dirty work. It's reasonable to assume that whoever has the money is the killer."

There was a new glint in Miss Withers' blue-gray eyes. "Go on."

"Also, Larsen's ex-wife—or do I mean ex-widow?—is aboard. I saw her. She is a lovely girl whose many friends agree that she would eat her young or sell her old mother down the river into slavery for a fast buck." He took out a cigar. "I'll go next door and have a smoke while you change, and then we'll go look for Lolly Larsen."

"I'm practically ready now," the schoolteacher agreed. "But take *that* with you!"

Malone hesitated, and then with a deep sigh reached down and took a firm grasp of all that was mortal of his late client. "Here we go again!"

A few minutes later Miss Hildegarde Withers was following Malone through the now-darkened train. The fact that this was somebody else's problem never occurred to her. Murder, according to her tenets, was everybody's business.

Malone touched her arm as they came at last to the door of the club car. "Here is where I saw Lolly last," he whispered. "She only got aboard at the last minute, and didn't have a reservation." He pointed down the corridor. "See that door, just this side of the pantry? It's a private lounge, used only for railroad officials or big-shots like governors or senators. Lolly bribed the steward to let her use it when she wanted to have a private talk with me. It just occurred to me that she might have talked him into letting her have it for the rest of the night. If she's still there—"

"Say no more," Miss Withers cut in. "I am a fellow passenger, also without a berth, seeking only a place to rest my weary head. After all, I have as much right in there as she has. But you will be within call, won't you?"

"If you need help, just holler," he promised. Malone watched as the school-teacher marched down the corridor, tried the lounge door gently, and then knocked. The door opened and she vanished inside.

The little lawyer had an argument with his conscience. It wasn't just that she re-minded him of Miss Hackett, it was that she had become a sort of partner. Besides, he was getting almost fond of that equine face.

Oh, well, he'd be within earshot. And if there was anything in the inspiration which had just come to him, she wasn't in any real danger anyway. He went on into the bar. It was half-dark and empty now, except for a little group of men in Navy uniforms at the far end, who were sleeping sprawled and entangled like a lit-ter of puppies.

"Sorry, Mr. Malone, but the bar is closed," a voice spoke up behind him. It was Horace Lee Randolph, looking drawn and exhausted. He caught Malone's glance toward the sleeping sailors and added, "Against the rules, but the conductor said don't bother 'em."

Malone nodded, and then said, "Horace, we're old friends and classmates. You know me of old, and you know you can trust me. *Where did you hide it?*"

"Where did I hide what?"

"You know what!" Malone fixed the man with the cold and baleful eye he used on prosecution witnesses. "Let me have it before it's too late, and I'll do my best for you."

The eyes rolled. "Oh, Lawdy! I knew I shouldn't a done it, Mista Malone! I'll show you!" Horace hurried on down through the car and unlocked a small closet filled with mops and brooms. From a box labeled *Soap Flakes* he came up with a paper sack. It was a very small sack to hold a hundred thousand dollars, Malone thought, even if the money was in big bills. Horace fumbled inside the sack.

"What's *that?*" Malone demanded.

"What would it be but the bottle of gin I sneaked from the bar? Join me?"

The breath went out of John J. Malone like air out of a busted balloon. He caught the doorknob for support, swaying like an aspen in the wind. It was at just that moment that they both heard the screams.

The rush of self-confidence with which Miss Hildegarde Withers had pushed her way into the lounge ebbed somewhat as she came face to face with Lolly Larsen. Appeals to sympathy, as from one supposedly stranded fellow passenger to another, failed utterly. It was not until the schoolteacher played her last card, reminding Lolly sharply that if there was any commotion the Pullman conductor would undoubtedly have them both evicted, that she succeeding in getting a toehold.

"Oh, *all right!*" snarled Lolly ungraciously. "Only shut up and go to sleep."

During the few minutes before the room went dark again, Miss Withers made a mental snapshot of everything in it. No toilet, no wardrobe, no closet. A small suitcase, a coat and a handbag were on the only chair. The money must be somewhere in this room, the schoolteacher thought. There was a way to find out.

As the train flashed through the moonlit night, Miss Withers busily wriggled out of her petticoat and ripped it into shreds. Using a bit of paper from her handbag for tinder—and inwardly praying it wasn't a ten-dollar bill—she did what had to be done. A few minutes later she burst out into the corridor, holding her handkerchief to her mouth.

She almost bumped into one of the sailors who came lurching toward her along the narrow passage, and gasped, "What do you want?"

He stared at her with heavy eyes. "If it's any of your business, I'm looking for the latrine," he said dryly.

When he was out of sight, Miss Withers turned and peeked back into the lounge. A burst of acrid smoke struck her in the face. Now was the time. "*Fire!*" she shrieked.

Thick billows of greasy smoke flooded out through the half-open door. Inside, little tongues of red flame ran greedily along the edge of the seat where Miss Withers had tucked the burning rags and paper.

Down the corridor came Malone and Horace Lee Randolph, and a couple of startled bluejackets appeared form the other direction. Somebody tore an extinguisher from the wall.

Miss Withers grabbed Malone's arm. "Watch her! She'll go for the money——"

The fire extinguisher sent a stream of foaming chemicals into the doorway just as Lolly Larsen burst out. Her mascara streaked down her face, already blackened by smoke, and her yellow hair was plastered unflatteringly to her skull. But she clutched a small leather case.

Somehow she tripped over Miss Withers' outstretched foot. The leather case flew across the corridor to smash against the wall, where it flew open, disclosing a multitude of creams, oils, and tiny bottles——a portable beauty parlor.

"She must have gone to sleep smoking a cigarette!" put in Miss Withers in loud clear tones. "A lucky thing I was there to smell the smoke and give the alarm——"

But John J. Malone seized her firmly by the arm and propelled her back through the train. "It was a good try, but you can stop acting now. She doesn't have the money." Back in her own compartment he confessed about Horace. "I had a wonderful idea, but it didn't pay off. The poor guy's career as a lawyer was busted by a City Hall chiseler. If Larsen was the one, Horace might have spotted him on the train and decided to get even."

"You were holding out on me," said Miss Withers, slightly miffed.

Malone unwrapped a cigar and said, "If anybody finds that money, I want it to be me. Because I've got to get my fee out of it or I can't even get back to Chicago."

"Perhaps you'll learn to like Manhattan," she told him brightly.

Malone said grimly, "If something isn't done soon, I'm going to see New York through those cold iron bars."

"We're in the same boat. Except," she added honestly, "that I don't think the Inspector would go so far as to lock me up. But he does take a dim view of anybody who finds a body and doesn't report it." She sighed. "Do you think we *could* get one of these windows open?"

Malone smothered a yawn and said, "Not in my present condition of exhaustion."

"Let's begin at the beginning," the schoolteacher said. "Larsen invited a number of people to a party he didn't plan to attend. He sneaked on this train, presumably disguised in a Navy enlisted man's uniform. How he got hold of it——"

"He was in the service for a while," said the little lawyer.

"The murderer made a date to meet his victim in your drawing room, hoping to set *you* up as the goat. He stuck a knife in him and then stripped him, looking for a money-belt or something."

"You don't have to undress a man to find a moneybelt," Malone murmured.

"Really? I wouldn't know." Miss Withers sniffed. "The knife was then hidden in your room, but the body was moved in here. The money——" She paused and studied him searchingly. "Mr. Malone, are you sure you didn't——?"

"We plead not guilty and not guilty by reason of insanity," Malone muttered. He closed his eyes for just five seconds' much-needed rest, and when he opened them a dirty-looking dawn was glaring in at him through the window.

"Good morning," Miss Withers greeted him, entirely too cheerfully. "Did you get any ideas while you were in dreamland?" She put away her toothbrush and added, "You know, I've sometimes found that if a problem seems insoluble, you can sleep on it and sometimes your subconscious comes up with the answer. Sometimes it's even happened to me in a dream."

"It does? It *has?*" Malone sat up suddenly. "Okay. Burglars can't be choosers. Sleep and the world sleeps——I mean, I'll just stand watch for a while and you try taking a nap. Maybe you can dream up an answer out of your subconscious. But dream fast, lady, because we get in about two hours from now."

But when Miss Withers had finally been comfortably settled against the pillows, she found that her eyelids stubbornly refused to stay shut.

"Try once more," John J. Malone said soothingly. She closed her eyes obediently, and his high, whispering tenor filled the little compartment, singing a fine old song. It was probably the first time in history, Miss Withers thought, that anyone had tried to use "Throw Him Down, McCluskey" as a lullaby, but she found herself drifting off....

Malone passed the time by trying to imagine what he would do with a hundred grand if he were the murderer. There must have been a desperate need for haste—— at any moment, someone might come back to the murder room. The money would have to be put somewhere handy——some obvious place where nobody would ever think of looking, and where it could be quickly and easily retrieved when all was clear.

There was an angry growl from Precious in his cage. "If you could only say something besides 'Meerow' and 'Fssst'!" Malone murmured wistfully. "Because you're the only witness. Now if it had been the parrot ..."

At last he touched Miss Withers apologetically on the shoulder. "Wake up, ma'am, we're coming into New York. Quick, what did you dream?"

She blinked, sniffed, and came wide awake. "My dream? Why——I was buying a hat, a darling little sailor hat, only it had to be exchanged because the ribbon was yellow. But first I wore it out to dinner with Inspector Piper, who took me to a Greek restaurant, and the proprietor was so glad to see us that he said dinner was on the house. But naturally we didn't eat anything because you have to beware of the Greeks when they come bearing gifts. His name was Mr. Roberts. That's all I remember."

"Oh, *brother!*" said John J. Malone.

"And there wasn't anyone named Roberts mixed up in this case, or anyone of Greek extraction, was there?" She sighed. "Pure nonsense. I guess a watched subconscious never boils."

The train was crawling laboriously up an elevated platform. "A drowning man will grasp at a strawberry," Malone said suddenly. "I've got a sort of an idea. Greeks bearing gifts—that means look out for somebody who wants to give you something for nothing. And that something could include gratuitous information."

She nodded. "Perhaps someone planned to murder Larsen aboard this train and wanted you aboard to be the obvious suspect."

The train shuddered to a stop. Malone leaped up, startled, but the schoolteacher told him it was only 125th Street. "Perhaps we should check and see who gets off." She glanced out the window and said, "On second thought, let's not. The platform is swarming with police."

They were interrupted by the porter, who brushed off Miss Withers, accepted a dollar from the gallant Malone, and then lugged her suitcases and the pet container down to the vestibule. "He'll be in your room next," she whispered to Malone. "What do we do now?"

"We think fast," Malone said. "The rest of your dream! The sailor hat with the wrong ribbon! And Mr. Roberts—"

The door burst open and suddenly they were surrounded by detectives, led by a grizzled sergeant in plain clothes. Lolly Larsen was with them. She had removed most of the traces of the holocaust, her face was lovely and her hair was gleaming, but her mood was that of a dyspeptic cobra. She breathlessly accused Miss Withers of assaulting her and trying to burn her alive, and Malone of engineering Steve Larsen's successful disappearance.

"So," said Malone. "You wired ahead from Albany, crying copper?"

"Maybe she did," said the sergeant. "But we'd already been contacted by the Chicago police. Somebody out there swore out a warrant for Steve Larsen's arrest . . ."

"Glick, maybe?"

"A Mr. Allen Roth, according to the teletype. Now, folks—"

But Malone was trying to pretend that Lolly, the sergeant, and the whole police department didn't exist. He faced Miss Withers and said, "About that dream! It must mean a sailor under false colors. We already know that Larsen was disguised in Navy uniform . . ."

"Shaddap!" said the sergeant. "Maybe you don't know, mister, that helping an embezzler to escape makes you an assessory after the fact."

"*Acc*essory," correct Miss Withers firmly.

237

"If you want Larsen," Malone said easily, "he's next door in my drawing room, wrapped up in the blankets."

"Sure, sure," said the sergeant, mopping his face. "Wise guy, eh?"

"Somebody helped Larsen escape—escape out of this world, with a shiv through the—throught the—?" Malone looked hopefully at Miss Withers.

"The *latissimus dorsi*," she prompted.

The sergeant barked, "Never mind the double-talk. Where is this Larsen?"

Then Lolly, who had pushed open the connecting door, let out a thin scream like tearing silk. "It *is* Steve!" she cried. "It's Steve, and he's dead!"

Momentarily the attention of the law was drawn elsewhere. "Now or never," said Miss Withers coolly. "About the Mr. Roberts thing—I just remembered that there was a play by that name a while back. All about sailors in the last war. I saw it, and was somewhat shocked at certain scenes. Their language—but anyway, I ran into a sailor just after I started that fire, and he said he was looking for the *latrine*. Sailors don't use Army talk—in *Mister Roberts* they called it the *head*!"

Suddenly the law was back, very direct and grim about everything. Miss Withers gasped with indignation as she found herself suddenly handcuffed to John J. Malone. But stone walls do not a prison make, as she pointed out to her companion-in-crime. "And don't you see? It means—"

"Madam, I am ahead of you. There was a *wrong* sailor aboard this train even after Larsen got his. The murderer must have taken a plane from Chicago and caught this train at Toledo. I was watching to see who got off, not who got on. The man penetrated Larsen's disguise—"

"In more ways than one," the schoolteacher put in grimly.

"And then after he'd murdered his victim, he took Larsen's sailor suit and got rid of his own clothes, realizing that nobody notices a sailor on a train! Madam, I salute your subconscious!" Malone waved his hand, magnificent even in chains. "The defense rests! Officer, call a cop!"

The train was crawling into one of the tunnels beneath Grand Central Station, and the harried sergeant was beside himself. "You listen to Mr. Malone," Miss Withers told their captor firmly, "or I'll hint to my old friend Inspector Oscar Piper that you would look well on a bicycle beat way out in Brooklyn!"

"Oh, no!" the unhappy officer moaned. "Not *that* Miss Withers!"

"That Miss Withers," she snapped. "My good man, all we ask is that you find the real murderer, who must still be on this train. He's wearing a Navy uniform . . ."

"Lady," the sergeant said sincerely, "you ask the impossible. The train is full of sailors, Grand Central is full of sailors."

"But this particular sailor," Malone put in, "is wearing the uniform of the man he killed. *There will be a slit in the back of the jumper*—just under the shoulder blade!"

"Where the knife went in," Miss Withers added. "Hurry, man! The train is stopping."

It might still have been a lost cause had not Lolly put in her five cents. "Don't listen to that old witch!" she cried. "Officer, you do your duty!"

The sergeant disliked being yelled at, even by blondes. "Hold all of 'em—her too," he ordered, and leaped out on the platform. He seized upon a railroad dick, who listened and then grabbed a telephone attached to a nearby pillar. Somewhere far off an alarm began to ring, and an emotionless voice spoke over the public address system. . . .

In less than two minutes the vast labyrinth of Grand Central was alerted, and men in Navy uniforms were suddenly intercepted by polite but firm railroad detectives who sprang up out of nowhere. Only one of the sailors, a somewhat older man who was lugging a pet container that wasn't his, had any real difficulty. He alone had a narrow slit in the back of his jumper.

Bert Glick flung the leather case down the track and tried vainly to run, but there was no place to go. The container flew open, and Precious scooted. Only a dumb Siamese cat, as Malone commented later, would have abandoned a lair that had a hundred grand tucked under its carpet of old newspapers.

"And to think that I spent the night within reach of that dough, and didn't grab my fee!" said Malone.

But it developed that there was a comfortable reward for the apprehension of Steve Larsen, alive or dead. Before John J. Malone took off for Chicago, he accepted an invitation for dinner at Miss Wither's modest little apartment on West 74th Street, arriving with four dozen roses. It was a good dinner, and Malone cheerfully put up with the screamed insults of Sinbad and the well-meant attentions of Talley, the apricot poodle. "Just as long as the cat stays lost!" he said.

"Yes, isn't it odd that nobody has seen hide nor hair of Precious! It's my idea that he's waxing fat in the caverns beneath Grand Central, preying on the rats who are rumored to flourish there. Would you care for another piece of pie, Mr. Malone?"

"All I really want," said the little lawyer hopefully, "is an introduction to your redheaded niece."

"Oh, yes, Joannie. Her husband played guard for Southern California, and he even made All-American," Miss Withers tactfully explained.

"On second thought, I'll settle for coffee," said John J. Malone.

Miss Withers sniffed, not unsympathetically.

Lawrence G. Blochman

(1900–1975)

Dr. Daniel Webster Coffee, pathologist of the Pasteur Hospital in mythical Northbank, New Jersey, and his Hindu assistant, Dr. Motilal Mookerji, on scholarship from Calcutta Medical College, were the first team of forensic sleuths in crime fiction, the forefathers of TV's *Quincy* and such contemporary detectives as Patricia Cornwell's Kay Scarpetta. Along with police lieutenant Max Ritter, Coffee and Mookerji were featured in numerous short stories published in *Collier's* and *Ellery Queen's Mystery Magazine* in the 1940s, 1950s, and 1960s. Their cases, which utilize modern (circa 1950) laboratory procedures in pathology, chemistry, serology, microscopy, and toxicology, have a uniform sense of realism, the result of the author's extensive research in forensic medicine.

Diagnosis: Homicide (1950), the first of two Dr. Coffee collections, was considered by Ellery Queen to be of sufficient import in the development of the detective short story that it became the 106th and final entry on the Queen's Quorum list of most influential collections. The team of pathologists also appears in *Clues for Dr. Coffee* (1964), and in a single novel, *Recipe for Homicide* (1952), a readable but minor work. The duo's talents, as Blochman himself seems to have realized, were better suited to the short-story form.

Although Dr. Mookerji speaks a sort of "babu" English, he is never portrayed as anything other than Dr. Coffee's equal professionally and as a human being. Lawrence Blochman lived in India for several years in the 1920s, while working as a foreign correspondent, and both understood and respected the Indian culture; his re-creation of an educated Hindu's English speech patterns may seem dubious by today's standards, but it carried no racist overtones. Dr. Mookerji's considerable forensic talents are prominently featured in several of the duo's investigations, among them "The Phantom Cry-Baby," the strange case of a woman who hears an infant crying in the night even though there is no baby in her house.

Lawrence G. Blochman created numerous other series characters during his four decades as a crime-story writer, many of these for the magazine markets at which most of his fiction was aimed. Inspector Leonidas Prike of the British Criminal Investigation Department is the featured performer in such excellent early novels as *Bombay Mail* (1934), set aboard a train bound from Calcutta to Bombay, and *Red Snow at Darjeeling* (1938), which takes place in the northern Indian tea-growing region in the shadow of the Himalayas. Other Blochman novels of note are *Blow-Down* (1939), a mystery-adventure tale set in a sleepy Central American banana port, and *See You at the Morgue* (1941), which concerns murder and a stolen shipment of valuable furs in New York City.

THE PHANTOM CRY-BABY

DR. DANIEL WEBSTER COFFEE AND DR. MOTILAL MOOKERJI
NEW JERSEY
C. 1950

D r. Daniel Webster Coffee was preparing a test for undulant fever. Intent on scraping the emulsion from a culture plate, he was not aware that he had a visitor in his laboratory until the man cleared his throat noisily.

"Dr. Coffee? I'm Leonard Philips. The Superintendent sent me to you." The visitor extended a big, muscular hand.

Dr. Coffee put down his platinum loop and shook hands with a gangling, white-haired, pick-faced man in a seersucker suit. Leonard Philips had the appearance of a country judge and the demeanor of a bass-voiced brush salesman. The aggressive smile and the long jaw above the black bow tie were vaguely familiar to Dr. Coffee.

"The Superintendent says you have a foreigner working in your lab," Philips said. "His name is Mookerji."

"Dr. Motilal Mookerji is our resident pathologist," Dan Coffee said. "He's a Hindu."

"I'm an attorney," Philips said. "Your Hindu friend has got himself in trouble with a client of mine. Do you know Mrs. Louise Gable?"

Dr. Coffee nodded. Then he laughed. The nod was for Mrs. Gable. Everyone in Northbank knew Louise Barzac Gable, a dark, handsome widow, the sole heir of the late Jacques Barzac, a Frenchman who had pyramided a side-street restaurant

241

and a tomato farm into a ten-million-dollar food cannery. The laugh was for Dr. Mookerji. Somehow Dan Coffee could not picture the round, brown, pink-turbaned Hindu in trouble with a beautiful young American widow.

"Is your Hindu friend an M.D.?" Philips asked.

"Dr. Mookerji is a graduate physician from Calcutta Medical College. He's continuing his studies here in America on a fellowship."

"You tell your Hindu resident that if he doesn't stay away from Mrs. Gable, I'll have him arrested for practicing medicine without a license," Philips declared. "He's been prescribing for my client."

Dr. Coffee frowned. This was serious—and puzzling. Dr. Mookerji was training for the laboratory, not the clinic. "Tell me about it," he said.

Leonard Philips carefully placed his straw hat on the centrifuge. "I guess you know that Mrs. Gable's husband was in the Air Force. The Japs killed him; shot him down over the Burma jungles a few days before V-J Day, the same day his son was born here in Northbank. The baby died a week later. Louise hasn't been quite right since. And lately she's been acting very strange indeed. She hears a baby crying at night in that big house of hers—and of course there isn't any baby."

"Where does Dr. Mookerji come in?" Dan Coffee asked.

Dr. Mookerji came in, the attorney said, when Philips urged Mrs. Gable to see a psychiatrist. Dr. Mookerji told her that there was nothing wrong with her except that she ought to remarry; that she needed a husband, not a psychiatrist.

"Damn it, Doctor," Philips said, "the woman can't get married if she's got a screw coming loose. It's not fair to the prospective husband or to a possible child. Don't you agree that she ought to see a psychiatrist?"

"I wouldn't prescribe without seeing the patient," said Dr. Coffee.

"She's completely goofy," Philips declared. "I'm executor of her father's estate, and I've never been able to settle the estate because she won't sign papers. She loses them. She gets mad and tears them up. She wants to turn that big house of hers into a foundlings' home, but she won't listen when I try to explain about titles and encumbrances. She's got to see a psychiatrist, Doctor. Will you tell this Mookerji to keep his advice to himself?"

"I'll speak to him," said Dr. Coffee. He handed Leonard Philips his hat.

Two hours later Dr. Motilal Mookerji returned to duty. The fat little Hindu waddled into the pathology laboratory, looking a little like a brown duck in a double-breasted suit and pink turban except that he stuck out in front instead of behind. His ready-made trousers settled in horizontal folds about his shoe-tops. He said, "Good afternoon, Doctor Sahib," took off his coat, and flipped up the tail of his turban so that it would fall outside the back of the white jacket he put on.

Dan Coffee looked up from his microscope. "Dr. Mookerji, what's this I hear about your trying to persuade a rich widow to marry you?"

"Widow? Marry?" The Hindu resident's mouth opened until his three brown chins made perfect accordion pleats. "Said statement is honeycombed with inaccuracies, Doctor Sahib. Item A: While Hindu widows no longer incinerate selves on funeral pyre of late husbands, widows still enjoy great disfavor in India regarding further matrimony. Item B: Am personally betrothed since age of nine years and married since seventeen. Having one wife and three assorted children currently residing with father in Bengal, am of opinion that bigamous courtship of American ladies would no doubt entail legal consequences."

"But you do know Mrs. Gable, Dr. Mookerji?"

"Quite." Dr. Mookerji's long black lashes drooped over his intelligent brown eyes. He looked at his hands—long, incongruously slim hands for one of his build. "Mrs. Gable's late deceased husband, Leftenant Gable, was semi-intimate friend of self while stationed Calcutta-side."

Lieutenant Gable, it seemed, had become quite chummy with Motilal Mookerji before he was moved to a forward base in Assam. Lieutenant Gable was more interested in the Hindu classics than in Karaiya Road, and even after he began flying combat missions, he spent his leaves in Calcutta and read *Bhagavad Gita* with the future Dr. Mookerji. On his last leave he had charged Mookerji with sending his annotated copy of *Bhagavad Gita* to his wife in case he did not come back. He had also counseled Mookerji to use his American fellowship by accepting a residency in Northbank. New York was too cosmopolitan. California was practically an independent country devoted to lotus-eaters, motion pictures, and citrus fruits. The South would not like the color of the Hindu's skin. The Middle West was the only place to learn about the real America. . . .

"Distinctly remember Leftenant Gable's parting words," said Dr. Mookerji. "'Come to Northbank,' he was advising, 'and we will eat cobbled corn and fried catfishes and strawberried brief-cake together—after the war.' After Leftenant Gable's heroic demise, was therefore honored to bring sad volume of *Bhagavad Gita* to Widow Gable with own hands."

About Louise Gable's sanity? Well, Dr. Mookerji wasn't a psychiatrist and he wasn't exactly sure. One couldn't be sure about any woman. All women were a little crazy, even Hindu women, and American women were particularly difficult for the Oriental to understand.

"American ladies appear somewhat schizophrenic," said Dr. Mookerji, "displaying stern male traits of boldness and commerce by day-time, while reverting to softish lures of timid female kitten at night-time."

About the baby she heard crying in the big house—the phantom baby that cried at night? Well, Louise Gable was a little crazy on the subject of babies. She had adopted —by absentee parenthood—a dozen European war orphans and a dozen Chinese babies. She wanted to make an orphans' home of the house which was much too big for her—and which Attorney Philips wanted to sell to a syndicate launching a new country club. Dr. Mookerji had never heard the baby which was supposed to cry in that house; nobody had; the servants lived in rooms over the garage and had never been in the house when the phantom baby cried. However, Dr. Mookerji was confident that the crying would stop if only Louise Gable would remarry and have another baby of her own. "According to Manu, Hindu lawgiver," said Dr. Mookerji, "women and oxen are superior creatures when yoked in team than when roaming at large. Therefore am enacting role of Kama, who is Hindu god somewhat resembling Cupid."

Louise Gable had two suitors, the Hindu said: Roger Gable, her late husband's brother, a former captain in the 101st Airborne who had been wounded at Bastogne, and who flew down from New York every weekend to court Louise; and Jim Stoneman, the handsome young manager of the Barzac Cannery. Roger Gable, it seemed, wanted to marry Louise whether she was crazy or not; the crazier, the better; he was a little crazy himself since that German shell fragment made a hole in his head. Jim Stoneman didn't say very much, but he did considerable courting of Louise five days a week and didn't mind the gossip about his courting the cannery.

"Am personally favoring suit of Captain Gable," the Hindu said. "Hindu tendency favors retaining betrothals in some family, if sufficient brothers survive. Besides, Captain Gable is splendid guy."

Unfortunately, Louise Gable seemed to favor Jim Stoneman. Stoneman was quietly serious, an excellent administrator, and the ideal man to look out for the family canning interests. Roger Gable was a big, irresponsible, irrepressible boy. Lovable, but—

Dr. Coffee interrupted to report the visit of Leonard Philips—and Philips' threat. "You will be careful about giving Mrs. Gable medical advice, won't you, Doctor?"

The Hindu wagged his bulky turban once to the left. He sighed. "Am of opinion that patent attorneys should remain glued to patents, even when canning inventions catapult same to position of power and glory. Am also of opinion that Barrister Philips is behaving like bulldog in cow-manger. Am desirous you should make acquaintance of Widow Gable, Doctor Sahib."

"Any time you say," Dan Coffee said—cheerfully. He could not know that within thirty hours he would not only have met the Widow Gable, but that she would be clinging to his arm with panic-clamped fingers, staring at a dead man.

•

None of it seemed quite real to Dr. Coffee except the wind and the rain outside, making the night lugubrious with sullen, stealthy, muted sounds. Yet the dead man on the stairs was real enough. So was the beautiful young woman he had met half an hour before, staring at the corpse with dark, fear-haunted eyes. Even the imaginary baby crying somewhere in the upper stories of the house must be real, since Dr. Coffee had heard the crying. Leonard Philips had said that Louise Gable was losing her mind, because she heard the baby. For a moment Dr. Coffee thought that perhaps he, too, was losing his sanity—until he reminded himself that this nightmare had begun prosaically and logically at his own front door that very evening.

It was a quiet Sunday evening, and Dr. Coffee had been exercising his weekly privilege of cluttering up the kitchen with what his wife called his "pathological culinary experiments." Dr. Coffee, who liked to eat, had a theory that a good trencherman should be a good cook. So far he had been only partially successful in proving his theory. For the past five Sundays he had been working on the problem of devising a cheese soufflé that would not collapse immediately upon being taken from the oven. Experiment No. 5 succeeded in delaying the collapse by forty-five seconds. He had wiped the flour from his eyebrow and the beaten egg-whites from the kitchen wall, recorded the oven temperature and recipe calibrations in a notebook, and, under the disapproving eye of his wife, stacked an amazing number of kitchen utensils in the sink. Then, since it was raining, he settled himself in an easy chair with a volume of Escoffier's cookbook.

Northbank's summer rains usually fell at night—steady enough to soak through the topsoil but never heavy enough to spoil the crops. Northbank owed its prosperity to its nocturnal rains which left the daylight hours to the ripening sunshine and flooded the canneries with fine vegetables from the surrounding farm lands. Dr. Coffee was reflecting that the nocturnal rains also made for cozy evenings at home when his doorbell rang—three long, loud peals that sent resounding echoes scurrying through the house.

A gust of cold rain blew into Dan Coffee's face as he opened the door. Dr. Motilal Mookerji stood outside. He wore a yellow slicker over his white uniform, giving him the general contours of a captive balloon. The rain-bedraggled tail of his turban clung to his slicker like a limp pink snake. Through the blur of the downpour, Dr. Coffee could see the gleam of a black coupe at the curb.

"Pardon unannounced intrusion, Doctor Sahib," the Hindu panted. "But am suddenly encumbered with subacute case of hysterical female jitters. Will you make social and professional acquaintance of Widow Gable at this time? Splendid. Then suggest attiring self in raincloak, since Widow Gable request escort to domicile. Phantom cry-baby presently engaged in habitual frightening vocal exercises."

Dr. Coffee got his first look at Louise Gable by the glow of the dashboard lights.

Her long, oriental-looking eyes peered straight ahead into the rainy night as she gripped the wheel of her car. The street lights whisking past made rhythmic patterns of chiaroscuro with her high, pale cheekbones and the blue-black hair she wore pulled back tightly from her broad forehead and twisted into a lustrous loop that caressed the nape of her neck. There was no doubt that she was very beautiful —and very frightened.

She apologized for taking Dr. Coffee away from his home on a night like this.

"But I simply couldn't go into that house alone," she said. "I'd just come back from driving Roger Gable—that's my brother-in-law—to the airport. As soon as I opened the door I heard the baby crying. I was terrified. My servants were out. I turned to Dr. Mookerji."

How long had this been going on? Two weeks exactly. Louise remembered the first time she had heard the crying—a Sunday night after returning from taking Roger Gable to the airport. For several days there had been nothing. Then the phantom baby had cried two nights running. The last time she had heard it was three nights ago—Thursday night. And then tonight. She had been particularly terrified tonight, perhaps because she was upset. She had quarreled violently with Roger Gable before leaving him at the airport. Perhaps her mind really was in a turmoil. She would know very soon now....

Louise Gable's house, a legacy from her father, stood back from the road at the end of a long, poplar-lined lane. It had the turrets, the long steep roofs, and the tall chimneys of a Burgundian château, and the general coziness of a mausoleum. The cedars and cypress banked in precise funereal masses were black against the fieldstone walls. The high Gothic windows were dark. Dr. Coffee held a flashlamp while Louise fumbled with her keys.

The massive oak door swung open. Dr. Coffee stood for a moment in the chill, musty silence of the vaulted foyer, wondering at the chill, musty silence of the vaulted foyer, wondering at the queer disquiet that ran through him like the first malaise of a fever. The very rustle of his raincoat seemed to echo in the darkness— peopled by some lurking evil, some nameless terror. Dr. Coffee held his breath while Louise groped for the light switch.

"Quite melancholy place, eh, Doctor Sahib?" The voice of the Hindu was shrill in the darkness.

When the great crystal chandelier finally burst into brilliance, Louise Gable was standing with her hand on the switch, her face uplifted anxiously, listening for something she dreaded to hear.

"There!" said Louise. "Can't you hear it?"

Dr. Coffee listened to the spatter of rain on the windows, to the wet rustle of the trees bending to the wind, to the throb of his own pulse beat in his ears. He began to shake his head. Suddenly he heard it—a faint, thin, reedy wail which seemed to come from far off. The high, inhuman monotone grew fainter and fainter, then stopped with a quick, sharp sound like the intake of breath, like a sob.

"I can hear it," Dr. Coffee said.

"Likewise," said Dr. Mookerji.

"Thank God!" Louise breathed. "Then I'm not really mad?"

"It's upstairs," Dr. Coffee said. "We'll trace it."

"Wait." Louise slammed the heavy front door. She tried the latch. Then she snapped on the upstairs lights.

The huge gilt-framed mirror on the landing reflected their ascent of the thick-carpeted stairs—the slim, dark girl between the pudgy Hindu and the tall, sandy-haired pathologist.

When they reached the landing, the phantom baby began crying again.

When they reached the top of the staircase, they found the dead man. He was lying face down, his head hanging over the edge of the top step, one arm poked grotesquely through the gilt-bronze balustrade.

Louise Gable drew back stiffly against the wall. She opened her mouth—but there was no scream in her throat.

Dr. Coffee stopped. He turned the dead man over.

Somewhere in the house the thin wail sobbed into silence.

Louise found her voice. She said: "It's Jim Stoneman." She asked no unnecessary questions. The glazed and bulging eyes, the swollen, blue-gray face spoke unequivocally of death.

Dr. Coffee tried to recall where he had heard the name of Jim Stoneman. Of course, Stoneman was manager of the Barzac Cannery and one of Louise Gable's suitors. The pathologist examined the marks on the swollen neck. He said: "The man's been strangled—not very long ago. Was he here when you left the house, Mrs. Gable?"

"I haven't seen him today." Louise gave a queer, short laugh. It was not a hysterical laugh. Louise was stunned, but she was not hysterical. Her voice was calm as she said: "Dr. Mookerji, do you know why Roger and I quarreled at the airport tonight?"

The question seemed irrelevant to Dr. Coffee, but the Hindu said: "Am without slightest intimation."

"Roger asked me again to marry him," Louise said. "I told him no—once and for all. I told him never to come back to Northbank, because I was going to marry Jim Stoneman. And now——" Louise put her hands to her temples. Two tears rolled down her cheeks as she stared at the dead man. "I've just found out I was going to marry a man I didn't love. I liked Jim a lot. He was comfortable and practical and reliable, and I guess I loved the security he represented. But now that he's dead I don't feel anything except that I love Roger. I love him terribly—the way I loved Ralph. I love him for all his craziness and irresponsibility and— whatever the war did to him. I even love that metal patch in his skull he's always joking about. I—"

"We'll have to call the police," Dr. Coffee interrupted.

Louise clutched his arm. "Doctor, you won't say anything to the police—about what I've just told you—about Jim and me and Roger? Because ... they ... might ... think ..."

The sentence died slowly. Louise was looking past Dan Coffee, looking down the stairs with unfocused eyes.

Dr. Coffee knew what the eyes were seeking. He, too, had heard the footstep on the floor below. He murmured: "Phone the police, Mrs. Gable. Dr. Mookerji will stay with you. I'm going down."

Dan Coffee gently removed the trembling hand from his arm and started down the stairs. From the landing he could see the front door gaping wide. The rain blowing in from the night spattered darkness on the Ispahan rug. There was no one in sight.

Standing under the crystal chandelier, Dr. Coffee was uneasily aware that he made an excellent target. There was already one dead man in the house. He snapped out the lights. He was not precisely invisible in the twilight from the up-stairs fixtures, but he felt better—until, above the sounds of wind and rain, he heard the creak of flooring.

The creak came from somewhere at his right. He moved noiselessly over the thick carpet toward the small Louis XV drawing room just off the foyer. He entered the drawing room, paused. Dark silence swirled around him. His hand explored the wall. Then the floor creaked again—very close by.

"Don't move!" Dr. Coffee was surprised at the peremptory tone of his own voice. "Put up your hands!"

His fingers touched the switch. Light flooded the room.

A husky, broad-shouldered man with shy gray eyes and a strong jaw stood with his arms crooked awkwardly over his head. He smiled sheepishly, as he said: "You're Dr. Coffee, aren't you? I've heard a lot about you from Dr. Mookerji. I'm Roger Gable."

Roger lowered his arms and held out his right hand. Dan Coffee hesitated a moment, then shook it. The handshake disturbed Dr. Coffee strangely. It was as limp and nerveless as a newly-dead corpse.

"I though you went back to New York tonight, Mr. Gable," Dr. Coffee said.

"My flight was washed out," Roger said. "I didn't want to bother Louise, so I took a taxi in from the airport."

"I didn't hear any taxi."

"He dropped me at the gate. I walked up the driveway. Say, is anything wrong? Where's Louise?"

"You must have heard Mrs. Gable talking upstairs," Dr. Coffee said. "Why didn't you come up, instead of sneaking off in here?"

Roger hesitated. "When I found the front door open, I was afraid something was wrong. Then, when I heard voices ... Well, I guess I was eavesdropping. Is Louise all right?"

Dr. Coffee's long fingers thoughtfully raked his unruly mop of straw-colored hair. He remembered Louise closing the front door. He looked at Roger Gable as though he were examining a section of tissue under the microscope, studying the cell pattern, seeking signs of malignancy. His lower jaw advanced slowly as he made his diagnosis. Then he jerked his head toward the door.

"Let's go up," he said.

Louise was standing in front of the gaudy mirror on the landing. Her lips parted when she recognized Roger.

"Captain Gable!" exclaimed Dr. Mookerji. "You are arriving in notch of time. What luck!"

"Bad luck, I'm afraid, Roger," said Louise Gable. She buried her face against Roger's shoulder and sobbed.

Outside the house the police sires were wailing.

It was two o'clock in the morning before Dan Coffee got to bed. There had been long, repetitious, and—to Dr. Coffee—stupid questioning by a dozen policemen, including the Chief of Police himself. Anything connected with the Barzac name was still political magic in Northbank, and even if Barzac's sole heir was not a political figure, she was young and female and beautiful and would probably make the front pages—a fact which the Chief could scarcely overlook.

There had been endless retelling of the story of the phantom cry-baby to explain Dr. Coffee's presence in the house—with no corroborative wailing from the upper floors.

There had been a bitter argument with the Coroner, because Dr. Coffee had said that proper thermometers might help establish the time of Stoneman's death, which could now only be estimated at less than two hours before the discovery of the body—since rigor mortis had not yet set in.

There had been one lucky break—the presence of Lieutenant of Detectives Max Ritter among the confused and determined police dragoons who tramped through the house in search of clues. Ritter had been conducting a one-man fight for a Northbank police laboratory; so far unsuccessful, he had contracted an unholy alliance with Dan Coffee for the unofficial use of the Pasteur Hospital pathology laboratory in puzzling cases demanding the scientific approach. Max Ritter was lavish with his friendly winks during the whole dreary preliminaries. He finally succeeded in getting Dr. Mookerji sent back to the hospital and Dr. Coffee to his home. But he could not prevent his Chief from bundling Louise and Roger Gable off to police headquarters.

At three in the morning, just as Dan Coffee was getting to sleep, his telephone rang.

"Hi, Doc," said Lieutenant Ritter. "I thought you'd want the score by innings. First of all, Mrs. Gable got her lawyer down here—that patent attorney who's been riding the gravy train ever since he put the legal fences around Barzac's canned tomato sauce. Name is Philips. Looks like he's going to have his fling at criminal law. He's talked the Chief into letting Mrs. Gable go.

"Second of all," Max Ritter continued, "the Chief is still holding this guy Roger Gable. The Chief sweat his story out of him—that he thought he was going to marry his sister-in-law until she told him tonight she was gong to ditch him for Stoneman. So the Chief's got it all pat—Gable killed Stoneman; motive, jealousy, and maybe one greedy eye on the Barzac estate. Do you think Gable did it, Doc?"

"I don't know, Max," Dan Coffee said sleepily. "I don't know what to think of his story of the front door being open."

"Neither do I," the detective said, "but somebody opened it—even if Mrs. Gable says she has the only key to the front door. How did Stoneman get in, Doc —unless she let him in herself? One more thing, Doc. Did you notice this guy Stoneman had both hands doubled up? Well, his right fist was full of little gray lumps, like coarse gravel. Maybe it's nothing, but maybe it's something. Anyhow, I sneaked out a few lumps before the Coroner took over, just in case you want to make with the test tubes. What time you due at your shop in the morning?"

"I'm driving over to Lycoville first thing," Dr. Coffee said. "They want me to sit in on an operation. Why don't you drop off the samples at my lab? Dr. Mookerji will be there."

"That Swami again?"

"You ought to know that Dr. Mookerji is a bank-up chemist, Max, after the job he did on the Starkey case."

"Sure, he's aces in chemistry," Ritter said. "Only we don't talk the same brand of English. Look, Doc, come right down to the morgue after Lycoville. I'll stall the autopsy till you get there."

"See you before noon, Max. Goodnight."

•

The autopsy revealed little except that Jim Stoneman had been strangled by a strong right hand. The marks on the throat—thumbmark on one side, the four fingers on the other—indicated only one hand had throttled Stoneman: the right one. A fractured thyroid cartilage and bleeding in the windpipe were index to the murderer's strength. Louise Gable was eliminated as the strangler because her right hand was too small to fit the marks on the dead man's throat. Roger Gable's hands were plenty big enough, so Roger remained in jail.

After the autopsy, Max Ritter asked Dr. Coffee: "Have you heard from Mrs. Gable?"

Dr. Coffee hadn't.

"Her lawyer, that guy Philips, calls me every hour on the hour to ask if I've seen her. Seems she walked out of the police station at three-thirty this morning and nobody's heard from her since. Philips is worried. But I guess she'll turn up. Say, I been talking to your Swami on the phone. I guess he knows what the gravel is, but you'll have to interpret for me, Doc. I'll drive you to the hospital."

The Hindu resident was bent over the autoclave when the two men entered the laboratory. As he straightened up, emerging like a rotund oriental Mephisto from a cloud of steam, the top of his turban came just to Dr. Coffee's shoulder.

"But Lieutenant Ritter received explanation of utmost lucidity," Dr. Mookerji protested. "Because of crystalline fracture, ventured opinion that dark, brittle substances were carbide of calcium. Suspicions confirmed by exposing same to contact with water, thereby causing decomposition into calcium hydroxide plus highly inflammable endothermic gas having somewhat stinking odor plus two atoms each of carbon and hydrogen. Gas is entitled acetylene. Correct, Doctor Sahib?"

"See what I mean, Doc? Ritter said.

"Your gravel is calcium carbide, which gives off acetylene gas when you add water," said Dr. Coffee. "You're just too young, Max. You're a child of the electric age. When I was a boy, I had a carbide lamp on my bicycle."

"I used to walk my paper route," the detective said. "I didn't have a bicycle. Neither did Stoneman when he was killed. The carbide mean anything, Doc?"

"Maybe." Dr. Coffee lighted a cigarette and thoughtfully watched the match burn down. "Max, did it rain last Thursday night?"

"I wouldn't know," Ritter answered.

"Dr. Mookerji, did it rain last Thursday night?"

The voluminous turban wagged back and forth. "Greatly fear am somewhat nincompoop regarding retention of meteorological data," the Hindu said.

"He doesn't remember either," Dr. Coffee interpreted. He turned to Doris Hudson, his chief technician. "Doris, call the weather bureau and ask if it rained in

Northbank Thursday night. Also find out if it rained two weeks ago Sunday night. Then phone Washington and locate General Barrington of the Veterans Administration. Ask the General to wire me collect the case history of Captain Roger Gable of the 101st Airborne, with a detailed description of head wounds ·received at Bastogne."

"Is that all?" asked Miss Hudson sweetly.

"After that, we get to work. Max, I've got a stack of slides to diagnose. I'll be tied up for about four hours, but I'd like to go out to Mrs. Gable's house with you late this afternoon. I think we may find out what makes Mrs. Gable's cry-baby cry."

In mid-afternoon Louise Gable herself appeared in the laboratory. She was pale and haggard and she wore the same blue dress she was wearing when Dr. Coffee last saw her. She had obviously been without sleep.

She was dry-eyed as she talked to Dan Coffee, but there were tears in her voice —the bitter, blind, hopeless tears of despair. She had been driving almost constantly since three-thirty in the morning, looking for the taxi that had picked up Roger at the airport and brought him to her home. She had hoped that the taxi driver could establish the exact time he had dropped Roger and that it would be later than the discovery of Jim Stoneman's body. She had finally found the driver, only to learn that he could not vouch for Roger's innocence. His watch had stopped. He did not know the exact time he had deposited Roger.

"Do you think Roger could have killed Jim, Doctor?" Louise asked. "Could that hole in his skull have affected his mind so that he really went mad after our fight at the airport—temporarily, I mean, just long enough to come back and kill Jim? Could it, Doctor?"

"I don't know," Dan Coffee said, "yet."

"Then I'll keep on looking. I must find someone who can say that Roger didn't come to my house until after Jim was dead. I must! I love him, Doctor. I've got to save him."

"You've got to get some sleep, Mrs. Gable."

"But I can't sleep. I can't possibly."

"I'll give you something to help." Dr. Coffee scribbled on a slip of paper. "Dr. Mookerji will go down the hall with you to the dispensary. They'll give you a bottle. When you get home, take one teaspoonful in a glass of water. You'll be asleep in no time. If you don't get a little rest, you'll come apart like a dandelion in a high wind. Promise you'll go home and sleep?"

"I'll try." Louise closed her eyes wearily. "I'll stop by to see if Len Philips has done anything for Roger. Then I'll go home."

•

At five that afternoon, driving to Louise's ancestral mansion in a police car, Max Ritter asked Dr. Coffee: "Think we'll find anything, Doc?"

"Yes. It rained on at least three nights that the baby cried."

"Whatever that means. Anything else?"

"Yes. I've got the Army medical report on Roger Gable's head wound. A tiny shell fragment was removed from the left frontal lobe of his brain, just anterior to the Rolandic fissure."

"You talk like the Swami," Ritter said. "Has Gable's brain got anything to do with Stoneman's murder?"

"Definitely. Have you charged Roger Gable with murder yet?"

"No, but if we don't book him today, that patent attorney Philips is going to spring him on a writ of habeas corpus. Did you read in the afternoon papers about how we're trying to locate the locksmith who made a duplicate key to Mrs. Gable's front door?"

"I didn't see the papers. Having any luck?"

"War of nerves." Ritter winked. "Just in case the strangler reads the papers. But maybe we can dig up the locksmith in time. It's an old French lock. Hey, here we are."

The plainclothesman on guard at the front door said Mrs. Gable had not come home yet. He was sure; he had been there all day.

Dr. Coffee led the way directly to the attic. He explained that he was looking for some sort of hose leading either from the roof or from the gutters under the eaves. After ten minutes of poking among dusty garden furniture, discarded walnut bedsteads, trunks, and cobwebs, Dr. Coffee found a piece of metal tubing that had been forced upward through the roofing. A long, thin rubber hose ran from the bottom of this to what seemed to be a pile of gardening tools.

"I'll be damned," said Ritter. "A watering can with a tin horn stuck on the spout."

"Damned ingenious!" Dan Coffee was examining the queer contraption. "Look, Max. This metal top seals the can hermetically when you fasten the bolts. There's an intake valve in this end here, where the rubber tube feeds in."

"What's that white stuff inside?" Ritter asked.

"Slaked lime—the residue after carbide breaks down in water. And look at the valve in the spout, Max. It has a rubber band as a spring to keep it closed."

"I don't get it, Doc. Is this thing supposed to blow the New Year's Eve horn?"

"Here's how it works. When it rains, water runs into the can from the tube connected to the roof. When the water hits the carbide, acetylene gas begins to form and closes the intake valve. When the gas pressure is high enough, it forces open the valve in the spout, and the gas rushes out through the little horn soldered to the end of the spout. When enough gas has escaped to reduce the pressure, the valve snaps shut, and the process begins again. Meanwhile the horn has given off a bleating wail that sounds like a squalling baby—from a distance. The baby cried only at night, Max, because it rains at night in Northbank in summer."

"I better go down and phone the boss about this," Ritter said.

"Take another look and see if Mrs. Gable is home yet," Dan Coffee said.

The pathologist was tinkering with the strange device when he heard Ritter call from the attic stairway: "She's not home, Doc."

Dan Coffee brushed the dust from his knees and went to the stairs. "That's funny, Max," he said. "She promised to go home to bed as soon as she talked to her lawyer. I wonder——?"

A moment later he was at the phone, dialing Leonard Philips' number.

The attorney's voice was vibrant with excitement as he said: "Coffee? Thank God you called! I've been trying to reach you everywhere. I finally called the police. She was asking for you before she lost consciousness. She——"

"Who? What happened?"

"Louise Gable. She's committed suicide . . . right here in my office!"

Max Ritter's siren screamed through traffic and traffic lights the entire five miles to Philips' office. Dr. Coffee perspired the whole way—about five miles to the gallon, according to Ritter.

A police emergency ambulance stood in front of Philips' office building. The elevator crawled to the seventh floor. Leonard Philips, his pink face mottled with white, his eyes wide, his hands fluttering like big, awkward birds, led the pathologist and the detective into his law library.

"I hope you're in time to save her," Philips said. "I think she's still alive."

Louise Gable was stretched out on a leather divan, her eyes closed, her face livid. An ambulance steward was working on her. Dr. Coffee felt her pulse, lifted one eyelid, and shone a pencil flashlight into the pupil. He listened to her breathing.

"I don't know what she took," said the ambulance steward, showing an empty bottle. "There was just a skull and cross-bones on the label. But I've been——"

"You're doing all right," Dr. Coffee said. "Now get a stretcher up here and take the girl to Pasteur Hospital. I'll phone ahead."

Dr. Coffee called his hospital and was connected with the pathology laboratory. "Dr. Mookerji? You were with Mrs. Gable when she had my prescription filled at the dispensary, weren't you? . . . You saw it made up? Exactly. And they put a poison label on the bottle? . . . Listen, Doctor, Mrs. Gable has swallowed the whole thing. I'm sending her to the hospital and I want you to meet her when she reaches emergency. Tell Dr. Green what she's taken and tell him she took three grams and has probably absorbed plenty. He'll know what to do. I'm in Philips' office now, but I'll be over within half an hour."

As Dr. Coffee hung up, he looked into the anxious face of Leonard Philips. "Tell me exactly what happened, Philips," Dr. Coffee said.

It seemed that Louise had come to the attorney's office shortly before Dr. Coffee phoned. Philips told her that he had abandoned his plan to ask for a writ of habeas corpus, because the police were convinced that Roger had killed Stoneman and were going to book him for murder. After talking to Roger in his cell, Philips, too, was reluctantly convinced that Roger was guilty. Then Louise broke down and cried and said that she was afraid all along that Roger had strangled Stoneman in a fit of jealousy. She was frantic with remorse—said it was all her fault for telling Roger she had jilted him for Stoneman, and that life was not worth living now, because she really loved Roger.

"She was in a frightful state of nerves," Philips said. "I offered to send her to the drugstore for some bromides to calm her, but she said she had a sedative and asked for a glass of water. When I brought the water, she took a bottle from her handbag, emptied it into the glass and swallowed it all. When I saw the poison label on the bottle, I tried to get one of the doctors in this building, but they'd all gone home. I tried to reach you, but—"

"How long was this before I phoned?" Dr. Coffee asked.

"About five minutes."

"Max." Dr. Coffee motioned to Lieutenant of Detectives Ritter. "I want you to arrest Leonard Philips for the murder of James Stoneman and the attempted murder of Louise Gable."

"Don't be ridiculous, Doctor." Philips smiled indulgently. "Roger Gable killed Stoneman. The police are charging him with murder...."

"Roger Gable is physically incapable of having strangled Stoneman," Dr. Coffee interrupted. "Stoneman was strangled by someone's right hand. Roger hasn't enough strength in the fingers of his right hand to strangle a day-old kitten. He has a scar in his left brain, in the motor area which controls the right hand. The muscles of his fingers are partially paralyzed. The medical records of the United States Army will back me up on this, Philips."

"And does the Army also accuse me because a mentally-deranged woman poisoned herself in my office, Dr. Coffee?"

"Louise Gable is no more deranged than you are, Philips, despite everything you've done to drive her crazy," Dr. Coffee said. "This afternoon Lieutenant Ritter and I discovered your ingenious crying machine in Mrs. Gable's attic which you intended to make her believe she was losing her mind. Did you really want her committed to an institution, Philips? Or were you just trying to prevent her marriage to someone who might pry into the finances of her father's estate? Max, you'd better subpoena the accounts of the Barzac estate and have them audited for shortages. They—Hello, Dr. Mookerji. Please sit down until I've finished."

The Hindu resident, who stood panting in the doorway, waddled to the nearest chair.

"Stoneman followed you into Louise's house last night, didn't he, Philips?" Dr. Coffee continued. "He discovered your crying machine. So Stoneman had to be killed. He died with the evidence clasped in his fist—a handful of carbide. And you were still in the house, Philips, when Mrs. Gable returned with Dr. Mookerji and me. You got out in such a hurry, just before Roger Gable arrived, that you left the front door open.

"But you still had to accomplish your original purpose—to get Louise Gable out of the picture. So when Louise told you she was going to take a sleeping mixture this afternoon, and you saw the skull and cross-bones on the bottle, you gallantly offered to mix it with water for her. You lied to me about the time. It wasn't five minutes before I arrived, but closer to two hours. I gave her the mixture, Philips, and I know that narcosis doesn't begin for about half an hour. When I saw her, she had been in a deep coma for at least an hour—without medical attention, because you wanted her to die.

"But she won't die. There were exactly three grams of barbiturate in the mixture —not quite enough to cause death. She'll be pretty sick for a while, but she's going to recover—to confirm the details of what I've just told you."

"Ridiculous!" Philips sprang up. He stood very erect, trembling with indignation. "Pure conjecture. You haven't a shred of proof."

"What nonsense, Barrister!" exclaimed Dr. Mookerji, wagging his pink turban from side to side. "Evidence abounds in great profusion. Item: Humble self witnessed Barrister's secret departure from Gable house prior to arrival of Captain Gable. Item: Microscopic examination of carbide in hand of late deceased Mr. Stoneman revealed crinkled threads from seersucker cloth composing jacket of Barrister Philips."

"You . . ." Philips gulped. "You have this evidence, Mookerji?"

"Am so stating," said the Hindu.

Philips dropped limply into his chair. He ran his big hands over his white hair. Then he laughed grimly. "I'm the one who must have been crazy," he said, "to kill a man for two hundred thousand dollars. With Louise out of the way for six months more, I could have made it up."

Max Ritter reached into his hip pocket for his handcuffs.

.

Roger Gable came to Pasteur Hospital as soon as he was released. Doctors Coffee and Mookerji accompanied him to Louise's bedside.

"Dr. Mookerji," Dan Coffee was saying as they entered the room, "if you really saw Philips leave the house last night, and if you really found seersucker threads under the microscope, why the devil didn't you tell me or Lieutenant Ritter this afternoon?"

The Hindu lowered his eyes. "Greatly fear am prevaricating fibber," he said. "Witnessed said evidence only with mind's eye. However, was of opinion that Barrister's confession was imperative and that all is fair in love and warfare against murderers. Moreover, since am enacting role of Hindu cupid— "

A white smile suddenly divided the Hindu resident's plump brown face as he saw Louise open her eyes. Roger Gable stooped to gather the girl into his arms.

The Hindu took Dr. Coffee's elbow and turned him around to face the door. "Please give opinion, Doctor Sahib," he said, "whether am making unlicensed medical prognosis by uttering hopeful prediction that house of Gable is destined to become house of Seven Gables?"

Lilian Jackson Braun

Lilian Jackson Braun's immensely popular novels featuring newspaperman Jim Qwilleran and his cats, Koko and Yum Yum, offer the most unusual of detecting partnerships. In the first book in the series (*The Cat Who Could Read Backwards*, 1966) Qwilleran appears as a somewhat seedy, down-on-his-luck former big-city crime reporter exiled to a small-town midwestern newspaper after an ugly divorce and a spell of hard drinking. His lively curiosity is still intact, however, and he is soon uncovering crimes, aided by his two likable Siamese cats, that his fellow townspeople would just as soon have allowed to remain covered. Given this scenario, many writers would sentimentalize Koko and Yum Yum to the point of cloying cuteness, but not Braun. Instead, she depicts them as intelligent animals (and possibly superior to many of the humans they encounter) who go about their catly business, thus providing their owner with insights that he uses to interpret human behavior.

Braun wrote two other books about this unlikely detecting trio in the 1960s: *The Cat Who Ate Danish Modern* (1967) and *The Cat Who Turned On and Off* (1968). After a hiatus of eighteen years, Qwilleran, Koko, and Yum Yum returned in the 1986 title *The Cat Who Saw Red*, and since then there have been yearly installments of their adventures. Braun has a gift for small-town milieu, and the fictional locale of Pickax City in Moose County is so well depicted that most readers would be able to find their way around if transported there. Similarly, the ongoing series characters—Alexander and Penelope Goodwinter, the town attorneys; Polly Duncan, the librarian and Qwilleran's romantic interest; Melinda Goodwinter, the town doctor—are well delineated in all their eccentricities. The backdrops for the stories are typical of small-town life: the local theater club (*The Cat Who Sniffed Glue*, 1988); the farm museum (*The Cat Who Talked to Ghosts*, 1990); and even a vendetta against the town's handymen (*The Cat Who Went Underground*, 1989).

Braun has also written more than a dozen short stories, collected in *The Cat Who Had FourteenTales* (1988). In the early story that follows, she departs from her usual detecting trio and presents a duo: Phut Phat, an elegant Siamese, whose "eight seal-brown points (there had been nine before that trip to the hospital) were as sleek as panne velvet" and the one of his two owners who is perceptive enough to understand his mental messages. It is interesting to note that the owners have no names as far as Phut Phat is concerned, and are merely ranked One and Two—testimony to Braun's in-depth understanding of cats, since One is the individual who feeds him.

PHUT PHAT CONCENTRATES

PHUT PHAT AND ONE AND TWO
A FASHIONABLE PART OF AN UNNAMED CITY
1963

Phut Phat knew, at an early age, that humans were an inferior breed. They were unable to see in the dark. They ate and drank unthinkable concoctions. And they had only five senses; the two who lived with Phut Phat could not even transmit their thoughts without resorting to words.

For more than a year, ever since he had arrived at the town house, Phut Phat had been attempting to introduce his system of communication, but his two pupils had made scant progress. At dinner time he would sit in a corner, concentrating, and suddenly they would say, "Time to feed the cat," as if it were their own idea.

Their ability to grasp Phut Phat's messages extended only to the bare necessities of daily living, however. Beyond that, nothing ever got through to them, and it seemed unlikely that they would ever increase their powers.

Nevertheless, life in the town house was comfortable enough. It followed a fairly dependable routine, and to Phut Phat, routine was the greatest of all goals. He deplored such deviation as tardy meals, loud noises, unexplained persons on the premises, or liver during the week. He always had liver on Sunday.

It was a fashionable part of the city in which Phut Phat lived. His home was a three-story brick house furnished with dark rugs and down-cushioned chairs and tall pieces of furniture from which he could look down on questionable visitors. He could rise to the top of the highboy in a single leap, and when he chose to scamper from first-floor kitchen to second-floor living room to third-floor bedroom, his ascent up the carpeted staircase was very close to flight, for Phut Phat was a Siamese. His fawn-colored coat was finer than ermine. His eight seal-brown points (there had been nine before that trip to the hospital) were as sleek as panne velvet, and his slanted eyes brimmed with a mysterious blue.

Those who lived with Phut Phat in the town house were a pair, identified in his consciousness as ONE and TWO. It was ONE who supplied the creature comforts—beef on weekdays, liver on Sunday, and a warm cuddle now and then. She also fed his vanity with lavish compliments and adorned his throat with jeweled collars taken from her own wrists.

TWO, on the other hand, was valued chiefly for games and entertainment. He said very little, but he jingled keys at the end of a shiny chain and swung them back and forth for Phut Phat's amusement. And every morning in the dressing room he swished a necktie in tantalizing arcs while Phut Phat leaped and grabbed with pearly claws.

These daily romps, naps on downy cushions, outings in the coop on the fire escape, and two meals a day constituted the pattern of Phut Phat's life.

Then one Sunday he sensed a disturbing lapse in the household routine. The Sunday papers, usually scattered all over the library floor for him to shred with his claws, were stacked neatly on the desk. Furniture was rearranged. The house was filled with flowers, which he was not allowed to chew. All day long ONE was nervous, and TWO was too busy to play. A stranger in a white coat arrived and clattered glassware, and when Phut Phat went to investigate an aroma of shrimp and smoked oysters in the kitchen, the maid shooed him away.

Phut Phat seemed to be in everyone's way. Finally he was deposited in his wire coop on the fire escape, where he watched sparrows in the garden below until his stomach felt empty. Then he howled to come indoors.

He found ONE at her dressing table, fussing with her hair and unmindful of his hunger. Hopping lightly to the table, he sat erect among the sparkling bottles, stiffened his tail, and fastened his blue eyes on ONE's forehead. In that attitude he concentrated—and concentrated—and concentrated. It was never easy to communicate with ONE. Her mind hopped about like a sparrow, never relaxed, and Phut Phat had to strain every nerve to convey his meaning.

Suddenly ONE darted a look in his direction. A thought had occurred to her.

"Oh, John," she called to TWO, who was brushing his hair in the dressing room, "would you ask Millie to feed Phuffy? I forgot his dinner until this very minute. It's after five o'clock, and I haven't fixed my hair yet. You'd better put your coat on; people will start coming soon. And please tell Howard to light the candles. You might stack some records on the stereo, too.... No, wait a minute. If Millie is still working on the canapes, would you feed Phuffy yourself? Just give him a slice of cold roast."

At this, Phut Phat stared at ONE with an intensity that made his thought waves almost visible.

"Oh, John, I forgot," she corrected. "It's Sunday, and he should have liver. Cut it in long strips or he'll toss it up. And before you do that, will you zip the back of my dress and put my emerald bracelet on Phuffy? Or maybe I'll wear the emerald myself, and he can have the topaz.... John! Do you realize it's five fifteen? I wish you'd put your coat on."

"And I wish you'd simmer down," said TWO, "No one ever comes on time. Why do you insist on giving big parties, Helen, if it makes you so nervous?"

"Nervous? I'm not nervous. Besides, it was *your* idea to invite my friends and your clients at the same time. You said we should kill a whole blasted flock of birds with one stone.... Now, *please*, John, are you going to feed Phuffy? He's staring at me and making my head ache."

Phut Phat scarcely had time to swallow his meal, wash his face, and arrange himself on the living room mantel before people started to arrive. His irritation at having the routine disrupted had been lessened somewhat by the prospect of being admired by the guests. His name meant "beautiful" in Siamese, and he was well aware of his pulchritude. Lounging between a pair of Georgian candlesticks, with one foreleg extended and the other exquisitely bent under at the ankle, with his head erect and gaze withdrawn, with his tail drooping nonchalantly over the edge of the marble mantel, he awaited compliments.

It was a large party, and Phut Phat observed that very few of the guests knew how to pay their respects to a cat. Some talked nonsense in a falsetto voice. Others made startling movements in his direction or, worse still, tried to pick him up.

There was one knowledgeable guest, however, who approached the mantel with a proper attitude of deference and reserve. Phut Phat squeezed his eyes in appreciation. The admirer was a man, who leaned heavily on a shiny stick. Standing at a respectful distance, he slowly held out his hand with one finger extended, and Phut Phat twitched his whiskers in polite acknowledgment.

"You are a living sculpture," said the man.

"That's Phut Phat," said ONE, who had pushed through the crowded room toward the fireplace. "He's the head of our household."

"He is obviously a champion," said the man with the shiny cane, addressing his hostess in the same dignified manner that had charmed Phut Phat.

"Yes, he could probably win a few ribbons if we wanted to enter him in shows, but he's strictly a pet. He never goes out, except in his coop on the fire escape."

"A coop? That's a splendid idea," said the man. "I should like to have one for my own cat. She's a tortoise-shell long-hair. May I inspect this coop before I leave?"

"Of course. It's just outside the library window."

"You have a most attractive house."

"Thank you. We've been accused of decorating it to complement Phut Phat's coloring, which is somewhat true. You'll notice we have no breakable bric-a-brac. When a Siamese flies through the air, he recognizes no obstacles."

"Indeed, I have noticed you collect Georgian silver," the man said in his courtly way. "You have some fine examples."

"Apparently you know silver. Your cane is a rare piece."

"Yes, it is an attempt to extract a little pleasure from a sorry necessity." He hobbled a step or two.

"Would you like to see my silver collection downstairs in the dining room?" asked ONE. "It's all early silver—about the time of Wren."

At this point Phut Phat, aware that the conversation no longer centered on him, jumped down from the mantel and stalked out of the room with several irritable flicks of the tail. He found an olive and pushed it down the heat register. Several feet stepped on him. In desperation he went upstairs to the guest room, where he discovered a mound of sable and mink and went to sleep.

After this upset in the household routine Phut Phat needed several days to catch up on his rest—so the ensuing week was a sleepy blur. But soon it was Sunday again, with liver for breakfast, Sunday papers scattered over the floor, and everyone sitting around being pleasantly routine.

"Phuffy! Don't roll on those newspapers," said ONE. "John, can't you see the ink rubs off on his fur? Give him the *Wall Street Journal*—it's cleaner."

"Maybe he'd like to go outside in his coop and get some sun."

"That reminds me, dear. Who was that charming man with the silver cane at our party? I didn't catch his name."

"I don't know," said TWO. "I thought he was someone you invited."

"Well, he wasn't. He must have come with one of the other guests. At any rate, he was interested in getting a coop like ours for his own cat. He has a long-haired torty. And did I tell you the Hendersons have two Burmese kittens? They want us to go over and see them next Sunday and have a drink."

Another week passed, during which Phut Phat discovered a new perch. He found he could jump to the top of an antique armoire—a towering piece of furniture in the hall outside the library. Otherwise, it was a routine week, followed by a routine weekend, and Phut Phat was content.

ONE and TWO were going out on Sunday to see the Burmese kittens, so Phut Phat was served an early dinner and soon afterward he fell asleep on the library sofa.

When the telephone rang and waked him, it was dark and he was alone. He raised his head and chattered at the instrument until it stopped its noise. Then he went back to sleep, chin on paw.

The second time the telephone started ringing, Phut Phat stood up and scolded it, arching his body in a vertical stretch and making a question mark with his tail. To express his annoyance, he hopped on the desk and sharpened his claws on Webster's Unabridged. Then he spent quite some time chewing on a leather bookmark. After that he felt thirsty. He sauntered toward the powder room for a drink.

No lights were burning, and no moonlight came through the windows, yet he moved through the dark rooms with assurance, sidestepping table legs and stopping to examine infinitesimal particles on the hall carpet. Nothing escaped him.

Phut Phat was lapping water, and the tip of his tail was wagging rapturously from side to side, when something caused him to raise his head and listen. His tail froze. Sparrows in the backyard? Rain on the fire escape? There was silence again. He lowered his head and resumed his drinking.

A second time he was alerted. Something was happening that was not routine. His tail bushed like a squirrel's, and with his whiskers full of alarm he stepped noiselessly into the hall, peering toward the library.

Someone was on the fire escape. Something was clawing at the library window. Petrified, he watched—until the window opened and a dark figure slipped into the room. With one lightening glide Phut Phat sprang to the top of the tall armoire.

There on his high perch, able to look down on the scene, he felt safe. But was it enough to feel safe? His ancestors had been watch-cats in Oriental temples centuries before. They had hidden in shadows and crouched on high walls, ready to spring on any intruder and tear his face to ribbons—just as Phut Phat shredded the Sunday paper. A primitive instinct rose in his breast, but quickly it was quelled by civilized inhibitions.

The figure in the window advanced stealthily toward the hall, and Phut Phat experienced a sense of the familiar. It was the man with the shiny stick. This time, though, his presence smelled sinister. A small blue light now glowed from the head of the cane, and instead of leaning on it, the man pointed it ahead to guide his way out of the library and toward the staircase. As the intruder passed the armoire, Phut Phat's fur rose to form a sharp ridge down his spine. Instinct said, "Spring at him!" But vague fears held him back.

With feline stealth the man moved downstairs, unaware of two glowing diamonds that watched him in the blackness, and Phut Phat soon heard noises in the dining room. He sensed evil. Safe on top of the armoire, he trembled.

When the man reappeared, he was carrying a bulky load, which he took to the library window. Then he crept to the third floor, and there were muffled sounds in the bedroom. Phut Phat licked his nose in apprehension.

Now the man reappeared, following a pool of blue light. As he approached the armoire, Phut Phat shifted his feet, bracing himself against something invisible. He felt a powerful compulsion to attack, and yet a fearful dismay.

"Get him!" commanded a savage impulse within him.

"Stay!" warned the fright throbbing in his head.

"Get him! ... Now ... *NOW!*"

Phut Phat sprang at the man's head, ripping with razor claws wherever they sank into flesh.

The hideous scream that came from the intruder was like an electric shock; it sent Phut Phat sailing through space—up the stairs—into the bedroom—under the bed.

For a long time he quaked uncontrollably, his mouth parched and his ears inside-out with horror at what had happened. There was something strange and wrong about it, although its meaning eluded him. Waiting for Time to heal his confusion, he huddled there in darkness and privacy. Blood soiled his claws. He sniffed with distaste and finally was compelled to lick them clean. He did it slowly and with repugnance. Then he tucked his paws under his warm body and waited.

When ONE and TWO came home, he sensed their arrival even before the taxicab door slammed. He should have bounded to meet them, but the experience had left him in a daze, quivering internally, weak and unsure. He heard the rattle of the front door lock, feet climbing the stairs, and the click of the light switch in the room where he waited in bewilderment under the bed.

ONE instantly gave a gasp, then a shriek. "John! Someone's been in this room. We've been robbed!"

TWO's voice was incredulous. "What! How do you know?"

"My jewel case. Look! It's open—and empty!"

TWO threw open a closet door. "Your furs are still here, Helen. What about money? Did you have any money in the house?"

"I never leave money around. But the silver! What about the silver? John, go down and see. I'm afraid to look. ... No! Wait a minute!" ONE's voice rose in panic. "Where's Phut Phat? What's happened to Phut Phat?"

"I don't know," said TWO with alarm. "I haven't seen him since we came in."

They searched the house, calling his name—unaware, with their limited senses, that Phut Phat was right there under the bed, brooding over the upheaval in his small world, and now and then licking his claws.

When at last, crawling on their hands and knees, they spied two eyes glowing red under the bed, they drew him out gently. ONE hugged him with a rocking embrace and rubbed her face, wet and salty, on his fur, while TWO stood by, stroking him with a heavy hand. Comforted and reassured, Phut Phat stopped trembling. He tried to purr, but the shock had constricted his larynx.

ONE continued to hold Phut Phat in her arms—and he had no will to jump down—even after two strange men were admitted to the house; they asked questions and examined all the rooms.

"Everything is insured," ONE told them, "but the silver is irreplaceable. It's old and very rare. Is there any chance of getting it back, Lieutenant?" She fingered Phut Phat's ears nervously.

"At this point it's hard to say," the detective said. "But you may be able to help us. Have you noticed any strange incidents lately? Any unusual telephone calls?"

"Yes," said ONE. "Several times recently the phone has rung, and when we answered it, there was no one on the line."

"That's the usual method. They wait until they know you're not at home."

ONE gazed into Phut Phat's eyes. "Did the phone ring tonight while we were out, Phuffy?" she asked, shaking him lovingly. "If only Phut Phat could tell us what happened! He must have had a terrifying experience. Thank heaven he wasn't harmed."

Phut Phat raised his paw to lick between his toes, still defiled with human blood.

"If only Phuffy could tell us who was here!"

Phut Phat paused with toes spread and pink tongue extended. He stared at ONE's forehead.

"Have you folks noticed any strangers in the neighborhood?" the lieutenant was asking. "Anyone who would arouse suspicion?"

Phut Phat's body tensed, and his blue eyes, brimming with knowledge, bored into that spot above ONE's eyebrows.

"No, I can't think of anyone," she said. "Can you, John?"

TWO shook his head.

"Poor Phuffy," said ONE. "See how he stares at me; he must be hungry. Does Phuffy want a little snack?"

Phut Phat squirmed.

"About these bloodstains on the window sill," said the detective. "Would the cat attack an intruder viciously enough to draw blood?"

"Heavens, no!" said ONE. "He's just a pampered little house pet. We found him hiding under the bed, scared stiff."

"And you're sure you can't remember any unusual incident lately? Has anyone come to the house who might have seen the silver or jewelry? Repairman? Window washer?"

"I wish I could be more helpful," said ONE, "but honestly, I can't think of a single suspect."

Phut Phat gave up.

Wriggling free, he jumped down from ONE's lap and walked toward the door with head depressed and hind legs stiff with disgust. He knew who it was. He knew! The man with the shiny stick. But it was useless to try to communicate. The human mind was closed so tight that nothing important would ever penetrate. And ONE was so busy with her own chatter that her mind . . .

The jingle of keys caught Phut Phat's attention. He turned and saw TWO swinging his key chain back and forth, back and forth, and saying nothing. TWO always did more thinking than talking. Perhaps Phut Phat had been trying to communicate with the wrong mind. Perhaps TWO was really Number One in the household and ONE was Number Two.

Phut Phat froze in his position of concentration, sitting tall and compact with tail stiff. The key chain swung back and forth, and Phut Phat fastened his blue eyes on three wrinkles just underneath TWO's hairline. He concentrated. The key chain swung back and forth, back and forth. Phut Phat kept concentrating.

"Wait a minute," said TWO, coming out of his puzzled silence. "I just thought of something. Helen, remember that party we gave a couple of weeks ago? There was one guest we couldn't account for. A man with a silver cane."

"Why, yes! The man was so curious about the coop on the fire escape. Why didn't I think of him? Lieutenant, he was terribly interested in our Georgian silver."

TWO said, "Does that suggest anything to you, Lieutenant?"

"Yes, it does." The detective exchanged nods with his partner.

"This man," ONE volunteered, "had a very cultivated voice and a charming manner."

"We know him," the detective said grimly. "We know his method. What you tell us fits perfectly. But we didn't know he was operating in this neighborhood again."

ONE said, "What mystifies me is the blood on the window sill."

Phut Phat arched his body in a long, luxurious stretch and walked from the room, looking for a soft, dark, quiet place. Now he would sleep. He felt relaxed and satisfied. He had made vital contact with a human mind, and perhaps—after all—there was hope. Some day they might learn the system, learn to open their minds and receive. They had a long way to go before they realized their potential—but there was hope.

Fredric Brown

(1906–1972)

Fredric Brown's vision of the world is paradoxical and slightly cockeyed. Things, in his eyes, are not always what one might think they are; elements of the bizarre spice the commonplace, and, conversely, elements of the commonplace leaven the bizarre. Madness and sanity are intertwined, so that it is often difficult to tell which is which; the same is true of tragedy and comedy. Brown seems to have felt that the forces, cosmic or otherwise, that control our lives are at best mischievous and at worse malign, that man has little to say about his own destiny, and that free will is a fallacy. The joke is on us, he seems to be saying in much of his work, and it is a joke that all too frequently turns nasty.

Brown employed a deceptively simple, chatty style that allows his fiction to be enjoyed as entertainment and also to be pondered by readers interested in the complex themes at its heart. *The Fabulous Clipjoint* (1947), the novel that introduced his detective duo of Ed and Am Hunter, and which also earned Brown a Mystery Writers of America Edgar for best first novel, is a prime example. On the one hand it is a tough, uncompromising mystery in which young and idealistic Ed Hunter joins forces with his pragmatic and jaded uncle Am, a retired circus performer, to solve the murder of Ed's father. On the other hand there are deeper meanings to the narrative—underlying themes of obsession, a young man's bitter and tragic coming of age, and the manipulation of those dark cosmic forces that the author believed control our lives.

Brown wrote six other Ed and Am Hunter books, in which the pair function as Chicago-based private eyes. None of these is as powerful or memorable as *The Fabulous Clipjoint*, though *Compliments of a Fiend* (1950), a mix of numbers racketeers, crystal gazers, and astrologers, and the kidnapping of Uncle Am, has some of the same obsessive intensity. The novelette that follows is the only Ed and Am Hunter short story—at once a straightforward medium hard-boiled detective tale and a complex character study in which Brown's skewed worldview may be glimpsed.

Even better than Brown's series mysteries are his nonseries suspense novels. *Knock Three-One-Two* (1959), a brilliantly constructed, frightening novel with a shocking and ironic climax, is the author at his most controlled while dealing with material at its most chaotic. *The Screaming Mimi* (1949) and *The Far Cry* (1951) are also outstanding. In addition to his crime fiction, Brown wrote fantasy and science fiction of comparable quality, and excellent short stories in both categories, including dozens of mordant short-shorts—a demanding form at which he proved himself a master. Many of these may be found in his 1961 collection, *Nightmares & Geezenstacks*.

BEFORE SHE KILLS

ED AND AM HUNTER
CHICAGO, ILLINOIS
1960

The door was that of an office in an old building on State Street near Chicago Avenue, on the near north side, and the lettering on it read Hunter & Hunter Detective Agency. I opened it and went in. Why not? I'm one of the Hunters; my name is Ed. The other Hunter is my uncle, Ambrose Hunter.

The door to the inner office was open and I could see Uncle Am playing solitaire at his desk in there. He's shortish, fattish and smartish, with a straggly brown mustache. I waved at him and headed for my desk in the outer office. I'd had my lunch—we take turns—and he'd be leaving now.

Except that he wasn't. He swept the cards together and stacked them but he said, "Come on in, Ed. Something to talk over with you."

I went in and pulled up a chair. It was a hot day and two big flies were droning in circles around the room. I reached for the fly swatter and held it, waiting for one or both of them to light somewhere. "We ought to get a bomb," I said.

"Huh? Who do we want to blow up?"

"A bug bomb," I said. "One of those aerosol deals, so we can get flies on the wing."

"Not sporting, kid. Like shooting a sitting duck, only the opposite. Got to give the flies a chance."

"All right," I said, swatting one of them as it landed on a corner of the desk. "What did you want to talk about?"

"A case, maybe. A client, or a potential one, came in while you were feeding your face. Offered us a job, but I'm not sure about taking it. Anyway, it's one you'd have to handle, and I wanted to talk it over with you first."

The other fly landed and died, and the wind of the swat that killed it blew a small rectangular paper off the desk onto the floor. I picked it up and saw that it was a check made out to Hunter & Hunter and signed Oliver R. Bookman—a name I didn't recognize. It was for five hundred dollars.

We could use it. Business had been slow for a month or so. I said, "Looks like you took the job already. Not that I blame you." I put the check back on the desk. "That's a pretty strong argument."

"No, I didn't take it. Ollie Bookman had the check already made out when he came, and put it down while we were talking. But I told him we weren't taking the case till I'd talked to you."

"Ollie? Do you know him, Uncle Am?"

"No, but he told me to call him that, and it comes natural. He's that kind of guy. Nice, I mean."

I took his word for it. My uncle is a nice guy himself, but he's a sharp judge of character and can spot a phony a mile off.

He said, "He thinks his wife is trying to kill him or maybe planning to."

"Interesting," I said. "But what could we do about it—unless she does? And then it's cop business."

"He knows that, but he's not sure enough to do anything drastic about it unless someone backs up his opinion and tells him he's not imagining things. Then he'll decide what to do. He wants you to study things from the inside."

"Like how? And why me?"

"He's got a young half brother living in Seattle whom his wife has never met and whom he hasn't seen for twenty years. Brother's twenty-five years old—and you can pass for that age. He wants you to come to Chicago from Seattle on business and stay with them for a few days. You wouldn't even have to change your first name; you'd be Ed Cartwright and Ollie would brief you on everything you'll be supposed to know."

I thought a moment and then said, "Sounds a little far out to me, but—" I glanced pointedly at the five-hundred-dollar check. "Did you ask how he happened to come to us?"

"Yes. Koslovsky sent him; he's a friend of Kossy's, belongs to a couple of the same clubs." Koslovsky is chief investigator for an insurance company; we've worked for him or with him on several things.

I asked, "Does that mean there's an insurance angle?"

"No, Ollie Bookman carries only a small policy—small relative to what his estate would be—that he took out a long time ago. Currently he's not insurable. Heart trouble."

"Oh. And does Kossy approve this scheme of his for investigating his wife?"

"I was going to suggest we ask Kossy that. Look, Ed, Ollie's coming back for our answer at two o'clock. I'll have time to eat and get back. But I wanted to brief you before I left so you could think it over. You might also call Koslovsky and get a rundown on Ollie, whatever he knows about him."

Uncle Am got up and got the old black slouch hat he insists on wearing despite the season. Kidding him about it does no good.

I said, "One more question before you go. Suppose Bookman's wife meets his half brother, his real one, someday. Isn't it going to be embarrassing?"

"I asked him that. He says its damned unlikely; he and his brother aren't at all close. He'll never go to Seattle and the chances that his brother will ever come to Chicago are one in a thousand. Well, so long, kid."

I called Koslovsky. Yes, he'd recommended us to Bookman when Bookman had told him what he wanted done and asked—knowing that he, Koslovsky, sometimes hired outside investigators when he and his small staff had a temporary overload of cases—to have an agency recommended to him.

"I don't think too much of his idea," Koslovsky said, "but, hell, it's his money and he can afford it. If he wants to spend some of it that way, you might as well have the job as anyone else."

"Do you think there's any real chance that he's right? About his wife, I mean."

"I wouldn't know, Ed. I've met her a time or two and—well, she struck me as a cold potato, probably, but hardly as a murderess. Still, I don't know her well enough to say."

"How well do you know Bookman? Well enough to know whether he's pretty sane or gets wild ideas?"

"Always struck me as pretty sane. We're not close friends but I've known him fairly well for three or four years."

"Just how well off is he?"

"Not rich, but solvent. If I had to guess, I'd say he could cash out at over one hundred thousand, less than two. Enough to kill him for, I guess."

"What's his racket?"

"Construction business, but he's mostly retired. Not on account of age; he's only in his forties. But he's got angina pectoris, and a year or two ago the medics told him to take it easy or else."

Uncle Am got back a few minutes before two o'clock and I just had time to tell him about my conversation with Kossy before Ollie Bookman showed up. Bookman was a big man with a round, cheerful face that made you like him at sight. He had a good handshake.

"Hi, Ed," he said. "Glad that's your name because it's what I'll be calling you even if it wasn't. That is, if you'll take on the job for me. Your Uncle Am here wouldn't make it definite. What do you say?"

I told him we could at least talk about it and when we were comfortably seated in the inner office, I said, "Mr. Bookman——" "Call me Ollie," he interrupted, so I said, "All right, Ollie. The only reason I can think of thus far, for not taking on the job, if we don't, is that even if you're right——if your wife does have any thoughts about murder——the chances seem awfully slight that I could find out about it, and how she intended to do it, in time to stop it."

He nodded. "I understand that, but I want you to try, anyway. You see, Ed, I'll be honest and say that I *may* be imagining things. I want somebody else's opinion——after that somebody has lived with us at least a few days. But if you come to agree with me, or find any positive indications that I'm maybe right, then——well, I'll do something about it. Eve——that's my wife's name——won't give me a divorce or even agree to a separation with maintenance, but damn it, I can always simply leave home and live at the club——better that than get myself killed."

"You have asked her to give you a divorce, then?"

"Yes, I—— Let me begin at the beginning. Some of this is going to be embarrassing to tell, but you should know the whole score. I met Eve ..."

2

He'd met Eve eight years ago when he was thirty-five and she was twenty-five, or so she claimed. She was a strip-tease dancer who worked in night clubs under the professional name of Eve Eden——her real name had been Eve Packer. She was a statuesque blonde, beautiful. Ollie had fallen for her and started a campaign immediately, a campaign that intensified when he learned that off-stage she was quiet, modest, the exact opposite of what strippers are supposed to be and which some of them really are. By the time he was finally having an affair with her, lust had ripened into respect and he'd been thinking in any case that it was about time he married and settled down.

So he married her, and that was his big mistake. She turned out to be completely, psychopathically frigid. She'd been acting, and doing a good job of acting, during the weeks before the marriage, but after marriage, or at least after the honeymoon, she simply saw no reason to keep on acting. She had what she wanted——security and respectability. She hated sex, and that was that. She turned Ollie down flat when he tried to get her to go to a psychoanalyst or even to a marriage consultant, who, he thought, might be able to talk her into going to an analyst. In every other way she was a perfect wife. Beautiful enough to be a showpiece that made all his friends envy him, a charming hostess, even good at handling servants and running the house. For all outsiders could know, it was a perfect marriage. But for a while it drove Ollie Bookman nuts. He offered to let her divorce him and make a generous settlement, either lump sum or alimony. But she had what she wanted, marriage and respectability, and she wasn't going to give them up and become a divorcee, even if doing so wasn't going to affect her scale of living in the slightest. He threatened to divorce her, and she laughed at him. He had, she pointed out, no grounds for divorce that he could prove in court, and she'd never give him any. She'd simply deny the only thing he could say about her, and make a monkey out of him.

It was an impossible situation, especially as Ollie had badly wanted to have children or at least a child, as well as a normal married life. He'd made the best of it by accepting the situation at home as irreparable and settling for staying sane by making at least occasional passes in other directions. Nothing serious, just a normal man wanting to live a normal life and succeeding to a degree.

But eventually the inevitable happened. Three years ago, he had found himself in an affair that turned out to be much more than an affair, the real love of his life—and a reciprocated love. She was a widow, Dorothy Stark, in her early thirties. Her husband had died five years before in Korea; they'd had only a honeymoon together before he'd gone overseas. Ollie wanted so badly to marry her that he offered Eve a financial settlement that would have left him relatively a pauper—this was before the onset of his heart trouble and necessary semiretirement; he looked forward to another twenty years or so of earning capacity—but she refused; never would she consent to become a divorcee, at any price. About this time, he spent a great deal of money on private detectives in the slim hope that her frigidity was toward him only, but the money was wasted. She went out quite a bit but always to bridge parties, teas or, alone or with respectable woman companions, to movies or plays.

Uncle Am interrupted. "You said you used private detectives before, Ollie. Out of curiosity, can I ask why you're not using the same outfit again?"

"Turned out to be crooks, Am. When they and I were finally convinced we couldn't get anything on her legitimately, they offered for a price to frame her for me." He mentioned the name of an agency we'd heard of, and Uncle Am nodded.

Ollie went on with his story. There wasn't much more of it. Dorothy Stark had known that he could never marry her but she also knew that he very badly wanted a child, preferably a son, and had loved him enough to offer to bear one for him. He had agreed—even if he couldn't give the child his name, he wanted one—and two years ago she had borne him a son, Jerry Stark. Ollie loved the boy to distraction.

Uncle Am asked if Eve Bookman knew of Jerry's existence and Ollie nodded.

"But she won't do anything about it. What could she do, except divorce me?"

"But if that's the situation," I asked him, "what motive would your wife have to want to kill you? And why now, if the situation has been the same for two years."

"There's been one change, Ed, very recently. Two years ago, I made out a new will, without telling Eve. You see, with angina pectoris, my doctor tells me it's doubtful if I have more than a few years to live in any case. And I want at least the bulk of my estate to go to Dorothy and to my son. So— Well, I made out a will which leaves a fourth to Eve, a fourth to Dorothy and half, in trust, to Jerry. And I explained, in a preamble, why I was doing it that way—the true story of my marriage to Eve and the fact that it really wasn't one, and why it wasn't. And I admitted paternity of Jerry. You see, Eve could contest that will—but would she? If she fought it, the newspapers would have a field day with the contents and make a big scandal out of it—and her position, her respectability, is the most important thing in the world to Eve. Of course, it would hurt Dorothy, too—but if she won, even in part, she could always move somewhere else and change her name. Jerry, if this happens in the next few years, as it probably will, will be too young to be hurt, or even to know what's going on. You see?"

"Yes," I said. "But if you hate your wife, why not—"

"Why not simply disinherit her completely, leave her nothing? Because then she *would* fight the will, she'd have to. I'm hoping by giving her a fourth, she'll decide she'd rather settle for that and save face than contest the will."

"I see that," I said. "But the situation's been the same for two years now. And you said that something recent—"

"As recent as last night," he interrupted. "I kept that will in a hiding place in my office—which is in my home since I retired—and last night I discovered it was missing. It was there a few days ago. Which means that, however she came to do so, Eve found it. And destroyed it. So if I should die now—she thinks—before I discover the will is gone and make another, I'll die intestate and she'll automatically get everything. She's got well over a hundred thousand dollars' worth of motive for killing me before I find out the will is gone."

Uncle Am asked, "You say 'she thinks.' Wouldn't she?"

"Last night she would have," Ollie said grimly. "But this morning, I went to my lawyer, made out a new will, same provisions, and left it in his hands. Which is what I should have done with the first one. But she doesn't know that, and I don't want her to."

It was my turn to question that. "Why not?" I wanted to know. "If she knows a new will exists, where she can't get at it, she'd know killing you wouldn't accomplish anything for her. Even if she got away with it."

"Right, Ed. But I'm almost hoping she will try, and fail. Then I'd be the happiest man on earth. I *would* have grounds for divorce—attempted murder should be grounds if anything is—and I could marry Dorothy, legitimize my son, and leave him with my name. I—well, for the chance of doing that, I'm willing to take the chance of Eve's trying and succeeding. I haven't got much to lose, and everything to gain. How otherwise could I ever marry Dorothy—unless Eve should predecease me, which is damned unlikely. She's healthy as a horse, and younger than I am, besides. And if she should succeed in killing me, but got caught, she'd inherit nothing; Dorothy and Jerry would get it all. That's the law, isn't it? That no one can inherit from someone he's killed, I mean. Well, that's the whole story. Will you take the job, Ed, or do I have to look for someone else? I hope I won't."

I looked at Uncle Am—we never decide anything important without consulting one another—and he said, "Okay by me, kid." So I nodded to Ollie. "All right," I said.

3

We worked out details. He'd already checked plane flights and knew that a Pacific Airlines plane was due in from Seattle at ten fifteen that evening; I'd arrive on that and meanwhile he'd pretend to have received a telegram saying I was coming and would be in Chicago for a few days to a week on business, and asking him to meet the plane if convenient. I went him one better on that by telling him we knew a girl who sometimes did part-time work for us as a female operative and I'd have her phone his place, pretend to be a Western Union operator, and read the telegram to whoever answered the phone. He thought that was a good idea, especially if his wife was the one to take it down. We worked out the telegram itself and then he phoned his place on the pretext of wanting to know if his wife would be there to accept a C.O.D. package. She was, so I phoned the girl I had in mind, had her take down the telegram, and gave her Ollie's number to phone it to. We had the telegram dated from Denver, since the real Ed, if he were to get in that evening, would already be on the plane and would have to send the telegram from a stop en route. I told Ollie I'd work out a plausible explanation as to why I hadn't decided, until en route, to ask him to meet the plane.

Actually, we arranged to meet downtown, in the lobby of the Morrison Hotel an hour before plane time; Ollie lived north and if he were really driving to the airport, it would take him another hour to get there and an hour back as far as the Loop, so we'd have two hours to kill in further planning and briefing. Besides another half hour or so driving to his place when it was time to head there.

That meant he wouldn't have to brief me on family history now; there'd be plenty of time this evening. I did ask what kind of work Ed Cartwright did, so if necessary I could spend the rest of the afternoon picking up at least the vocabulary of whatever kind of work it was. But it turned out he ran a printing shop—which was a lucky break since after high school and before getting with my Uncle Am, I'd spent a couple of years as an apprentice printer myself and knew enough about the trade to talk about it casually.

Just as Ollie was getting ready to leave, the phone rang and it was our girl calling to say she'd read the telegram to a woman who'd answered the phone and identified herself as Mrs. Oliver Bookman, so we were able to tell Ollie the first step had been taken.

After Ollie had left, Uncle Am looked at me and asked, "What do you think, kid?"

"I don't know," I said. "Except that five hundred bucks is five hundred bucks. Shall I mail the check in for deposit now, since I won't be here tomorrow?"

"Okay. Go out and mail it if you want and take the rest of the day off, since you'll start working tonight."

"All right. With this check in hand, I'm going to pick me up a few things, like a couple shirts and some socks. And how about a good dinner tonight? I'll meet you at Ireland's at six."

He nodded, and I went to my desk in the outer office and was making out a deposit slip and an envelope when he came and sat on the corner of the desk.

"Kid," he said. "This Ollie just *might* be right. We got to assume that he could be, anyway. And I just had a thought. What would be the safest way to kill a man with bad heart trouble, like angina pectoris is? I'd say conning him into having an attack by giving him a shock or by getting him to overexert himself somehow. Or else by substituting sugar pills for whatever he takes—nitroglycerin pills, I think it is—when he gets an attack."

I said, "I've been thinking along those lines myself, Uncle Am. I thought maybe one thing I'd do down in the Loop is have a talk with Doc Kruger." Kruger is our family doctor, sort of. He doesn't get much business from either of us but we use him for an information booth whenever we want to know something about forensic medicine.

"Wait a second," Uncle Am said. "I'll phone him. Maybe he'll let us buy him dinner with us tonight to pay him for picking his brains."

He went in the office and used his phone; I heard him talking to Doc. He came out and said, "It's a deal. Only at seven instead of six. That'll be better for you, anyway, Ed. Bring your suitcase with you and if we take our time at Ireland's, you can go right from there to meet Ollie and not have to go home again."

So I did my errands, went to our room, cleaned up and dressed, and packed a suitcase. I didn't think anybody would be looking in it to check up on me, but I thought I might as well be as careful as I could. I couldn't provide clothes with Seattle labels but I could and did avoid things with labels that said Chicago or were from well-known Chicago stores. And I avoided anything that was monogrammed, not that I particularly like monograms or have many things with them. Then I doodled around with my trombone until it was time to head for Ireland's.

I got there exactly on time and Doc and Uncle Am were there already. But there were three Martinis on the table; Uncle Am had known I wouldn't be more than a few minutes late, if any, so he'd ordered for me.

Without having to be asked, since Uncle Am had mentioned it over the phone, Doc started telling us about angina pectoris. It was incurable, he said, but a victim of it might live a long time if he took good care of himself. He had to avoid physical exertion like lifting anything heavy or climbing stairs. He had to avoid overtiring himself by doing even light work for a long period. He had to avoid over indulgence in alcohol, although an occasional drink wouldn't hurt him if he was in good physical shape otherwise. He had to avoid violent emotional upsets as far as was possible, and a fit of anger could be as dangerous as running up a flight of stairs.

Yes, nitroglycerin pills were used. Everyone suffering from angina carried them and popped one or two into his mouth any time he felt an attack coming on. They either prevented the attack or made it much lighter than it would have been otherwise. Doc took a little pillbox out of his pocket and showed us some nitro pills. They were white and very tiny.

There was another drug also used to avert or limit attacks that was even more effective than nitroglycerin. It was amyl nitrite and came in glass ampoules. In emergency, you crushed the ampoule and inhaled the contents. But amyl nitrate, Doc told us, was used less frequently than nitroglycerin, and only in very bad cases or for attacks in which nitro didn't seem to be helping, because repeated use of amyl nitrite diminished the effect: the victim built up immunity to it if he used it often.

Doc had really come loaded. He'd brought an amyl nitrite ampoule with him, too, and showed it to us. I asked him if I could have it, just in case. He gave it to me without asking why, and even showed me the best way to hold it and crush it if I ever had to use it.

We had a second cocktail and I asked him a few more questions and got answers to them, and that pretty well covered angina pectoris, and then we ordered. Ireland's is famous for sea food; it's probably the best inland sea-food restaurant in the country, and we all ordered it. Doc Kruger and Uncle Am wrestled with lobsters; me, I'm a coward—I ate royal sole.

4

Doc had to take off after our coffee, but it was still fifteen or twenty minutes too early for me to leave—I'd have to take a taxi to the Morrison on account of having a suitcase; otherwise, I'd have walked and been just right on the timing—so

Uncle Am and I had a second coffee apiece and yakked. He said he felt like taking a walk before he turned in, so he'd ride in the taxi with me and then walk home from there.

I fought off a bellboy who tried to take my suitcase away from me and made myself comfortable on one of the overstuffed chairs in the lobby. I'd sat there about five or ten minutes when I heard myself being paged. I stood up and waved to the bellboy who'd been doing the paging and he came over and told me I was wanted on the phone and led me to the phone I was wanted on. I bought him off for four bits and answered the phone. It was Ollie Bookman, as I'd known it would be. Only he and Uncle Am would have known I was here and Uncle Am had left me only ten minutes ago.

"Ed," he said. "Change of plans. Eve wasn't doing anything this evening and decided to come to the airport with me, for the ride. I couldn't tell her no, for no reason. So you'll have to grab a cab and get out there ahead of us."

"Okay," I said. "Where are you now?"

"On the way south, at Division Street. Made an excuse to stop in a drugstore; didn't know how to get in touch with you until the time of our appointment. You can make it ahead of us if you get a cabby to hurry. I'll stall—drive as slow as I can without making Eve wonder. And I can stop for gas, and have my tires checked."

"What do I do at the airport if the plane's late?"

"Don't worry about the plane. You take up a spot near the Pacific Airlines counter; you'll see me come toward it and intercept me. Won't matter if the plane's in yet or not. I'll get us the hell out of there fast before Eve can learn if the plane's in. I'll make sure not to get there *before* arrival time."

"Right," I said. "But, Ollie, I'm not supposed to have seen you for twenty years —and I was five then, or supposed to be. So how would I recognize you? Oh, for that matter, you recognize me?"

"No sweat, Ed. We write each other once a year, at Christmas. And several times, including last Christmas, we traded snapshots with our Christmas letters. Remember?"

"Of course," I said. "But didn't your wife see the one I sent you?"

"She may have glanced at it casually. But after seven months she wouldn't remember it. Besides, you and the real Ed Cartwright are about the same physical type, anyway—dark hair, good looking. You'll pass. But don't miss meeting us before we reach the counter or somebody there might tell us the plane's not in yet, if it's not. Well, I better not talk any longer."

I swore a little to myself as I left the Morrison lobby and went to the cab rank. I'd counted on the time Ollie and I would have had together to have him finish my briefing. This way I'd have to let him do most of the talking, at least tonight. Well, he seemed smart enough to handle it. I didn't even know my parent's names, whether either of them was alive, whether I had any other living relatives besides Ollie. I didn't even know whether I was married or not—although I felt reasonably sure Ollie would have mentioned it if I was.

Yes, he'd have to do most of the talking—although I'd better figure out what kind of business I'd come to Chicago to do; I'd be supposed to know that, and Ollie wouldn't know anything about it. Well, I'd figure that out on the cab ride.

Barring accidents, I'd get there well ahead of Ollie, and I didn't want accidents, so I didn't offer the cabby any bribe for speed when I told him to take me to the airport. He'd keep the meter ticking all right, since he made his money by the mile and not by the minute.

I had my cover story ready by the time we got there. It wasn't detailed, but I didn't anticipate being pressed for details, and if I was, I knew more about printing equipment than Eve Bookman would know. I was a good ten minutes ahead of plane time. I found myself a seat near the Pacific Airlines counter and facing in the direction from which the Bookmans would come. Fifteen minutes later—on time, as planes go—the public-address system announced the arrival of my flight from Seattle, and fifteen minutes after that—time for me to have left the plane and even to have collected the suitcase that was by my feet—I saw them coming. That is, I saw Ollie coming, and with him was a beautiful, *soignée* blonde who could only be Eve Bookman, nee Eve Eden. Quite a dish. She was, with high heels, just about two inches short of Ollie's height, which made her just about as tall as I, unless she took off her shoes for me. Which, from what Ollie had told me about her, was about the last thing I expected her to do, especially here in the airport.

I got up and walked toward them and—remembering identification was only from snapshot—didn't put too much confidence in my voice when I asked, "Ollie?" and I put out my hand but only tentatively.

Ollie grabbed my hand in his big one and started pumping it. "Ed! Gawdamn if I can believe it, after all these years. When I last saw you, not counting pictures, you looked—Hell, let's get to that later. Meet Eve. Eve, meet Ed."

Eve Bookman gave me a smile but not a hand. "Glad to meet you at last, Edward. Oliver's talked quite a bit about you." I hoped she was just being polite in making the latter statement.

I gave her a smile back. "Hope he didn't say anything bad about me. But maybe he did; I was probably a pretty obstreperous brat when he saw me last. I would have been—let's see—"

"Five," said Ollie. "Well, what are we waiting for? Ed, you want we should go right home? Or should we drop in somewhere on the way and hoist a few? You weren't much of a drinker when I knew you last but maybe by now—"

Eve interrupted him. "Let's go home, Oliver. You'll want a nightcap there in any case, and you know you're not supposed to have more than one or two a day. Did he tell you, Edward, about his heart trouble in any of his letters?"

Ollie saved me again. "No, but it's not important. All right, though. We'll head home and I'll have my daily one or two, or maybe, since this is an occasion, three. Ed, is that your suitcase back by where you were sitting?"

I said it was and went back and got it, then went with them to the parking area and to a beautiful cream-colored Buick convertible with the top down. Ollie opened the door for Eve and then held it open after she got in. "Go on, Ed. We can all sit in the front seat." He grinned. "Eve's got an MG and loves to drive it, but we couldn't bring it tonight. With those damn bucket seats, you can't ride three in the whole car." I got in and he went around and got in the driver's side. I was wishing that I could drive it—I'd never piloted a recent Buick—but I couldn't think of any reasonable excuse for offering.

Half an hour later, I wished that I'd not only offered but had insisted. Ollie Bookman was a poor driver. Not a fast driver or a dangerous one, just sloppy. The way he grated gears made my teeth grate with them and his starts and stops were much too jerky. Besides, he was a lane-straddler and had no sense of timing on making stop lights.

But he was a good talker. He talked almost incessantly, and to good purpose, briefing me, mostly by apparently talking to Eve. "Don't remember if I told you, Eve, how come Ed and I have different last names, but the same father—not the same mother. See, I was Dad's son by his first marriage and Ed by his second—Ed was born Ed Bookman. But Dad died right after Ed was born and Ed's mother, my stepmother, married Wilkes Cartwright a couple years later. Ed was young enough that they changed his name to match his stepfather's, but I was already grown up, through high school anyway, so I didn't change mine. I was on my own by then. Well, both Ed's mother and his stepfather are dead now; he and I are the only survivors. Well . . ." And I listened and filed away facts. Sometimes he'd cut me in by asking me questions, but the questions always cued in their own answers or were ones that wouldn't be giveaways whichever way I answered them, like, "Ed, the house you were born in, out north of town—is it still standing, or haven't you been out that way recently?"

I was fairly well keyed in on family history by the time we got home.

5

Home wasn't as I'd pictured it, a house. It was an apartment, but a big one—ten rooms, I learned later—on Coleman Boulevard just north of Howard. It was the fourth floor, but there were elevators. Now that I thought of it, I realized that Ollie, because of his angina, wouldn't be able to live in a house where he had to climb stairs. But later I learned they'd been living there ever since they'd married, so he hadn't had to move there on account of that angle.

It was a fine apartment, nicely furnished and with a living room big enough to contain a swimming pool. "Come on, Ed," Ollie said cheerfully. "I'll show you your room and let you get rid of your suitcase, freshen up if you want to—although I imagine we'll all be turning in soon. You must be tired after that long trip. Eve, could we talk you into making a round of Martinis meanwhile?"

"Yes, Oliver." The perfect wife, she walked toward the small but well-stocked bar in a corner of the room.

I followed Ollie to the guest room that was to be mine. "Might as well unpack your suitcase while we talk," he said, after he closed the door behind us. "Hang your stuff up or put it in the dresser there. Well, so far, so good. Not a suspicion, and you're doing fine."

"Lots of questions I've still got to ask you, Ollie. We shouldn't take time to talk much now, but when will we have a chance to?"

"Tomorrow. I'll say I have to go downtown, make up some reasons. And you've got your excuse already—the business you came to do. Maybe you can get it over with sooner than you thought—but then decide, since you've come this far anyway, to stay out the week. That way you can stick around here as much as you want, or go out only when I go out."

"Fine. We'll talk that out tomorrow. But about tonight, we'll be talking, the three of us, and what can I safely talk about? Does she know anything about the size of my business, or can I improvise freely and talk about it?"

"Improvise your head off. I've never talked about your business. Don't know much about it myself."

"Good. Another question. How come, at only twenty-five, I've got a business of my own? Most people are still working for somebody else at that age."

"You inherited it from your stepfather, Cartwright. He died three years ago. You were working in the shop and moved to the office and took over. And as far as I know, or Eve, you're doing okay with it."

"Good. And I'm not married?"

"No, but if you want to invent a girl you're thinking about marrying, that's another safe thing you can improvise about."

I put the last of the contents of my suitcase in the dresser drawer and we went back to the living room. Eve had the cocktails made and was waiting for us. We sat around sipping at them, and this time I was able to do most of the talking instead of having to let Ollie filibuster so I wouldn't put my foot into my mouth by saying something wrong.

Ollie suggested a second round but Eve stood up and said that she was tired and that if we'd excuse her, she'd retire. And she gave Ollie a wifely caution about not having more than one more drink. He promised he wouldn't and made a second round for himself and me.

He yawned when he put his down after the first sip. "Guess this will be the last one, Ed. I'm tired, too. And we'll have plenty of time to talk tomorrow."

I wasn't tired, but if he was, that was all right by me. We finished our nightcaps fairly quickly.

"My room's the one next to yours," he told me as he took our glasses back to the bar. "No connecting door, but if you want anything, rap on the wall and I'll hear you. I'm a light sleeper."

"So am I," I told him, "So make it vice versa on the rapping. I'm the one that's supposed to be protecting you, not the other way around."

"And Eve's room is the one on the other side of mine. No connecting door there, either. Not that I'd use it, at this stage, even if it stood wide open with a red carpet running through it."

"She's still a beautiful woman," I said, just to see how he'd answer it.

"Yes. But I guess I'm by nature monogamous. And this may sound corny and be corny, but I consider Dorothy and me married in the sight of God. She's all I'll ever want, she and the boy. Well, come on, and we'll turn in."

I turned in, but I didn't go right to sleep. I lay awake thinking, sorting out my preliminary impressions. Eve Bookman—yes, I believed Ollie's story about their marriage and didn't even think it was exaggerated. Most people would think her sexy as hell to look at her, but I've got a sort of radar when it comes to sexiness. It hadn't registered with a single blip on the screen. And Koslovsky is a much better than average judge of people and what had he said about her? Oh, yes, he'd called her a cold potato.

Some women just naturally hate sex and men—and some of those very women become things like strip teasers because it gives them pleasure to arouse and frustrate men. If one of them breaks down and has an affair with a man, it's because the man has money, as Ollie had, and she thinks she can hook him for a husband, as Eve did Ollie. And once she's got him safely hog-tied, he's on his own and she can be her sweet, frigid self again. True, she's given up the privilege of frustrating men in audience-size groups, but she can torture the hell out of one man, as long as he keeps wanting her, and achieve respectability and even social position while she's doing it.

Oh, she'd been very pleasant to me, very hospitable, and no doubt was pleasant to all of Ollie's friends. And most of them, the ones without radar, probably thought she was a ball of fire in bed and that Ollie was a very lucky guy.

But murder—I was going to take some more convincing on that. It could be Ollie's imagination entirely. The only physical fact he'd come up with to indicate even the possibility of it was the business of the missing will. And she could have taken and destroyed that but still have no intention of killing him before he could make another like it; she could simply be hoping he'd never discover that it was missing.

But I could be wrong, very wrong. I'd met Eve less than three hours ago and Ollie had lived with her eight years. Maybe there was more than met the eye. Well, I'd keep my eyes open and give Ollie a run for his five hundred bucks by not assuming that he was making a murder out of a molehill. I went to sleep and Ollie didn't tap on my wall.

6

I woke at seven but decided that would be too early and that I didn't want to make a nuisance of myself by being up and around before anybody else, so I went back to sleep and it was half past nine when I woke the second time. I got up, showered and shaved—my bedroom had a private bath so all of them must have—dressed and went exploring. I went back to the living room and through it, and found a dining room. The table was set for breakfast for three but no one was there yet.

A matronly-looking woman who'd be a cook or housekeeper—I later learned that she was both and her name was Mrs. Ledbetter—appeared in the doorway that led through a pantry to the kitchen and smiled at me. "You must be Mr. Bookman's brother," she said. "What would you like for breakfast?"

"What time do the Bookmans come down for breakfast?" I asked.

"Usually earlier than this. But I guess you talked late last night. They should be up soon, though."

"Then I won't eat alone, thanks. I'll wait till at least one of them shows up. And as for what I want—anything; whatever they will be having. I'm not fussy about breakfasts."

She smiled and disappeared into the kitchen and I disappeared into the living room. I took a chair with a magazine rack beside it and was leafing through the latest *Reader's Digest*, just reading the short items in it, when Ollie came in looking rested and cheerful. "Morning, Ed. Had breakfast?"

I told him I'd been up only a few minutes and had decided to wait for company. "Come on, then," he said. "We won't wait for Eve. She might be dressing now, but then again she might sleep till noon."

But she didn't sleep till noon; she came in when we were starting our coffee, and told Mrs. Ledbetter that she'd just have coffee, as she had a lunch engagement in only two hours. So the three of us sat drinking coffee and it was very cozy and you wouldn't have guessed there was a thing wrong. You wouldn't have guessed it, but you might have felt it. Anyway, I felt it.

Ollie asked me if I wanted a lift downtown to do the business I'd come to do, and of course I said that I did. We discussed plans. Mrs. Ledbetter, I learned, had the afternoon and evening off, starting at noon, so no dinner would be served that evening. Eve would be gone all afternoon, playing bridge after her lunch date, and she suggested we all meet in the Loop and have dinner there. I wasn't supposed to know Chicago, of course, so I let them pick the place and it came up the Pump Room at seven.

Ollie and I left and on the way to the garage back of the building, I asked him if he minded if I drove the Buick. I said I liked driving and didn't get much chance to.

"Sure, Ed. But you mean you and Am don't have a car?"

I told him we wanted one but hadn't got around to affording it as yet. The few times we needed one for work, we rented one and simply got by without one for pleasure.

The Buick handled wonderfully. With me behind the wheel, it shifted smoothly, didn't jerk in starting or stopping; it timed stop lights and didn't straddle lanes. I asked how much it cost and said I hoped we'd be able to afford one like it someday. Except that we'd want a sedan because a convertible is too noticeable to use for a tail job. When we rented cars, we usually got a sedan in some neutral color like gray. Detectives used to use black cars, but nowadays a black car is almost as conspicuous as a red one.

I asked Ollie where he wanted me to drive him and he said he'd like to go to see Dorothy Stark and his son, Jerry. They lived in an apartment on LaSalle near Chicago Avenue. And did I have any plans or would I like to come up to meet them? He said he would like that.

I told him I'd drop up briefly if he wanted me to, but that I had plans. I wanted him to lend me the key to his apartment and I was going back there, after I could be sure both Mrs. Ledbetter and Mrs. Bookman had left. Since it was the former's afternoon off, it would be the best chance I'd have to look around the place in privacy. He said sure, the key was on the ring with the car keys and I might as well keep the keys, car and all, until our dinner date at the Pump Room. It would be only a short cab ride for him to get there from Mrs. Stark's. I asked him if there was any danger that Eve would go back to the apartment after her lunch date and before her bridge game. He was almost sure that she wouldn't, but her bridge club broke up about five thirty and she'd probably go back then to dress for dinner. That was all right; I could be gone by then.

When I parked the car on LaSalle, I remembered to ask him who I was supposed to be when I met Mrs. Stark—Ed Hunter or Ed Cartwright. He suggested we stick to the Cartwright story; if he told Dorothy the truth, she'd worry about him being in danger. Anyway, it would be simpler and take less explanation.

I liked Dorothy Stark on sight. She was small and brunette, with a heart-shaped face. Only passably pretty—nowhere near as stunning as Eve—but she was warm and genuine, the real thing. And really in love with Ollie; I didn't need radar to tell me that. And Jerry, age two, was a cute toddler. I can take kids or let them alone, but Ollie was nuts about him.

I stayed only half an hour, breaking away with the excuse of having a business-lunch date in the Loop, but it was a very pleasant half hour, and Ollie was a completely different person here. He was at home in this small apartment, much more so than in the large apartment on Coleman Boulevard. And you had the feeling that Dorothy was his wife, not Eve.

I was only half a dozen blocks from the office and I didn't want to get out to Coleman Boulevard before one o'clock, so I drove over to State Street and went up to see if Uncle Am was there. He was, and I told him what little I'd learned to date and what my plans were.

"Kid," he said, "I'd like a ride in that chariot you're pushing. How about us having an early lunch and then I'll go out with you and help search the joint. Two of us can do twice as good a job."

It was tempting but I thumbed it down. If a wheel did come off and Eve Bookman came back unexpectedly, I could give her a song and dance as to what I was doing there, but Uncle Am would be harder to explain. I said I'd give him a ride, though. We could leave now and he could come with me out as far as Howard Avenue and we'd eat somewhere out there; then he could take the el back south from the Howard station. It would amount only to his taking a two-hour lunch break and we did that any time we felt like it. He liked the idea.

I let him drive the second half of the way and he fell in love with the car, too. After we had lunch, I phoned the apartment from the restaurant and let the phone ring a dozen times to make sure both Mrs. Bookman and Mrs. Ledbetter were gone. Then I drove Uncle Am to the el station and myself to the apartment.

7

I let myself in and put the chain on the door. If Eve came back too soon, that was going to be embarrassing to explain; I'd have to say I'd done it absent-mindedly and it would make me look like a fool. But it would be less embarrassing than to have her walk in and find me rooting in the drawers of her dresser.

First, I decided, I'd take a look at the place as a whole. The living room, dining room, and the guest bedroom were the only rooms I'd been in thus far. I decided to start at the back. I went through the dining room and the pantry into the kitchen. It was a big kitchen and had the works in the way of equipment, even an automatic dishwasher and garbage disposal. A room on one side of it was a service and storage room and on the other side was a bedroom; Mrs. Ledbetter's, of course. I looked around in all three rooms but didn't touch anything. I went back to the dining room and found that the door from it led to a room probably intended as a den or study; there was a desk—an old-fashioned roll-top desk that was really an antique—two file cabinets, a bookcase filled mostly with books on construction and business practice with a few novels on one shelf, mostly mysteries, a typewriter on a stand, and a dictating machine. This was Ollie's office, from which he conducted whatever business he still did. And the dictating machine meant he must have a part-time secretary, however many days or hours a week. He'd hardly dictate letters and then transcribe them himself.

The roll-top desk was closed but not locked. I opened it and saw a lot of papers and envelopes in pigeonholes, but I didn't study any of them. Ollie's business was no business of mine. But I wondered if he'd used the "Purloined Letter" method of hiding his missing will by having it in plain sight in one of those pigeonholes. And if so, what had Eve been looking for when she found it? I made a mental note to ask him about that.

There was a telephone on top of the desk and I looked at the number on it; it wasn't the same number as that on the phone in the living room, which meant it wasn't an extension but a private line.

I closed the desk and went back to the living room and through its side doorway to the hall from which the bedrooms opened. Another door from it turned out to be a linen closet.

Ollie's bedroom was the same size as mine and furnished in the same way. I walked over to the dresser. A little bottle on it contained nitro-glycerin pills. It held a hundred and was about half full. Beside it were three glass ampoules of amyl nitrite like the one in my pocket, the one I'd got from Doc Kruger last night at dinner. I looked at the ampoules and decided that they hadn't been tampered with. Couldn't be tampered with, in fact. But I took a couple of the nitro pills out of the bottle and put them in my pocket. If I had a chance to get them to Uncle Am, I'd ask him to take them to a laboratory and have them checked to make sure they were really what the label claimed them to be.

I didn't search the room thoroughly, but I looked through the dresser drawers and the closet. I wasn't sure what I was looking for, unless maybe a gun. If Ollie kept a gun, I wanted to know it. But I didn't find a gun or anything else more dangerous than a nail file.

Eve Bookman's room was, of course, the main object of my search, but I wasn't in any hurry and decided I'd do a little thinking before I tackled it. I went back to the living room and since it occurred to me that if Eve was coming back between lunch and bridge, this would be about the time, I took the chain off the door. It wouldn't matter if I was found here, as long as I was innocently occupied. I could just say that I was unable to see the man I'd come to see until tomorrow. And that Ollie—Oliver to her—had had things to do in the Loop and had lent me his car and his house key.

I made myself a highball at the bar and sat down to sip it and think, but the thinking didn't get me anywhere. I knew one thing I'd be looking for—pills the size and color of nitro pills but that might turn out to be something else. Or a gun or any other lethal weapon, or poison—if it could be identified as such. But that was all and it didn't seem very likely to me that I'd find any of those things, even if Eve did have any designs on her husband's life. One other thing I thought of: I might as well finish my search for a gun by looking for one in Ollie's office. If he had one, I wanted to know it, and he might keep it in his study instead of his bedroom.

I made myself another short drink and did some more thinking without getting any idea except that if I could reach Ollie by phone at the Stark apartment, I could simply ask him about the gun, and another question or two I'd thought of.

I rinsed out and wiped the glass I'd used and went to the telephone. I checked the book and found a *Stark, Dorothy* on LaSalle Street and called the number. Ollie answered and when I asked him if he could talk freely, he said sure, that Dorothy had gone out shopping and had left him to baby-sit.

I asked him about guns and he said no, he didn't own any.

I told him I'd noticed the ampoules and pills on his dresser and asked him if he carried some of both with him. He said the pills yes, always. But he didn't carry ampoules because the pills always worked for him and the ampoules he just kept on hand at home in case his angina should get worse. He told me the same thing about them the doctor had, that if one used them often they became ineffective. He'd used one only once thus far, and wouldn't again until and unless he had to.

After I'd hung up, I remembered that I'd forgotten to ask him where the will had been hidden in his office, but it didn't seem worth while calling back to ask him. I wanted to know, if only out of curiosity, but there wasn't any hurry and I could find out the next time I talked to him alone.

I put the chain bolt back on the door—I was pretty sure by now that Eve wasn't coming back before her bridge-club session, as it was already after two, but I thought I might as well play safe—and went to her room.

8

It was bigger than any of the other bedrooms—had originally, no doubt, been intended as the master bedroom—and it had a dressing room attached and lots of closet space. It was going to be a lot of territory to cover thoroughly, but if Eve had any secrets, they'd surely be here, not in Ledbetter territory like the kitchen or Ollie's office or neutral territory like the living room. Apparently she spent a lot of time here; besides the usually bedroom furniture and a vanity table, there was a bookcase of novels and a writing desk that looked used. I sighed and pitched in. Two hours later, all I knew that I hadn't known—but might have suspected—before was that a woman can have more clothes and more beauty preparations than a man would think possible.

I'd looked in everything but the writing desk; I'd saved that for last. There were three drawers and the top one contained only raw materials—paper and envelopes, pencils, ink and such. No pens, but she probably used a fountain pen and carried it with her. The middle one contained canceled checks, neatly in order and rubber-banded,. used stubs of checkbooks similarly banded, and bank statements. No current checkbook; she must have had it with her. The bottom drawer was empty except for a dictionary, a Merriam-Webster *Collegiate*. If she corresponded with anyone, beyond sending out checks to pay bills, she must have destroyed letters when she answered them and not owed any at the moment; there was no correspondence at all.

I still had almost an hour of safe time, since her bridge club surely wouldn't break up before five, so for lack of anything else to go through, I started studying the bank statements and the canceled checks. One thing was immediately obvious: this was her personal account, for clothes and other personal expenses. There was one deposit a month for exactly four hundred dollars, never more or never less. None of the checks drawn against this amount would have been for household expenses. Ollie must have handled them, or had his hypothetical part-time secretary (that was another thing I hadn't remembered to ask him about, but again it was nothing I was in a hurry to know) handle them. This account was strictly a personal one. Some of the checks, usually twenty-five- or fifty-dollar ones, were drawn to cash. Others, most of them for odd amounts, were made out to stores. There was one every month to a Howard Avenue Drugstore, no doubt mostly for cosmetics, most of the others to clothing stores, lingerie shops and the like. Occasional checks to some woman or other for odd amounts up to twenty or thirty dollars were, I decided, probably bridge losses or the like, at times when she didn't have enough cash to pay off. From the bank statements I could see that she lived up to the hilt of her allowance; at the time each four-hundred-dollar check was deposited, always on the first of the month, the balance to which it was added was never over twenty or thirty dollars.

I went through the stack of canceled checks once more. I didn't know what I was looking for, but my subconscious must have noticed something my conscious mind had missed. It had. Not many of the checks were over a hundred dollars, but all of the checks to one outfit, Vogue Shops, Inc., were over a hundred and some were over two hundred. At least half of Eve's four hundred dollars a month was being spent in one place. And other checks were dated at different times, but the Vogue checks were all dated the first of the month exactly. Wondering how much they did total, I took paper and pencil and added the amounts of six of them, for the first six months of the previous year. The smallest was $165.50 and the largest $254.25, but the total—it jarred me. The total of the six checks came to $1,200. Exactly. Even. On the head. And so, I knew a minute later, did the checks for the second half of the year. It certainly couldn't be coincidence, twice.

Eve Bookman was paying somebody an even two hundred bucks a month— and disguising the fact, on the surface at any rate, by making some of the amounts more than that and some less, but making them average out. I turned over some of the checks to look at the endorsements. Each one was rubber-stamped *Vogue Shops, Inc.*, and under the rubber stamp was the signature *John L. Littleton*. Rubber stamps under that showed they'd all been deposited or cashed at the Dearborn Branch of the Chicago Second National Bank.

And that, whatever it meant, was all the checks were going to tell me. I re-banded them and put them back as I'd found them, took a final look around the room to see that I was leaving everything else as I'd found it, and went back to the living room. I was going to call Uncle Am at the office—if he wasn't there, I could reach him later at the rooming house—but I took the chain off the door first. If Eve walked in while I was talking on the phone, I'd just have to switch the subject of conversation to printing equipment. Uncle Am would understand.

He was still at the office. I talked fast and when I finished, he said, "Nice going, kid. You've got something by the tail and I'll find out what it is. You stick with the Bookmans and let me handle everything outside. We've got two lucky breaks on this. One, it's Friday and that bank will be open till six o'clock. Two, one of the tellers is a friend of mine. When I get anything for sure, I'll get in touch with you. Is there an extension on the phone there that somebody could listen in on?"

"No," I said. "There's another phone in Ollie's office, but it's a different line."

"Fine, than I can call openly and ask for you. You can pretend it's a business call, if anyone's around, and argue price on a Miehle vertical for your end of the conversation."

"Okay. One other thing." I told him about the two alleged nitro pills I'd appropriated from Ollie's bottle. I told him that on my way in to town for dinner, I'd drop them off on his desk at the office and sometime tomorrow he could take them to the lab. Or maybe, if nitro had a distinctive taste, Doc Kruger could tell by touching one of them to his tongue.

9

It was five o'clock when I hung up the phone. I decided that I'd earned a drink and helped myself to a short one at the bar. Then I went to my room, treated myself to a quick shower and a clean shirt for the evening.

I was just about to open the door to leave when it opened from the other side and Eve Bookman came home. She was pleasantly surprised to find me and I told her how I happened to have the house key and Ollie's car, but said I'd been there only half an hour, just to clean up and change shirts for the evening.

She asked why, since it was five thirty already, I didn't stay and drive her in in Ollie's car. That way we wouldn't be stuck, after dinner, with having both the Buick and the MG downtown with us and could all ride home together.

I told her it sounded like an excellent idea. Which it was, except for the fact that I wanted to get the pills to Uncle Am. But there was a way around that. I asked if she could give me a piece of paper, envelope and stamp. She went to her room to get them and after she'd gone back there to dress, I addressed the envelope to Uncle Am at the office, folded the paper around the pills and sealed them in the envelope. All I'd have to do was mail it, on our way in, at the Dearborn Post Office Station and it would get there in the morning delivery.

I made myself comfortable with a magazine to read and Eve surprised me by taking not too long to get ready. And she looked gorgeous, and I told her so, when she came back to the living room. It was only six fifteen and I didn't have to speed to get us to the Pump Room by seven. Ollie wasn't there, but he'd reserved us a table and left word with the maître d' that something had come up and he'd be a bit late.

He was quite a bit late and we were finishing our third round of Martinis when he showed up, very apologetic about being detained. We decided we'd have one more so he could have one with us, and then ate a wonderful meal. As an out-of-town guest who was presuming on their hospitality already, I insisted on grabbing the check. A nice touch, since it would go on Ollie's bill anyway.

We discussed going on to a night club, but Eve said that Ollie looked tired—which he did—and if we went clubbing, would want to drink too much. We could have a drink or two at home—if Ollie would promise to hold to two. He said he would.

Since Ollie admitted that he really was a little tired, I had no trouble talking him into letting me do the driving again. Eve seemed more genuinely friendly than hitherto. Maybe it was the Martinis before dinner or maybe she was getting to like me. But it was an at-a-distance type of friendliness; my radar told me that.

Back home, I offered to do the bartending, but Eve overruled me and made our drinks. We were drinking them and talking about nothing in particular when I saw

Ollie suddenly put down his glass and bend forward slightly, putting his right hand under his left arm.

Then he straightened up and saw that we were both looking at him with concern. He said, "Nothing. Just a little twinge, not an attack. But maybe to be on the safe side, I'll take one——"

He took a little gold pillbox out of his pocket and opened it.

"Good Lord," he said, standing up. "Forgot I took my last one just before I got to the Pump Room. Just as well we didn't go night-clubbing, after all. Well, it's okay now. I'll fill it."

"Let me——" I said.

But he looked perfectly well now and waved me away. "I'm perfectly okay. Don't worry."

And he went into the hallway walking confidently, and I heard the door of his room open and close so I knew he'd made it all right.

Eve started to make conversation by asking me questions about the girl in Seattle whom I'd talked about, and I was answering and enjoying it, when suddenly I realized Ollie had been gone at least five minutes and maybe ten. A lot longer than it would take to refill a pillbox. Of course he might have decided to go to the john or something while he was there, but just the same, I stood up quickly, excused myself without explaining, headed for his room.

The minute I opened the door, I saw him and thought he was dead. He was lying face down on the rug in front of the dresser and on the dresser there wasn't any little bottle of pills and there weren't any amyl nitrite ampoules, either.

I bent over him, but I didn't waste time trying to find out whether he was dead or not. If he was, the ampoule I'd got from Doc Kruger wasn't going to hurt him. And if he was alive, a fraction of a second might make the difference of whether it would save him or not. I didn't feel for a heartbeat or look at his face. I got hold of a handful of hair and lifted his head a few inches off the floor, reached in under it with my hand and crushed the ampoule right under his nose.

Eve was standing in the doorway and I barked at her to phone for an ambulance, right away quick. She ran back toward the living room.

10

Ollie didn't die, although he certainly would have if I hadn't had the bright idea of appropriating that ampoule from Doc and carrying it with me. But Ollie was in bad shape for a while, and Uncle Am and I didn't get to see him until two days later, Sunday evening.

His face looked gray and drawn and he was having to lie very quiet. But he could talk, and they gave us fifteen minutes with him. And they'd told us he was definitely out of danger, as long as he behaved himself, but he'd still be in the hospital another week or maybe even two.

But bad as he looked, I didn't pull any punches. "Ollie," I said, "it didn't work, your little frame-up. I didn't go to the police and accuse Eve of trying to murder you. On the other hand, I've given you this break, so far. I didn't go to them and tell them you tried to commit suicide in a way to frame her for murder. You must love Dorothy and Jerry awfully much to have planned that."

"I—I do," he said. "What—made you guess, Ed?"

"Your hands, for one thing," I said. "They were dirtier than they'd have been if you'd just fallen. That and the fact that you were lying face down told me how you managed to bring on that attack at just that moment. You were doing push-ups — about as strenuous and concentrated exercise as a man can take. And just kept doing them till you passed out. It *should* have been fatal, all right.

"And you knew the pills and ampoules had been on your dresser that afternoon, and that Eve had been home since I'd seen them and could have taken them. Actually you took them yourself. You came out in a taxi—and we could probably find the taxi if we had to prove this—and got them yourself. You had to wait till you were sure Eve and I would be en route downtown, and that's why you were so late getting to the Pump Room. Now Uncle Am's got news for you—not that you deserve it."

Uncle Am cleared his throat. "You're not married, Ollie. You're a free man because your marriage to Eve Packer wasn't legal. She'd been married before and hadn't got a divorce. Probably because she had no intention of marrying again until you popped the question to her, and then it was too late to get one.

"Her legal husband, who left her ten years ago, is a bartender named Littleton. He found her again somehow and when he learned she'd married you illegally, he started blackmailing her. She's been paying him two hundred a month, half the pin-money allowance you gave her, for three years. They worked out a way she could mail him checks and still have her money seemingly accounted for. The method doesn't matter."

I took over. "We haven't called copper on the bigamy bit, either, because you're not going to prosecute her for it, or tell the cops. We figure you owe her something for having tried to frame her on a murder charge. We've talked to her. She'll leave town quietly, and go to Reno, and in a little while you can let out that you're divorced and free. And marry Dorothy and legitimize Jerry.

"She really will be getting a divorce, incidentally, but from Littleton, not from you. I said you'd finance that and give her a reasonable stake to start out with. Like ten thousand dollars—does that sound reasonable?"

He nodded. His face looked less drawn, less gray now. I had a hunch his improvement would be a lot faster now.

"And you fellows," he said. "How can I ever——?"

"We're even," Uncle Am said. "Your retainer will cover. But don't ever look us up again to do a job for you. A private detective doesn't like to be made a patsy, be put in the spot of helping a frame-up. And that's what you tried to do to us. Don't ever look us up again."

We never saw Ollie again, but we did hear from him once, a few months later. One morning, a Western Union messenger came into our office to deliver a note and a little box. He said he had instructions not to wait and left.

The envelope contained a wedding announcement. One of the after-the-fact kind, not an invitation, of the marriage of Oliver R. Bookman to Dorothy Stark. On the back of it was scribbled a note. "Hope you've forgiven me enough to accept a wedding present in reverse. I've arranged for the dealer to leave it out front. Papers will be in glove compartment. Thanks for everything, including accepting this." And the little box, of course, contained two sets of car keys.

It was, as I'd known it would be, a brand-new Buick sedan, gray, a hell of a car. We stood looking at it, and Uncle Am said, "Well, Ed, have we forgiven him enough?"

"I guess so," I said. "It's a sweet chariot. But somebody got off on his time, either the car dealer or the messenger, and it's been here too long. Look."

I pointed to the parking ticket on the windshield. "Well, shall we take our first ride in it, down to the City Hall to pay the fine and get right with God?"

We did.

Jack Webb

(1920–)

Given the social and political climates of the early 1950s, and the tendency in mystery and detective fiction in those days toward noncontroversial protagonists (Mickey Spillane's Mike Hammer being a prominent exception), the launching of a series about a Jewish policeman and a Roman Catholic priest whose parish is located in a poor Hispanic neighborhood was a calculated risk for both author and publisher. Reader response to Detective-Sergeant Sammy Golden and Father Joseph Shanley turned out to be quite favorable, however, though critical reaction was mixed. One reason for the duo's success was the gritty, semi-hard-boiled style employed by Jack Webb; another was inherent in the fact that he chose to downplay the religious and ethnic differences of his heroes, while focusing on their developing friendship and on the various good and evil characters who inhabit the Los Angeles barrio where both men work. Father Shanley is the much better drawn of the two; he and his Church of St. Anne parishioners come across realistically as both individuals and practicing Catholics. Golden's ethnic background is never explored and is referred to only in generalities. Whether this sketchiness was intentional is a matter of conjecture.

The series encompassed nine novels published over a twelve-year span, originating with *The Big Sin* (1952), in which Shanley and Golden meet and join forces to bring to justice the murderer of a Latina showgirl. *The Brass Halo* (1957) has a moody jazz theme, a subject on which Webb was an expert and about which he wrote with such passion that his prose becomes almost lyrical at times. The last of the nine, *The Gilded Witch* (1963), concerns a sordid, *Peyton Place*–style roman à clef that precipitates several homicides among the St. Anne flock.

The creator of Father Shanley and Sammy Golden is not the same Jack Webb who starred in the TV series *Dragnet* and who wrote the mainstream police novel *The Badge*, despite some critical claims to the contrary (the entry on Webb in the first volume of *Twentieth Century Crime and Mystery Writers*, for instance). Nor were the two men related in any way. The mystery-writing Jack Webb was a technical writer who once worked for the San Diego Zoo and served in the army during World War II in the unusual capacity of trainer of a unit of carrier pigeons. His first novel, a

Western as by Tex Grady, was published in 1952. He also wrote four crime novels as John Farr; two of these have zoo backgrounds (*Don't Feed the Animals*, 1955, and *The Lady and the Snake*, 1957). Under his own name, in addition to the nine Shanley–Golden mysteries, he published two nonseries suspense novels and more than a score of short stories. "And Start with a Blonde" is the only one of his shorter works to feature his detecting duo; despite flawed construction and a plot that is too easily resolved, it demonstrates the qualities of characterization and evocative mean-streets atmosphere that made the series popular and helped to pave the way for the religious and ethnically mixed teams (such as Barbara D'Amato's Figueroa and Bennis) who followed.

AND START WITH A BLONDE

FATHER SHANLEY AND SAMMY GOLDEN
LOS ANGELES, CALIFORNIA
1960

The first time Father Shanley saw the blonde, he shared the experience with every male parishioner over the age of fourteen and under seventy. It was true that her black dress was smart, and that the black bit of lace with little bows all caught like fish in a net was quite the proper hat for one of the more fashionable parishes, but she did not belong in St. Anne's. Not among the Marquezes, and Gonzalezes, the Alejandros and the Cervantes. Moreover, even though she sat quietly through the early Mass, she was that sort of woman who made the mere fact of her sex a most disturbing element.

The second time he saw the blonde, she was dead—remarkably and brutally dead. Nor was there any question of what the murder weapon had been. The shards of the tall, dark Scotch bottle were strewn on the cheap carpet from wall to wall and the reek of expensive whiskey filled the shabby room.

It was after midnight when Sergeant Golden reached the parish house beside the church of St. Anne.

At nine o'clock, when Father had phoned Homicide from the dead woman's apartment, Sammy Golden had been down on South Center on a case of little interest to anyone excepting the medical examiner.

Lieutenant Adams had gone out on the priest's urgent call. He had been preceded by Officers Gault and Savage, whose radio car had been in the Royal Heights area. The initial inquiry had been completed.

Now, Sammy had come to St. Anne's because he was a friend, and also because Dan Adams had not been satisfied with Father's story.

Adams had said, "You know I don't doubt Father, Sammy, but ... it's just, well ..." He had paused and run distracted hands through his short-cropped red hair. "Hell, look at the facts. Forget it's Shanley for a minute. He says he's seen the girl once, in his church last Sunday, that when he spoke to her after the services, she didn't even answer him, yet when she called tonight, she knew all about him, refused to see him at the parish house in the morning and insisted that he come to the Vista del Sur Apartments right away."

"Why?"

"Yeah, why?" Dan grinned briefly. "From the way Father spoke, I had the feeling that he didn't like the sound of it at all, that he actually was quite upset at going to *that woman's* apartment alone, and would have gotten out of it if she hadn't said that she had been told he was the one man she could trust, that if she ever needed him he would come."

"Told by who?" Sammy demanded.

"Whom," said Adams. "You go find out."

So he had, and the light was on over the front door. Golden climbed from his car and opened the gate under the arbor overburdened with pale pink roses.

Father Shanley was at the door before he could ring. "Come in, Sammy. Come in."

Sammy followed him into the house. "I'm sorry I was out when you called. I was attending a wake down on South Center. Dan Adams filled me in when he got back. I came as soon as I could."

"Then you've talked to Dan. Good. Heaven knows I've been over the details often enough tonight. I've got some coffee ready. You go on into the study. Are you still on duty?"

"Officially," Sammy said carefully, "the night watch ended twenty minutes ago. So far as I know, nobody's paying me any overtime."

"Good, I'll bring a little brandy, then. I wouldn't admit it to anyone but you, Sammy, but this has been a night and I could use a drop of something." Father paused with his hand against the kitchen door. "Yes, Sammy, I sure could!"

Sergeant Golden went on down the hall past the dining room and into the familiar surroundings of the study where he spent so many, many hours and where talk hadn't always been a crime. He wore a puzzled frown. It was nearly ten years now since he and Father had clashed and then joined forces, and he never had seen his friend so nervous. Sure, he had been through a shocking experience, but the shock of violent death was nothing new to Joseph Shanley.

The opposite door swung open to the pressure of Father's toe and he came in bearing a tray in both hands. He carried a coffeepot, cups, saucers, a bottle of Christian Brothers, two small snifters and paper napkins on the tray. Sammy helped him arrange things on the small table beside the big chair.

Sammy straightened up, shoving his hands into his pockets. "All right, Father, what is it? Let's get rid of it."

Father Shanley set the pot down carefully and met the detective's glance steadily. "You heard how she was killed?"

"Whiskey bottle."

"That's right. Dan tell you that the bottle hadn't been emptied?" Sammy waited.

The priest handed him a drink. "Upstairs in my closet," he said soberly, "is one of my black suit coats, stained across the lapels and rather damp. It smells strongly of whiskey."

"What in the devil—"

"Precisely my own thoughts," Father agreed. "Incidentally," he added dryly, "it's not the coat I was wearing when I paid my call."

Sammy tasted his brandy, felt the warmth of it on his tongue and then finished it off quickly. The priest reached for the bottle. Golden shook his head. "Maybe I needed one, too."

Shanley said quietly, "It's rather frightening, isn't it? That they knew when I found the girl I'd report her death. That they knew when I found the coat I'd report it rather than clean it or otherwise dispose of it—either of which would have been relatively simple. Being sure of these things when I was the only witness to my own actions."

"Don't let it spook you," Sammy said. "It may be our one break."

"Break?"

"The fellow knows you. Chances are, you know him." He grinned without humor. "Also, Father, he doesn't like you very much."

"No, Sammy." The pain was clear in Father's glance. "Not that, not *murder* because of hatred of me!"

It was nine o'clock the following morning when the big man left the Carlton Plaza and walked ten blocks to Center Street. He turned south into the Latin-American district a few blocks above skid row. In the foyer of a theater the billboards advertised *Cuattro contra el imperio* and *Dos diabolitos en aduros*. With his back to the girl in the tiny cubicle of the box office, he removed his tie and slipped it in his jacket pocket. Then he unbuttoned the two top buttons of his shirt and ran his hand roughly through his gray-flecked hair. These small actions, plus the fact he had not shaved, were enough to put him on Center Street without attracting undue attention.

On down the street, he paused before a hole in the wall called La Fiesta. But there were only two young men at the bar, so he walked on until he came to El Charro. Here, there were quite a number along the shabby bar. The big man went in. He paid for his first beer with a twenty-dollar bill. He left the change carelessly on the damp wood before him. A great many glances evidenced more interest in his money than he did.

He was on his second beer when the husky voice inquired, "You like to buy Lupe a little drink, *si?*"

"Why not?"

Her brassy hair had dark roots. There was a gold cap on one front tooth and her smile was enormous. She more than covered the stool beside him.

The bartender glanced at them sourly.

"Bring Lupe a drink," the big man said.

"Sure, Joe," Lupe agreed. "I gotta friend. What's your name, friend?" Her left hand rested on his knee. "Whiskey and soda, Joe."

The friendship prospered through five whiskeys and soda.

"Fren'," Lupe said, her soft body rocking, "good fren' with no name. You wanna good time, good fren'?"

The man let his gaze wander the joint. Joe was at the far end emptying a case of beer into the cooler under the back bar. The stools on either side of them were empty. He leaned closer. "You want to earn twenty bucks, Lupe?"

"Twenty bucks, *por Dios!*"

"Good. Now listen to me, Lupe." He lowered his voice to a harsh whisper. "I'm going to make a phone call and you're going to do the talking. Okay?"

"Okay. . . ."

It was a little after noon when Captain Bill Cantrell and Sergeant Golden climbed from the official sedan at the curb in front of the parish house. Father Shanley laid down the shears with which he was trimming the flamboyant pillar of Gladiator roses beside the small front porch and then peeled off his gloves.

"Captain Cantrell, Sammy, I'm delighted to see you." The priest's smile was genuine.

"Are you, Father?" Cantrell growled. He threw the remnants of a tattered cigar at a rosebush. "Mind if we come in?"

His face sobering, Joseph Shanley swung upon the gate. "Sammy's told you about the coat?"

"Yeah," Cantrell admitted. "Funny thing, that coat."

"I don't find it so," Father said gravely. "I expect you would like to have it."

The captain from Homicide nodded. He didn't look any happier about it than Sammy did, and Sammy hadn't even spoken. Bill Cantrell said, "This isn't easy for us, Father. We have a search warrant. Would you like us to serve it?"

The priest's strong, tanned hands gripped the top of the fence. "Please," he said quietly, "would you mind telling me what this is all about?"

"Father," Sammy began, "this is——"

"I'll do the talking," Cantrell said abruptly. He returned to Shanley. "We have received some information. In it certain allegations were made. If you would like to be represented by an attorney, we'll permit you to call one."

"But, why?"

"Then we may make the search?"

The priest nodded without speaking. As they started up the front steps, he said, "One favor. It might benefit all of us if I were to find an errand for Mrs. Mulvaney outside the house before you go to work."

The priest returned to the front hall. "I've convinced her that the Fuertes need her pepper-pot soup more than I do. They've all had a virus this last week. And after that, she's going to do some shopping to replace the soup and she's been wanting new curtains for the kitchen windows. So, if we could start upstairs while she's putting on her bonnet, that should give you ample time. . . ."

They began their search in the priest's sparse, almost Spartan bedroom beneath the still, watching eyes of the dusty gold crucifix.

Father Shanley never forgot Sergeant Golden's expression as he turned from the bottom dresser drawer, his hands coming up from the bleached Navy suntans that were now the priest's old work clothes. In his grasp was a pair of flimsy nylons.

"Well, Father?" It was Cantrell who spoke, not Golden.

Joseph Shanley came out of the shock slowly. "Her legs were bare," he said with a hollow detachment. "I remember because the door was open and the light was on and I could see her calves and ankles and feet and those new shoes with the clean, clean soles. So, of course, I hurried in. What else could I do? She was on the floor, you see. Not at all in a proper position and, of course, I could smell the liquor."

The two policemen stared at him.

"Sammy," Father said, "Sammy . . ."

Before Golden could reply, Cantrell caught his arm and squeezed. Sammy looked down at the stockings in his hand. The Captain's bloodshot eyes never left the priest.

Father spoke quickly, a sudden, bitter anger rising in his voice. "Good heavens, you two don't think ..."

"Sometimes we have to," Captain Cantrell said soberly. "You'd better come downtown with me for awhile, Father."

"Is this an arrest?"

"I didn't say that." He turned his glance to Sammy, rubbing the back of his neck. "You stay here, Sergeant. I'm going to have a team from the lab comb the place. Somebody might have been careless. After they arrive, you can beat it home. Report as regularly for the night watch."

Sammy had watched them go and felt like Judas. An involuntary Judas, sure, but then, what Judas is not? And even if he had not carried the story of Father's liquor-spattered coat to headquarters, the phone call this morning would have done the job. It had been an anonymous call, but not a crank one, a call from an exceedingly nervous woman with a Spanish accent who insisted that she had seen *a priest* hurrying from the Vista del Sur Apartments where the "mystery blonde" had been killed at *eight-thirty*.

It had been nine when Father had called Homicide to report the murder and, according to Shanley, eight-thirty when the blonde had called him to come to her.

So, somebody was lying. Sammy backed up and started over; so the woman was a liar. Why? Last night he had suggested that someone did not like Father. True as that might be, it was not half enough by far. Because you had to go back to the beginning and start with a blonde, an expensive blonde who had moved into a cheap apartment in a neighborhood where she didn't belong, who attended a church where she didn't fit and who had died most violently only last night.

According to her driver's license, she was Sally M. Cox, five foot four inches tall, weighed one hundred and thirty pounds and lived at the Vista del Sur address. Inasmuch as she had moved to that address less than three weeks ago, the driver's license was brand new. It said exactly what she wanted it to say and no more. There was no previous record of the State of California's having issued a driver's permit to one Sally M. Cox. She had a checking account at the Royal Heights branch of the Bank of Southern California. She had made an initial deposit of three thousand dollars in cash. The currency had been in old bills of varying denominations. There had been nothing irregular about it except that the amount was startling in Royal Heights.

Insofar as anyone could determine, Sally Cox had been born three weeks ago, when she had made a bank deposit, rented a furnished apartment and taken a driver's test. She had lived a short life and there was little evidence that it had been happy.

When the Crime Lab crew arrived, Sammy left.

He walked down to Ney and caught a bus into town. It wasn't like Cantrell to leave any of his men without transportation. But nobody had been like nobody this morning. Or last night, for that matter.

Off the bus, he headed for the garage under the big white police-department building and then changed his mind. It wasn't much farther to the morgue.

"Cox," he said, "Sally M. Cox."

The attendant led the way. It was cold in the morgue. Quiet.

"Don't often get a looker," he said. He pulled back the covering from her head and shoulders. "Right pretty," he said. "If you forget what was done to her. A few years ago, I bet she was something terrific."

Sammy glanced at the attendant, coming out of his study of the face before him. "What did you say?"

"I just said that a few years ago . . ."

"Where's your phone?"

"Back there on the desk where you came in."

Sammy swung away from the man and headed out.

"Put her away?" the attendant shouted after him.

"You stay put," Golden said over his shoulder. "Both of you," he added rather needlessly.

"Jack York'll be right down," the detective said when he returned. York was the best artist on the force.

"You onto something, Sergeant?" the attendant said.

"I don't know," Sammy said honestly.

"You think the priest had anything to do with it?"

Golden's right hand flashed out and caught a fistful of shirt front. His eyes were bleak. "Where did you hear anything like that?"

"Say, who do you think . . ." The man's voice trailed off, suddenly frightened.

"I asked you a question."

"I don't know nothin', just what the night man told me when I come on."

Sammy let go of the shirt. "Your friend's got a lousy mouth."

"Sure, Sergeant, sure. Say, I just remember, you and that priest . . ."

"That's right," Sammy agreed quietly, "me and *that* priest . . ."

Office York arrived with pencils and pad. Sammy grinned crookedly. "You bring some imagination, Jack?"

"What's on your mind?"

Sergeant Golden nodded at Sally Cox. "Can you do her face as though she were twenty pounds lighter, seven or eight years younger and wearing her hair loose to her shoulders?"

York frowned and studied the full, sensuous, sleeping expression. Then, rapidly, he went to work. Before he was halfway through, Sammy sighed. Then his expression grew thoughtful. In twenty minutes, the sketch was complete.

The police artist held it up for inspection. "Somebody you know, if I may ask?"

"Sari Angel," Sammy said softly. "The Naked Angel." He stared down at the mortal remains on the table. *Good afternoon*, he thought; *good afternoon and goodby....* There was a certain justice in her final violence.

Sammy took the picture from York. "You can put her to bed," he said to the attendant.

The two officers left together.

"Naked Angel," York said.

"A stripper once. Sensational. Also the girl friend of a guy named Gerald Dempsy. He had his wife killed because of her. Father Shanley brought him back from Mexico single-handed. We sent him up...." Sammy paused, frowning.

"I don't get it," York said.

"Neither do I," Golden admitted.

Captain William Cantrell made the call to Folsom Prison from his office.

Gerald Dempsy had been released five weeks ago after serving seven years and nine months. He had been a model prisoner. He had corresponded with a Sara Engel while he was there and a woman who had identified herself as the same had visited him a number of times during the last two years.

"That would be after she stopped being the Angel," Sammy said.

Cantrell nodded, his burned-out eyes watching the sergeant.

Sammy switched from the girl then and came back to Dempsy. "And he did hate Father," he said. "He had more reason to than any other human being."

"But he wouldn't kill *her*," Cantrell growled.

"Eight years of hating," Sammy said grimly, "is a hell of a long time."

"No proof." Cantrell threw his cigar at a basket in the corner.

"We'll get it."

"How?"

"Find Dempsy."

"Sure." The Captain's voice was sour. "In a week, a month, a year. He's a smart boy. He's not broke. He'll be a thousand miles from here."

"He wasn't when he made that phone call this morning."

"That was a Mexican woman."

"Sure," Sammy said, "who did the talking. But Sally Cox was created to frame Father, to disgrace him."

Cantrell slapped his hands hard on the desk before him. His voice was rough. "You did a good job identifying the Angel—I'll give you that. And we'll get an all-points out on Dempsy—I'll give you that, too. But we've got a murderer to find, not a two-bit lousy frame. Now you take the night off and go on home. You've done a day's work and I'll pull somebody in to handle your spot on the night watch."

Sammy's nails bit into the palms of his hands. He relaxed them with an effort. "Where's Father, Bill?"

"Down the hall having a talk with Dan and Ed Haggerty—a long talk."

Silently, Sergeant Golden turned to walk from the room.

"And you leave 'em alone," Cantrell shouted.

"Sure," Sammy said, "sure, Bill."

He knew what Cantrell had said with never saying a word about it. Identifying the Angel and proving Dempsy was loose hadn't helped Father. If Dempsy had murdered his girl friend, it had to be proved. And if it were not ... *Booze on the priest's coat, torn nylon stockings hidden in a drawer ...*

He got off the elevator opposite RECORDS.

He signed for two photos from the Dempsy file.

He started with the Biltmore Hotel. Dempsy had always lived high. Dempsy had money. Dempsy had been a tipper.

After the Biltmore, he hit the Statler.

It was seven-thirty in the evening when he walked into the Carlton Plaza. There was no Dempsy on the register. The registration clerk wasn't "very good about faces." The bell captain started to shake his head, and then hesitated.

"Seven, eight years older," Sammy said quickly. "Probably has put on weight. None of the tan that's in these shots. Been in prison."

The man nodded abruptly. "I'm not certain," he said. He didn't mean it.

They started through the bellhops.

The third bellhop said, "That would be nine eighteen, sir. I took his bags up myself."

The hotel detective's name was Grierson. They rode up together.

Outside nine eighteen Grierson glanced up and down the hall and then slipped a snub-nosed .38 from a shoulder holster into his right jacket pocket. He used his left hand to insert the pass key into the lock. The door opened silently.

A single lamp was burning beside the easy chair. Newspapers were scattered around it. The big man on the bed had an arm cocked across his face. He was not aware of them until they were in the room with the door closed behind them.

"All right, Dempsy," Sammy said.

The big man swung his legs from the bed and sat up. When the light hit the planes of his face, his cheeks were shining. He stared at the two men with swollen eyes. *Lord,* Sammy thought, *he's been crying like a baby.* It wasn't the victory Sammy'd expected. It was somehow shameful, somehow embarrassing. There was a framed photograph on the chest of drawers. The slim blond girl in it looked like an angel. It had been taken many years ago.

Grierson broke the strange charade. "This your man?"

"This is the man," Sammy repeated. He crossed the room to the phone. Cantrell was still in his office.

"I've picked up Dempsy," Sergeant Golden said. "We're in room nine eighteen at the Carlton Plaza." His own voice sounded hollow.

Eight-thirty, nine-thirty, ten-thirty. Gerald Dempsy talked. All the hatred Sammy had guessed came spilling out. A nursed hatred, a nurtured hatred, all aimed at one man. It had coiled and grown through the prison years, it had blossomed with the invention of Sally Cox. Two individuals getting even for the wasted years. For the years Father Joseph Shanley had lost them when he captured Dempsy. Sari Angel and Gerald Dempsy, planning, scheming, thinking, forming an antichrist out of a man most considered nearly a saint.

But it hadn't worked, Dempsy said, hadn't worked, because Sari Angel was dead.

And he wept again.

It was a closed-door session. The captain and the sergeant together in Cantrell's office.

"The man's a psychopath," Sammy said viciously.

"Is he?" Cantrell rubbed at the corners of his burning eyes.

"You don't believe him, Bill?"

"Somebody killed the Angel."

"Dempsy."

"You sure he did, Sammy?" Cantrell worked the cellophane wrapper off a cigar.

"God," Sammy said, "I don't know."

"We've sent Shanley home," Cantrell said, his rough voice almost gentle. "I think you'd better go and pay him another call."

"Me!" Sammy raised a tortured glance. "I've crucified him already."

"Sure," Cantrell agreed. "I can send Prouty and Mendez. We have to talk to him again."

"I'll go."

"Dan Adams better go with you."

"Alone," Sammy said. He took a deep breath. "It's better that way."

"Yeah," Bill said. He watched Sergeant Golden walk to the door. It was a damned long walk. The truth was hard to come by sometimes.

Golden took his own car. He drove out West Ney in the backwash of the big east-west freeway through the dirty shirttails of the city.

I could use a drink, Sammy thought. He kept driving.

The Chino Poblano was just three blocks from the parish house.

Sammy parked in front of the joint. *After tonight*, he thought, *I'm going to get drunk and stay drunk*. It would be better than thinking. Anything would.

It was an old bar, shiny from a thousand damp cloths, worm-eaten with the marks of careless cigarettes. The light inside was dusty and the electric fan made a quiet music. The men spoke mostly in the gentle cadence of their native tongue and even at this late hour there was a table of dominoes. Sammy ordered a double shot with a water chaser.

The bartender brought his drink. Sammy paid.

"It is the *rubia*," the bartender said. "That is why you are here, Sergeant?"

"I'm here for a drink," Sammy said. He tried to remember the man's name, but he had met so many of Father's people. *Father's people*—the phrase was like an open wound.

The bartender scowled. "Even dead, such a one makes trouble. I could have told you that from the first time I saw her."

"In church?"

The man thumped his forefinger on the bar. "In here. Upon the same stool as the one you occupy. Before God!" The domino players had turned their heads and were watching.

"Here?" Sammy repeated. He tried to stop the excitement curling inside him.

"*Pues*, and why not?" The bartender shrugged. "It is the nearest place."

"Alone?"

"That I will give her. She came alone. She left alone. In this place, that is not an easy thing. I speak in confidence, Sergeant, because you are a friend of *el padre*."

"About the woman," Sammy snapped.

"*Sí*," said the bartender, "*muy guapa*, that one. She was not unfriendly, you understand. But she could handle men. All fire and ice. And when it was cold, Sergeant"—he grinned—"it was very, very cold. Even such a pig as Miguel could see that."

"Miguel?"

"Miguel Milpas. A fool. A chaser. Big in the stomach, bigger in the head. A big trouble in here. A bad drunk."

Sammy leaned forward. "This Milpas, where would I find him?"

The bartender called to the domino players, "*¿Dónde está la casa de Miguel?*"

There was a quick flutter of consideration in Spanish.

"Around the corner on Mercado," the bartender translated. "Fourth house on the right."

"Thanks." Sammy left his drink unfinished.

In a poor district, Mercado was the poorest street. Dark, leaning houses, broken fences. Sammy went up the walk and onto a warped and sagging porch. He knocked. He pounded. In the house next door, a child began to cry. Across the street, a window went up.

The door before him swung open. "Wha' do you wan'?" A big shadow in the greater shadow behind it.

"Are you Miguel Milpas?"

"Who wan's to know?"

"I'm a police officer. I want—"

The door slammed toward him. Sammy met it with his shoulder. The man was running through the house. The detective stumbled after him, following the clatter of footsteps. Then the footsteps stopped and he heard the squeal of wood against wood as when a badly fitted drawer is pulled.

It came from the left and Sammy crouched as he moved down a dark, narrow hall toward the dark room at the end. The shot exploded over his head.

From the memory of the flash, he dived for Miguel. His head smashed into the gross barrel of Miguel's belly.

Sammy got up first. He lit a match, caught the gleam of the nickel-plated pistol and kicked it across the room before he found the finger switch on the old brass fixture. The light showed a fat, ugly drunk, holding his stomach and moaning.

Golden stood over him. "Get up, Milpas."

"*¡Por Dios!* I am broken in two."

Sammy grabbed a handful of hair and pulled the man's head up and back. "The blonde woman, Sally Cox, last night!"

Miguel groaned.

"The blonde woman!" Sammy repeated.

"I did not mean to. She open the door when I knock. She is angry to see me. She grab a bottle, a wild cat, *gata, gatoda!*" He closed his eyes and tried to rock forward. Golden let go of the man and stepped back.

"Well, now, if that isn't a picture!"

Sammy swung toward the door. Lieutenant Adams leaned against the frame, a broad grin on his freckled face. "Bill thought somebody should tag along and pick up your stitches."

"You heard?" Sammy demanded.

"I heard."

Golden felt his own grin growing. "Well, what are we waiting for?"

Adams jerked a thumb at the man on the floor. "For him to get well," he said.

It was late the next afternoon when Sammy finally reached the parish house of St. Anne's. He had had ten hours sleep, a shave, a shower, and a quart of beer to celebrate rejoining the human race.

Father Joseph Shanley took him into the study with an arm about his shoulders. The priest had heard enough to know that he was clear of the tall cloud, but he had not heard the details.

"Miguel Milpas," Father shook his head. "One of my failures . . ."

"A big trouble," Sammy quoted the bartender, "a bad drunk."

"Nevertheless . . ." the priest said.

"You were darned lucky we found him. Maybe you were even lucky he did it. Dempsy and the Angel were out to get you and get you good. The night before last you were bound for an assignation. After you arrived at the apartment you were to be doused with liquor, and she was going to run from the apartment, her clothes torn, screaming at the top of her lungs. A lot of people would have seen you. Then Dempsy was to have picked her up and they would have vanished into the night. One phone call, and the police would have found an apartment abandoned by a terror-stricken woman, witnesses and you wandering around smelling of whiskey."

Father shuddered.

"He almost made it at that. Because even with Sari dead, he had enough hatred left to improvise."

"That poor man . . ." Joseph Shanley stared at Sammy Golden. "What will you people do to him?"

"Not much, actually. Aside from entering the parish house, it's hard to put a finger on anything he did that's strictly illegal."

The detective shrugged. "One thing I can tell you, though, we'll put the fear of God in him where you're concerned."

A ghost of a smile touched the corners of Father's eyes. "Isn't that a little outside of your bailiwick, Sergeant?"

"You go to . . ." Sammy began and stopped. There was too little logic in the last word, and besides, they had been there only last night.

Michael Gilbert

(1912–)

Mr. Calder and Mr. Behrens are not quite what they seem. They are not detectives in the strict sense of the term, nor are they, as everyone in their village of Lamperdown believes, two mild-mannered gentleman friends of independent means. They are in fact professional counterintelligence agents attached to the External Branch of the Joint Services Standing Intelligence —a pair of very quiet and very deadly spies working at a Cold War job in which, as Mr. Calder has said, "there is neither right nor wrong. Only expediency."

No one is better at expedient action than Daniel Joseph Calder and Samuel Behrens. In "The Road to Damascus," the team utilize the twin discoveries of a World War II hidey-hole containing the skeleton of a murdered man, and the fact that a former army colonel has been selling secrets to the Russians, to fashion a trap that at once explains the mystery and eliminates the spy. Gilbert's style is wry, restrained, penetrating, and ironic, and his plotting is impeccable—qualities that make for stimulating reading and overshadow the fact, apparent in this story, that the two "gentlemen" are nothing of the kind. They and the world they inhabit are amoral; there is a good deal of casual killing in their adventures, much of it coolly and professionally done by Mr. Calder and Mr. Behrens themselves. Nevertheless, the stories collected in *Game Without Rules* (1967) and *Mr. Calder & Mr. Behrens* (1982) are uniformly excellent and justify Ellery Queen's claim that they are "the most important series of spy stories since Somerset Maugham's pioneering *Ashenden*."

Michael Gilbert has created several other series characters, among them Inspector Hazelrigg of Scotland Yard, who is featured in such novels as *Smallbone Deceased* (1950), considered by many to be a classic, and *Death Has Deep Roots* (1951); and police detective Patrick Petrella, hero of the 1959 novel *Blood and Judgement* and the 1977 collection of short stories, *Petrella at Q*. Much of Gilbert's fiction deals with courtroom tactics and other legal matters, the consequence of his many years as a London solicitor. His work also reflects a wide range of other interests that have resulted in intellectual puzzles and romantic thrillers as well as police procedurals and tales of espionage.

THE ROAD TO DAMASCUS

E veryone in Lamberdown knew that Mr. Behrens, who lived with his aunt at
the Old Rectory and kept bees, and Mr. Calder, who lived in a cottage on
the hilltop outside the village and was the owner of a deerhound called
Rasselas, were the closest of close friends. They knew, too, that there was something out of the ordinary about both of them.

Both had a habit of disappearing. When Mr. Calder went he left the great dog in
charge of the cottage; and Mr. Behrens would plod up the hill once a day to talk to
the dog and see to his requirements. If both men happened to be away at the same
time, Rasselas would be brought down to the Old Rectory where, according to
Flossie, who did for the Behrenses, he would sit for hour after hour in one red
plush armchair, staring silently at Mr. Behrens' aunt in the other.

There were other things. There was known to be a buried telephone line connecting the Old Rectory and the cottage; both houses had an elaborate system of
burglar alarms; and Mr. Calder's cottage, according to Ken who had helped to build
it, had steel plates inside the window shutters.

The villagers knew all this and, being countrymen, talked very little about it, except occasionally among themselves toward closing time. To strangers, of course,
they said nothing.

That fine autumn morning Rasselas was lying, chin on ground, watching Mr. Calder
creosote the sharp end of a wooden spile. He sat up suddenly and rumbled out a
warning.

"It's only Arthur," said Mr. Calder. "We know him."

The dog subsided with a windy sigh.

Arthur was Mr. Calder's nearest neighbor. He lived in a converted railway car-
riage in the company of a cat and two owls, and worked in the woods which cap
the North Downs from Wrotham Hill to the Medway—Brimstone Wood, Molchil
Wood, Long Gorse Shaw, Whitehorse Wood, Tom Lofts Wood and Leg of Mutton
Wood. It was a very old part of the country and, like all old things, it was full of
ghosts. Mr. Calder could not see them, but he knew they were there. Sometimes
when he was walking with Rasselas in the woods, the dog would stop, cock his

head on one side and rumble deep in his throat, his yellow eyes speculative as he followed some shape flitting down the ride ahead of them.

"Good morning, Arthur," said Mr. Calder.

"Working, I see," said Arthur. He was a small, thick man, of great strength, said to have an irresistible attraction for women.

"The old fence is on its last legs. I'm putting this in until I can get it done properly."

Arthur examined the spile with an expert eye and said, "Chestnut. That should hold her for a season. Oak'd be better. You working too hard to come and look at something I found?"

"Never too busy for that," said Mr. Calder.

"Let's go in your car, it'll be quicker," said Arthur. "Bring a torch, too."

Half a mile along a rutted track they left the car, climbed a gate and walked down a broad ride, forking off it onto a smaller one. After a few minutes the trees thinned, and Mr. Calder saw that they were coming to a clearing where wooding had been going on. The trunks had been dragged away and the slope was a litter of scattered cordwood.

"These big contractors," said Arthur. "They've got no idea. They come and cut down the trees, and lug 'em off, and think they've finished the job. Then I have to clear it up. Stack the cordwood. Pull out the stumps where they're an obstruction to traffic."

What traffic had passed, or would ever pass again through the heart of this secret place, Mr. Calder could hardly imagine. But he saw that the workmen had cleared a rough path which followed the contour of the hill and disappeared down the other side, presumably joining the track they had come by somewhere down in the valley. At that moment the ground was a mess of tractor marks and turned earth. In a year the raw places would be skimmed over with grass and nettles and blue bells and kingcups and wild garlic. In five years there would be no trace of the intruders.

"In the old days," said Arthur, "we done it with horses. Now we do it with machinery. I'm not saying it isn't quicker and handier, but it don't seem altogether right." He nodded at his bulldozer, askew on the side of a hummock. Rasselas went over and sneered at it, disapproving of the oily smell.

"I was shifting this stump," said Arthur, "when the old cow slipped and came down sideways. She hit t'other tree a proper dunt. I thought I bitched up the works, but all I done was shift the tree a piece. See?"

Mr. Calder walked across to look. The tree which Arthur had hit was no more than a hollow ring of elm, very old and less than three feet high. His first thought was that it was curious that a heavy bulldozer crashing down onto it from above should not have shattered its frail shell altogether.

"Ah! You have a look inside," said Arthur.

The interior of the stump was solid concrete.

"Why on earth," said Mr. Calder, "would anyone bother——?"

"Just have a look at this."

The stump was at a curious angle, half uprooted so that one side lay much higher than the other.

"When I hit it," said Arthur, "I felt something give. Truth to tell, I thought I'd cracked her shaft. Then I took another look. See?"

Mr. Calder looked. And he saw.

The whole block—wooden ring, cement center and all—had been pierced by an iron bar. The end of it was visible, thick with rust, sticking out of the broken earth. He scraped away the soil with his fingers and presently found the U-shaped socket he was looking for. He sat back on his heels and stared at Arthur, who stared back, solemn as one of his own owls.

"Someone," said Mr. Calder slowly, "—God knows why—took the trouble to cut out this tree stump and stick a damned great iron bar right through the middle of it, fixed to open on a pivot."

"It would have been Dan Owtram who fixed the bar for 'em, I don't doubt," said Arthur. "He's been dead ten years now."

"Who'd Dan fix it for?"

"Why, for the military."

"I see," said Mr. Calder. It was beginning to make a little more sense.

"You'll see when you get inside."

"Is there something inside?"

"Surely," said Arthur. "I wouldn't bring you out all this way just to look at an old tree stump, now would I? Come around here."

Mr. Calder moved round to the far side and saw, for the first time, that when the stump had shifted it had left a gap on the underside. It was not much bigger than a badger's hole.

"Are you suggesting I go down *that*?"

"It's not so bad, once you're in," said Arthur.

The entrance sloped down at about forty-five degrees and was only really narrow at the start, where the earth had caved in. After a short slide Mr. Calder's feet touched the top of a ladder. It was a long ladder. He counted twenty rungs before his feet were on firm ground. He got out his torch and switched it on.

He was in a fair-sized chamber, cut out of the chalk. He saw two recesses, each containing a spring bed on a wooden frame; two or three empty packing cases, upended as table and seats; a wooden cupboard, several racks, and a heap of disintegrating blankets. The place smelled of lime and dampness and, very faintly, of something else.

A scrabbling noise announced the arrival of Arthur.

"Like something outer one of them last-war films," he said.

"*Journey's End!*" said Mr. Calder. "All it needs is a candle in an empty beer bottle and a couple of gas masks hanging up on the wall."

"It was journey's end for him all right." Arthur jerked his head toward the far corner, and Mr. Calder swung his torch round.

The first thing he saw was a pair of boots, then the mildewy remains of a pair of flannel trousers, through gaps in which the leg bones showed white. The man was lying on his back. He could hardly have fallen like that; it was not a natural position. Someone had taken the trouble to straighten the legs and fold the arms over the chest after death.

The light from Mr. Calder's torch moved upward to the head, where it stayed for a long minute. Then he straightened up. "I don't think you'd better say much about this. Not for the moment."

"That hole in his forehead," said Arthur. "It's a bullet hole, ennit?"

"Yes. The bullet went through the middle of his forehead and out at the back. There's a second hole there."

"I guessed it was more up your street than mine," said Arthur. "What'll we do? Tell the police?"

"We'll have to tell them sometime. Just for the moment, do you think you could cover the hole up? Put some sticks and turf across?"

"I could do that all right. 'Twont really be necessary, though. Now the wooding's finished you won't get anyone else through here. It's all preserved. The people who do the shooting, they stay on the outside of the covers."

"One of them didn't," said Mr. Calder, looking down at the floor and showing his teeth in a grin.

Mr. Behrens edged his way through the crowd in the drawing room of Colonel Mark Bessendine's Chatham quarters. He wanted to look at one of the photographs on the mantelpiece.

"That's the *Otrango*," said a girl near his left elbow. "It was Grandfather's ship. He proposed to Granny in the Red Sea. On the deck-tennis court, actually. Romantic, don't you think?"

Mr. Behrens removed his gaze from the photograph to study his informant. She had brown hair and a friendly face and was just leaving the puppy-fat stage. Fifteen or sixteen he guessed. "You must be Julia Bessendine," he said.

"And you're Mr. Behrens. Daddy says you're doing something very clever in our workshops. Of course, he wouldn't say what."

"That was his natural discretion," said Mr. Behrens. "As a matter of fact, it isn't hush-hush at all. I'm writing a paper for the Molecular Society on Underwater Torque Reactions and the Navy offered to lend me its big test tank."

"Gracious!" said Julia.

Colonel Bessendine surged across.

"Julia, you're in dereliction of your duties. I can see that Mr. Behrens' glass is empty."

"Excellent sherry," said Mr. Behrens.

"Tradition," said Colonel Bessendine, "associates the Navy with rum. In fact, the two drinks that it really understands are gin and sherry. I hope our technical people are looking after you?"

"The Navy have been helpfulness personified. It's been particularly convenient for me, being allowed to do this work at Chatham. Only twenty minutes' run from Lamperdown, you see."

Colonel Bessendine said, "My last station was Devonport. A ghastly place. When I was posted back here I felt I was coming home. The whole of my youth is tied up with this part of the country. I was born and bred not far from Tilbury and I went to school at Rochester."

His face, thought Mr. Behrens, was like a waxwork. A clever waxwork, but one which you could never quite mistake for human flesh. Only the eyes were truly alive.

"I sometimes spent a holiday down here when I was a boy," said Mr. Behrens. "My aunt and uncle—he's dead now—bought the Old Rectory at Lamperdown after the First World War. Thank you, my dear, that was very nicely managed." This was to Julia, who had fought her way back to him with most of the sherry still in the glass. "In those days your school," he said to the girl, "was a private house. One of the great houses of the county."

"It must have been totally impracticable," said Julia Bessendine severely. "Fancy trying to *live* in it. What sort of staff did it need to keep it up?"

"They scraped along with twenty or thirty indoor servants, a few dozen garden-ers and gamekeepers, and a cricket pro."

"Daddy told me that when he was a boy he used to walk out from school, on half holidays, and watch cricket on their private cricket ground. That's right, isn't it, Daddy?"

"That's right, my dear. I think, Julia—"

"He used to crawl up alongside the hedge from the railway and squeeze through a gap in the iron railings at the top and lie in the bushes. And once the old lord walked across and found him, and instead of booting him out, he gave him money to buy sweets with."

"Major Furlong looks as if he could do with another drink," said Colonel Bessendine.

"Colonel Bessendine's father," said Mr. Behrens to Mr. Calder later that evening, "came from New Zealand. He ran away to sea at the age of thirteen, and got himself a job with the Anzac Shipping Line. He rose to be head purser on their biggest ship, the *Otrango*. Then he married. An Irish colleen, I believe. Her father was a landowner from Cork. That part of the story's a bit obscure, because her family promptly disowned her. They didn't approve of the marriage at all. They were poor but proud. Old Bessendine had the drawback of being twice as rich as they were."

"Rich? A purser?"

"He was a shrewd old boy. He bought up land in Tilbury and Grays and leased it to builders. When he died, his estate was declared for probate at £85,000. I expect it was really worth a lot more. His three sons were all well educated and well behaved. It was the sort of home where the boys called their father 'sir,' and got up when he came into the room."

"We could do with more homes like that," said Mr. Calder. "Gone much too far the other way. What happened to the other two sons?"

"Both dead. The eldest went into the Army: he was killed at Dunkirk. The second boy was a flight lieutenant. He was shot down over Germany, picked up and put into a prison camp. He was involved in some sort of trouble there. Shot, trying to escape."

"Bad luck," said Mr. Calder. He was working something out with paper and pencil. "Go away." This was to Rasselas, who had his paws on the table and was trying to help him. "What happened to young Mark?"

"Mark was in the Marines. He was blown sky high in the autumn of 1940—the first heavy raid on Gravesend and Tilbury."

"But I gather he came down in one piece."

"Just about. He was in hospital for six months. The plastic surgeons did a wonderful job on his face. The only thing they couldn't put back was the animation."

"Since you've dug up such a lot of his family history, do I gather that he's in some sort of a spot?"

"He's in a spot all right," said Mr. Behrens. "He's been spying for the Russians for a long time and we've just tumbled to it."

"You're sure?"

"I'm afraid there's no doubt about it at all. Fortescue has had him under observation for the last three months."

"Why hasn't he been put away?"

"The stuff he's passing out is important, but it's not vital. Bessendine isn't a scientist. He's held security and administrative jobs — where a project has run smoothly, or where it got behind time, or flopped. There's nothing the other side likes more than a flop."

"How does he get the information out?"

"That's exactly what I'm trying to figure out. It's some sort of post-office system, no doubt. When we've sorted that out, we'll pull him in."

"Has he got any family?"

"A standard pattern Army-type wife. And a rather nice daughter."

"It's the family who suffer in these cases," said Mr. Calder. He scratched Rasselas' tufted head, and the big dog yawned. "By the way, we had rather an interesting day, too. We found a body."

He told Mr. Behrens about this, and Mr. Behrens said, "What are you going to do about it?"

"I've telephoned Fortescue. He was quite interested. He's put me on to a Colonel Crawston, who was in charge of Irregular Forces in this area in 1940. He thinks he might be able to help us."

Colonel Crawston's room was littered with catalogs, feeding charts, invoices, paid bills and unpaid bills, seed samples, gift calendars, local newspapers, boxes of cartridges, and buff forms from the Ministry of Agriculture, Fisheries and Food.

Mr. Calder said, "It's really very good of you to spare the time to talk to me, Colonel. You're a pretty busy man, I can see that."

"We shall get on famously," said the old man, "if you'll remember two things. The first is that I'm deaf in my left ear. The second, that I'm no longer a colonel. I stopped being that in 1945."

"Both points shall be borne in mind," said Mr. Calder, easing himself round onto his host's right-hand side.

"Fortescue told me you were coming. If that old bandit's involved, I suppose it's Security stuff?"

"I'm not at all sure," said Mr. Calder. "I'd better tell you about it. . . ."

"Interesting," said the old man, when he had done so. "Fascinating, in fact."

He went across to a big corner cupboard, dug into its cluttered interior and surfaced with two faded khaki-colored canvas folders, which he laid on the table. From one of them he turned out a thick wad of papers, from the other a set of quarter- and one-inch military maps.

"I kept all this stuff," he said. "At one time, I was thinking of writing a history of Special Operations during the first two years of the war. I never got round to it, though. Too much like hard work." He unfolded the maps, and smoothed out the papers with his bent and arthritic fingers.

"Fortescue told me," said Mr. Calder, "that you were in charge of what he called 'Stay-put Parties.'"

"It was really a very sound idea," said the old man. His frosty blue eyes sparkled for a moment, with the light of unfought battles. "They did the same thing in Burma. When you knew that you might have to retreat, you dug in small resistance groups, with arms and food and wireless sets. They'd let themselves be overrun, you see, and operate behind the enemy lines. We had a couple of dozen posts like that in Kent and Sussex. The one you found would have been—Whitehorse Wood you said?—here it is, Post Six. That was a very good one. They converted an existing dene-hole—you know what a dene-hole is?"

"As far as I can gather," said Mr. Calder, "the original inhabitants of this part of the country dug them to hide in when *they* were overrun by the Angles and Saxons and such. A sort of pre-Aryan Stay-put Party."

"Never thought of it that way." The old man chuckled. "You're quite right, of course. That's exactly what it was. Now then. Post Six. We had three men in each —an officer and two NCOs." He ran his gnarled finger up the paper in front of him. "Sergeant Brewer. A fine chap that. Killed in North Africa. Corporal Stubbs. He's dead, too. Killed in a motor crash, a week after VE Day. So your unknown corpse couldn't be either of *them*."

There was a splendid inevitability about it all, thought Mr. Calder. It was like the unfolding of a Greek tragedy, or the final chord of a well-built symphony. You waited for it. You knew it was coming. But you were still surprised when it did.

"Bessendine," said the old man. "Lieutenant Mark Bessendine. Perhaps the most tragic of the lot, really. He was a natural choice for our work. Spoke Spanish, French and German. Young and fit. Front-line experience with the Reds in Spain."

"What exactly happened to him?"

"It was the first week in November 1940. Our masters in Whitehall had concluded that the invasion wasn't on. I was told to seal up all my posts and send the men back to their units. I remember sending Mark out that afternoon to Post Six——it hadn't been occupied for some weeks—told him to bring back any loose stores. That was the last time I saw him—in the flesh, as you might say. You heard what happened?"

"He got caught in the German blitz on Tilbury and Gravesend."

"That's right. Must have been actually on his way back to our HQ. The explosion picked him up and pushed him through a plate-glass window. He was damned lucky to be alive at all. Next time I saw him he was swaddled up like a mummy. Couldn't talk or move."

"Did you see him again?"

"I was posted abroad in the spring. Spent the rest of the war in Africa and Italy. ... Now you happen to mention it, though, I thought I did bump into him once—at the big reception center at Calais. I went through there on my way home in 1945."

"Did he recognize you?"

"It was a long time ago. I can't really remember." The old man looked up sharply. "Is it important?"

"It might be," said Mr. Calder.

"If you're selling anything," said the old lady to Mr. Behrens, "you're out of luck."

"I am neither selling nor buying," said Mr. Behrens.

"And if you're the new curate, I'd better warn you that I'm a Baptist."

"I'm a practicing agnostic."

The old lady looked at him curiously, and then said, "Whatever it is you want to talk about, we shall be more comfortable inside, shan't we?"

She led the way across the hall, narrow and bare as a coffin, into a surprisingly bright and cheerful sitting room.

"You don't look to me," she said, "like the sort of man who knocks old ladies on the head and grabs their life's savings. I keep mine in the bank, such as they are."

"I must confess to you," said Mr. Behrens, "that I'm probably wasting your time. I'm in Tilbury on a sentimental errand. I spent a year of the war in the Air Force prison camp in Germany. One of my greatest friends there was Jeremy Bessendine. He was a lot younger that I was, of course, but we had a common interest in bees."

"I don't know what you were doing up in an airplane, at your time of life. I expect you dyed your hair. People used to do that in the 1914 war. I'm sorry, I interrupted you. Mr. ....?"

"Behrens."

"My name's Galloway. You said Jeremy Bessendine."

"Yes. Did you know him?"

"I knew *all* the Bessendines. Father and mother, and all three sons. The mother was the sweetest thing, from the bogs of Ireland. The father, well, let's be charitable and say he was old-fashioned. Their house was on the other side of the road to mine. There's nothing left of it now. Can you see? Not a stick nor a stone."

Mr. Behrens looked out of the window. The opposite side of the road was an open space containing one row of prefabricated huts.

"Terrible things," said Mrs. Galloway. "They put them up after the war as a temporary measure. Temporary!"

"So that's where the Bessendines' house was," said Mr. Behrens, sadly. "Jeremy often described it to me. He was so looking forward to living in it again when the war was over."

"Jeremy was my favorite," said Mrs. Galloway. "I'll admit I cried when I heard he'd been killed. Trying to escape, they said."

She looked back twenty-five years, and sighed at what she saw. "If we're going to be sentimental," she said, "we shall do it better over a cup of tea. The kettle's on the boil." She went out into the kitchen but left the door open, so that she could continue to talk.

"John, the eldest, I never knew well. He went straight into the Army. He was killed early on. The youngest was Mark. He was a wild character, if you like."

"Wild? In what way?" said Mr. Behrens.

Mrs. Galloway arranged the teapot, cups, and milk jug on a tray and collected her thoughts. Then she said, "He was a rebel. Strong or weak?"

"Just as it comes," said Mr. Behrens.

"First two brothers, they accepted the discipline at home. Mark didn't. Jeremy told me that when Mark ran away from school—the second time—and his father tried to send him back, they had a real set-to, the father shouting, the boy screaming. That was when he went off to Spain to fight for the Reds. Milk and sugar?"

"Both," said Mr. Behrens. He thought of Mark Besssendine as he had seen him two days before. An ultracorrect, poker-backed, poker-faced regular soldier. How deep had the rebel been buried?

"He's quite a different sort of person now," he said.

"Of course, he would be," said Mrs. Galloway. "You can't be blown to bits and put together again and still be the same person, can you?"

"Why, no," said Mr. Behrens. "I suppose you can't."

"I felt very strange myself for a week or so, after it happened. And I was only blown across the kitchen and cracked my head on the stove."

"You remember that raid, then?

"I most certainly do. It must have been about five o'clock. Just getting dark, and a bit misty. They came in low, and the next moment—*crump, bump*—we were right in the middle of it. It was the first raid we'd had—and the worst. You could hear the bombs coming closer and closer. I thought, I wish I'd stayed in Saffron Walden—where I'd been evacuated, you see—I'm for it now, I thought. And it's all my own fault for coming back like the posters told me not to. And the next moment I was lying on the floor, with my head against the stove, and a lot of warm red stuff running over my face. It was tomato soup."

"And that was the bomb that destroyed the Bessendines' house—and killed old Mr. and Mrs. Bessendine?"

"That's right. And it was the same raid that nearly killed Mark. My goodness!" The last exclamation was nothing to do with what had gone before. Mrs. Galloway was staring at Mr. Behrens. Her face had gone pale. She said, "Jeremy! I've just remembered! When it happened they sent him home, on compassionate leave. He *knew* his house had been blown up. Why would he tell you he was looking forward to living in it after the war—when he must have known it wasn't there?"

Mr. Behrens could think of nothing to say.

"You've been lying, haven't you? Who are you? What's it all about?"

Mr. Behrens put down his teacup, and said, gently, "I'm sorry I had to tell you a lot of lies, Mrs. Galloway. Please don't worry about it too much. I promise you that nothing you told me is going to hurt anyone."

The old lady gulped down her own tea. The color came back slowly to her cheeks. She said, "Whatever it is, I don't want to know about it." She stared out of the window at the place where a big house had once stood, inhabited by a bullying father and a sweet Irish mother, and three boys. She said, "It's all dead and done with, anyway."

As Mr. Behrens drove home in the dusk, his tires on the road hummed the words back at him. *Dead and done with.*

Mr. Fortescue, who was the manager of the Westminster branch of the London and Home Counties Bank, and a number of other things besides, glared across his broad mahogany desk at Mr. Calder and Mr. Behrens and said, "I have never encountered such an irritating and frustrating case."

He made it sound as if they, and not the facts, were the cause of his irritation.

Mr. Behrens said, "I don't think people quite realize how heavily the scales are weighted in favor of a spy who's learned his job and keeps his head. All the stuff that Colonel Bessendine is passing out is stuff he's officially entitled to know. Progress of existing work, projects for new work, personnel to be employed, Security arrangements. It all comes into his field. Suppose he *does* keep notes of it. Suppose we searched his house, found those notes in his safe. Would it prove anything?"

"Of course it wouldn't," said Mr. Fortescue, sourly. "That's why you've got to catch him actually handing it over. I've had three men—apart from you—watching him for months. He behaves normally—goes up to town once or twice a week, goes to the cinema with his family, goes to local drink parties, has his friends in to dinner. All absolutely above suspicion."

"Quite so," said Mr. Behrens. "He goes up to London in the morning rush hour. He gets into a crowded Underground train. Your man can't get too close to him. Bessendine's wedged up against another man who happens to be carrying a briefcase identical with his own. . . ."

"Do you think that's how it's done?"

"I've no idea," said Mr. Behrens. "But I wager I could invent half a dozen other methods just as simple and just as impossible to detect."

Mr. Calder said, "When exactly did Mark Bessendine start betraying his country's secrets to the Russians?"

"We can't be absolutely certain. But it's been going on for a very long time. Back to the Cold War which nearly turned into a hot war—1947, perhaps.

"Not before that?"

"Perhaps you had forgotten," said Mr. Fortescue, "that until 1945 the Russians were on our side."

"I wondered," said Mr. Calder, "if before that he might have been spying for the Germans. Have you looked at the 'Hessel' file lately?"

Both Mr. Fortescue and Mr. Behrens stared at Mr. Calder, who looked blandly back at them.

Mr. Behrens said, "We never found out who Hessel was, did we? He was just a code name to us."

"But the Russians found out," said Mr. Calder. "The first thing they did when they got to Berlin was to grab all Admiral Canaris' records. If they found the Hessel dossier there—if they found out that he had been posing successfully for more than four years as an officer in the Royal Marines—"

"Posing?" said Mr. Fortescue, sharply.

"It occurred to me as a possibility."

"If Hessel is posing as Bessendine, where's Bessendine?" said Mr. Fortescue.

"At the bottom of a pre-Aryan chalk pit in Whitehorse Wood, above Lamperdown," said Mr. Calder, "with a bullet through his head."

Mr. Fortescue looked at Mr. Behrens, who said, "Yes, it's possible. I had thought of that."

"Lieutenant Mark Bessendine," said Mr. Calder, slowly, as if he was seeing it all as he spoke, "set off alone one November afternoon, with orders to close down and seal up Post Six. He'd have been in battle dress and carrying his Army pay book and identity papers with him, because in 1940 everyone did that. As he was climbing out of the post, he heard, or saw, a strange figure. A civilian, lurking in the woods, where no civilian should have been. He challenged him. And the answer was a bullet, from Hessel's gun. Hessel had landed that day, or the day before, on the South Coast, from a submarine. Most of the spies who were landed that autumn lasted less than a week. Right?"

"They were a poor bunch," said Mr. Fortescue. "Badly equipped, and with the feeblest cover stories. I sometimes wondered if they were people Canaris wanted to get rid of."

"Exactly," said Mr. Calder. "But Hessel was a tougher proposition. He spoke excellent English—his mother was English, and he'd been to an English public school. And here was a God-sent chance to improve his equipment and cover. Bessendine was the same size and build. All he had to do was to change clothes and instead of being a phoney civilian, liable to be questioned by the first constable he met, he was a properly dressed, fully documented Army officer. Provided he kept on the move, he could go anywhere in England. No one would question him. It wasn't the sort of cover that would last forever. But it didn't matter. His pickup was probably fixed for four weeks ahead—in the next no-moon period. So he put on Bessendine's uniform, and started out for Gravesend. Not, I need hardly say, with any intention of going back to Headquarters. All he wanted to do was to catch a train to London."

"But the Luftwaffe caught him."

"They did indeed," said Mr. Calder. "They caught him—and they set him free. Free of all possible suspicion. When he came out of that hospital six months later, he had a new face. More. He was a new man. If anyone asked him anything about his past, all he had to say was, 'Oh, that was before I got blown up. I don't remember very much about that.'"

"But surely," said Mr. Fortescue, "it wasn't quite as easy as that. Bessendine's family—" He stopped.

"You've seen it too, haven't you?" said Mr. Calder. "He had no family. No one at all. One brother was dead, the other was in a prison camp in Germany. I wonder if it was a pure coincidence that he should later have been shot when trying to escape. Or did Himmler send a secret instruction to the camp authorities? Maybe it was just another bit of luck. Like Mark's parents being killed in the same raid. His mother's family lived in Ireland—and had disowned her. His father's family—if it existed—was in New Zealand. Mark Bessendine was completely and absolutely alone."

"The first Hessel messages went out to Germany at the end of 1941," said Mr. Fortescue. "How did he manage to send them?"

"No difficulty there," said Mr. Calder. "The German short-wave transmitters were very efficient. You only had to renew the batteries. He'd have buried his in the wood. He only had to dig it up again. He had all the call signals and codes."

Mr. Behrens had listened to this in silence, with a half-smile on his face.

Now he cleared his throat and said, "If this—um—ingenious theory is true, it does—um—suggest a way of drawing out the gentleman concerned, does it not?"

"I was very interested when you told me about this dene-hole," said Colonel Bessendine to Mr. Behrens. "I had heard about them as a boy, of course, but I've never actually seen one."

"I hope we shan't be too late," said Mr. Behrens. "It'll be dark in an hour. You'd better park your car here. We'll have to do the rest of the trip on foot."

"I'm sorry I was late," said Colonel Bessendine. "I had a job I had to finish before I go off tomorrow."

"Off?"

"A short holiday. I'm taking my wife and daughter to France."

"I envy you," said Mr. Behrens. "Over the stile here and straight up the hill. I hope I can find it from this side. When I came here before I approached it from the other side. Fork right here, I think."

They moved up through the silent woods, each occupied with his own, very different, thoughts.

Mr. Behrens said, "I'm sure this was the clearing. Look. You can see the marks of the workmen's tractors. And this—I think—was the stump."

He stopped, and kicked at the foot of the elm bole. The loose covering pieces of turf on sticks, laid there by Arthur, collapsed, showing the dark entrance.

"Good Lord!" said Colonel Bessendine. He was standing, hands in raincoat pockets, shoulders hunched. "Don't tell me that people used to live in a place like that?"

"It's quite snug inside."

"Inside? You mean you've actually been inside it?" He shifted his weight so that it rested on his left foot and his right hand came out of his pocket and hung loose.

"Oh, certainly," said Mr. Behrens. "I found the body, too."

There was a long silence. That's the advantage of having a false face, thought Mr. Behrens. It's unfair. You can do your thinking behind it, and no one can watch you actually doing it.

The lips cracked into a smile.

"You're an odd card," said Colonel Bessendine. "Did you bring me all the way here to tell me that?"

"I brought you here," said Mr. Behrens, "so that you could explain one or two things that have been puzzling me." He had seated himself on the thick side of the stump. "For instance, you must have known about this hideout, since you and Sergeant Brewer and Corporal Stubbs built it in 1940. Why didn't you tell me that when I started describing it to you?"

"I wasn't quite sure then," said Colonel Bessendine. "I wanted to make sure."

As he spoke his right hand moved with a smooth unhurried gesture into the open front of his coat and out again. It was now holding a flat blue-black weapon which Mr. Behrens, who was a connoisseur in such matters, recognized as a *Zyanidpistole* or cyanide gun.

"Where did they teach you that draw?" he said. "In the *Marineamt?*"

For the first time he thought that the colonel was genuinely'surprised. His face still revealed nothing, but there was a note of curiosity in his voice.

"I learned in Spain to carry a gun under my arm and draw it quickly," he said. "There were quite a few occasions on which you had to shoot people before they shot you. Your own side, sometimes. It was rather a confused war in some ways."

"I imagine so," said Mr. Behrens. He was sitting like a Buddha in the third attitude of repose, his feet crossed, the palms of his hands pressed flat, one on each knee. "I only mentioned it because some of my colleagues had a theory that you were a German agent called Hessel."

In the colonel's eyes a glint of genuine amusement appeared for a moment, like a face at a window, and ducked out of sight again.

"I gather that you were not convinced by this theory?"

"As a matter of fact, I wasn't."

"Oh. Why?"

"I remember what your daughter told me. That you used to crawl up alongside a hedge running from the railway line to the private cricket ground at the big house. I went along and had a look. You couldn't crawl up along the hedge now. It's too overgrown. But there *is* a place at the top—it's hidden by the hedge, and I scratched myself damnably getting into it—where two bars are bent apart. A boy could have got through them easily."

"You're very thorough," said the colonel. "Is there anything you *haven't* found out about me?"

"I would be interested to know exactly when you started betraying your country. And why. Did you mean to do it all along and falling in with Hessel and killing him gave you an opportunity —the wireless and the codes and the call signs—?"

"I can clearly see," said the colonel, "that you have never been blown up. Really blown to pieces, I mean. If you had been, you'd know that it's quite impossible to predict what sort of man will come down again. You can be turned inside out, or upside down. You can be born again. Things you didn't know were inside you can be shaken to the top."

"Saul becoming Paul, on the road to Damascus."

"You *are* an intelligent man," said the colonel. "It's a pleasure to talk to you. The analogy had not occurred to me, but it is perfectly apt. My father was a great man for disciplining youth, for regimentation, and the New Order. Because he was my father, I rebelled against it. That's natural enough. Because I rebelled against it, I fought for the Russians against the Germans in Spain. I saw how those young Nazis behaved. It was simply a rehearsal for them, you know. A rehearsal for the struggle they had dedicated their lives to. A knightly vigil, if you like. I saw them fight, and I saw them die. Any that were captured were usually tortured. I tortured them myself. If you torture a man and fail to break him, it becomes like a love affair. Did you know that?"

"I, too, have read the works of the Marquis de Sade," said Mr. Behrens. "Go on."

"When I lay in hospital in the darkness with my eyes bandaged, my hands strapped to my sides, coming slowly back to life, I had the strangest feeling. I *was* Hessel, I *was* the man I had left lying in the darkness at the bottom of the pit. I had closed his eyes and folded his hands, and now I was him. His work was my work. Where he had left it off, I would take it up. My father had been right and Hitler had been right and I had been wrong. And now I had been shown a way to repair the mistakes and follies of my former life. Does that sound mad to you?"

"Quite mad," said Mr. Behrens. "But I find it easier to believe than the rival theory—that the accident of having a new face enabled you to fool everyone for twenty-five years. You may have had no family, but there were school friends and Army friends and neighbors. But I interrupt you. When you got out of the hospital and decided to carry on Hessel's work, I suppose you used his wireless set and his codes?"

"Until the end of the war, yes. Then I destroyed them. When I was forced to work for the Russians I began to use other methods. I'm afraid I can't discuss them, even with you. They involve too many other people."

In spite of the peril of his position, Mr. Behrens could not suppress a feeling of deep satisfaction. Not many of his plans had worked out so exactly. Colonel Bessendine was not a man given to confidences. A mixture of carefully devised forces was now driving him to talk. The time and the place; the fact that Mr. Behrens had established a certain intellectual supremacy over him; the fact that he must have been unable, for so many years, to speak freely to anyone; the fact that silence was no longer important, since he had made up his mind to liquidate his audience. On this last point Mr. Behrens was under no illusions. Colonel Bessendine was on his way out. France was only the first station on a line which led to Eastern Germany and Moscow.

"One thing puzzles me," said the colonel, breaking into his thoughts. "During all the time we have been talking here—and I cannot tell you how much I have enjoyed our conversation—I couldn't help noticing that you have hardly moved. Your hands, for instance, have been lying cupped, one on each knee. When a fly annoyed you just now, instead of raising your hand to brush it off you shook your head violently."

Mr. Behrens said, raising his voice a little, "If I were to lift my right hand a very well-trained dog, who has been approaching you quietly from the rear while we were talking, would have jumped for your throat."

The colonel smiled. "Your imagination does you credit. What happens if you lift your left hand? Does a genie appear from a bottle and carry me off?"

"If I raise my left hand," said Mr. Behrens, "you will be shot dead."

And so saying, he raised it.

The two men and the big dog stared down at the crumbled body. Rasselas sniffed at it, once, and turned away. It was carrion and no longer interesting.

"I'd have liked to try to pull him down alive," said Mr. Behrens. "But with that foul weapon in his hand I dared not chance it."

"It will solve a lot of Mr. Fortescue's problems," said Mr. Calder. He was unscrewing the telescopic sight from the rifle he was carrying.

"We'll put him down beside Hessel. I've brought two crowbars along with me. We ought to be able to shift the stump back into its original position. With any luck they'll lie there, undisturbed, for a very long time."

Side by side in the dark earth, thought Mr. Behrens. Until the Day of Judgement, when all hearts are opened and all thoughts known.

"We'd better hurry, too," said Mr. Calder. "It's getting dark and I want to get back in time for tea."

Reginald Hill

(1936–)

Superintendent Andrew Dalziel (pronounced Dee-ell) and Sergeant (later Inspector) Peter Pascoe are a pair of Yorkshire police detectives—"two men who are absolutely contrasted in background, attitudes, and approach, but who are forced to admit grudging respect for each other," in the author's own capsule description. Dalziel is a coarse, old-fashioned policeman whose stated philosophy is: "Life's a series of wrecks. Make sure you get washed up with the survivors." The much-younger Pascoe is both well-educated (he has a degree in social science and is an omnivorous reader) and the possessor of liberal ideas about life, which he considers "a sorrow and a mystery," and police work. Despite growth and change in both characters over the course of thirteen novels, their fundamental differences remain the same, and it is their sometimes prickly, sometimes comic relationship that forms the central appeal of the series.

Reginald Hill's adroit plotting skills are another strong point, which combined with a darkening vision of the world have kept him from writing the same book twice. His first novel and the first to feature Dalziel and Pascoe, *A Clubbable Woman* (published in England in 1970 but not in the United States until 1984), is a bawdily amusing look at the rugby world of northern England. In *Exit Lines* (1984), investigation into the deaths of three old men on the same winter night provides a forum for serious philosophical commentary on the aging process and the nature of life and death. *Bones and Silence* (1990), the recipient of a British Crime Writers Association Gold Dagger award for best novel of its year, is concerned with medieval Yorkshire mystery plays, in one of which Dalziel acts the part of God. The novelette that follows, one of five in the 1979 collection, *Pascoe's Ghost and Other Brief Chronicles of Crime,* also demonstrates Hill's shrewd characterizations and unique blend of comedy, tragedy, and philosophy.

In addition to the Dalziel and Pascoe series, Reginald Hill has published two novels about black private detective Joe Sixsmith (*Blood Sympathy* and *Born Guilt*, 1994 and 1995, respectively); thrillers such as *A Very Good Hater* (1974), which deals with a pair of former servicemen who come upon a man they suspect is a Nazi war criminal whom they have sworn to kill, and which is distinguished by several surprising plot twists; and eight nonseries novels under the pseudonym Patrick Ruell, some lighthearted (*Red Christmas,* 1972) and some quite serious in tone (*The Only Game,* 1991).

DALZIEL'S GHOST

SUPERINTENDENT DALZIEL AND SERGEANT PASCOE
YORKSHIRE, ENGLAND
1979

"**W**ell, this is very cosy," said Detective-Superintendent Dalziel, scratching his buttocks sensuously before the huge log fire.

"It is for some," said Pascoe, shivering still from the frosty November night.

But Dalziel was right, he thought as he looked round the room. It *was* cosy, probably as cosy as it had been in the three hundred years since it was built. It was doubtful if any previous owner, even the most recent, would have recognized the old living-room of Stanstone Rigg farm-house. Eliot had done a good job, stripping the beams, opening up the mean little fireplace and replacing the splintered uneven . floorboards with smooth dark oak; and Giselle had broken the plain white walls with richly coloured, voluminous curtaining and substituted everywhere the ornaments of art for the detritus of utility.

Outside, though, when night fell, and darkness dissolved the telephone poles, and the mist lay too thick to be pierced by the rare headlight on the distant road, then the former owners peering from their little cube of warmth and light would not have felt much difference.

Not the kind of thoughts a ghost-hunter should have! he told himself reprovingly. Cool calm scepticism was the right state of mind.

And his heart jumped violently as behind him the telephone rang.

Dalziel, now pouring himself a large scotch from the goodly array of bottles on the huge sideboard, made no move towards the phone though he was the nearer. Detective-Superintendents save their strength for important things and leave their underlings to deal with trivia.

"Hello," said Pascoe.

"Peter, you're there!"

"Ellie love," he answered. "Sometimes the sharpness of your mind makes me feel unworthy to be married to you."

"What are you doing?"

"We've just arrived. I'm talking to you. The super's having a drink."

"Oh God! You did warn the Eliots, didn't you?"

"Not really, dear. I felt the detailed case-history you doubtless gave to Giselle needed no embellishment."

326

"I'm not sure this is such a good idea."

"Me neither. On the contrary. In fact, you may recall that on several occasions in the past three days I've said as much to you, whose not such a good idea it was in the first place."

"All you're worried about is your dignity!" said Ellie. "I'm worried about that lovely house. What's he doing now!"

Pascoe looked across the room to where Dalziel had bent his massive bulk so that his balding close-cropped head was on a level with a small figurine of a shepherd chastely dallying with a milkmaid. His broad right hand was on the point of picking it up.

"He's not touching anything," said Pascoe hastily. "Was there any other reason you phoned?"

"Other than what?"

"Concern for the Eliots' booze and knick-knacks."

"Oh, Peter, don't be so half-witted. It seemed a laugh at The Old Mill, but now I don't like you being there with him, and I don't like me being here by myself. Come home and we'll screw till someone cries *Hold! Enough!*"

"You interest me strangely," said Pascoe. "What about *him* and the Eliots' house?"

"Oh, sod him and sod the Eliots! Decent people don't have ghosts!" exclaimed Ellie.

"Or if they do, they call in priests, not policemen," said Pascoe. "I quite agree. I said as much, remember . . .?"

"All right, all right. You please yourself, buster. I'm off to bed now with a hot-water bottle and a glass of milk. Clearly I must be in my dotage. Shall I ring you later?"

"Best not," said Pascoe. "I don't want to step out of my pentacle after midnight. See you in the morning."

"Must have taken an electric drill to get through a skirt like that," said Dalziel, replacing the figurine with a bang. "No wonder the buggers got stuck into the sheep. Your missus checking up, was she?"

"She just wanted to see how we were getting on." said Pascoe.

"Probably thinks we've got a couple of milkmaids with us," said Dalziel, peering out into the night. "Some hope! I can't even see any sheep. It's like the grave out there."

He was right, thought Pascoe. When Stanstone Rigg had been a working farm, there must have always been the comforting sense of animal presence, even at night. Horses in the stable, cows in the byre, chickens in the hutch, dogs before the fire. But the Eliots hadn't bought the place because of any deep-rooted love of nature. In fact Giselle Eliot disliked animals so much she wouldn't even have a guard dog, preferring to rely on expensive electronics. Pascoe couldn't understand how George had got her even to consider living out here. It was nearly an hour's run from town in good conditions and Giselle was in no way cut out for country life, either physically or mentally. Slim, vivacious, sexy, she was a star-rocket in Yorkshire's sluggish jet-set. How she and Ellie had become friends, Pascoe couldn't work out either.

But she must have a gift for leaping unbridgeable gaps for George was a pretty unlikely partner, too.

It was George who was responsible for Stanstone Rigg. By profession an accountant, and very much looking the part with his thin face, unblinking gaze, and a mouth that seemed constructed for the passage of bad news, his unlikely hobby was the renovation of old houses. In the past six years he had done two, first a Victorian terrace house in town, then an Edwardian villa in the suburbs. Both had quadrupled (at least) in value, but George claimed this was not the point and Pascoe believed him. Stanstone Rigg Farm was his most ambitious project to date, and it had been a marvellous success, except for its isolation, which was unchangeable.

And its ghost. Which perhaps wasn't.

It was just three days since Pascoe had first heard of it. Dalziel, who repaid hospitality in the proportion of three of Ellie's home-cooked dinners to one meal out had been entertaining the Pascoes at The Old Mill, a newly opened restaurant in town.

"Jesus!" said the fat man when they examined the menu. "I wish they'd put them prices in French, too. They must give you Brigitte Bardot for afters!"

"Would you like to take us somewhere else?" enquired Ellie sweetly. "A fish and chip shop, perhaps. Or a Chinese takeaway?"

"No, no," said Dalziel. "This is grand. Any road, I'll chalk what I can up to expenses. Keeping an eye on Fletcher."

"Who?"

"The owner," said Pascoe. "I didn't know he was on our list, sir."

"Well, he is and he isn't," said Dalziel. "I got a funny telephone call a couple of weeks back. Suggested I might take a look at him, that's all. He's got his finger in plenty of pies."

"If I have the salmon to start with," said Ellie, "it won't be removed as material evidence before I'm finished, will it?"

Pascoe aimed a kick at her under the table but she had been expecting it and drawn her legs aside.

Four courses later they had all eaten and drunk enough for a kind of mellow truce to have been established between Ellie and the fat man.

"Look who's over there," said Ellie suddenly.

Pascoe looked. It was the Eliots, George dark-suited and still, Giselle ablaze in clinging orange silk. Another man, middle-aged but still athletically elegant in a military sort of way, was standing by their table. Giselle returned Ellie's wave and spoke to the man, who came across the room and addressed Pascoe.

"Mr. and Mrs. Eliot wonder if you would care to join them for liqueurs," he said. Pascoe looked at Dalziel enquiringly.

"I'm in favour of owt that means some other bugger putting his hand in his pocket," he said cheerfully.

Giselle greeted them with delight and even George raised a welcoming smile.

"Who was that dishy thing you sent after us?" asked Ellie after Dalziel had been introduced.

"Dishy? Oh, you mean Giles. He *will* be pleased. Giles Fletcher. He owns this place."

"Oh my! We send the owner on errands, do we?" said Ellie. "It's great to see you, Giselle. It's been ages. When am I getting the estate agent's tour of the new house? You've promised us first refusal when George finds a new ruin, remember?"

"I couldn't afford the ruin," objected Pascoe. "Not even with George doing our income tax."

"Does a bit of the old tax fiddling, your firm?" enquired Dalziel genially.

"I do a bit of work privately for friends," said Eliot coldly. "But in my own time and at home."

"You'll need to work bloody hard to make a copper rich," said Dalziel.

"Just keep taking the bribes, dear," said Ellie sweetly. "Now when can we move into Stanstone Farm, Giselle?"

Giselle glanced at her husband, whose expression remained a blank.

"Any time you like, darling," she said. "To tell you the truth, it can't be soon enough. In fact, we're back in town."

"Good God!" said Ellie. "You haven't found another place already, George? That's pretty rapid even for you."

A waiter appeared with a tray on which were glasses and a selection of liqueur bottles.

"Compliments of Mr Fletcher," he said.

Dalziel examined the tray with distaste and beckoned the waiter close. For an incredulous moment Pascoe thought he was going to refuse the drinks on the grounds that police officers must be seen to be above all favour.

"From Mr Fletcher, eh?" said Dalziel. "Well, listen, lad, he wouldn't be best pleased if he knew you'd forgotten the single malt whisky, would he? Run along and fetch it. I'll look after pouring this lot."

Giselle looked at Dalziel with the round-eyed delight of a child seeing a walrus for the first time.

"Cointreau for me please, Mr Dalziel¹," she said.

He filled a glass to the brim and passed it to her with a hand steady as a rock.

"Sup up, love," he said, looking with open admiration down her cleavage. "Lots more where that comes from."

Pascoe, sensing that Ellie might be about to ram a pepper-mill up her host's nostrils, said hastily, "Nothing wrong with the building, I hope, George? Not the beetle or anything like that?"

"I sorted all that out before we moved," said Eliot. "No, nothing wrong at all."

His tone was neutral but Giselle responded as though to an attack.

"It's all right, darling," she said. "Everyone's guessed it's me. But it's not really. It's just that I think we've got a ghost."

According to Giselle, there were strange scratchings, shadows moving where there should be none, and sometimes as she walked from one room to another 'a sense of emptiness as though for a moment you'd stepped into the space between two stars."

This poetic turn of phrase silenced everyone except Dalziel, who interrupted his attempts to scratch the sole of his foot with a bent coffee spoon and let out a raucous laugh.

"What's that mean?" demanded Ellie.

"Nowt," said Dalziel. "I shouldn't worry, Mrs. Eliot. It's likely some randy yokel roaming about trying to get a peep at you. And who's to blame him?"

He underlined his compliment with a leer straight out of the old melodrama. Giselle patted his knee in acknowledgement.

"What do *you* think, George?" asked Ellie.

George admitted the scratchings but denied personal experience of the rest.

"See how long he stays there by himself," challenged Giselle.

"I didn't buy it to stay there by myself," said Eliot. "But I've spent the last couple of nights alone without damage."

"And you saw or heard nothing?" said Ellie.

"There may have been some scratching. A rat perhaps. It's an old house. But it's only a house. I have to go down to London for a few days tomorrow. When I get back we'll start looking for somewhere else. Sooner or later I'd get the urge anyway."

"But it's such a shame! After all your work, you deserve to relax for a while," said Ellie. "Isn't there anything you can do?"

"Exorcism," said Pascoe. "Bell, book and candle."

"In my experience," said Dalziel, who had been consuming the malt whisky at a rate which had caused the waiter to summon his workmates to view the spectacle, "there's three main causes of ghosts."

He paused for effect and more alcohol.

"Can't you arrest him, or something?" Ellie hissed at Pascoe.

"One: bad cooking," the fat man continued. "Two: bad ventilation. Three: bad conscience."

"George installed air-conditioning himself," said Pascoe.

"And Giselle's a super cook," said Ellie.

"Well then," said Dalziel. "I'm sure your conscience is as quiet as mine, love. So that leaves your randy yokel. Tell you what. Bugger your priests. What you need is a professional eye checking on things."

"You mean a psychic investigator?" said Giselle.

"Like hell!" laughed Ellie. "He means get the village bobby to stroll around the place with his truncheon at the ready."

"A policeman? But I don't really see what he could do," said Giselle, leaning towards Dalziel and looking earnestly into his lowered eyes.

"No, hold on a minute," cried Ellie with bright malice. "The Superintendent could be right. A formal investigation. But the village flatfoot's no use. You've got the best police brains in the county rubbing your thighs, Giselle. Why not send for them?"

Which was how it started. Dalziel, to Pascoe's amazement, had greeted the suggestion with ponderous enthusiasm. Giselle had reacted with a mixture of high spirits and high seriousness, apparently regarding the project as both an opportunity for vindication and a lark. George had sat like Switzerland, neutral and dull. Ellie had been smilingly baffled to see her bluff so swiftly called. And Pascoe had kicked her ankle savagely when he heard plans being made for himself and Dalziel to spend the following Friday night waiting for ghosts at Stanstone Farm.

As he told her the next day, had he realized that Dalziel's enthusiasm was going to survive the sober light of morning, he'd have followed up his kick with a karate chop.

Ellie had tried to appear unrepentant.

"You know why it's called Stanstone, do you?" she asked. "Standing stone. Get it? There must have been a stone circle there at some time. Primitive worship, human sacrifice, that sort of thing. Probably the original stones were used in the building of the house. That'd explain a lot, wouldn't it?"

"No," said Pascoe coldly. "That would explain very little. It would certainly not explain why I am about to lose a night's sleep, nor why you who usually threaten me with divorce or assault whenever my rest is disturbed to fight *real* crime should have arranged it."

But arranged it had been and it was small comfort for Pascoe now to know that Ellie was missing him.

Dalziel seemed determined to enjoy himself, however.

"Let's get our bearings, shall we?" he said. Replenishing his glass, he set out on a tour of the house.

"Well wired up," he said as his expert eye spotted the discreet evidence of the sophisticated alarm system. "Must have cost a fortune."

"It did. I put him in touch with our crime prevention squad and evidently he wanted nothing but the best," said Pascoe.

"What's he got that's so precious?" wondered Dalziel.

"All this stuff's pretty valuable, I guess," said Pascoe, making a gesture which took in the pictures and ornaments of the master bedroom in which they were standing. "But it's really for Giselle's sake. This was her first time out in the sticks and it's a pretty lonely place. Not that it's done much good."

"Aye," said Dalziel, opening a drawer and pulling out a fine silk underslip. "A good-looking woman could get nervous in a place like this."

"You reckon that's what this is all about, sir?" said Pascoe. "A slight case of hysteria?"

"Mebbe," said Dalziel.

They went into the next room, which Eliot had turned into a study. Only the calculating machine on the desk reminded them of the man's profession. The glass-fronted bookcase contained rows of books relating to his hobby in all its aspects from architectural histories to do-it-yourself tracts on concrete mixing. An old grandmother clock stood in a corner, and hanging on the wall opposite the bookcase was a nearly lifesize painting of a pre-Raphaelite maiden being pensive in a grove. She was naked but her long hair and the dappled shadowings of the trees preserved her modesty.

For a fraction of a second it seemed to Pascoe as if the shadows on her flesh shifted as though a breeze had touched the branches above.

"Asking for it," declared Dalziel.

"What?"

"Rheumatics or rape," said Dalziel. "Let's check the kitchen. My belly's empty as a football."

Giselle, who had driven out during the day to light the fire and make ready for their arrival, had anticipated Dalziel's gut. On the kitchen table lay a pile of sandwiches covered by a sheet of kitchen paper on which she had scribbled an invitation for them to help themselves to whatever they fancied.

Underneath she had written in capitals BE CAREFUL and underlined it twice.

"Nice thought," said Dalziel, grabbing a couple of the sandwiches. "Bring the plate through to the living-room and we'll eat in comfort."

Back in front of the fire with his glass filled once again, Dalziel relaxed in a deep armchair. Pascoe poured himself a drink and looked out of the window again.

"For God's sake, lad, sit down!" commanded Dalziel. "You're worse than a bloody spook, creeping around like that."

"Sorry," said Pasco

"Sup your drink and eat a sandwich. It'll soon be midnight. That's zero hour, isn't it? Right, get your strength up. Keep your nerves down."

"I'm not nervous!" protested Pascoe.

"No? Don't believe in ghosts, then?"

"Hardly at all," said Pascoe.

"Quite right. Detective-inspectors with university degrees shouldn't believe in ghosts. But tired old superintendents with less schooling than a pit pony, there's a different matter."

"Come off it!" said Pascoe. "You're the biggest unbeliever I know!"

"That may be, that may be," said Dalziel, sinking lower into his chair. "But sometimes, lad, sometimes..."

His voice sank away. The room was lit only by a dark-shaded table lamp and the glow from the fire threw deep shadows across the large contours of Dalziel's face. It might have been some eighteenth-century Yorkshire farmer sitting there, thought Pascoe. Shrewd; brutish; in his day a solid ram of a man, but now rotting to ruin through his own excesses and too much rough weather.

In the fireplace a log fell. Pascoe started. The red glow ran up Dalziel's face like a flush of passion up an Easter Island statue.

"I knew a ghost saved a marriage once," he said ruminatively. "In a manner of speaking."

Oh Jesus! thought Pascoe. It's ghost stories round the fire now, is it?

He remained obstinately silent.

"My first case, I suppose you'd call it. Start of a meteoric career."

"Meteors fall. And burn out," said Pascoe. "Sir."

"You're a sharp bugger, Peter," said Dalziel admiringly. "Always the quick answer. I bet you were just the same when you were eighteen. Still at school, eh? Not like me. I was a right Constable Plod I tell you. Untried. Untutored. Hardly knew one end of my truncheon from t'other. When I heard that shriek I just froze."

"Which shriek?" asked Pascoe resignedly.

On cue there came a piercing wail from the dark outside, quickly cut off. He half rose, caught Dalziel's amused eye, and subsided, reaching for the whisky decanter.

"Easy on that stuff," admonished Dalziel with all the righteousness of a temperance preacher. "Enjoy your supper, like yon owl. Where was I? Oh aye. I was on night patrol. None of your Panda-cars in those days. You did it all on foot. And I was standing just inside this little alleyway. It was a dark narrow passage running between Shufflebotham's woolmill on the one side and a little terrace of back-to-backs on the other. It's all gone now, all gone. There's a car park there now. A bloody car park!

"Any road, the thing about this alley was, it were a dead end. There was a kind of buttress sticking out of the mill wall, might have been the chimneystack, I'm not sure, but the back to backs had been built flush up against it so there was no way through. No way at all."

He took another long pull at his scotch to help his memory and began to scratch his armpit noisily.

"Listen!" said Pascoe suddenly.

"What?"

"I thought I heard a noise."

"What kind of noise?"

"Like fingers scrabbling on rough stone," said Pascoe.

Dalziel removed his hand slowly from his shirt front and regarded Pascoe malevolently.

"It's stopped now," said Pascoe. "What were you saying, sir?"

"I was saying about this shriek," said Dalziel. "I just froze to the spot. It came floating out of this dark passage. It was as black as the devil's arsehole up there. The mill wall was completely blank and there was just one small window in the gable end of the house. That, if anywhere, was where the shriek came from. Well, I don't know what I'd have done. I might have been standing there yet wondering what to do, only this big hand slapped hard on my shoulder. I nearly shit myself! Then this voice said, 'What's to do, Constable Dalziel?' and when I looked round there was my sergeant, doing his rounds.

"I could hardly speak for a moment, he'd given me such a fright. But I didn't need to explain. For just then came another shriek and voices, a man's and a woman's, shouting at each other. 'You hang on here,' said the sergeant. 'I'll see what this is all about.' Off he went, leaving me still shaking. And as I looked down that gloomy passageway, I began to remember some local stories about this mill. I hadn't paid much heed to them before. Everywhere that's more than fifty years old had a ghost in them parts. They say Yorkshiremen are hard-headed, but I reckon they've got more superstition to the square inch than a tribe of pygmies. Well, this particular tale was about a mill-girl back in the 1870s. The owner's son had put her in the family way which I dare say was common enough. The owner acted decently enough by his lights. He packed his son off to the other end of the country, gave the girl and her family a bit of cash and said she could have her job back when the confinement was over."

"Almost a social reformer," said Pascoe, growing interested despite himself.

"Better than a lot of buggers still in business round here," said Dalziel sourly. "To cut a long story short, this lass had her kid premature and it soon died. As soon as she was fit enough to get out of bed, she came back to the mill, climbed through a skylight on to the roof and jumped off. Now all that I could believe. Probably happened all the time."

"Yes," said Pascoe. "I've no doubt that a hundred years ago the air round here was full of falling girls. While in America they were fighting a war to stop the plantation owners screwing their slaves!"

"You'll have to watch that indignation, Peter," said Dalziel. "It can give you wind. And no one pays much heed to a preacher when you can't hear his sermons for farts. Where was I, now? Oh yes. This lass. Since that day there'd been a lot of stories about people seeing a girl falling from the roof of this old mill. Tumbling over and over in the air right slowly, most of 'em said. Her clothes filling with air, her hair streaming behind her like a comet's tail. Oh aye, lovely descriptions some of them were. Like the ones we get whenever there's an accident. One for every pair of eyes, and all of 'em perfectly detailed and perfectly different."

"So you didn't reckon much to these tales?" said Pascoe.

"Not by daylight," said Dalziel. "But standing there in the mouth of the dark passageway at midnight, that was different."

Pascoe glanced at his watch.

"It's nearly midnight now," he said in a sepulchral tone.

Dalziel ignored him.

"I was glad when the sergeant stuck his head through that little window and bellowed my name. Though even that gave me a hell of a scare. 'Dalziel!' he said. 'Take a look up this alleyway. If you can't see anything, come in here.' So I had a look. There wasn't anything, just sheer brick walls on three sides with only this one little window. I didn't hang about but got myself round to the front of the house pretty sharply and went in. There were two people there besides the sergeant. Albert Pocklington, whose house it was, and his missus, Jenny. In those days a good bobby knew everyone on his beat. I said hello, but they didn't do much more than grunt. Mrs Pocklington was about forty. She must have been a bonny lass in her time and she still didn't look too bad. She'd got her blouse off, just draped around her shoulders, and I had a good squint at her big round tits. Well, I was only a lad! I didn't really look at her face till I'd had an eyeful lower down and then I noticed that one side was all splotchy red as though someone had given her a clout. There were no prizes for guessing who. Bert Pocklington was a big solid fellow. He looked like a chimpanzee, only he had a lot less gumption."

"Hold on," said Pascoe.

"What is it now?" said Dalziel, annoyed that his story had been interrupted.

"I thought I heard something. No, I mean really heard something this time."

They listened together. The only sound Pascoe could hear was the noise of his own breathing mixed with the pulsing of his own blood, like the distant sough of a receding tide.

"I'm sorry," he said. "I really did think. . ."

"That's all right, lad," said Dalziel with surprising sympathy, "I know the feeling. Where'd I got to? Albert Pocklington. My sergeant took me aside and put me in the picture. It seems that Pocklington had got a notion in his mind that someone was banging his missus while he was on the night shift. So he'd slipped away from his work at midnight and come home, ready to do a bit of banging on his own account. He wasn't a man to move quietly, so he tried for speed instead, flinging open the front door and rushing up the stairs. When he opened the bedroom door, his wife had been standing by the open window naked to the waist, shrieking. Naturally he thought the worst. Who wouldn't? Her story was that she was getting ready for bed when she had this feeling of the room suddenly becoming very hot and airless and pressing in on her. She'd gone to the window and opened it, and it was like taking a cork out of a bottle, she said. She felt as if she was being sucked out of the window, she said. (With tits like you and a window that small, there wasn't much likelihood of that! I thought.) And at the same time she had seen a shape like a human figure tumbling slowly by the window. Naturally she shrieked. Pocklington came in. She threw herself into his arms. All the welcome she got was a thump on the ear, and that brought on the second bout of shrieking. She was hysterical, trying to tell him what she'd seen, while he just raged around, yelling about what he was going to do to her fancy man."

He paused for a drink. Pascoe stirred the fire with his foot. Then froze. There it was again! A distant scratching. He had no sense of direction.

The hairs on the back of his neck prickled in the traditional fashion. Clearly Dalziel heard nothing and Pascoe was not yet certain enough to interrupt the fat man again.

"The sergeant was a good copper. He didn't want a man beating up his wife for no reason and he didn't want a hysterical woman starting a ghost scare. They can cause a lot of bother, ghost scares," added Dalziel, filling his glass once more with the long-suffering expression of a man who is being caused a lot of bother.

"He sorted out Pocklington's suspicions about his wife having a lover first of all. He pushed his shoulders through the window till they got stuck to show how small it was. Then he asked me if anyone could have come out of that passageway without me spotting them. Out of the question, I told him.

"Next he chatted to the wife and got her to admit she'd been feeling a bit under the weather that day, like the 'flu was coming on, and she'd taken a cup of tea heavily spiked with gin as a nightcap. Ten minutes later we left them more or less happy. But as we stood on the pavement outside, the sergeant asked me the question I'd hoped he wouldn't. Why had I stepped into that alley in the first place? I suppose I could have told him I wanted a pee or a smoke, something like that. But he was a hard man to lie to, that sergeant. Not like the wet-nurses we get nowadays. So after a bit of humming and hawing, I told him I'd seen something, just out of the corner of my eye, as I was walking past. 'What sort of thing?' he asked. Like something falling, I said. Something fluttering and falling through the air between the mill wall and the house end.

"He gave me a queer look, the sergeant did. 'I tell you what, Dalziel,' he said. 'When you make out your report, I shouldn't say anything of that. No, I should keep quiet about that. Leave ghosts to them that understands them. You stick to crime.' And that's advice I've followed ever since, till this very night, that is!"

He yawned and stretched. There was a distant rather cracked chime. It was, Pascoe realized, the clock in Eliot's study striking midnight.

But it wasn't the only sound.

"*There!* Listen," urged Pascoe, rising slowly to his feet. "I *can* hear it. A scratching. Do *you* hear it, sir?"

Dalziel cupped one cauliflower ear in his hand.

"By Christ, I think you're right, lad!" he said as if this were the most remote possibility in the world. "Come on! Let's take a look."

Pascoe led the way. Once out of the living-room they could hear the noise quite clearly and it took only a moment to locate it in the kitchen.

"Rats?" wondered Pascoe.

Dalziel shook his head.

"Rats gnaw," he whispered. "That sounds like something bigger. It's at the back door. It sounds a bit keen to get in."

Indeed it did, thought Pascoe. There was a desperate insistency about the sound. Sometimes it rose to a crescendo, then tailed away as though from exhaustion, only to renew itself with greater fury.

It was as though someone or something was caught in a trap too fast for hope, too horrible for resignation. Pascoe had renewed his acquaintance with Poe after the strange business at Wear End and now he recalled the story in which the coffin was opened to reveal a contorted skeleton and the lid scarred on the inside by the desperate scraping of fingernails.

"Shall I open it?" he whispered to Dalziel.

"No," said the fat man. "Best one of us goes out the front door and comes round behind. I'll open when you shout. OK?"

"OK" said Pascoe with less enthusiasm than he had ever OK'd even Dalziel before.

Picking up one of the heavy rubber-encased torches they had brought with them, he retreated to the front door and slipped out into the dark night.

The frost had come down fiercely since their arrival and the cold caught at his throat like an invisible predator. He thought of returning for his coat, but decided this would be just an excuse for postponing whatever confrontation awaited him. Instead, making a mental note that when he was a superintendent he, too, would make sure he got the inside jobs, he set off round the house.

When he reached the second corner, he could hear the scratching quite clearly. It cut through the still and freezing air like the sound of a steel blade against a grinding-stone.

Pascoe paused, took a deep breath, let out a yell of warning and leapt out from the angle of the house with his torch flashing.

The scratching ceased instantly, there was nothing to be seen by the rear door of the house, but a terrible shriek died away across the lawn as though an exorcized spirit was wailing its way to Hades.

At the same time the kitchen door was flung open and Dalziel strode majestically forward; then his foot skidded on the frosty ground and, swearing horribly, he crashed down on his huge behind.

"Are you all right, sir?" asked Pascoe breathlessly.

"There's only one part of my body that feels any sensitivity still," said Dalziel. "Give us a hand up."

He dusted himself down, saying, "Well, that's ghost number one laid."

"Sir?"

"Look."

His stubby finger pointed to a line of paw prints across the powder frost of the lawn.

"Cat," he said. "This was a farmhouse, remember? Every farm has its cats. They live in the barn, keep the rats down. Where's the barn?"

"Gone," said Pascoe. "George had it pulled down and used some of the stones for an extension to the house."

"There you are then," said Dalziel. "Poor bloody animal wakes up one morning with no roof, no rats. It's all right living rough in the summer, but comes the cold weather and it starts fancying getting inside again. Perhaps the farmer's wife used to give it scraps at the kitchen door."

"It'll get precious little encouragement from Giselle," said Pascoe.

"It's better than Count Dracula anyway," said Dalziel.

Pascoe, who was now very cold indeed, began to move towards the kitchen, but to his surprise Dalziel stopped him.

"It's a hell of a night even for a cat," he said. "Just have a look, Peter, see if you can spot the poor beast. In case it's hurt."

Rather surprised by his boss's manifestation of kindness to animals (though not in the least at his display of cruelty to junior officers), Pascoe shivered along the line of paw prints across the grass. They disappeared into a small orchard, whose trees

338

seemed to crowd together to repel intruders, or perhaps just for warmth. Pascoe peered between the italic trunks and made cat-attracting noises but nothing stirred. "All right," he said. "I know you're in there. We've got the place surrounded. Better come quietly. I'll leave the door open, so just come in and give a yell when you want to give yourself up."

Back in the kitchen, he left the door ajar and put a bowl of milk on the floor. His teeth were chattering and he headed to the living-room, keen to do full justice to both the log fire and the whisky decanter. The telephone rang as he entered. For once Dalziel picked it up and Pascoe poured himself a stiff drink.

From the half conversation he could hear, he gathered it was the duty sergeant at the station who was ringing. Suddenly, irrationally, he felt very worried in case Dalziel was going to announce he had to go out on a case, leaving Pascoe alone.

The reality turned out almost as bad.

"Go easy on that stuff," said Dalziel. "You don't want to be done for driving under the influence."

"What?"

Dalziel passed him the phone.

The sergeant told him someone had just rung the station asking urgently for Pascoe and refusing to speak to anyone else. He'd claimed what he had to say was important. "It's big and it's tonight" were his words. And he'd rung off saying he'd ring back in an hour's time. After that it'd be too late.

"Oh shit," said Pascoe. "It sounds like Benny."

Benny was one of his snouts, erratic and melodramatic, but often bringing really hot information.

"I suppose I'll have to go in," said Pascoe reluctantly. "Or I could get the Sarge to pass this number on."

"If it's urgent, you'll need to be on the spot," said Dalziel. "Let me know what's happening, won't you? Best get your skates on."

"Skates is right," muttered Pascoe. "It's like the Arctic out there."

He downed his whisky defiantly, then went to put his overcoat on.

"You'll be all right by yourself, will you, sir?" he said maliciously. "Able to cope with ghosts, ghouls, werewolves and falling mill girls?"

"Never you mind about me, lad," said Dalziel jovially. "Any road, if it's visitors from an old stone circle we've got to worry about, dawn's the time, isn't it? When the first rays of the sun touch the victim's breast. And with luck you'll be back by then. Keep me posted."

Pascoe opened the front door and groaned as the icy air attacked his face once more.

"I am just going outside," he said. "And I may be some time."

To which Dalziel replied, as perhaps Captain Scott and his companions had, "Shut that bloody door!"

It took several attempts before he could persuade the frozen engine to start and he knew from experience that it would be a good twenty minutes before the heater began to pump even lukewarm air into the car. Swearing softly to himself, he set the vehicle bumping gently over the frozen contours of the long driveway up to the road.

The drive curved round the orchard and the comforting silhouette of the house soon disappeared from his mirror. The frost-laced trees seemed to lean menacingly across his path and he told himself that if any apparition suddenly rose before the car, he'd test its substance by driving straight through it.

But when the headlights reflected a pair of bright eyes directly ahead, he slammed on the brake instantly.

The cat looked as if it had been waiting for him. It was a skinny black creature with a mangled ear and a wary expression. Its response to Pascoe's soothing noises was to turn and plunge into the orchard once more.

"Oh no!" groaned Pascoe. And he yelled after it, "You stupid bloody animal! I'm not going to chase you through the trees all bloody night. Not if you were a naked naiad, I'm not!"

As though recognizing the authentic tone of a Yorkshire farmer, the cat howled in reply and Pascoe glimpsed its shadowy shape only a few yards ahead. He followed, hurling abuse to which the beast responded with indignant miaows. Finally it disappeared under a bramble bush.

"That does it," said Pascoe. "Not a step further."

Leaning down he flashed his torch beneath the bush to take his farewell of the stupid animal.

Not one pair of eyes but three stared unblinkingly back at him, and a chorus of howls split the frosty air.

The newcomers were young kittens who met him with delight that made up for their mother's wariness. They were distressingly thin and nearby Pascoe's torch picked out the stiff bodies of another two, rather smaller, who hadn't survived.

"Oh shit," said Pascoe, more touched than his anti-sentimental attitudes would have permitted him to admit.

When he scooped up the kittens, their mother snarled in protest and tried to sink her teeth into his gloved hand. But he was in no mood for argument and after he'd bellowed, "Shut up!" she allowed herself to be lifted and settled down comfortably in the crook of his arm with her offspring.

It was quicker to continue through the orchard than to return to the car. As he walked across the lawn towards the kitchen door he smiled to himself at the prospect of leaving Dalziel in charge of this little family. That would really test the fat man's love of animals.

The thought of ghosts and hauntings was completely removed from his mind. And that made the sight of the face at the upstairs window even more terrifying. For a moment his throat constricted so much that he could hardly breathe. It was a pale face, a woman's he thought, shadowy, insubstantial behind the leaded panes of the old casement. And as he looked the room behind seemed to be touched by a dim unearthly glow through which shadows moved like weed on a slow stream's bed. In his arms the kittens squeaked in protest and he realized that he had involuntarily tightened his grip.

"Sorry," he said, and the momentary distraction unlocked the paralysing fear and replaced it by an equally instinctive resolve to confront its source. There's nothing makes a man angrier than the awareness of having been made afraid.

He went through the open kitchen door and dropped the cats by the bowl of milk which they assaulted with silent delight. The wise thing would have been to summon Dalziel from his warmth and whisky, but Pascoe had no mind to be wise. He went up the stairs as swiftly and as quietly as he could.

He had calculated that the window from which the "phantom" peered belonged to the study and when he saw the door was open he didn't know whether he was pleased or not. Ghosts didn't need doors. On the other hand it meant that *something* was in there. But the glow was gone.

Holding his torch like a truncheon, he stepped inside. As his free hand groped for the light switch he was aware of something silhouetted against the paler darkness of the window and at the same time of movement elsewhere in the room. His left hand couldn't find the switch, his right thumb couldn't find the button on the torch, it was as if the darkness of the room was liquid, slowing down all movement and washing over his mouth and nose and eyes in wave after stifling wave.

Then a single cone of light grew above Eliot's desk and Dalziel's voice said, "Why're you waving your arms like that, lad? Semaphore, is it?"

At which moment his fingers found the main light switch.

Dalziel was standing by the desk. Against the window leaned the long painting of the pre-Raphaelite girl, face to the glass. Where it had hung on the wall was a safe, wide open and empty. On the desk under the sharply focused rays of the desk lamp lay what Pascoe took to be its contents.

"What the hell's going on?" demanded Pascoe, half relieved, half bewildered.

"Tell you in a minute," said Dalziel, resuming his examination of the papers.

"No, sir," said Pascoe with growing anger. "You'll tell me now. You'll tell me exactly what you're doing going through private papers without a warrant! And how the hell did you get into that safe?"

"I've got you to thank for that, Peter," said Dalziel without looking up.

"*What?*"

"It was you who put Eliot in touch with our crime prevention officer, wasn't it? I did an efficiency check the other morning, went through all the files. There it was. Eliot, George. He really wanted the works, didn't he? What's he got out there? I thought. The family jewels? I checked with the firm who did the fitting. I know the manager, as it happens. He's a good lad; bit of a ladies' man, but clever with it."

"Oh God!" groaned Pascoe. "You mean you got details of the alarm system and a spare set of keys!"

"No, I didn't!" said Dalziel indignantly. "I had to work it out for myself mainly."

He had put on his wire-rimmed National Health spectacles to read the documents from the safe and now he glared owlishly at Pascoe over them.

"Do you understand figures?" he asked. "It's all bloody Welsh to me."

Pascoe consciously resisted the conspiratorial invitation.

"I"ve heard nothing so far to explain why you're breaking the law, sir," he said coldly. "What's George Eliot supposed to have done?"

"What? Oh, I see. It's the laws of hospitality and friendship you're worried about! Nothing, nothing. Set your mind at rest, lad. It's nowt to do with your mate. Only indirectly. Look, this wasn't planned, you know. I mean, how could I plan all that daft ghost business? No, it was just that the Fletcher business was getting nowhere . . ."

"Fletcher?"

"Hey, here's your income tax file. Christ! Is that what your missus gets just for chatting to students? It's more than you!"

Pascoe angrily snatched the file from Dalziel's hands. The fat man put on his sympathetic, sincere look.

"Never fret, lad. I won't spread it around. Where was I? Oh yes, Fletcher. I've got a feeling about that fellow. The tip-off sounded good. Not really my line, though. I got Inspector Marwood on the Fraud Squad interested, though. All he could come up with was that a lot of Fletcher's business interests had a faint smell about them, but that was all. Oh yes, and Fletcher's accountants were the firm your mate Eliot's a partner in."

"That's hardly a startling revelation," sneered Pascoe.

"Did you know?"

"No. Why should I?"

"Fair point," said Dalziel. "Hello, hello."

He had found an envelope among the files. It contained a single sheet of paper which he examined with growing interest. Then he carefully refolded it, replaced it in the envelope and began to put all the documents read or unread back into the safe.

"Marwood told me as well, though, that Fletcher and Eliot seemed to be pretty thick at a personal level. And he also said the Fraud Squad would love to go over Fletcher's accounts with a fine-tooth comb."

"Why doesn't he get himself a warrant then?"

"Useless, unless he knows what he's looking for. My tipster was too vague. Often happens with first-timers. They want it to be quick and they overestimate our abilities."

"Is that possible?" marvelled Pascoe.

"Oh aye. Just. Are you going to take that file home?"

Reluctantly, Pascoe handed his tax file back to Dalziel, who thrust it in with the others, slammed the safe, then did some complicated fiddling with a bunch of keys.

"There," he said triumphantly, "all locked up and the alarm set once more. No harm to anyone. Peter, do me a favour. Put that tart's picture back up on the wall. I nearly did my back getting it down. I'll go and mend the fire and pour us a drink."

"I am not involved in this!" proclaimed Pascoe. But the fat man had gone.

When Pascoe came downstairs after replacing the picture, Dalziel was not to be found in the living-room. Pascoe tracked him to the kitchen, where he found him on his hands and knees, feeding pressed calves-tongue to the kittens.

"So you found 'em," said Dalziel. "That's what brought you back. Soft bugger."

"Yes. And I take it I needn't go out again. There's no snout'll be ringing at one o'clock. That was you while I was freezing outside, wasn't it?"

"I'm afraid so. I thought it best to get you out of the way. Sorry, lad, but I mean, this fellow Eliot is a mate of yours and I didn't want you getting upset."

"I *am* upset," said Pascoe. "Bloody upset."

"There!" said Dalziel triumphantly. "I was right, wasn't I? Let's get that drink. These buggers can look after themselves."

He dumped the rest of the tongue on to the kitchen floor and rose to his feet with much wheezing.

"There it is then, Peter," said Dalziel as they returned to the living-room. "It was all on the spur of the moment. When Mrs Eliot suggested we spend a night here to look for her ghosts, I just went along to be sociable. I mean, you can't be rude to a woman like that, can you? A sudden shock, and that dress might have fallen off her nipples. I'd no more intention of really coming out here than of going teetotal! But next morning I got to thinking. If we could just get a bit of a pointer where to look at Fletcher ... And I remembered you saying about Eliot doing your accounts at home."

"Income tax!" snorted Pascoe. "Does that make me a crook? Or him either?"

"No. It was just a thought, that's all. And after I'd talked to Crime Prevention, well, it seemed worth a peek. So come down off your high horse. No harm done.

Your mate's not in trouble, OK? And I saw nowt in his safe to take action on. So relax, enjoy your drink. I poured you brandy, the scotch is getting a bit low. That all right?"

Pascoe didn't answer but sat down in the deep old armchair and sipped his drink reflectively. Spur of the moment, Dalziel had said. Bloody long moment, he thought. And what spur? There was still something here that hadn't been said.

"It won't do," he said suddenly.

"What's that?"

"There's got to be something else," insisted Pascoe. "I mean, I know you, sir. You're not going to do all this *just* on the off-chance of finding something to incriminate Fletcher in George's safe. There *has* to be something else. What did you expect to find, anyway? A signed confession? Come to that, what *did* you find?"

Dalziel looked at him, his eyes moist with sincerity.

"Nowt, lad Nowt. I've told you. There'll be no action taken as a result of anything I saw tonight. None. There's my reassurance. It was an error of judgement on my part. I admit it. Now does that satisfy you?"

"No, sir, to be quite frank it doesn't. Look, I've got to know. These people are my friends. You say that they're not mixed up in anything criminal, but I still need to know exactly what is going on. Or else I'll start asking for myself."

He banged his glass down on the arm of his chair so vehemently that the liquor slopped out.

"It'll burn a hole, yon stuff," said Dalziel, slandering the five-star cognac which Pascoe was drinking.

"I mean it, sir," said Pascoe quietly. "You'd better understand that."

"All right, lad," said Dalziel. "I believe you. You might not like it though. *You'd* better understand *that*."

"I'll chance it," replied Pascoe.

Dalziel regarded him closely, then relaxed with a sigh.

"Here it is then. The woman Giselle is having a bit on the side with Fletcher."

Pascoe managed an indifferent shrug.

"It happens," he said, trying to appear unsurprised. In fact, why was he surprised? Lively, sociable, physical Giselle and staid, self-contained, inward-looking George. It was always on the cards.

"So what?" he added in his best man-of-the-world voice.

"So if by and chance, Eliot did have anything which might point us in the right direction about Fletcher . . ."

Pascoe sat very still for a moment.

"Well, you old bastard!" he said. "You mean you'd give him good reason to do the pointing! You'd let him know about Giselle . . . Jesus wept! How low can you get?"

"I could have just let him know in any case without checking first to see if it was worthwhile," suggested Dalziel, unabashed.

"So you could!" said Pascoe in mock astonishment. "But you held back, waiting for a chance to check it out! Big of you! You get invited to spend the night alone in complete strangers' houses all the time! And now you've looked and found nothing, what are you going to do? Tell him just on the off-chance?"

"I didn't say I'd found *nothing*," said Dalziel.

Pascoe stared at him.

"But you said there'd be no action!" he said.

"Right," said Dalziel. "I mean it. I think we've just got to sit back and wait for Fletcher to fall into our laps. Or be pushed. What I did find was a little anonymous letter telling Eliot what his wife was up to. Your mate *knows*, Peter. From the postmark he's known for a few weeks. He's a careful man, accountants usually are. And I'm sure he'd do a bit of checking first before taking action. It was just a week later that my telephone rang and that awful disguised voice told me to check on Fletcher. Asked for me personally. I dare say you've mentioned my name to Eliot, haven't you, Peter?"

He looked at the carpet modestly.

"Everyone's heard of you, sir," said Pascoe. "So what happens now?"

"Like I say. Nothing. We sit and wait for the next call. It should be a bit more detailed this time, I reckon. I mean, Eliot must have realized that his first tip-off isn't getting results and now his wife's moved back into town to be on Fletcher's doorstep again, he's got every incentive."

Pascoe looked at him in surprise.

"You mean the ghosts . . ."

"Nice imaginative girl, that Giselle! Not only does she invent a haunting to save herself a two hours' drive for her kicks, but she cons a pair of thick bobbies into losing their sleep over it. I bet Fletcher fell about laughing! Well I'm losing no more! It'll take all the hounds of hell to keep me awake."

He yawned and stretched. In mid-stretch there came a terrible scratching noise and the fat man froze like a woodcut of Lethargy on an allegorical frieze.

Then he laughed and opened the door.

The black cat looked up at him warily but her kittens had no such inhibitions and tumbled in, heading towards the fire with cries of delight.

"I think your mates have got more trouble than they know." said Dalziel.

Next morning Pascoe rose early and stiffly after a night spent on a sofa before the fire. Dalziel had disappeared upstairs to find himself a bed and Pascoe assumed he would still be stretched out on it. But when he looked out of the living-room he saw he was wrong.

The sun was just beginning to rise behind the orchard and the fat man was standing in front of the house watching the dawn.

A romantic at heart, thought Pascoe sourly.

A glint of light flickered between the trunks of the orchard trees, flamed into a ray and began to move across the frosty lawn towards the waiting man. He watched its progress, striking sparks off the ice-hard grass. And when it reached his feet he stepped aside.

Pascoe joined him a few minutes later.

"Morning, sir," he said. "I've made some coffee. You're up bright and early."

"Yes," said Dalziel, scratching his gut vigorously. "I think I've picked up a flea from those bloody cats."

"Oh," said Pascoe. "I thought you'd come to check on the human sacrifice at dawn. I saw you getting out of the way of the sun's first ray."

"Bollocks!" said Dalziel, looking towards the house, which the sun was now staining the gentle pink of blood in a basin of water.

"Why bollocks?" wondered Pascoe. "You've seen one ghost. Why not another?"

"One ghost?"

"Yes. The mill-girl. That story you told me last night. Your first case."

Dalziel looked at him closely.

"I told you that, did I? I must have been supping well."

Pascoe, who knew that drink had never made Dalziel forget a thing in his life, nodded vigorously.

"Yes, sir. You told me that. You and your ghost."

Dalziel shook his head as though at a memory of ancient foolishness and began to laugh.

"Aye, lad. My ghost! It really is my ghost in a way. The ghost of what I am now, any road! That Jenny Pocklington, she were a right grand lass! She had an imagination like your Giselle!"

"I don't follow," said Pascoe. But he was beginning to.

"Believe it or not, lad," said Dalziel. "In them days I was pretty slim. Slim and supple. Even then I had to be like a ghost to get through that bloody window! But if Bert Pocklington had caught me, I really would have been one! Aye, that's right. When I heard that scream, I was coming out of the alley, not going into it!"

And shaking with laughter the fat man headed across the lacy grass towards the old stone farmhouse where the hungry kittens were crying imperiously for their breakfast.

Edward D. Hoch

(1930–)

In a career that has spanned more than forty years, Edward D. Hoch has probably created more series detective characters than any other writer past or present—some twenty-five at last count. While most do their sleuthing alone or with others in minor roles, two of his most successful series feature duos. One is the "Computer Cops," Carl Crader and Earl Jazine, who investigate crimes for the Federal Computer Investigation Bureau in the early twenty-first century; the team appears in three of Hoch's four novels— *The Transvection Machine* (1971), *The Fellowship of the Hand* (1973), and *The Frankenstein Factory* (1975), all of which are expert blends of detection, science fiction, and social commentary.

Hoch's second detective duo appears solely in short stories. Former Scotland Yard agent Sebastian Blue and his partner, Laura Charme, a pair reminiscent of John Steed and Emma Peel of *Avengers* fame, work for Interpol in the investigation of international crimes involving more than one country. Their adventures have been chronicled in close to a score of stories published in *Ellery Queen's Mystery Magazine,* beginning in 1973. "The Case of the Modern Medusa," in which Blue and Charme journey to Geneva to contend with the seemingly impossible murder of a beautiful gold smuggler during a Mythology Fair, is among the most satisfying of their joint efforts.

Edward D. Hoch's true metier is the short story, as evidenced by the fact that he has written exclusively in this form for the past two decades and made a living doing so. His amazingly fecund imagination has resulted in nearly eight hundred published stories since his first sale in 1955. Outstanding among his other series characters are Police Captain Leopold, whose cases are generally of the procedural variety; Dr. Sam Hawthorne, a New England country doctor who solves "impossible" rural mysteries in the early years of this century; Simon Ark, a shadowy figure who claims to be a 2000-year-old Coptic priest and whose detections are flavored with elements of the occult; Jeffrey Rand, a retired spy and an expert at decrypting baffling codes and ciphers; Ben Snow, who may or may not be a reincarnation of Billy the Kid and whose bailiwick is the Old West; and Nick Velvet, a master thief with a peculiar code of honor —he will risk his life and freedom to steal any object, no matter how difficult the challenge, so long as the item has no monetary value.

Many of Hoch's series stories have been collected. *The Thefts of Nick Velvet* (1978), *The Quests of Simon Ark* (1984), *Leopold's Way* (1985), and *Diagnosis: Impossible, the Problems of Dr. Sam Hawthorne* (1996) are particularly noteworthy. Twenty-two of his equally excellent nonseries crime stories appear in the 1992 collection *The Night My Friend.*

INTERPOL: THE CASE OF THE MODERN MEDUSA

SEBASTIAN BLUE AND LAURA CHARME
GENEVA, SWITZERLAND
1973

She was too beautiful to make a convincing Medusa, even with the terrible wig and its writhing plastic serpents. Gazing at herself in the mirror, Gretchen could only wonder at the chain of events that had caused Dolliman to hire her in the first place. Then the buzzer sounded and it was time to make her entrance.

She rose through a trap door in the floor, effectively masked by a cloud of chemically produced mist. As the mist cleared enough for the audience to see her, there were the usual startled exclamations. Then Toby, playing the part of Perseus, came forward with his sword and shield to slay her. It wasn't exactly according to mythology, but it seemed to please the audience of tourists.

As Toby lifted his sword to strike, her mind was on other things. She was remembering the charter flights to the Far East, the parties and the fun. But most of all she was remembering the gold. It was a great deal to give up, but she'd made her decision.

Toby, following the script they'd played a hundred times before, pushed her down into the swirling mists and grabbed the dummy head of Medusa that was hidden there. The sight of the bloody head always brought a gasp from the crowd, and this day was no exception. Gretchen felt for the trap door and opened it. While the crowd applauded and Toby took his bows, she made her way down the ladder to the lower level.

That was where they found her, an hour later. She was crumpled at the foot of the ladder, her Medusa wig a few feet away. Her throat had been cut with a savage blow, as if by a sword.

The advertisement, in the Paris edition of the English-language *Herald-Tribune,* read simply: *New Medusa wanted for Mythology Fair. Apply Box X-45.*

Laura Charme read it twice and asked, "Sebastian, what's a Mythology Fair?"

Turned around in his chair, Sebastian Blue replied, "An interesting question. The Secretary-General would like an answer, too. A Swiss citizen named Otto Dolliman started it in Geneva about two years ago. On the surface it's merely a tourist attraction, but it might be a bit more underneath."

They were in Sebastian's office on the top floor of Interpol headquarters in Saint-Cloud, a suburb of Paris. It was the sort of day when the girls in the translating department ignored the calendar and wore their summer dresses one last time. Laura had started out in the translating department herself, before the Secretary-General teamed her with Sebastian, a middle-aged Englishman formerly of Scotland Yard, and set them to investigating airline crimes around the globe.

"What happened to the old Medusa?" she asked Sebastian.

"She was a West German airline stewardess named Gretchen Spengler. It seems she was murdered two weeks ago."

"Oh, great, and I'll bet I'm supposed to take her place! I've been through this sort of thing before!"

Sebastian smiled across the desk at her. "Blame the Secretary-General. It was his idea. Seems Miss Spengler was believed to be a key link in a gold-smuggling operation which in turn is part of the world-wide narcotics network."

"You'd better explain that to me," Laura said, tossing her long reddish-blonde hair. "Especially if I'm supposed to take her place at this Mythology Fair."

"It seems that a good deal of Mob money—skimmed off the receipts of gambling casinos—finds its way into Swiss banks. It's used to make purchases on the international gold market, and the gold in turn is smuggled from Switzerland to the Far East, where it's then used to buy morphine base and raw opium for the making of heroin. The heroin is then smuggled into the United States, completing the world-wide circle."

"And how was Gretchen Spengler smuggling the gold?"

"Interpol's suspicion is that it traveled in the large metal food containers along with the hot meals for the passengers. Such a hiding place would need the cooperation of a stewardess, of course, so the gold wouldn't be accidentally discovered. Gretchen worked at Otto Dolliman's Mythology Fair in Geneva during her spare time, between flights, and Interpol believes Dolliman or someone else connected with the Fair recruited her for the gold smuggling. Chances are she was murdered because we were getting too close to her."

Laura nodded. "I can imagine how they'll welcome me if they discover I work for Interpol. And what are you going to be doing while I'm shaking my serpents?"

"I won't be far away," Sebastian promised. "I never am, you know."

Geneva is a city of contrasts—small in size even by Swiss standards, yet still an important world crossroads and headquarters for a half-dozen specialized agencies of the United Nations, plus the International Red Cross and the World Council of Churches. The bustle at the airport reflected this cosmopolitan atmosphere, and Laura Charme was all but swallowed up in a delegation of arriving ministers.

Finally she fought her way to a taxi and gave the address of the Mythology Fair. "I take a great many tourists there," the driver informed her, speaking French. "Are you with a tour?"

"No. I'm looking for a job."

His eyes met hers in the mirror. "French?"

"French-English. Why do you ask?"

"I just wondered. The other girl was German."

"What happened to her?"

The driver shrugged. "She was killed. Such a shame—she was a lovely girl. Like you."

"Who killed her?"

"The police don't know. Some madman, certainly."

He was silent then, until at last he deposited her in front of a large old house overlooking Lake Geneva. Much of the front yard had been paved over and marked off for parking, and a big green tour bus sat empty near the entrance. Laura paid the driver and went up the steps to the open door.

The first person she saw was a gray-haired woman of slender build who seemed to be selling tickets. "Four francs, please," she said in French.

"I answered the advertisement for a new Medusa. I was told to come here for an interview."

"Oh, you must be Laura Charme. Very well, come this way." The woman led her past the ticket table and down a long corridor past framed portraits of various mythic heroes. She recognized Zeus and Jason and even the winged horse, Pegasus, but was stumped when it came to the women.

The gray-haired woman turned to her and said, in belated introduction, "I'm Helen Dolliman. My husband owns this." She gestured with her hand to include, apparently, the house and entire countryside.

"It's a beautiful place," Laura said. "I do hope I'll be able to work here."

The woman smiled slightly. "Otto liked the picture you sent. And it's difficult to get just the girl we want. I think you'll get the job." She paused before a closed door of heavy oak. "This is his office."

She knocked once and opened the door. The room itself was quite small, with only a single window covered by heavy wire mesh. The furnishings, too, were small and ordinary. But what set the room apart at once was the eight-foot-tall statue of King Neptune that completely dominated the far wall, crowding even the desk behind which a thin-haired middle-aged man was working.

"Otto," his wife announced, "this is Miss Charme, from Paris."

The man put down his pen and looked up, smiling. His face was drawn and his skin chalky-white, but the smile helped. "Ah, so good of you to come all this distance, Miss Charme! I do think you'll make a perfect Medusa."

"Thank you, I guess." Her eyes left his face and returned to the statue.

"You're admiring my Neptune."

"It's certainly . . . large."

He got up and stood beside it. "This is one of a series of the Roman gods, sculptured in the style of Michelangelo's Moses by the Italian Compoli in the last century. The trident that Neptune holds is very real, and quite sharp."

He lifted it from the statue's grasp and held it out to Laura. She saw the three spear-points aimed at her stomach and shuddered inwardly. "Very nice," she managed as he returned the weapon to its resting place with Neptune. "But tell me, just what is the Mythology Fair?"

"It is an exhibit, my dear girl—a live-action exhibit, if you will. All the gods and heroes and demons of myth are represented here—Greek, Roman, even Norse and Oriental. Our workrooms and dressing rooms are on the lower level. This level and the one above are open to the public for a small admission charge. They view paintings and statues representing the figures of myth—but more than that, they are entertained by live-action tableaux of famous scenes from mythology. Thus we have Ulysses returning to slay the suitors, the wooden horse at the walls of Troy, Perseus slaying Medusa, Cupid and Psyche, King Midas, Venus and Adonis, the labors of Hercules, and many others."

"Quite a bit of violence in some of those."

Otto Dolliman shrugged. "The public buys violence. And if some of our goddesses show a bit of bosom, the public buys that, too."

"I was wondering how someone like me could land the job of Medusa. I always thought she was quite ugly."

"It was the snakes in her hair that turned men to stone, my dear girl. And we will furnish those." He reached into the bottom drawer of his desk and produced a dark wig with a dozen plastic serpents hanging from it. As he held it out to Laura, the snakes began to move, seeming to take on a life of their own. Laura gasped and jumped back.

"They're alive!" she screeched.

"Not really," Mrs. Dolliman said, stepping forward to take the wig from her husband's hand. "We have little magnets in the snakes' heads, positioned so that the heads repel one another. They produce some quite realistic effects at times. See?"

Laura took a deep breath and accepted the wig. It seemed to fit her head well, though the weight of the magnetized serpents was uncomfortably heavy. "How long do I have to wear this thing?" she asked.

"Not more than a few minutes at a time," Dolliman assured her. "You come up through a trap door, hidden by some chemical mist, and Toby kills you with his sword. You fall back into the mist clouds, Toby reaches down, and holds a fake papier-mâché head aloft for the spectators to gasp at. I know it isn't exactly according to the myth—Medusa was asleep at the time of her death, for one thing—but the public enjoys it this way."

"Who's Toby?"

"What?"

"Who's Toby?" Laura repeated. "This fellow with the sword."

"Toby Marchant," Dolliman explained. "He's English, a nice fellow, really. He plays Perseus, and quite well, too. Come on, you might as well meet him."

Laura followed Otto and his wife out of the office and down the corridor to a wing of the great house. They passed a group of tourists, probably from the green bus out front, being guided through the place by a handsome young man, dressed in a black blazer, who bowed slightly as they passed.

"That's Frederick, one of our guides," Helen Dolliman explained. "With the guides and the actors, and a few workmen, we employ a staff of thirty-four people here. Of course many of the actors in the tableaux work only part time, between other jobs."

They paused before one stage, standing behind a dozen or so customers before a curtained stage. As the curtains parted Laura saw a bare-chested man who seemed to have the legs and body of a horse. She could tell it was a fake, but a clever one. "The centaur," Dolliman said. "Very popular with the tours. Ah, here is Toby."

A muscular young man about Laura's age, with shaggy black hair and a beard, came through a service door in the wall. He smiled at Laura, looking her up and down. "Would this be my new Medusa?"

"We have just hired her," Dolliman confirmed. "Laura Charme, meet Toby Marchant."

"A pleasure," she replied, accepting his hand. "But tell me, what have you been doing for a Medusa all these weeks?"

Toby Marchant shook his head sadly. "Venus has been filling in, but it's not the same. She has to run back and forth between the two stages. But she was doing it while Gretchen was flying, so she was the logical one to fill in." He glanced at Dolliman and brought his hand out from behind his back, revealing a paper bag. "Speaking of Gretchen—"

"Yes" Dolliman asked.

Toby opened the bag reluctantly and brought out the head of a young girl, covered with blood. Laura took one look and screamed.

Helen Dolliman motioned her to silence, glancing around to see who had heard the outburst. "It's only the papier mâché head we told you about," she explained quickly. You'll have to learn to control yourself better!"

"What is this place—a chamber of horrors?" Laura asked.

"No, no," Toby said, embarrassed and trying to calm her. "I shouldn't have pulled it out like that. It's just that the head was made to look like Gretchen and now she's dead. We can't use Venus' head. We'll need a new one made for Laura here, or the illusion will be ruined."

"I'll take care of it," Dolliman assured him. "Give me the bag."

Laura took a deep breath. "The taxi driver told me Gretchen was murdered. Did the police find her killer?"

"Not yet," Toby admitted. "But it must have been some sex fiend with one of the tours. Apparently he slipped downstairs and was waiting when she came through the trap door. I was right above her, but I never heard a thing."

"Toby was busy taking bows," Helen Dolliman snorted. "He wouldn't have heard a thing."

They went downstairs, showing Laura the dressing room that would be hers, the ladder leading to the trap door, the stage where she'd be beheaded five or six times daily, depending on the crowds. "Think you can do it?" Toby asked at the conclusion of a quick run-through.

"Sure," Laura said bravely. "Why not?"

A tall redhead wearing too much makeup came by, glancing up at the stage. "Better close that. Another bus just pulled up."

"This is our Venus and part-time Medusa," Toby said, making introductions. "Hilda Aarons."

Hilda grunted something meant to be a greeting and sauntered off. Laura was rapidly deciding that the Mythology Fair wasn't the friendliest place to work.

Sebastian Blue arrived two days after Laura started her chores as Medusa. He came with a group of touring Italians, but managed to separate himself from them, wandering off by himself down one of the side corridors.

"Can I help you?" a pleasant young man in a black blazer asked.

"Just looking around," Sebastian told him.

"I'm Frederick Braun, one of the tour guides. If you've become separated from your group I'd be glad to show you around."

Sebastian thought his blond good looks were strongly Germanic. He was a Hitler Youth, born thirty years too late. "I was looking for the director. I believe his name is Dolliman."

"Certainly. Right this way."

Otto Dolliman greeted Sebastian with a limp handshake and said, "No complaints, I hope."

"Not exactly. I represent the International Criminal Police Organization in Paris."

If possible, Dolliman's face grew even whiter. "Interpol? Is it about that girl's murder?"

"Yes, it is," Sebastian admitted. "We've had her under limited surveillance in connection with some gold-smuggling activities."

"Gretchen a gold smuggler? I can't believe that!"

"Nevertheless it seems to have been true. Didn't it ever strike you as strange that she continued working as an airline stewardess even after you hired her for your Mythology Fair?"

"Not at all, Mr. Blue. Both positions were essentially part-time. She worked charter flights and nonscheduled trips to the Far East mainly. And of course the bulk of her work here was during the vacation season and on weekends."

"Have you replaced her in the Fair?"

Dolliman nodded. "I hired a French girl just the other day. It's almost time for the next performance. Would you like to see it?"

"Very much."

Sebastian followed him down a hallway to the exhibit proper, where a string of little stages featured recreations of the more spectacular events of mythology. After watching a bearded Zeus hurl a cardboard thunderbolt, they moved on to the Medusa exhibit.

"That's Toby Marchant. He plays Perseus," Dolliman explained. The young man in a brief toga carried a sword and shield in proper Medusa-slaying tradition. He moved carefully through the artificial mist that rose from unseen pipes and acted out his search for the serpent-headed monster. Presently she appeared through the mist, up from the trap door. Sebastian thought Laura looked especially lovely in her brief costume. The snakes in her hair writhed with some realism, but otherwise she was hardly a convincing monster.

Toby Marchant, holding the shield protectively in front of him, swung out wildly with his sword. It was obvious he came nowhere near her, but Laura fell back into the mist with a convincing gasp. Toby reached down and lifted a bloody head for the spectators to gasp at.

"It was after this that Gretchen was killed," Dolliman explained in a whisper. "She slipped down through the trap door, and somebody was waiting at the foot of the ladder. Hilda found her about an hour later."

"Is it possible that Toby might have actually killed her in full view of the spectators?"

Dolliman shook his head. "The police have been all through this. The throat wound would have killed her almost instantly. She could never have gone through that trap door and down the ladder. Besides, the people would have seen it. There'd have been blood on the stage. She bled a great deal. Besides, his sword is a fake."

"That mist could have washed the blood away."

"No. Whoever killed her, it wasn't Toby. It was someone waiting for her below."

"The police report says the weapon was probably a sword."

"Unfortunately there are nearly fifty swords of various shapes and sizes on the premises. Some are fakes, like Toby's but some are the real thing."

"I'd like to speak to your new Medusa if I could," Sebastian said.

"Certainly. I'll call her."

After a few moments Laura appeared, devoid of snakes and wearing a robe over her Medusa costume. Sebastian motioned her down the corridor, where they could talk in privacy. "How's it going?"

"Terrible," she confessed. "I've had to do that silly stunt five times a day. Yesterday when I came through the trap door that guide, Frederick, was waiting down below to grab my leg. I thought for a minute I was going to be the next victim."

"Oh?"

"He seems fairly harmless, though. I chased him away and he went. How much longer do I have to be here?"

"Till we find out something. Has anyone approached you about smuggling gold?"

She shook her head. "And I even mentioned over breakfast yesterday that I'd once been an airline stewardess. I think the gold smugglers have switched to a different gimmick, but I don't know what it is."

They'd almost reached Otto Dolliman's office, and suddenly Toby Marchant hurried out. "Have you seen Otto?" he asked Laura. "He's not in his office and I can't find him anywhere."

"We left him not five minutes ago, down by the tableaux."

"Thanks," Toby said, and hurried off in that direction.

"He seemed quite excited," Sebastian remarked.

"He usually is," Laura said. "But he's a good sort."

They paused by the open door of Dolliman's office, and he asked, "Do you think Dolliman is the gold smuggler? Is there any way all this could be going on without his knowledge?"

"It seems unlikely," she admitted. "But if he's behind it, would he kill Gretchen right on the premises and risk all the bad publicity?"

"These days bad publicity can be good publicity. I'll wager the crowds have picked up since the killing."

At that moment Otto Dolliman himself came into view, hurrying along the corridor. "Excuse me," he said. "I have to place an important call."

Toby came along behind him and seemed about to follow him into the office, but Dolliman slammed the big oak door. Toby glanced at Sebastian and Laura, shrugged, and went on his way.

"Now what was that all about?" Laura wondered aloud.

"It's your job to find out, my dear," Sebastian reminded her.

They were just moving away from the closed office door when they heard a sound from inside. It was like a gasp, followed by the beginning of a scream.

"What's that?" Laura asked.

"Come on, something's happening in there!" Sebastian reached the office door and opened it.

Otto Dolliman was sprawled in the center of the little office, his eyes open and staring at the ceiling. The trident from King Neptune's statue had been driven into his stomach. There was little doubt that he was dead.

"My God, Sebastian!" Laura gasped.

He'd drawn the gun from his belt holster. "Stay here in the doorway," he cautioned. "Whoever killed him must be still in the room."

His eyes went from the partly open window with its wire-mesh grille to the cluttered desk and the statue of Neptune beside it. Then he stepped carefully back and peered behind the door, but there was no one.

The room was empty except for Otto Dolliman's body . . .

"The thing is impossible," Sebastian Blue said later, after the police had come again to the Mythology Fair with their cameras and their questions. "We were outside that door all the time and no one entered or left. The killer might have been hiding behind the desk when Dolliman entered the room, but how did he get out?"

"The window?"

He walked over to examine it again, but he knew no one could have left that way. Though the window itself had been raised a few inches, the wire-mesh grille was firmly bolted in place and intact. Sebastian could barely fit two fingers through the openings. The window faced the back lawn, with a cobblestone walk about five feet below. Obviously the grille was to keep out thieves.

"Nothing here," Sebastian decided. "It's an impossible crime—a locked room, except that the room wasn't actually locked."

"You must have had those at Scotland Yard all the time."

"Only in books, my dear." He frowned at the floor where the body had rested, then looked up at the mocking statue of Neptune.

"An arrow could pass through this grillework," Laura remarked, still studying the window. "And they use arrows in the Ulysses skit."

"But he wasn't killed with an arrow," Sebastian reminded her. "He was killed with a trident, and it was right here in the room with him." He'd examined the weapon at some length before the police took it away, and had found nothing except a slight scratch along its shaft. There were no fingerprints, which ruled out the remote possibility of suicide.

"A device of some sort," she suggested next. "An infernal machine rigged up to kill him as soon as he entered the office."

"A giant rubber band?" Sebastian said with a dry chuckle. "But he was in there for a few minutes before the murderer struck, remember? And besides, what happened to this machine of yours? There's no trace of it now."

"A secret passage? We know there are trap doors in the floors around here."

"The police went over every square inch. No, it's nothing like that."

"Then how was it done?"

Sebastian was staring up at Neptune's placid face. "Unless that statue came alive long enough to kill him, I don't see any solution." He turned and headed for the door. "But one person I intend to speak to is Toby Marchant."

They found Toby talking with Frederick and Hilda and some of the others in a downstairs dressing room. While Laura still tried to keep up the pretense that Sebastian Blue had merely been questioning her, he turned his attention to Toby, calling him aside.

"All right, Toby, it's time to quit playing games. Two people are dead now, and with Dolliman gone chances are you'll be out of a job anyway. What do you know about this?"

"Nothing, I swear!"

"But you were looking for Dolliman just before he was killed. You told him something that sent him hurrying to his office to make a phone call."

Toby Marchant hesitated. "Yes," he said finally. "I suppose I'll have to tell you about that, Mr. Blue. You see, I came across some information regarding Gretchen's death—information I thought he should know."

"And now he's dead, so should I know it."

Another hesitation. "It's about Hilda Aarons. I caught her going through some of Gretchen's things, apparently looking for something."

Sebastian glanced past his shoulder toward the tall redhead. She was watching them intently. "And you told Otto Dolliman about this?"

Toby nodded. "He asked us to watch out for anything suspicious. What I told him about Hilda seemed to confirm some information he already had. He said he had to make a phone call at once."

"But not to the police, apparently. He walked right by me and went into his office.

"He may not have trusted an outsider. Sometimes he acted as if he trusted only his wife."

"Have you seen Helen Dolliman recently?" Sebastian asked. He'd had only a few words with her before the police arrived.

"She's probably up in her room. Second floor, the far wing."

Sebastian found Helen Dolliman alone in her room, busy packing a single suitcase. Her eyes were red, as if from tears.

"You're leaving?"

"Do I have anything to stay here for?" she countered. "The police will shut us down now. And even if they don't, I have no intention of spending another night in the same house with a double murderer. He killed Otto and I'm probably next on his list."

"Do you have any idea why your husband was murdered?"

The little woman swept a wisp of hair from her eyes. "I suppose for the same reason the girl was."

"Which was?"

"The gold."

"Yes, the gold. What do you know about it?"

"About a year ago Otto caught a man with some small gold bars. He fired him on the spot, but we've always suspected there were others involved."

"Gretchen Spengler?"

"Yes. Before she died she told Otto she was getting out of it."

"Toby says he caught Hilda Aarons going through Gretchen's things after she was killed. He told Otto about it."

She nodded. "My husband discussed it with me. We were going to fire Hilda."

"Might that have caused her to kill him?"

"It might have, if she's a desperate person."

"Apparently he was trying to call someone about it just before he was killed."

"Perhaps," she said with a shrug, subsiding into a sort of willing acceptance.

He could see there was no more to be learned from her. He excused himself and went back down in search of Laura.

She was talking with Frederick Braun at the foot of the stairs, but the blond tour guide excused himself as Sebastian approached. "What was all that?"

"He's still after me," she said with a shrug. "I really think he's a frustrated Pan, speaking in mythological terms."

Sebastian frowned at the young man's retreating back, watching him go out the rear door of the house. Then he said, "We're going to have to move fast. Helen Dolliman is preparing to close the place and leave. Once everybody scatters we'll never get to the bottom of this thing."

"How can we get to the bottom of it anyway, Sebastian? We've got two murders, one of them an impossibility."

"But we've got a lead, too. Gretchen was killed and the smuggling by aircraft apparently ended. Yet the murderer has stayed on here at the Mythology Fair. We know that because he killed Dolliman, too. I reject for the moment the idea of two independent killers. So what have we? The gold smugglers still at work, but not using aircraft. They have found a new route for their gold, and we must find it, too."

"Let me work on it," Laura Charme said. Staring at an approaching group of tourists, she suddenly got an idea.

Night came early at this time of year, with the evening sun vanishing behind the distant Alps by a little after six. One of the tour groups was still inside the big house when Laura slipped out the rear door and moved around the cobblestone walk past the window to Dolliman's office. She came out at the far end of the paved parking area, near the single green tour bus that still waited there.

If the Mythology Fair was really closing down, she knew the smuggler should have to move fast to dispose of any remaining gold. And if she'd guessed right about these tour buses, she might see something very interesting as darkness fell.

She'd been standing in the shadows for about twenty minutes when the bus driver appeared from the corner of the building, carrying something heavy in both hands. He paused by the side of the vehicle and opened one of the luggage compartments. But he wasn't stowing luggage. Instead he seemed to be lifting up a portion of the compartment floor, shifting baggage out of the way.

Laura stepped quickly from the shadows and moved up behind him. "What do you have there?" she asked.

The man whirled at the sound of her voice. He cursed softly and grabbed an iron bar that was holding open the luggage compartment door. As the door slammed shut she saw him coming at her with the bar, raising it high overhead. She dipped, butting him in the stomach, and grabbed his wrist for a quick judo topple that sent him into the bushes by the house.

As he tried to untangle himself and catch his breath, she ripped the wrapper from the object he'd been carrying. Even in the near-darkness she could see the glint of gold.

Then she heard footsteps, and another man rounded the corner of the building. It was Toby Marchant. She rose to her feet and hurried to meet him. "Toby, that bus driver had a bar of gold. He was trying to hide it beneath the luggage compartment."

"What's this?" He hurried over to the bushes with her.

"Toby, I'll keep him here. You go find that Englishman, Sebastian Blue."

Toby turned partly away from her as the bus driver struggled to his feet. "Oh, I don't think we need Blue."

"Of course we need him! He's from Interpol, and so am I."

"That's interesting to know," Toby said. "But I already suspected it." He turned back toward her and now she saw the gun in his hand. "Don't make a sound, my dear, or you'll end up the way Gretchen and Otto did."

"I—"

"Tie her up, Gunter," he told the driver. "And gag her. We'll stow her in the luggage compartment and take her along for security."

Laura felt rough hands yank her wrists behind her. Then, suddenly, the parking area was flooded with light from overhead. Toby whirled and fired a shot without aiming. There was an answering shot as the bus driver dropped her wrists and started to run. He staggered and went down hard.

"Drop the gun, Toby," Sebastian called out from beyond the spotlights. "We want you alive."

Toby Marchant hesitated, weighing his chances, and then let the gun fall from his fingers.

It was some time later before Laura could get all the facts out of Sebastian Blue. They were driving back to the airport, after Toby Marchant had been turned over to the local police and the bus driver rushed to the hospital.

"How did you manage to get there in the nick of time?" she asked him. "I didn't tell you of my suspicions about the tour buses."

"No, but you didn't have to. I had my own suspicions of Toby, and I was watching him. I saw him meet the driver and get the gold bar from its hiding place. When I saw him point the gun at you, I switched on the overhead lights and then the shooting started. Luckily for us both, Toby had no idea how many guns were against him, so he chose to surrender."

"But how did you know Toby was involved in the smuggling?"

"I didn't, but I was pretty sure he'd committed both murders, which made him the most likely candidate."

"He killed Otto Dolliman in that locked room? But how?"

"There's only one way it could have been done, ruling out secret passages and invisible men. Remember that scratch along the shaft of the trident? Toby entered the office prior to Dolliman's arrival, removed the trident from the statue of Neptune, and thrust the shaft of it through the wire grating on the window. Remember, the window itself was open a few inches. Thus, the pronged head of the trident was inside the office, but the shaft was sticking out the window.

"Toby then got Otto to enter the office on some pretext—probably telling him to phone for urgent supplies of some sort—left the house, walked around the cobblestone path just outside, and positioned himself at the window. Perhaps Dolliman saw the trident sticking through the grillework and walked over to investigate. Or perhaps Toby called him to the window, pretending to find it like that. In either event, as Dolliman reached the window, Toby drove the trident into his stomach, killing him. He then pushed the shaft all the way through the wire grillework, so the trident remained in Dolliman's body and made it appear that the killer must have been in the room with him."

"But why did he want to kill him in a locked room?"

"He didn't. He was just setting up an alibi for himself, since we saw him leave Dolliman alive. He couldn't forsee that we'd remain outside the door and hear Dolliman's dying gasps. You see, once I figured out the method, Toby had to be the killer. We'd seen him come out of that office ourselves. And the killer had to be in the office prior to the killing to push the trident through the screen. He couldn't have it sticking out the window for long, risking discovery, so he had to lure Dolliman back to his office.

"That was where Toby made his big mistake. When we surprised him coming out of the office, he had to act as if he was frantically seeking Dolliman to tell him something. Later, when I asked what it was all about, he had to come up with a good lie. He said he'd told Dolliman he caught Hilda going through Gretchen's things. I suspect that was true, and that it involved your friend Frederick, the guide, but—Helen Dolliman later told me her husband had discussed the matter with her."

"Which meant," Laura said, "he must have told Dolliman about it much earlier."

"Exactly. Early enough for Dolliman to discuss it with his wife. And if Toby lied about the reason for luring Dolliman to his office, it figured that he also prepared the trident and killed him with it."

"What about Gretchen?"

"She wanted out of the gold smuggling, so he had to kill her—she knew too much. I suppose Dolliman was suspicious that Toby killed her, so Dolliman had to die, too. Either that, or Dolliman discovered that Toby was now using the tour buses to smuggle the gold out of Switzerland."

"But I thought we decided Toby couldn't have done it because he was still on stage when Gretchen went through the trap door to her death. Don't tell me we have another impossible crime?"

Sebastian shook his head. "Not really. Our mistake was in jumping to the conclusion that the killer was waiting for her. Actually, Toby went downstairs after the act was over and killed her then. I suppose he swung the sword at her in jest, just as he did on stage, only this time it was for real. She wouldn't even have screamed when she saw it coming at her."

"How awful!"

"But what about you? How did you tumble to the fact the tour buses were being used?"

Laura shrugged. "Partly intuition, I suppose. We figured the gold was still leaving the country, and not by plane. It just seemed a likely method. Tour buses cross boundary lines all the time, and they're not usually searched too carefully."

They came in sight of the airport and Sebastian said, "I imagine Paris will look good to you after this. Or did you enjoy playing Medusa?"

She grinned and held up the wig with its writhing snakes. "I brought it along as a souvenir. Just so we'll know the whole thing wasn't a myth."

Marcia Muller

(1944–)

Marcia Muller's series private investigator, Sharon McCone (who first appeared in 1977 in *Edwin of the Iron Shoes*), generally flies and detects solo. However, thoughout more than eighteen novel-length cases and more than a dozen short stories (most of which are collected in the 1995 Anthony Award–winning *The McCone Files*), McCone has amassed a large cast of ongoing series characters, the details of whose lives frequently are difficult for Muller to keep track of.

One of the foremost of these ongoing characters is McCone's assistant, Rae Kelleher, who was introduced in *There's Something in a Sunday* (1989). At first Kelleher is a young, insecure woman with a disordered life, but in later books she matures into a confident, capable investigator and finally takes a pivotal role in the 1996 novel *The Broken Promise Land*. In this, the second story narrated by Kelleher, Sharon McCone assigns her to a particularly obnoxious client, then finds herself enlisted by Rae to assist in a daring rescue.

Sharon McCone was the first of a vast number of contemporary American female private investigators. She began her career with the now-defunct All Souls Legal Cooperative, a San Francisco–based organization having its roots in the 1970s poverty law movement. In her fifteenth novel-length case, *Till the Butchers Cut Him Down* (1994), McCone went out on her own, establishing her agency while retaining office space in the co-op's Victorian, but she was soon to relocate to a renovated pier on the city's waterfront. McCone—who can alternately be compassionate, intuitive, highly professional, somewhat pompous, and exceedingly stubborn—has investigated cases set against such backgrounds as the aviation industry (*Both Ends of the Night,* 1997), the country music scene (*The Broken Promise Land,* 1996), terrorist bombings (*A Wild and Lonely Place,* 1995), and the ecology movement (*Where Echoes Live,* 1991), and is possibly the first of the current crop of female investigators to earn her private pilot's license. In 1993 the Private Eye Writers of America gave her creator their Life Achievement Award in recognition of her contribution to the genre.

THE HOLES IN THE SYSTEM

RAE KELLEHER AND SHARON McCONE
SAN FRANCISCO, CALIFORNIA
1996

T here are some days that just ought to be called off. Mondays are always hideous: The trouble starts when I dribble toothpaste all over my clothes or lock my keys in the car and doesn't let up till I stub my toe on the bedstand at night. Tuesdays are usually when the morning paper doesn't get delivered. Wednesdays are better, but if I get to feeling optimistic and go to aerobics class at the Y, chances are ten to one that I'll wrench my back. Thursdays—forget it. And by five on Friday, all I want to do is crawl under the covers and hide.

You can see why I love weekends.

The day I got assigned to the Boydston case was a Tuesday.

Cautious optimism, that was what I was nursing. The paper lay folded tidily on the front steps of All Souls Legal Cooperative—where I both live and work as a private investigator. I read it and drank my coffee, not even burning my tongue. Nobody I knew had died, and there was even a cheerful story below the fold in the Metro section. By the time I'd looked at the comics and found all five strips that I bother to read were funny, I was feeling downright perky.

Well, why not? I wasn't making a lot of money, but my job was secure. The attic room I occupied was snug and comfy. I had a boyfriend, and even if the relationship was about as deep as a desert stream on the Fourth of July, he could be taken most anyplace. And to top it off, this wasn't a bad hair day.

All that smug reflection made me feel charitable toward my fellow humans—or at least my coworkers and their clients—so I refolded the paper and carried it from the kitchen of our big Victorian to the front parlor and waiting-room so others could partake. A man was sitting on the shabby maroon sofa: bald and chubby, dressed in lime green polyester pants and a strangely patterned green, blue, and yellow shirt that reminded me of drawings of sperm cells. One thing for sure, he'd never get run over by a bus while he was wearing that getup.

He looked at me as I set the paper on the coffee table and said, "How ya doin', little lady?"

Now, there's some contention that the word "lady" is demeaning. Frankly, it doesn't bother me; when I hear it I know I'm looking halfway presentable and haven't got something disgusting caught between my front teeth. No, what rankled was the word "little." When you're five foot three the word reminds you of things

364

you'd just as soon not dwell on—like being unable to see over people's heads at parades, or the little-girly clothes that designers of petite sizes are always trying to foist on you. "Little," especially at nine in the morning, doesn't cut it.

I glared at the guy. Unfortunately, he'd gotten to his feet and I had to look up.

He didn't notice I was annoyed; maybe he was nearsighted. "Sure looks like it's gonna be a fine day," he said.

Now I identified his accent—pure Texas. Another strike against him, because of Uncle Roy, but that's another story.

"It *would've* been a nice day," I muttered.

"Ma'am?"

That did it! The first—and last—time somebody had gotten away with calling me "ma'am" was on my twenty-eighth birthday two weeks before, when a bagboy tried to help me out of Safeway with my two feather-light sacks of groceries. It was not a precedent I wanted followed.

Speaking more clearly, I said, "It would've been a nice day, except for you."

He frowned. "What'd I do?"

"Try 'little,' a Texas accent, and 'ma'am'!"

"Ma'am, are you all right?"

"Aaargh!" I fled the parlor and ran up the stairs to the office of my boss, Sharon McCone.

Sharon is my friend, mentor, and sometimes—heaven help me—custodian of my honesty. She's been all those things since she hired me a few years ago to assist her at the co-op. Not that our association is always smooth sailing: She can be a stern taskmaster and she harbors a devilish sense of humor that surfaces at inconvenient times. But she's always been there for me, even during the death throes of my marriage to my pig-selfish, perpetual-student husband, Doug Grayson. And ever since I've stopped referring to him as "that bastard Doug" she's decided I'm a grown-up who can be trusted to manage her own life—within limits.

That morning she was sitting behind her desk with her chair swiveled around so she could look out the bay window at the front of the Victorian. I've found her in that pose hundreds of times: sunk low on her spine, long legs crossed, dark eyes brooding. The view is of dowdy houses across the triangular park that divides the street, and usually hazed by San Francisco fog, but it doesn't matter; whatever she's seeing is strictly inside her head, and she says she gets her best insights into her cases that way.

I stepped into the office and cleared my throat. Slowly Shar turned, looking at me as if I were a stranger. Then her eyes cleared. "Rae, hi. Nice work on closing the Anderson file so soon."

"Thanks. I found the others you left on my desk; they're pretty routine. You have anything else for me?"

"As a matter of fact, yes." She smiled slyly and slid a manila folder across the desk. "Why don't you take this client?"

I opened the folder and studied the information sheet stapled inside. All it gave was a name—Darrin Boydston—and an address on Mission Street. Under the job description Shar had noted "background check."

"Another one?" I asked, letting my voice telegraph my disappointment.

"Uh-huh. I think you'll find it interesting."

"Why?"

She waved a slender hand at me. "Go! It'll be a challenge."

Now, that *did* make me suspicious. "If it's such a challenge, how come you're not handling it?"

For an instant her eyes sparked. She doesn't like it when I hint that she skims the best cases for herself—although that's exactly what she does, and I don't blame her. "Just go see him."

"He'll be at this address?"

"No, he's downstairs. I got done talking with him ten minutes ago."

"Downstairs? *Where* downstairs?"

"In the parlor."

Oh, God!

She smiled again. "Lime green, with a Texas accent."

"So," Darrin Boydston said, "did y'all come back down to chew me out some more?"

"I'm sorry about that." I handed him my card. "Ms. McCone has assigned me to your case."

He studied it and looked me up and down. "You promise to keep a civil tongue in your head?"

"I said I was sorry."

"Well, you damn near ruint my morning."

How many more times was I going to have to apologize?

"Let's get goin', little lady." He started for the door.

I winced and asked, "Where?"

"My place. I got somebody I want you to meet."

Boydston's car was a white Lincoln Continental—beautiful machine, except for the bull's horns mounted on the front grille. I stared at them in horror.

"Pretty, aren't they?" he said, opening the passenger's door.

"I'll follow you in my car," I told him.

He shrugged. "Suit yourself."

As I got into the Ramblin' Wreck—my ancient, exhaust-belching Rambler American—I looked back and saw Boydston staring at *it* in horror.

Boydston's place was a storefront on Mission a few blocks down from my Safeway —an area that could do with some urban renewal and just might get it, if the upwardly mobile ethnic groups that're moving into the neighborhood get their way. It shared the building with a Thai restaurant and a Filipino travel agency. In its front window red neon tubing spelled out THE CASH COW, but the bucking outline below the letters was a bull. I imagined Boydston trying to reach a decision: call it the Cash Cow and have a good name but a dumb graphic; or call it the Cash Bull and have a dumb name but a good graphic; or just say the hell with it and mix genders.

But what kind of establishment was this?

My client took the first available parking space, leaving me to fend for myself. When I finally found another and walked back two blocks he'd already gone inside.

Chivalry is dead. Sometimes I think common courtesy's obit is about to be published too.

When I went into the store, the first thing I noticed was a huge potted barrel cactus, and the second was dozens of guitars hanging from the ceiling. A rack of worn cowboy boots completed the picture.

Texas again. The state that spawned the likes of Uncle Roy was going to keep getting into my face all day long.

The room was full of glass showcases that displayed an amazing assortment of stuff: rings, watches, guns, cameras, fishing reels, kitchen gadgets, small tools, knickknacks, silverware, even a metronome. There was a whole section of electronic equipment like TVs and VCRs, a jumble of probably obsolete computer gear, a fleet of vacuum cleaners poised to roar to life and tidy the world, enough exercise equipment to trim down half the population, and a jukebox that just then was playing a country song by Shar's brother-in-law, Ricky Savage. Delicacy prevents me from describing what his voice does to my libido.

Darrin Boydston stood behind a high counter, tapping on a keyboard. On the wall behind him a sign warned CUSTOMERS MUST PRESENT TICKET TO CLAIM MERCHANDISE. I'm not too quick most mornings, but I did manage to figure out that the Cash Cow was a pawnshop.

"Y'all took long enough," my client said. "You gonna charge me for the time you spent parking?"

I sighed. "Your billable hours start now." Then I looked at my watch and made a mental note of the time.

He turned the computer off, motioned for me to come around the counter, and led me through a door into a warehouse area. Its shelves were crammed with more of the kind of stuff he had out front. Halfway down the center aisle he made a right turn and took me past small appliances: blenders, food processors, toasters, electric woks, pasta makers, even an ancient pressure cooker. It reminded me of the one the grandmother who raised me used to have, and I wrinkled my nose at it, thinking of those sweltering late-summer days when she'd make me help her with the yearly canning. No wonder I resist the womanly household arts!

Boydston said, "They buy these gizmos 'cause they think they need 'em. Then they find out they don't need and can't afford 'em. And then it all ends up in my lap." He sounded exceptionally cheerful about this particular brand of human folly, and I supposed he had good reason.

He led me at a fast clip toward the back of the warehouse—so fast that I had to trot to keep up with him. One of the other problems with being short is that you're forever running along behind taller people. Since I'd already decided to hate Darrin Boydston, I also decided he was walking fast to spite me.

At the end of the next-to-last aisle we came upon a thin man in a white T-shirt and black work pants who was moving boxes from the shelves to a dolly. Although Boydston and I were making plenty of noise, he didn't hear us come up. My client put his hand on the man's shoulder, and he stiffened. When he turned I saw he was only a boy, no more than twelve or thirteen, with the fine features and thick black hair of a Eurasian. The look in his eyes reminded me of an abused kitten my boyfriend Willie had taken in: afraid and resigned to further terrible experiences. He glanced from me to Boydston, and when my client nodded reassuringly, the fear faded to remoteness.

Boydston said to me, "Meet Daniel."

"Hello, Daniel." I held out my hand. He looked at it, then at Boydston. He nodded again, and Daniel touched my fingers, moving back quickly as if they were hot.

"Daniel," Boydston said, "doesn't speak or hear. Speech therapist I know met him, says he's prob'ly been deaf and mute since he was born."

The boy was watching his face intently. I said, "He reads lips or understands signing, though."

"Does some lip reading, yeah. But no signing. For that you gotta have schooling. Far as I can tell, Daniel hasn't. But him and me, we worked out a personal kind of language to get by."

Daniel tugged at Boydston's sleeve and motioned to the shelves, eyebrows raised. Boydston nodded, then pointed to his watch, held up five fingers, and pointed to the front of the building. Daniel nodded and turned back to his work. Boydston said, "You see?"

"Uh-huh. You two communicate pretty well. How'd he come to work for you?"

My client began leading me back to the store—walking slower now. "The way it went, I found him all huddled up in the back doorway one morning 'bout six weeks ago when I opened up. He was damn near froze but dressed in clean clothes and a new jacket. Was in good shape, 'cept for some healed-over cuts on his face. And he had this laminated card . . . wait, I'll show you." He held the door for me, then rummaged through a drawer below the counter.

The card was a blue three-by-five encased in clear plastic; on it somebody had typed I WILL WORK FOR FOOD AND A PLACE TO SLEEP. I DO NOT SPEAK OR HEAR, BUT I AM A GOOD WORKER. PLEASE HELP ME.

"So you gave him a job?"

Boydston sat down on a stool. "Yeah. He sleeps in a little room off the warehouse and cooks on a hotplate. Mostly stuff outta cans. Every week I give him cash; he brings back the change—won't take any more than what his food costs, and that's not much."

I turned the card over. Turned over my opinion of Darrin Boydston, too. "How d'you know his name's Daniel?"

"I don't. That's just what I call him."

"Why Daniel?"

He looked embarrassed and brushed at a speck of lint on the leg of his pants. "Had a best buddy in high school down in Amarillo. Daniel Atkins. Got killed in 'Nam." He paused. "Funny, me giving his name to a slope kid when they were the ones that killed him." Another pause. "Of course, this Daniel wasn't even born then, none of that business was his fault. And there's something about him . . . I don't know, he just reminds me of my buddy. Don't suppose old Danny would mind none."

"I'm sure he wouldn't." Damn, it was getting harder and harder to hate Boydston! I decided to let go of it. "Okay," I said, "My case-file calls for a background check. I take it you want me to find out who Daniel is."

"Yeah. Right now he doesn't exist—officially, I mean. He hasn't got a birth certificate, can't get a social security number. That means I can't put him on the payroll, and he can't get government help. No classes where he can learn the stuff I can't teach him. No SSI payments or Medicare, either. My therapist friend says he's one of the people that slip through the cracks in the system."

The cracks are more like yawning holes, if you ask me. I said, "I've got to warn you, Mr. Boydston: Daniel may be in the country illegally."

"You think I haven't thought of that? Hell, I'm one of the people that voted for Prop One-eighty-seven. Keep those foreigners from coming here and taking jobs from decent citizens. Don't give 'em nothin' and maybe they'll go home and quit using up my tax dollar. That was before I met Daniel." He scowled. "*Damn*, I hate moral dilemmas! I'll tell you one thing, though: This is a good kid, he deserves a chance. If he's here illegally ... well, I'll deal with it somehow."

I liked his approach to his moral dilemma, I'd used it myself a time or ten. "Okay," I said, "tell me everything you know about him."

"Well, there're the clothes he had on when I found him. They're in this sack; take a look." He hauled a grocery bag from under the counter and handed it to me.

I pulled the clothing out: rugby shirt in white, green, and navy; navy cords; navy-and-tan down jacket. They were practically new, but the labels had been cut out.

"Lands' End?" I said. "Eddie Bauer?"

"One of those, but who can tell which?"

I couldn't, but I had a friend who could. "Can I take these?"

"Sure, but don't let Daniel see you got them. He's real attached to 'em, cried when I took 'em away to be cleaned the first time."

"Somebody cared about him, to dress him well and have this card made up. Laminating like that is a simple process, though; you can get it done in print shops."

"Hell, you could get it done *here*. I got in one of those laminating gizmos a week ago; belongs to a printer who's having a hard time of it, checks his shop equipment in and out like this was a lending library."

"What else can you tell me about Daniel? What's he like?"

Boydston considered. "Well, he's proud—the way he brings back the change from the money I give him tells me that. He's smart; he picked up on the warehouse routine easy, and he already knew how to cook. Whoever his people are, they don't have much; he knew what a hotplate was, but when I showed him a microwave it scared him. And he's got a tic about labels—cuts 'em out of the clothes I give him. There's more, too." He looked toward the door; Daniel was peeking hesitantly around its jamb. Boydston waved for him to come in and added, "I'll let Daniel do the telling."

The boy came into the room, eyes lowered shyly—or fearfully. Boydston looked at him till he looked back. Speaking very slowly and mouthing the words carefully, he asked, "Where are you from?"

Daniel pointed at the floor.

"San Francisco?"

Nod.

"This district?"

Frown.

"Mission district? Mis-sion?"

Nod.

"Your momma, where is she?"

Daniel bit his lip.

"Your momma?"

He raised his hand and waved.

"Gone away?" I asked Boydston.

"Gone away or dead. How long, Daniel?" When the boy didn't respond, he repeated, "How long?"

Shrug.

"Time confuses him," Boydston said. "Daniel, your daddy—where is he?"

The boy's eyes narrowed and he made a sudden violent gesture toward the door.

"Gone away?"

Curt nod.

"How long?"

Shrug.

"How long, Daniel?"

After a moment he held up two fingers.

"Days?"

Headshake.

"Weeks?"

Frown.

"Months?"

Another frown.

"Years?"

Nod.

"Thanks, Daniel." Boydston smiled at him and motioned to the door. "You can go back to work now." He watched the boy leave, eyes troubled, then asked me, "So, what d'you think?"

"Well, he's got good linguistic abilities; somebody bothered to teach him words —probably the mother. His recollections seem scrambled. He's fairly sure when the father left, less sure about the mother. That could mean she went away or died recently and he hasn't found a way to mesh it with the rest of his personal history. Whatever happened, he was left to fend for himself."

"Can you do anything for him?"

"I'm sure going to try."

My best lead on Daniel's identity was the clothing. There had to be a reason for the labels being cut out—and I didn't think it was because of a tic on the boy's part. No, somebody had wanted to conceal the origins of the duds, and when I found out where they'd come from I could pursue my investigation from that angle. I left the Cash Cow, got in the Ramblin' Wreck, and when it finally stopped coughing, drove to the six-story building on Brannan Street south of Market where my friend Janie labors in what she calls the rag trade. Right now she works for a T-shirt manufacturer—and there've been years when I would've gone naked without her gifts of overruns—but during her career she's touched on every area of the business; if anybody could steer me toward the manufacturer of Daniel's clothes, she was the one. I gave them to her and she told me to call later. Then I set out on the trail of a Mission district printer who had a laminating machine.

Print and copy shops were in abundant supply there. A fair number of them did laminating work, but none recognized—or would own up to recognizing—Daniel's three-by-five card. It took me nearly all day to canvass them, except for the half-hour when I had a beer and a burrito at La Tacqueria, and by four o'clock I was totally discouraged. So I stopped at my favorite ice-cream shop, called Janie and found she was in a meeting, and to ease my frustration had a double-scoop caramel swirl in a chocolate chip cookie cone.

No wonder I'm usually carrying five spare pounds!

The shop had a section of little plastic tables and chairs, and I rested my weary feet there, planning to check in at the office and then call it a day. If turning the facts of the case over and over in my mind all evening could be considered calling it a day. . . .

Shar warned me about that right off the bat. "If you like this business and stick with it," she said, "you'll work twenty-four hours a day, seven days a week. You'll think you're not working because you'll be at a party or watching TV or even in bed with your husband. And then all of a sudden you'll realize that half your mind's thinking about your current case and searching for a solution. Frankly, it doesn't make for much of a life."

Actually it makes for more than one life. Sometimes I think the time I spend on stakeouts or questioning people or prowling the city belongs to another Rae, one who has no connection to the Rae who goes to parties and watches TV and—now—sleeps with her boyfriend. I'm divided, but I don't mind it. And if Rae-the-investigator intrudes on the off-duty Rae's time, that's okay. Because the off-duty Rae gets to watch Rae-the-investigator make her moves—fascinated and a little envious.

Schizoid? Maybe. But I can't help but live and breathe the business. By now that's as natural as breathing air.

So I sat on the little plastic chair savoring my caramel swirl and chocolate chips and realized that the half of my mind that wasn't on sweets had come up with a weird little coincidence. Licking ice-cream dribbles off my fingers, I went back to the phone and called Darrin Boydston. The printer who had hocked his laminating machine was named Jason Hill, he told me, and his shop was Quick Prints, on Mission near Geneva.

I'd gone there earlier this afternoon. When I showed Jason Hill the laminated card he'd looked kind of funny but claimed he didn't do that kind of work, and there hadn't been any equipment in evidence to brand him a liar. Actually, he wasn't a liar; he didn't do that kind of work *anymore*.

Hill was closing up when I got to Quik Prints, and he looked damned unhappy to see me again. I took the laminated card from my pocket and slipped it into his hand. "The machine you made this on is living at the Cash Cow right now," I said. "You want to tell me about it?"

Hill—one of those bony-thin guys that you want to take home and fatten up —sighed. "You from Child Welfare or what?"

"I'm working for your pawnbroker, Darrin Boydston." I showed him the ID he hadn't bothered to look at earlier. "Who had the card made up?"

"I did."

"Why?"

"For the kid's sake." He switched the Open sign in the window to Closed and came out onto the sidewalk. "Mind if we walk to my bus stop while we talk?"

I shook my head and fell in next to him. The famous San Francisco fog was in, gray and dirty, making the gray and dirty Outer Mission even more depressing than usual. As we headed toward the intersection of Mission and Geneva, Hill told me his story.

"I found the kid on the sidewalk about seven weeks ago. It was five in the morning—I'd come in early for a rush job—and he was dazed and banged up and bleeding. Looked like he'd been mugged. I took him into the shop and was going to call the cops, but he started crying—upset about the blood on his down jacket. I sponged it off, and by the time I got back from the restroom, he was sweeping the print-room floor. I really didn't have time to deal with the cops, so I just let him sweep. He kind of made himself indispensable."

"And then?"

"He cried when I tried to put him outside that night, so I got him some food and let him sleep in the shop. He had coffee ready the next morning and helped me take out the trash. I still thought I should call the cops, but I was worried: He couldn't tell them who he was or where he lived; he'd end up in some detention center or foster home and his folks might never find him. I grew up in foster homes myself; I know all about the system. He was a sweet kid and deserved better than that. You know?"

"I know."

"Well, I couldn't figure *what* to do with him. I couldn't keep him at the shop much longer—the landlord's nosy and always on the premises. And I couldn't take him home—I live in a tiny studio with my girlfriend and three dogs. So after a week I got an idea: I'd park him someplace with a laminated card asking for a job; I knew he wouldn't lose it or throw it away, because he loved the laminated stuff and saved all the discards."

"Why'd you leave him at the Cash Cow?"

"Mr. Boydston's got a reputation for taking care of people. He's helped me out plenty of times."

"How?"

"Well, when he sends out the sixty-day notices saying you should claim your stuff or it'll be sold, as long as you go in and make a token payment, he'll hang onto it. He sees you're hurting, he'll give you more than the stuff's worth. He bends over backwards to make a loan." We got to the bus stop and Hill joined the rush-hour line. "And I was right about Mr. Boydston helping the kid, too," he added. "When I took the machine in last week, there he was, sweeping the sidewalk."

"He recognize you?"

"Didn't see me. Before I crossed the street, Mr. Boydston sent him on some errand. The kid's in good hands."

Funny how every now and then when you think the whole city's gone to hell, you discover there're a few good people left. . . .

Wednesday morning: cautious optimism again, but I wasn't going to push my luck by attending an aerobics class. Today I'd put all my energy into the Boydston case.

First, a call to Janie, whom I hadn't been able to reach at home the night before.

"The clothes were manufactured by a company called Casuals, Incorporated," she told me. "They only sell by catalogue, and their offices and factory are on Third Street."

"Any idea why the labels were cut out?"

"Well, at first I thought they might've been overstocks that were sold through one of the discounters like Ross, but that doesn't happen often with the catalogue outfits. So I took a close look at the garments and saw they've got defects—nothing major, but they wouldn't want to pass them off as first quality."

"Where would somebody get hold of them?"

"A factory store, if the company has one. I didn't have time to check."

It wasn't much of a lead, but even a little lead's better than nothing at all. I promised Janie I'd buy her a beer sometime soon and headed for the industrial corridor along Third Street.

Casuals, Inc. didn't have an on-site factory store, so I went into the front office to ask if there was one in another location. No, the receptionist told me, they didn't sell garments found to be defective.

"What happens to them?"

"Usually they're offered at a discount to employees and their families."

That gave me an idea, and five minutes later I was talking with a Mr. Fong in personnel. "A single mother with a deaf-mute son? That would be Mae Jones. She worked here as a seamstress for … let's see … a little under a year."

"But she's not employed here anymore?"

"No. We had to lay off a number of people, and those with the least seniority are the first to go."

"Do you know where she's working now?"

"Sorry, I don't."

"Mr. Fong, is Mae Jones a documented worker?"

"Green card was in order. We don't hire illegals."

"And you have an address for her?"

"Yes, but I can't give that out."

"I understand, but I think you'll want to make an exception in this case. You see, Mae's son was found wandering the Mission seven weeks ago, the victim of a mugging. I'm trying to reunite them."

Mr. Fong didn't hesitate to fetch her file and give me the address, on Lucky Street in the Mission. Maybe, I thought, this was my lucky break.

The house was a Victorian that had been sided with concrete block and painted a weird shade of purple. Sagging steps led to a porch where six mailboxes hung. None of the names on them was Jones. I rang all the bells and got no answer. Now what?

"Can I help you?" an Asian-accented voice said behind me. It belonged to a stooped old woman carrying a fishnet bag full of vegetables. Her eyes, surrounded by deep wrinkles, were kind.

"I'm looking for Mae Jones."

The woman had been taking out a keyring. Now she jammed it into the pocket of her loose-fitting trousers and backed up against the porch railing. Fear made her nostrils flare.

"What?" I asked. "What's wrong?"

"You are from them!"

"Them? Who?"

"I know nothing."

"Please don't be scared. I'm trying to help Mrs. Jones's son."

"Tommy? Where is Tommy?"

I explained about Jason Hill finding him and Darrin Boydston taking him in.

When I finished the woman had relaxed a little. "I am so happy one of them is safe."

"Please, tell me about the Joneses."

She hesitated, looking me over. Then she nodded as if I'd passed some kind of test and took me inside to a small apartment furnished with things that made the thrift-shop junk in my nest at All Souls look like Chippendale. Although I would've rather she tell her story quickly, she insisted on making tea. When we were finally settling with little cups like the ones I'd bought years ago at Bargain Bazaar in Chinatown, she began.

"Mae went away eight weeks ago today. I thought Tommy was with her. When she did not pay her rent, the landlord went inside the apartment. He said they left everything."

"Has the apartment been rented to someone else?"

She nodded. "Mae and Tommy's things are stored in the garage. Did you say it was seven weeks ago that Tommy was found?"

"Give or take a few days."

"Poor boy. He must have stayed in the apartment waiting for his mother. He is so quiet and can take care of himself."

"What d'you suppose he was doing on Mission Street near Geneva, then?"

"Maybe looking for her." The woman's face was frightened again.

"Why there?" I asked.

She stared down into her teacup. After a bit she said, "You know Mae lost her job at the sewing factory?"

I nodded.

"It was a good job, and she is a good seamstress, but times are bad and she could not find another job."

"And then?"

" . . . There is a place on Geneva Avenue. It looks like an apartment house, but it is really a sewing factory. The owners advertise by word of mouth among the Asian immigrants. They say they pay high wages, give employees meals and a place to live, and do not ask questions. They hire many who are here illegally."

"Is Mae an illegal?"

"No. She was married to an American serviceman and has her permanent green card. Tommy was born in San Francisco. But a few years ago her husband divorced her and she lost her medical benefits. She is in poor health, she has tuberculosis. Her money was running out, and she was desperate. I warned her, but she wouldn't listen."

"Warned her against what?"

"There is talk about that factory. The building is fenced and the fences are topped with razor wire. The windows are boarded and barred. They say that once a worker enters she is not allowed to leave. They say workers are forced to sew eighteen hours a day for very low wages. They say that the cost of food is taken out of their pay, and that ten people sleep in a room large enough for two."

"That's slavery! Why doesn't the city do something?"

The old woman shrugged. "The city has no proof and does not care. The workers are only immigrants. They are not important."

I felt a real rant coming on and fought to control it. I've lived in San Francisco for seven years, since I graduated from Berkeley, a few miles and light years across the Bay, and I'm getting sick and tired of the so-called important people. The city is beautiful and lively and tolerant, but there's a core of citizens who think nobody and nothing counts but them and their concerns. Someday when I'm in charge of the world (an event I fully expect to happen, especially when I've had a few beers), they'll have to answer to *me* for their high-handed behavior.

"Okay," I said, "tell me exactly where this place is, and we'll see what we can do about it."

"Slavery, plain and simple," Shar said.

"Right."

"Something's got to be done about it."

"Right."

We were sitting in a booth at the Remedy Lounge, our favorite tavern down the hill from All Souls on Mission Street. She was drinking white wine, I was drinking beer, and it wasn't but three in the afternoon. But McCone and I have found that some of our best ideas come to us when we tilt a couple. I'd spent the last four hours casing—oops, I'm not supposed to call it that—conducting a surveillance on the building on Geneva Avenue. Sure looked suspicious—trucks coming and going, but no workers leaving at lunchtime.

"But what can be done?" I asked. "Who do we contact?"

She considered. "Illegals? U.S. Immigration and Naturalization Service. False imprisonment? City police and district attorney's office. Substandard working conditions? OSHA, Department of Labor, State Employment Development Division. Take your pick."

"Which is best to start with?"

"None—yet. You've got no proof of what's going on there."

"Then we'll just have to get proof, won't we?"

"Uh-huh."

"You and I both used to work in security. Ought to be a snap to get into that building."

"Maybe."

"All we need is access. Take some pictures. Tape a statement from one of the workers. Are you with me?"

She nodded. "I'm with you. And as backup, why don't we take Willie?"

"*My* Willie? The diamond king of northern California? Shar, this is an investigation, not a date!"

"Before he opened those discount jewelry stores Willie was a professional fence, as you may recall. And although he won't admit it, I happen to know he personally stole a lot of the items he moved. Willie has talents we can use."

"My tennis elbow hurts! Why're you making me do this?"

I glared at Willie. "Shh! You've never played tennis in your life."

"The doc told me most people who've got it have never played."

"Just be quiet and cut that wire."

"How d'you know there isn't an alarm?"

"Shar and I have checked. Trust us."

"I trust you two, I'll probably end up in San Quentin."

"Cut!"

Willie snipped a fair segment out of the razor wire topping the chain-link fence. I climbed over first, nearly doing myself grievous personal injury as I swung over the top. Shar followed, and then the diamond king—making unseemly grunting noises. His tall frame was encased in dark sweats tonight, and they accentuated the beginnings of a beer belly.

As we each dropped to the ground, we quickly moved into the shadow of the three-story frame building and flattened against its wall. Willie wheezed and pushed his longish hair out of his eyes. I gave Shar a look that said, *Some asset you invited along.* She shrugged apologetically.

According to plan we began inching around the building, searching for a point of entry. We didn't see any guards. If the factory employed them, it would be for keeping people in; it had probably never occurred to the owners that someone might actually *want* in.

After about three minutes Shar came to a stop and I bumped into her. She steadied me and pointed down. A foot off the ground was an opening that had been boarded up; the plywood was splintered and coming loose. I squatted and took a look at it. Some kind of duct—maybe people-size. Together we pulled the board off.

Yep, a duct. But not very big. Willie wouldn't fit through it—which was fine by me, because I didn't want him alerting everybody in the place with his groaning. I'd fit, but Shar would fit better still.

I motioned for her to go first.

She made an after-you gesture.

I shook my head.

It's your case, she mouthed.

I sighed, handed her the camera loaded with infrared film that I carried, and started squeezing through.

I've got to admit that I have all sorts of mild phobias. I get twitchy in crowds, and I'm not fond of heights, and I hate to fly, and small places make my skin crawl. This duct was a *very* small space. I pushed onward, trying to keep my mind on other things—such as Tommy and Mae Jones.

When my hands reached the end of the duct I pulled hard, then moved them around till I felt a concrete floor about two feet below. I wriggled forward, felt my foot kick something, and heard Shar grunt. *Sorry.* The room I slid down into was pitch black. I waited till Shar was crouched beside me, then whispered, "D'you have your flashlight?"

She handed me the camera, fumbled in her pocket, and then I saw streaks of light bleeding around the fingers she placed over its bulb. We waited, listening. No one stirred, no one spoke. After a moment Shar took her hand away from the flash and began shining its beam around. A storage room full of sealed cardboard boxes, with a door at the far side. We exchanged glances and began moving through the stacked cartons.

When we got to the door I put my ear to it and listened. No sound. I turned the knob slowly. Unlocked. I eased the door open. A dimly lighted hallway. There was another door with a lighted window set into it at the far end. Shar and I moved along opposite walls and stopped on either side of the door. I went up on tiptoe and peeked through the corner of the glass.

Inside was a factory: row after row of sewing machines, all making jittery up-and-down motions and clacking away. Each was operated by an Asian woman. Each woman slumped wearily as she fed the fabric through.

It was twelve-thirty in the morning, and they still had them sewing!

I drew back and motioned for Shar to have a look. She did, then turned to me, lips tight, eyes ablaze.

Pictures? she mouthed.

I shook my head. *Can't risk being seen.*

Now what?

I shrugged.

She frowned and started back the other way, slipping from door to door and trying each knob. Finally she stopped and pointed to one with a placard that said STAIRWAY. I followed her through it and we started up. The next floor was offices —locked up and dark. We went back to the stairwell, climbed another flight. On the landing I almost tripped over a small, huddled figure.

It was a tiny gray-haired woman, crouching there with a dirty thermal blanket wrapped around her. She shivered repeatedly. Sick and hiding from the foreman. I squatted beside her.

The woman started and her eyes got big with terror. She scrambled backwards toward the steps, almost falling over. I grabbed her arm and steadied her; her flesh felt as if it was burning up. "Don't be scared," I said.

Her eyes moved from me to Shar. Little cornered bunny-rabbit eyes, red and full of the awful knowledge that there's noplace left to hide. She babbled something in a tongue that I couldn't understand. I put my arms around her and patted her back —universal language. After a bit she stopped trying to pull away.

I whispered, "Do you know Mae Jones?"

She drew back and blinked.

"Mae Jones?" I repeated.

Slowly she nodded and pointed to the floor off the next landing.

So Tommy's mother *was* here. If we could get her out, we'd have an English-speaking witness who, because she had her permanent green card, wouldn't be afraid to go to the authorities and file charges against the owners of this place. I glanced at Shar. She shook her head.

The sick woman was watching me. I thought back to yesterday morning and the way Darrin Boydston had communicated with the boy he called Daniel. It was worth a try.

I pointed to the woman. Pointed to the door. "Mae Jones." I pointed to the door again, then pointed to the floor.

The woman was straining to understand. I went through the routine twice more. She nodded and struggled to her feet. Trailing the ratty blanket behind her, she climbed the stairs and went through the door.

Shar and I released sighs at the same time. Then we sat down on the steps and waited.

It wasn't five minutes before the door opened. We both ducked down, just in case. An overly thin woman of about thirty-five rushed through so quickly that she stumbled on the top step and caught herself on the railing. She would have been beautiful, but lines of worry and pain cut deep into her face; her hair had been lopped off short and stood up in dirty spikes. Her eyes were jumpy, alternately glancing at us and behind her. She hurried down the stairs.

"You want me?"

"If you're Mae Jones." Already I was guiding her down the steps.

"I am. Who are—"

"We're going to get you out of here, take you to Tommy."

"Tommy! Is he—"

"He's all right, yes."

Her face brightened, but then was taken over by fear. "We must hurry. Lan faked a faint, but they will notice I'm gone very soon."

We rushed down the stairs, along the hall toward the storage room. We were at its door when a man called out behind us. He was coming from the sewing room at the far end.

Mae froze. I shoved her, and then we were weaving through the stacked cartons. Shar got down on her knees, helped Mae into the duct, and dove in behind her. The door banged open.

The man was yelling in a strange language. I slid into the duct, pulling myself along on its riveted sides. Hands grabbed for my ankles and got the left one. I kicked out with my right foot. He grabbed for it and missed. I kicked upward, hard, and heard a satisfying yelp of pain. His hand let go of my ankle and I wriggled forward and fell to the ground outside. Shar and Mae were already running for the fence.

But where the hell was Willie?

Then I saw him: a shadowy figure, motioning with both arms as if he were guiding an airplane up to the jetway. There was an enormous hole in the chain-link fence. Shar and Mae ducked through it.

I started running. Lights went on on the corners of the building. Men came outside, shouting. I heard a whine, then a crack.

Rifle, firing at us!

Willie and I hurled ourselves to the ground. We moved on elbows and knees through the hole in the fence and across the sidewalk to the shelter of a van parked there. Shar and Mae huddled behind it. Willie and I collapsed beside them just as sirens began to go off.

"Like 'Nam, all over again," he said.

I stared at him in astonishment. Willie had spent most of the war hanging out in a bar in Cam Ranh Bay.

Shar said, "Thank God you cut the hole in the fence!"

Modestly he replied, "Yeah, well, you gotta do something when you're bored out of your skull."

Because a shot had been fired, the SFPD had probable cause to search the building. Inside they found some sixty Asian women—most of them illegals—who had been imprisoned there, some as long as five years, as well as evidence of other sweatshops the owners were running, both here and in southern California. The INS was called in, statements were taken, and finally at around five that morning Mae Jones was permitted to go with us to be reunited with her son.

Darrin Boydston greeted us at the Cash Cow, wearing electric-blue pants and a western-style shirt with the bucking-bull emblem stitched over its pockets. A polyester cowboy. He stood watching as Tommy and Mae hugged and kissed, wiped a sentimental tear from his eye, and offered Mae a job. She accepted, and then he drove them to the house of a friend who would put them up until they found a place of their own. I waited around the pawnshop till he returned.

When Boydston came through the door he looked down in the mouth. He pulled up a stool next to the one I sat on and said, "Sure am gonna miss that boy."

"Well, you'll probably be seeing a lot of him, with Mae working here."

"Yeah." He brightened some. "And I'm gonna help her get him into classes, stuff like that. After she lost her Navy benefits when that skunk of a husband walked out on her, she didn't know about all the other stuff that's available." He paused, then added, "So what's the damage?"

"You mean, what do you owe us? We'll bill you."

"Better be an honest accounting, little lady," he said. "Ma'am, I mean," he added in his twangiest Texas accent. And smiled.

I smiled, too.

Bill Pronzini

(1943-)

While professional women detectives proliferate in the 1990s and have inspired contemporary writers to create numerous fictional counterparts, such role models were few and far between in the nineteenth century. Those women who managed to defy the odds acquitted themselves admirably, a few so well that they have become historical footnotes; it is only fitting that they should also inspire modern fiction writers. For instance, Ed Gorman's 1990 novel, *Night of Shadows*, celebrates the achievements of Anna Tolan, the first uniformed policewoman, who began service with the Cedar Rapids, Iowa, police department in 1895. And Sabina Carpenter, one-half of the 1890s detective duo of Carpenter and Quincannon, is loosely based on the first woman private investigator, Kate Warne, who was a trusted employee of Allen Pinkerton in Baltimore in the years following the Civil War.

Sabina Carpenter and John Quincannon were introduced in *Quincannon* (1985), though each held a different job at that time—she as an undercover Pinkerton operative in Denver, he as a troubled U.S. Secret Service agent attached to the San Francisco office. The friendship that developed between them led, in the 1986 collaboration with Marcia Muller, *Beyond the Grave,* to the establishment of Carpenter & Quincannon, Professional Detective Services—something of a radical partnership for the Victorian era, and a platonic one despite Quincannon's best efforts to the contrary. Since then, the duo have been featured in a series of short stories, most of which deal with odd and seemingly impossible crimes; these are scheduled to be collected by Crippen & Landru in late 1998, under the title *Carpenter & Quincannon, Professional Detective Services*. Although Quincannon is the viewpoint character throughout the series and does much of the team's sleuthing, Sabina plays no small role and in fact provides the solution to more than one investigation, as she does in "The Desert Limited," the tale of a wanted felon's baffling disappearance from a fast-moving train.

Bill Pronzini is best known as the creator of the "Nameless Detective," a modern San Francisco private eye whose career began with *The Snatch* in 1971 and has continued to the present. The most recent "Nameless" novel, *Illusions* (1997), is his twenty-fourth full-length case; he also appears in numerous short stories, most of which have been collected in *Casefile* (1983) and *Spadework* (1996). Pronzini has also written virtually every other kind of popular fiction, including a mainstream political novel with columnist Jack Anderson, *The Cambodia File* (1981). Among his best work are two recent nonseries suspense novels, *Blue Lonesome* (1995), which was a *New York Times* Notable Book of the Year, and *A Wasteland of Strangers* (1997).

THE DESERT LIMITED

SABINA CARPENTER AND JOHN QUINCANNON
CALIFORNIA DESERT, 1890s
1995

Across the aisle and five seats ahead of where Quincannon and Sabina were sitting, Evan Gaunt sat looking out through the day coach's dusty window. There was little enough to see outside the fast-moving Desert Limited except sun-blasted wasteland, but Gaunt seemed to find the emptiness absorbing. He also seemed perfectly comfortable, his expression one of tolerable boredom: a prosperous businessman, for all outward appearances, without a care or worry, much less a past history that included grand larceny, murder, and fugitive warrants in three western states.

"Hell and damn," Quincannon muttered. "He's been lounging there nice as you please for nearly forty minutes. What the devil is he planning?"

Sabina said, "He may not be planning anything, John."

"Faugh. He's trapped on this iron horse and he knows it."

"He does if he recognized you, too. You're positive he did?"

"I am, and no mistake. He caught me by surprise while I was talking to the conductor; I couldn't turn away in time."

"Still, you said it was eight years ago that you had your only run-in with him. And at that, you saw each other for less than two hours."

"He's changed little enough and so have I. A hard case like Gaunt never forgets a lawman's face, any more than I do a felon's. It's one of the reasons he's managed to evade capture as long as he has."

"Well, what *can* he be planning?" Sabina said. She was leaning close, her mouth only a few inches from Quincannon's ear, so their voices wouldn't carry to nearby passengers. Ordinarily the nearness of her fine body and the warmth of her breath on his skin would have been a powerful distraction; such intimacy was all too seldom permitted. But the combination of desert heat, the noisy coach, and Evan Gaunt made him only peripherally aware of her charms. "There are no stops between Needles and Barstow; Gaunt must know that. And if he tries to jump for it while we're traveling at this speed, his chances of survival are slim to none. The only sensible thing he can do is to wait until we slow for Barstow and then jump and run."

"Is it? He can't hope to escape that way. Barstow is too small and the surroundings too open. He saw me talking to Mr. Bridges; it's likely he also saw the Needles station agent running for his office. If so, it's plain to him that a wire has been sent to Barstow and the sheriff and a complement of deputies will be waiting. I was afraid he'd hopped back off then and there, those few minutes I lost track of him shortly afterward, but it would've been a foolish move and he isn't the sort to panic. Even if he'd gotten clear of the train and the Needles yards, there are too many soldiers and Indian trackers at Fort Mojave."

"I don't see that Barstow is a much better choice for him. Unless...."

"Unless what?"

"Is he the kind to take a hostage?"

Quincannon shifted position on his seat. Even though this was October, usually one of the cooler months in the Mojave Desert, it was near-stifling in the coach; sweat oiled his skin, trickled through the brush of his freebooter's beard. It was crowded, too, with nearly every seat occupied in this car and the other coaches. He noted again, as he had earlier, that at least a third of the passengers here were women and children.

He said slowly, "I wouldn't put anything past Evan Gaunt. He might take a hostage, if he believed it was his only hope of freedom. But it's more likely that he'll try some sort of trick first. Tricks are the man's stock-in-trade."

"Does Mr. Bridges know how potentially dangerous he is?"

"There wasn't time to discuss Gaunt or his past in detail. If I'd had my way, the train would've been held in Needles and Gaunt arrested there. Bridges might've agreed to that if the Needles sheriff hadn't been away in Yuma and only a part-time deputy left in charge. When the station agent told him the deputy is an unreliable drunkard, and that it would take more than an hour to summon soldiers from the fort, Bridges balked. He's more concerned about railroad timetables than he is about the capture of a fugitive."

Sabina said, "Here he comes again. Mr. Bridges. From the look of him, I'd say he's very much concerned about Gaunt."

"It's his own blasted fault."

The conductor was a spare, sallow-faced man in his forties who wore his uniform and cap as if they were badges of honor. The brass buttons shone, as did the heavy gold watch chain and its polished elk's-tooth fob; his tie was tightly knotted and his vest buttoned in spite of the heat. He glanced nervously at Evan Gaunt as he passed, and then mournfully and a little accusingly at Quincannon, as if he and not Gaunt was to blame for this dilemma. Bridges was not a man who dealt well with either a crisis or a disruption of his precise routine.

When he'd left the car again, Sabina said, "You and I *could* arrest Gaunt ourselves, John. Catch him by surprise, get the drop on him . . . "

"He won't be caught by surprise—not now that he knows we're onto him. You can be sure he has a weapon close to hand and won't hesitate to use it. Bracing him in these surroundings would be risking harm to an innocent bystander."

"Then what do you suggest we do?"

"Nothing, for the present, except to keep a sharp eye on him. And be ready to act when he does."

Quincannon dried his forehead and beard with his handkerchief, wishing this was one of Southern Pacific's luxury trains—the Golden State Limited, for instance, on the San Francisco–Chicago run. The Golden State was ventilated by a new process that renewed the air inside several times every hour, instead of having it circulated only slightly and cooled not at all by sluggish fans. It was also brightly lighted by electricity generated from the axles of moving cars, instead of murkily lit by oil lamps; and its seats and berths were more comfortable, its food better by half than the fare served on this southwestern desert run.

He said rhetorically, "Where did Gaunt disappear to after he spied me with Bridges? He gave me the slip on purpose, I'm sure of it. Whatever he's scheming, that's part of the game."

"It was no more than fifteen minutes before he showed up here and took his seat."

"Fifteen minutes is plenty of time for mischief. He has more gall than a roomful of senators." Quincannon consulted his turnip watch; it was nearly two o'clock. "Four, is it, that we're due in Barstow?"

"Four oh five."

"More than two hours. Damnation!"

"Try not to fret, John. Remember your blood pressure."

Another ten minutes crept away. Sabina sat quietly, repairing one of the grosgrain ribbons that had come undone on her traveling hat. Quincannon fidgeted, not remembering his blood pressure, barely noticing the way light caught Sabina's dark auburn hair and made it shine like burnished copper. And still Evan Gaunt peered out at the unchanging panorama of sagebrush, greasewood, and barren, tawny hills.

No sweat or sign of worry on *his* face, Quincannon thought with rising irritation. A bland and unmemorable countenance it was, too, to the point where Gaunt would all but become invisible in a crowd of more noteworthy men. He was thirty-five, of average height, lean and wiry; and although he had grown a thin mustache and side-burns since their previous encounter, the facial hair did little to individualize him. His lightweight sack suit and derby hat were likewise undistinguished. A human chameleon, by God. That was another reason Gaunt had avoided the law for so long.

There was no telling what had brought him to Needles, a settlement on the Colorado River, or where he was headed from there. Evan Gaunt seldom remained in one place for any length of time—he was a predator constantly on the prowl for any illegal enterprise that required his particular brand of guile. Extortion, confidence swindles, counterfeiting, bank robbery—Gaunt had done them all and more, and served not a day in prison for his transgressions. The closest he'd come was that day eight years ago when Quincannon, still affiliated with the U.S. Secret Service, had led a raid on the headquarters of a Los Angeles-based counterfeiting ring. Gaunt was one of the koniakers taken prisoner after a brief skirmish and personally questioned by Quincannon. Later, while being taken to jail by local authorities, Gaunt had wounded a deputy and made a daring escape in a stolen milk wagon—an act that had fixed the man firmly in Quincannon's memory.

When he'd spied Gaunt on the station platform in Needles, it had been a much-needed uplift to his spirits: he'd been feeling less than pleased with his current lot. He and Sabina had spent a week in Tombstone investigating a bogus mining operation, and the case hadn't turned out as well as they'd hoped. And after more than twenty-four hours on the Desert Limited, they were still two long days from San Francisco. Even in the company of a beautiful woman, train travel was monotonous—unless, of course, you were sequestered with her in the privacy of a drawing room. But there were no drawing rooms to be had on the Desert Limited, and even if there were, he couldn't have had Sabina in one. Not on a train, not in their Tombstone hotel, not in San Francisco—not anywhere, it seemed, past, present, or future. Unrequited desire was a maddening thing, especially when you were in such close proximity to the object of your desire. His passion for his partner was exceeded only by his passion for profitable detective work; Carpenter and Quincannon, Lovers, as an adjunct to Carpenter and Quincannon, Professional Detective Services, would have made him a truly happy man.

Evan Gaunt had taken his mind off that subject by offering a prize almost as inviting. Not only were there fugitive warrants on Gaunt, but two rewards totaling five thousand dollars. See to it that he was taken into custody and the reward money would belong to Carpenter and Quincannon. Simple enough task, on the surface; most of the proper things had been done in Needles and it seemed that Gaunt was indeed trapped on this clattering, swaying iron horse. And yet the man's audacity, combined with those blasted fifteen minutes—

Quincannon tensed. Gaunt had turned away from the window, was getting slowly to his feet. He yawned, stretched, and then stepped into the aisle; in his right hand was the carpetbag he'd carried on board in Needles. Without hurry, and without so much as an eye flick in their direction, he sauntered past where Quincannon and Sabina were sitting and opened the rear door.

Close to Sabina's ear Quincannon murmured, "I'll shadow him. You wait here." He adjusted the Navy Colt he wore holstered under his coat before he slipped out into the aisle.

The next car back was the second-class Pullman. Gaunt went through it, through the first-class Pullman, through the dining car and the observation lounge, into the smoker. Quincannon paused outside the smoker door; through the glass he watched Gaunt sit down, produce a cigar from his coat pocket, and snip off the end with a pair of gold cutters. Settling in here, evidently as he'd settled into the day coach. Damn the man's coolness! He entered as Gaunt was applying a lucifer's flame to the cigar end. Both pretended the other didn't exist.

In a seat halfway back Quincannon fiddled with pipe and shag-cut tobacco, listening to the steady, throbbing rhythm of steel on steel, while Gaunt smoked his cigar with obvious pleasure. The process took more than ten minutes, at the end of which time the fugitive got leisurely to this feet and started forward again. A return to his seat in the coach? No, not yet. Instead he entered the gentlemen's lavatory and closed himself inside.

Quincannon stayed where he was, waiting, his eye on the lavatory door. His pipe went out; he relighted it. Two more men—a rough-garbed miner and a gaudily outfitted drummer—came into the smoker. Couplings banged and the car lurched slightly as its wheels passed over a rough section of track. Outside the windows a lake shimmered into view on the southern desert flats, then abruptly vanished: heat mirage.

The door to the lavatory remained closed.

A prickly sensation that had nothing to do with the heat formed between Quincannon's shoulder blades. How long had Gaunt been in there? Close to ten minutes. He tamped the dottle from his pipe, stowed the briar in the pocket of his cheviot. The flashily dressed drummer left the car; a fat man with muttonchop whiskers like miniature tumbleweeds came in. The fat man paused, glancing around, then turned to the lavatory door and tried the latch. When he found it locked he rapped on the panel. There was no response.

Quincannon was on his feet by then, with the prickly sensation as hot as a firerash. He prodded the fat man aside, ignoring the indignant oath this brought him, and laid an ear against the panel. All he could hear were train sounds: the pound of beating trucks on the fishplates, the creak and groan of axle play, and the whisper of the wheels. He banged on the panel with his fist, much harder than the fat man had. Once, twice, three times. This likewise produced no response.

"Hell and damn!" he growled aloud, startling the fat man, who turned quickly for the door and almost collided with another just stepping through. The newcomer, fortuitously enough, was Mr. Bridges.

When the conductor saw Quincannon's scowl, his back stiffened and alarm pinched his sallow features. "What is it?" he demanded. "What's happened?"

"Evan Gaunt went in here some minutes ago and he hasn't come out."

"You don't think he — ?"

"Use your master key and we'll soon find out."

Bridges unlocked the door. Quincannon pushed in first, his hand on the butt of his Navy Colt — and immediately blistered the air with a five-jointed oath.

The cubicle was empty.

"Gone, by all the saints!" Bridges said behind him. "The damned fool went through the window and jumped."

The lone window was small, designed for ventilation, but not too small for a man Gaunt's size to wiggle through. It was shut but not latched; Quincannon hoisted the sash, poked his head out. Hot, dust-laden wind made him pull it back in after a few seconds.

"Gone, yes," he said, "but I'll eat my hat if he jumped at the rate of speed we've been traveling."

"But — but he must have. The only other place he could've gone — "

"Up atop the car. That's where he did go."

Bridges didn't want to believe it. His thinking was plain: If Gaunt had jumped, he was rid of the threat to his and his passengers' security. He said, "A climb like that is just as dangerous as jumping."

"Not for a nimble and desperate man."

"He couldn't hide up there. Nor on top of any of the other cars. Do you think he crawled along the roofs and then climbed back down between cars?"

"It's the likeliest explanation."

"Why would he do such a thing? There's nowhere for him to hide *inside*, either. The only possible places are too easily searched. He must know that, if he's ridden a train before."

"We'll search them anyway," Quincannon said darkly. "Every nook and cranny from locomotive to caboose, if necessary. Evan Gaunt is still on the Desert Limited, Mr. Bridges, and we're damned well going to find him."

The first place they went was out onto the platform between the lounge car and the smoker, where Quincannon climbed the iron ladder attached to the smoker's rear wall. From its top he could look along the roofs of the cars, protecting his eyes with an upraised arm: the coal-flavored smoke that rolled back from the locomo-

389

tive's stack was peppered with hot cinders. As expected, he saw no sign of Gaunt. Except, that was, for marks in the thin layers of grit that coated the tops of both lounge car and smoker.

"There's no doubt now that he climbed up," he said when he rejoined Bridges. "The marks on the grit are fresh."

The conductor's answering nod was reluctant and pained.

Quincannon used his handkerchief on his sweating face. It came away stained from the dirt and coal smoke, and when he saw the streaks, his mouth stretched in a thin smile. "Another fact: No matter how long Gaunt was above or how far he crawled, he had to be filthy when he came down. Someone may have seen him. And he won't have wandered far in that condition. Either he's hiding where he lighted, or he took the time to wash up and change clothes for some reason."

"I still say it makes no sense. Not a lick of sense."

"It does to him. And it will to us when we find him."

They went to the rear of the train and began to work their way forward, Bridges alerting members of the crew and Quincannon asking questions of selected passengers. No one had seen Gaunt. By the time they reached the first-class Pullman, the urgency and frustration both men felt were taking a toll: preoccupied, Quincannon nearly bowled over a pudgy, bonneted matron outside the women's lavatory and Bridges snapped at a white-maned, senatorial gent who objected to having his drawing room searched. It took them ten minutes to comb the compartments there and the berths in the second-class Pullman: another exercise in futility.

In the first of the day coaches, Quincannon beckoned Sabina to join them and quickly explained what had happened. She took the news stoically; unlike him, she met any crisis with a shield of calm. She said only, "He may be full of tricks, but he can't make himself invisible. Hiding is one thing; getting off this train is another. We'll find him."

"He won't be in the other two coaches. That leaves the baggage car, the tender, and the locomotive; he has to be in one of them."

"Shall I go with you and Mr. Bridges?"

"I've another idea. Do you have your derringer with you or packed away in your grip?"

"In here." She patted her reticule.

"Backtrack on us, then; we may have somehow overlooked him. But don't take a moment's chance if he turns up."

"I won't," she said. "And I'll warn you the same."

The baggage master's office was empty. Beyond, the door to the baggage car stood open a few inches.

Scowling, Bridges stepped up to the door. "Dan?" he called. "You in there?" No answer.

Quincannon drew his revolver, shouldered Bridges aside, and widened the opening. The oil lamps were lighted; most of the interior was visible. Boxes, crates, stacks of luggage, and express parcels—but no sign of human habitation.

"What do you see, Mr. Quincannon?"

"Nothing. No one."

"Oh, Lordy, I don't like this, none of this. Where's Dan? He's almost always here, and he never leaves the door open or unlocked when he isn't. Gaunt? Is he responsible for this? Oh, Lordy, I should've listened to you and held the train in Needles."

Quincannon shut his ears to the conductor's babbling. He eased his body through the doorway, into an immediate crouch behind a packing crate. Peering out, he saw no evidence of disturbance. Three large crates and a pair of trunks were belted into place along the near wall. Against the far wall stood a wheeled luggage cart piled with carpetbags, grips, and war bags. More luggage rested in neat rows nearby; he recognized one of the larger grips, pale blue and floral-patterned, as Sabina's. None of it appeared to have been moved except by the natural motion of the train.

Toward the front was a shadowed area into which he couldn't see clearly. He straightened, eased around and alongside the crate with his Navy at the ready. No sounds, no movement ... until a brief lurch and shudder as the locomotive nosed into an uphill curve and the engineer used his air. Then something slid into view in the shadowy corner.

A leg. A man's leg, bent and twisted.

Quincannon muttered an oath and closed the gap by another half dozen paces. He could see the rest of the man's body then—a sixtyish gent in a trainman's uniform, lying crumpled, his cap off and a dark blotch staining his gray hair. Quincannon went to one knee beside him, found a thin wrist, and pressed it for a pulse. The beat was there, faint and irregular.

"Mr. Bridges! Be quick!"

The conductor came running inside. When he saw the unconscious crewman he jerked to a halt; a moaning sound vibrated in his throat. "My God, Old Dan! Is he —?"

"No. Wounded but still alive."

"Shot?"

"Struck with something heavy. A gun butt, like as not."

"Gaunt, damn his eyes."

"He was after something in here. Take a quick look around, Mr. Bridges. Tell me if you notice anything missing or out of place."

"What about Dan? One of the drawing-room passengers is a doctor."

"Fetch him. But look here first."

Bridges took a quick turn through the car. "Nothing missing or misplaced, as far as I can tell. Dan's the only one who'll know for sure."

"Are you carrying weapons of any kind? Boxed rifles, handguns? Or dynamite or black powder?"

"No, no, nothing like that."

When Bridges had gone for the doctor Quincannon pillowed the baggage master's head on one of the smaller bags. He touched a ribbon of blood on the man's cheek, found it nearly dry. The assault hadn't taken place within the past hour, after Gaunt's disappearance from the lavatory. It had happened earlier, during his fifteen-minute absence outside Needles—the very first thing he'd done, evidently, after recognizing Quincannon.

That made the breaching of the baggage car a major part of his escape plan. But what could the purpose be, if nothing here was missing or disturbed?

The doctor was young, brusque, and efficient. Quincannon and Bridges left Old Dan in his care and hurried forward. Gaunt wasn't hiding in the tender; and neither the taciturn engineer nor the sweat-soaked fireman had been bothered by anyone or seen anyone since Needles.

That took care of the entire train, front to back. And where the bloody hell was Evan Gaunt?

Quincannon was beside himself as he led the way back down-train. As he and Bridges passed through the forward day coach, the locomotive's whistle sounded a series of short toots.

"Oh, Lordy," the conductor said. "That's the first signal for Barstow."

"How long before we slow for the yards?"

"Ten minutes."

"Hell and damn!"

They found Sabina waiting at the rear of the second coach. She shook her head as they approached: her backtracking had also proven fruitless.

The three of them held a huddled conference. Quincannon's latest piece of bad news put ridges in the smoothness of Sabina's forehead, her only outward reaction. "You're certain nothing was taken from the baggage car, Mr. Bridges?"

"Not absolutely, no. Every item in the car would have to be examined and then checked against the baggage manifest."

"If Gaunt did steal something," Quincannon said, "he was some careful not to call attention to the fact, in case the baggage master regained consciousness or was found before he could make good his escape."

"Which could mean," Sabina said, "that whatever it was would've been apparent to us at a cursory search."

"Either that, or where it was taken from would've been apparent."

Something seemed to be nibbling at her mind; her expression had turned speculative. "I wonder ... "

"What do you wonder?"

The locomotive's whistle sounded again. There was a rocking and the loud thump of couplings as the engineer began the first slackening of their speed. Bridges said, "Five minutes to Barstow. If Gaunt is still on board—"

"He is."

"—do you think he'll try to get off here?"

"No doubt of it. Wherever he's hiding, he can't hope to avoid being found in a concentrated search. And he knows we'll mount one in Barstow, with the entire train crew and the authorities."

"What do you advise we do?"

"First, tell your porters not to allow anyone off at the station until you give the signal. And when passengers do disembark, they're to do so single file at one exit only. That will prevent Gaunt from slipping off in a crowd."

"The exit between this car and the next behind?"

"Good. Meet me there when you're done."

Bridges hurried away.

Quincannon asked Sabina, "Will you wait with me or take another pass through the cars?"

"Neither," she said. "I noticed something earlier that I thought must be a coincidence. Now I'm not so sure it is."

"Explain that."

"There's no time now. You'll be the first to know if I'm right."

"Sabina ... " But she had already turned her back and was purposefully heading forward.

He took himself out onto the platform between the coaches. The Limited had slowed to half speed; once more its whistle cut shrilly through the hot desert stillness. He stood holding onto the handbar on the station side, leaning out to where he could look both ways along the cars—a precaution in the event Gaunt tried to jump and run in the yards. But he was thinking that this was another exercise in futility. Gaunt's scheme was surely too clever for such a predictable ending.

Bridges reappeared and stood watch on the offside as the Limited entered the railyards. On Quincannon's side the dun-colored buildings of Barstow swam into view ahead. Thirty years ago, at the close of the Civil War, the town—one of the last stops on the old Mormon Trail between Salt Lake City and San Bernardino—

had been a teeming, brawling shipping point for supplies to and high-grade silver ore from the mines in Calico and other camps in the nearby hills. Now, with Calico a near-ghost town and most of the mines shut down, Barstow was a far tamer and less populated settlement. In its lawless days, Evan Gaunt could have found immediate aid and comfort for a price, and for another price, safe passage out of town and state; in the new Barstow he stood little enough chance—and none at all unless he was somehow able to get clear of the Desert Limited and into a hidey-hole.

A diversion of some sort? That was one possible gambit. Quincannon warned himself to remain alert for anything—anything at all—out of the ordinary.

Sabina was on his mind, too. Where the devil had she gone in such a hurry? What sort of coincidence—

Brake shoes squealed on the sun-heated rails as the Limited neared the station platform. Less than a score of men and women waited in the shade of a roof overhang; the knot of four solemn-faced gents standing apart at the near end was bound to be Sheriff Hoover and his deputies.

Quincannon swiveled his head again. Steam and smoke hazed the air, but he could see clearly enough: No one was making an effort to leave the train on this side. Nor on the offside, else Bridges would have cut loose with a shout.

The engineer slid the cars to a rattling stop alongside the platform. Quincannon jumped down with Bridges close behind him, as the four lawmen ran over through a cloud of steam to meet them. Sheriff Hoover was burly and sported a tobacco-stained mustache; on the lapel of his dusty frock coat was a five-pointed star, and in the holster at his belt was a heavy Colt Dragoon. His three deputies were also well-armed.

"Well, Mr. Bridges," the sheriff said. "Where's this man, Evan Gaunt? Point him out and we'll have him in irons before he can blink twice."

Bridges said dolefully, "We don't have any idea where he is."

"You don't— What's this? You mean to say he jumped somewhere along the line?"

'I don't know what to think. Mr. Quincannon believes he's still on board, hiding."

"Does he now." Hoover turned to Quincannon, gave him a quick appraisal. "So you're the flycop, eh? Well, sir? Explain."

Quincannon explained, tersely, with one eye on the sheriff and the other on the rolling stock. Through the grit-streaked windows he could see passengers lining up for departure; Sabina, he was relieved to note, was one of them. A porter stood between the second and third day coaches, waiting for the signal from Bridges to put down the steps.

"Damn strange," Hoover said at the end of Quincannon's recital. "You say you searched everywhere, every possible hiding place. If that's so, how could Gaunt still be on board?"

"I can't say yet. But he is — I'll stake my reputation on it."

"Well, then, we'll find him. Mr. Bridges, disembark your passengers. All of 'em, not just those for Barstow."

"Just as you say, Sheriff."

Bridges signaled the porter, who swung the steps down and permitted the exodus to begin. One of the first passengers to alight was Sabina. She came straight to where Quincannon stood, took hold of his arm, and drew him a few paces aside. Her manner was urgent, her eyes bright with triumph.

"John," she said, "I found him."

He had long ago ceased to be surprised at anything Sabina said or did; she was his equal as a detective in every way. He asked, "Where? How?"

She shook her head. "He'll be getting off any second."

"Getting off? How could he — ?"

"There he is!"

Quincannon squinted at the passengers who were just then disembarking: two women, one of whom had a small boy in tow. "Where? I don't see him — "

Sabina was moving again. Quincannon trailed after her, his hand on the Navy Colt inside his coat. The two women and the child were making their way past Sheriff Hoover and his deputies, none of whom was paying any attention to them. The woman towing the little boy was young and pretty, with tightly curled blond hair; the other woman, older and pudgy, powdered and rouged, wore a gray serge traveling dress and a close-fitting Langtry bonnet that covered most of her head and shadowed her face. She was the one, Quincannon realized, that he'd nearly bowled over outside the women's lavatory in the first-class Pullman.

She was also Evan Gaunt.

He found that out five seconds later, when Sabina boldly walked up and tore the bonnet off, revealing the short-haired male head and clean-shaven face hidden beneath.

Her actions so surprised Gaunt that he had no time to do anything but swipe at her with one arm, a blow that she nimbly dodged. Then he fumbled inside the reticule he carried and drew out a small-caliber pistol; at the same time, he commenced to run. Sabina shouted, Quincannon shouted, someone else let out a thin scream; there was a small scrambling panic on the platform. But it lasted no more than a few seconds, and without a shot being fired. Gaunt was poorly schooled on the mechanics of running while garbed in women's clothing: the traveling dress's long skirt tripped him before he reached the station office. He went down in a tangle of arms, legs, petticoats, and assorted other garments that he had wadded up and tied around his torso to create the illusion of pudginess He still clutched the pistol when Quincannon reached him, but one well-placed kick and it went flying. Quincannon then dropped down on Gaunt's chest with both knees, driving the wind out of him in a grunting hiss. Another well-placed blow, this one to the jaw with Quincannon's meaty fist, put an end to the skirmish.

Sheriff Hoover, his deputies, Mr. Bridges, and the Limited's passengers stood gawping down at the now half-disguised and unconscious fugitive. Hoover was the first to speak. He said in tones of utter amazement, "Well, I'll be damned."

Which were Quincannon's sentiments exactly.

"So that's why he assaulted Old Dan in the baggage car," Bridges said a short while later. Evan Gaunt had been carted off in steel bracelets to the Barstow jail, and Sabina, Quincannon, Hoover, and the conductor were grouped together in the station office for final words before the Desert Limited continued on its way. "He was after a change of women's clothing."

Sabina nodded. "He devised his plan as soon as he recognized John and realized his predicament. A quick thinker, our Mr. Gaunt."

"The stolen clothing was hidden inside the carpetbag he carried into the lavatory?"

"It was. He climbed out the window and over the tops of the smoker and the lounge car to the first-class Pullman, waited until the women's lavatory was empty, climbed down through that window, locked the door, washed and shaved off his mustache and sideburns, dressed in the stolen clothing, put on rouge and powder that he'd also pilfered, and then disposed of his own clothes and carpetbag through the lavatory window."

"And when he came out to take a seat in the forward day coach," Quincannon said ruefully, "I nearly knocked him down. If only I had. It would've saved us all considerable difficulty."

Hoover said, "Don't chastise yourself, Mr. Quincannon. You had no way of suspecting Gaunt had disguised himself as a woman."

"That's not quite true," Sabina said. "Actually, John did have a way of knowing —the same way I discovered the masquerade, though at first notice I considered it a coincidence. Through simple familiarity."

"Familiarity with what?" Quincannon asked.

"John, you're one of the best detectives I've known, but honestly, there are times when you're also one of the least observant. Tell me, what did I wear on the trip out to Arizona? What color and style of outfit? What type of hat?"

"I don't see what that has to do with—" Then, as the light dawned, he said in a small voice, "Oh."

"That's right," Sabina said, smiling. "Mr. Gaunt plundered the wrong woman's grip in the baggage car. The gray serge traveling dress and Langtry bonnet he was wearing are mine."

Barbara D'Amato

(1938-)

Barbara D'Amato's detecting duo of Chicago police officers Suze Figueroa and Norm Bennis made their first appearance in the short-story form. The half Italian, half Mexican policewoman and the black policeman are well-matched partners, and the often amusing interplay between them and the other members of their squad realistically mirrors police work. In 1996 the pair proved their ability to sustain a full-length work in the novel *Killer.app.* "Stop, Thief!" displays both their detecting abilities and their compassion as they go about their usual (and not so usual) daily business.

In addition to Figueroa and Bennis, D'Amato has created two other series characters: forensic pathologist Gerritt DeGraaf and freelance investigator Cat Marsala. The DeGraaf books (*The Hands of Healing Murder,* 1980; *The Eyes on Utopia Murders,* 1981) are traditional mysteries respecting all the conventions of the genre, while the Cat Marsala novels are broader in scope, examining various aspects of contemporary society.

The Marsala series had its genesis in an actual case that D'Amato researched for her true-crime book, *The Doctor, the Murder, the Mystery* (1992), for which she exhaustively researched the case of a Chicago physician convicted of murdering his wife in spite of a preponderance of evidence to the contrary. The author undertook many of the same tasks her fictional heroine works at and came away with the idea for *Hardball* (1990), in which Marsala investigates a campaign to legalize drugs in Illinois. Subsequent titles delve into similarly interesting areas, such as prostitution (*Hard Women,* 1993) and hospital trauma centers (*Hard Case,* 1994). The six Marsala novels, while hard-edged, are leavened by cynical good humor, and their protagonist conveys a strong moral sense without indulging in heavy-handed sermonizing.

STOP, THIEF!

SUSANNAH (SUZE) MARIA FIGUEROA AND NORM BENNIS
CHICAGO, ILLINOIS
1991

O fficer Susannah Maria Figueroa lounged back against one of the desks in the roll-call room. She was five feet one, which made her just the right height to be able to rest both buttocks on the desktop.

"See—this woman in a Porsche was driving along, minding her own business, on the way to an afternoon of serious shopping," she said to Officers Hiram Quail and Stanley Mileski, while her partner, Norm Bennis, taller than she was, lounged with one thigh against a neighboring desk, "and *whump*! she hits a cat in the street."

"I would think *moosh*! Not *whump*!" Mileski said. he was a skinny white guy, slightly stooped.

"She gets out," Figueroa said, "looks at the cat, head's okay, tail's okay, but it's flat as a wafer in the middle. Well, it's about three o'clock in the afternoon and she figures the kids'll be coming outa school soon and it's gonna upset the little darlings to see a squashed cat."

"Would," said Mileski. "Some. Then again, some of 'em would love it."

"So she picks it up real careful by the tail and puts it in a Bloomingdale's bag she had in the car and drives on to the mall with it."

"Type o' woman," said Norm Bennis, "who has lotsa extra Bloomie's bags." Bennis was a black man of medium height, built like a wedge. He had slender legs, broad chest, and very, very muscular shoulders.

"Right," said Figueroa, shrugging a little to settle her walkie-talkie more comfortably. "So she pulls up into the mall. Gets out to go in, she should hit Nieman Marcus before the rush starts, but the sun's shinin' down hard and she figures the car's gonna heat up and the cat's gonna get hot and smell up her car."

"Which it would," said Mileski.

"So she takes the bag and puts it up on the hood of the car to wait there while she's shopping. She goes in the mall. Meanwhile, along comes this other woman—"

"Nice lookin' lady," Bennis said. "Named Marietta."

"—who sees the bag there, thinks hah! Fine merchandise unattended, and takes it. Then this woman Marieta with the Bloomie's bag goes into the mall. She's a shoplifter. She's truckin' through the jewelry department at Houston's lookin' for something worth boostin', sees a pearl necklace some clerk didn't put back, picks it up, opens the Bloomie's bag, drops the necklace in, sees the cat, screams like a train whistle, and falls down in a dead faint. The store manager or some other honcho runs over, tries to revive her, slaps her face, but she sits up once, glances at the bag and falls over again in a dead faint, so they call the paramedics. The EMTs arrive, chuck her onto a gurney, put her Bloomie's bag between her feet, which is SOP with personal belongings, and whisk her out to the ambulance."

"Meanwhile," Bennis said, "the clerk at the jewelry counter's seen the pearls are missin'."

"Which is where we come in. By this time the woman's at the hospital, but by astute questioning of the store personnel, we put two and two together—"

"*Experience* and astute questioning, Suze my man," Bennis said. Bennis was thirty-five. Suze was twenty-six.

"—we figure out where the pearls are. So we roll on over to the hospital with lights and siren. Woman's in the emergency room and we just mosey on in and ask if we can dump out the bag. Orderly doesn't know enough to say no—"

"Sometimes you luck out," said Bennis.

"—so we turn the bag upside down and out flops the pearls plus the dead cat. At which point, the *orderly* faints."

"We were kinda surprised ourselves," Bennis said. "Didn't faint, though."

"Too tough," said Figueroa.

"Macho," said Bennis.

"Spent the next two hours in the district on the paper," Figueroa said.

"Odd, you know, when a supposed victim turns into a perp. Kinda felt sorry for her."

Figueroa said, "Not me, Bennis. She's a crook."

Mileski said, "Don't suppose they managed to revive the cat?"

Sergeant Touhy strode in and the third watch crew faded into seats.

Sergeant Touhy said, "Bennis? Figueroa? We've had a complaint from the hospital. Seems they don't like cat guts on their gurneys."

Bennis started to say, "We didn't know about the cat—" but Figueroa kicked him and muttered, "Probable cause!" so he shut up. "But we got our offender, Sarge," Suze Figueroa said.

"Yeah," Bennis said. "Boosts our solved record."

Touhy ignored them. "Next time, look in the bag first. Now let's read some crimes."

"You really need *three* ammo pouches?" Quail whispered at Figueroa. "You expecting a war?"

She whispered back. "Hey! You get in serious shit and I come in as backup you'll kiss my pouches."

Each ammo pouch held six rounds of .38 ammunition for the standard service revolver. You could fit three pouches, max, on your Sam Browne, though most officers didn't. Privately, Figueroa wished she could carry her ammo like the cowboys did, in loops all around the belt. But the department had a regulation that all ammo had to be concealed. Takes half the fun out, Figueroa thought.

She also thought it would be nice if Maintenance would wait to turn on the heat in here until the weather got cold. The roll-call room for the First District was never going to be a photo opportunity for *Architectural Digest*. But why not livable? The smell of hot wool and sweat was practically thick enough to see.

After ten minutes or so Touhy finished up with, "Pick up the new runaway list at the desk. Now, we've been getting more and more complaints from the senior-citizen groups in the neighborhood, and I'll tell you now I don't want the Gray Panthers on my ass. We got a lot of older people out there, they think they're under siege. From teenagers, more than our serious nasties. These are people who're specifically trying to get their grocery shopping done before the schools let out. Get back in their houses before the teenagers are set free. I mean, it's like three-thirty to them is when the Draculas come out. They get pushed, hassled. Yelled at. Called bad names. Get their groceries stolen."

"It happens," Mileski said.

"Not in *my* district it don't, Mileski!"

"Right, boss."

"Okay. Now hit the bricks and clear."

Norm and Suze were in an early car today, so they were on the street by three in the afternoon. They were beat car 1-33, patrolling the north end of the district.

Chicago's First District is unique among the twenty-five district stations in that it operates out of the big central cop-shop at 11th and State. It is also one of the most varied districts. It has world-class hotels of mind-boggling elegance and enough marble to stress the bedrock. It has the most soul-deadening public housing. It has staggeringly expensive jewelry emporiums and meretricious underwear stores where lewd sayings are embroidered on bras and panty bottoms. It has grade schools and premier medical schools and on-the-job training in crime and prostitution.

"One thirty-one?"

One thirty-one was Mileski and his partner, Hiram Quail. Suze and Norm heard Mileski's voice come back, "Thirty-one."

"I've got a car parked on a fire hydrant at 210 W. Grand."

"Ten-four, squad."

A new voice. "One twenty-seven."

"Twenty-seven. Go."

"I need an RD number for an attempted strongarm robbery."

"Uh—your number's gonna be 660932."

"Thanks much."

Norm and Suze rolled south on Wells, Norm driving and Suze doing a good eyeballing of the street. This part of Wells was a patchwork retail mix of run-down cigar and miscellany stores, trendy boutiques, newsstands that specialized in stroke magazines, cheap shoe stores, a Ripley's Believe It or Not Museum, coffee shops with early-bird special dinners and upscale yuppie restaurants where you could pay fifty bucks for a hundred calories. Four black teenagers, three of them boys with Gumby haircuts and one leotard-clad girl, cutting school and throwing shots at each other, lingered around a newsstand. They glanced at the squad car and looked away. A skinny white guy with a wispy beard passed them, cowboy-walking. "One of our known felons," Norm said.

"Brace him?" Suze said.

"He's not breakin' a law."

"Not right *now*."

"Be mellow, my man."

Coming the other way were two women in high heels, wearing fur coats that were hardly necessary, given the mild weather, the coats open in front, heavy gold chains swinging, very high heels, and purses dangling by their straps from one hand. Norm slowed. The white guy and the black kids watched the women peck their way along the street.

"Volunteer victims," Norm said.

The radio said, "Twenty-seven, your VIN is coming back clear."

"Ten-four."

"Thirty-one?"

"Thirty-one."

"We got a maroon Chevy blew the stoplight at—"

Norm shrugged as the women achieved the next block unharmed. He accelerated away from the curb. The radio said, "One thirty-three."

Suze picked up the mike. "Thirty-three."

"We got a shoplifting, Sounds of the Times, 279 Wells, two male whites, fifteen to eighteen years old."

"Somebody holding them?" Suze said.

"Nope. Fled on foot, knocked over an old man. Check on the man, plus see the manager. Mr. Stone."

The address was a block north of their car's beat boundary, but thirty-one was tied up, so it was reasonable for them to slide on over.

Sounds of the Times was one of the seriously trendy ones. The double window display, with glossy chrome-and-ebony frames around the windows and the entry between them, was laid out on sheets of casually rumpled blue denim. "Dance through the Decades" was spelled out in letters cut from sheet music that hung from barely visible threads above the display. There were rows of CDs, and beneath them rows of shoes of the period when the music was popular, starting in the left window with the 1890s, Strauss waltzes and kid pumps with little seed pearls, through Cuban heels and Friml with a gap where a CD had been taken out, and Billy Rose with T-strap dancing shoes, through the early fifties, saddle shoes then penny loafers and Nat "King" Cole. In the right windows the late fifties segued into Elvis and then the Beatles, with strap sandals, then Earth shoes, and acid rock, up to 2 Live Crew, and MC Hammer and in front of these a pair of inflatable Reeboks. A pretty nice window, Figueroa thought, although it would have been nicer-looking if the display hadn't been in such rigid rows.

The old man sat on a bench outside the store, trembling. Like many old men, his face looked like a peach—a three-day growth of soft white beard against an old pink skin. He was dressed in an aged windbreaker. He looked bitterly cold, despite the pleasant weather.

"See if he's hurt. I'll check with the manager," Norm said. The manager was striding toward the front door already. He wore a white shirt with navy and red sleeve garters and a navy vest and pants.

Suze sat down on the bench. "You okay?" she asked.

"I guess."

"What's your name, sir?"

"Minton. Raymond Minton."

"What happened to you, Mr. Minton?"

"Um—" He shook his head as if he wasn't sure.

"How old are you, Mr. Minton?"

"Eighty-seven," he said with some pride and complete clarity.

"And where do you live?"

"Fassbinder House."

Something less than a nursing home, more than a residence hotel. Figueroa knew it. Supervised living it was called, for the indigent elderly. About a block and a half west of here. She had been inside with a walkaway a couple of weeks before. It was functional.

Minton's head bobbed up and down on a skinny neck. The hair was thin and white on top of his head and hadn't been cut recently. Wisps of it moved in the breeze. The man needed a hat, Suze Figueroa thought. A wool hat.

"What happened here?" she said.

"Pushed me down." He was, sadly, not at all amazed. It had probably happened before.

"How? Where?"

"I was going out of the store. Under that alarm arch thing. One of 'em was just ahead of me. The other one was coming through and gave me a shove. Pushed me right down. Like I was—a door or something like that in his way. Just shoved me away. And then the alarm went off."

"You fell?"

"Mmm-mm." He pointed at his knee. The pants leg was roughed and a little blood soaked into the fabric from underneath. Thin blood, Figueroa thought.

"Can you stand on it?"

"Oh sure!" he said and got up to show her. He sat down immediately, a little sheepish at his weakness. But not as if anything was broken, Suze thought with some relief. The hand that lay in his lap was skinned on the palm and the ball of the thumb was bleeding. Caught himself on the hand and knee. Better that than break an elbow. She'd had one of them last week, and he'd screamed so much she could hardly hear the dispatcher to call for an ambulance.

"Wait here, please, Mr. Minton."

Bennis had got the manager calmed down. It wasn't that the guy was scared. Mr. Stone was angry, bright red in the face.

"Slouching around the store! I gotta keep my eyes on all of 'em at once!" he said. "I hate kids. Punks!"

"I guess *mosta* your customers are kids, though, huh?" Bennis said.

"Shit! Yeah!"

Bennis sighed; his mild suggestion that the store profited from teenagers had done nothing to honey up Mr. Stone. "So let me get a description."

"Punks!"

"Yeah, I know. Black punks or white punks?"

"I told you guys that when I called in!"

"Tell me again."

"White, and by the way—"

"Height?"

"Medium. Like five ten. One was maybe a little shorter than that."

"Weight?"

"Skinny. Both of 'em. Brown hair. And skinheads."

"Skinheads! Really?" Chicago didn't have many skinheads. Yet. Let's keep our fingers crossed, Bennis thought.

"Well, not *real* skinheads, but their hair was cut right to the scalp up to here," he said, indicating an inch above the tops of his ears. "I hate that bald haircut they wear."

"Eye color?"

"Hey! How'm I gonna see a thing like that? Sneaky little monsters keep their eyes squinted anyhow!"

Bennis said, "Clothes?"

"Black leather jackets, running shoes, Levi's. Jackets must've cost more than I make in a *week*."

At the clothing description, which narrowed it to maybe eighty percent of the teenagers in the city, Bennis sighed again, loud enough for Stone to hear him and frown. "Distinguishing features?"

"Ugly bastards. One was pimply. Other one was trying to grow a mustache. Hah! Smirking at me with five hairs on his upper lip!"

Bennis got on the radio and put out the description. Figueroa sidled over to the window displays. She looked at the gap.

"See which way they went?" Bennis asked Stone.

"Nah. Right into the crowd out there and zip!"

"Mr. Minton," Figueroa said, walking out the door, "did *you* see which way they went?"

"There."

Minton pointed south.

"Fled southbound," Bennis said. "Mr. Stone?"

"Yeah?"

"How many CDs did they have on 'em when they took off?"

"How do I know? Didn't even know there was a problem until the door alarm went off. There's the one missin' outa the window, but probably they loaded up before they boogied. Shit! Anyhow, by the time the alarm goes off they're outa here. Fat lot of good the alarm is. And that old guy's lyin' on the sidewalk. You don't think he's gonna sue us, do ya? The old guy?"

"I wouldn't know, Mr. Stone."

"Better not. His own fault, gettin' in the way."

Figueroa strolled around while Bennis told the dispatcher that the teens could have one or more stolen CDs on them.

"Never catch 'em now," Stone said. "Took you guys five minutes to get here."

"Two," Bennis said. "You called at 3:11. We rolled up at 3:13."

"Well, it's five minutes *now*. They could be anywhere."

Bennis shrugged. Too true.

Outside, Figueroa sat down on the bench next to the old man. "How's that knee now, Mr. Minton?" she said.

"Don't know." He stretched the leg out. The thin fabric of his worn pants pulled back from the blood-stained knee and he winced. He dragged his pants leg up a few inches with one blue-veined hand, picking the fabric loose from the skin. His shinbone looked sharp above the sagging sock.

"Are you married, Mr. Minton?" Figueroa said.

"Was. Her name was Helen. She's dead."

"How long have you been living at Fassbinder House?"

"Four years."

"How do you like it? Pretty Spartan?" For a second she wondered if he'd know what Spartan meant. Or would remember if he had once known. When he answered, she felt as chagrined as if she had been visibly condescending.

"It isn't bad. The food's warm."

And how basic that was, Figueroa thought.

"Mr. Minton, I guess you and your wife used to dance," Figueroa said. "To Friml."

He didn't answer.

"Do they have a CD player at the Fassbinder?"

He didn't answer.

"What do they play on it?"

The old man groaned. "Show tunes," he said. "Broadway shows. From the Forties and Fifties."

"I see."

"Do you? They think—the nice children who run the Fassbinder think—we were young in the Forties and Fifties. They can't imagine anybody being older than that. Young! I was forty-seven in 1950!" He started to laugh, laughed and laughed, showing missing teeth and an old tongue, creased and bluish-pink, laughed until he started to cough. But he caught himself then and quieted.

Figueroa said, "I'll tell the manager it was a mistake."

"Fourteen dollars for one disc!" he said. It could have been fourteen thousand.

"Give it to me, Mr. Minton, and I'll take it back."

He grabbed her arm in a bony grip. "I wouldn't have said the kids did it. I really wouldn't have. If they hadn't pushed me."

Bennis said, "How'd you know?"

"With a missing Friml? Kids these days aren't into that."

"Some could be, Suze my man."

"The kind wearing that sort of outfit? That kind of haircut?"

"Not likely."

"Scholarly types maybe. Plus, these kids were out of here by 3:11."

"So?"

"School's out at 3:30. They were cutting school. These are not your scholars, Bennis. If MC Hammer had been lifted, okay. But Rudolf Friml?"

Bennis nodded. They got back in the squad car.

"He gonna just skate, Figueroa?"

"Yeah, I cut him loose."

"Um——"

"Hey, Bennis, you figure he's gonna go on to a life of crime? He's eighty-seven years old."

"How we gonna put it down?"

"Unfounded."

"Okay."

"What's the matter?"

"I saw you buy the CD from Stone. For the old guy."

"Shit, don't look at me like that. I saved us two hours in the district handling the paper."

"Figueroa, my man, climb down. You are preaching to the converted. I already called in for fifteen minutes' personal time. I'm gonna buy you a cup of coffee."

"Why me?"

"I figure it'll take you that long to get over bein' human."

Ellen Dearmore

pseudonym of Erlene Hubly

(1936–1996)

"The Adventure of the Perpetual Husbands" combines two increasingly popular subgenres: the historical mystery and the lesbian mystery. In her tale of Gertrude Stein and Alice B. Toklas joining forces as a detecting duo, Ellen Dearmore evokes a strong sense of place and time; the political and social nuances of Paris and its expatriate American community in the 1920s are clearly reflected, and the presence of Ernest Hemingway as one of the story's focal characters adds authenticity. Dearmore published a second Stein–Toklas detective collaboration, "The Adventure of the Gioconda Smile," in which the pair investigate the theft of the *Mona Lisa*.

While the historical mystery, often using actual historical figures as protagonists, has long been a staple of the genre, the lesbian mystery has only recently gained acceptance. Novels with gay male protagonists, such as Joseph Hansen's Dave Brandstetter and George Baxt's Pharoah Love, have appeared from mainstream publishers since the mid-1960s, but most lesbian mysteries have been brought out by small presses, such as Crossing (which published the anthology in which "The Adventure of the Perpetual Husbands" first appeared) or Naiad. Sandra Scoppetone's 1991 novel, *Everything You Have Is Mine*, featuring lesbian private investigator Lauren Laurano, marked a watershed for the subgenre when it was published by Little, Brown, and Katherine V. Forrest's Los Angeles policewoman, Kate Delafield, has made the transition from small press to mainstream with publication of *Liberty Square* by Berkley in 1997. Mary Wings' Emma Victor novels, previously published by Crossing in the United States and The Women's Press in England, are also scheduled for mainstream publication.

THE ADVENTURE OF
THE PERPETUAL HUSBANDS

GERTRUDE STEIN AND ALICE B. TOKLAS
PARIS, FRANCE
1988

t was hard that fall of 1921, I remember, not to get interested in the Landru case. It was all everyone was talking about. "The Bluebeard of Paris," they were calling Henri Désiré Landru, because he had had so many wives and had murdered them all except one. And of course there were his lovers; all Paris knew of them. I would go into my favorite butcher shop, up on the rue de l'Odeon, and Monsieur Renard would greet me.

"Good morning, Mademoiselle Al-leece," he would say. "We have some nice tongue today. And what do you think of Landru? Two hundred eighty-three lovers! What a man! French to be sure!"

I did not like tongue and I did not like Landru and I most certainly did not like all those lovers. So I would say, "Monsieur Renard, the quality of your meat has fallen off since you became interested in the Landru case."

"Oh, no, Mademoiselle Al-leece," he would assure me. "I will not allow that!"

But, of course, he did.

All Paris did.

Gertrude was no exception.

Gertrude, of course, loved to read murder mysteries—sometimes as many as three a week. She also liked to think of herself as a detective. "It's the perfect crime," she said. "He murdered eleven people, and yet not one body has been found! What did he do with the bodies?"

The newspaper *Le Monde*, I remember, was asking the same question, and offering 5000 francs for the best answer.

"I have never won 5000 francs before," Gertrude said. "That would take us quite nicely to the south of France next summer. With that much money we could even stay through the fall. It's definitely worth my time."

So all of Paris went mad over Landru and Gertrude went mad over Landru and then finally, I am sorry to say, I did too. The day I found out about the *petite annonce*.

Four years earlier, in 1917, the year that Gertrude had bought her first Ford car and learned how to drive, Gertrude and I had been helping out in the war effort.

We were working for the American Fund for the French Wounded, delivering hospital supplies to a number of French cities. We were in and out of Paris all that year, first down to Perpignam, then back to Paris, and then on to Nîmes. But before we went to Nîmes I decided to get rid of the heavy old Smith Premier typewriters that I had been using for years. So I placed a *petite annonce* in the newspaper.

I remember my advertisement quite well. *For Sale: Smith Premier typewriter, excellent condition. Contact Alice Toklas, 27, rue de Fleurus, 6e.* It was during the war when people still trusted one another and thought nothing of placing a *petite annonce* in the newspaper, even mentioning their names and the fact that they were women, although after the war and the Landru case they thought twice about doing such a thing. But I placed my advertisement in the paper and several people came by and inquired about the typewriter. But none of them bought it. One thought it was too heavy and old—which it was—that's why I was trying to get rid of it. Another wanted a French typewriter with the cedilla and the circumflex and the Smith Premier was an English typewriter. I began to realize that selling this typewriter was going to take some time, and Gertrude and I didn't have much time then. So I withdrew the advertisement, put the Smith Premier back into the closet, and thought no more about it. Until the day four years later when Gertrude reminded me.

"Alice!" Gertrude came into the kitchen one afternoon, early in the case, while I was preparing dinner. She was obviously excited and out of breath and had a newspaper in her hand.

"Listen to this," she said, opening the newspaper. "It's about Landru."

"*It is by now quite clear that the way this most monstrous of murderers met his victims was through the means of the* petite annonce. *The unsuspecting woman would place her small classified in the newspaper, sometimes offering for sale items of jewelry or clothing, sometimes pieces of furniture. Answering her advertisement, presenting himself at her door, would be the pleasant, smiling, polite, soft-spoken, always confident Landru, ready to make an offer all the more liberal than the woman was asking, since his intention was to pay in other than cash. And how could these honest, but guileless starved-for-affection, middle-aged women know that this man who had suddenly appeared so innocently on their doorsteps, who was to flatter them and court them and who would marry ten of them, how could they know that it would be he who would take them on the darkest journey of all, to a death more horrible than any of them could imagine?*"

Gertrude looked up from the paper.

"Do you remember, during the war, when you were trying to sell the Smith Premier? You placed a *petite annonce* in the paper."

"I remember."

"What year was that?"

"Nineteen-seventeen. The year you bought the Ford.

"I thought so. Who answered the ad?"

"Three people—two men and a woman."

"Did either of the men have a beard?"

"No."

"Are you sure?"

"I always remember a beard."

"Then it wasn't Landru," Gertrude said, laying her paper down. "That's a relief! But don't you see how close you came? That's the way Landru met his victims— through the *petite annonce*. Nineteen-seventeen was his busiest year—he met and murdered five of his victims then. Don't you see? Landru could have come to this very house! One of the things he bought from one of the women he murdered was a *typewriter!*"

Gertrude looked at me, and I looked at her, but neither of us said another word.

That was when I became interested in the Landru case.

I am sure that if I had let her, Gertrude would have been content to spend the rest of her life in her chintz-covered chair by the fireplace, just thinking thoughts. I called her Sherlock Holmes on several occasions, but I could just as easily have called her Ralph Waldo Emerson or Sigmund Freud. For of all things in the world, Gertrude loved to think most of all.

I once said this to Picasso, her closest friend for many years.

"No," he said, "you're mistaken. Gertrude likes to move best of all. I think of Gertrude always in her car, driving through the countryside."

"Don't let that fool you," I said. "She moves in order to find things to think about."

Picasso was not sure of that but I was. Of all the things in the world, Gertrude liked to think best of all. And her favorite kind of thinking was the kind I could not understand.

I once read a book about some medieval monks who were called Scholastics and who spent their lives thinking about such things as how many angels could sit on the head of a pin or how many teeth a horse had. As for myself I have never been much interested in how many angels could sit on the head of a pin. And if I needed to know how many teeth a horse had, although I can't imagine why I would ever need to know such a thing, I certainly would not think about it. I would simply go find a horse, open its mouth, and count its teeth. But Gertrude was different. Gertrude liked to think about that horse, while sitting in her chintz-covered chair, and try to imagine how many teeth it had.

I once accused Gertrude of being a Scholastic, the last of the medieval monks, and she said, "That's not true. Thinking is essential to me, it is not an intellectual game. Every thought I have is another attempt for me to understand the world. I think so that I may live. I think so that I will know who I am and by knowing who I am know who others are too. I cannot exist without thoughts.

And so Gertrude thought.

So whereas most people would have started right off with the problem at hand, the one Le Monde was offering 5000 francs for, the one the police had not yet been able to solve—how Landru had disposed of the bodies of his eleven victims, ten wives and the son of one of the wives—Gertrude started off with something else. What kind of crime it was.

"It's a French crime," Gertrude said to me one night after dinner as we were sitting in the atelier. "French crimes are between men and their lovers and American crimes are between fathers and their children. Lizzie Borden is an American crime and Landru is a French crime. That's too bad. I understand American crimes much better. I must think about that."

So Gertrude thought about it and then, several nights later, brought up the subject again.

"Do you remember our discussion about French crimes and American crimes?"

"Yes."

"Well, I've written something. It's called An American Crime. I'd like to read it to you."

Gertrude began.

"An American Crime

Lizzie Borden took an axe
And gave her Mother forty whacks
When she saw what she had done
She gave her Father forty-one

I have thought about it often, that rhyme.

And who wrote it.

Some say a man wrote it and some say a woman wrote it but no one knows for sure.

It may be the most important part about the whole thing, that rhyme and who wrote it, surpassed only by the fact that Lizzie Borden was guilty but not in the eyes of a jury only in the eyes of God.

There is guilt and there is guilt, big guilt and little guilt and the question becomes who does the big guilt belong to and who does the little guilt belong to.

Some say the big guilt belongs to fathers and mothers but especially to fathers and I do not disagree. And some say the little guilt belongs to sons and daughters but most especially to daughters as they have fathers while sons mostly have mothers. And I do not disagree.

So there is big guilt and little guilt and fathers and daughters and mothers and sons but mostly fathers and daughters.

And daughters.

And daughters must be daughters until they marry or until their fathers die at which time they can become women. This in some respects is as difficult as being a daughter only not as difficult because you no longer have a father. Only some women even when they are women are still daughters so much did they have fathers. So it is difficult being a woman but it is more difficult being a daughter.

I know.

And by now I also know something else.

About the rhyme.

Who wrote it.

Most certainly a daughter."

Gertrude finished reading and then looked up.

"Do you understand what I am saying?

"You are writing about your father. And yourself. And, of course, the fact that Lizzie's father got one more whack than her mother. It's a nice piece, Gertrude, and I'm glad you wrote it. But I don't see what it has to do with the Landru case."

"It has nothing to do with the Landru case," Gertrude said, raising her voice. "But it was important for me to have that thought. Now I know about American crimes."

Somewhere early in the case Gertrude began keeping a file on Landru. She would go out once a day, sometimes even more, when the events of the trial had been especially sensational, and buy the latest newspaper accounts. I also remember the cheap pamphlets that were sold on the street. There was a biography of the one wife, Fernande Segret, who had somehow managed not to be murdered, although Landru had taken her out to the villa at Gambais where he had killed the others. She was only eighteen years old, and so the pamphlet was not very long. But it did, according to Gertrude, shed some light on the case. So bit by bit Gertrude began to put together a file on the Landru case.

"I've made a list," Gertrude said one night, as we were sitting in the studio, "of some of the things I want to think about in the Landru case. I must see it in words —if I am going to solve it."

Gertrude began reading from her list.

"Number One: the fact that Landru had 283 lovers.

"He had ten wives, too, but he also had 283 lovers. That may be the most startling fact about the whole case. Can you imagine?"

"I would prefer not to try."

"It would certainly take a lot of energy."

"To say nothing of deception."

"That's one way to look at it. Anther is to think that maybe he brought them some happiness, that but for him 283 women might possibly have never been loved."

"*Gertrude!* But we are talking about murder."

"Perhaps. But perhaps we are also talking about love."

"I think not."

"Maybe so."

"Number Two: his name: Henri Désiré Landru.

"His Christian name, Henri, which turned out not to be so Christian, after all. But *Henri.* Doesn't that bring to mind Henry VIII, who had six wives and murdered two of them? To this unfortunate name of *Henri* was added the even more difficult name Désiré. To desire. That explains the 283 lovers. You know my theory about names: to name is to claim, to name is to blame, to name is to determine. In this case it obviously determined.

"Number Three: Landru's appearance

"He's fifty-two years old, short—only five feet, six inches—bald, has a sallow complexion, and a long pointed beard. How then do we explain the uncanny attraction that women felt for him? There were his eyes, several of his lovers mentioned his eyes. 'Mesmerizing,' 'serpent-like,' 'charming.' But was that enough to cast such a spell? There is, of course, his car. Many of his women mention that. And there is no doubt that a car makes one more attractive to women. But does that car explain the whole attraction? Probably not."

"What's his sign?" I interrupted.

"What?"

"His astrological sign."

"Is that important?"

"It could be. It might even give us just the clue we need."

"You know I don't believe in that. We've got to stick *to the facts*, Alice."

Gertrude looked back at her list.

"Number Four: the famous death carnet.

"This notebook, of course, is the evidence that will finally send Landru to the guillotine. In it he lists the names of all his victims. The name is followed by a date, then by a time.

For example: 27th December 1916, Madame Collomb, 4:30 a.m.
12th April 1917, Mademoiselle Babelay, at 4 a.m.
1st September, 1917, Madame Buisson, 10:15 p.m.
26th November, 1917, Madame Jaume, at 5 a.m.

"The time is the time he murdered them, but how strange to record it. There is also this inscription beside each name: 'one single, one round-trip to Gambais.' He would buy himself a round-trip train ticket to Gambais, knowing that he would return to Paris. But as he also knew the woman who was with him would not return, he would buy her only a one-way ticket. How curious, and how curious to record it."

"And how mindful of his memory," I said. "He is obviously not a wasteful man."

Number Five: the question of what Landru did with the bodies of his eleven victims.

"This is, of course, the great mystery. The police speculate that he burned parts of the bodies—the most identifiable parts, heads and such—in the kitchen stove at Gambais. A pile of ashes, presumably some of the remains, was found in the shed in the back of his house. They also found teeth and bones belonging to three women in the shed. But where are the rest of the bodies, and how did he get rid of them? That is the question everyone would like to know."

Gertrude looked up from her list.

"These are the things I would like to think about. But before I can do that, I must think about something else. The man himself. What kind of man is Henri Désiré Landru? And how does his mind work? If I can understand the way his mind works, I will know what he did with the bodies."

"It's quite simple," I said. "He's a husband."

"A *husband?* I didn't think of that. But if so, a very peculiar one."

"A perpetual one."

Gertrude laughed.

"Is that a husband then? Or is that a contradiction in terms? One can be a husband once, but can one be a husband ten different times?"

"Eleven times. Landru had one legal wife. He didn't kill her."

"Can one be a husband eleven different times? I need to know what a husband is. I think I know, but maybe I don't. I will ask Hemingway."

Hemingway, of course, was the other perpetual husband in this adventure—he had four different wives before he was through, although at the time when Gertrude and I first knew him he had only one, his first, Hadley.

"There are two ways of looking at that," Gertrude used to say, referring to Hemingway's wives. "Either he liked marriage so much he wanted to keep experiencing it, only with a different wife each time. Or he didn't like marriage at all."

I was inclined to believe the latter.

Gertrude had just met Hemingway when this adventure took place, through her friend Sherwood Anderson. Gertrude was immediately taken with Hemingway; I was not. From the first I didn't trust him.

Most people think of Hemingway as a great boisterous man who hunted lions in Africa and fought bulls in Spain and who was afraid of nothing. But the Hemingway I knew in his early twenties was anything but that. He was so shy, in fact, that sometimes he couldn't even look me in the eye. That is because I frightened him, Gertrude used to say. But if that is so then everyone must have frightened him. Because I never saw him look anyone in the eye. Except, of course, Gertrude.

Perhaps the problem with Hemingway—of course there were several problems with Hemingway—but perhaps the first one was his wife, Hadley. Not that there was anything wrong with her. She was lovely and sweet and adored Hemingway in spite of what he later did to her and was probably doing to her all along. But the problem with Hadley was that Hemingway never brought her to the rue de Fleurus, as the other men brought their wives.

One of my jobs at the rue de Fleurus was to sit with the wives. This would free Gertrude to sit with the husbands and they would laugh and talk and have intellectual discussions while I would sit with the wives and talk about perfumes and hats and exchange recipes. I did not mind sitting with the wives. Sometimes they were interesting but most of the time they were not. But I did not mind. But the problem with Hemingway was that he never brought his wife and so I had no one to sit with. Hemingway would sit with Gertrude and they would laugh and talk, and all the time I would wonder what am I supposed to do? There is no one for me to sit with. So should I sit at all or should I just move around, pretending to sit, or should I just leave the room altogether?

There was no such problem with Picasso. When Picasso would come to visit Gertrude he would always bring Fernande and I would sit with Fernande and talk about hats and perfumes and exchange recipes, although Fernande was not much of a cook—rice was her specialty. And Gertrude would sit with Picasso and talk about art and artists. And then after a while Picasso would leave. But Hemingway never left.

So Hemingway was a husband although he didn't bring his wife and Gertrude wanted to know what that was like.

"What does it mean to be a husband?" she would ask Hemingway as they sat in the studio with their knees almost touching—although that was later, their knees almost touching. At first it was bottom on the floor, Hemingway sitting at Gertrude's feet, looking up. "I think I know, I almost know, but it is important for me to know. If I am to solve the Landru case."

"Do you want me to be frank?" I remember Hemingway asking one day. Of course Gertrude did.

"Well, then, it means that I can have sex with Hadley. Before I was married, I couldn't do that. I could have, but I didn't."

"That's quite interesting," Gertrude said. "But let me ask you this. If I were to have sex with you, Hemingway, would that make me your wife?"

"Yes, you would be, as long as we had gone through a marriage ceremony. No, wait. Can't a marriage be annulled—if the two people haven't slept together?"

"I think it can. So we would have to have sex in order to be husband and wife."

"Yes."

"Well, that gets us somewhere. But aren't there other considerations besides the legal ones? If you were my husband, for example, wouldn't that mean that you would feel some kind of emotional commitment toward me?"

"I wouldn't have to be your husband to feel that. I could feel it before we were married."

"Then we are back to the question of legality. All being a husband means is that one can, and must, have sex with one's wife."

"It looks like it."

I did not like to hear them talking this way, about what it meant to be a husband. Because I could hear the other conversation that was going on between them, the real one, and I disliked that one even more than the one they were saying out loud. That's when I started feeding Hemingway. I would go into the studio—because, of course, most of the time Hemingway was there I was in the kitchen—and would say to him, would you like some homemade plum liqueur—Hemingway loved my homemade liqueurs—or would you like a fresh scone, I have just baked them. Although I knew that I was feeding Hemingway and thus encouraging him to come again I also knew that I was keeping them from talking about what it meant to be a husband. Hemingway had that effect on some people. I have a *faiblesse* for Hemingway, a weakness, Gertrude would say. And while I most certainly did *not* have a *faiblesse* for Hemingway, I had to acknowledge him for Gertrude's sake. So I fed him scones and more scones until finally Gertrude said, "Thank you, Alice, but Hemingway has had quite enough scones."

But Hemingway was not much help with that question, I remember, about what it was like to be a husband. Of course he knew nothing about it. Gertrude was later to say, after her *faiblesse* had passed—he having never really been one. But at the time she thought Hemingway was one. He was everything, the sun, the moon, and oh, those eyes! she would say, *extraordinaire!*

"You are barking up the wrong tree," I said one day after a particularly exhausting session with Hemingway. "You are never going to get anywhere with the

Landru case as long as you think it's about husbands. Landru is a husband, but the case is about wives.

"*Wives?*"

"Yes. How all those women could have fallen for such a man, how not one of them ever suspected a thing, not even his real wife, the legal one. Didn't she ever wonder why he never came home, or what he was doing all the time he was away from her? And the others — the ten that he murdered. Didn't any of them wonder what kind of work he did? He didn't have a job. Didn't any of them wonder where he got his money from? And the one who got away. What was it she said when the police came to talk to her? I would do it all over again, I love him so. See? It's about wives."

"I hadn't thought of that."

Gertrude paused.

"Are you angry?" she asked. "You sound angry."

"No, it's just. . . ."

"What?"

"Hemingway. I wish he had a home of his own."

Gertrude laughed. "He's just young. And away from home for the first time."

"First time? He came to Europe years ago."

"Hemingway's just young, and a little frightened. And no matter how old he gets, it'll always be the same. He'll still be away from home for the first time. Don't be too hard on Hemingway."

It was hard not to be hard on Hemingway. Because almost every day there was something else.

Early in their relationship Gertrude had decided that she would teach Hemingway how to write. "I can do it one of two ways," she told him. "Either in the abstract or the concrete. Which would you prefer?"

"The concrete," he said.

"All right, then," Gertrude answered. "Bring over some of your stories."

"Yes," she said to him one day after she had read them. "Some of them are good but most of them are bad. I will say why in a minute but first I must say this. No one writes a story, Hemingway, in which a woman complains about the size of a man's sexual organ. You can, of course, but if you do you will be one kind of writer and I don't think you want to be that kind. You must define yourself from the first."

"I was just trying to portray reality as I see it."

Or as you wish it were, I thought.

"Well, don't," Gertrude said. "It's simply not done. It's *inaccrochable.* Nobody likes to be offended when they read."

"Now, then," Gertrude continued. "Let's talk about your writing. You need to learn many things, Hemingway, so many that I don't know where to begin. Perhaps with description. You seem fond of that."

"It's my favorite kind of writing."

"That may be so. But like all beginners you have tried to put in too much. When you describe the river you once went fishing in, for example. There's so much here that I can't see the river. You must start over, and concentrate."

Hemingway began describing the river to Gertrude, concentrating, and I thought here is a safe place for me to leave, I had to run some errands. I was gone for an hour or so and when I returned I went straight to the kitchen, as was my habit, and began to prepare dinner.

I hadn't been in the kitchen five minutes when I heard laughing and scuffling coming from the studio. Uh, oh, I thought, that does not sound like description. "That's not fair, Hemingway," I heard Gertrude cry out, "it's below the belt!" What is below the belt I wondered as I started for the studio. The scuffling got louder and louder and when I came to the studio door I saw why.

Gertrude and Hemingway were boxing!

"Hemingway didn't believe me," Gertrude called out, "when I told him I used to box when I was in medical school. We have a bet that I can't go three rounds with him. I'm winning!"

"Only because I'm letting you!"

They both dropped their gloves and looked at me.

"Don't let me interrupt anything important," I said.

Gertrude turned to Hemingway. "Put up your dukes," she said. "Or have you conceded defeat?"

Hemingway put up his dukes.

"OK, Hemingway," Gertrude said. "Prepare for a right to the jaw!"

I left the room.

I went back into the kitchen and started with dinner again although I must admit it was hard to concentrate on the brussel sprouts. I hadn't known that Gertrude had boxed when she was in medical school.

I said this to her later that night, after dinner.

"I was sure I had told you," Gertrude said. "At Johns Hopkins. I was a little overweight then and I thought the exercise would do me good. So I hired a sparring partner—Buzz Gleason. A welterweight. We boxed every night after dinner in the living room. It was when I was on East Eager Street. I've told you of East Eager Street?"

"Yes."

"But it didn't do any good, so I gave it up."

"Gertrude," I said. "I think you should tell Hemingway about us. He doesn't seem to know. I get the feeling he thinks you're available to anyone who comes along."

"That's hardly possible!" Gertrude laughed. "I'm old enough to be his mother! He's twenty-two years old!"

"That's why you should tell him."

"I can't, Alice. I don't know him well enough yet, and besides, I don't think he'd want to hear. No, we'll stay as we are. Hemingway and I need each other now. He needs to learn how to write and I need to teach him. And there's the Landru case. Perhaps later I'll tell him. But for now you'll just have to be patient about Hemingway. And you'll just have to trust me."

That was the trouble, I thought. I wasn't sure I could.

I remember quite well when it was that Gertrude began the second part of her investigation — the part, I might add, that she should have began with first — what Landru had done with the bodies of his eleven victims.

"Of course," Gertrude said one night as she was going through her file, "there are several questions about the bodies. An interesting one came up at the trial today. The defense brought up the fact that no blood had ever been found anywhere at Gambais — either in the kitchen where, supposedly, Landru burned some of the bodies, or out in the shed where he cut some of them up. That one's easy to answer. I know from my medical studies that if you let a dead body set for several days, then when you cut it up it will not bleed. So that problem is solved. Now we come to the difficult part — how he got rid of the bodies once he cut them up. *If* he cut them up. We know that he burned parts of them. They found one hundred kilos of ashes out in the shed. One hundred kilos — over two hundred pounds! That's a lot of ashes! How many bodies would that make?"

Gertrude thought about that for several days and then she seemed to stop thinking about it. And Hemingway didn't come around for a while and so I let my guard down and began to think that things had returned to normal.

That was my mistake.

I had been out shopping one day and returned to the rue de Fleurus around four in the afternoon. I opened the door and walked into the pavilion and knew immediately that something was wrong. I could see smoke in the hallway and I thought, the place is on fire!

I ran toward the kitchen and the smoke became thicker and there was a terrible smell and I thought what on earth is burning? Did I leave something in the oven? Then I got into the kitchen and saw that they were both there, Gertrude and Hemingway, standing next to my stove.

"Don't be alarmed," Gertrude said. "We are watching it closely."

"What on earth are you cooking?" I asked, running toward the stove. "The temperature is up to seven hundred degrees! You'll destroy my oven!"

419

"No," Gertrude said. "It's made of cast iron. It comes from America. It'll burn anything."

"What are you doing?"

"We're almost through," Gertrude said. "It won't be much longer. We're going to completely reduce a body to ashes, and then weigh them."

"A *body?*"

"Not a real body. A sheep's head. But the principle's the same. We've worked out a formula for converting the weight of the sheep's ashes to human bone density."

I turned to Hemingway. "*You* put her up to this!"

"No," Gertrude said. "I thought of it myself. But Hemingway's helping me. He's especially good at math."

I couldn't help it, as I stood there with my oven on fire and the smoke pouring out and Hemingway there, *in my kitchen,* I was so angry that I started to cry. There were so many tears that I finally had to leave the kitchen and go up to my bedroom. Gertrude came after me.

"Alice," she said, knocking on my door. "I'm sorry about the oven. But I'm sure we haven't destroyed it."

I didn't answer.

"I know how you feel about your kitchen. But it'll be the same again—as soon as it's aired."

I said nothing.

"I've asked Hemingway to leave. He's gone now."

Silence.

"I know when Landru was born," Gertrude said, changing the subject. "You asked me that once. His astrological sign."

I almost spoke, but caught myself.

"Pussy?" Gertrude said. "Please speak to me."

"Go away. I don't want to talk now."

Gertrude went away.

I sat there on the edge of the bed trying to calm myself and slowly I did. Then I thought this is the second time Landru has caused me trouble—first with my typewriter and now with my kitchen. There's only one thing left to do. I'll have to solve the case myself, and put an end to all this.

I am sick and tired of perpetual husbands!

The next morning while Gertrude was still asleep I went into the atelier and began going through her Landru file. I wasn't sure what I was looking for but I knew I would know when I saw it. I thumbed through the newspaper clippings, paused over a genealogical chart that traced Landru's ancestry back five generations, looked at the notes Gertrude had made along the margins of the chart, then went on. Near the bottom of the file, there was a pamphlet that caught my eye: "The Making of a Murderer: An Astrological Reading of the Mass Murderer Henri Désiré Landru." It was Landru's horoscope!

I quickly opened the pamphlet and saw there, on the first page, Landru's chart. Beneath the chart was a listing of the positions the planets had been in at the moment of Landru's birth.

Henri Désiré Landru, born 17 April 1869, 6 a.m. at
2° Latitude, 49° Longitude
Positions of Planets by Signs

Sun	22°	Aries
Moon	24°	Aries
Mercury	5°	Aries
Venus	15°	Aries
Mars	16°	Leo
Jupiter	26°	Aries
Saturn	26°	Aries
Uranus	13°	Cancer
Neptune	17°	Aries
Pluto	15°	Taurus
Ascendant	10°	Taurus

The first thing I noticed, as I looked at Landru's chart, was the large number of planets that had been in the sign of Aries when he was born. Seven of the ten planets were there—an amazing concentration! That figures, I thought. Aries are the bullies of the zodiac. Once would be enough, but to have it in your chart *seven different times!* No wonder all those women were murdered! As I continued to look at the chart I saw something even more amazing. Landru's ascendant was Taurus. My sun sign was Taurus so I knew about Taurus and I also knew that the ascendant could be as dominant a force as the sun sign itself. And if that were true and it was then I knew what that could mean.

So Landru's ascendant was Taurus.

Hmmmmm.

There was only one thing to do, I realized, as I lay the pamphlet down. Go to Gambais and check things out for myself.

Now that I knew what to look for.

•

I was taking no chances as I arose the next morning. I had suspected that Landru was an early riser. Most Tauruses are, having been born in late April or most of May when the weather starts to get nice and people want to be out of doors—just the opposite of Aquarians, who are born in the dead of winter and so never want to get up at all. But if Landru was an early riser then it might be important for me to get up even earlier than he had. So I had gotten up extra early, around four, and began to dress for my journey.

Gertrude, of course, was still asleep, having just gone to bed, and wouldn't be up until noon. I debated for a moment whether to leave her a note telling her where I was going, and then decided against it. With any luck, I would be back before noon and there would be no need to explain anything. Except, of course, the solution to the case.

I took a taxi to the Gare Montparnasse and got on the fast electric train that went to Versailles and got off halfway there at the town of Gambais. I call it a town but it was only a village, maybe not even that, just ten or twelve houses in a row along a cobblestone road. I walked through the town fairly quickly—it does not take long to pass ten houses—and I thought, where is Landru's villa? It was still very early, a little past five, and not many people were up yet. But I did manage to find one man who was delivering milk in a little cart he pushed over the cobblestones. "Landru's *villa?*" he snorted, after he had told me how to get there. "More like a broken-down pig sty."

I walked to the edge of town and started down the dirt road that led toward Landru's villa, all the time coming closer and closer to a forest that seemed to circle the edge of town. That forest was tempting to think about, with all those dark and hidden places to bury bodies in. But I thought no, forests belong to Sagittarians, not to Tauruses. I'm looking for something else.

I finally came to Landru's villa at the end of the road and saw what the milkman had meant. It was a small stone house, so small it looked more like the servant's quarters than the main house itself. The front gate was chain-locked and had a sign hanging across it: KEEP OUT, BY ORDER TO THE VERSAILLES POLICE. So much for going to the front door and looking in the windows, I thought, although it wasn't doors or windows I wanted, or even rooms. I walked around to the back of the house and saw the small shed that Gertrude had mentioned—where they had found the bones and teeth—and I thought I have seen enough here, but I have not seen it yet.

I walked back to town and walked around for another half-hour or so and found the cemetery and thought about that for a while. Then as I was walking back up the road toward the train station I saw a long line of lorries coming toward town and then turning off and going down a road. I watched them for some time. Then I walked back to town and found the local postman—by now the town was waking up—and talked to him. Then I walked back to the train station and got on the train and started back for Paris.

As the train pulled out of the station I looked at the clock above the station door. Seven forty-five, it said. It's a good thing I did get up extra early this morning, I thought, or I wouldn't have seen it.

So Landru *is* a Taurus, after all.

He, too, got up very early, in order to do his business.

I didn't see much of Gertrude that day. She had gotten up extra late, around two in the afternoon while I was out shopping, and by the time I had returned she was in the studio. I hadn't had time to go in and talk to her, as I usually did, having lost some of the morning hours and so having to work extra hard to make them up. It was not until dinner that we finally saw one another.

"I've been thinking about the Landru case all day," Gertrude said as we sat down to dinner.

"Oh? So have I."

"I've been thinking that perhaps I've gotten ahead of myself, that maybe I should go back to some of the earlier items on my list. My experiment with the sheep's head wasn't as successful as I had hoped."

"There's no need for that," I said. "I wanted to tell you earlier. I've solved the case."

Gertrude looked up.

"What?"

"I went to Gambais this morning—while you were asleep. I know what he did with the bodies."

"You've said nothing of this to me."

"I'm saying it now."

"But now?"

"I can't tell you. But I can show you—if you'll come to Gambais. But we'll have to get up early. We've got to be there before six."

"Six? *In the morning?* You know I can't do that!"

"That's up to you."

"Well, I could do this. I just won't go to bed tonight. That way I won't have to get up early—if I don't go to bed."

"That's one way of looking at it."

Gertrude and I left very early the next morning for Gambais. Gertrude, of course, didn't drive at night and as it was still dark we decided to take the electric train. Once we got to the station, however, there was a brief skirmish—Gertrude didn't like to ride public conveyances. But when it became obvious that the only way she was going to get to Gambais was on one—unless, of course, she wanted to walk—the skirmish was over. We got on the train and were in Gambais by five.

At first Gertrude was excited about being in Gambais, "the scene of the crime," as she called it.

"Why didn't I think of this before?" she said. "It's so much easier to visualize it when I'm here."

But once we got out to the villa and stood before it, she began to have doubts.

"It may have been easier," she said, "not seeing it. The villa is beginning to get in the way of my thoughts. It's becoming bigger than my thoughts and so I'm not having any thoughts. Maybe we should leave."

On the way back to town Gertrude began to feel better.

"I'm beginning to have thoughts again," she said. "I need to find a lake. He probably dumped the bodies in a lake."

"You're an Aquarius and so you thought of a lake. But he didn't. He thought of something better. Come and I'll show you."

We walked back through town and reached its eastern edge and that was when I saw them again, regular as clockwork, coming down the road, the long line of lorries.

"Do you see those?" I asked Gertrude.

"Sure. Trucks."

"*Garbage* trucks," I corrected. "Making their morning run in from Paris. They start coming in each morning around six."

"Very interesting. But I've seen garbage trucks before."

"Not *these* garbage trucks. Come with me."

We started walking down the road, following the lorries. It was no a long walk but it was a dusty one and by the time Gertrude and I had reached the quarry pits we were both coughing.

"You know I don't like to cough," Gertrude said, coughing.

"It's not much farther."

We came to the quarry pits and stopped.

"These pits go back for miles," I said. "Right up to the edge of the Rambouillet Forest. For the past six years the city of Paris has been dumping some of its garbage here."

"What are you saying?"

"That Landru knew of these pits, that he knew the trucks came here early each morning and dumped tons of garbage into them, and that he brought the bodies of his victims here and threw them into the pits. What better place to put dead bodies —than in a garbage pit, where he knew they would soon be covered with tons of garbage?"

"Ummmm," Gertrude said. "It's possible. Where were you standing when you first had this idea?"

"Over there." I pointed to a promontory that jutted out over one of the pits. Gertrude walked over to the promontory and stood on it.

"Yes," she said. "I'm beginning to see what you mean. But there are many pits. Wouldn't that have been a problem?"

"Why?"

"Surely the trucks do not get to each pit each day. Wouldn't there have been the risk that the body might not be covered up right away?"

"But didn't you say he cut the bodies up?"

"Yes—into small pieces. Of course! That would solve the problem! They'd blend in with all the other garbage and not be noticed."

"Yes."

"There's this as well," Gertrude said, stepping down off the promontory. "The smell. I like that even less than I like to cough and so we must leave soon. But the smell of this place would have kept all but the garbage men away. It's certainly not the kind of place where people would come for picnics. So Landru was safe there too. No one would be here to see him dump the bodies.

We began to walk back toward town.

"What made you think of these pits?" Gertrude asked.

"Landru's horoscope. Of course, I saw the lorries. But before I saw them I knew what I was looking for. Landru is a Taurus—or at least his ascendant is Taurus."

"You know I don't believe in that."

"Some people do. And show me a Taurus and I'll show you a garden—or in Landru's case, a garbage pit. I knew he'd try to bury the bodies somewhere—Tauruses love to dig in the earth. So I looked for some graves at the villa. Of course there weren't any—that would have been too obvious. It's the first place the police would have looked. Then I found the cemetery in town. What a clever place to bury a few extra bodies—in a place already full of them. But when I talked to the postman at Gambais, he said that the police had already checked the cemetery. In fact, all the cemeteries in the province have been checked. That was when I saw the lorries and found the pits."

"Yes," Gertrude said. "It was a very clever plan. Nearly perfect, in fact."

By the time we had gotten back to Gambais Gertrude liked Landru's plan so much that she thought we should tell someone else about it. There was no police station at Gambais. But Gertrude remembered that the Versailles Police Department had carried out the initial investigation of the case, and so we went to Versailles. Once there we found the police station and Gertrude introduced herself to the Prefect of Police.

"I am Gertrude Stein," she said, "and I have something to tell you about the Landru case."

Of course the Prefect of Police had never heard of Gertrude Stein. But I am happy to say that by the end of the day he had. He was so taken, in fact, with what she had to say that he called the Prefect of Police in Paris and they had a long talk. Then several newspaper reporters came out to Versailles and we all went back to Gambais, again in a public conveyance, but this time one about which there was no skirmish at all—a police car. Gertrude was delighted with that.

We went out to the quarry pits and Gertrude explained it all again—this time standing on the very spot where she had first gotten the idea. The story appeared in the newspapers the next day, several with pictures, which made Gertrude even happier than the police car. The next day she received a letter of commendation from the Prefect of Police at Versailles, praising her for her fine detective work, which pleased her even more. Then she wrote up her solution to the Landru case, telling how Landru had disposed of the bodies in the garbage pits, and sent it to *Le Monde*. Her entry was judged to be the best they received and so she won the prize. Again there were newspaper stories and again more photographs and, of course, a check for 5000 francs, which pleased Gertrude most of all.

"Now we can have our summer in the south of France," she said. "This is the way I have always wanted to be able to provide for you, Alice. Someday we will be rich, I promise."

So in the end everyone was happy.

Gertrude was happy because she had gotten her name in the newspapers and because the Prefect of the Versailles Police had sent her a letter of commendation and, of course, because she won the 5000 francs. Monsieur Godefroy, the chief prosecutor in the case, was happy because the jury found Landru guilty of eleven counts of murder and sentenced him to death. And all of France, except, of course, the one wife who had gotten away, was happy because there was soon to be one less murderer in their midst.

But perhaps I was the happiest of all.

For on the morning of February 22, 1922, Henri Désiré Landru was led from his prison cell at Versailles and marched out into the courtyard, where, at exactly five a.m., his head was cut off.

I, of course, being an early riser, was up at that hour. And having read of the execution time in the newspapers the day before, I noted it on the clock in the studio.

I will not say that I was smiling, as I looked at the clock, at exactly five a.m., and observed the moment of death. But I will say that I felt a moment of great relief.

That now there was one less man amongst us to have 283 lovers.

And one less husband to be unfaithful to eleven wives.

And, of course, one less subject for Gertrude and Hemingway to talk about.

Julie Smith

(1944-)

While Julie Smith is best known for her richly textured novels of the contemporary South featuring New Orleans policewoman Skip Langdon, she has demonstrated her versatility with two earlier series and numerous short stories. The five Rebecca Schwartz mysteries, which debuted with *Death Turns a Trick* (1982), are fast-paced comic tales of the exploits of a San Francisco Jewish feminist attorney. Paul McDonald, a freelance San Francisco editor (an occupation Smith once pursued) appeared in two novels, *True-Life Adventure* (1985) and *Huckleberry Fiend* (1987); his strong first-person voice proves Smith's ability to portray authentically a member of the opposite gender.

In the late 1980s Smith, a Savannah native who admits to never having felt at home in the South, began to examine her roots fictionally; the resultant novel, *New Orleans Mourning* (1990), earned her the Edgar Allan Poe Award for Best Novel and introduced Skip Langdon. The tall, somewhat overweight policewoman is a product of New Orleans society who has never conformed to the genteel image; an outsider on her home turf, she draws upon her wide contacts to plumb the dark underside of the city, while relying on her objectivity to understand and mesh the facts of her investigations. Smith weaves intricate tales of treachery and deceit on every level of society, and surrounds her heroine with a well-drawn and eccentric cast of ongoing characters. Her examination of Southern society in *The Axeman's Jazz* (1991), *Jazz Funeral* (1993), *New Orleans Beat* (1994), *House of Blues* (1995), and *The Kindness of Strangers* (1996) makes New Orleans, in all its flawed beauty, as much of a character as Langdon herself.

While Skip usually detects on her own, here she is joined by her male friend, Steve Steinman, in an original story that may very well be the only short mystery set in Antarctica. It is a fitting last entry for this anthology, as Langdon and Steinman epitomize the detecting duo in the 1990s, and deal with issues that will last well into the twenty-first century.

THE END OF THE EARTH

SKIP LANGDON AND STEVE STEINMAN
ANTARCTICA
1997

She sat on a rock, boots digging into the snow, binoculars trained on the lone bird trudging up the hill. It waddled absurdly, poorly adapted for walking, much less long-distance hiking. She knew some penguins had to walk as far as a hundred miles to the sea and back to their nests. They could, of course, just stay at sea, but the species continued because they opted instead for the uphill trudge.

She felt hands come to rest on her shoulders. "Some say the world will end in ice."

The voice was so familiar it might as well have been her own. She completed the thought. "From what I've tasted of desire, I hold with those who favor fire."

"You know the poem."

"Yes. Were you thinking of the penguin?"

"Can you imagine being so driven?"

That was the day before Toby's body was found. He was their favorite person on the ship.

They had wondered who'd be crazy enough to take a cruise to the end of the earth—to actually pay for it, which they hadn't—and had looked forward to grand eccentrics, screwball adventurers. Yet plain vanilla was the flavor of the month. Everyone seemed tediously normal, except for some of the guides, of whom Toby was one.

They might have known this would be the case if they'd been the sorts of people who traveled much themselves. They'd have liked to be—and certainly intended to be—but right now they were a little young and not quite successful enough. In other words, being a police officer (Detective Skip Langdon, New Orleans P.D.) and a much-in-demand film editor (Steve Steinman, self-employed), she didn't have the money and he didn't have the time. The Antarctica trip was a gift.

Skip's good friend Jimmy Dee Scoggin won it in a charity drawing, but didn't feel he could leave his adopted children at Christmas.

"But Dee-Dee," Skip said, "why don't you just go another time?"

"Because winter is summer Down There—good God, that sounds like what's in your pants. It's the only time the ocean thaws, comprenez? Anyway, I don't *want* to go. I hate ice. I hate snow. I hate penguins. I only bought the ticket to be nice."

"How could anyone hate penguins?"

"They make me feel like a shabby dresser."

The appealing thing to Skip and Steve, who weren't all that fond of ice and snow themselves, was that this was no luxury cruise, but adventure travel. Getting there was half the trip, if not half the fun. You had to fly to Miami, then to Santiago, then to Tierra del Fuego, where you boarded an ice-class ship that would hold some thirty-eight passengers and about as many crew members. Then you spent two days in Drake Passage, the roughest water in the world, and if you weren't seasick, you were as rare a bird as a condor.

Once in Antarctic waters, you landed on the continent several times a day, wherever there were penguins and scenery, in rubber dinghies that could hold a dozen people.

The guides drove the dinghies, led hikes, and lectured on such topics as Antarctic history and wildlife. They were the usual semi-loners—as close to cowboys as a twentieth-century man can get—young, well-educated, contrarian in every way. Toby had wild blond hair, a quick clever tongue, and an air of competence that Skip liked. In water so icy it could kill in minutes, she wanted a dinghy-driver who could patch a leak.

"After the guides," she said to Steve as they hunkered in their bunks during the Drake crossing, "the crew's the most interesting."

"Do tell. You never mentioned you speak Estonian."

"Andre's English isn't that bad."

"It is so. But he's a great-looking guy."

"He was a scientist when this was a research ship. He even helped design it."

"Start from the beginning, okay?"

"In the days of the Soviet Union, there were lots of research vessels, studying various things about the climate and the ice and the wildlife—Antarctic Studies, you might say."

"Ha. Spy ships."

"Oh, I'm sure. But they did provide employment for guys like Andre. And this was one of them. You didn't know?"

"As a matter of fact, I did. While you were getting the mad scientist's life story, I happened to retaliate by chatting up the waitress in the shorts."

"Oh, yeah. Shorty. I guess that's how she got her name. But really! Who wears shorts in the Antarctic?"

"There's nothing short about her legs."

Skip ignored him, answering her own question. "A waitress looking for a better life, that's who."

"Well, in that case she shouldn't have picked Toby. He'll probably spend his whole life traveling and never make a nickel."

"She's Toby's girlfriend?"

"Are you jealous?"

That was how they spent the two days on the Drake, sometimes not even making it to meals, having soup sent in instead, gossiping because there was little else to do.

Sometimes the ship rolled and sometimes it pitched. The sky was overcast, and the waves were grayish mountains that shattered over the bow, reaching seven on the Beaufort Scale, something, as Skip understood it, rather like a Richter Scale that measured fractious water instead of cranky land. Eleven was cyclone strength.

The change, when it came, was almost instant. Skip was napping when she heard Steve jump from the top bunk. "What?"

"Feel it?"

"Feel what?"

"It's like the curious incident of the dog in the night—from the Holmes story."

"The dog did nothing in the night."

"Exactly. The ship's like a friendly pup. I'm going on deck."

He was back in ten minutes. "Come on. You've got to see this. You won't believe it."

The sea was as blue as its reputation, except where the sun turned it gold. The sky was a clearer, more exaggerated hue than even seemed possible. A black-browed albatross glided at the stern. That was all.

Except that it was about the most beautiful sight she'd ever beheld.

It could have been any seascape, but it was far more vivid, seemed somehow in tighter focus than anything in life—more like an artist's notion of nature.

"Must be the Dramamine," she murmured. "Or was there something in the soup?"

"Clean air," said Steve. "I guess we've never really looked through it before."

Except for one freezing morning at a place ironically named Paradise Bay, the weather held for the entire five days they sailed the Southern Ocean.

Their first landing was at a place called Bailey's Head, which housed a rookery comprised of anywhere from 80,000 to a million penguins, depending on who you believed. Waiting excitedly to board the dinghy, in two sets of expedition-weight underwear under waterproof trousers, Skip and Steve reacquainted themselves with their fellow passengers. Some they hadn't yet met. One or two they avoided.

Like the red-faced man who kept making dumb jokes. "You think I'm getting in that thing?" he yelled as the guide lowered the first dinghy. "What if we get a flat?"

His wife was much younger, as slender and polished as he was sloppy and rough. "Oh, Hal," she said, obviously embarrassed. Skip thought she'd said it before. Hal turned to her, annoyance all over his face, but caught sight of Skip, who was six feet tall. "Well, good morning. How's the weather up there?" It was a phrase she hadn't heard in so long she thought it had disappeared from the language.

"Hal!" said his wife.

He ignored her, extending his hand. "Hal Travis. Norman, Oklahoma. This is my wife, Anna. Haven't seen you two."

"Little mal de mer."

He nodded. "Gets 'em every time. See my daughter over there? Dale the Whale? Wouldn't you know she had it too? The bigger they are, the harder they fall, I always say." He turned back toward the water. "Hey, Toby, you got that inner tube going yet?"

"You're in Andre's boat. Dale, come on. You're with me."

Hal said, "Good thing. She'll probably sink it."

"Hal, please," said Anna. "She'll hear you."

"Oh, come on. I've been kidding her all her life. She loves it."

Hundreds of penguins were lined up on the shore, four or five deep, each awaiting its turn to dive in. Not only were they patiently permitting the ones in front to go first, their progress was hampered by the returning ones, for whom they also waited. At one end of the beach was a veritable penguin highway, the wet black backs of the birds coming home on the right, the dry white fronts of the ones going to sea on the left.

The bustle was continual, deadly serious intent apparent in every sure-footed step. Though Skip had been too sick to make it to the penguin lecture, Andre had filled her in. She knew that both mates sat on the nests, taking turns going to sea. In the crowded rookery, where each penguin looked exactly like each other one, mates found each other by the sounds of each other's voices. After a curious recognition dance, involving much bowing and bobbing, the sitting mate would stand by while the returning one fed the chick regurgitated fish or squid.

The other animals, the more shabbily dressed ones, trudged up a steep hill to the rookery, keeping the mandated fifteen feet away from the birds. On top, they had both a stunning panorama and a bird's-eye view of bird life—birds with other birds, birds feeding their young, and birds waddling, ever waddling.

"Hey, look. There's an egg hatching. Look—little pecker's coming out *now*." Hal edged in front of everyone else, camera clicking, about a foot from the hatching chick.

"So much," said Skip, "for the fifteen-foot rule. Who is that asshole, anyway?"

"He has the suite," said a woman named Carol, a Texan with a brisk climbing style.

"Wouldn't you know." There was only one suite aboard the ship, and it was nearly double the cost of a cabin.

"He's my dad," said Toby.

A day later Toby was dead.

Andre found him lying on deck, his head caved in as if he had fallen while running, smashing his skull on the steel—a daredevil laid low by the most prosaic of accidents. The deck had been wet, and a rope had been carelessly left out of place. He could have tripped or slipped—perhaps both.

Or so it seemed until the ship's doctor came forward. Skip had thought the man was a senior sailor of some sort, the first mate perhaps, by the elegant way he looked and the casual way he behaved. He was the very personification of "Nordic," a man so white he resembled a statue. He'd probably started life as a towhead and turned golden blond. Now his hair was once again the color of a sail. He had surgeons' hands—lovely ones with prominent veins and knuckles. Skip had noticed him often, noticed that he never missed a landing and always carried a backpack. Some detective, she thought, that she hadn't put it together.

She watched as he heaved himself to his feet after examining the body, and conferred with the captain. There was a lot of head-shaking and gesturing. And then, to her surprise, the Nordic man approached her. "Please, the captain would like to see you."

The captain wore blue. She wondered if it was a rule. He had a craggy face and an air of such authority that if she'd seen him on the street she'd have known he was used to being obeyed. Now he did his best to seem her supplicant. "Miss Langdon. That is, *Detective* Langdon. We have a small problem. The doctor here says our late friend Toby has more than one injury, inconsistent with slipping and falling. We have reason to believe there has been foul play. And frankly, we don't know what to do.... We wonder if you would be kind enough to help us?"

"Of course. Let's get everyone off the deck and rope it off. Wake up everyone who isn't here and have them go to the conference room—sailors, staff, passengers, everybody. I'll have to question each person separately. Don't give anyone time alone—or alone with a friend or spouse. Get them all in there together except the people absolutely necessary to sailing the ship."

"Yes, of course," said the captain. He looked taken aback, as if he hadn't expected quite such decisiveness.

She wasn't at all sure what laws were eventually going to apply—Estonian, possibly, since the ship was Estonian—but then Toby was American and who knew what nationality the murderer was. All she could do was gather and preserve what evidence she could—in other words, follow the only procedure she knew.

She turned to the doctor. "What have we got?"

"There seem to be a number of head injuries." He shrugged. "Does one's head bounce when one falls? And if so, how many times? Anyway, he was young, he had good balance—and so there is common sense as well. Most people who fall down get up and walk away."

"But the medical sticking point is multiple injuries?"

"Yes."

"Time of death?"

"Very recently. Within the hour."

It was after one A.M., but nowhere near dark—in the South, the season of the midnight sun is reversed. Steve and Skip had gone for a stroll in the eerie light, but most people were probably in bed. Someone up to no good would have the run of the ship.

Skip said to the captain, "What about the wet deck and the rope? That doesn't seem exactly shipshape."

"It happens."

She thought it was awfully convenient.

"What about the family?" asked the captain.

"What indeed. I wonder what Dale the Whale's story is? While you're getting people organized, may I have permission to search the ship?"

"Of course, but—I don't know about people's cabins."

Skip knew nothing about maritime law, but she wasn't prepared to go any further than she normally would—just in case.

She nodded. "I'll stay out of them. Steve, could you go? I need to get started with the interviews."

"Sure. One murder weapon coming up."

She talked to Andre first. He was officially a sort of liaison between the crew and the passengers, his title being "Passenger Mate." Toby had told Skip all about it —it was more or less a made-up position meant simply to give him a job. He knew everything there was to know about the ship and was considered far too valuable to be permitted to slip away.

She knew the rest of his story too. He'd once been at a research station, when the power source had been lost. He and his fellow scientists had been forced to spend the Antarctic winter with neither heat nor light. Survival would have seemed a full-time job—Skip couldn't even imagine it—but every day Andre had gone to his lab, and had worked. "He was the one who got the group through. He won't admit it," Toby had said, "because he hates the Communists so much—but he was awarded the Order of Lenin for what he did."

He was obviously no ordinary man. He was very handsome, yet awkward, both socially and in the way he moved, as if he were made of some durable substance that simply wasn't pliable. There was something heroic about him, yet it was something more dogged than swashbuckling. Hercules he wasn't; he was more like the Little Engine That Could.

"If I'd gotten there earlier," he was saying. "If only I'd gotten there earlier."

"Why do you say that?"

"Maybe I could have helped him."

"How did you happen to find him?"

"I have a lecture tomorrow—you remember? 'My Twenty Years in the Antarctic.' I was up, preparing for it. I was nervous—I went outside for a smoke."

"And?"

He shrugged. "I found him. It was too late."

His English was minimal, but he had little to say, anyway—he hadn't heard or seen anything. All he had done was find the body. He seemed distraught and also nervous, writhing underneath, as if being deprived of heroism this time was eating him up.

"Do you know of anyone who might have wanted to kill Toby?"

"He was . . . " He shook his head. "No. No. Toby. No."

He and Toby, she thought, had been close. Toby had spoken of him often and always with admiration. I'll try him again, she decided, and moved on to Dale the Whale.

Dale wasn't really fat, but she was no lithe, perfect Anna. Since Skip herself was six feet tall and overweight by some standards, she had sympathy for the Dales of the world. Also, she didn't get along that great with her own dad.

Dale kept her brown hair short and wore no makeup, almost as if she didn't much care what anyone thought, but since her skin was smooth and her color good, it merely looked casual rather than careless. At the moment, her face was puffy from crying.

"He was twenty-nine—tomorrow would have been his thirtieth birthday."

"You were close to your brother?"

Dale nodded.

"How did your family happen to be traveling together?"

"We weren't supposed to be. Dad and Anna were coming to be with Toby on his birthday. And he called up and said—well, frankly . . . " She hesitated. "I don't want you to take this the wrong way, but he said he was afraid."

"Afraid of what?"

"Dad. He has . . ." Again she stopped, apparently unsure what to say. Or playacting. "He has a history of violence."

"What sort?"

"Oh, just with us. He used to beat us when we were kids."

Skip was puzzled. Toby had been well over six feet tall—surely he could protect himself. "There must be more."

"Yeah. Mom—he used to knock her around as well. One day she took some pills."

"Are you saying your mother killed herself?"

Dale nodded. "Oh, yes. And Dad was married again six months later." She had that defiant look people get when they're trying to cover up something that hurts.

"Still, I don't see why Toby was afraid of him."

"Well, it's this way. Granddaddy McAvoy, my mom's dad, made a fortune in bottle caps—do you love it? Somebody's gotta make them. Dad married Mom and took over the company, and Granddad, in his infinite wisdom, didn't leave Mom any money. And didn't leave me any. On the McAvoy side, the money is passed strictly to the male heirs. Toby gets his on his thirtieth birthday, but *only* if he's working for the company—and on that date, the same amount goes to the company.

"Matching funds, you might say."

"Granddad was a piece of work. But, anyhow, you've probably guessed it—Toby had absolutely no interest in bottle caps, and Dad wanted the money. So, if you want to know the truth, he really came to the end of the earth to persuade Toby to come to work for the company. Toby was afraid there'd be trouble, so he made me promise I'd never leave him alone with Dad—and then he made Dad pay for my ticket."

"Are you saying he was physically afraid of your dad?"

She looked confused. "I don't know. I honestly don't know. All I know is he didn't want to be alone with him."

"Did you see Toby earlier tonight?"

"Oh, yes. He came to my cabin a little before . . . I guess, before he was killed." She snapped her fingers. "Shorty! Damn, I forgot about that."

"Back up a little—you lost me."

"He was upset. He came to tell me she broke up with him. They had a huge fight because he turned Dad down—in other words, because he wasn't going to be a rich American. Naturally he thought she'd just been using him, and that made him feel bad. He'd lost girlfriends before, but he just rode with it, you know what I mean? All smiles, there'll-be-another-one-soon kind of thing. Last night he seemed really depressed—it wasn't like Toby, but he could get that way around Dad."

"What time did he leave?"

"About an hour and a half ago." Her eyes brimmed, as the reality of it hit her.

Skip called in the girlfriend. "I understand you were involved with Toby."

And then *she* burst into tears.

"You must have been in love with him."

"Oh, yes. Oh, yes, I am in love with him."

"So why did you dump him, Shorty?"

"How you know about that?"

"You want to tell me about it?"

She seemed almost relieved. "Yes. Yes, I tell you about it. You never know it to look at me, but I am a responsible woman. I have a daughter in kindergarten and a son in diapers and I love my children. I care about my children. Toby have a very wonderful opportunity to make a lot of money and he turn it down. Like he don't care about me, he don't care about my children." The woman spoke angrily, apparently forgetting her grief. "He turn it down and we have a big fight—huge fight."

"When?"

"Tonight. Right after dinner."

"I tell him my children come first, and I'm sorry I must move on, and he beg me not to, but that is the way it is. My children *must* come first."

"Tell me about the offer."

"His father—you know? The man in the suite—his father ask him to come to work for a huge bonus. Toby is afraid of his father, you know that? He is an angry man —a nasty man—Toby said he does not know what will happen if he turn his father down." She squinched up her eyes, but Skip couldn't tell if real tears came out or not. "And now his father kill him. What a waste! He could have made me so happy."

"Why do you say his father killed him?"

She look surprised. "Who else would do that?"

"You, maybe. If you were very angry."

"Hey, wait a minute. I dump *him*. I told you that. I am a responsible woman. I don't need to kill nobody. I just move on, that's all."

Skip could believe that. Probably, she thought, two or three times a trip.

"When was the last time you saw him?"

"When he leave my cabin. I sob myself to sleep, then I find out he is dead."

There were no witnesses to the fight, and Shorty had no alibi for the ensuing hours.

That's two votes for Dad, Skip thought, *I wonder if I should just get his side of the story.*

She looked at her watch. It had been an hour and still no word from Steve. She went out and gestured for the captain. "Is Steve back yet? From searching?"

Confused, he surveyed the crowded room. "I don't think so."

Odd, she thought, but since everyone was in the room, she wasn't particularly worried.

"Has anyone left the room at all?"

"Only to go to the lavatory—and we've been careful to watch. Only one at a time, and for only a few moments."

"Okay. Send in the father next."

In grief, Hal Travis resembled a child for whom things have gone wrong—more sullen than sorrowful, Skip thought.

She said: "I'm sorry for your loss, Mr. Travis. I understand Toby was about to celebrate a birthday."

"Who the hell told you that?"

She liked his defensiveness—it gave her a nice advantage.

"His thirtieth. Was anything special supposed to happen then?" Purposely, she phrased her question like a prosecutor—not leading, yet clearly conveying the idea that she already knew the answer.

"My daughter told you, I presume. He was going to inherit money. What's that got to do with anything?"

"You tell me."

"Don't you give me orders! I've had about enough of you bullying me and my family. Let me tell you and tell you right now: Dale's got her faults, but she's not a murderer. She and Toby were as close as a brother and sister can be. You just get any ideas about her out of your head. Anyway, it doesn't make sense. If she were a murderer, she wouldn't kill him, she'd kill me."

Skip thought, *You're not kidding it doesn't make sense.* She said, "Why would she kill you?"

"For wanting to replace her." He spoke crossly, obviously unable to understand how she could be so dense.

"I think you'd better start at the beginning, Mr. Travis."

"Fool board made her CEO of the damn company, and she's just about run it in the ground. I wanted to replace her with Toby—so why wouldn't she kill me instead of him?"

"Did he accept your offer?"

"He was going to."

"Why do you say that?"

"He said he'd let me know tomorrow."

"Tell me something. If the board has the power to appoint the CEO, how could you replace Dale with Toby?"

He sunk his head into his shoulders, more like a sullen kid than ever. "I could have talked them into it."

I'll bet. Skip read it this way: Either because of poor performance or worse personality, the company had fired Hal and replaced him with Dale. He thought he could set up a puppet named Toby.

No matter who was running the company, Hal had a history of violence when angry and—despite his face-saving story—he'd probably been turned down.

But Skip couldn't help but notice that candid, good-sister Dale, who'd somehow failed to mention her cushy job at the bottle cap factory, just might have a motive herself.

Maybe Toby *had* said he'd think about the offer, and not just to get his dad off his back. Or maybe that was the original idea, then he'd had the fight with Shorty and decided to reconsider. He'd gone by to tell Dale and she'd quickly squashed that plan—along with his skull.

The captain knocked.

"Yes?"

"Steve is back."

"Okay, Mr. Travis. We'll continue this later."

The minute Steve came in, she could see he'd found something good. "The weapon? You found the weapon?"

"I wish. What would you do with a blunt instrument you happen to murder somebody with in the middle of the Southern Ocean?"

She sighed. "Toss it overboard."

"Yeah."

"Well? If it wasn't the weapon, what?"

"The motive."

"Oh, great."

"Hey, what's wrong?"

"I found a few of those, too. But I'm still impressed—don't get me wrong. Shoot."

"There's three decks below this one, did you know that? One for the crew and two others, where I was strictly forbidden to go, but did anyhow. Guess what's down there? Labs."

"What kind of labs?"

"Abandoned, locked-up labs full of dusty old beakers and things. From the research days."

Her interest was piqued. "Really?"

"All except for two. One of those is a working chemical lab of some kind—I couldn't tell you what's being made there, but I've got an idea. Because the one next door is all fitted out with fluorescent lights."

"Yep. A mini pot farm. And whatever they're doing, they're doing it right. There's a lot of good-looking weed in there."

"So they're probably making drugs in the chemical lab—a little diversification."

"Ecstasy maybe. Something like that."

"But who's doing it? That's the question."

"Well, it would be if not for your faithful servant. I don't know yet, but I do have the key. As it happens, in the chemistry lab there's also an ancient computer. I mean we're talking dinosaur. You may recall I'm pretty good with these things."

"A genius, practically."

"The only problem is, I don't speak Estonian."

"But surely you rose above that." His whole manner was so smug she was sure he had something.

"Well the only recent file in it had exactly two words in it I could recognize:

'Toby' and 'Shorty.' Someone's keeping a log, I think—Toby's name came up about a week ago, and Shorty's—get this—tonight. Followed by exclamation marks. What do you think?"

"I think everybody lies, and just when you think you've got the hang of something it flies out of control." She filled him in on her interviews. "Let's get the Antarctic Sex Queen in here again. You want to stick around and be the good cop? I'm sure she'll probably respond to your charm and magnetism."

"Sure. I'll be gentle as a penguin."

Shorty was tearing at a tissue. Skip said, "Okay, Shorty. We found the pot farm and the chemistry lab. Start talking."

She stared at Steve, eyes opening up like a couple of beach umbrellas. Finally she turned them on Skip. "I don't know what you mean."

"You were there tonight, weren't you?"

"No! You're crazy. You talk stuff I don't understand. I don't know nothin' about no drugs. I don't know *nothing*."

"We have proof you're involved in the drug ring. You know what that means? It means you're going to jail unless you cooperate. It means your children are going to spend the rest of their lives in foster care."

"No! No. You can't do this. This is supposed to be about Toby. Why don't you investigate something important?"

Steve said, "Hey, Skip, give her a minute to think, okay? Can't you see she's upset?"

A tiny ray of hope flamed up in Shorty's eyes.

He said, "You didn't kill Toby, did you? She thinks you did. She knows he was involved in the drug ring and. . . ."

"He was not! There is no drug ring—this is crazy."

"Look, Shorty, I'm trying to help you. If you weren't involved and he wasn't involved, what's the big deal?"

"Oh, God." Her body fell forward, heaving with ragged, tearing sobs, her head down on the table.

Skip gave Steve the thumbs-up sign.

The curly head finally rose, the face below all pink and wet. "I'm so ashamed."

"Of what, Shorty?"

"Toby knew about the drugs. He found out last week, and he knew he shouldn't, but he have to tell me—he just have to—you know? Because he was so upset he couldn't be quiet."

"Why was he so upset?"

"Because Andre was his best friend."

"Andre."

"Oh, yes, Andre. There is no ring, no nothing. We find out everything. When the ship stops at this American research station—it does every trip, you know?—Andre unloads to this one guy. That's it—just one other guy who gets the stuff out on supply ships. We know, but we tell nobody, you understand? Because Andre and Toby are ... like this." She put two fingers together. "You know Toby. He put friendship above everything."

"Why did you say you were ashamed?"

"Because I go there last night—after our fight. I figure Andre has money now —I move on to him. I lie, I say I go to bed and cry, because I am so ashamed."

The rest was easy. Confronted, Andre broke into a thousand pieces. Toby had told him he knew about the drugs, but Andre trusted him to keep quiet. When he found out Shorty knew, he panicked. He no longer felt his friend could be trusted. So he killed Toby, and Skip suspected Shorty would soon have taken a long, cold swim under the shining Southern Cross.

But Shorty was so sure the father was the perp it never occurred to her where the real danger was.

Andre was eager not to be seen as a common drug manufacturer. He was utterly matter-of-fact, as if he were telling the story of going to his lab with no light and no heat in sub-zero weather. "I did what was necessary," he said, as if it made sense.

"Necessary for what?"

"I wanted to buy the ship."

"Buy the *ship*? What on earth for?"

"To return it to research. To science! As before."

Skip thought she was finally getting it. "It must be hard driving dinghies when you used to be a nationally respected. . . ."

"No, no, you don't understand. What we did was *important*. It could solve the world's food problem some day. Or perhaps. . . ."

"Perhaps what?"

"Weather ... global warming. The ocean is in trouble. We can't just stop. . . ."

He reminded Skip of nothing so much as the lone penguin climbing the hill—utterly focused, but rather like a machine that's not even sure why it has to keep running. She could see how he'd gotten those men through the Antarctic winter—through pure, plain blind ambition, stubborn and awkward, but kind of heroic nonetheless. His innate doggedness, his absolute refusal to be beaten, had taken a tiny turn somewhere, twisted into grim desire, and turned dangerous.

Fire, she thought. Robert Frost knew what he was talking about. The world was sure to end in fire.

AUTHOR INDEX

Names in bold belong to authors who have stories included.